Miss Read

* * * *

THREE GREAT NOVELS

CHRONICLES of FAIRACRE

Village School

Village Diary

Storm in the Village

Illustrated by J. S. Goodall

ORION

Village School © Miss Read 1955
Village Diary © Miss Read 1957
Storm in the Village © Miss Read 1958

This omnibus first published by Michael Joseph, 1964
Published in Penguin Books, 1982
Copyright © Miss Read 1982

Published in 2005 by Orion,
an imprint of the Orion Publishing Group Ltd.

A CIP catalogue record for this book is
available from the British Library.

ISBN 0 75287 280 X (trade paperback)

Typeset at the Spartan Press Ltd,
Lymington, Hants
Printed in Great Britain by
Clays Ltd, St Ives plc

The Orion Publishing Group
Orion House
5 Upper Saint Martin's Lane
London, WC2H 9EA

www.orionbooks.co.uk

Miss Read, or in real life Dora Saint, was a teacher by profession who started writing after the Second World War, beginning with light essays written for *Punch* and other journals. She then wrote on educational and country matters and worked as a scriptwriter for the BBC. Miss Read was married to a schoolmaster for sixty-four years until his death in 2004, and they have one daughter.

In the 1998 New Year Honours list Miss Read was awarded an MBE for her services to literature. She is the author of many immensely popular books, including two autobiographical works, but it is for her novels of English rural life for which she is best known. The first of these, *Village School*, was published in 1955, and Miss Read continued to write about the fictitious villages of Fairacre and Thrush Green until her retirement in 1996. She lives in Berkshire.

Contents

* * * *

Village School

PART ONE
Christmas Term

* * * *

1. Early Morning

The first day of term has a flavour that is all its own; a whiff of lazy days behind and a foretaste of the busy future. The essential thing, for a village schoolmistress on such a day, is to get up early.

I told myself this on a fine September morning, ten minutes after switching off the alarm clock. The sun streamed into the bedroom, sparking little rainbows from the mirror's edge; and outside the rooks cawed noisily from the tops of the elm trees in the churchyard. From their high look-out the rooks had a view of the whole village of Fairacre clustered below them; the village which had been my home now for five years.

I had enjoyed those five years – the children, the little school, the pleasure of running my own school-house and of taking a part in village life. True, at first, I had had to walk as warily as Agag; many a slip of the tongue caused me, even now, to go hot and cold at the mere memory, but at last, I believed, I was accepted, if not as a proper native, at least as 'Miss Read up the School,' and not as 'that new woman pushing herself forward!'

I wondered if the rooks, whose clamour was increasing with the warmth of the sun, could see as far as Tyler's Row at the end of the village. Here lived Jimmy Waites and Joseph Coggs, two little boys who were to enter school today. Another new child was also coming, and this thought prodded me finally out of bed and down the narrow stairs.

I filled the kettle from the pump at the sink and switched it on. The new school year had begun.

Tyler's Row consists of four thatched cottages and very pretty they look. Visitors always exclaim when they see them, sighing ecstatically and saying how much they would like to live there. As a realist I am always constrained to point out the disadvantages that lurk behind the honeysuckle.

The thatch is in a bad way, and though no rain has yet dripped through into the dark bedrooms below, it most certainly will before long. There is no doubt about a rat or two running along the ridge, as spry as you please, reconnoitring probably for a future home; and the starlings and sparrows find it a perfect resting-place.

'They ought to do something for us,' Mrs Waites told me, but as 'They,' meaning the landlord, is an old soldier living with his sister in the next village on a small pension and the three shillings he gets a week from each cottage (when he is lucky), it is hardly surprising that the roof is as it is.

There is no drainage of any sort and no damp-course. The brick floors sweat and clothes left hanging near a wall produce a splendid crop of prussian blue mildew in no time.

Washing-up water, soap-suds and so on are either emptied into a deep hole by the hedge or flung broadcast over the garden. The plants flourish on this treatment, particularly the rows of Madonna lilies which are the envy of the village. The night-cart, now a tanker-lorry, elects to call in the heat of the day, usually between twelve and one o'clock, once a week. The sewerage is carried through the only living-room and out into the road, for the edification of the school-children who are making their way home to dinner, most probably after a hygiene lesson on the importance of cleanliness.

In the second cottage Jimmy Waites was being washed. He stood on a chair by the shallow stone sink, submitting meekly to his mother's ministrations. She had twisted the corner of the face-flannel into a formidable radish and was turning it remorselessly round and round inside his left ear. He wore new corduroy trousers, dazzling braces and a woollen vest. Hanging on a line which was slung across the front of the mantelpiece, was a bright blue-and-red-checked shirt, American style. His mother intended that her Jimmy should do her credit on his first day at school.

She was a blonde, lively woman married to a farm-worker as fair as herself. 'I always had plenty of spirit,' she said once, 'Why, even during the war when I was alone I kept cheerful!' She did, too, from all accounts told by her more puritanical neighbours;

and certainly none of us is so silly as to ask questions about Cathy, the only dark child of the six, born during her husband's absence in 1944.

Cathy, while her brother was being scrubbed, was feeding the hens at the end of the garden. She threw out handfuls of mixed wheat and oats which she had helped to glean nearly a year ago. This was a treat for the chickens and they squawked and screeched as they fought for their breakfast.

Their noise brought one of the children who lived next door to a gap in the hedge that divided the gardens. Joseph was about five, of gipsy stock, with eyes as dark and pathetic as a monkey's. Cathy had promised to take him with her and Jimmy on this his first school morning. This was a great concession on the part of Mrs Waites as the raggle-taggle family next door was normally ignored.

'Don't you play with them dirty kids,' she warned her own children, 'or you'll get Nurse coming down the school to look at you special!' And this dark threat was enough.

But today Cathy looked at Joseph with a critical eye and spoke first.

'You ready?'

The child nodded in reply.

'You don't look like it,' responded his guardian roundly. 'You wants to wash the jam off of your mouth. Got a hanky?'

'No,' said Joe, bewildered.

'Well, you best get one. Bit of rag'll do, but Miss Read lets off awful if you forgets your hanky. Where's your mum?'

'Feeding baby.'

'Tell her about the rag,' ordered Cathy, 'and buck up. Me and Jim's nearly ready.' And swinging the empty tin dipper she skipped back into her house.

Meanwhile, the third new child was being prepared. Linda was eight years old, fat and phlegmatic, and the pride of her fond mother's heart. She was busy buttoning her new red shoes while her mother packed a piece of chocolate for her elevenses at playtime.

The Moffats had only lived in Fairacre for three weeks, but we had watched their bungalow being built for the last six months.

7

'Bathroom and everything!' I had been told, 'and one of those hatchers to put the dishes through to save your legs. Real lovely!'

The eagle eye of the village was upon the owners whenever they came over from Caxley, our nearest market-town, to see the progress of their house. Mrs Moffat had been seen measuring the windows for curtains and holding patterns of material against the distempered walls.

'Thinks herself someone, you know!' I was told later. 'Never so much as spoke to me in the road!'

'Perhaps she was shy.'

'Humph!'

'Or deaf, even.'

'None so deaf as those that won't hear,' was the tart rejoinder. Mrs Moffat, alas! was already suspected of that heinous village crime known as 'putting on side.'

One evening, during the holidays, she had brought the child to see me. I was gardening and they both looked askance at my bare legs and dirty hands. It was obvious that she tended to cosset her rather smug daughter and that appearances meant a lot to her, but I liked her and guessed that the child was intelligent and would work well. That her finery would also excite adverse comment among the other children I also surmised. Mrs Moffat's aloofness was really only part of her town upbringing, and once she realized the necessity for exchanging greetings with every living soul in the village, no matter how pressing or distracting one's own business, she would soon be accepted by the other women.

Linda would come into my class. She would be in the youngest group, among those just sent up from the infants' room where they had spent three years under Miss Clare's benign rule. Joseph and Jimmy would naturally go straight into her charge.

At twenty to nine I hung up the tea towel, closed the back door of the school-house and stepped across the playground to the school.

Above me the rooks still chattered. Far below they could see, converging upon the school lane, little knots of children from all quarters of the village. Cathy had Jimmy firmly by the hand: Joseph's grimy paw she disdained to hold, and he trailed behind her, his dark eyes apprehensive.

Linda Moffat, immaculate in starched pink gingham, walked primly beside her mother; while behind and before, running, dawdling, shouting or whistling, ran her future school fellows.

Through the sunny air another sound challenged the rooks' chorus. The school bell began to ring out its morning greeting.

2. OUR SCHOOL

The school at Fairacre was built in 1880, and as it is a church school it is strongly ecclesiastical in appearance. The walls are made of local stone, a warm grey in colour, reflecting summer light with honeyed mellowness, but appearing dull and dejected when the weather is wet. The roof is high and steeply-pitched and the stubby bell-tower thrusts its little Gothic nose skywards, emulating the soaring spire of St Patrick's, the parish church, which stands next door.

The windows are high and narrow, with pointed tops. Children were not encouraged, in those days, to spend their working time in gazing out at the world, and, sitting stiffly in the well of the room, wearing sailor suits or stout zephyr and serge frocks, their only view was of the sky, the elm trees and St Patrick's spire. Today their grandchildren and great-grandchildren have exactly the same view; just this lofty glimpse of surrounding loveliness.

The building consists of two rooms divided by a partition of glass and wood. One room houses the infants, aged five, six and seven years of age, under Miss Clare's benevolent eye. The other room is my classroom where the older children of junior age stay until they are eleven when they pass on to a secondary school, either at Caxley, six miles away, or in the neighbouring village of Beech Green, where the children stay until they are fifteen.

A long lobby runs behind these two rooms, the length of the building; it is furnished with pegs for coats, a low stone sink for the children to wash in, and a high new one for washing-up the dinner things. An electric copper is a recent acquisition, and very handsome it is; but although we have electricity installed here there is no water laid on to the school.

This is, of course, an appalling problem, for there is no water to drink – and children get horribly thirsty – no water for washing hands, faces, cleansing cuts and grazes, for painting, for mixing paste or watering plants or filling flower vases; and, of course, no water for lavatories.

We overcome this problem in two ways. A large galvanized iron tank on wheels is filled with rainwater collected from the roof, and this, when we have skimmed off the leaves and twigs and rescued the occasional frog, serves most of our needs. The electric copper is filled in the morning from this source and switched on after morning playtime to be ready for washing not only the crockery and cutlery after dinner but also the stone floor of the lobby.

I bring two buckets of drinking water across the playground from the school-house where there is an excellent well, but we must do our own heating, so that a venerable black kettle stands on my stove throughout the winter months, purring in a pleasantly domestic fashion, ready for emergencies. The electric kettle, in my own kitchen, serves us at other times.

The building is solid structurally and kept in repair by the church authorities whose property it is. One defect, however, it seems impossible to overcome. A skylight, strategically placed over the headmistress's desk, lets in not only light, but rain. Generations of local builders have clambered over the roof and sworn and sawn and patched and pulled at our skylight – but in vain. The gods have willed otherwise, and year after year Pluvius drops his pennies into a bucket placed below for the purpose, the clanging muffled by a dishcloth folded to fit the bottom.

The school stands at right angles to the road and faces across the churchyard to the church. A low dry-stone wall runs along by the road dividing it from the churchyard, school playground and the school-house garden. Behind this the country slopes away, falling slightly at first, then rising, in swelling folds, up into the full majesty of the downs which sweep across these southern counties for mile upon mile. The air is always bracing, and in the winter the wind is a bitter foe, and that quality of pure light, which is peculiar to downland country, is here very noticeable.

The children are hardy and though, quite naturally, they take their surroundings for granted, I think that they are aware of the fine views around them. The girls particularly are fond of flowers, birds, insects and all the minutiae of natural life, guarding jealously any rare plant against outsiders' prying eyes, and having a real knowledge of the whereabouts and uses of many plants and herbs.

The boys like to dismiss such things as 'girls' stuff,' but they too can find the first mushrooms, sloes or blackberries for their mothers or for me; and most of the birds' nests are known as soon as they are built. Luckily, stealing eggs and rifling nests seem to be on the wane, though occasional culprits are brought to stern judgment at my desk. They suffer, I think, more from the tongues of the girls in the playground in matters like this, for there is no doubt about it that the girls are more sympathetic to living things and pour scorn and contumely on any young male tyrants.

In one corner of the small, square playground is the inevitable pile of coke for the two slow combustion stoves. These coke piles seem to be a natural feature of all country schools. This is considered by the children, a valuable adjunct to playtime activities. A favourite game is to run scrunchily up the pile and then to slither down in gritty exhilaration. Throwing it at each other, or at a noisy object such as the rainwater tank, is also much enjoyed, hands being wiped perfunctorily down the fronts of jackets or on the seats of trousers before the beginning of writing lessons. All these joys are strictly forbidden, of course, which adds to the fearful delight.

Furthest from the wall by the road at the other side of the playground grows a clump of elm trees, and their gnarled roots, which add to the hazards of the playground's surface, are a favourite place to play.

The recesses are rooms, larders, cupboards or gardens, and the ivy leaves from the wall are used for plates and provisions, and twigs for knives and forks. Sometimes they play shops among the roots, paying each other leaves and bearing away conkers, acorns and handfuls of gravel as their purchases. I like to hear the change in their voices as they become shopkeepers or customers. They affect a high dictatorial tone of voice when they assume adult status, quite unlike the warm burr of their everyday conversations.

The fields lie two or three feet below the level of the playground and a scrubby hedge of hazel and hawthorn marks this boundary. The sloping bank down is scored by dozens of little bare paths, worn by generations of sturdy boots and corduroy breeches.

Altogether our playground is a good one – full of possibilities for resourceful children and big enough to allow shopkeepers, mothers and fathers, cowboys and spacemen to carry on their urgent affairs very happily together.

On this first morning of term Miss Clare had already arrived when I walked over at a quarter to nine. Her bicycle, as upright and as ancient as its owner, was propped just inside the lobby door.

The school had that indefinable first-morning smell compounded of yellow soap, scrubbed floorboards and black-lead. The tortoise stove gleamed like an ebony monster; even the vent-pipe which soared aloft towards the pitch-pine roof was blackened as far as Mrs Pringle, the school cleaner, could reach. Clean newspaper covered the freshly-hearthstoned surroundings of the stove – which officially remained unlit until October – and the guard, just as glossy, was neatly placed round the edges of the outspread *News of the World*.

My desk had that bare tidy look that it only wears for an hour or so on this particular morning of term; and the inkstand, an imposing affair of mahogany and brass, shone in splendour. I wondered as I walked through to Miss Clare's room just how quickly its shelf would remain unencumbered by the chalk, beads, raincoat buttons, paper clips, raffia needles and drawing pins that were its normal burden.

Miss Clare was taking a coat-hanger out of her big canvas hold-all. She is very careful of her clothes, and is grieved to see the casual way in which the children sling their coats, haphazard, on to the pegs in the lobby. Her own coat is always smoothed methodically over its hanger and hung on the back of the class-room door. The children watch, fascinated, when she removes her gloves, for she blows into them several times before folding them neatly together. Her sensible felt hat has a shelf to itself inside the needlework cupboard.

Miss Clare has taught here for nearly forty years, with only one break, when she nursed her mother through her last illness twelve years ago. She started here as a monitress at the age of thirteen, and was known officially, until recently, as 'A Supplementary Uncertificated Teacher.' Her knowledge of local family history is far-reaching and of inestimable value to the teaching of our present pupils. I like to hear the older people talk of her. 'Always a stickler for tidiness,' the butcher told me, 'the only time I was smacked in the babies' class was when Miss Clare found me kicking another boy's cap round the floor.'

Miss Clare is of commanding appearance, tall and thin, with beautiful white hair, which is kept in place with an invisible hair-net. Even on the wildest day, when the wind shrieks across the downs, Miss Clare walks round the play-ground looking immaculate. She is now over sixty, and her teaching methods have of late been looked upon by some visiting inspectors with a slightly pitying eye. They are, they say, too formal; the children should have more activity, and the classroom is unnaturally quiet for children of that age. This may be, but for all that, or perhaps because of that, Miss Clare is a very valuable teacher, for in the first place the children are happy, they are fond of Miss Clare, and she creates for them an atmosphere of serenity and quiet which means that they can work well and cheerfully, really laying the foundations of elementary knowledge on which I can build so much more quickly when they come up into my class.

Her home is two miles away, on the outskirts of the next village of Beech Green. She has lived there ever since she was six, a solemn little girl in high-buttoned boots and ringlets, in the cottage which her father thatched himself. He was a thatcher by trade, and many of the cottages in the surrounding villages are decorated with the ornate criss-crossing and plaiting which he loved to do. He was much in demand at harvest time for thatching ricks, and Miss Clare often makes 'rick-dollies' of straw for the children like the ones her father used to put on top of the newly-thatched stacks.

In the corner of the room John Burton was pulling lustily at the bell-rope. He stopped as I came in.

'Five minutes' rest,' I said, 'then another pull or two to tell the others that it's time to get into lines in the playground.'

Miss Clare and I exchanged holiday news while she unlocked her desk and took out her new register, carefully shrouded in fresh brown paper. She had covered mine for me too, at the end of last term, and written in the names of our new classes in her sloping copper-plate hand.

We should have forty children altogether this term; eighteen in the infants' room and twenty-two in mine; and though our numbers might seem small, compared with the monstrous regiments of forty and fifty to a class in town schools, the age range, of course, would be a considerable handicap.

I should have five children in my lowest group who would be nearly eight years old and these would still have difficulty in reading fluently and with complete understanding. At the other end of the classroom would be my top group, consisting of three children, including Cathy Waites, who would be taking the examination which would decide their future schooling at eleven. These children would need particular care in being shown how to tackle arithmetical problems, how to understand written questions and, more important still, how to set out their answers and express themselves generally, in clear and straightforward language.

Miss Clare's youngest group would consist of the two new little boys, Jimmy Waites and Joseph Coggs, as well as the twins, Diana and Helen, who had entered late last term owing to measles and had learnt very little. Miss Clare was of the opinion, knowing something of their family history, that they might well be in her bottom group for years.

'What can you expect,' she said, looking at the hieroglyphics that passed for writing on their blackboards, 'their grandfather never stuck at one job for more than a week and the boy took after him. Added to that he married a girl with as much sense as himself, and these two are the result.'

'I'll get the doctor to look at them specially, when she comes,' I comforted her,'I think if they had their adenoids removed they might be much brighter.'

Miss Clare's snort showed what good she thought this would do two of the biggest duffers who had ever come into her hands.

Her aim with the top group in her class will be, first, to see that they can read, and also write legibly, know their multiplication tables up to six times at least, and be able to do the four rules of addition, subtraction, multiplication and division, working with tens and units and shillings and pence. They should also have a working knowledge of the simple forms of money, weight and length, and be able to tell the time.

John, who had had his gaze fixed on the ancient wall-clock, now gave six gigantic tugs on the rope, for it said five minutes to nine, and then, leaping up on to the corner desk, looped it up, out of temptation's way, on to a hook high on the wall.

Outside, we could hear the scuffle of feet and cries of excited children. Together Miss Clare and I walked out into the sunshine to meet our classes.

3. The Pattern of the Morning

My desk was being besieged by children, all eager to tell me of their holiday adventures.

'Miss, us went to Southsea with the Mothers' Union last week, and I've brought you back a stick of rock,' announced Anne.

Eric flapped a long rubbery piece of seaweed like a flail.

'It's for us to tell the weather by,' he explained earnestly. 'You hangs it up – out the lobby'l' do – and if it's wet it's going to rain – or is it if it's been wet it feels wet? I forgets just which, miss, but anyhow if it's dry it ain't going to rain.'

'Isn't,' I corrected automatically, rummaging in the top drawer of the desk for the dinner book.

'I know where there's mushrooms, miss. I'll bring you some for your tea s'afternoon.'

'They's not mushrooms, miss,' warned Eric. 'They's toadstools – honest, miss! Don't you eat 'em, miss! They's poison!'

I waved them away to their desks. Only the new children stood self-consciously in the front, looking at their shoes or at me for support. Linda Moffat's immaculate pink frock and glossy curls were getting a close scrutiny from the other children, but, unperturbed, she returned their round-eyed stares.

The children sit two in a desk and Anne, a cheerful nine-year-old, seemed Linda's best desk-mate.

'Look after Linda, Anne,' I said, 'she doesn't know anyone yet.'

Holding her diminutive red handbag, Linda settled down beside Anne. They gave each other covert looks under their lashes, and when their glances met exchanged smiles.

The four young ones, just up from Miss Clare's class, settled in two desks at the front. Once sitting in safety their shyness vanished, and they looked cheerfully about, grinning at their friends. They were at that engaging stage of losing their front milk teeth, and their gappy smiles emphasized their tender years. I went over to the piano.

'As we haven't given out the hymn books yet, we'll sing one we know by heart.'

They scrambled to their feet, desk seats clanging up behind

them, and piped 'The King of Love my Shepherd is,' rather sharp with excitement.

Our piano is made of walnut, and is full of years. The front has an intricate fretwork design and through the openings pleated red silk can be seen. The children look upon its venerable beauties with awed admiration. It has a melancholy, plangent tone, and two yellow keys which are obstinately dumb. These keys give a curiously syncopated air to the morning hymns.

Usually the whole school comes into this one classroom for prayers, but on the first morning of term it always seems best to stay in our own rooms and settle in quickly.

After the hymn we had a short prayer. With eyes screwed up tightly and hands solemnly folded beneath their chins the children looked misleadingly angelic. Patrick, the smallest, with head bowed low, was busily sucking his thumb, and I made a mental note that here was a habit to be corrected or otherwise his new second teeth would soon be in need of a brace. As I watched, a shilling fell from his clasped hands and rolled noisily towards me. Patrick opened one eye. It swivelled round like a solitaire marble, following the shilling's journey, then, catching my own eye upon it, it shut again with a snap.

After prayers we usually have a scripture lesson, or learn a new hymn or a psalm, until half-past nine, when arithmetic lesson begins; but on this morning we settled to more practical matters and the children came out in turn with their dinner money for the week. This was ninepence a day. Some children had also brought National Savings money, and this was entered in a separate book and stamps handed over to the child, if it possessed a safe place to put them, or put in a special Oxo tin until home time.

All but four children, who went home for their dinners, brought out their dinner money, and as they put it on my desk I looked at their hands. Sometimes they arrive at school so filthy, either through playing with mud on the way, or through sheer neglect in washing, that they are not fit to handle their books, and then out they are sent to the stone sink in the lobby, to wash in rainwater and carbolic soap. In this way too I can keep a watch on the nail-biters, and those culprits who, after a week's self-control, can show a proud sixteenth of an inch, are rewarded with sweets and flattery. Scabies, too, which first shows itself between the fingers, is a thing to watch for, though, happily, it is rare here; but it spreads quickly and is very aggravating to the sufferer.

While I was busy with all this, Miss Clare came through the partition door.

'May I speak to Cathy?' she asked. 'It's about Joseph's dinner money. Does his mother want him to stay?'

'Yes, miss,' said Cathy, looking rather startled, 'but she never gave me no money for him.'

'Didn't give me any money,' said Miss Clare automatically.

' "Didn't-give-me-any-money," I mean,' repeated Cathy, parrot-wise.

'I'll write a note for you to take to Mrs Coggs when you go home,' said Miss Clare, and lowering her voice to a discreet whisper, turned to me. 'May be difficult to get the money regularly from that family – a feckless woman!' And shaking her white head she returned to the infants.

The children were now beginning to get restless, for, normally, when I was busy they would take out a library book, or a notebook of their own making, which we called a 'busy book,' in which they could employ themselves in writing lists of birds, flowers, makes of cars, or any other things which interested them. They could, if they liked, copy down the multiplication tables, or the weekly poem or spelling list which hung upon the wall; but, at the moment, their desks were empty.

'Let me see who would like to come out and play "Left and Right," ' I said.

Peace reigned at once. Chests were flung out and faces assumed a fierce air of responsibility and trustworthiness.

'Patrick!' I called, choosing the smallest new boy, and he flushed a deep pink with pleasure.

'Left and Right' is the simplest and most absorbing game for occasions when a teacher is busy with something else. All that is needed is a small object to hide in one hand, a morsel of chalk, a bead or a halfpenny, any one, in fact, of the small things that litter the inkstand. The child in front, hands behind him, changes the treasure from one to the other; then, fists extended before him, he challenges someone to guess which hand it is in. Here the teacher, with half an eye on the game, one and a half on the business in hand, and her main object peace in which to carry it out, can say, 'Choose someone really quiet, dear. No fussy people; and, of course, no one who asks!' This deals a severe blow to the naughty little boys who are whispering 'Me! Choose me! Or else—!'

'Richard!' called Patrick to his desk-mate.

'Left!'

'No, right!' said Patrick, opening a sticky palm.

'That's left! Miss, that was left!' went up the protesting cry.

Patrick turned round to me indignantly.

'But you're facing the other way now!' I point out, and the age-long problem, which puzzles all children, had to be explained yet again.

At last the game continued its even tenor. Dinner money and savings money were both collected, checked and put in their separate tins. The register was called for the first time, and a neat red stroke in every square showed that we were all present.

The clock on the wall said twenty-past ten when we had finished handing out a pink exercise book each for English, a blue for arithmetic and a green for history and geography. Readers, pens, pencils, rulers and all the other paraphernalia of daily school life were now stored safely, and at the moment tidily, in their owner's possession.

The children collected milk and straws and settled down to refreshment. Luckily this term there were no milk-haters and all twenty-two bottles were soon emptied. When they had finished they went joyfully out to play.

I went across to my own quiet house and switched on the kettle. Two cups and saucers were already set on the tray in the kitchen, and the biscuit tin stood on the dresser. Miss Clare would be over in a minute. We took it in turns to do playground duty, guarding the coke pile from marauders, watching out for any sly teasing, and routing out the indoor-lovers who would prefer to sit in their desks even on the loveliest day. I went back to the playground while the kettle boiled.

Linda was undoing her packet of chocolate and Anne was trying to look unconcerned. Anne was always rather hungry, the child of a mother who went by early morning bus to the atomic research works some miles away, and who had little time to leave such niceties as elevenses for her daughter. There was no shortage of money in this home, but definitely a shortage of supervision. Anne's shoes were good, but dirty; her dinner money was often forgotten, and her socks frequently sported a hole. Her suspense now was shortlived, for Linda broke off a generous piece of her slab, handed it over, and cemented the friendship which had already begun.

'D'you mind being new?' asked Anne squelchily.

'Not now,' answered Linda, 'once all that staring's stopped, I don't mind; and if anyone tries hitting me my mum said I was to tell her.' She eyed the noisy children around her complacently. 'Not that they will, probably – and anyway,' she added, dropping her voice to a sinister whisper, 'I bites horrible!' Anne looked properly impressed.

Cathy, between bites of apple, was encouraging Joseph Coggs and her young brother to visit the boys' lavatory behind its green corrugated iron screen. At the other end of the playground, similarly screened, were two more bucket-type lavatories with well-scrubbed wooden seats, for the girls' use.

Mr Willet is our caretaker, and has the unenviable job of emptying the buckets three times a week; and this he does into deep holes which are dug on a piece of waste ground, some hundred yards away, behind his own cottage. Mrs Pringle, the school cleaner, scrubs seats and floors, and everything is kept as spotless as is possible with this deplorable and primitive type of sanitation.

Above the shouting of the children came the sound of the school gate clanging shut, and across the playground, his black suit glossy in the sunlight, came the vicar. Miss Clare hurried in to fetch another cup and saucer from the dresser and I went to meet him.

The Reverend Gerald Partridge has been vicar of Fairacre, and its adjoining parish of Beech Green, for only four years, and so is looked upon as a foreigner by most of his parishioners. His energetic wife is as brisk and practical as he is gentle and vague. He is chairman of the managers of Fairacre school and comes in every Friday morning to take a scripture lesson with the older children.

On this morning, he carried a list of hymns, which he asked me to teach the children during the term, and I said I would look through them. He sighed at my guarded answer, for he knew as well as I did that not all the hymns would be considered suitable by me for teaching to children. His weakness for the metaphysical poets led him into choosing quite inexplicable hymns about showers and brides, with lines like:

'Rend each man's temple-veil and bid it fall.'

or, worse still, Milton's poems set as hymns, containing such lines as:

'And speckled vanity
Will sicken soon and die,
And leprous sin will melt from earthly mould,'

all of which may be very fine in its way but is quite beyond the comprehension of the pupils here. The vicar smiles and nods his mild old head when I protest.

'Very well, my dear, very well. Just as you think best. Let us leave that hymn until they are older.' And then he meanders away to talk to the children, leaving me feeling a bully and browbeater.

He drank his tea and then started up his car, setting off, very slowly and carefully, down the road to his vicarage.

4. THE PATTERN OF THE AFTERNOON

One of the most difficult things to teach young children is to express themselves in sentences. When you listen to them talking you realize why. There is hardly a complete sentence in the whole conversation.

'Coming up shop?' says one.
'Can't! Mum's bad.'

'What's up with her?'

'Dunno.'

'Doctor come?'

'Us rung up. May come, s'pose,' and so on. There is a sure exchange of thought and some progress in this staccato method, but it does not make for any literary style when it comes to writing a composition.

The children in these parts are not, as a whole, great readers. A neighbouring schoolmaster, Mr Annett, put it succinctly: 'Most parents take the viewpoint of "What the devil are you doing wasting your time with a trashy book, when the carrots want thinning!" Or the beans want picking, or the wood wants chopping, or the snow wants sweeping – any of the urgent outdoor matters which beset a country child more than the town one. So out they are sent, with a clump on the ear to help them, and it almost seems wrong to some of them to read.'

Because of this attitude, and the children's own very understandable desire to help in outside activities in an agricultural area, they do not get accustomed to seeing or hearing thought expressed in plain English. A great number of them have great difficulty in spelling, other than phonetically, for they are not readers by habit and not familiar with the look of words. However, phonetically, they make the most gallant efforts, one of the nicest I ever received being the information that 'Donkeys like ssos' (thistles).

So, after play, we settled down to writing together on the blackboard a composite account of the holidays.

'John, tell me something that you did.'

'Went to the seaside, miss.'

'How?'

'Bus.'

'By yourself?'

'No. Lot of us kids went. Us went with the Mothers' Union, miss.'

'Right. Now put all that into sentences that I can write on the blackboard.'

There was a horrified silence. It was one thing to answer leading questions, but quite another thing to put them into even the simplest English.

'Well, come along. You can start by saying, "During the holidays I went to the seaside." '

John repeated this with some relief, hoping that left to my own devices I would do the whole composition for him. The first sentence was put up.

'What shall we put next?'

'I went in a bus,' said Anne.

I put it up.

'Now what?'

'I went with the Mothers' Union.'

'I went with some others.'

'I went on a Saturday.'

'I went with my sister.'

I pointed out that although these were all good sentences in themselves, it became a little monotonous to start every one with 'I went.' It was while we were wrestling with different wordings of the sentences that footsteps and clankings were heard. Sylvia rushed to the door and revealed Mrs Crossley, or, as the children call her, 'The Dinner Lady.'

She was balancing three tin boxes in an unsteady pile against her cardigan, and willing hands relieved her of them.

'Only two canisters today,' she said, and the children sat rigidly, hoping to be the lucky person chosen to fetch them from the mobile dinner-van at the school gate. Anne and Linda were chosen for this envied task and while they were gone, I signed the daily chit for Mrs Crossley, to say that I had received the number of dinners ordered. Then I gave her the slip showing how many dinners I estimated that I should need for the next day.

Mrs Crossley drives the dinner-van, loaded up about ten in the morning at the depot, and delivers dinners at about a dozen schools on her round of about twenty miles. Each school has a plate-heating oven which is switched on just before the dinners are due, and the tins are put in to keep warm with the plates. The big canisters are heat-retaining and very heavy to handle. Stews, hot potatoes and other vegetables, custard or sauces, are delivered in these and the meals are usually very good indeed. In the summer, salads are frequent, and the children eat most things heartily except fish. This, even when fried, is not relished, and recently it has been struck off the menu as there was so much wasted.

Cathy was sent through to the infants' room to see if the tables were ready. Miss Clare's class had gone out for the last period of the morning to have their physical training lesson, leaving the classroom empty for the arrangement of three trestle-tables for the dinner children. Miss Clare had switched on the oven, which was in her room, and Cathy laid the tables for thirty. Those who went home to dinner were sent off; the others washed their hands and then we all took our places at the tables. It was ten past twelve and we were all hoping for something good in the tins.

Miss Clare and I served out slices of cold meat, mashed potatoes and salad, and Sylvia and Cathy and Anne carried them round. Miss Clare sat at the head of one table and I at another, and when we had finished the first course two big boys, John and Ernest, cleared away. It was followed by plums and custard. Jimmy Waites was still rather awed by his new surroundings and ate very little, but Joseph Coggs, who, I suspected, very seldom had a dinner as well-prepared as this, ate a prodigious amount, coming up for a third helping of plums and custard with the older children.

When we had stacked the dirty crockery and cutlery ready for Mrs Pringle, and cleared the tables of their checked mackintosh tablecloths, the children went out to play and Miss Clare and I went over to the school-house to wash ourselves and tidy up ready for afternoon school.

Mrs Pringle was surrounded by clouds of steam when I returned to the lobby.

'Did you have a good holiday?' I asked her.

'Not much of a holiday for me, scrubbing this whole place out!' was the rejoinder.

'Well, it all looks very nice, anyway.'

'How long for?' said Mrs Pringle acidly. She is one of the happy martyrs of this world, hugging her grudges to her and relishing every insult as a toothsome morsel. Why she carries on the job of school caretaker I can't think, unless its very nature, that of work quickly undone, appeals to her warped spirit. Children she looks upon as conspirators against cleanliness and order; and the idea of any sort of mess of their making being accidental, or, worse still, legitimate, is unbelievable to her.

Her great loves are the two slow-burning tortoise stoves. These two ugly monsters she polishes till they gleam like jet, and it gives her real pain to see them lit, with the ashes dropping untidily round them. The coke cauldrons are a torture to her, for these make more mess, and during the winter months relations are more than usually strained between us.

There is almost a battle when it comes to starting up the stoves at the approach of the cold weather. I refuse to have the children sitting in a cold schoolroom, incapable of work and the prey of any germs at large, when the stoves are there and mountains of coke stand between us and misery.

Mrs Pringle's methods are subtle when I have given firm orders for the stove to be lit. For a day or two she stalls with 'Ran out of matches,' or 'Mr Willet did say he'd bring up the kindling wood, but he ain't done it yet,' but finding that I have lit the fire myself she gives in and continues, most reluctantly, to renew it each day. This does not mean to say that the matter is closed. Far from it; for should she have occasion to enter the room she will fan herself ostentatiously with her hand – often mauve with the cold – and say, 'Phew! How can you stick this heat, I don't know! Makes me come over real faint meself!' Sometimes the attack is on a broader front and the ratepayers are brought in as support.

'Coke's going down pretty smartish. Shouldn't be surprised if we don't get a letter from the Office the way we gets through it. Stands to reason the Office has to keep upsides the ratepayers!'

'The Office' is, of course, the local education office and the only real link between it and Mrs Pringle is the cheque which arrives from it for her services at the end of every month. Mrs Pringle, consequently, looks upon 'The Office' in rather the same way as she looks upon the Almighty, invisible and omnipotent.

This afternoon I beat a retreat into my classroom, but was closely pursued by Mrs Pringle, dripping from the elbows.

'What's more,' she said malevolently, 'we're a spoon short. You been mixing up paste again?'

'No,' I said shortly, 'you'd better count them again.' This is an old feud, dating from five years ago when I once committed the unforgivable crime of borrowing a school spoon because I had mislaid the usual wooden one. Mrs Pringle has never allowed me to forget this deplorable lapse.

At a quarter past one the children came back into their desks, breathless and cheerful, and after we had marked the register we tackled our joint composition again. After a while afternoon somnolence began to descend upon them, and when I thought they had studied the example of fair English, which they had been driven into producing, long enough, I went to the piano and we sang some of the songs which they had learnt the term before.

After play large sheets of paper were given out and the boxes of wax crayons; and the children were asked to illustrate either their day at the seaside or any other particular day that they had enjoyed during the past few weeks.

Industriously they set to work, blue crayons were scrabbled furiously along the bottom of the papers for the sea and yellow suns like daisies flowered on all sides. The room was quiet and happy, the afternoon sun beat in through the Gothic windows and the clock on the wall stepped out its measured tread to home-time at half-past three. As most of the children stay to dinner, and those that do go home live so very near, it seems wiser to have a short break at midday, start afternoon school early and finish early. In the summer this means that the children get a long spell of sunshine outdoors, and in the winter they can be safely home before it becomes dark.

We collected up our pictures and crayons and tidied up the room. The first day at school is always a long one, and the children looked sleepy.

The infants, who had been let out earlier, could be heard calling to each other as they ran up the road.

We stood and sang grace, wished each other 'Good afternoon' and made our way into the lobby. Jimmy and Joseph were standing there, anxiously waiting for Cathy.

'Did you enjoy school?' I asked them. Jimmy nodded.

'What about you, Joseph?'

'I liked the dinner,' he answered diplomatically in his husky gipsy voice. I left it at that.

Miss Clare was wheeling her bicycle across the playground. It struck me suddenly that she was looking old and tired.

She mounted carefully and rode slowly away down the road, upright and steady, but it seemed to me, as I stood watching her progress, that it needed more effort than usual; and this was only the first day of term.

How long, I wondered, would she be able to continue?

I had my tea in the warm sunshine of the garden at the back of my school-house. The schoolmaster who had lived here before me was a great gardener, and had planted currant bushes, black and red, raspberries and gooseberries. These were safely enmeshed in a wire run to keep the birds off, and I bottled the crops or made jelly and jam in the evenings or in the holidays.

I had planted two herbaceous borders, one on each side of the garden, both edged with Mrs Sinkins' pinks which liked the chalky soil. Vegetables I did not bother to plant, not only because of the lack of room, but also because kind neighbours gave me more than I could really cope with, week after week. Broad beans, shallots, peas, carrots, turnips, brussels sprouts, cabbage, they all came in generous supplies to my doorstep. Sometimes the donors were almost too generous, forgetting, I suppose, how relatively little one woman can eat. I have found before now no less than five rotund vegetable marrows, like abandoned babies, on my doorstep in one week.

The difficulty is in handing these over to someone who might like them, without offending the giver. In a village this is doubly difficult as almost all are related, or close neighbours, or know exactly what is going on in the cottages nearby. I have been driven to digging dark, secret holes, under cover of night, and shovelling in many an armful of lettuce or several mammoth parsnips that have beaten my appetite.

I made some jam in the evening with a basket of early black plums which John Pringle, Mrs Pringle's only son, and a near neighbour of mine, had brought me.

The kitchen was very pleasant as I stirred. The window over the stone sink looks out on to the garden. A massive lead pump with a long handle stands by the side of the sink, and it is from this that I fill the buckets for the school's drinking water. When the water supply is laid on through the village, which may be in a few years' time, I have been promised a new deep sink by the managers.

In one corner stands a large brick copper and my predecessors used this to heat water for their baths, lighting a fire each time, but I have an electric copper which saves much time and trouble. The bath is a long zinc one, which hangs in the porch outside the back door, and it is put on the kitchen floor at bath time and filled from the tap at the bottom of the copper and cooled with buckets from the pump. With a bath towel warming over the hot copper and the kitchen well steamed up it is very snug.

The rest of the house downstairs consists of a large dining-room with a brick fireplace, a small hall and a small sitting-room. I rarely use this room as it faces north, but live mainly in the dining-room which is warmer, has a bigger fireplace and is convenient for the kitchen.

Upstairs there are two bedrooms, both fairly large, one over the kitchen and sitting-room, and the other, in which I sleep, directly above the dining-room. Throughout the house the walls are distempered a dove grey and all the paintwork is white. It is a solidly-built house of red brick, with a red-tiled roof, and in its setting of trees it looks most attractive. I am very fond of it indeed, and luckier, I realize, than many country headmistresses.

5 · First Impressions

In their adjoining cottages at Tyler's Row the two new pupils at Fairacre School were safely in bed, but not yet asleep.

Jimmy Waites lay on his lumpy flock mattress in a big brass bedstead which had once been his grandmother's. It had been the pride of her heart, and she had slept in it as a bride and until her death. The brass knobs at each corner, and the little ones across the head and the foot of the bed, had been polished so often that they were loose. His grandmother had told Jimmy that when she was a young woman she had tied a fresh blue bow at each bed-post, and the sides had been decently draped in white starched valances reaching to the floor. The edges of these she had crimped with a goffering iron. With a patchwork quilt on top, the bed must have been a thing of great beauty.

These refinements had long since passed away. The remains of the patchwork quilt were still in use as an ironing cloth; but the bows and the valances had vanished. Even so, Jimmy was very proud of the brass bedstead. In one of the loose knobs he kept his treasures: a very old piece of chewing gum, a glass marble, and a number of leather discs which he had cut secretly from the flock mattress. This operation had, in part, contributed to the general lumpiness.

Cathy shared this bed with him on the landing-bedroom. The stairs came straight up from the living-room to this room of theirs, and it was inclined to be draughty. A small window gave what light it could, but an old pear tree growing close against the side of the house spread its branches too near to allow much illumination. In the summer the light filtered through its thick green foliage gave a curiously under-water effect to the room, as the shadows wavered against the walls. In the winter the skinny branches tapped and scraped the glass, like bony questing fingers, and Jimmy buried his head under the clothes to muffle his terror.

His two older sisters slept downstairs, for they had to be up first, and were out of the house and waiting at the top of the road for the first bus to Caxley at seven each morning.

His father and mother slept in the only other bedroom that

opened out from the landing and was situated over the living-room. Until recently Jimmy had slept with them in his cot in the corner, but this he had now outgrown, and so he had been promoted to the brass bedstead. When one of his sisters married, which was to be this summer, the remaining one would probably take his place with Cathy in grandmother's bed, and he instead would have to sleep downstairs on the sofa. He did not like the idea of sleeping in a room of his own and resolutely put this fear from him at nights, determined to enjoy his present comforts.

As he lay there, sucking his thumb, drifting between sleeping and waking, the sights and sounds and smells of his first day at school crowded thick upon him. He saw the orderly rows of desks; some of them, including his own, had a twelve-inch square carved on to the lid, and he had enjoyed rubbing his fat forefinger along the grooves.

He remembered Miss Clare's soft voice; her big handbag and the little bottle of scent which she had taken from it. The top had rolled away towards the door and he had run to pick it up for her. She had dabbed a drop of cold scent into his palm for payment, but its fragrance had soon been lost in the ball of plasticine which he pummelled and rolled into buttons and marbles and, best of all, a long sinuous snake. He remembered the feel of it in his hand, dead, but horribly writhing as he swung it to and fro. Holding his stub of chalk, when he had tried to copy his letters from the blackboard, had not been so pleasurable. His fingers had clenched so tightly that they had ached.

He remembered the clatter of the milk bottles when the children returned them to the steel crate in the corner. He had enjoyed his milk largely because he had drunk it through a straw and this was new to him. It was gratifying to see the milk sink lower and lower in the bottle and to feel the cold liquid trickling down in his stomach.

He sighed, and wriggled down more closely into the lumpy mattress. Yes, he liked school. He'd have milk tomorrow with a straw, and play with plasticine snakes, and perhaps go and see Cathy again in the next room. Cathy . . . he was glad Cathy was there too. School was all very nice but there was nothing quite like home, where everything was old and familiar. Still sucking his thumb, Jimmy fell asleep.

Next door Joseph Coggs lay on a decrepit camp bed and listened to his parents talking downstairs. Their voices carried clearly up the stairs to the landing-bedroom, and he knew that his father was angry.

'Ninepence a day! Lot of nonsense! Pay four bob a week, near enough, for Joe's dinners alone? Not likely! You give 'un a bit o' bread and cheese same as you gives me, my girl.'

Arthur Coggs also went on the early bus to Caxley. He was employed as an unskilled labourer with a building firm, and he spent his days mixing cement, carrying buckets and wheeling barrows. At twelve o'clock he sat down with his mates to eat the bread and cheese, and sometimes a raw onion, which his wife had packed for him. Joseph knew those packed dinners by sight – thick slabs of bread smeared with margarine and an unappetizing hunk of dry cheese – and his spirits drooped at the thought of having to take such victuals to school, and, worse still, of having to eat them within sight and smell of the luscious food such as he had enjoyed that day.

Beside his own bed, so close that he could touch the grey army blanket that covered it, was an iron bedstead containing his two younger sisters. They slept soundly, their matted heads close together on the striped ticking of a dirty pillow which boasted no such effete nonsense as a pillowslip. Their small pink mouths were half open and they snored gently.

Next door, in his parents' bedroom, he could hear the baby whimpering. He was devoted to this youngest child and suffered dreadfully in sympathy when it cried. Its small red fists and bawling mouth affected him deeply and he would do anything to appease its wants. He wished his mother would let him hold it more often, but she was impatient of his offers of help and pushed him out of her way.

'Mind now,' he heard his father shout, 'you do as I say. He can pay for what he's had, but you put him up summat same as me!'

To Joseph, listening aloft, these were sad words, for although he too had dwelt on the new experiences of the day, as had the boy next door, and though the plasticine, milk bottles, desks and children had all made their lasting impression on his young mind, it was the dinner, warm and plentiful, the plums and, most of all, those three swimming platefuls of golden custard, that had meant most to young Joseph Coggs.

Two fat tears coursed down his face as, philosophically, he turned on his creaking bed and settled down to sleep.

Mr and Mrs Moffat were making a rug together, one at each end. It was an intricate pattern of roses in a basket on a black background.

It was designed to lie before the shiny tiled fireplace of the small drawing-room, which was Mrs Moffat's new joy. When they had lived above their shop in Caxley, she had thought long and often about the furnishing of a drawing-room when she should have such a luxury, and she had cut out of the women's magazines, that she loved, many pictures and diagrams of suggested layouts for such rooms, as well as actual photographs of film stars' apartments.

If she had had her real wish she would have had a tiger skin as a hearth-rug, but she realized that her present drawing-room, which was only twelve feet by ten, would be hopelessly dwarfed by this extravagance, and that dream was put away with the others.

As their hooks flashed in and out of the canvas, Mr Moffat inquired about his daughter's debut at the village school.

'She didn't say much,' said Mrs Moffat, 'and she kept her clothes nice and clean. She's sitting by Anne Someone-or-other. Her mother works up the Atomic.'

'I know her dad. Nice chap he is; works for Heath the farmer. I met him at the pub.'

'Well, that's something! I don't want Linda picking up anything. Those ringlets take enough time without anything else.'

'She'll pick up nothing from that family she didn't ought!' replied Mr Moffat shortly. 'Won't hurt her to rough it a bit. You make a sissy of her.'

Mrs Moffat went pink. She realized the rough truth of this remark, but she resented the fact that all her striving and ambition for their only daughter should go unrecognized, and simply be dismissed as feminine vanity. It was more than that, but how to express it was beyond her powers.

She relapsed into hurt silence. If it hadn't been for her efforts they would still have been living over that poky shop, she thought to herself. She wanted Linda to have a better chance than she had had herself. She wanted her daughter to have all the things that she had wanted so dreadfully herself when she was young. A dance frock, with a full skirt and ruched bodice, a handbag to go with each change of clothes; she wanted Linda to join a tennis club, even perhaps go riding in immaculate jodhpurs and a hard hat. What Mrs Moffat's fierce maternal love ignored was the fact that Linda might be very well content without these social trappings that meant so much to her mother.

Mr Moffat sensed that he had upset his wife again. In silence they thrust the wool through the canvas and Mr Moffat thought, not for the first time, what kittle-cattle women were.

Linda, in her new pale-blue bed in the little back bedroom was thinking about her new friend Anne. It was a pity she was so untidy; her mother would mind about that if she invited her to play one Saturday, but nevertheless she would do so. She liked this new school; the children had admired her frock and red shoes and she realized that she could queen it here far more easily than at the little private school which she had attended in Caxley. There had been too many other mothers of the same calibre as Mrs Moffat there, all vying with each other in dressing up their children and exhorting them to speak in refined voices. It had been an effort, Linda realized now, all the time. At the village school, despite her mother's warnings, she knew that she would be able to relax in the other children's company.

The thing that worried Linda most, as she looked back upon her first day at school, was the lavatories. She was appalled at this primitive sanitation. Caxley had had main drainage, and her own new bathroom at the bungalow was fitted with a water-closet. She had never before come across a bucket-type lavatory and the memory of her few minutes there that morning, with her nose firmly pressed into her hands which smelt of lavender soap, made her shudder. She made a mental note that she would sprinkle toilet water on her handkerchief tomorrow against the perils of the day; and while she was debating which of her two minute bottles, lavender or carnation, she would use, she dropped suddenly into sleep.

While Miss Clare and I were enjoying our tea one morning at the school-house, the telephone rang. It was Mr Annett's high-pitched voice that assaulted my ear with a torrent of words. He is the schoolmaster at Beech Green, a quick, impatient man, a widower, living with an old Scotch housekeeper in the school-house there. He had only been married for six months when his young wife was killed in an air-raid at Bristol, near where his London school had been evacuated. Very soon afterwards he had sold most of their possessions and taken the little headship at Beech Green. He spends his life fighting a long, losing battle against the country child's slowness of wits and leisurely tempo of progress. He is also the choirmaster of St Patrick's.

'Look here,' he gabbled, 'it's about the Harvest Festival. Mrs Pratt can't get along to play the organ tonight – one of the children's down with chicken-pox – and I wondered if you could step in. We want to practise the anthem, "The Valleys Stand so Thick with Corn." D'you know it? You must do; we've had it every Harvest Festival since the war ended and still they don't know it!'

There was the sound of a scuffle at the end of the telephone.

'Well, get out of the way, you fool!' shouted Mr Annett exasperated. 'Not you, of course, Miss Read, the cat! Well, can you? At half-past seven? Thanks, I'll see you then.' The telephone dropped with a clatter and I could imagine Mr Annett sprinting on to the next job, quivering with nervous energy.

I finished my tea reviewing the evening's work before me. One thing, I was certain of plenty of amusement.

6. CHOIR PRACTICE

The heavy church door groaned open, and the chill odour, a mixture of musty hymn-books and brass polish, greeted me as I tiptoed down the shining aisle for choir practice.

Mr Annett was already there, flitting about the chancel from one side to the other, putting out copies of the anthem, for all the world like an agitated wren. His fingers flickered to his mouth, and back to his papers, as he separated them impatiently.

'Good evening, good evening! This is good of you. Anyone in sight? No sense of time, these people! Nearly half-past now! Enough to drive you mad!' His words jerked out as he darted breathlessly about. A leaflet fluttered down to the hideous lozenge-patterned carpet which covers the chancel floor.

As he was scrabbling it up wildly, we heard the sound of country voices at the door, and a little knot of people entered. Mr Willet and his wife were there, two or three of my older pupils, looking sheepish at seeing me in an unusual setting, and Mrs Pringle brought up the rear. Mrs Pringle's booming contralto voice tends to drown the rest of the choir with its peculiarly strong carrying qualities. As her note reading is far from accurate, and she resents any sort of correction, Mrs Pringle is rather more of a liability than an asset to St Patrick's church choir; but her aggressive piety, expressing itself in the deepest genuflections, the most military sharp-turns to the east and the raising of eyes to the chancel roof, is an example to the fidgety choir-boys, and Mr Annett bears with her mannerisms with commendable fortitude.

I went through to the vestry to see if Eric, my organ blower, was at his post. The vestry was warm and homely. The table was covered with a red serge cloth with a fringe of bobbles. On it stood a massive ink bottle containing an inch of ink, which had dried to the consistency of honey. Leaning negligently against the table was Eric, looking unpleasantly grubby, and blowing gum bubbles from his mouth in a placid way.

'For pity's sake, Eric,' I protested, 'not in here, please!'

He turned pink, gobbled, and then, to my consternation, gave an enormous gulp, his eyes bulging.

'Gorn!' he announced with relief.

'I didn't intend you to *swallow* it, Eric—' I began, while dreadful visions of acute internal pains, ambulances, distracted parents and awful recriminations crowded upon me.

'It don't hurt you,' Eric reassured me. 'I often eats it – gives you the hiccups sometimes. That's all!'

Shaken, I returned to the organ and set out the music. Four or five more choir members had arrived and Mr Annett was fidgeting to begin. Snatches of conversation drifted over to me.

'But a *guinea*, mark you, just for killing an old pig!'

'Ah! But you got all the meat and lard and that, look! I knows you has to keep 'un all the year, and a guinea do seem a lot, I'll own up, but still—'

'Well, well!' broke in Mr Annett's staccato voice. 'Shall we make a start?'

'Young Mrs Pickett said to tell you she'd be along presently when she'd got the baby down. He's been a bit poorly—'

This piece of news started a fresh burst of comment, while Mr Annett raised and lowered himself impatiently on his toes.

'Poor little crow! Teeth, I don't wonder!'

'She called in nurse.'

'Funny, that! I see her only this morning up the shop—'

Mr Annett's patience snapped suddenly. He rattled his baton on the reading desk and flashed his eyes.

'Please, please! I'm afraid we must begin without Mrs Pickett. Ready, Miss Read? One, two!' We were off.

Behind me the voices rose and fell, Mrs Pringle's concentrated lowing vying with Mrs Willet's nasal soprano. Mrs Willet clings to her notes so cloyingly that she is usually half a bar behind the rest. Her voice has that penetrating and lugubrious quality found in female singers' renderings of 'Abide With Me' outside public houses on Saturday nights. She has a tendency to over-emphasize the final consonants and draw out the vowels to such excruciating lengths, and all this executed with such devilish shrillness, that every nerve is set jangling.

This evening Mrs Willet's time-lag was even worse than usual. Mr Annett called a halt.

'This,' he pleaded, 'is a cheerful lively piece of music. The valleys, we're told, laugh and sing. Lightly, please, let it trip, let it be merry! Miss Read, could you play it again?'

As trippingly and as nimbly as I could I obliged, watching Mr Annett's black, nodding head in the mirror above the organ. The tuft of his double crown flicked half a beat behind the rest of his head.

'Once more!' he commanded, and obediently the heavy, measured tones dragged forth, Mr Annett's baton beating a brisk but independent rhythm. Suddenly he flung his hands up and gave a slight scream. The choir slowed to a ragged halt and pained glances were exchanged. Mrs Pringle's mouth was buttoned into its most disapproving lines, and even Mr Willet's stolid countenance was faintly perturbed.

'The *time*! The *time*!' shouted Mr Annett, baton pounding on the desk. 'Listen again!' He gesticulated menacingly at my mirror and I played it again. 'You hear it? It goes:

'They *dance*, bong-bong,
 They *sing*, bong-bong,
 They *dance*, BONG and BONG, *sing* BONG-BONG!

It's just as simple as that! Now, with me!'

With his hair on end and his eyes gleaming dangerously, Mr Annett led them once more into action. Gallantly they battled on, Mr Annett straining like an eager puppy at the leash, while the slow voices rolled steadily along behind.

The lights had been put on in the chancel, but the rest of the church was cavernous and shadowy, making an age-old back-cloth, aloof and beautiful, for this one hour's rustic comedy.

On the wall of the chancel stood the marble bust of Sir Charles Dagbury, once lord of the manor of this parish, staring with sightless eyes across the scene. On each side of his proud, disdainful face fell symmetrical cascades of curls, and his nostrils were curved as though with distaste for the rude mortals busking below.

The furious tapping of Mr Annett's baton broke the spell.

'David,' he was saying to the smallest choir-boy, 'get up on a hassock, child! Your head's hardly showing.'

'But I'm up on one, sir,' protested David, looking aggrieved.

'Sorry, sorry! Never met such badly-designed choir-stalls in my life,' announced Mr Annett, with the fine disregard of the towns-man for the dangers this sort of remark incurs. 'Much too tall, and hideous at that!'

There was a sharp hiss as Mrs Pringle drew an outraged breath.

'My old grandfather,' she began heavily, 'though a trying old gentleman at the last, and should by rights have gone to the infirmary, such a dance as he led his poor wife, was as fine a carpenter as you could wish to meet in a day's march, and these choir-stalls here,' she leant forward menacingly and slapped one of them with a substantial hand – 'these here very choir-stalls was reckoned one of his best bits of work! Ain't that right?' she demanded of her abashed neighbours.

There were awkward mutterings and shufflings. Mr Annett had the grace to flush and look ashamed.

'I do apologize, Mrs Pringle,' he said handsomely. 'I meant no offence to the craftsman who made the choir-stalls. First-class work, obviously. It was the design I was criticizing.'

'My grandfather,' boomed Mrs Pringle, with awful intensity, 'DESIGNED THEM TOO!'

'I can only apologize again,' said Mr Annett, 'and hope that you will forgive my unfortunate remarks.' He coughed nervously. 'Well, to continue! Next Sunday we shall have "Pleasant are Thy Courts Above" and I thought we'd try the descant in the second verse only. All agreeable?'

There was a murmur of assent from all except Mr Willet, who has a somewhat Calvinistic attitude to church affairs.

'I likes to hear a hymn sung straightforward myself,' he said, blowing out his tobacco-stained moustache, 'these fiddle-faddles takes your mind off the words, I reckon.'

'I'm sorry to hear that you think so,' said Mr Annett. 'What's the general feeling?' He looked round at the company, baton stuck through his hair.

Nobody answered, as nobody wanted to fall out with either Mr Willet or Mr Annett. In the silence Eric could be heard creaking about in the vestry. There was suddenly a shattering hiccup.

'Then we'll carry on,' said Mr Annett, jerked back to life by this explosion. 'Descant verse two only. The psalms we've practised and – oh, yes – before I forget! We'll have the seven-fold Amen at the end of the service.'

Mr Willet snorted and muttered heavily under his moustache.

'Well, what now?' snapped Mr Annett irritably. 'What's the objection to the seven-fold Amen?'

'Popish!' said Mr Willet, puffing out the moustache. 'I'm a plain man, Mr Annett, a plain man that's been brought up God-fearing; and to praise the Lord in a bit of respectable music is one thing, but seven-fold Amens is taking it too far, to my way of thinking. And my wife here,' he said, rounding fiercely on the shrinking Mrs Willet, 'agrees with me! Don't you?' he added, thrusting his face belligerently to hers.

'Yes, dear,' said Mrs Willet faintly.

'It's a pity—' began Mr Annett.

'And while we're at it,' continued Mr Willet loudly, brushing aside this interruption, 'what's become of them copies of the hymn-books done in atomic-sulphur?'

Mr Annett looked bewildered, as well he might.

'You know the ones, green covers they had, with the music and atomic-sulphur written just above. I'm used to 'em. We was all taught atomic-sulphur years ago at the village school, when schooling WAS schooling, I may say – and all us folks my age gets on best with it!'

'I believe they are in a box in the vestry,' said Mr Annett, pulling himself together, 'and of course you can use the copies with tonic solfa if you prefer them. They'd become rather shabby, that's why the vicar put them on one side.'

Mr Willet, having had his say, was now prepared to be mollified, and grunted accordingly.

Mr Annett began to shovel music back into his case.

'Thank you, ladies and gentlemen. Next week, at the same time? Good evening, everybody. Yes, I think the anthem will go splendidly on the day – good night, good night.'

They drifted away into the shadows of the church, past the empty pews, the font, and the memorial tablets and tombs of their forefathers. Quietness came flooding back again. I locked the organ and went out to the vestry.

Eric, glistening from his exertions, was still struggling with recalcitrant hiccups, but seemed otherwise in excellent health. Mr Annett was giving him a shilling for his labours.

'And if you buy any more of that horrible gum,' I told him, 'eat it at home. If I see any in school it goes into the waste-paper basket, my boy!'

Grinning cheerfully he clattered off down the vestry steps and we followed him into the soft evening air.

The choir members were gossiping at the church gate, hidden from us by the angle of the wall. Their voices floated clearly across the graveyard.

'I believes in speaking my mind,' Mr Willet was saying firmly, ' "Speak the truth and shame the devil!" There's plenty o' sense in that. That young Annett'd have us daubed with incense, like Ancient Britons, if he had his way!'

''Tis nothing to do with him – incense and that. 'Tis the vicar's job and he's all right,' asserted a woman's voice.

Mrs Pringle had the last word. 'I trounced him proper about my grandpa! What if he was a sore trial at times? He was my own flesh and blood, wasn't he? Fair made me boil to hear him spoke of so low—' The booming voice died away as the footsteps grew fainter and fainter on the flinty road.

7. MISS CLARE FALLS ILL

Term was now several weeks old. Jimmy, Joseph and Linda had settled down and played schools, space-ships and shops in the playground as noisily as the rest.

Mrs Coggs had taken a job at the public house down the lane. Each morning she spent two hours there, washing glasses and scrubbing out the bar parlour, while the baby slept in its pram in the garden where she could keep an eye on it.

This arrangement had happy results for Joseph. For three or four weeks he had brought craggy slices of bread to school for his lunch, with an occasional apple or a few plums to enliven it; and this dreary meal he had eaten sadly, his dark eyes fixed upon the school dinners that his more fortunate fellows were demolishing.

But now, with money of her own in her pocket, Mrs Coggs was able to rebel against her husband's order of 'No school dinner for our Joe!' and to everyone's satisfaction Joseph returned to the dinner table, a broad smile on his face and a three-helping appetite keener than ever.

The weather had been mellow and golden all through September. The harvest had been heavy, the stacks were already being thatched, and housewives were hard at it bottling and jamming a bumper crop of apples, plums and damsons. Even Mrs Pringle admitted that the weather was lovely, and looked with gratification at the two unsullied stoves.

But one morning I awoke to a changed world. A border of scarlet dahlias, as brave as guardsmen the afternoon before, drooped, brown and clammy; and the grass was grey with frost.

The distant downs had vanished behind a white mist and

below the elm trees the yellow leaves were thickening fast into an autumn carpet.

After breakfast I went across to the school to face Mrs Pringle. She was rubbing the desks with a blue-check duster. Her expression was defensive.

'Mrs Pringle,' I began bravely, 'if it is like this tomorrow we must put the stoves on.'

'The *stoves*!' said Mrs Pringle, opening her eyes with amazement. 'Why, miss, we shan't need those for a week or so yet. This 'ere's a heat mist. You'll see – it'll clear to a real hot day!'

'I doubt it,' I replied shortly. 'Get firewood and coke in tonight in case this weather has set in. I'll listen to the forecast this evening and let you know definitely first thing tomorrow morning.'

I returned to the school-house feeling that the preliminary skirmish had gone well. Mrs Pringle I had left, muttering darkly, as she flicked the window-sills.

During the morning a watery sun struggled through, its rays falling across the children's down-bent heads as they struggled with their arithmetic. It was very quiet in the classroom. There was a low buzzing from the infants' side of the partition and the measured ticking of the ancient clock on the wall.

Suddenly, we were all frightened out of our wits by a heavy banging at the door. It was Mr Roberts the farmer, and one of his men, Tom Bates. Each carried a stout sheaf of corn. Behind me, the children chattered excitedly.

'Vicar said you'd be needing this for decorating the church for Harvest Festival on Sunday,' said Mr Roberts in his cheerful bellow. He is one of our more energetic school managers, as well as our near neighbour, so that he comes in to see us very often. He stamped into the room followed by Tom Bates and put the corn down by a long desk which stands at the side of the room. The floor-boards shook with the tremor of their heavy boots and the thud of corn.

The children always like Mr Roberts to come into the schoolroom. He is an enormous man with hands like hams and legs as thick as tree trunks. Once when he visited us he stepped back into the easel, capsizing the blackboard, a pot of catkins and a small boy who had been hovering in the vicinity. The children are always hopeful that this glorious confusion may happen again; and certainly their eyes light up at Mr Roberts' advent.

'If you want any more,' said Mr Roberts, stepping perilously near the milk crate, 'just you let me know. Plenty where that came from!' He skirted the easel adroitly and vanished into the lobby after Tom.

Hubbub broke out; long division, shopping bills, pounds and ounces were all neglected as the children surveyed the riches on the floor.

'Can us do 'em this afternoon, miss?'

'You said us boys could make the bunches this time.'

'The girls done it all last time.'

'Vicar said all us schoolchildren could do the altar rail.'

'No, he never then! The Guides always does the altar rail.'

I interposed. 'Nothing will be done until this afternoon. Get on with your arithmetic.'

Sadly they bent to their task again. Pens scratched in ink-wells, fingers were surreptitiously counted under desks, brows were furrowed and lips moved, as if in prayer, as the work went on again.

It has always been the custom in this parish for the children of Fairacre School to decorate certain parts of the church for Harvest Festival. The pew ends are always in our care and, this year, the altar rail had been given into our charge too. Last year we had been allowed to adorn the font steps, and striped marrows had jostled with mammoth cooking apples for a foot-hold. The corn is divided up into small bunches to be tied to the pew ends, the rest being left for the other decorators to use in other parts of the church.

Mrs Pringle snorted with disgust as she passed through the room after dinner, on the way to her steaming boiler.

'Fine old mess, that's all's to be said about corn! Fancy bringing that ol' stuff in here all over my clean floor! No more than a pighole this room'll be for two days, I can see! Shan't waste me strength on it till the lot's cleared out.'

She kicked the sheaf contemptuously to one side with her black laced boot to show her disgust of the whole concern.

*

The children squatted among the straw like so many clucking hens, their fingers busily arranging the corn into neat bunches. They chatted to each other as they scratched about the floor.

Next door the infants were employed in the same way. There was always a great surge of happiness in the school as they prepared for Harvest Festival. Tomorrow they would bring their own offerings from home: scrubbed carrots, bronzed onions, cabbages like footballs, and any other fruits of the earth that they could cajole from their parents. These, with our bunches of corn we would carry to the church, and this was the excitement to which they were now looking forward so eagerly.

While they were busily employed the door of the partition opened a crack and a dark eye appeared. I waited to see what would happen.

Gradually the crack widened and Joseph Coggs, finger in mouth, gazed silently at me. I gazed back, amused, wondering if he would come in or scamper away. He did neither. He stood stock-still and then beckoned to me urgently.

'Say!' he called in his husky voice, 'Miss Clare's been and fallen over!'

Panic gripped me as I fled into the infants' room. The chattering of my own class continued unconcernedly behind me as I closed the dividing door.

It was very quiet in Miss Clare's room. The children stood round her chair gaping, while slumped across the table, her white hair lying in a pool of water from an overturned vase, lay their teacher. Her lips were blue and she moaned in a terrifying rhythm.

'Take your bunches,' I said hastily, 'and go into my room.' They moved away slowly as I bent over her. At this moment she gave a little sigh and raised her head. Voices floated through the door.

'Look at all them babies coming in our room!'

'Here, what's up?'

'You git back in your own place!'

'You are all to work together,' I ordered from the door. 'And quietly! Miss Clare's not very well. There will be sweets for people who work best!' This shameless piece of bribery was justified by the occasion, I felt.

I shut the door firmly. Miss Clare looked at me with a wan smile.

'A drink,' she whispered.

The floor of the lobby was still damp from Mrs Pringle's scrubbing brush and the windows covered in steam. I whipped the clean cloth from the top of the drinking bucket and filled a mug.

The colour gradually crept back into Miss Clare's cheeks as she sipped. I sat on the front desk and watched her anxiously.

'Will you be all right for a minute while I go across to fill a hot bottle? Then I will help you over there.'

'There's no need,' protested Miss Clare, flushing pink at the thought of leaving her post in the middle of the afternoon, 'I can manage now. This isn't the first time this has happened; but luckily it's never happened in school.'

'Just sit still for a few minutes and I'll be back,' I told her, and went through to the children, my legs wobbling under me in the most cowardly fashion. It was a relief to enter this normal buzzing atmosphere and to breathe the homely smell of straw.

'Get on quietly,' I said as I tottered through. 'I'll be back soon.'

I switched on the kettle and rang Miss Clare's doctor. By a miracle he was in and promised to come at once. I helped Miss Clare across to the school-house and Dr Martin arrived as I was tucking the rug round her on the sofa. I poured them some tea and returned to school.

It is a funny thing, but faced with a crisis, children always suffer a sea-change for the better. When they might well be resentful at changes of plan and deprivation of their liberty they become instead soft-voiced and unnervingly angelic. Perhaps the sudden removal of adult supervision lessens the tension, and they feel relaxed and happy. I can't account for it, but it has happened to me many times. On the occasions when an accident has befallen one child and I have imagined rioting and mayhem breaking out among the others in my absence, I have always tortured myself unnecessarily, and returned to find as meek a flock of lambs as ever rejoiced a teacher's heart.

This afternoon was no exception, and thankfully I passed round the sweet tin.

Cathy collected the bundles of straw; dozens of them, ranging from sleek beauties to ragged mops; the floor looked like a chicken run, littered with straw and some bright specks of grain which Jimmy Waites was picking up with his fat fingers.

'For me bantam cock,' he explained, 'and if he lays an egg I'll bring it for you, miss.' Cathy gave me a sidelong smile, as one woman to another in the presence of innocent childhood.

As they sang grace I pondered on the best message to send by the children about their early home-coming. It was inevitable that the news of Miss Clare's illness would get about rapidly, but I did not want a succession of visitors during the next hour or so. The majority would, no doubt, be anxious to be of use, but there were one or two whose ghoulish desire for any grisly details would bring them to my door, and these I felt I could not face for a little while.

'Tell your mothers,' I announced, 'that you are home early as Miss Clare is not very well this afternoon. I expect she will be back tomorrow.'

This white lie I hoped would keep the more avid newsmongers at bay.

A spiteful little wind had sprung up, spattering the windows with the flying elm leaves, as the children straggled away. A tiny whirlwind chased the dead leaves rustling round and round by the door-scraper. With a rush they rattled suddenly over the threshold. Winter was forcing its way in.

'Stoves alight tomorrow, Mrs Pringle,' I said aloud.

Dr Martin, I noticed with some annoyance as I entered the kitchen, was drying his hands on my clean tea towel. He was whistling tunelessly to himself.

'How is she?'

'She'll be all right now; but I'd like her to stay here for the night if you can have her.'

'Of course.'

'I'll call in to see her sister on my way back. It might be as well if she stayed with her for a week or two, though I doubt if she will go there. It's a pity they don't hit it off better.'

Dr Martin is now in his seventies and knows the histories of the village families intimately. Twice a week, on Wednesdays and Saturdays, he comes to Fairacre to hold his surgery in the drawing-room of Mr Roberts' farmhouse. His enormous white cupboard, smelling of drugs and ointments, dominates this room, which is set aside for his use.

'Has she needed to call you in before?' I asked. 'She's said nothing to me about these attacks.'

'Had them off and on for two years now, the silly girl,' said Dr Martin, folding the tea-towel into a very small damp square that would never dry and putting it carefully on the window-sill. He faced me across the kitchen table.

'She will have to give this up, you know. Should have done so last year, but she's as obstinate as her father was. Do your best to make her see it. I'll call in tomorrow morning.'

He put his head round the door of the living-room.

'Now, Dolly, stay there and rest. You'll do, my dear, you'll do!'

Outside the back door he checked, and I thought he had some last minute instructions to give me, but he was staring at a climbing rose, that nodded in the wind.

'Now, that's a nice one,' he said intently, and carefully picked a bloom. Tucking it into his buttonhole he trotted briskly across to his car, and I remembered with amusement what I had heard the villagers say about him. 'That ol' Dr Martin – can't never resist a rose, nor a glass of home-made wine. They're his failings, see?'

Dr Martin must have put a match to the fire for its cheerful light was the first thing I noticed in the quiet living-room. Miss Clare was lying back on the sofa with her eyes shut, and I thought that she slept.

'I heard,' she said, without opening her eyes; and for the life of me I could say nothing – nothing of comfort to an old tired woman who was facing the end of more than forty years' service – that would not sound presumptuous or patronizing. For a minute I hated my own boisterous good health that seemed to put up a barrier between us. She must have thought from my silence that I had not heard her, for she sat up and said again: 'I heard what Dr Martin said. He's right, you know. I shall go at Christmas.'

Now, although I could have spoken, I was afraid to do so, lest she should hear from the tremor in my voice how much I was moved. She looked anxiously at me.

'Or do you think I should go at once? Is that what you think? Do you wish I'd gone before? You must have noticed that I was not doing my job as I should.'

This had the effect of loosening my tongue, and I told her how groundless were these thoughts.

'Don't think about plans tonight,' I urged her. 'We'll see what the doctor says about you tomorrow and talk it over then.'

But although she acquiesced with surprising meekness about the postponement of her own arrangements, her mind returned to school affairs.

'Should you phone to the office, do you think, dear? It closes at five, you know, and if you need a supply teacher—'

'I shall manage easily tomorrow on my own,' I assured her, 'we shall go over to the church to get it ready, and I can ring the office when I've seen Dr Martin. Don't worry about a thing.' I got up from the end of the sofa to go upstairs to get the spare room ready for her. She sat very still with her head downbent. There were tears on her cheek, glistening in the light from the fire.

'I always loved Harvest Festival,' she said, in a small shaken voice.

8. HARVEST FESTIVAL

Mrs Pringle greeted me in a resigned way when I went over to the school soon after eight the next morning. She was limping ostentatiously – a bad sign – for it meant that she expected to be 'put upon' and so her leg, as she expresses it, 'had flared up again.' This combustible quality of Mrs Pringle's leg obliges one to be careful of expecting any extra effort – such as lighting the stoves, the present fear.

'I haven't got round to the stoves yet,' breathed Mrs Pringle painfully. She winced as she moved the inkwell on the desk. It was apparent that this morning's 'flare-up' was more than usually fierce.

'Don't bother!' I said, 'I shall have all the children in here today, and in any case we shall spend quite a time over at the church.' At this her face relaxed and there was a marked improvement in the afflicted limb as she walked quite briskly to open a window.

'Sad about Miss Clare,' said Mrs Pringle, arranging her features in a series of down-turned crescents. 'A fit, so Mr Willet understood.'

'No, not a fit—' I said, nettled.

'Can't hardly ever do anything about fits,' Mrs Pringle went on complacently. She folded her arms and settled down for a cosy gossip. 'My sister's boy, what's due to be called up any time, why he's had 'em since a dot. Just after whooping-cough it started; my sister had a terrible time with him over whooping-cough. Tried everything! Dr Martin's stuff never helped – all that did was to take the varnish off the mantelshelf where the bottle stood; and Mrs Willet's old mother – who was a wise old party though she lost her hair terrible towards the end – she recommended a fried mouse, eaten whole if possible, to stop the cough!'

'Surely not!' I exclaimed, feeling that a fried mouse, in my case, would successfully stop respiration altogether, let alone a cough.

'Ain't you ever heard of that? Oh, a good old-fashioned cure, that is – though it never done Perce much good. These 'ere fits come on after that. It's the swallering of the tongue that makes it more trying like.'

I said I was sure it was and beat an ignoble retreat before fresh horrors were thrust upon me.

There were several bunches of flowers for Miss Clare when the children trickled into school and these I took over to her as she lay breakfasting in bed. She seemed better, and awaited Dr Martin's visit with composure.

The work of making straw bunches proceeded briskly. Dust thickened the golden bars of sunshine and every time the door opened a little eddy of chaff would whisper round the floor. The long desk at the side was packed high with apples, marrows, giant parsnips and a fine bright orange pumpkin that Linda Moffat's grandfather had brought for her from his Caxley back-garden. It was much admired, as an exotic bloom from foreign parts.

In the midst of the hubbub a visitor arrived. A tall cadaverous woman, dressed in a fawn overcoat and fawn hat, came round the door and stood gazing down upon the squatting children with an expression of strong distaste.

I hastened to welcome her, noticing that her complexion was as fawn as her attire and wondering, not for the first time, why sallow people are so magnetically drawn to this colour. Even her teeth were a subdued shade of yellow, and had I been capable of seeing her aura I have no doubt that that too would have been in the beige range.

'I am Miss Pitt, the new needlework inspector,' she said, revealing the teeth a little more. 'This doesn't appear to be a very convenient time to call.'

I explained that we were about to go over to the church, but that it was no bother to show her our work.

Ankle deep in straw, I pushed across to the needlework cupboard and returned with girls' bags.

'The bigger ones are making aprons with cross-over straps. That brings in buttonholes,' I enlarged, pulling one or two specimens into view, 'and the small girls are making bibs or hankies.'

I left her to look at them while I broke up a quiet but vicious fight which had started in a corner. Someone's special pile of extra-large-eared corn was being purloined and there were stealthy recriminations going on.

'Oh, dear!' said Miss Pitt, scrutinizing an apron, 'oh, dear! I'm afraid this is very out-of-date.'

'Out-of-date?' I repeated, bewildered. 'But children can always do with pinafores!'

Miss Pitt passed a fawn hand across her brow, as one suffering fools, but not gladly.

'We just don't,' she began wearily, as though addressing a very backward child, 'we just don't expect young children like this to do such fine, close work. Pure Victoriana, this!' she went on, tossing Anne's apron dangerously near an inkwell. 'All this HEMMING and OVERSEWING and BUTTONHOLING – it just isn't done these days. Plenty of thick bright wool, crewel needles, not too small, and coarse crash, or better still, hessian to work on, and THE VERY SIMPLEST stitches! As for these poor babies with their hankies—!' She gave a high affected laugh, 'Canvas mats, or a simple pochette is the sort of thing that they should be attempting. Eyestrain, you know!'

'But not one of them wears glasses,' I protested, 'and they've always been perfectly happy making these things for themselves or their families. And surely they should learn the elementary stitches!'

'No; I'm not criticizing—' I felt I should like to know just what she was doing then, but restrained myself, 'it's all a matter of APPROACH! Have you any hessian in the school?'

'Only a very small amount for the babies,' I replied firmly, 'and as I've used up all our money on this cotton material I'm afraid the aprons and so on will have to go forward.'

'A pity,' said Miss Pitt, sadly. She sighed bravely. 'Ah well! I will call in again some time next term and see if I can give you some more help. We do so want to bring Colour and Life into these rather drab surroundings, don't we?'

I could have suggested that a more colourful wardrobe might help towards this end, but common courtesy forbade it.

'One meets such hardworking people in this job,' she continued smiling graciously at me – she might have been slumming – 'such really worthy fellow-creatures. It's a great privilege to be able to guide them, I find.'

She gave a last look round the room, averting her eyes quickly from the outcast aprons. 'Good-bye, Miss Annett,' she said, consulting a list. 'This is Beech Green School, isn't it?'

'This is Fairacre School,' I pointed out. 'Mr Annett is headmaster at Beech Green School.'

'Then he's next on my list,' replied the imperturbable Miss Pitt, her self-esteem not a bit ruffled. She stepped out into the sunshine.

'Turn right here,' I told her, 'and it's about two or three miles along the Caxley road.' I watched her turn her car and drive off. 'And what Mr Annett will have to say to that fawn fiend I should dearly love to know!' I thought.

The church seemed very tranquil after the bustle of the schoolroom. The children tiptoed in with their treasures and set to work lashing the bunches of corn to the pew heads with strands of raffia. The four biggest children, John, Sylvia, Cathy and Anne were in charge of the altar rail, and, full of importance, they arranged beetroots, marrows and apples in magnificent pyramids, standing back with their heads on one side, every now and again, to admire the effect.

Sir Charles Dagbury looked down as disdainfully as ever upon them, as they enlivened his cold home, while, in the body of the church, more sightless eyes gazed down upon the young children from the church walls.

The troubles and vexations of the last twenty-four hours suddenly seemed less oppressive. It is difficult, I reflected, to take an exaggerated view of any personal upheaval when standing in a building that has witnessed the joys, the hopes, the griefs and all the spiritual tremors of mortal men for centuries.

These walls had watched the parishioners of Fairacre revealing the secrets of their hearts from the time when those kneeling men had worn doublets and hose. Some of the effigies had been here when Cromwell's men had burst in, as the mutilated marble bodies on two magnificent tombs testified. Bewigged papas, and later, crinolined mamas had sat in these pews with rows of nicely-graded children beside them, and these had been followed, in their turn, by their grandchildren and great-grandchildren, some of whom now chattered and scurried up and down the aisle.

In the presence of this ancient, silent witness, it was right that personal cares should assume their own insignificant proportions. They were, after all, as ephemeral as the butterflies that hovered over the Michaelmas daisies on the graves outside. And, hurt as they might do at the moment, they could not endure.

Dr Martin had prescribed at least three weeks' rest for Miss Clare.

'But she's so anxious to clear up her affairs properly at school that I see no reason why she shouldn't have the last two weeks of term here, if she makes the progress I think she will,' he added. 'It will be a wrench for her after all these years – perhaps this break may help the parting a little.'

Her sister came to fetch her after tea. Miss Clare had agreed to stay with her for a week, although it was quite obvious that her independent spirit rebelled against submitting to a younger sister's ministrations.

My problem now was to find a substitute for Miss Clare for the next few weeks, and I rang up the local education office at Caxley to see if there was a supply teacher available.

Supply teachers are a rarity in country districts, but I was in luck.

'Have you come across Mrs Finch-Edwards?' asked Mr Taylor, officially the Divisional Organizer, at the other end of the line.

'No, does she live near here?'

'They live in Springbourne.' This is a hamlet two miles away from Fairacre, further from Caxley. 'Only been there two or three months. She's had experience with infants in London. I'll see if she can be with you on Monday.'

'That's wonderful!' I said thankfully, putting down the receiver.

Mrs Finch-Edwards turned out to be a large, boisterous young woman, with a high colour, a high voice and a high coiffure done in masses of helped-auburn curls. Her hearty efficiency and superb self-confidence made me feel quite timid and anaemic by contrast. All through the few weeks of her sojourn at Fairacre School the partition rattled with the vibrations of her cheerful voice and the innumerable nursery rhymes and jingles, all, it seemed, incorporating deafening hand-clapping at frequent intervals, which the infants learnt eagerly. They all adored her, for she had an energy that matched their own, and her extensive wardrobe, of many colours, intrigued them.

The girls in my class were full of admiration for Mrs Finch-Edwards.

'She's real pretty,' said Anne to Linda as they hung over the fireguard that surrounded the roaring stove. 'Even if she is a bit fat.'

'Didn't ought to wear mauve, though,' said Linda judicially, smoothing her new grey skirt. 'It's too old for her. You have to be very fair or very dark for mauve, my mum says.'

We worked well together, although I missed Miss Clare's tranquil presence sorely. Mrs Finch-Edwards could not resist pointing out the deficiencies of Fairacre School as compared with the palatial palaces she had known, strewn, it would appear, with such luxurious equipment as individual beds for afternoon rest, sliding-chutes, dolls' houses, sand pits, paddling pools and – the acme of civilization – several drinking fountains. She was appalled by the jug-mug-and-drinking-pail apparatus in her outside lobby.

'I should never have *dreamt*—!' she told me, 'when I think of Hazel Avenue Infants' or Upper Eggleton's Nursery School with their own towels, each one appliquéd with each child's motif, you know, a toy soldier, say, or an apple – and when I think of the stock they had – well, it does just *show*, doesn't it? How you struggle on here, year after year, dear, I don't know. It must be truly frustrating for you. Tells on your looks in the end, too,' she added, taking a quick look at herself in the murky background of 'The Angelus' behind my desk. She pinned up a fat curl thoughtfully. 'I thought at one time I might fancy a country headship; that was before I met my hubby, of course. He wouldn't let me do that now.'

She always spoke of 'hubby' as though he were a hulking caveman and she a clinging little wisp dependent on him for everything. This 'trembling-with-fear-at-his-frown' attitude was all the more absurd when one had seen 'hubby,' who stood five-foot-six in his dove-grey socks, had next to no chin and a pronounced lisp. His wife's magnificent physique completely overshadowed his own modest appearance and it was obvious that in any action she dashingly led the way. I bore her comments on the poverty of equipment at Fairacre School, and the poverty of looks of its headmistress with all the humility I could muster.

'We usually give a concert at Christmas,' I told her, 'and I think we could manage one this year. Could you teach the infants two or three songs with actions or perhaps a very short play? Miss Clare could cope with the carols when she comes back, and my class are going to do "Cinderella." What do you think about it?'

Mrs Finch-Edwards was most enthusiastic and bubbled over with suggestions for costumes which she offered to make, with some help. An idea struck me, as I saw Linda Moffat twirling round and round in the playground showing off the two and a half yards of flannel in her new skirt.

'I'll call on Linda's mother. I know she's clever with clothes, and has a machine. She may help too.' I was glad that I had thought of this opportunity of seeing Mrs Moffat again, for I suspected that she was not very happy in the village yet, and despite the beauties of her bungalow, a lonely woman.

'Come with me,' I urged Mrs Finch-Edwards, 'we'll go one evening next week and see what happens.'

I little realized that that evening was going to begin a strong friendship between the two women that would flourish for the rest of their lives.

9. Getting Ready for Christmas

Winter had really come. The milk saucepans, which lived under my kitchen sink for the warm months of the year, were now at school and put on the hot stoves, one in my room and the other in the infants'.

Woolly scarves, thick coats and wellingtons decked the lobby. Gloves were constantly getting lost; children vanished, in the wrong wellingtons, on foggy afternoons, and others had to hobble home in those that were left, or pick their way through the puddles, to their mothers' wrath, in inadequate plimsolls. The classroom resounded to coughs, sniffs and shattering sneezes, and toes were rubbed up and down legs to ease chilblains.

The vicar, on his weekly visits, wore his winter cloak, green with age but dramatic in cut, and a pair of very old leopard-skin gloves, to which he was much attached. They had been left to him, 'more years ago than he cared to remember,' by an old lady who had embroidered no less than seven altar-fronts for him. His voice became so soft, and his eye so liquid, when he spoke of his departed friend, that it was impossible not to suspect a romantic attachment; and, in fact, this can have been the only reason for clinging, year after year, to a pair of gloves that had become so very odorous, moth-eaten and generally nasty. Altogether, during the winter months, the cloak, the gloves, and a biretta worn at a rakish angle, combined to give the vicar of St Patrick's a somewhat bizarre, but dashing appearance.

He had gone through to see Miss Clare, who was now back with us, to tell her how sorry he was to accept her notice of resignation at the end of the term.

'I shall put the advertisement in *The Teachers' World* and possibly *The Times Educational Supplement* this week,' he said on his way back. 'I doubt if we shall get anyone to start in January, but Mrs Finch-Edwards may be willing to come until we get suited.' He paused and stroked the gloves nervously. Loose fur, I noted with distaste, began to settle heavily on *The Wind in the Willows* lying ready for the English Literature lesson on my desk. 'How do you get on with her?'

'Very well,' I said firmly, and he departed, looking relieved. I blew my desk clean and called peremptorily for a little less noise from my class.

During these last few weeks of term preparations for the concert kept us in a bustle. Mrs Finch-Edwards called in one afternoon a week to coach the infants in the plays and the action songs she had chosen for them. She and Mrs Moffat were spending almost every afternoon snipping and sewing the costumes, shouting cheerfully above the hum of their machines and becoming fast friends in the process.

'What I should like better than anything,' confessed Mrs Moffat one day to this new friend, who had banished the bogey of loneliness, 'would be to have a dress shop!'

'Me too!' rejoined Mrs Finch-Edwards, and they looked at each other with a wild surmise. There was a vibrating moment as their thoughts hovered over this mutual ambition.

'If it weren't for the family, and the house, and that,' finished Mrs Moffat, her eyes returning rather sadly to her seam.

'If it weren't for hubby,' echoed Mrs Finch-Edwards, gazing glumly at a gusset. They sewed in silence.

John Burton, Sylvia Long and Cathy Waites, who were all ten, sat for the first part of the examination which would determine their future schooling, one bitterly cold morning. The rest of the class were in Miss Clare's room, and the solemnity of the occasion and the need for complete quietness so that the three entrants would do their best, had been impressed upon the whole school.

It was very peaceful as the three children tackled the problems. It was an intelligence test, intended to sort out the children capable of attempting the papers to be set next February, from those who were not capable of attempting any further effort at all.

A wicked draught blew under the door, stirring the nature chart on the wall. The clock ticked ponderously, cinders clinked into the ash pan, and a rustling in the raffia cupboard sounded suspiciously like a mouse.

Cathy, frowning hard, went steadily through the paper; but John and Sylvia sighed, chewed their pens and occasionally gave a groan. At half-past eleven they finished, handed in their papers and smiled with relief at each other and vanished into the playground. John's paper, as I suspected, was sadly unfinished; Sylvia's was no better, but Cathy's looked much more hopeful.

The only dark child among the Waites' family had certainly more intelligence than her flaxen-haired brothers and sisters.

The day of the concert dawned and the afternoon was spent in getting the school ready for the hundred or so parents and friends we expected to be in the audience at seven o'clock.

The partition was pushed back, groaning and creaking, and Mr Willet, John Pringle, Mrs Pringle, Miss Clare and I erected the stage at the end of the infants' room and piled desks outside in the playground, praying that the weather would stay fine until the next morning.

The children had been sent home early, theoretically to rest, but a knot of them clustered open-mouthed in the playground to watch the preparations, despite increasingly sharp requests to go home and stay there.

Mrs Pringle, with a nice regard for social strata, had arranged the first row of chairs for the school managers and their friends. Armchairs from my house and her own, some tall, some squat, stood cheek by jowl with a settee that Mr Roberts had lent from the farm opposite. All this cushioned comfort would be shared by the vicar, who was chairman of the managers, his wife, Mr and Mrs Roberts, Colonel Wesley – very shaky and deaf but one of the more zealous managers – and wealthy Miss Parr, the only female manager.

'You'd better put two or three more comfortable chairs in case Mrs Moffat and Mrs Finch-Edwards get time to come in,' I told Mrs Pringle.

'This row's for the gentry,' pointed out Mrs Pringle. 'There's plenty of ordinary chairs for the rest.'

At the back of the hall, which was the side of my classroom, were rows of plain benches on which I knew the boys would stand and gape at the distant stage. We had never yet got through a concert without several deafening crashes, but so far we had had no injuries. I hoped our luck would hold.

The children were dressing in the lobby superintended by Mrs Moffat and Mrs Finch-Edwards, their mouths puckered up with holding pins. The air quivered with excitement.

Miss Clare, resolutely refusing to sit in the gentry's row, had her own chair set by the side of the stage and instituted herself as prompter and relief pianist.

Mr Annett had come over to help and I could hear him at the further lobby door collecting the shillings which were going to swell the school funds. The rows gradually filled and the air became thick with shag tobacco smoke.

A twittering row of fairies creaked excitedly up on to the platform behind the drawn curtain and I spoke to the vicar through the crack. He struggled up from the depths of Mr Roberts' settee, still clutching his leopard-skin gloves, and gave everyone present a warm welcome.

The fairies took a deep breath and up went the curtain in spasmodic jerks. The concert had begun.

It was a most successful evening. No one was hurt when three benches overturned, though a very loud word which was uttered at the time caused Joseph Coggs to look at me with eyes like saucers.

'You hear that man?' he whispered. 'He swored!'

Mr Annett told me that he had collected nearly five pounds at the door and that everyone had been most complimentary about the costumes. Mrs Moffat and Mrs Finch-Edwards bridled with pleasure when they heard this in the lobby where they were packing clothes wearily into baskets and boxes. The vicar took Miss Clare home and I reminded him of the Christmas party on the last day of term during the next week.

The night sky was thick with stars as the people dwindled away into the darkness.

'What about them desks, miss?' said Mr Willet at my elbow. 'They might get wet.'

'Forget them!' I said, turning the key in the school door. It had been a very long day.

On the last Saturday of term I caught the bus to Caxley to buy presents for the children with some of the concert money. I struggled round Woolworth's buying little dolls, balls, coloured pencils, clockwork mice and decorations for the Christmas tree, and spent the next hour searching the rest of the town for more elusive toys. In the market-place I came across Mr Annett.

'Do you want a lift?' he asked. 'I'm just off.'

I consulted my shopping list. There seemed nothing more of extreme urgency and I gratefully climbed into the car.

'I sometimes wonder about Christmas,' said Mr Annett meditatively, looking at my feet which I was resting, in an unlovely way, on their outer edges. We edged gingerly down the crowded High Street, demented shoppers darting before us, screaming at their children to 'Stay there – Lor' the traffic – Stay there!'

'The thing to do,' I said as we gained the lane that leads to Beech Green and Fairacre, 'is to get absolutely everything in the summer and lock it in a cupboard. Then order every scrap of food from a shop the week before Christmas and sit back and enjoy watching everyone else go mad. I've been meaning to do it for years.'

'Come and have tea with me,' said Mr Annett, swerving into the school playground before I had a chance to answer. His school-house was bigger than mine and also had a bathroom, but poor Mr Annett's towels were grey, I noticed, and the floor needed cleaning. The dust of several days lingered on the banisters, and it was quite obvious that his housekeeper did not overwork herself.

His sitting-room, however, though dusty, was light and sunny, with an enormous radiogram in one corner and two long shelves above it stacked with gramophone records. In the other corner was his 'cello, and I remembered that Mr Annett was a keen member of the Caxley orchestra.

Mrs Nairn, a wispy little Scotswoman, brought in the tea, and smiled upon me graciously.

'Your brother rang up while you was out,' she said to Mr Annett, 'and said to tell you he'll be down next Friday tea-time, and he's bringing two bottles of whisky and a bird ready cooked.'

This news delighted Mr Annett. 'Good, good!' he said, dropping four lumps of sugar carefully into my cup. 'That's wonderful! He's here with me for a week or more over Christmas. He's just had a book published in America, you know, and he's expecting big sales.'

As I knew that his brother was a professor of mathematics at one of the northern universities and occasionally brought out books with such titles as *The Quadrilateral Theory and its Relation to the Quantitative Binomial Cosine*, I felt unequal to any cosy chit-chat about the new publication, and contented myself with polite noises at this good news.

I did not get back until seven and spent the rest of the evening packing presents in blue tissue paper for boys and pink for girls and thanking my stars that there were only forty children in Fairacre School.

It was the last afternoon and the Christmas party was in full swing. Lemonade glasses were empty, paper hats askew, and the children's faces flushed with excitement. They sat at their disordered tables, which were their workaday desks pushed up together in fours and camouflaged with Christmas tablecloths. Their eyes were fixed on the Christmas tree in the centre of the room, glittering and sparkling with frosted baubles and tinsel.

Miss Clare had insisted on dressing it on her own, and had spent all the previous evening in the shadowy schoolroom alone with the tree and her thoughts. The pink and blue parcels dangled temptingly and a cheer went up as the vicar advanced with the school cutting-out scissors.

Round the room were parents and friends, who had come to share the fun of the party and to see the presentation of a clock and a cheque to Miss Clare on this her last school day.

The children had all brought a penny or two for a magnificent bouquet which was now hidden under the sink in the lobby, out of harm's way. The youngest little girl, John Burton's sister, was already in a fine state of nerves at the thought of presenting it at the end of the proceedings.

The floor was a welter of paper, bent straws and crumbs, and I saw Mrs Pringle's mouth drooping down, tortoise-fashion, as she surveyed the wreckage. Luckily the vicar clapped his hands for silence before she had a chance for any damping remark.

The room was very quiet as he spoke, simply and movingly, of all that Miss Clare had meant in the lives of those of us there that afternoon. It was impossible to repay years of selfless devotion, but we would like her to have a token of our affection. Here, he looked helplessly round for the parcel and envelope, which Mrs Pringle found for him and thrust hastily into his hand as though they were hot potatoes.

Miss Clare undid them with shaking fingers, while a little whisper of excitement ran round the room. There was the sudden clang of the paint bucket from the lobby, and little Eileen Burton emerged triumphantly with the bouquet and presented it with a commendable curtsey, amid a storm of clapping.

Miss Clare replied with composure, and I never admired her more than on this occasion. A reserved woman herself, I think that this was the first time that she realized how warmly we all felt towards her. She thanked us simply and quietly, and only the brightness of her eyes as she looked at the happy children told of the tears that could so easily have come to a less courageous woman.

PART TWO
Spring Term

* * * *

10. Winter Fevers

The Christmas holidays had slid away all too quickly. On the morning after we had broken up, I was busy writing Christmas cards, when a hammering had come at the front door.

On the step stood Linda and Anne. Linda carried a small parcel with much care, and when I invited them in she put it on the table among the half-finished cards.

'It's from both of us,' she announced proudly.

It turned out to be a bottle of scent called 'Dusky Allure.' A female of mature charms pranced on the label, inadequately clad in what looked like a yard of cheese-muslin. A palm tree and a few stars added point to the title. The children beamed at me as I unscrewed the top.

'It's simply wonderful!' I told them, when I had got over the coughing attack. 'And very, very kind of you.'

I pressed biscuits and lemonade upon them, and they sat on the edges of their chairs, demure and gratified, while I finished off the cards. In the quiet room one's lemonade went down with a gurgle, and they exchanged mirthful looks and turned pink.

We parted with various good wishes for Christmas and they skipped away taking with them my cards to post.

On Christmas Eve I had had more visitors. The carol-singers arrived on a clear, frosty night, bearing three hurricane lamps on long poles, and pushing a little harmonium which Mrs Pratt played. Mr Annett conducted them with vigour, and in the light of one of the lamps I saw that brother Ted had been prevailed upon to bring his flute. The fresh country voices were at their best in the cold night air, and even Mr Annett seemed pleased with his choir's efforts.

'Splendid!' he said vigorously, as 'Hark, the herald angels sing' dwindled to a close, and he beamed upon them all with such goodwill that I wondered if brother Ted's two bottles had been broached before they had set off, or whether it was indeed the spirit of Christmas that had softened him to include even Mrs Pringle in his expansive smile.

The new term found a depleted school, for measles had broken out in the village. In the infants' room Mrs Finch-Edwards had only twelve children to teach, out of eighteen, and I had only twenty out of twenty-two.

The weather was bitterly cold, with an east wind that flattened the grass and shrivelled the wallflower plants against the school wall. The skylight had undergone its usual repairs during the holiday, and though we had had no rain yet to test its endurance to the weather, it certainly let in a more fiendish draught than usual, which gave me a stiff neck.

The children did not want to go out into the playground, and with the weather as it was I doubted whether they would gain much from the airing; but being school-bound made them quarrelsome and cantankerous. Tempers were short and Mrs Pringle more annoying than ever with her fancied grievances and nagging at the children.

We all longed for the spring, for sunshine and flowers, and the thought that we were only in January made that prospect all the more hopeless.

It was during arithmetic one morning, when I had been teaching the middle group to multiply with two figures, that John Burton came out with the astonishing remark: 'I'm done! Can't do no more!'

He threw his pen down on to the desk, leant back and closed his eyes. He, as a top group member, had been working quietly at some problems from the blackboard, and this outburst made us all stop and stare.

'If you can't do any more of those, John,' I said, 'try some from Exercise Six.'

'I've said, ain't I, that I can't do no more?' shouted John, glaring at me. This was quite unlike his usual docile manner and I felt annoyed.

'What nonsense—' I began, when, to my amazement, he burst into tears, resting his head on his arms on the desk.

The children were much shocked that John, the head boy, the school bellringer, the biggest boy there, should indulge in such childish weakness! Their eyes and mouths were like so many O's.

I went over to him and raised his head. It was difficult to tell from the tears and congestion if he were feverish or not, but his forehead was burning.

'Have you had measles?'

'No, miss.'

'Is your mother at home?'

'No, miss. She's got a job at Caxley this week.'

'Anyone at home?'

'Not till four o'clock.'

I went to see Mrs Finch-Edwards.

'I'll leave the door open while I take him over to the house, if you'll keep an eye on them. What about Eileen?'

His little sister looked perfectly normal. She had not had measles, but technically she was now in quarantine if, as was fairly obvious, her brother had got it. We decided to compromise by putting her desk in front, away from the others, for the rest of the day.

John looked very sorry for himself as he lay on the sofa under a rug, with the thermometer protruding from his mouth.

'Did you say your mother was serving at Sutton's the fish-shop?'

John nodded, as he was effectively gagged with the thermo-meter. I looked up the telephone number as we waited, thinking, not for the first time, how sad it is when mothers with young children have to take full-time jobs, and how impossible it is to try and be a substitute.

The thermometer stood at 102 degrees when I took it from his mouth. I tucked him up more securely in his rug, poked up the fire and went out into the hall to telephone to his mother.

'Speak to Mrs Burton?' said a voice, which I supposed to be the fishmonger's. 'She's serving at the moment.'

'Then I'll hang on,' I said, 'but this is urgent. Her little boy is ill and she will have to come immediately.'

'It's most inconvenient,' said the fishmonger severely, 'but I'll tell her.'

Mrs Burton was sensible and practical. She would be on the next bus, and intimated that if Mr S. didn't like it he could lump it. I went back to tell John the good news, but he had fallen asleep, breathing heavily, his forehead damp with sweat, so I crept out and across to the school.

It is this sort of occasion that makes one realize how absolutely necessary it is for every school, however small, to have two people who can take charge. Without Mrs Finch-Edwards there to superintend the children, any sort of accident might have happened; and I thought of several schoolmistresses that I knew, in the charge of perhaps twenty or more children, with no adult help within call, who might be coping at this very moment with such an emergency and with all the added mental distress of their lonely circumstances. It is a position in which no teacher should have to find herself, and yet it is, alas, a common one in our country areas.

It was during this bleak and plague-ridden period that Mr Willet appeared one morning with his hand heavily swaddled in strips of shirt-tail.

'We 'ad a very rough night, miss, very rough! Very rough indeed!' he said in reply to my inquiries. 'That Arthur Coggs, miss, is nothing more than a crying disgrace to Fairacre.'

It had all begun, evidently, at Caxley during the dinner hour. It was market day, and a member of one of the more rabid and obscure evangelical sects had set up his rostrum between a fishmonger with lungs of brass, and a purple-faced gentleman who threatened to smash up teapots and repair them again, with the aid of the miraculous paste which he held in his hand.

When twelve o'clock struck, Mr Willet told me, 'This 'ere 'eathen-jelly was as hoarse as a crow and took his tracts and that round to the building site where Arthur Coggs and his mates had just knocked off. They was sitting about on wheelbarrows and such, having their grub.'

So blood-curdling, evidently, were the ''eathen-jelly's descriptions of the after-life that they could confidently look forward to, that Arthur was seriously perturbed. Early memories of his stern old father, who had held much the same beliefs as the earnest soul before him, came flooding back, and he resolved in a flash to give up drinking, swearing, wife-and-child beating, and to become an example of right-living to all Fairacre.

During the afternoon, as he stacked bricks in a leisurely way, he decided that his new life might profitably begin on the morrow. This evening he would have a farewell round of drinks with his cronies at 'The Beetle and Wedge,' and tell them of his changed ways. Who knows, he might even per-suade some of those lost, black sheep to return to the fold with him?

He was, of course, chipped unmercifully by the hardened sinners in the pub that night. Spirits were high, language ripe and fruity, and beer flowed more generously than usual, as 'This was poor old Arthur's last drink!' By closing-time Arthur was decidedly drunk, and inflamed with his mission for reclaiming lost souls.

'You better save old Willet,' suggested one boisterous reveller, as they approached the Willets' prim cottage.

Mr and Mrs Willet had been in what Mr Willet called 'a lovely sleep,' when the rumpus began. Afire with good works, Arthur belaboured the paint-encrusted knocker, with all the might of the righteous. His companions were divided between mirth and shame. Some egged him on, while the more sober did their best to get him away from the door.

'What the Hanover!' said Mr Willet, creaking out of bed. He leant out of the window. 'Get off home! Waking up sleeping folks! Get off with you!'

'You come on down!' rejoined Arthur, 'I got something to ask you urgent!'

Mr Willet pulled on his socks, using language that Mrs Willet had never heard him use before in all their twenty-eight years of married life and regular church-going. She followed him timidly down to the last few steps of the box staircase, holding the door at the bottom open a chink to see that no harm came to her husband.

'Well, what is it?' asked Mr Willet testily, as he unbolted the front door. The cat, so recently put out, now streaked in, with a cry of alarm, followed by Arthur Coggs.

His companions melted rapidly away into the darkness. It appeared to them that Mr Willet, standing there in his billowing flannel shirt that served him by night and day for six days of the week, and with his sturdy legs bristling like gooseberries in the night air, could well cope alone with his visitor.

Arthur came very close to Mr Willet and scrutinized his unwelcoming visage.

'Mr Willet,' he said with something between a sob and a hiccup, 'I got something to ask you.'

'Well, git on with it,' said Mr Willet sharply. The draught from the door was cruel.

Arthur Coggs looked behind him furtively, then advanced another step. 'Willet, are you saved?' he pleaded earnestly.

Mr Willet's patience snapped at this insult to as steady-going a churchman as the village boasted.

'Saved?' he echoed. 'I'm a durn sight more saved than you are, you gobbering great fool!' And he attempted to push Arthur through the door. But, with the strength of one who burns with nine pints of beer and religious convictions, Arthur thrust him aside, closed the door with a backward kick, and came further into the room. He leant heavily on the table and looked across at the incensed Mr Willet.

'But 'ave you seen the light?' he persisted. 'Do your limbs tremble when you think of what's to come?'

Mr Willet's limbs were trembling enough, as it was, with cold and fury. He opened his mouth to speak, but was shouted down.

'Gird on your armour, Willet!' bellowed Arthur, his breath coming in beery waves across the table. He brandished his arms wildly, knocking down a very old fly-paper, that fell glutinously across the red serge tablecloth.

'Gird on your sword! Gird on your 'elmet, Willet!' His eye lit upon two stuffed owls that dominated the dresser by the fireplace. Carefully he lifted the heavy glass cover from them, and, with a glad cry, dropped it over his own head. The stuffed owls swayed on their dead branch, and Mrs Willet gave a little wail, and came down the last three stairs.

Like some enormous goldfish Arthur rounded on her, eyes gleaming through the cover.

'You saved?' he bellowed suspiciously to the newcomer, steaming up the glass as he spoke.

'Yes, thank you,' murmured Mrs Willet faintly, shrinking behind her husband.

'Then put on your 'elmet,' advised Arthur, tapping the glass by his right ear. 'Gird your loins—!'

''Ere, that's enough of that!' shouted Mr Willet, enraged. He caught hold of the dome above Arthur's shoulders and attempted to force it off; but so heavy was it, and so much taller was his visitor, that he found it impossible to accomplish.

'Sit you down, will 'ee?' screamed Mr Willet, giving the glass a vicious slap and Mr Coggs a most unorthodox blow in the stomach. Arthur folded up neatly and sat, winded, on the horse-hair sofa.

Speechless with fury Mr Willet pulled the cover off and handed it to his wife, who tiptoed across the room and replaced it lovingly over the owls.

'If I wasn't in me night-shirt,' said Mr Willet wrathfully, 'I'd 'old your fat 'ead under the pump! You git off home to your poor wife!'

Arthur's militant spirit had evaporated suddenly, and at the mention of his wife a maudlin smile curved his moist mouth.

'Me poor wife!' he repeated, and sat considering this for a full minute. 'Me *only* wife,' he said, looking up in some surprise. He lurched to his feet and caught Mr Willet by the neck of his shirt.

'And do you know what?' he boomed, his face thrust close to his host's, 'she ain't saved, poor weasel! Me *only* wife, and she ain't saved!'

Mr Willet broke away and flung open the door.

'Then you can dam' well clear off 'ome and save her! Coming in 'ere kicking up like this! Be off with you, Arthur Coggs!'

With inexpressible dignity Arthur drew himself up and crossed the threshold.

'I 'opes,' he said coldly, swaying on the doorstep, 'that I knows when I'm not welcome. Arthur Coggs ain't the sort that pushes in where 'e's not wanted!'

And with a shattering hiccup, he passed out into the night.

This dreadful scene had direct repercussions on our school life, for Joseph Coggs was absent the next morning, spoiling the week's record of attendance for the infants' room. 'Me dad overdone it,' he explained in the afternoon, 'and we was all late up.'

Worse still, Mr Willet had been 'so shook up by the rough night' that he cut his thumb badly as he was opening a tin of baked beans for breakfast and, as I have told, had to attend to his school duties with a heavily-bandaged hand for the rest of the week.

So discouraged was Arthur Coggs by the unpopularity of his mission work, that he lapsed into his normal regrettable ways, much to the relief of the whole village.

11. THE NEW TEACHER

There were only three applicants for the post advertised at Fairacre School, although the advertisement had appeared in both *The Teachers' World* and *The Times Educational Supplement* for several weeks.

The vicar had called a managers' meeting to interview the three applicants on a Thursday afternoon, late in January. It was to be held at two-thirty in the vicar's dining-room, and I was invited to be present. I appreciated this courtesy, which is not always extended to the headmaster or headmistress when new staff is being appointed, and arranged with Mrs Finch-Edwards a combined crayoning class of the whole school. As an added incentive to good behaviour I produced a box of small silver stars to be gummed on the best work, and from the children's rapt expressions when I told them of these joys I fully expected that Mrs Finch-Edwards would have a peaceful afternoon while I was at the vicarage.

I walked across the churchyard to the meeting. Mr Partridge's vicarage stands in an enormous garden which abuts on to the graveyard. Mr Willet, who is St Patrick's sexton as well as our caretaker, was tidying up the graves, straightening a loose kerb-stone, breaking off a dead rose or setting an overturned flower vase upright again.

'Snow on the way, miss,' he greeted me. 'Look at them clouds!' He pointed to the gilded weathercock that gleamed like gold against a pile of heavy, ominous clouds behind St Patrick's. 'Wind's dropped too.'

He fell into step beside me and we walked across to the wicket-gate that opened into a shrubbery in the vicar's garden.

'The graves look very nice and tidy,' I said, making conversation.

Mr Willet looked gratified. He stopped by a particularly ugly memorial cross made from pinkish polished granite. It reminded me of brawn. 'My uncle Alf,' he said, patting it lovingly. 'Stands the weather well.'

The vicarage is a large Georgian house of warm red brick, standing among sloping lawns and looking out upon two fine cedar trees. It has a square, pillared porch and a beautiful fanlight over the door. I was glad to see that the iron bell-pull which I had rung on my first visit there, and which had disconcerted me by coming away in my hand, had been replaced by a bell-push on the jamb of the door.

The dining-table was set out with the applicants' papers at the head of it, and chairs set primly round. The vicar, as chairman, welcomed us and resumed his place at the head of the table. Miss Parr was already there, an old lady of nearly eighty, who lives at the other end of Fairacre in a house built in the reign of Queen Anne. The villagers maintain that she is fabulously wealthy. Certainly she is generous, and none going to her for financial help is disappointed. She says that she is fond of children, 'even these modern ones that do nothing but eat gum,' but so far as I know, she has never set foot in the school of which she has been a manager for nearly thirty years, during a school session.

Colonel Wesley, also nearing his eightieth birthday, sat beside her. He calls in to see the children on occasions, and is, of course, invited to all school functions, as are all the managers.

Both Miss Parr and the Colonel, despite their age and frequent indispositions, attend managers' meetings regularly. It will be difficult when these two leave the board of managers to find two people in the village who will come forward to take their place. Neither Miss Parr's nieces and nephews, nor Colonel Wesley's three sons and numerous grandchildren have ever used the state schools for any part of their education. Few people nowadays, even if they have close ties with their local school, have either the time or the desire to take on these voluntary duties which an earlier generation shouldered with the feeling of *noblesse oblige.*

Mr Roberts the youngest school manager had attended an elementary school in Caxley as a small boy, and gone on from there to the local grammar school. He has a first-hand knowledge of elementary education and he, with the vicar, has a close understanding of the practical needs of the school in their care.

Behind the vicar's chair, on the wall, hangs a portrait of one of his ancestors. He has a peevish expression and is holding out a piece of paper as though he were saying petulantly, 'Now, could you read this writing? Isn't it appalling?'

The vicar is inordinately proud of this picture and the letter, he claims, was written by Charles II to his ancestor to thank him for services rendered during his exile. Be that as it may, the old gentleman would not appear to be overjoyed at its perusal.

I was studying it again when the vicar said, 'I think we should begin. The applicants are Mrs Davis, who has come from Kent . . .' He paused, and looked at us over his glasses. 'Er . . . this lady has not had experience with infants, but would like to try. She has two children of her own, I believe.' From his tone it was clear that her application had not impressed him very favourably.

'The second applicant,' he went on, 'is a little older and has had experience in infant and junior schools in several towns in the Midlands. She is, at the moment, teaching in Wolverhampton. She could begin in March.'

'What's the last like?' asked Mr Roberts, stretching his long legs out under the table suddenly.

'A Miss Gray, very much younger, still in her twenties. She left the teaching profession last summer—'

'No disgrace, I hope?' said Miss Parr.

'Oh, no, indeed, no, no, no! Nothing of that sort,' the vicar assured her hastily. 'I understand she nursed her mother for some months, but is now free to take a post.'

'Does she come from a distance?' asked the Colonel. 'Any chance of her living at home, I mean; or will she have to have digs in the village?'

'I expect it will have to be Mrs Pratt's,' answered the vicar. 'I have approached her and she has a very nice bedroom—'

'Well, let's see these gals,' said Miss Parr, putting her gloves down on the table with an impatient slap. I suspected that she had given up an afternoon nap for this meeting, for she seemed restless and had stifled yawns.

'Well, there we are,' said the vicar, gazing round at us all. 'I rather feel that Miss Gray will be our best choice, judging from her application; but we will ask them in and see for ourselves. Shall we have the lady from Kent in first?'

There were grunts of approval and the vicar went across the hall to ask Mrs Davis in.

They returned together. The vicar took his place at the end of the table again and Mrs Davis sat nervously at the other. We all wished her 'Good afternoon,' and smiled at her encouragingly.

She was a large woman with a shiny face. Her neck was flushed red with embarrassment and she answered the vicar's questions breathlessly.

'May I ask something?' she said. 'Where is the nearest station?'

'Why, Caxley!' said Mr Roberts in surprise.

'And what sort of bus service?' she asked. The Colonel told her and her mouth dropped open.

'I'm afraid that quite settles it,' she said with decision. 'I thought, coming along, how far away from everything it was; but if that's the situation – well, I'm sorry, but I would rather withdraw my application. I've got my two girls to think of, you know. We can't be buried miles from anywhere!'

The vicar looked regretful.

'Well, Mrs Davis,' he began, 'I know Fairacre is a little remote but—'

'I'm sorry, I'm sure, for all the trouble I've given; but my mind's made up. I had a look round the village this morning and it's not a bit like Kent, you know.' Her tone was reproachful.

The vicar said he was sorry, but if Mrs Davis was quite decided . . . He paused, his voice a query.

Mrs Davis rose from the dining-room chair and said, 'I'm afraid I must say "No," but I'm grateful to you for calling me up for interview.'

She smiled round at us; we made sounds of regret, and the vicar escorted her into the hall inviting her to stop for tea before she faced her long journey, but, like a freed bird, Mrs Davis was anxious to fly back to her nest in Kent and we heard her steps on the gravel path as she hurried to catch the three o'clock bus.

'Well, well,' said the vicar, with a note of relief in his voice as he sorted out the next application form, 'a pity about Mrs Davis, but of course she must consider her family.'

'Would never have done, anyway,' said Miss Parr flatly, voicing the secret thoughts of us all.

The vicar cleared his throat noisily. 'I'll fetch Miss Winter now. The lady from Wolverhampton,' he reminded us, as he set off across the hall again.

Miss Winter was as pale as Mrs Davis had been rosy. Grey wisps of hair escaped from a grey hat, her gloved hands fluttered and her pale lips twitched with nervousness. She did not heed our greetings nor our smiles, as she was quite incapable of meeting our eyes.

It transpired that she was run-down. She had had very large classes for many years and found them too much for her. It was quite apparent that they would be. Her discipline, I suspected, was non-existent, and even our local children, docile and amenable as they are by most standards, would soon take advantage of this poor, fluttering soul.

'I think I could manage young children,' she said, in answer to the vicar. 'Oh, yes, a small class of *good* young children . . . I should enjoy that! And I'm sure my health would improve in the country! The doctor himself suggested that I needed a much less trying post. Town children can be very unruly, you know!'

The managers asked a few more questions. The Colonel asked his stock one: 'A communicant, of course?'; and Miss Parr her stock one: 'I do so hope you are interested in needlework? Good, *plain* needlework – the number of girls these days with no idea of simple stitchery—'

Miss Winter was asked to wait again in the drawing-room while we interviewed the last applicant.

Miss Isobel Gray was twenty-nine, tall and dark. She was not good-looking, but had a pleasant pale face and a fine pair of grey eyes. We all felt more hopeful as she answered the vicar's questions calmly and concisely.

'I see that you gave up teaching to nurse your mother. I gather that she is well enough for you to feel that you can apply for a permanent post?'

'My mother, I'm afraid, died in the autumn. I did not feel like going back to teaching immediately, but I should like to now.'

We all made noises of sympathy and the vicar made a kind little speech.

Yes, she was a communicant, she replied to the Colonel, and yes, she was most interested in plain needlework and made many of her own garments, she told Miss Parr. There were a few more practical questions before the vicar escorted her back to the drawing-room.

'Well?' he asked, when he returned.

'Best of the bunch,' said Mr Roberts, stretching his legs again.

'A very nice, ladylike gal,' said Miss Parr approvingly.

'I liked her,' said the Colonel.

The Vicar turned to me. 'Miss Read, you have to work with our choice – what do you feel about it?'

'I like her too,' I said; and the vicar, nodding happily, made his final trip across the hall to acquaint Miss Gray with her good fortune and offer Miss Winter solace in a cup of tea.

Soon after five o'clock that day the vicar called at my house, bringing Miss Gray with him.

'Could you show Miss Gray over the school?' he asked, 'and I wondered if you would be able to go down to Mrs Pratt's with her to arrange about board and lodging. I wish there were more choice,' he added, turning to the new teacher, 'but accommodation in a village is always difficult – very difficult!' He stroked his leopard-skin gloves sadly, and some stray fur fluttered down with his sigh. 'But I'm sure you will be very happy here with us,' he went on, bracing up, 'Fairacre is an example of cheerful living to our neighbouring villages. Don't you agree, Miss Read?'

I assured him truthfully that I had been happy in Fairacre, but I wondered if Mrs Pringle and a few other such gloomy sprites could fairly be called examples of cheerful living.

The vicar said good-bye and went off down the path with a swirl of his cloak. A few snowflakes fluttered in the light from the porch.

'You haven't got to make the journey home tonight, I hope?' I asked Miss Gray.

'No, I'm staying with friends in Caxley. If I catch the 6.15 bus that will suit them very well.'

I put on my coat and we went across to the dark school.

'I wish you could have seen it in sunshine,' I said, 'it looks much better.'

'But I have,' she said, to my surprise. 'When I thought of applying I came over from Caxley and looked at the school and the village. I liked it all so much that that made up my mind for me. I know the neighbourhood fairly well through staying with friends. They have a good deal to do with the orchestra in Caxley.'

'Do you play at all?'

'Yes, the violin and the piano. I should like to join the orchestra if it is easy to get in and out of Caxley.'

The school was very still and unreal. The tidy rows of desks, the children's drawings, the pot of Roman hyacinths in flower on my desk all looked like stage properties awaiting the actor's presence to lend them validity. The artificial light heightened this effect.

Our shoes echoed noisily on the boards as we went through to the infants' room that would be Miss Gray's own.

'I wonder *why* they built the windows so horribly high!' exclaimed Miss Gray, looking at the narrow arches set up in the wall. 'Well, I know they didn't want the children to look out, but really – such a peculiar mentality!'

She walked round her new domain, examining pictures and

looking at books in the cupboards. Her pale face had grown quite pink with excitement and she looked almost pretty. It seemed a pity to take her away from it all, but if she had to catch the Caxley bus and we had to face Mrs Pratt first, there was no time to spare.

'You are coming to us on the first of February, I believe?' I asked.

'Yes, it seems best. I've no notice to give in, but it means that I shall have just over a week to settle in the village, and it gives your supply teacher a little notice.'

So we arranged that she would come over one day before the beginning of February to see about syllabuses, schemes of work, children's records, reading methods and all the other interesting school matters, but that now, with time pressing, we must hurry down the road to Mrs Pratt's house, before that lady began putting her two little children to bed.

Jasmine Villa had been built some eighty years ago by a prosperous retired tradesman from Caxley. His grandson still ran the business there, but let this property to Mr and Mrs Pratt for a rental so small that it was next to impossible for him to keep the house in adequate repair.

It was square and grey with a slated roof. A verandah ran across its width, and over this in the summer-time grew masses of the shrub which gave the house its name. So dilapidated was this iron verandah that its curling trellis-work and the jasmine appeared to give each other much-needed mutual support. A neat black and white tiled path, edged with undulating grey stone coping, like so many penny buns in rows, led from the iron gate to the front door. It was an incongruous house to find in this village. It might have been lifted bodily from Finsbury Park or Shepherd's Bush and dropped down between the thatched row of cottages belonging to Mr Roberts' farm on the one side, and the warm red bulk of 'The Beetle and Wedge' on the other.

Mrs Pratt, a plain cheerful woman in her thirties, opened the door to us. Her face always gleams like a polished apple, so tight and shiny is her well-scrubbed skin.

'Come into the front room,' she invited us, 'I'm afraid the fire's not in – we live at the back mostly, and my husband's just having his tea out there.' An appetizing smell of grilled herring wreathed around us as she spoke.

I explained why I had come and introduced the two to each other. Mrs Pratt began to rattle away about cooked breakfasts, bathing arrangements, washing and ironing, retention fees, door keys and all the other technical details that landladies need to discuss with prospective tenants, while Miss Gray listened and nodded and occasionally asked a question.

The room was lit by a central hanging bulb. It was very cold and I was glad that Mrs Pratt's business methods were so brisk that I might reasonably get back to my fire within half an hour.

Against one wall stood an upright piano on which Mrs Pratt practised her church music. A copy of 'The Crucifixion' was open on the stand. Mr Annett evidently started practising his Good Friday oratorio in good time. Two large photographs dominated the top. One showed a wasp-waisted young woman, with a bustle, leaning against a pedestal, in a sideways-bend position which must have given her ribs agony as her corsets could not have failed to dig in cruelly at the top. The same young woman appeared in the second photograph. She was in a wedding dress, and stood behind an ornately carved chair, in which sat a bewildered little man with a captured expression. One large capable hand rested on his shoulder, the other grasped the chair-back, and on her face was a look of triumph. Between the two photographs was a long green dish of thick china, shaped like a monstrous lettuce leaf, with three china tomatoes clustering at one end.

I turned my fascinated gaze to the sideboard as Mrs Pratt's voice rose and fell. Here there was more distorted pottery to the square foot of sideboard top than I have ever encountered. Toby jugs jostled with teapots shaped like houses, jam pots shaped like beehives, apples and oranges, jugs like rabbits and other animals, and one particularly horrid one taking the form of a bird – the milk coming from the beak as one grasped the tail for a handle. A shiny black cat, with a very long neck, supported a candle on its head and leered across at a speckled china hedgehog whose back bristled with coloured spills. A bloated white fish with its mouth wide open had 'ASHES' printed down its back and faced a frog who was yawning, I imagine, for the same purpose. At any minute one imagined that Disneyish music would start to play and these fantastic characters would begin a grotesque life of their own, hobbling, squeaking, lumbering, hinnying – poor deformed players in a nightmare.

'I do like pretty things,' said Mrs Pratt complacently, following my gaze. 'Shall we go up and see the bedroom?'

It was surprisingly attractive, with white walls and velvet curtains – 'bought at a sale,' explained Mrs Pratt – which had faded to a gentle blue. The room, like the one below it which we had just left, was big and lofty, but much less cluttered with furniture. Miss Gray seemed pleased with it. There were only three drawbacks, and they were all easily removed; a plaster statuette of a little girl with a pronounced spinal curvature and a protruding stomach, who held out her skirts winsomely as she gazed out of the window; and two pictures, equally distressing.

One showed a generously-proportioned young woman with eyes piously upraised. She was lashed securely to a stake set in the midst of a raging river, for what reason was not apparent. There were some verses, however, beneath this picture and I determined to read them when visiting Miss Gray in the future. The other picture was even more upsetting, showing a dog lying in a welter of blood, the whites of its eyes showing frantically. Its young master, in a velvet suit, was caressing it in farewell. I knew I should never hope for a wink of sleep in the presence of such scenes and only prayed that Miss Gray might not be so easily affected.

We followed Mrs Pratt down the stairs to the front door. Snow-flakes whirled in as she opened it.

'I will let you know definitely by Monday,' said Miss Gray. 'Will that do?'

'Perfectly, perfectly!' answered Mrs Pratt happily, 'and we can always alter anything you know – I mean, if you want to bring your own books or pictures we could come to some arrangement—'

We nodded and waved our way through the snowflakes down

to the gate and into the lane. The snow was beginning to settle and muffled the sounds of our footsteps.

'I suppose,' Miss Gray began diffidently, 'that there is nowhere else to go?'

'I don't know of any other place,' I replied, and went on to explain how difficult it is to get suitable lodgings for a single girl in a village. The cottages are too small and are usually overcrowded as it is, and the people who have large houses would never dream of letting a room to a school-teacher. It is a very serious problem for rural schools to face. It is not easy for a girl to find suitable companionship in a small village, and if it is any considerable distance from a town there may be very little to keep her occupied and happy in such a restricted community. It is not surprising that young single women, far from their own homes, do not stay for any length of time in country schools.

'Those pictures must go!' said Miss Gray decidedly, as we stood sheltering against Mr Roberts's wall waiting for the bus.

'They must,' I agreed, with feeling.

'She's asking two pounds ten a week,' pursued Miss Gray, 'which seems fair enough I think.' I thought so too, and we were busy telling each other how much better it would all look with a fire going and perhaps some of the china tactfully removed 'for safety's sake,' and one's own books and possessions about, when the bus slithered to a stop in the snow. Miss Gray boarded it, promising to telephone to me, and was borne away round the bend of the lane.

12. Snow and Skates

It snowed steadily throughout the night and I woke next morning to see a cold pallid light reflected on the ceiling from the white world outside. It was deathly quiet everywhere. Nothing moved and no birds sang. The school garden, the playground, the neighbouring fields and the distant majesty of the downs were clothed in deep snow; and although no flakes were falling in the early morning light, the sullen grey sky gave promise of more to come.

Mrs Pringle was spreading sacks on the floor of the lobby when I went over to the school.

'Might save a bit,' she remarked morosely, 'though with the way children throws their boots about these days, never thinking of those that has to clear up after them, I expect it's all love's labour lost.' She followed me, limping heavily, into the schoolroom. I prepared for the worst.

'This cold weather catches my bad leg cruel. I said to Pringle this morning, "For two pins I'd lay up today, but I don't like to let Miss Read down." He said I was too good-hearted, always putting other people first – but I'm like that. Have been ever

83

since a girl; and a good thing I did come!' She paused for dramatic effect. I knew my cue.

'Why? What's gone wrong?'

'The stove in the infants' room.' Her smile was triumphant. 'Something stuck up the flue, shouldn't wonder. That Mrs Finch-Edwards does nothing but burn paper, paper, paper on it! Never see such ash! And as for pencil sharpenings! Thick all round the fireguard, they are! Miss Clare, now, always sharpened on to a newspaper, and put it all, neat as neat, in the basket, but I wouldn't like to tell you some of the stuff I've riddled out of that stove at nights since madam's been in there!'

She buttoned up her mouth primly and gave me such a dark look that one might have thought she'd been fishing charred children's bones out of the thing.

I assumed my brisk tone. 'It won't light at all?'

'Tried three times!' attested Mrs Pringle, with maddening complacency. 'Fair belches smoke, pardon the language! Best get Mr Rogers to it. Mr Willet's got no idea with machinery. Remember how he done in the vicar's lawn-mower?'

I did, and said we must certainly get Mr Rogers to come and look at the stove. Mrs Pringle noticed the use of the first person plural and hastened to extricate herself.

'If my leg wasn't giving me such a tousling I'd offer to go straight away, miss, as you well know. For as Pringle says, never was there such a one for doing a good turn to others, but it's as much as I can do to drag myself round now. As you can see!' she added, moving crabwise to straighten the fire-irons, and flinching as she went.

'The children will all have to be in here together this morning, so I shall go down myself,' I said. 'With this weather, and the epidemic still flourishing, I doubt if we shall get many at school in any case.'

'If only he was on the 'phone,' said Mrs Pringle, 'it would save you a walk. But there, when you're young and spry a walk in the snow's a real pleasure!'

She trotted briskly back to the lobby, the limp having miraculously vanished, as she heard children's voices in the distance.

'And don't bring none of that dirty old snow in my clean school,' I heard her scolding them. 'Look where you're treading now – scuffling about all over! Anyone'd think I was made of sacks.'

There were only eighteen children in school that day. Little wet gloves, soaked through snowballing, and a row of wet socks and steaming shoes lined the fire-guard round the stove in my room.

I left Mrs Finch-Edwards to cope with a test on the multiplication tables and set out to see Mr Rogers who is the local blacksmith and odd-job man.

His forge is near Tyler's Row and I walked down the deserted village street thinking how dirty the white paint, normally immaculate, of Mr Roberts' palings looked against the dazzle of the snow. I passed Mrs Pratt's house and 'The Beetle and Wedge,' where I caught a glimpse of Mrs Coggs on her knees, with a stout sack for an apron and a massive scrubbing-brush in her hand.

'Sut!' said Mr Rogers, when I told him. 'Corroded sut!' He was hammering a red-hot bar, as he spoke, and his words jerked from him to an accompanying shower of sparks. 'That's it, you'll see! Corroded sut in the flue-pipe!' He suddenly flung the bar into a heap of twisted iron in a dark recess, and drawing a very dirty red handkerchief from his pocket, he blew his nose violently. I waited while he finished this operation, which involved a great deal of polishing, mopping and finally flicking of the end of his flexible nose, from side to side.

At last he was done, and he stuffed his handkerchief away, with some post-operative sniffs, saying: 'Be up there during your dinner hour, miss; clobber and all! Nothing but sut, I'll lay!'

The schoolroom was cheerful and warm to return to. There was a real family feeling in the air this morning, engendered by the small number of children and the wider range of age, from the five-year-olds like Joseph and Jimmy to the ten-year-old Cathy and John Burton.

They were sitting close to the stove, on which the milk saucepan steamed, with their mugs in their hands. After the bleak landscape outside this domestic interior made a comforting picture. They chattered busily to each other, recounting their adventures on the perilous journey to school, and tales grew taller and taller.

'Why, up Dunnett's there's a tractor buried, and you can't see nothing of it, it's that deep!'

'You ought to see them ricks up our way! Snow's right up the top, one side!'

'Us fell in a drift outside the church where that ol' drain is! Poor ol' Joe here he was pretty near up to his armpits, wasn't you? Didn't half make me laugh!'

'They won't run no more Caxley buses today, my dad said. It's higher'n a house atween here and Beech Green!'

Their eyes were round and shining with excitement as they sought to impress each other. Sipping and munching their elevenses, they gossiped away, heroes all, travellers in a strange world today, whose perils they had overcome by sheer intrepidity.

Playtime over, I brought out the massive globe from the cupboard and set it on the table. I told them about hot countries and cold, about tropical trees and steaming jungles, and about vast tracts of ice and snow, colder and more terrifying than any sights they had seen that morning. Together we ranged the world, while I tried to describe the diverse glories of tropic seas and majestic mountain ranges, the milling vivid crowds of the Indian cities and the lonely solitude of the trapper's shack; all the variety of beauty to be found in our world, here represented by this fascinating brass-bound ball in a country classroom.

'And all the time,' I told them, 'the world is going round and round, like this!' I twirled the globe vigorously, with one finger on the Russian Steppes. 'Which accounts for the night and the day,' I added. I regretted this remark as soon as I saw the bewildered faces before me, for this meant a further lesson, and one, as I knew from bitter experience, that was always difficult.

'How d'you mean – night and day?' came the inevitable query.

I looked at the clock. Ten minutes before the dinner van was due to arrive – I launched into the deep.

'Come and stand over here, John, and be the sun. Don't move at all. Now watch!' I twirled the globe again. 'Here's England, facing John – the sun, that is. It's bright and warm here, shining on England, but as I turn the globe what happens?'

There was a stupefied silence. The older children were thinking hard, but the babies, very sensibly, had ceased to listen to such dull stuff and were sucking thumbs happily, their eyes roving round the unaccustomed pictures of their older brothers' and sisters' room.

'England moves away?' hazarded one groping soul.

'Yes, it moves further and further round, until it is in darkness. It's night-time now for us.'

'Well, who's got the sun now?' asked someone who was really getting the hang of this mystery.

'Australia, New Zealand, all the countries on this side of the globe. Then, as the world turns, they gradually revolve back into darkness and we come round again. And so on!' I twisted the globe merrily, and they watched it spin with silent satisfaction.

'You know,' said John at last, summing up the wonder succinctly, 'someone thought that out pretty good!'

The dinner van was twenty minutes late and I began to feel worried. Throughout the geography lesson the clang and scrape of Mr Willet's spade had been heard as he cleared a path through the playground. I went out now to see if he had any news.

He stumped off to the road for me and I heard voices in the distance. His face was alight with the importance of bad news when he returned.

'They've just rung Mr Roberts, miss. He's taking his tractor out to Bember's Corner to try and right the van. It come off the road into the ditch, they says!' He puffed his moustache in and out in pleasurable excitement.

'Is Mrs Crossley all right?'

'Couldn't say, I'm sure; but not likely, is it? I mean, bound to be shook up, if there ain't nothing broken, which is only to be expected.' He fairly glowed with the countryman's morbid delight in someone elses's misfortune. I thought of my hungry family.

'Mr Willet,' I begged, 'do please go to the shop and get some bread for the children and tins of stew.' I made rapid mental calculations. About six would be able to go home and find their mothers there, but I should have at least twelve to provide for.

'Yes,' I continued, 'two loaves, six tins of stewed steak and two pounds of apples. And half a pound of toffees, please.' It seemed a good mixed diet and I doubted whether the vitamin content would be as well balanced as it should be; but it would be nourishing and quickly prepared. I provided him with money and a basket and returned to send home the children that I could and to break the news to the others.

Dinner was a huge success. Mrs Finch-Edwards and the children had heaved one of the long tables from the infants' room and set it by the stove, while I opened tins of steak and mixed up Oxo cubes and cut bread, over in my kitchen, with Cathy Waites and little Jimmy as awed assistants. Jimmy wandered round the kitchen inspecting the equipment.

'And what's this, miss?'

'That's for mashing potatoes.'

'My mum uses a fork. What's this?'

'A tea-strainer. Pass the salt, Cathy.'

'What for?'

'To catch the tea-leaves. And the pepper, dear.'

'What do you want to catch tea-leaves for?'

'Because I don't like them in my teacup. I think we'll start the other loaf now.'

'What do you do with them when you've caught them?'

'Throw them away.'

'Well, why catch them if you throws them out after?'

'Cathy,' I said firmly, 'take the tea-strainer to the sink and show him with water and bits of bread crumb, while I finish this off!'

The demonstration was successful, and when I presented Jimmy with an old strainer, to keep the tea-leaves out of his own cup at home, he was enraptured.

Dinner was eaten amid great good-humour and to the accompaniment of metallic hammerings from next door, where Mr Rogers, complete with 'clobber' was attacking the flue-pipe. It was, as he had foretold, simply corroded soot which had flaked away and fallen across a turn in the pipe, preventing a draught, and he departed in a comfortable glow of self-esteem.

The snow had begun to fall again, and Mrs Pringle, when she arrived to wash-up, was plastered with snow where she had faced the wind. Her expression was martyred and her limp much accentuated.

'If it's no better by half-past two,' I said to Mrs Finch-Edwards, as we watched the snow whirling in eddies across Mr Willet's newly-made path, 'we'll close school and get them home early.'

'I shall have to wheel my bicycle most of the way to Spring-bourne,' said Mrs Finch-Edwards. 'My hubby was awfully wor-ried about me coming on it this morning. Like a hen with one chick, he is!' She dusted her massive torso down with a gratified smirk. 'I sometimes wonder how he ever got along before he met me – with nothing to worry over, the silly boy!'

I was about to say that, surely, she had told me herself that he used to keep pigs, but thinking that this might be misconstrued, I held my tongue.

At half-past two the weather was even worse, and we buttoned children into coats, turned up collars, crossed woolly scarves over bulging fronts and tied them into fringed bustles behind, sorted out gloves and wellingtons and with final exhortations to keep together, to go *straight* home and (forlorn hope!) to desist from snowballing each other on the way, we sent the little band out into the wind and storm.

For three days and three nights the countryside was swept by snowstorms. Only three children arrived one morning and I rang the local education office for permission to close school. The snow-ploughs came out from Caxley to clear the main roads and a breakdown lorry was able to get to the abandoned dinner van and tow it back to the garage. Mrs Crossley, despite blood-curdling rumours, was luckily unhurt.

At last the snow stopped, and on the fourth day the sun shone from a sky as limpid as a June morning's. The snow glittered like sugar icing, but the temperature remained so low that there was no hope of a thaw. Mr Roberts had his duck-pond swept clear of snow and invited the village to skate. As the pond is a large one, and nowhere deeper than two feet, mothers were only too delighted to send the children who had been milling about their feet for the past few days, and once school was over – for we opened again when the snowstorms stopped – the children raced joyfully across the road to a superb slide at one edge of the pond.

The older generation dug out skates, and so keen were they that Mr Roberts switched on the headlights of his lorry and evening parties swirled and skimmed like rare winter swallows while the ice held.

Dr Martin and his wife brought Miss Clare, and the vicar, in a dashing red and white ski-ing jacket over his clerical greys and the inevitable leopard-skin gloves encasing his hands, brought his wife. Miss Parr came, with a sister who must have been eighty, and all these elderly people came into their own. They waltzed, they glided, they swerved magnificently in figures-of-eight, while we younger ones tottered tensely round on borrowed skates, or, more ignobly still, pushed old kitchen chairs before us and marvelled at the grace and beauty of those who were our seniors by thirty years or more.

Mrs Roberts, with true farmhouse hospitality, threw open her great kitchen, and sizzling sausages and hard-boiled eggs and hot dripping toast were offered to the hungry skaters, with beer or cocoa to wash down the welcome food. For a week the fun continued; then the church weathercock slewed round, a warm west wind rushed to us across the downs, the roofs began to drip and little rivers trickled and gurgled along the lanes of Fairacre.

The thaw had come; we packed away our skates, and Mr Roberts' ducks went back to their pond again.

13. SAD AFFAIR OF THE EGGS

Joseph Coggs sidled round the half-shut door of his cottage. The baby's pram was just inside and wedged the door securely. After the February sunshine the little house was dark, and smelt of babies' washing and burnt potatoes.

Joseph put the cap that he was carrying very carefully on the table.

'Mum!' he shouted hopefully. There was no reply. He went through to the lean-to scullery and saw his mother through the open door feeling baby clothes against her cheek. Around her, on the ragged hedge and on the unkempt gooseberry bushes were innumerable tattered garments, drying as best they could.

'Got something for you!' said Joseph, in his hoarse cracked voice. His eyes gleamed with excitement.

'What? Some old trash from school again?' queried his mother crossly.

'Ah! I got a little house I done a's'afternoon – but I got something special for you!' He tugged at her arm, and, snatching a few garments from the bushes as she went, his mother submitted to being pulled back to the house.

Proudly Joseph displayed the contents of his cap – five brown eggs, with the bloom of that day's laying still upon them.

'Where d'you get'em?' inquired his mother suspiciously.

'Mrs Roberts give 'em to me,' said her son, but his fingers drummed uncomfortably on the table edge and his eyes remained downcast. His mother thought quickly. Five eggs would be a godsend with things as they were. Now that Arthur was back regular at 'The Beetle and Wedge,' there was mighty little handed over to her for food.

It was a pity they'd stopped teasing her husband about that night at Willet's, for while that had been going on Arthur had only dared to call in for a quick one and had escaped from their ribald tongues as hastily as he could. She'd noticed the difference in her housekeeping money. She looked again at the tempting eggs. Why, she could make something real nice for the kids with them, and Mrs Roberts wasn't likely to miss them anyway. She spoke kindly to her son.

'That was nice of her – a real lady, Mrs Roberts! I'll put 'em safe in the cupboard.' And she whisked them hastily away. She didn't want awkward questions from Arthur anyway, and somehow, well – out of sight was out of mind, wasn't it? And least said, soonest mended! Sensible sayings, both of 'em!

'And this is what I done today,' Joseph's voice broke in on her thoughts. 'Miss Gray done the door for me, but I cut up the lines myself.' He held up a small paper house, grubby and woefully askew. His face glowed with the pride of creation. 'Ain't it lovely?'

'Pity they don't learn you nothing better than that stuff,' said his mother shortly, still smarting from a guilty conscience. 'Them new teachers don't half fill you up with rubbish. Time you was learnt something useful.' But she suffered him to prop it on the window-sill and there he leant, gazing through the tiny open door, at the window beyond. Tomorrow he'd cut out little men and women from the paper, he told himself happily, and they could all live together in his house, his very own house. He sighed blissfully at the thought of all the joy ahead.

Next door Jimmy and Cathy Waites were at tea. This was what Mrs Waites called 'A scratch meal,' as they would be having high tea soon after six when the rest of the family returned from Caxley.

As the children chattered together and munched bread and shop honey, she studied an advertisement in her favourite women's weekly magazine.

'I've half a mind to,' she murmured to herself, 'only one and three! It's a saving really; that last lot of nail-varnish was never rightly my colour.' She inspected her hands minutely. Despite housework and vegetable peeling they were still pretty.

'Don't want to let myself go,' she told herself peering down at her reflection in the glass-bottomed tray. 'Be as slummocky as the creature next door!' And with one of her sharp nails she began to claw out 'This Week's Amazing Offer To Our Readers.'

Jimmy was intent on the label on the honey jar. He now knew his sounds and was beginning to find that, by piecing them together, real words sometimes evolved. He was agog to read, to be able to sit, as Cathy did, with her head in a book, sometimes looking sad, sometimes laughing, flicking over the magic pages that unrolled a story for her.

'MAD FROM—' he began painfully.

'It's got an E on it,' said Cathy exasperatedly. 'You know what Miss Gray said! It says its *name* not its sound! Not "MAD," silly, "MADE!"'

'MADE FROM' repeated Jimmy meekly, and began maddeningly on 'PURE' with all its phonetic pitfalls.

Cathy fidgeted restlessly, as he struggled. A thought struck her. 'Mum, I never told you yesterday! I've got to do the next bit of that exam, next week, Miss Read says. If I gets through I can go to Caxley.'

Mrs Waites looked up from the scraps of paper, round-eyed.

'Well, aren't you a one! My, I'm glad, Cath! You do your best, love, and if you gets it we'll let you go somehow.'

Visions of uniforms, hockey sticks, satchels and other paraphernalia flickered before her. It would cost a mint of money. But
there, others managed, didn't they? And if the kid was clever
enough to get to Caxley High School, or whatever its new-
fangled name was, she'd see she was turned out nice. She looked
again at her daughter's dark head, close to Jimmy's flaxen one, as
she explained the intricacies of 'SUGAR' to him; and let herself
dwell, for an indulgent minute, on the memory of the dark good
looks of Cathy's father.

'He was a card, and no mistake,' she thought, blushing slightly.
She pulled herself together and rose to clear the table. No good
thinking on things past. Some people would say she'd been bad,
but she didn't believe anything that could make you so happy
could be *all* bad. She stood still, butter-dish in hand, puzzling
over the niceties of moral conduct.

'Ah, well!' she said, at length, giving up the struggle to
straighten the tangled skein, 'I've got a real good husband to
think about now!' And shutting the memory away in the secret
drawer that all pretty women have, she went to put on the
potatoes for his supper.

Mrs Finch-Edwards was sitting on Mrs Moffat's couch, admiring
the new rug which lay before the tiled hearth, and listening to
Mrs Moffat's account of Linda's progress under Miss Read.

'She can read anything, you know. Never had any difficulty
with that; but surely she ought to know all her tables by eight
years old! Didn't you teach them that in your room?'

'Only a few,' said Mrs Finch-Edwards. 'These days they don't
expect children to start all that stuff as young as we did.'

'Then it's time things were altered,' said Mrs Moffat decidedly.
'How's Linda going to tackle the arithmetic paper in the exam, if
she's still feeling her way round stuff she should have learnt in the
infants' room? What we'll do if she doesn't get through to Caxley
High School, I don't know. You know my husband's not one to
worry, but I know money's short. This house took more than we
thought, and the shop's not doing too well.'

Mrs Finch-Edwards studied her friend's worried countenance
and offered what comfort she could.

'You don't have to worry about Linda. She's got a couple of

years yet, and she's bright enough. As for money, well, we all worry about that, don't we?'

'Yes, but this is worse than usual! I've promised Linda she shall have dancing lessons next term at Caxley and now – well, I really don't know how we can do it! And she's that set on it!'

And so are you, thought Mrs Finch-Edwards, torn between pity and exasperation at this exhibition of maternal ambition.

'Can't you take in a bit of dressmaking?' she asked dubiously.

Mrs Moffat looked slightly offended.

'It's not quite the thing, is it? A little shop, now – the sort of idea we've talked about – that's different! But there again, you need capital. I don't like to say too much to Len, he always takes me up so short, saying other people can do on what we get. I tell him maybe they've no desire to better themselves.'

There were footsteps outside and Linda burst in.

'Hello, auntie, hello, mum!' She stood there, panting and sniffing.

'Wipe your nose!' said her mother, rather put out at her daughter's tousled appearance before a visitor. Linda rubbed her nose along her knuckles in a perfunctory way.

Mrs Moffat's voice rose to a horrified scream. 'For pity's sake, Linda! Where do you pick up such ways? That common school—!' She turned a scandalized glance at Mrs Finch-Edwards. 'Where's your hanky?'

'Lost it!' returned her daughter.

'Then go and get one!' said her mother, 'and wash yourself and do your hair!' she called after the retreating child. 'You see what I mean?' she appealed to her friend. 'She's getting as bad as the rest of them, and what can I do about it? If only I could get her to those dancing classes – she might meet some better-class children there.'

She rose to get the tea ready. At the door she turned with a refined shudder. 'I never thought to see a daughter of mine – COMMON!' she said.

It was arithmetic lesson and the classroom was quiet. Both blackboards were covered with sums, and the three groups groaned over such diverse problems as '½ lb. butter at 4s. lb.' in the lowest group, to '6d. as a decimal of £' in the highest one.

Beside me sat Cathy who was being shown once again the mysteries of long multiplication. She had some difficulty with this type of sum, though normally intelligent enough, and with the examination so near I felt we really must master this particular problem.

We were interrupted by the clang of the paint-bucket and heavy footsteps in the lobby, Mr Roberts' large head came round the door.

'Sorry to interrupt,' he said, in what he fondly imagined was a whisper. The children looked up, delighted at this welcome interruption. Who knows, Mr Roberts might have the old black-board down again, their eyes sparkled to each other! And what could be more delightful than that, in the middle of an arithmetic test?

'Can I have a word with you alone?' he asked.

I sent Cathy back to her desk, with a long multiplication sum to attempt, and followed him into the lobby.

His big face was distressed. 'Look here!' he began, 'I don't like suspecting people, as you know.' He stopped and studied his boot so long that I felt he needed some assistance.

'Well, come on! Out with it!' I said peremptorily, 'they'll be copying wholesale in there if I don't get back quickly.'

Mr Roberts shifted uncomfortably, took a deep breath and rattled it all out. It appeared that he had been missing eggs from the hen-house and had marked some very early that morning and put them back in the nest. He went to collect them at half-past nine and they had vanished. Would I mind . . . (here he peered earnestly at me and turned a deep red) if he looked through the children's pockets?

I said I thought we should ask the children first if they knew anything about the missing eggs; then they would have the chance to own up.

An unhappy silence greeted my inquiries. No, no one knew anything about the eggs. Blue eyes, brown eyes, hazel eyes, met mine in turn as I looked at their upturned faces. I nodded to Mr Roberts who returned miserably to the lobby. This was obviously hurting him as much as it hurt us, I thought with some amusement.

'Get on with your work again,' I said, and pens were resumed abstractedly, tongues twirled from the corners of mouths, and superficially, at least, all seemed normal; but there was a tension in the air. The door opened again and Mr Roberts beckoned me out with an enormous forefinger.

'Oh, miss!' came a choked cry as I went towards the door. It was Eric who had called out – his normally pale face suffused with a pink flush. Tears stood in his eyes.

'What is it, Eric?'

'Nothing, miss, nothing!' he said with a sob. And putting his head down in his arms his shoulders began to shake. His neighbours looked at him in astonishment and pity.

Out in the lobby Mr Roberts held open the pocket of Eric's raincoat. There, carefully wrapped in dock-leaves were three eggs. Each had a tiny cross on its side from Mr Roberts' pencil.

'Will you deal directly with this,' I asked, 'or shall I make it a caning job?'

Mr Roberts' unhappy face became aghast. 'Oh, by no means! Not caning! Such little children—' he began incoherently.

'They're quite big enough to know the difference between right and wrong,' I said firmly, 'but if you feel that way about it I shall hand him over to you and content myself with a short lecture about this.'

Mr Roberts twisted his great hands together and I felt a twinge of compunction for his soft heart as I opened the classroom door.

'Eric,' I called, 'come here a moment!'

With a dreadful shuddering sigh Eric lifted his mottled face. Slowly he came towards the lobby where Mr Roberts awaited him with quite as much agitation of spirit. I looked at them both as the distance between them dwindled, and then returned to the classroom, leaving the coats and hats to witness the meeting between accuser and accused.

'And I give a few to little Joe Coggs,' Eric had sniffed to me later, "cos he saw me taking 'em and I never wanted him to say nothing.'

History lesson, about a little Roman boy, to whom the children were becoming much attached, was sacrificed to a lecture on respect for other people's property, common honesty, the power of example and the evil of leading others into bad ways. It was a much-chastened class that settled down to its nature lesson about the common newt, several of which disported themselves in a glass tank at the side of the room. I left them drawing sharply-spiked backs and starfish feet, and went into the next room to bring home to Joseph Coggs the wickedness of his crime.

'And another two?' Miss Gray was asking, stacking milk bottles in pairs into the crate.

'Four!' chorused the group clustered round her.

'And another two?'

'Six!'

'And two more?' The milk bottles clinked again.

'Eight!' This rather more doubtfully. Miss Gray left them to count again, and straightened her back to greet me. I told her the story and asked if I might take Joseph out into her lobby.

'I wanted to see you about my digs,' said Miss Gray, who had been with us now for about a fortnight.

'Us makes it seven!' shouted one of the mathematicians by the milk crate.

'Count again,' advised Miss Gray. 'We're getting ready for the two times table tomorrow, but heavens, what murder it is!'

'What is the matter at Mrs Pratt's?' I asked.

'Well, you know how it is—' she began uncomfortably.

'Tell me later,' I said taking Joseph's sticky hand and leading him from the class to the quiet order of the lobby.

Mrs Pringle's copper was humming merrily as I drew from Joseph the sorry tale of his part in the egg crime. Fat tears coursed down his face and splashed on to his dirty jersey.

'And my mum put 'em in the cupboard and we had one each for breakfast when our dad 'ad gone to work.' His tears flowed afresh as he burst out, 'Nothing ain't nice today! My little house, what I took home . . . my dad used it to light his pipe this morning . . . he never cared, he never cared!'

Truly Joseph Coggs suffered much. When the storm had spent itself I gave what tardy consolation I could by telling him that it was treacle tart for dinner and he might make another little house. The tears dried miraculously.

'But mind,' I added, in a firm school-marm voice, 'there's to be no more stealing. You understand?'

'Yes, miss,' answered Joseph with a repentant sniff; but I noticed that his eyes were on the school oven.

14. The Jumble Sale

For the past week, posters announcing the jumble sale to be held in the schoolroom in aid of the Church Roof Fund had fluttered from the wall by the bus stop, the grocer's window, and from a hook in the butcher's shop.

At the end of afternoon school, Miss Gray and I pushed back the creaking partition between our rooms, and trundled the heavy desks into a long L-shaped counter, in readiness for the people who were coming to price the jumble before the public were admitted at seven o'clock.

'I wish I could help you with the pricing,' Miss Gray said, puffing slightly with her exertions, 'but I do so want to go to the orchestra practice and it begins at 6.30.'

'How are you getting into Caxley?'

'Mr Annett said he would fetch me and bring me back. I knew him a little through the people I used to stay with in Caxley. They play in the orchestra too.'

We sat down on the desks to get our breath and surveyed our filthy hands.

'Miss Clare's coming to tea,' I said, 'she's helping with the jumble sale. Can you stop for tea with us?'

'I'd rather not, many thanks. I must collect my violin and music; and I shall need to change. Which reminds me . . . It looks as though I shall have to leave Mrs Pratt's, I'm afraid.'

'Isn't it working out well? I know it's not ideal, but digs are hopeless in a village.'

'It's partly that; although I hadn't thought of complaining.' She gave me a sidelong smile, 'I hang a towel over the nymph in the river each night, and my petticoat over the dying dog – I really haven't the heart to say anything to Mrs Pratt about removing them.'

'Is it the food?'

'Lord, no! I get more than I want. No . . . Mrs Pratt's mother has just died over at Springbourne and they'll want my room for her father. He's evidently going to make his home with them. In a way, it solves my problem – but what on earth shall I do about other digs? I feel I can't live too far away. I can't afford a car and the buses from Caxley just don't fit in with school hours.'

'You can have my spare bedroom until you find somewhere that you really like. I'll make more inquiries, but don't worry unduly. If Mrs Pratt wants you out quickly, come to me for a time.'

Her thanks were cut short by the arrival of Miss Clare who was propping up her venerable bicycle in its old accustomed spot by the stone sink in the lobby. She looked well and rested and greeted us in her gentle voice.

'We don't begin pricing until five o'clock,' I told her, 'so we've plenty of time to go and build our strength up with tea!'

Miss Gray made her farewells and hastened off to Mrs Pratt's to get ready for Mr Annett, and Miss Clare and I dawdled, arm in arm, in the playground to watch the rooks as they wheeled about the elms, sticks in beaks, busily furbishing up their nests for the arrival of the new young occupants.

Mrs Pringle and the vicar's wife, Mrs Partridge, were already shaking out vests and sorting out shoes when Miss Clare and I went over to the school. We each carried a blue marking-pencil, shamelessly purloined from the school stock cupboard, paper, scissors and pins.

'Good evening, good evening!' Mrs Partridge greeted us, bustling along the line of desks with a pair of antique dancing shoes in her hand. They were pale grey in colour, with a strap and two buttons. The toes were sharply pointed with heels of the Louis type, and they looked about size two. It would be interesting to see who bought them.

'Such lovely things,' continued Mrs Partridge, with professional enthusiasm, 'so very good of people to give so generously.' Mrs Partridge, from years of experience, knew the necessity of praising everything sent to a jumble sale, for, to be sure, any adverse comment is bound to be overheard, if not by the donor, then by some dear friend who feels impelled to impart the tidings. Life in a village demands a guard on the tongue, and none knows this better than the vicar's wife.

'Now shall we put the things out first? Men's clothing here, women's there, and children's at the end? We thought shoes on this form near the door, and hats – such an attractive collection, don't you think? – in the far corner.'

'What about admission money?' asked Mrs Pringle. 'Who's taking that?'

Mrs Partridge looked a little flummoxed. 'The posters haven't said anything about admission. I think we must let the people in free.'

'A great mistake, in my opinion,' rejoined Mrs Pringle heavily. Her mouth began to turn down ominously. 'At Caxley last week the Baptists charged threepence; and no ill-feeling. But there, if you don't want the money—' Mrs Pringle shrugged her massive shoulders, as one who washes her hands of the whole affair, and began worrying at the tape that bound several pairs of men's corduroy trousers together.

'Well, well, well, well!' clucked Mrs Partridge in a conciliatory way, 'and this shall be the junk stall – china, you know, and jewellery and any odds and ends. Mr Willet has very kindly offered to sell raffle tickets for this basket of eggs. Mr Roberts sent them over – so kind, so kind!'

We all trotted to and fro, carrying everything, from derelict footstools to babies' binders, to their appointed places. A particularly hideous table, with three and a half legs and a top so mutilated with Indian carving as to render it quite useless, impeded us seriously in our movements.

'Who on earth,' said Mrs Partridge, shaken from her normal caution, 'sent that dreadful thing?'

Mrs Pringle's breathing became more stertorous than usual and her eyes glittered dangerously. Trembling, our fingers fluttering with the price tickets and our heads down bent, Miss Clare and I awaited the breaking of the storm.

'That table,' began Mrs Pringle, with awful deliberation, 'that *beautiful* table, was a wedding present to Pringle's mother, from her mistress that she worked for from the age of twelve. And as loyal a girl her mistress could never have wished for!'

Mrs Partridge was beginning her apologies, but they were brushed aside.

'*And furthermore*,' went on Mrs Pringle, very loudly indeed, and with one hand upraised as though taking the oath, 'the dear old lady had it stood by her bedside till her dying day. She had her Bible on it, close to her hand, and all her other needs.'

She paused for breath, and Mrs Partridge hastened in with: 'I'm sure, Mrs Pringle, I meant nothing derogatory—'

'*Such as*,' continued Mrs Pringle in a fearsome boom, 'her indigestion tablets, her teeth, her glasses and a very fine clock given her by Pringle and myself on the occasion of her eightieth birthday, and much admired by all her visitors. As well it might be, considering the shocking price that shark in Caxley asked for it!'

'Well, I'm sorry that you should be upset,' persisted Mrs Partridge, 'and I hope you will accept my apology.'

Mrs Pringle bared her teeth for a moment and inclined her head graciously.

'It has *associations*, that table, and I don't like to hear ill spoke of it. A friend of the family, you might say.'

'Quite, quite!' said the vicar's wife in a final kind of way, and she and Mrs Pringle continued in silence to pin tickets along the men's stall, while Miss Clare and I, who had retired in a cowardly way with our blue pencils to the hat department, tried to appear unconcerned and efficient, and failed, I fear, to look either.

*

At seven o'clock the door was opened and a gratifyingly large crowd swarmed in. Capacious shopping bags of every shape and colour dangled from the women's arms. The first rush, as always, was for the children's clothes.

'Do nice for my sister's youngest.'

'Ah, that's just right for our Edna for next summer! Always liked a bit of frilling on knickers for little girls, myself!'

'Hold up, Annie, and let's try this for size! Pull your stummick back, child! How's a body to tell, else?'

The clothes were churned over by busy hands, snatched from one to the other, admired, deprecated and subjected to close and searching scrutiny. Pennies, sixpences, shillings and half-crowns changed hands, and the pudding basins provided by the vicar's wife on each stall were soon filling with contributions to Fairacre Church Roof Fund.

Prominent in the mob of women jostling for position was Mrs Bryant, a tall, imposing gipsy, wearing a man's trilby hat squarely upon her coiled greasy plaits. Heavy gold earrings gleamed against her dusky cheeks and she carried a formidable ebony stick. Behind hovered the lesser fry of her family, daughters, young wives and a bevy of dark-eyed children who watched everything in solemn silence. Mrs Bryant was known to strike a hard bargain and when she approached the men's stall, where Miss Clare and I were struggling to find change for a pound note and sell waistcoats and socks at the same time, we girded ourselves for the fray.

With the end of her ebony stick Mrs Bryant lifted a pair of grey flannel trousers. She gazed at the dangling objects with contempt, and then said: 'Give you sixpence for these.'

'The price is marked on them, Mrs Bryant,' replied Miss Clare, without looking up from her counting.

'They's only rubbish! Not fit for nothing but dusters!' persisted Mrs Bryant.

'In that case I advise you not to buy them,' answered Miss Clare politely, handing change to a customer and not bothering to glance in the gipsy's direction.

'Shillun!' snapped Mrs Bryant. Several of the women had paused in their buying to watch with amusement and also with some admiration for Miss Clare's handling of the situation.

'What price are they?' asked one, looking aloft at the suspended garments. In one swift movement Miss Clare twitched them free, surveyed the ticket, and handed them over to the questioner, saying, 'Half a crown.' There were sly smiles all round at this neat manoeuvre. Mrs Bryant said, 'Some folks buys any old rags, I sees!' and strode off with a face like thunder.

Mr Roberts towered above the throng and his mighty laugh could be heard above all the hubbub. He was present in his triple role of school manager, churchwarden and donor of the raffle prize.

'How are you doing, Mr Willet?' I heard him shout cheerfully.

Mr Willet was laboriously writing out the counterfoil of a raffle ticket, licking his pencil frequently, and, as it was an indelible one, gradually dyeing the edge of his ragged moustache a sinister purple. His tongue, by now an awe-inspiring sight, would have done credit to a prize chow.

'Made ten shillings already,' answered Mr Willet, with some pride.

'Fine, fine! You'll be able to buy one of my tickets for the Grand National draw. Come on now, Mr Willet,' said Mr Roberts tugging a book from his pocket, 'All in a good cause – Caxley Old Folks' Outing.'

'Mr Roberts,' he answered with dignity, 'you should know I'm not a betting man! It's the devil's work! I promised my poor old mother, years ago – and I hope she can hear me now wherever she may be – that I would never have no hand in betting and lottery!'

'Then what the blazes are you doing with the raffle tickets?' demanded Mr Roberts, trying to control his mirth.

Mr Willet's purple mouth opened and shut once or twice.

'As a sidesman, Mr Roberts, I hope I know my duty to the church,' he answered with fine illogicality, 'I'm putting my personal feelings on one side. The church must come first!'

'Well said!' replied Mr Roberts, 'and I'll have two tickets for my own eggs.' Mr Willet's pencil returned to his mouth as he settled the book of tickets more conveniently on the basket-handle.

'In that case, sir, I'm sure my poor old mother would wish me to contribute to the Caxley Old Folks,' said Mr Willet as he tore out the tickets. And fishing in their pockets the two men found each a shilling and exchanged them with due civility.

One blue and white spring morning, soon after the jumble sale, the sunlight streamed so temptingly through our high Gothic windows and the rooks cawed so encouragingly from the elm trees, that I decided that it was cruelty to children – and teachers – to coop ourselves up any longer.

'Put your books away,' I told the delighted class, 'and we'll go out for a nature walk and see how many exciting things we can find.'

They bustled into the lobby, chattering busily, while they put on their coats. I went through to Miss Gray's room.

'This is too good to miss,' I said, indicating the window. 'Would you like to bring them out for half an hour?'

We buttoned coats and tied shoelaces amidst cheerful confusion; then two by two, with John Burton and Cathy Waites as leaders, we took our excited family out into the spring sunshine.

Mr Roberts was laying a hedge with expert strokes of a chopping knife. He straightened up and smiled at the procession as it dawdled by him. There was a chorus of greeting.

'Morning, sir. Hello, sir. We's out for a walk! Too good to stop in, Miss Read says!'

'Never heard of such a thing!' said Mr Roberts, trying to appear deeply shocked at this news. 'No slipping out of school when I was a boy! Where are you going?'

'I thought I'd take them down to the wood to see if there are any early primroses and violets. We should get some catkins; but I don't want to be too long in case the managers find out!'

Mr Roberts' mighty laugh at this mild sally made little Eileen Barton run to the side of her big brother in alarm, and we left him, still smiling, to continue his work.

Our progress down the village street was greeted by cries and friendly shouts from windows and gardens. Mothers, making beds and dusting window-sills, called to us, the toddlers, fingers in mouths, watched us round-eyed. Mr Willet, who was inspecting a row of young broad beans, waved to us from his garden, and we all bounded along quite heady with this unwonted freedom, feeling devil-may-care at having escaped from school and revelling in the surprise we were occasioning by our incursion into the morning life of Fairacre.

We turned left at 'The Beetle and Wedge' along a narrow lane that led to a small copse at the foot of the downs. Beyond the copse the lane rose, becoming narrower and grassier, until it petered out into an indistinct footpath on the bare heights. A fresh wind tossed the children's hair and the catkins that streamed, like banners, from the hazels in the hedge.

In the dry fine grass of the banks, the violets' heart-shaped leaves were showing, and the little girls searched industriously for the blue and white blossoms, holding their thread-like stems tightly in their small cold fingers, and sniffing at their bunches hungrily. Starved of flowers through the long winter months, now the full joy of this sensuous feast broke upon them.

High above us, in a fold of the windy downs, we could see the shepherd's hut and the lambing pens made from square bales of straw set together to make a shelter from the weather. Now and again we could hear the distant tinkle of a sheep-bell, and the children would stop short, heads cocked sideways to listen.

'It's my grandpa, up there with the sheep,' John Burton told me. 'I takes his tea up sometimes after school. He give me this yesterday.' Fishing in his pocket he drew out a little boat fashioned from half a cork. By its odour, the cork had once served to seal a bottle of sheep disinfectant. Three masts adorned it and sets of paper sails, and rigging contrived, I guessed, from unravelled binder twine, completed the ship.

'He give Eileen the other one,' went on John, 'but she floated hers out in the road last night and it went down the drain.' His voice was full of scorn.

By now we had reached the copse, and some of the children sat in the shelter of the trees to rest, while others picked early primroses and anemones, or found other treasures . . . birds' feathers, oak-apples, coloured stones, or the large, pale-grey shells of the Roman snails that frequent the downlands.

I leant against a post and watched a tractor, looking like a toy in the distance, creeping slowly across a field. Half the field was already ploughed, and behind the tractor wheeled and fluttered a flock of hungry rooks, scrutinizing the fresh-turned ribs of earth for food. They were too far away to hear, but their black shapes rose and scattered like flakes of burnt paper from a bonfire.

Reluctantly, we returned bearing our trophies with us, with flushed faces and tangled hair. As we turned the bend of the lane I saw the school nurse's car outside our gate.

Nurse Barham, a plump motherly woman, with a Yorkshire brogue, calls periodically to inspect heads and keep an eye open for any other infection.

I watched her as she parted locks and ruffled the boys' hair, keeping up a comforting monologue the whole time.

'Beautiful hair, dear, keep it brushed well. Now your hands. Spread out your fingers. Nice nails, not bitten, I see. Don't forget to wash them before dinner.'

The children do not seem to mind being subjected to this examination. Only the nail-biters look rather fearfully at Nurse's face as they proffer their stubby fingers for inspection. Nurse's main concern, when she looks at hands, is for scabies, but she is also a foe to nail-biters.

'You don't know of anyone who could put our new young teacher up, I suppose?' I asked her, as she worked. Nurse Barham knows the neighbourhood well and realizes the difficulty of getting digs. 'Miss Clare suggested Mrs Moffat – a newcomer here. I don't know whether she will be able to, I'm sure.'

'I can't think of anyone suitable,' said Nurse thoughtfully, 'but I'll remember to let you know if I come across anyone. I've met Miss Gray at music practices. She seems very nice indeed. Mr Annett seems to think so, anyway,' she added mischievously and whisked off to her duties in the infants' room.

I felt vaguely annoyed by this last remark. Really, village gossip is downright irritating, I thought. The poor girl has only to be given a lift home by a neighbour and the village has them wedded, bedded and all the children named for them. It was too bad, and I was a little cool with Nurse when she bustled back.

'Only the new little boy, Joseph Coggs,' she informed me, 'I'll go and call on his mother now if she'll be in.'

I glanced at the clock. Mrs Coggs would be back from her floor-scrubbing at 'The Beetle and Wedge,' I told Nurse.

'What sort of home?' she asked. I told her what I knew of the Coggs family and she departed to Tyler's Row to see what advice and help she could give, and to leave a large bottle of noxious-smelling liquid for the anointing of Joseph's head.

Miss Gray had liked the idea of going to Mrs Moffat's bungalow if it could be arranged. Miss Clare, with true village caution, had advised us against going to Mrs Moffat too precipitately.

'Let me mention it to Mrs Finch-Edwards,' she had said, 'and let her sound Mrs Moffat. Then we can follow her lead.'

I was glad about this arrangement, for although I was willing to have Miss Gray at my house, I realized that it was not an ideal plan. We had to work together during school hours and I felt it would be better for both of us to have our leisure times apart. Our relationship at school could not be happier, and I did not want to subject it to too rigorous a trial.

Mrs Finch-Edwards had approached the subject of Miss Gray's future occupation of the spare bedroom with some wariness, but Mrs Moffat welcomed the idea.

'It would be a help with the housekeeping,' she said gratefully, 'and I only use that room for my needlework and the machine. All those things could easily go in the dining-room cupboard.' She pondered for a while. 'And she's a real lady-like girl,' she added, 'set a good example to Linda, and that sort of thing. I'll talk it over with Len tonight and let you know tomorrow.'

And so it had been settled. Miss Gray had called at the bungalow and inspected the bedroom, happily picture-free, and admired the bathroom – a refinement which Mrs Pratt's house lacked, and which had meant two trips a week to the friends in Caxley – they had discussed terms, to their mutual satisfaction, and Miss Gray was to move into her new home in a fortnight's time, with a very much lighter heart.

15. The Bell Tolls

Three energetic little girls were skipping in the playground. Two took it in turns to twist the rope, arms flailing round, while the third bobbed merrily up and down, hair and skirts dancing, in the twirling rope.

'Salt, mustard, vinegar, pepper!
One, two, three, four, five . . .'

they chanted breathlessly, until the skipping child caught a foot
or stopped from sheer exhaustion.

The rest of the children played more quietly, for the spell of fine
weather continued and the spring sunshine beating back from the
school walls sent most of them to the shade of the elm trees. Here
they crouched, some playing with marbles, beautiful, whorled,
glass treasures kept carefully in little bags of strong calico or
striped ticking; some tossing five-stones, red, blue, green, orange
and white, up into the air and catching them expertly on the back
of their hands before going on to further complicated manoeuvres. These movements had old quaint names like 'Nelson,
Crabses and Lobsters,' and involved much dexterity, patience and
quickness of eye.

Among the roots, the little ones played the timeless make-
believe games: mothers-and-fathers, hospitals, schools and keeping house. Above them the tight, rosy buds of the elms were
beginning to break out into tiny green fans, and in the school
garden the polyanthus, which the children here call 'spring
flowers,' and early daffodils and grape hyacinths all nodded
gently in the warm sunshine.

Against the north wall, in the cool shade, Cathy played two-
ball intently by herself. Her cotton skirt was stuffed inelegantly
into her knickers, for some of the seven movements of this game
involved bouncing the balls and catching them between one's
legs, and a skirt was a severe obstruction. She counted aloud, her
dark eyes fixed on the two flying balls, and as she twirled and
threw, and bounced and caught, she thought about the examination papers that she had attempted that morning . . . papers
that would decide her future.

She had sat at her usual desk, with only Miss Read for silent
company, while the rest of the class had taken their work into
Miss Gray's room next door. She had felt lonely, but important,
left behind, with only the clock's heavy ticking and the rustle of
her papers to break the silence; but once begun she had forgotten
everything in her steady work. If this was the way to get to
Caxley High School with its untold joys and games, gymnastics,

acting and never-ending supply of library books, why, then she'd work hard and get there! That determination, which set her apart from the other members of her family, whose sweet placidity she lacked, carried her triumphantly through that morning's labours; and when, at last, she put down her pen and stretched her cramped fingers, she was conscious of work well done.

In all the schools around Caxley preparations were going forward for the annual Caxley Musical Festival, which is held in the Corn Exchange each May.

Miss Gray and I had spent a long singing lesson picking our choir. This was not an easy task, as all the children were bursting to take part, but Miss Gray, with considerable tact, managed to weed out the real growlers, with no tears shed.

'A little louder,' she said to Eric, 'now once again,' And Eric would honk again, in his tuneless, timeless way, while Miss Gray listened solemnly and with the utmost attention. Then, 'Yes,' she said, in a considering way, 'it's certainly a *strong* voice, Eric dear, and you do *try*: but I'm afraid we must leave you out this time. We must have voices that blend well together.'

'He really is the Tuneless Wonder!' she said to me later, with awe in her voice. 'I've never known any child quite so tone-deaf.'

I told her that Eric was also quite incapable of keeping in step to music; the two things often going together. Miss Gray had not come across this before and was suitably impressed.

'When you think how hard it is NOT to prance along the pavement in time with a barrel-organ,' she remarked, 'it seems almost clever!'

I handed over the choir to her care as she was a much more competent musician than I was, and for weeks the papers on the walls rustled to the vibrations of 'Over the Sea to Skye' and 'I'll Go No More A-Roving,' and the horrid intricacies of the round 'Come, Follow, Follow, Follow, Follow, Follow, Follow Me.' This last was usually punctuated with dreadful crashings of Miss Gray's ruler and despairing cries from the children who had failed to come in at the right bar, battled against overwhelming odds, faltered to a faint piping, and finally finished with a wail of lamentation. The thought that this sort of thing was going on in dozens of neighbouring schools was enough to daunt the stoutest heart; but Miss Gray, with youth and ardour to sustain her, struggled bravely on.

One afternoon, while the choir was carolling away with Miss Gray at the piano, and I was watching the infants and 'growlers' drawing pictures of any scene they liked from 'Cinderella' in the next room, the bells gave out a muffled peal from St Patrick's spire close by. The peal was followed by solemn tolling. Next door the music continued cheerfully enough, but in my room the children looked up with startled faces, pencils held poised in their hands.

On and on tolled the great bell, beating out its slow measure over the listening village. Out across the sunny fields floated the sound and men looked up from their hedging and harrowing to count the strokes. In the cottages housewives paused in their ironing or cooking, and stood, tools in hand, as the tolling went on. Sixty . . . seventy . . . still the bell tolled . . . and little children squatting by backdoor steps suddenly became conscious of the tension in the air and ran in, fearfully, to seek the comfort of familiar things.

'Come follow, follow, follow . . .' the children's voices stumbled next door; and Mrs Pringle's face appeared at the window opposite. I heard her in the lobby and went out to see her.

'Forgot my apron,' she volunteered. 'They say poor Miss Parr's passed on.' She stuffed her checked apron into a black shiny bag and I noticed that her hands, wrinkled and puffy with her recent washing-up, were trembling slightly. 'I was in service with her, as a girl . . . just for a bit, you know . . . she was good to me, very good.'

I said I was sure she had been, and it was sad to hear the bell tolling. Mrs Pringle appeared not to hear these lame remarks. She was gazing, with unseeing eyes, at the pile of coke in the playground.

'Always paid well too, and was generous with her clothes, and that. I've still got a scarf she give me . . . mauve, it is. Yes, never grudged nothing to me, I must say—' Her voice faltered, and she turned hastily away to pick up the black bag from the draining board. When she faced me again it was with her usual dour expression.

'Ah, well! No good grieving over times past, I suppose. And after all, if she couldn't afford to be generous with the lot she'd got, who could?'

This uncharitable comment seemed to give Mrs Pringle some comfort; but I could see that this seeming indifference, this harshly-expressed philosophy, was Mrs Pringle's challenge to something which had shaken her more than she cared to show. Her parting comment was a truer indication of her feelings.

'I suppose we've all got to go, but somehow . . . that old bell! I mean, it brings it home to you, don't it? It brings it home!' As she stumped off, the black bag swaying on her arm, I felt for Mrs Pringle, my old sparring partner, a rare pang of pity.

Miss Parr's funeral was held on an afternoon as glorious as that on which she had died.

The children had brought bunches of cottage flowers, daffodils, polyanthus, wallflowers, and little posies from the woods and banks, primroses, blue and white violets and early cowslips. We put them all in my gardening trug, which was lined with moss, and Cathy wrote on a card, 'With love from the children at Fairacre School,' in her most painstaking hand, and we laid it among the blooms. Mr Willet was entrusted with it, and he set off to deliver it at the house.

As the playground is in full view of the churchyard, I decided to let the children have an early playtime, and then be comfortably indoors while the service was going on.

We had begun *The Wind in the Willows*, and I thought, as I waited for the children to settle down after playtime, what a perfect afternoon it was to hear about the adventures of Water Rat and Mole. An exhilarating wind was blowing the rooks about the blue and white sky. Somewhere, in the vicarage garden, a blackbird whistled, and an early bee, bumbling lazily up and down the window-pane, gave a foretaste of summer joys.

Together, the children and I set out into that enchanted world where the river laps eternally and the green banks form the changeless setting for Mole's adventures. The sun dappled the children's heads as it shone through the tossing boughs into the schoolroom. Around them lay the sunshine, and within them too, as they contemplated, with their mind's eye, the sunlit landscape conjured up by magic words.

I was conscious, as I read steadily on, of ominous sounds from the churchyard, slow footsteps on the scrunching gravel, a snatch or two of solemn phrase in Mr Partridge's gentle voice, blown this way by the exuberant breeze, and the muffled thumpings of heavy wood lowered into the earth. Very near at hand a lark soared madly upwards, singing in a frenzy of joy, with the sun warm on its little back. It seemed hard, I thought, to have to be buried on such an uprushing afternoon.

Out there, in the churchyard, the black silent figures would be standing immobile around the dark hole. Above them, no less black, the rooks would be wheeling and crying, unheeded by the mourners. They would stand there, heads downbent, with who knows what emotions stirring them . . . pity, regret, the realization of the swiftness of life's passage, the inevitability of death. While here, in the classroom, sitting in a golden trance, our thoughts were of a sun-dappled stream, of willows and whiskers, of water-bubbles and boats . . . and, I venture to think, that of all those impressions which were being made on that spring afternoon, ours, for all their being transmitted, as it were, second-hand, would be more lasting in their fresh glory.

Thoughts by a graveside are too dark and deep to be sustained for any length of time. Sooner or later the hurt mind turns to the sun for healing, and this is as it should be, for otherwise, what future could any of us hope for, but madness?

16. APRIL BIRTHDAY PARTY

April had come; one of the most beautiful within living memory. The long spell of sunshine and the unusually warm nights had brought early rows of carrots and peas and sturdy broad beans into all the cottage gardens.

'Unseasonable!' announced Mr Willet. 'We'll pay for it later, mark me, now! Just get the fruit blossom out and there'll be a mort of frosts. Seen it happen time without number!' He seemed to gain some morbid satisfaction from this augury.

The children were glorying in it and were already tanned and freckled. They came in from the playground and spreading their hot arms along the cool wood of the desks, they sniffed luxuriously at the warm, biscuity smell that the sun had drawn from their scorched skins.

In a week's time the Easter holidays would begin, and I hoped that the fine weather would hold, for my garden was weedy and the hedges, usually clipped at the beginning of May, were already needing attention.

On this particular afternoon the girls were busy with their sewing and the boys were making raffia mats or cane baskets or bowls according to their ability. The last few stitches were being put, by Linda Moffat, into a kettle-holder of especial importance; and as the other children worked they watched Linda with excitement.

The kettle-holder was their own present to Miss Clare who celebrated her birthday that day. All the children in the school had put several stitches in it – some, I fear, which Miss Clare would privately think of as 'cat's teeth' – and I had promised to take it to her when I went to her tea-party that afternoon.

Linda cut the cotton with a satisfying snip of the scissors and came out to the front of the class, bearing it as if it were the Holy Grail itself. It certainly was a magnificent object, made of a piece of vivid material, in deep reds and blues of a paisley pattern. It was edged with scarlet binding and had a rather bumpy loop to hang it by.

Linda held it up for the children to admire and they looked at it with reverence.

'Us've done it real nice!'

'Don't it look good!'

'Miss Clare'll like that all right!'

'Ah! Even if she's got a little old kettle-holder, she can always do with another one!'

They nodded wisely to each other, exchanging sagacious remarks like old women at a market stall.

John Burton, who was the neatest-fingered child, had the enviable task of wrapping it in tissue paper and tying it with a piece of red raffia. The children, handwork neglected, clustered round his desk to watch the delicate operation and to give advice.

'You pulls it too tight, mate!'

'He's right, you know . . . you'll have it all twizzled up inside!'

'If you leaves it to me,' said John soberly and without any rancour, 'I'll do it all right. It ain't no good getting excited-like when you doos parcels.' He tied a neat bow with unhurrying fingers, and I put it in a prominent position on top of the piano, so that they could gloat over it until it was time to go home.

There were four of us sitting at Miss Clare's round table that afternoon.

A cloth of incredible whiteness, bordered with a deep edging of Miss Clare's mother's crocheting, covered the table, and in the middle stood a bowl of primroses. The best tea-service, patterned with pansies, was in use, and cut-glass dishes held damson cheese and lemon curd of Miss Clare's own making. The bread and butter was cut so thin as to be almost transparent.

'I've a special old carving-knife,' explained Miss Clare earnestly, 'and I always sharpen it on the bottom step up to the lawn. It's really quite simple.'

The kettle-holder had been much admired and hung on a hook by the fire-place. Miss Clare glanced at it fondly from time to time.

'I shan't dirty it, you know. I've an old one I shall use . . . no, I really don't feel I could soil that one!'

Miss Gray and Mrs Finch-Edwards were with us and the conversation turned to Miss Gray's new home.

'No complaints anywhere!' announced Miss Gray. 'Except perhaps over-feeding. She's a wonderful cook.'

'And dressmaker,' added Miss Clare, peering into the depths of the teapot.

'She's making me some silk frocks,' began Mrs Finch-Edwards, then stopped suddenly. Her face became a warm red and she crumbled her cake.

'For any special occasion?' asked Miss Gray, who seemed unaware of her neighbour's sudden shyness.

Mrs Finch-Edwards looked up from her crumbling. 'I want them in September. I . . . that is, my hubby and I . . . are looking forward to a baby then.'

We were all delighted and a hubbub of questioning broke out

about knitting needs, the desirability of real wool for first-size vests, no matter what time of the year the baby was born . . . the advantages of high prams over low prams, and draped cots over plain ones . . . until it dawned on us three spinsters how fervent we were being with our advice to the only member of the party, who, presumably, knew more about the business than the rest of us put together.

The tea-party gained immensely in hilarity and animation after this disclosure, Miss Clare even going so far as to scold her guest for cycling over 'in her present state . . . very naughty indeed!' And she was inclined to get her brother to take her back in his car!

While we were thus cosily gossiping Mr Annett came up the path with a basket of eggs.

Mrs Partridge helped at the Women's Institute stall for two hours each market day, and I used to see the vicar's ancient car nosing its way round the bend by the school just before ten each Thursday morning. In the back would be piled Fairacre Women's Institute's contributions. During the holidays, Miss Clare had always enjoyed helping the vicar's wife, and now, having retired, she helped regularly at the stall.

On their way they would stop at Beech Green School. Mr Annett's older boys produced a weekly supply of eggs, vegetables, herbs and flowers which were sold on a stall in the market, belonging to a local market gardener. With the proceeds they bought seeds, plants, netting, tools and so on to carry on this good work. By the time the boys had loaded up their products Miss Clare and Mrs Partridge would be seated in a bower of greenery, peering above bunches of scrubbed carrots and turnips, and feeling for the gears among the cabbages.

At this time of year the school garden was not producing enough to be sent in, so that Mr Annett brought the eggs to Miss Clare to pack with hers overnight to save the car stopping again.

He sat himself down by Miss Gray and ate birthday cake. He looked very much more relaxed and happy, and could be called almost good-looking, I decided, when he smiled at his neighbour. If only he were fed properly and did not drive himself so hard at everything . . . if only he could find a thoroughly nice wife . . . I found myself looking at Miss Gray speculatively and pulled myself up sharply. Really, I was quite as bad as Nurse!

But for all that I was glad to see how very much at ease they were in each other's company, and although I didn't go so far as to name their children for them, I must admit that I was favouring a draped creamy wedding-dress for Miss Gray, rather than a white, when Miss Clare brought me back to earth by inquiring kindly if I had found the cake perhaps a trifle too rich.

The children were busy copying a notice from the blackboard. It said:

> 'Spring term ends on April 9th.
> School will reopen on Tuesday, April 28th.'

Pens were being wielded with especial care for their parents would receive these joyous communications and the children were aware that criticism, kindly or adverse, would greet their handwriting.

My class had to do two copies apiece; the best writers might even have the honour of writing a third, for Miss Gray's children could not yet be relied upon for a fair copy and the older children would supply theirs.

As they rattled their nibs in the inkwells and thumped their blotting paper with fat fists, I marked the compositions which had been written that morning. The subject was 'A Hot Day.' John Burton who has a maddening habit of transposing letters had written:

A HOT DAY

I feels tried when it is hot. I likes it best to be just rihgt not to hot not to clod. I wears my thin clothes when it is hot and my shaddy linen hat we bouhgt at a jumble sale it is a treat.

I called him to my desk and corrected this piece of work while he watched.

'You must make an effort with these "ght" words,' I told him, writing 'bought' and 'right' for him to copy three times. I explained, yet again, the intricacies of 'to, too and two' and wrote 'too hot and too cold' to be copied thrice.

There has been much discussion recently on the methods of marking compositions. Some hold that the child should be allowed to pour out its thoughts without bothering overmuch about spelling and punctuation. Others are as vehement in their assurances that each word misspelt and incorrectly used should be put right immediately. I think a middle course is best. On most occasions I correct and mark the work with the child by me, explaining things as I did to John, but sometimes I tell the children before they begin that I want to see how much they can write, and although I should appreciate correct spelling, I would rather they got on with the narrative and spelled phonetically than hold up their good work by inquiring how to spell a particular word. In this way I can assess any literary ability more easily and encourage that fluency, both written and spoken, which is so sorely lacking in this country school.

As a rule, the girls find it easier to express themselves than the boys. Their pens cover the page more quickly, they use a wider choice of adjective, and make use too of imagery, which the boys seldom do. The boys' essays are usually short, painstakingly dull and state facts. John Burton's account of a hot day is a fair example of the boys' attempts.

Cathy's contribution on the same subject made much more interesting reading:

A Hot Day

There are no clouds today and we shall have P.T. in the playground which I like. I like to run and jump and feel the wind through my hair. But I hope Miss Read does not make us sit with our legs crossed up for our exsersises because my knees get all sticky at the back on a hot day.

On the way home we all walk in the shade by the hedge. The cows stand under the trees and swish their tails to keep the flies off.

My mother likes hot days because her washing bleeches

white as snow, much whiter than the flowers on the elder bush where she always spreads out our hankys.

Everyone is happy when the sun shines on a hot day.

The glorious weather continued unbroken and here in the school-room were all the tokens of an early spring. The nature table against the wall bore primroses, cowslips and bluebells. The tadpoles were growing their legs with alarming rapidity and were due to depart, any day now, for the pond.

The weather chart pinned on the wall above the table showed a succession of yellow suns, bright as daisies, and out in the lobby a few cotton hats and light cardigans were an indication of the heat. To Mrs Pringle's well-disguised gratification the stoves had been unlit for two or three weeks and the most that she could find to grumble at was the wallflower petals that fluttered from the jug on the window-sill to the floor.

After the hard winter it seemed an enchanted time, and the reading of *The Wind in the Willows* on those blissful afternoons matched both the freshness and youth of the listeners and the spring world outside.

Through the partition I could hear the hum of Miss Gray's class at work. She seemed happy and in better health than when she arrived. Mrs Moffat had turned out to be the perfect landlady, and was herself much happier now that she had an appreciative lodger to admire her cooking, needlework and the other domestic virtues which her husband was apt to take for granted.

I hoped very much that Miss Gray would stay with me at Fairacre School. The children adored her and responded well to her quiet but cheerful manner. I could see that she was providing for them, as Miss Clare had done, an atmosphere of security and peaceful happiness in which even the most nervous child could put forth its best. With her top group's reading, particularly, she had worked well, and I was looking forward to having them in September in my class, confident that they would be able to hold their own with the older children. It was a fortunate day indeed, I told myself, when Miss Gray was appointed to Fairacre School and I hoped that she would stay with us for many years. A small doubt arose in my mind – wordless, but shaped like a question mark.

'Well, naturally . . . if that happened—' I answered aloud, and had to change the mutter to a cough, as the children's eyes met mine in some bewilderment.

April 9th came at last, and the excitement of the last day of term kept the children chattering like starlings.

As I was giving out the hymn books for morning prayers, Eric appeared at the door, with his father behind him. Mr Turner was carrying in his arms a small girl, who could not have been more than three years old. He looked dishevelled and agitated, and motioning Eric to his desk, I went into the lobby with his father.

'I've come to ask a favour, miss,' he began anxiously, dumping the child by his knees. She put one arm round his legs and looked up at me wonderingly.

'If you want me to have your daughter for the day,' I answered – this sort of emergency crops up occasionally and I always enjoy these diversions – 'I shall be very pleased indeed.'

Mr Turner looked relieved and grinned down at the upturned face.

'Hear that, duck? You can stop at school along of Eric, like a big girl, and I'll fetch you as soon as I gets back from Caxley.'

'What's happened?' I asked.

'It's my wife. I had to get Mrs Roberts to ring up Doctor at five this morning, and she's been took to hospital. Appendix, they thinks it is, and I'm to go in early this afternoon. Mrs Roberts would have had the little 'un but for it being market day. Ah! She's a good sort – been real kind, give us breakfast in her kitchen and all. And you too, miss,' he added hastily, fearful lest I should take umbrage at his praise of Mrs Roberts and his neglect of me, 'I'm truly thankful, miss . . . you knows that!' He fumbled in his pocket and brought out some coppers. 'For Lucy's dinner, if that's all right.' He counted out the money carefully, promised to fetch his daughter before the end of afternoon school, if he could get away from the hospital in time, and, with a final knuckle-grinding shake of my hand, made his farewell.

All through the morning Lucy sat perched up on the seat by her brother. Eric had been sent through to Miss Gray's room for a box of bricks, a doll and a picture book and these she played with very happily, keeping up a soft running commentary on her activities.

The children were enchanted to have a baby in the classroom and made a great fuss of her, offering her their sweets at playtime and picking up the stray bricks that crashed to the floor.

They reflected the attitude of the grown-up village people in their relationship to young children. I am always amazed at the servitude of the parents in these parts to their children, particularly the little rascals between two and five years old. These engaging young scoundrels can twist their doting parents round their fingers by coaxing, whining or throwing a first-class tantrum. The parents thoroughly spoil them, and the older children are also encouraged to pander to their lightest whim. Sweets, ice-cream, apples, bananas, cakes and anything else edible that attracts the child's fancy flow in an uninterrupted stream down the child's throat, as well as normal meals and the quota of orange juice and cod liver oil which is collected from the monthly clinic at the village hall, and, I must say in all honesty, that a more healthy set of children it would be hard to find. They seem to stay up until the parents themselves go to bed, and I see them playing in their gardens, or more frequently in the lane outside their cottages, until dusk falls. Then, sometimes as late as ten o'clock on a summer's evening, they finally obey the calls to 'Come on in!' which have been issuing from the cottage unheeded for an hour or more, and dragging reluctant feet they resign themselves, still protesting, to bed.

And yet, as I have said, under these methods which are a direct violation of the rules of a well-regulated nursery, these children thrive. Furthermore, when they enter school at the age of five, one might reasonably expect some trouble in maintaining discipline; but this is not so.

They prove to be docile and charming, obedient and happy in their more restricted mode of life. The truth of the matter is, I think, that they feel the need for direction and authority, and if this is offered them with interest and kindness they are more than ready to co-operate.

They love to have an outlet for their creative ability. To be shown how to make a paper windmill, or a top that really works, to learn to sing a song with actions, to make a bead necklace for themselves, or a rattle for a baby at home, or best of all, something for their mothers – a paper mat with their own bright patterns adorning it – all these things give them infinite pleasure because they have had an aim and they can see something for their labours. Their pre-school play has on the whole been aimless. Their parents buy for them expensive toys, dolls' prams, tricycles, model cars and the like which have restricted scope in a child's hands. Sand, water, clay and other creative media are not encouraged. 'Too messy . . . don't you go mucking up that clean frock now with that old mud,' you hear the parents call. 'Leave them old stones be and come and nurse your dolly! What's the good of me giving a pound for it if you never plays with it, eh?' What indeed?

In the infants' room Miss Gray was unpinning the Easter frieze of yellow chicks which had been the apple of the children's eyes for the past fortnight. Her cupboards were packed full of the objects which normally were stored in individual boxes under each child's desk. Counters, plasticine, chalk, felt dusters, first readers, boxes of letters and all the paraphernalia of infants' work had been sorted, checked and repacked.

The dregs of powder paint had been poured away and gleaming jam jars awaited next term's mixture-as-before. Vases were stacked on one shelf, and below them the great black clay tin, weighing half a hundredweight, had been packed with moist flannel to keep the balls in good condition for three weeks.

The babies were busy polishing their desks, on top and underneath, with pieces of rag brought from home and a dab from Miss Gray's furniture polish tin.

'Waste of time and good polish!' was Mrs Pringle's sour comment as she carried in the clean crockery to put away in the tall cupboard. On top of this stood a mysterious cardboard box, out of reach of prying hands. The label said 'Milk Chocolate Easter Eggs' and was carefully turned to face away from the class. Each one had a small label tied on, either blue or pink, and each child had to find the one with his own name on it. Miss Gray was going to hide them about the classroom while the children were out at afternoon play.

'Which reminds me,' she said to me, grovelling painfully under a low desk for a stray drawing-pin, 'I must see that they bring the eggs to me to check up on the names. It will never do to eat the wrong egg!'

In my room there was an equally interesting container, but mine was a round moss-lined basket, like an enormous nest, filled with eggs wrapped in bright tinfoil. The arrival of Lucy in our midst would mean a trip across to the schoolhouse to fetch one more for the basket.

We too were in a fine bustle of clearing-up when the vicar came in at the door. His cloak and leopard-skin gloves had been put away with his other winter garments, and he presented a summery appearance in his pale grey flannel suit and panama hat.

'I wanted to remind you all of one or two things,' began the vicar, when the children had settled back into their desks and he went on to explain to them the significance of the next Sunday, Palm Sunday, and invited offerings of pussy-willow and spring flowers for the church.

He followed this by a brief homily on Easter, the significance of the eggs which they would receive, and the hope that they would be at church with their parents on both these days.

He then spent a few minutes looking at the Easter cards which the children had crayoned ready to take home to their parents, and deciding that this was as good a time as any to present the eggs, I fetched two extra from the house and then passed the basket round.

The children's faces were alight with joy as they chose their eggs, little Lucy having to be restrained from scooping all that were left into her pinafore.

When it was found that there was one left and I asked them if they could think who might like it, the children rose to their cue, and, as one man, chorused: 'The vicar, miss! The vicar!'

And so, with great cheerfulness we broke up, and the children of Fairacre School, clutching their treasures to them, clattered out into the spring sunshine – free for three weeks!

PART THREE
Summer Term

* * * *

17. ANCIENT HISTORY, DOCTOR AND THE FILMS

In the bottom drawer of my desk are three massive books, with leather covers and mottled edges. Embossed on their fronts are the words 'Log Book' and they cover, between them, the history of this school.

The third one, which is nearly filled, has been in use for the past twenty years. If anything of note happens, such as a visit from an inspector, the outbreak of an epidemic, or the early closing of school through bad weather, illness or any other reason, then I make a note to that effect in the book, following in the tradition of the former heads of Fairacre School.

The log books thus form a most interesting account of a school's adventures; the early ones are particularly fascinating and should, I sometimes feel, be handed over to the local archivist who would find them a valuable contribution to the affairs of the district.

Our first entry at Fairacre School is at the latter end of 1880 when the first headmistress set down the details of her appointment and that of her sister as 'An assistant in the Babies' Class.' It has thus been a two-teacher school since its inception.

These two ladies would appear to have been kindly, conscientious and religious. Their discipline seems to have been maintained with some difficulty, and the rule, laid down by the local authority and still in force, that canings must be entered in the log book, leads to several poignant entries. The ink has faded to fawn in this first battered book, but there, in rather agitated handwriting, we can read:

'February 2nd, 1881. Had occasion to cane John Pratt (3) for Disobedience.'

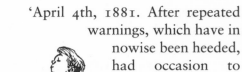

And a little later on:

'April 4th, 1881. After repeated warnings, which have in nowise been heeded, had occasion to punish Tom East (2), William Carter (2) and John Pratt (3) the Ringleader, for Insolence and Damage to School Property.'

The figures in brackets refer to the number of strokes of the cane, usually (2) or (3) seemed to be the rule, but gentle Miss Richards was evidently driven to distraction by John Pratt, for before long we read, in a badly-shaking hand:

'July, 1882. Found John Pratt standing on a Stool, putting on the Hands of the Clock with the greatest Audacity, he imagining himself unobserved. For this Impudence received six (6).'

During the following two years there are several entries about the sisters' ill-health and in 1885 a widow and daughter took over the school. Their first entry reads:

'April, 1885. Found conditions here in sore confusion. Children very backward and lacking, in some cases, the first Rudiments of Knowledge. Behaviour, too, much to be deplored.'

This is interesting because it is echoed, at every change of head, throughout the seventy-odd years of Fairacre School's history. The new head confesses himself appalled and shocked at his predecessor's slackness, sets down his intention of improving standards of work and conduct, runs his allotted time and goes, only to be replaced by just such another head, and just such another entry in the log book.

After a number of changes the headmistresses were replaced by a series of headmasters. One, Mr Hope, had his wife as assistant and their only child, Harriet, figures in the log book as the star pupil for several years.

'16th June, 1911. The Vicar presented the Bishop's prize to the best pupil, Harriet Hope. The Bishop was pleased to say that this child's ability and endeavour were outstanding.'

I like to think of Harriet accepting her prize Bible in this old schoolroom, her hair smoothed down and her pinafore dazzling white over a clean zephyr frock, while her classmates, resplendent in Norfolk or sailor suits for the occasion, clapped heartily.

But in 1913 come two tragic entries.

'January 20th, 1913. Have to record sad death of pupil (and only daughter) Harriet Hope,' and

'January 25th, 1913. School closed today on the occasion of the funeral of late pupil, Harriet Hope, aged twelve years and four months.'

Mr Hope's entries go on until 1919. He records his wife's long illness, his work throughout the Great War in the village, the school's War Savings accounts, the return of old pupils in uniform, the deaths of some in battle, and finally:

'May 18th, 1919. Have now to enter this last. My resignation having been accepted I leave Fairacre School for an appointment in Leicestershire.'

Mrs Willet filled in some of the gaps for me when I went down there to buy some rhubarb for bottling.

'I remember him well, of course, though I was only a child at the time; Harriet was a year or two older than I was. He went all to pieces after the child died. They both took it very hard. Mrs Hope was never well after it, and the headmaster – well, he just took to the bottle. I can remember him now bending down to mark something on my desk, his hand shaking like a leaf and his breath heavy with liquor. As soon as the school clock said ten, he'd put up another few sums on the blackboard, dare us to make a racket and then saunter down to 'The Beetle' for a drink. Us kids used to stand up on the desk seats and watch him go. The boys used to pretend to be upending the bottle and hiccup and that – all very naughty, I suppose, but you couldn't hardly blame them with that example set them, could you, miss?'

She wrapped the rhubarb securely in two of its own great leaves and tied the bundle with bass. From the dresser the owls gazed unblinkingly from under their glass case and I remembered the affair of Arthur Coggs.

As if she knew what was in my mind, Mrs Willet spoke: 'And I believe that's partly why my husband's so set against the drink. He saw what it done to poor Mr Hope – he was asked to leave the school you know, becoming too much of a byword – and took up some job up north as an ordinary teacher. They say he was never a headmaster again; which was a pity really, he being so clever. He wrote some lovely poetry and used to read it to us. Of course some of the boys laughed about it, but us girls liked it.'

'Was Mr Willet at school when you were?'

'Oh, yes, miss. He was always sweet on me. Pushed a little stone heart through the partition to me when I was still in the babies' room. There's a biggish gap in one part, you know.'

I did know. The children still poke odd things through to the adjoining room. The last object confiscated had been a stinging-nettle leaf cunningly gummed on to a long strip of cardboard.

Mrs Willet crossed to the dresser and brought back an oval china box. The lid bore a picture of Sandown and inside it was lined with red plush. She turned out the contents on to the serge tablecloth – jet brooches, military buttons, clasps, a gold locket and chain, and, among these trinkets, a small pebble, shaped like a heart, which had been picked up in the playground by the ardent young Willet so many years ago.

After admiring the treasures I made my farewells and set off up the lane with the heavy cold bundle on my bare arm.

'I suppose you're thinking of a full store-cupboard,' shouted Mr Roberts across the hedge. But my thoughts were of the man who had lived once in my house, whose daughter had died, whose wife had ailed, whose poems had been laughed at by the only people he had found to listen to them. The log books, with their sparse entries, tell truly of 'old, unhappy, far-off things, and battles long ago.'

Dr Ruth Curtis, who is our school doctor, employed by the County Council, is a man-hater. Or perhaps it would be better to say that she is a man-despiser, for she would scorn to whip up so much emotion against the lowly creatures as hatred. The men maintain, with their habitual modesty, that this is because she has not been lucky enough to secure one of them for a husband.

'Stands to reason,' they assert, soberly, 'that she feels frustrated! "Unfulfilled" is the word, isn't it?' And I try and look as solemn as they do, as I listen to them.

We women hold different views, but we don't air them quite so readily in front of the men. After all, as we say to each other, we all have to live together, don't we? No good making bad blood.

Dr Curtis arrived early in the summer term to examine the new children, Joseph, Jimmy and Linda, and the children who would be leaving at the end of the term, Cathy, Sylvia and John Burton.

The parents of these children had been notified of the time of the appointment and had been invited to be present. Chairs had been set in the lobby and Doctor had my room for the examination. The chart for sight testing was pinned up on to the partition, the scales were in evidence, and the wooden measure was fixed to the back of the door to record the heights of the six children.

Doctor was busy sorting out the cards which record each child's medical history throughout its school life. Cathy's, John's and Sylvia's would be forwarded to their new schools at the end of this term.

'Sorry I'm late,' growled Dr Curtis. 'My brother's staying with me and wanted me to change an adhesive dressing on his leg before I came away. Really, the fuss! I'd just started to pull it when he made enough noise for six stuck pigs! "Here!" I said, "take the scissors and hot water and get it off yourself!" So I've left him soaking the stuff, trying not to hurt himself. I told him one good sharp tear would soon get it off, but what can you do with men?'

I assumed that this question was rhetorical and asked her if she would like to see Mrs Coggs first with Joseph, as I knew she would want to get down to 'The Beetle and Wedge' for her scrubbing.

Joseph's eyes were wide with alarm throughout his examination. His apprehension, as he stood with his back to the door and felt the wooden marker descending on to his head, was pitiful to see. But no tears fell, even when Doctor stood him on a desk to see if his feet were flat.

'A very nice arch,' she said, squinting at Joseph's grubby foot. 'Very nice!' she added, and I caught the note of disappointment in her voice. Obviously flat feet were going to be 'the thing' this year, and I imagined half the children in the county walking about on the sides of their feet, as they did remedial exercises for the next few months.

Last year, hollow backs had been our doctor's obsession, and the year before, I remember, we were all exhorted to swim whenever possible to improve our physique. I could imagine the conversation when a few headmasters and mistresses met together later on in the term:

'And how many flat feet in your school?'

'Ten out of twenty.'

'Oh, we did better than that! We scored five out of six!'

Sure enough, the true fanatic gleam came into the doctor's eye only when she approached the feet this time. She left these to the last, in each case, working conscientiously on sight, hearing, hearts, posture, throats, height and weight, rather as a child works steadily through its pudding keeping the chocolate sauce intact to eat at the end.

John Burton was the only child who obliged Doctor on this day, but his feet were so triumphantly flat as to make up for the disappointingly springy feet of the other five. Mrs Burton was asked to take him to the clinic at Caxley where she would be shown the exercises he would need to do; and so Doctor's visit came to a successful close.

The lobby was empty, the chairs returned to the schoolroom

and the smell of disinfectant from the tumbler on Doctor's desk, which had held the spatula that she used when inspecting throats, gradually faded away.

'A really bad case, that last one,' said Doctor with much gratification, snapping her case closed. 'I'll keep an eye on that boy. I really don't think I've ever seen anything flatter!'

Quite exhilarated, she waved good-bye from her little car, and I returned to the schoolroom reflecting that we do indeed take our pleasures variously.

Mrs Pringle's bad leg always took a turn for the worse on the first Wednesday of each month.

On this afternoon the mobile film van called at Fairacre School to the joy of all but Mrs Pringle.

I could never quite understand the grounds for Mrs Pringle's dislike of these educational films. She had hinted darkly once of a terror-laden afternoon when her sister had heard the shout of 'Fire!' go up at the Caxley cinema and had had a corn trodden on painfully in the general stampede to the exit. But this second-hand adventure could not have accounted entirely for the regular monthly 'flare-up' of her own afflicted member. I think the general disorganization upset her, for we had to trundle back the partition and arrange the chairs in rows at the infants' end, leaving my part free for the screen to stand. The black-out curtains were drawn and, except for the unbiddable skylight which defied all attempts to shroud it, very little light penetrated. The children loved this mysterious twilight, and excitement always ran high, until the purring of the projector quietened them.

'Waste of the ratepayers' money,' snorted Mrs Pringle as, limping heavily, she clattered plates into the crockery cupboard. 'Do the children more good, I'd say, to be learnt something useful. Spelling, for instance. We always had spelling lists every Wednesday afternoon in Mr Hope's time. And he knew how to spell them himself without having to look 'em up!'

Mrs Pringle had been scandalized to see me looking up a word in the dictionary the week before. I think she had seriously considered reporting me to the omnipotent 'office' for inefficiency.

'Never see Mr Hope with a rubbishy thing like a dictionary,' continued Mrs Pringle, shooting forks with quick-fire precision into their box, and shouting above the racket.

'Perhaps he kept it at home,' I replied amiably.

'And another thing,' boomed Mrs Pringle, 'some of these films are downright improper. I saw one once at Caxley, with two people kissing each other, and though I daresay they were well on the road to a straightforward wedding, I didn't care for it myself and come out at once. Very unpleasant remarks I had to put up with too, I may say, from other people in the row who should have known better by the flashy way they were dressed up.'

I wondered whether it was worth while shouting myself hoarse against the clatter by explaining that the afternoon's programme consisted of a film about the building of a Norman castle, which would link up with the history lessons of this term, a second film about the herring industry, which might widen the outlook of some of these children who had only just seen the sea, although it lay less than eighty miles away; and a short film about the animals at the London Zoo. I decided to save my breath, and, leaving Mrs Pringle to her dark mutterings, I went to welcome Mr Pugh who was staggering in carrying heavy equipment. Behind him followed a train of admiring children who had had strict orders to stay in the playground until called, but were drawn to Mr Pugh's imposing collection of tin cases, cables, stands, the rolled-up screen and so on, like needles to a magnet.

Mr Pugh is a small, volatile Welshman who takes his work very seriously. His job is really to bring the films and to show them, but he takes such a passionate interest in every one of them that any sort of adverse criticism throws him into Celtic protestations. One would imagine that he had produced, directed and acted in all the films that flicker in our murky classroom, so quick is he in their defence. Luckily, he is soothed by cups of tea, and I make sure that the tray is set and the kettle filled in readiness, on the first Wednesday afternoon of each month.

At last the room was ready, the children were called in and exhorted by me in the playground to step carefully over the cable, and by Miss Gray inside to sit down and sit still. Mr Pugh flicked a switch, the projector purred, the pictures wavered before us and the old magic had begun again. After each film the children clapped energetically. The most popular, of course, was the animal film. Some of the children had already been to the Zoo and I knew that others might go in the near future with the Mothers' Union outing.

A satisfied sigh went up from the school as the last film ended. Miss Gray and I drew back the curtains and surveyed our family, sitting in rows and blinking like little owls in the unaccustomed light.

While Mr Pugh dismantled his paraphernalia, Miss Gray went to switch on the kettle and I led the children out to play, their heads buzzing with castles, herrings and hippopotami. Tomorrow I should have to sort out these troubled images for them, as best I could, and I made a mental note that another trip across to the church to see the Norman window there, would be a good thing to do in the morning.

These visits from the film unit are of inestimable value to the country school. The choice of films is wide and gives an added fillip to the classroom lessons which follow them.

Perhaps the welcome that the children give to Mr Pugh and his fellows is the surest indication of their success.

18. THE MUSICAL FESTIVAL

There was a bus drawn up in the lane outside Fairacre School. It quivered and vibrated in the May sunlight; and beside it, in their best clothes, the children clustered hopping with excitement. It was the great day of the Caxley Musical Festival and Miss Gray, who was to conduct the choir, was doing her best to fight down her own stage-fright and calm her charges.

She wore a pale-green linen frock which had been much admired by the children.

'Real smashing!' said John Burton.

'It suits her lovely!' said the girls, head on one side; and Linda Moffat said, with much pride: 'My mum helped her with it. You never saw so many darts in the bodice! That's what makes it fit so good.'

'Now you understand,' I addressed the children when they were finally seated, 'you are to be on your best behaviour. All the other schools will be there at the Corn Exchange. Let them see how polite and helpful you are!'

Whether these admonitions were heeded I doubt, for the excitement of the occasion was almost unendurable, but the driver climbed in, was greeted cheerfully by the children, for he was a local boy, and the bus began to grind along the flower-starred lanes to Caxley.

'Miss,' said Eric, 'what happens when we want a drink?'

'Or we feels sick?' added Ernest.

'Or wants to be excused?' asked Linda in a prim, but anxious whisper.

We assured them that Caxley Corn Exchange offered facilities which could cope with all these contingencies, and we begged them to cease to worry, to relax, to rest their throats or otherwise they would forget their songs or sing horribly sharp with anxiety.

At last we chugged into the market-place. There, outside the Corn Exchange which dominates one side of the square, were queues of excited children slowly edging through the wide doorway.

Shepherding their flocks were determinedly patient teachers, the women with their hair freshly set, wearing undramatic summer dresses and their best sandals, and the men almost unrecognizable in formal suits . . . their beloved shapeless grey flannels and jejune hacking jackets mercifully left behind on the backs of their bedroom chairs.

We collected our twittering children and joined the mob.

Caxley Corn Exchange is described as 'an imposing pile' by the local guide-book and perhaps it is as well to leave it at that. Certainly one's feelings on first catching sight of it are incredulity and then pity for so much misapplied labour.

Inside, the walls are of bare brick. The windows are glazed with a greenish glass and these admit a curious underwater light which adds to the general feeling of submersion. On each side of the windows are brick curlicues, like gigantic barley-sugar sticks, and at the end of the hall looms a massive statue of one of the benefactors of the town. This forbidding person, who is twelve feet high, gazes with bewhiskered severity at the crowd below him, and holds in his hand a watch, for all the world as if he is saying: 'Late again, eh? This must be reported!'

The hall was rapidly filling with schoolchildren from more than twenty schools. We found our places and gazed about us.

In the centre of the hall was a dais with a large table, a microphone, masses of papers and a handbell. Here the judges were to sit. Near the stage was the grand piano with banks of hydrangeas at its feet.

'Real beautiful, ain't it?' said Sylvia in an awed whisper – her eyes on the barley sugar sticks.

'Been here often!' announced John Burton casually, with a cosmopolitan air. 'Come with my dad for the chrysanthemum show last autumn. There's a bigger place than this up London.'

A respectful silence greeted this piece of news.

At last Eric spoke. 'Show off!' he said witheringly, and had the satisfaction of seeing John turn pink, but whether from rage or discomfiture no one knew.

The morning wore on. We sailed over the sea to Skye at various paces from staccato to near-static. We follow-follow-followed till we were dizzy and our heads throbbed. The air inside the Corn Exchange grew thicker despite the open windows, which had yielded grudgingly, with dreadful groanings, to much heavy battering.

But the Fairacre children looked bright-eyed as squirrels as they waited on the stage to begin their songs. Miss Gray's green linen back registered acute anxiety and her baton trembled when she raised it first, but once they were launched all went well and they beamed smugly at the applause which followed their efforts. Swaggering slightly, they simpered back to their places. Mr Annett, who had somehow managed to seat himself near our school, murmured congratulations into Miss Gray's ear as she returned, and hitched his chair a foot closer.

The chairman rose on the dais.

'We'll stop now for lunch. Everyone back here please at one-thirty sharp. Thank you all very much,' This welcome announcement brought the biggest clap of the morning.

After lunch Miss Gray and I took the children to a nearby park. They made a rush for the paddling pool, for in the downland village of Fairacre there is very little water to play in.

The sun was warm and a dragon-fly hovered, vibrating and iridescent over the water. I sat on the grass to watch our children as they gazed at the lucky owners of toy boats who were running importantly round the edge with long sticks.

At the other end of the park I could see the Beech Green children, with Miss Young and Mr Annett. He appeared to be scanning the horizon in a purposeful way, and at length he detached himself from his school and, leaving poor Miss Young to cope with the entire school, advanced rapidly upon Miss Gray who was sitting composedly upon a bench under a poplar tree.

'There's fish here!' screamed Joseph Coggs, across the pond, in great excitement. 'Little 'uns, miss. You come and see!'

'There's real fish what you can eat in that ditch behind you,' a tall boy told him, in a voice that trembled between soprano and baritone, indicating a little stream that slips along the side of the park to join the river that flows through Caxley. At this moment hubbub broke forth behind me and there, emerging dripping from the pool, with hair sleeked down like a seal and mouth agape for bawling, stood Jimmy Waites.

His beautiful white shirt and grey flannel shorts were soaking, and spattered with flotsam from the surface. In fact, the only dry things about him were his socks and sandals which Cathy had helped him to remove for a surreptitious paddle while my eye was averted. Crying herself, with vexation and shock, she knelt beside her little brother.

I halloed to Miss Gray who was still sitting on the bench studying her shoes demurely while Mr Annett chattered away beside her. Really, I thought with some exasperation, it was too bad of them to be so blissfully removed from the vexations of this life. Somewhat peremptorily, I told Miss Gray that I was taking Jimmy to the lavatory to mop him up and would she keep an eye on the others. Mr Annett returned hastily to this world from the elysium where he had been floating, and had the good sense to offer to run the child home in his car when I had dried him.

'Lord!' said the attendant with relish, 'he hasn't half got his clothes mucked up! Won't your mother say something to you, my lad!' At which, the hideous bawling which I had calmed with much difficulty, broke forth anew.

Between us we rubbed the shivering child dry and Cathy was despatched to fetch Mr Annett's car rug to wrap him in.

We emerged from the shrubbery, which decently drapes our Caxley lavatories, with Jimmy looking like a little Red Indian, the fringe of the rug trailing behind him. We gathered the rest of the children together and with Mr Annett carrying Jimmy, and Miss Gray beside him, leading the way, we returned to the Corn Exchange.

As we crossed the market square I noticed John Burton walking closely behind Mr Annett. He was mimicking the schoolmaster's springy steps, and with eyes crossed and mouth idiotically open he was giving a striking and hideous representation of a love-sick swain, much to the admiration of his companions.

'John Burton!' I called sharply. He hastily returned to normal. 'What on earth,' I continued, using that tone of shocked bewilderment that comes so easily to any teacher, 'what on earth, boy, are you supposed to be doing?'

'Nothing, miss!' he answered meekly, and, lamb-like, walked with decorous steps back to his place in the Corn Exchange. We watched Mr Annett and his bundle drive away towards Fairacre and followed the children for the afternoon session.

'Well, we've had enough excitement to last us today,' I commented to Miss Gray, as we subsided into our seats. She smiled at me in reply, with such sweet and lunatic vagueness, that I realized that she was still many miles away, on the road to Fairacre, in fact. Love, I thought crossly, can be very tiresome; and, looking to the stage for some relief, found none; for, with awful purpose writ large upon their youthful faces, twenty children were there assembled, and each bore a violin.

It was not until after Mr Annett's return that the second shock of the day fell. He had assured me, in a tickling whisper, that Jimmy was safely with his mother and I had whispered back my gratitude and allowed my tense muscles to relax with some relief. At that moment I thought of Joseph Coggs, scanned the rows before and behind me and could see nothing of him. On the stage the excruciating sawing went on, and under the cover of its discord I sent agitated messages to Miss Gray. Had she seen him? Had he slipped out to the lavatory? Did he come back with us? Had she counted the children when she collected them in the park? How many were there then?

Miss Gray's gentle gaze rested upon me without a hint of perturbation. She wore the expression of one who, returning from an anaesthetic, leaves some bright world behind with infinite regret. Only the fact that she turned her eyes in my direction gave any hint that she had heard me.

No help there, I thought to myself, and added in a savage whisper: 'I'm going out to look for him.' Several shocked glances from my more musically-conscious colleagues were cast at me as I retreated from the hall, and a look, more in sorrow than in anger, from the only female judge.

'Are you all right? Can I fetch you some water?' inquired a kindly headmaster near the door. I felt inclined to tell him that I was on the verge of an apoplectic fit, brought on through exasperation, and that nothing less than half a tumbler of neat brandy could touch me – but, knowing how these things get misconstrued in a small community, I restrained myself, thanked him, and escaped into the market square.

The park was much less crowded now and presented a peaceful appearance. Mothers sat beside prams, knitting or gossiping, while their infants slept or hurled toys blissfully to the ground.

The paddling pool had only a few small female occupants, who were wading with their frocks tucked into bulging knickers. Joseph was not among them.

In the distance the park-keeper was spearing odd pieces of paper with a spiked stick. I hurried towards him.

'I've lost a child—' I began breathlessly.

'No need to take on so, ma!' replied the man. 'You ain't the first to mislay your kiddy, believe me. The mothers we get, coming up here to me, hollering same as you—'

'I am unmarried—' I said with what dignity I could muster.

'Well, well,' soothed the insufferable fellow comfortingly, 'we all makes mistakes sometimes.'

'I mean,' I said with emphasis, wondering how long my sanity could stand up to these repeated bludgeonings of an unkind fate, 'that I am a schoolteacher.'

'That accounts for it, miss,' the man assured me. 'School-teachers, unless they're caught very young, never hardly gets married. Funny when you come to think of it!'

His eyes became glazed as he dwelt upon this natural phenom-enon, and I adopted a brisk tone to bring him round.

'One of my children . . . my class . . . a little boy, was left behind when we went back to the Corn Exchange this afternoon. A dark child – about five.'

'About five,' repeated the man slowly, stropping his chin with a dirty hand. He thought for a few minutes and then looked up brightly. 'He's probably lost!' he said.

Controlling myself with a superhuman effort, I told him to take the child if he found him to Miss Gray at the Corn Exchange, where he would be suitably rewarded. Turning my back on him, with some relief, I set out to the little stream where I guessed that those 'fish big enough to eat' had probably drawn the truant from Fairacre School.

The stream was bordered with dense reeds, lit here and there by yellow irises and kingcups. The early swallows and swifts flashed back and forth, squealing, the sun glinting on their dark-blue backs. On any other afternoon I should have thought this willow-lined retreat a paradise, but anxiety dulled its beauties, as I squelched by the water's edge to the detriment of my white shoes.

'Joseph! Joseph!' I called, but the only answering cry was from the birds around me. Somehow I felt sure that the child was near here . . . that the stream had attracted him.

Supposing, I thought suddenly, something dreadful had happened to him! Morbid pictures of a small body awash among the duckweed, or entangled among willow roots, or, worse still, gradually being sucked down into the treacherous mud at the stream's edge, all flitted through my mind.

'For pity's sake,' I begged myself crossly, 'don't add to it! You'll be choosing the hymns for the funeral next.'

The stream made a sharp right-angled bend by a fine black poplar tree whose white fluff blew about the grass beneath it. Huddled against its trunk, terrifyingly still, lay Joseph.

Unable to speak, and with mounting agitation, I approached him. To my infinite relief I could hear him snoring.

His cheeks were flushed with sleep, but there were shiny streaks, like snail tracks, where the salt tears had dried. His long black lashes were still wet and his pink mouth slightly open. Beside him, in a jam jar, swam two frenzied minnows in about half an inch of water.

I sat down on the grass beside the sleeping figure to regain my composure. Tears of relief blurred the shining landscape, my legs ached and I felt, suddenly, very old and shaky.

While I was recovering, Joseph stirred. He opened his eyes and stared straight above him at the rustling leaves. Then, without moving his body, he rolled his head over and looked long and solemnly at me. Slowly a very loving smile curved his lips, he put out a grubby hand and held fast to my clean dress.

'Oh, Joseph!' was all I could say, giving him a hug.

'I got lost,' growled Joseph, 'and a boy give me this jar to go fishing with. Ain't they lovely?' He held the jar up to the sunshine while the two unhappy occupants flapped more madly than before.

I rose to my feet, and we went to the water's edge to fill the jar. There was no doubt about it . . . the minnows were destined to spend the rest of their short lives in Joseph's doting care.

Together we wandered back along the stream, hand in hand, Joseph pausing from time to time to croon over the top of the jar. His sandals oozed black slime at every step, his eyes were still swollen with crying, but he was a very happy little boy, safe again, and with two new playmates.

The market square was dazzling in the sunlight and it was good to get back to the cool under-water gloom of the Corn Exchange. Thankfully, I realized that the violins had finished during my absence, but my relief was short-lived.

'And now,' announced the chairman, with misplaced enthusiasm, as we regained our seats, 'we begin the percussion classes!'

The children sang on the way home in the bus. They sang all the songs that they had learnt for the Festival, some they had heard on the wireless, and some regrettable numbers that someone's father had taught them in an expansive moment. Miss Gray and I sat silent, I with exhaustion and she, it seemed, with unmodified rapture. Occasionally a happy little sigh escaped her lips. Occasionally, when my feet obtruded their discomfort particularly, I sighed too.

At Mrs Moffat's bungalow we stopped and she spoke.

'Shall I come on to the school with you? Can I be of any help?'

'No,' I answered, 'I can manage. It's been a long day – you'll want your tea and a rest I expect.'

'It's been a heavenly day,' replied Miss Gray ardently, 'and I'm not a bit tired. In fact, I've arranged to go out for the evening with Mr Annett . . . we thought . . . well, yes! I'm going out with Mr Annett.'

I said that would be very nice indeed and that I would see her in the morning.

John Burton, who had overheard this conversation, and fondly imagined that he was unobserved, now saw fit to repeat his famous dying-duck-in-a-thunderstorm act and began to blow languid kisses about the bus to his delighted friends.

The door closed behind Linda and Miss Gray. I leant forward and, without any warning, gave John Burton a sharp box on the ear.

It was, I found, the best moment of the day.

19. THE FÊTE

In the infants' room a crayoning lesson was in progress. Joseph Coggs, now recovering from his adventure, was busily drawing little boys dancing. They all had three buttons down their egg-shaped bodies, large teeth and hands like rakes. From their trunks up they presented a wooden and fearsome appearance; but their legs were thrown about in attitudes of wild abandonment.

'Be very careful,' Miss Gray warned them, 'the best ones will be pinned up on the blackboard, and put in the tent for everyone to see, on the day of the Fête.'

'Will we get prizes?' asked Jimmy Waites.

'Very likely; and even if you don't, you want your parents to see how well you can draw. Keep them clean,' added Miss Gray, and went back to her cupboard-tidying, humming to herself.

Joseph liked to hear her humming. She hummed a lot these days, and seemed, he thought, to be kinder than ever. As he drew a large yellow circle for the sun, he thought of all the things she had taught him.

He could add up numbers up to ten and take them away too, though this was hard sometimes. He knew all the sounds the letters made and some words as well. He could copy his name from the card Miss Gray had made for him, and he knew lots of songs and poems that he sang and recited to his little sisters at home. And as for making paper houses, like the first one his father had used for a pipe lighter, why, he'd made dozens since then and each better than the last. Yes, he decided, he liked school and . . . blow it all, he'd bust his crayon!

'Lend us yer yaller,' he hissed to Eileen Burton beside him, but she was uppish this afternoon, and shook her head.

'I wants it,' she said firmly, putting down the green one she had been using for grass. The subject was 'A Summer's Day,' and all the green crayons were wearing down fast. She snatched up her yellow crayon close to her chest. 'I wants it,' she repeated, and then leaning over surveyed Joseph's picture closely. 'I wants it for the sun,' she announced triumphantly, and began to draw a yellow circle, exactly like Joseph's, on her paper.

This annoyed him, and, gripping Eileen's fragile wrist, he tried to prise the crayon from her fingers. Miss Gray, humming still, and sitting on her heels with her head in the cupboard, remained oblivious of the gathering storm.

'You ol' devil!' breathed Joseph, scarlet in the face. 'You copycat! You give it here!'

With a wrench, Eileen gained possession of the crayon again, and holding it above her head, she put out an impudent pink tongue at her pursuer. Maddened, Joseph lowered his dark head and butted her on the shoulder, and then, fastening his teeth in her arm he bit as hard as he could.

A terrible screaming broke out from Eileen and cries from the rest of the class. Miss Gray, rushed into action, slapped Joseph and released Eileen who inspected her wounds and howled afresh at the neat teeth marks on her tender flesh.

'He swored, Miss,' volunteered Jimmy Waites, 'he said "Devil," Miss, didn't he? Didn't he swear, then?'

Yes, he had, agreed everybody, rather smugly. Joseph Coggs had swored and tried to take Eileen's crayon and bit her when she wouldn't let him have it. Joseph Coggs was a naughty boy, wasn't he? Joseph Coggs wouldn't be allowed to go to the Fête, would he? Joseph Coggs, in the opinion of his self-righteous classmates, was not fit to mix with them.

Miss Gray silenced them peremptorily, sent Joseph to stand by her desk and Eileen to wash her arm in the lobby.

The artists continued in comparative silence, but there were many accusing nods towards the culprit, who was having his version of the incident drawn from him by Miss Gray.

'It doesn't excuse you, Joseph,' said Miss Gray finally, 'you must say you are sorry to her and never do such a dreadful thing again. I shall have to write a note to Eileen's mother to explain her hurt arm, and you must sit on your own until we can trust you again.'

So Joseph sat in splendid isolation to finish his picture, and a few sad tears mingled with the daisies that he drew in the grass.

But once the hated apology was over, the crayons collected, and Miss Gray's *Mother Goose Nursery Rhymes* appeared again on her desk, his spirits revived.

Who cared what ol' Eileen Burton's mother said? She couldn't hurt him, and anyway it served her right for copying his sun. And he didn't call 'Devil' swearing – why, it was in the Bible the vicar read to them! Swearing indeed! With a glow of pride Joseph thought of all the real swear words his father used. He bet he knew more than anybody in the class, if it came to that!

Much heartened, he turned an attentive face to Miss Gray, who thought what a dear little boy he was, despite everything. And there she was right.

The fête was held on the first Saturday in May, in the Vicarage garden; 'Proceeds' said the posters, that fluttered from vantage points in the village, 'in aid of the Church Roof Fund.'

'And how slowly it grows!' sighed the vicar. 'We need another three hundred pounds at least, and the roof is deteriorating every day.'

He was in his shirt-sleeves, his mild, old face screwed up against the sunshine. He bore a wooden mallet for driving in the stakes which were to hold the various notices. In the distance we could hear the clatter of the lawn mower which Mr Willet was pushing over the tennis court.

This, the only flat piece of the vicar's garden, which lay on the slope of the downs, was to be used for bowling for the pig. Golden bales of straw were stacked at the side, ready to make an enclosure for the great skittles, when Mr Willet had finished his ministrations.

A breeze fluttered the crêpe paper along the edge of the stalls. Miss Clare was busy setting out dozens of crêpe paper dorothy bags filled with home-made candy, and tempting bottles and boxes of toffee, humbugs and boiled sweets. Rows of lollipops lined the edge of the stall and it was obvious that Miss Clare's old pupils would soon be flocking round her again.

She was having lunch with me; cold meat, new potatoes and salad, with gooseberry fool for sweet – a meal which, I surmised, would be echoed in most Fairacre homes that day – a direct result of a bumper gooseberry crop coupled with hectic last-minute preparations for the fête.

In Linda Moffat's house, Mrs Moffat, her mouth full of pins, was putting the final touches to her daughter's flowered head-dress. Linda was going to the fête dressed as a shepherdess, complete with blue satin panniers, sprigged apron and a shepherd's crook, borrowed from old Mr Burton and decked for the occasion with bunches of blue ribbons. Miss Gray stood by admiring. 'Sweet!' she said.

'Hold ftill!' said Mrs Moffat, much impeded in her speech by pins 'Ftand ftraight for juft a fecond more!'

And Linda, sighing deeply, but submitting to the fuss, only hoped that her long suffering might result in a prize in the fancy-dress competition that afternoon.

In Tyler's Row, at the Waites' cottage, there was great excitement, for a letter had come, with the education committee's seal on its envelope, bringing the good news that Cathy had been deemed fit for a place next September at Caxley County Grammar School for Girls.

'But I wanted to go to the High School!' protested Cathy, when this was read out to her.

'Same thing!' her mother assured her. 'Cathy, my love, you've done real well.'

Her father beamed at her, and feeling in his pocket, presented her with half a crown.

'Here, duck, that's for the fête this afternoon. I reckon you deserves a bit of a spree!'

The letter was propped carefully behind the tea-tin on the mantelpiece, and Cathy, rushing into the little garden turned cartwheel after cartwheel, her red checked knickers bright in the sunshine, letting off some of the high spirits that fizzed and bubbled within her.

Joseph Coggs, squatting on the ash path next door, watched these antics through the hedge. Beside him sat his two little sisters, crop-headed since Nurse's visit, busily stirring stones and mud together for a delightful dolls' pudding.

'Going up the fête?' asked Cathy, standing upright at last and staggering slightly as the garden slowed down around her.

'Dunno,' answered Joseph gruffly. The two little girls ceased their stirring, and advanced towards the gap in the hedge, wiping their hands down their bedraggled skirts.

'What fête?'

'Up the vicar's. You know, what we been practising for at school.'

Joseph suddenly remembered all he had been told about races, fancy-dress competitions, sweet-stalls, prizes and his own beautiful picture which had been pinned on to the board for the judges to see. Without a word he pounded up to the house, the sisters scampering, squeaking, behind him.

In the stuffy kitchen his mother was shaking the baby's bottle and looking at it with some impatience. The baby cried fitfully.

'Can us go to the fête?'

'Do let's, Mum; let's go! Say us can go, Mum!' they clamoured above the baby's crying.

'Oh, we'll see,' said their mother testily. 'You get off in the garden while I feeds baby. This bottle don't draw right.'

She sucked at it lustily and then turned it upside down, watching it critically.

'Oh, Mum, you might! Just for a bit. Please, Mum!' they pleaded.

The bottle was thrust into the baby's mouth, and peace reigned.

'I'll see how I gets on,' said Mrs Coggs grudgingly. 'I don't know as I've got enough clean clothes for you all to go up to the vicar's, with all the rain this week. You get on outside and play quiet for a bit. Perhaps we can.'

She joggled the baby on her arm. The children still waited.

'Oh, buzz off!' shouted Mrs Coggs with exasperation. 'I've said us might go, haven't I?'

And with this unsatisfactory answer ringing in their ears, the Coggs children returned reluctantly to the garden.

The vicar had prevailed upon a well-known novelist, Basil Bradley, who lived locally, to open the fête, and this he had done in a speech of charm and brevity.

Beside him, accommodated in the vicar's best armchair, sat his mother, an old lady in her ninety-third year, so wayward and so eccentric in her behaviour as to cause her celebrated son many moments of anxiety.

She was the widow of a brewer and was said to be very wealthy indeed.

It was common knowledge that her son had none of this money. He lived, comfortably enough, however, upon his earnings, and was wont to smile patiently when his mother said, as she did frequently, 'Why the dickens should the boy have any of my money? He'll have it when I'm gone – do him good to wait for it!'

It was her habit, however, to give him expensive, and often useless, presents at odd times, which he did his best to receive gratefully, for he was devoted to this maddening despot. Only this morning he had accepted, with well-simulated gratification, a quite hideous paper-rack, made of black bog-wood, which his mother had purchased from an antique dealer who should have known better.

'Speak up, Basil,' she had commanded, in a shrill pipe, towards the end of his speech, 'Mumble-mumble-mumble! Use your teeth and your tongue, boy! Where are your consonants!'

She was now at Miss Clare's stall inquiring the price of sweets, and expressing her horror at such outrageous charges.

'As a gel,' she said to the imperturbable Miss Clare, 'I bought pure home-made fig toffee for a halfpenny a quarter. Good wholesome food, with a wonderful purging property. Not this sort of rubbish!' She waved an ebony stick disdainfully at Miss

Clare's stall and turned away in disgust. Her son, smiling apologetically, bought humbugs and lollipops in such enormous quantities that Miss Clare wondered where on earth he would get rid of them.

Dr Martin, holding a large golliwog which he had won at hoop-la, was admiring the rose which climbed over the vicarage porch.

'That's a nice rose,' said the old lady, coming up behind him. 'A good old-fashioned rose. A nice flat face on it, you can get your nose into!'

The vicar basked in this sudden approval. 'A great favourite of mine, isn't it, Doctor? I planted it the autumn that my son was born.'

'Can't beat a Gloire de Dijon,' agreed the doctor, 'splendid scent!' And he bent a spray for the old lady to sniff.

'Allow me to pick you some,' said the vicar, and vanished into the house for the scissors.

'Most sensible man I've seen for a long time,' commented Mrs Bradley. 'Knows a good rose and gives you some too. Don't often get a bunch of flowers these days. Old people get neglected,' she added, squeezing a tear of quite unnecessary self-pity into her eye. Doctor Martin and poor Basil Bradley exchanged understanding looks. Doctor Martin thought of the numerous well-kept hothouses in the Bradley grounds and forbore to make any comment; but taking the old lady's hand in his he patted it comfortingly.

The vicar bustled back and snipped energetically, taking great pains to cut off any thorns. He was very proud of his rose and delighted to find an admirer in this crusty old lady.

'And now,' she said, when the bouquet was tied with bass, 'I must give you something for your funds before my son takes me home. Go away, Basil,' she ordered the poor man, who had stepped forward to take her arm. 'Go away, boy, while I go into the vicarage to write a cheque. And don't fuss round me as though I were incapable!'

Her son meekly sat on the edge of the stone urn while the vicar, expostulating politely, led his visitor to the drawing-room. There, in a spiky handwriting, reminiscent of the French governess of her childhood, Mrs Bradley wrote a cheque and gave it to the vicar.

'But, my dear Mrs Bradley, I simply can't accept—' began that startled man.

'Stuff!' snapped Mrs Bradley, 'I haven't been given a bunch of roses like that for years. Stop fussing, man, and let me get home for my rest.'

She stepped out into the sunshine again and set off for the car.

Mr Partridge, much bewildered, held out the cheque for Basil Bradley's inspection.

'Your mother, so kind, but I feel perhaps . . . her great age, you know,' babbled the vicar incoherently.

The son reassured him. 'I'm so glad that she has given generously to such a good cause. Believe me, you have made her very happy this afternoon.'

'Hurry up, boy,' came a shrill voice from the car, 'don't waste the vicar's time when he's busy!' And, waving a claw-like hand, she was driven off.

Over on the tennis court, bowling-for-the-pig was doing a roaring trade. Mr Willet was in charge, perched up on the top of the straw bales, and hopping down, every now and again, to roll the heavy balls back to John Burton's father, who was taking the sixpences and handing out the balls.

Away, in the corner of the walled kitchen garden, stood the pigsty, usually empty, but now housing a small black Berkshire pig, who was accepting such dainties as apple cores, and even an occasional toffee-paper, from the children who stood round admiring him.

Mrs Bryant, her trilby hat a landmark, sat on the grass at the side of the tennis court, with several of her sons and daughters around her. All her boys were noted marksmen, and very few pigs from the local fêtes found other homes than with the Bryant tribe.

Malachi, a swarthy six-footer, in a maroon turtle-neck sweater, had just knocked seven of the nine skittles down with his three balls, and Ezekiel was now about to try his luck.

All Mrs Bryant's boys had Biblical names and as she had mastered the reading of capital letters, but had never gained the ability to read small ones, their names had been garnered from the headings of the books of the Bible. Her fifth son she had decided to call 'Acts' but was gently dissuaded from this by the vicar who had suggested that 'Amos' might be a happy substitute, and in this the old lady had concurred.

The tale got round, however, and Amos was nicknamed 'Acts' or rather, 'Axe,' from an early age. Now a man in his thirties, Axe Bryant ran a thriving fish and chip shop in Caxley, and was too busy this afternoon preparing his potatoes for the Saturday night rush to join his brothers at Fairacre in bowling for the pig.

After Ezekiel had had his turn, John Pringle arrived on the scene. He was popular, and everyone hoped he would give the Bryants a run for their money. With great cunning he bowled his three balls, and the last one, by some distortion of the pitch, knocked down three out of the remaining four standing.

'Eight!' went up the triumphant cry, 'Good old John! Eight!' And delighted glances were exchanged and much back-slapping. Even Mrs Pringle managed a faint congratulatory smile at her son, basking in his reflected glory. But the Bryant tribe looked grim.

'Malachi!' ordered Mrs Bryant in a voice of thunder, with a jerk of the trilby hat towards the balls. With his black brows drawn together, Malachi advanced with another sixpence, and after spitting on his hands, he sent down his first ball in answer to the challenge.

Mrs Moffat was receiving congratulations from the vicar's wife on her daughter's dress. Linda had won first prize of five shillings which she was now ploughing back into the fête funds by treating several small friends to ice-cream.

Several of the mothers had spoken to her and had said how pretty Linda looked. Fairacre, Mrs Moffat suddenly thought, was a very pleasant place, and, with an uprush of spirits, she remembered how gloomy she had been a year ago as a newcomer to the village. No, she decided, things were not too bad. Money was easier with Miss Gray boarding with her, Linda was happy at school, the house and garden were settled and she had made a staunch friend in Mrs Finch-Edwards. She moved among the crowd on the lawn, now one of Fairacre's inhabitants, accepted and content.

The schoolchildren in my class performed their play. John Burton's opening line, 'I am the Spirit of Summer,' which I had practised with him until it rang in my head from dawn to dusk, was, as I had feared, delivered in the perfunctory, off-hand mutter, that I had sweated blood to change to an arresting declamation. Everyone applauded heartily, however, and the infants gambolled on to perform their singing games under Miss Gray's direction.

In the vicar's drawing-room, Miss Clare sat at the piano, which had been pulled close to the french windows, and there she played the old nursery tunes, 'Here we go round the Mulberry Bush' and 'Poor Jenny is a-weeping,' and 'There was a Jolly Miller,' as she had done so many times for their fathers and mothers.

The babies clapped and sang, very delighted with themselves, gazing cheerfully over their shoulders at their parents all the time. The circle occasionally set off in the wrong direction and had to be steered by Miss Gray now and again, but the whole show was an enormous success, and I felt that Fairacre School had covered itself with glory.

A cold little wind sprang up after tea, rustling the leaves of the rhododendrons and sending the people back to their cottages. The stall-holders began to sell their wares at half-price, and the people in charge of Aunt Sally, fishing with a magnet, and rolling pennies, began to collect their paraphernalia and the pudding basins, heavy with money.

'It seems incredible,' said the vicar later, as he sat with neat piles of coins before him, 'but we seem to have made a hundred and fifty pounds! Of course, I know that that includes Mrs Bradley's most generous contribution, but even so . . . it is quite wonderful!' His face was glowing with happiness. He adored his church and the parlous state of the roof had afforded him much sorrow for some time. Now, well before the winter gales began, a start could be made.

Through the french windows he could see the bigger children, under Mr Willet's supervision, clearing up the debris. Mrs Coggs, with her young family, had made her appearance very late, but was now busily stuffing lettuces, gooseberries and spring cabbage into a string bag.

'It will be a relief to get rid of it,' the vicar's wife was assuring her. 'We can't keep it here and it will come in useful for the children, I hope.' She caught sight of Joseph's monkey eyes fixed mournfully upon her. 'Here, my dear, run over to Miss Clare and see if she has anything left on the sweet stall.' And to Joseph's speechless amazement he found himself on his way to Miss Clare with a sixpence warm in his hand.

John Pringle was trundling a wheelbarrow covered with a net out of the vicarage gate. Loud squealing accompanied him as he wheeled his pig home, and on each side of the barrow trotted admiring children.

Outside 'The Beetle and Wedge' lounged the Bryant menfolk. Mrs Bryant had stalked home in disgust some half-hour earlier, and the men were loth to face her acid tongue when they returned.

They watched the pig and its escort go by them, with hostile glances, but in stony silence. As the cavalcade turned the bend, Ezekiel spoke.

'Come and 'ave one, mates,' he muttered, and the brothers turned silently in at the pub door to gain consolation for past tribulations and strength to face those to come.

20. PERPLEXED THOUGHTS ON RURAL EDUCATION

'Heard about Springbourne?' asked Mr Willet. He was sheltering in the school doorway from a sharp spattering of hail. Beside him was propped a besom with which he had been sweeping the coke back to the pile. An outbreak of Cowboys-and-Indians, involving ambushes behind the pile and wild sorties over it, had spread the crunching mess far and wide.

'What about it?' I said, peering out to see if I could make a dash for the kettle. The spasmodic spatterings suddenly turned to a heavy bombardment. Hailstones danced frenziedly on the asphalt, so thick and fast, that it seemed as though a mist were rising. I leant against the stone sink in the lobby, ready to gossip.

'They say the school's closing down,' said Mr Willet. 'You heard that?'

I said I had.

'Well, it ain't good enough by half. The people over Spring-bourne are proper wild about it. After all, it's been there pretty near as long as this one.'

'But it's so expensive to keep up. Only fifteen children, I believe and the building in need of repair.'

'What about it? Got to go to school somewhere, ain't they? Can't walk this far, some of 'em only babies; now, can they? Besides, every village wants its own school. Stands to reason you wants your own children to run round the corner to where you went yourself.'

He blew out his stained moustache with vexation.

'And another thing,' he said, nodding like a mandarin, 'the bus'll cost a pretty penny to cart 'em over here. And what about poor old Miss Davis? Been there donkey's years. She and Miss Clare was pupil teachers together as girls. Where's she to go? Pushed off to some ol' school in Caxley, I've heard tell, with great ol' classes that'll shout her down, I shouldn't wonder!' He paused for breath, glowering out across the veiled playground.

'Mark my words, Miss Read,' he continued, wagging a finger, 'this'll be the death of that poor soul. Give her life up, she has, to Springbourne – and the people there won't let her go without a tussle. Run the cubs, played the organ, done the savings – Oh! I reckons it's cruel!'

I agreed that it was.

'And where's the poor ol' gel to live? There's rumours going that she'll be turned out of the school-house, where she's lived all these years. Look at the garden she's made! A real picture – and took her all her life! And that's another thing!' Mr Willet moved closer to me to emphasize his point. The ragged moustache was thrust aggressively near.

'Suppose these school people up the office ever wants to open that school again? Who's coming there, if they've sold the house? Tell me that?' he demanded. 'You know, miss, we've seen it time and time again – no house, no schoolteacher! And in the end it's the kids and the village what suffers. No one living there to take an interest and know everybody. "Yank 'em off in a bus," says the high-ups!' Mr Willet's tone changed to one of mincing refinement. ' "Push 'em all into one big school – it's economy we've got to think of!" '

I laughed, and was immediately sorry, for Mr Willet was so burning with righteous indignation that I could not explain that I was laughing at his impersonations and not at his sentiments.

'Economy!' Mr Willet spat out, with disgust. 'I don't call that economy! Economy's taking care of what you've got and making good use of it. And if shutting up the village schools for the sake of a bit of hard cash is what the high-ups call economy, they just wants to sit down quiet for a minute and think what real value means – not ol' money – that's the least of it – and then to think again and ask themselves "What are we throwing away?"'

The hail stopped with dramatic suddenness, and with Mr Willet's wisdom ringing in my ears I sped across to the kettle.

While Mrs Pringle was still flicking her duster the next morning. Miss Gray beckoned me into her empty room to show me a very beautiful sapphire ring snug in its little satin-lined box.

'I can't tell you how pleased I am!' I said, kissing her heartily, 'you'll suit each other so well—' A thought struck me. 'It is Mr Annett, I suppose?'

Miss Gray laughed, although her eyes were wet and she was rather tremulous. 'Yes, indeed, who else would it be?'

'I'm so glad. He deserves to be happy at last.'

'Poor man!' agreed Miss Gray, with a sigh so fraught with sympathy and pity that I foresaw a very maudlin few minutes. 'He has suffered terribly,' she went on, looking at me with anguished grey eyes. I composed my features and prepared to listen to the harrowing account of Mr Annett's past love-life and the hopes, declared with becoming downcast modesty, for his future. But luck was with me. The door burst open, and a gaggle of small children entered.

'Miss,' said Jimmy Waites breathlessly, 'Eileen Burton's knicker elastic's busted, and she won't come out of the lavatory she says, until you brings a pin!'

Miss Gray put the ring in her bag and hastened away, while I returned to my room to choose the morning hymn, observing, as I went, how seldom one can indulge in the inflation of any sort of emotion without life's little pin-pricks bursting the balloon.

'And a very good thing too,' I was moralizing to myself,

'emotions cannot be enjoyed without them becoming dangerous to one's sense of proportion,' and I was about to develop this lofty theme, when I caught sight of Ernest, and was obliged to break off to direct him to wipe his nose.

On Tuesday the *Caxley Chronicle* carried the announcement of the engagement and all the village was agog.

'Not that it wasn't plain to see for weeks,' was the general verdict. 'Let's hope they'll be happy.'

Mrs Pringle was at the top of her form when she heard the news.

'That poor girl!' she said, dragging her leg slightly, 'he's got through one wife and now he's setting about another!'

'Oh, come!' I protested, 'you make him sound a Bluebeard! It wasn't Mr Annett's fault, merely his misfortune, that his first wife was killed in an air-raid!'

'That's his story,' replied Mrs Pringle, darkly, 'and anyway who's to say we shan't get more air-raids?'

This piece of reasoning was quite beyond me, but I determined to let some light into the gloom of Mrs Pringle's argument.

'You are saying, in effect, Mrs Pringle, that anyone marrying Mr Annett lays themselves open either to slow-death-by-matrimony or sudden-death-by-air-raid.'

'What a wicked lie!' boomed Mrs Pringle indignantly, bristling and breathless. 'I simply said Mr Annett had got a good wife in Miss Gray and I hope she's got some idea of the state of the house she's taking over before she goes to it as a bride.'

Before this *volte-face* I was silent.

'And if she wants to know of a real good scrubber, my husband's niece over at Springbourne would be the one for the job, but would need to be supplied with old-fashioned bar soap, these new sudses, she says, brings her up all of a nettle-rash!' She paused for breath and assumed the look of piety which the choir-boys mimic so well.

'May she be very happy,' she said lugubriously, 'and I only pray she doesn't have her confinements in that front bedroom of Mr Annett's! Mortal damp, it is, mortal damp!'

'Delightful news,' said the vicar, beaming, 'so very suitable – a most charming pair! But, my dear Miss Read, Annett's gain must, of course, be Fairacre's loss, I fear. Has she mentioned anything to you? Whether she is willing to continue here I mean? At any rate for a few months, shall we say? Just until – well, in any case – does she want to go on teaching?'

I said that I had no idea.

'I must set about drafting another advertisement if she decides to leave us, I suppose. Such a short time since our last interviews. I wonder now if Mrs Finch-Edwards would help us out again?'

I pointed out that Mrs Finch-Edwards would be busy looking after a young baby by that time.

'Of course, of course,' nodded the vicar. 'More good news! I never can quite decide which I find the pleasanter – news of a wedding or a birth. Well, who can we think of?'

'Let's find out if Miss Gray is planning to leave or stay first,' I suggested.

At the back of the class I could see a picture, drawn by Ernest, being displayed secretly to his neighbour, under the desk. From a distance it looked remarkably like a caricature of the vicar and I felt the matter should be investigated immediately. I did my best to catch the malefactor's eye, but he was much too engrossed with his handiwork to bother about me.

'I'll call again,' said the vicar, setting off for the door, so preoccupied that he forgot his farewells to the children. At the door, he paused: 'Perhaps Miss Clare?' he suggested. His face was illuminated. He looked like a child who has just remembered that it is Christmas morning. With a happy sigh, he vanished round the door.

The warm weather had returned. On the window-sills, pinks, so tightly packed that they looked like cauliflowers, sent down warm waves of perfume to mingle with the scent of roses on my desk.

The elm trees in the corner of the playground cast comforting cool shadows, and beyond them, in the lower field that stretched away to the foot of the downs, the hay was being cut.

Vetch, marguerite and sorrel had coloured the thick grass and now they were falling together before the cutting-machine. Behind Mr Roberts' house was a field of beans in flower and every now and again we would take in a heady draught from that direction.

The pace of school work inevitably slowed down. The children were languid, their thoughts outside in the sunshine. It was the right time for day-dreaming, and I took as many lessons as possible in the open air.

One afternoon of summer heat we were disposed at the edge of the half-cut field under the elm trees' shade. The air was murmurous with the noise of the distant cutter and with myriads of small insects. Far away the downs shimmered in the heat, and little blue chalk butterflies hovered about us. In a distant cottage garden I could see an old woman bending down to tie lace curtains over her currant bushes to protect the fruit from the birds.

The lesson on the time-table was 'Silent Reading' and in various attitudes, some graceful and some not, the children sat or lay in the grass with their books propped before them. Some read avidly, flicking over the pages, their eyes scampering along the lines. But others lay on their stomachs, legs undulating, with their eyes fixed dreamily on the view before them, a grass between their lips, and eternity before them.

With so little encouragement to read at home, in overcrowded cottages and with young brothers and sisters clamouring round them until bedtime and after, these schoolchildren at Fairacre desperately need peace and an opportunity to read. But on this particular afternoon I wondered how much reading was being done and how much day-dreaming. My marking pencil slowed to a standstill and the geography test papers lay neglected in my lap. What an afternoon, I mused! When these boys and girls are old and look back to their childhood, it is the brightest hours that they will remember. This is one of those golden days to lay up as treasure for the future, I told myself, excusing our general idleness.

There were footsteps on the high playground behind us and one of the infants came to the edge and looked down upon us. He spoke importantly: 'Miss Gray says to tell you a man's come.'

'Oh, then I'll come and see him,' I said, putting down my papers reluctantly. The children hardly noticed my going, but lay docile and languorous as though a spell were upon them.

The child and I crossed the baking playground. The sun

beat here unmercifully and I spread my hand over the child's head.

'Do you know the man?' I asked him.

'It's not exactly a man,' he answered thoughtfully, and paused. I began to wonder what sort of monster had called.

'It's just John Burton's dad,' he added.

Alan Burton had called to discuss his son's future schooling. He was very disappointed that John had not been accepted for the Grammar School at Caxley, and did not want the boy to go on to Beech Green next term.

'Not that I've anything against Mr Annett. He's all right – but there's not the stuff there for training a boy like John who wants to do something with his hands. There's no woodwork shop and no metalwork place, and as far as I can see the building's just the same as it was years ago. Where's this technical school we were promised when young John was a baby in arms?'

I agreed that there was no sign of it.

'A man like me can't afford to send a boy away to school even if he wanted to. I could have managed the Grammar School in the old days and John would have been a credit to the place. He's good at games and he can make anything. I want something better than Beech Green for him now. Mr Annett has to take all sorts, and there's some among them downright vicious. And some thick-headed ones that are bound to hold the others back.'

All this was sound good sense and I felt very sorry for Alan Burton. It certainly was a calamity that the Caxley area had no technical school for boys of John's calibre. I could only suggest that he let him go to Beech Green where he would get a certain amount of handicraft training and then apprentice him at fifteen to a trade that he would enjoy.

'I suppose that's what it'll be,' he sighed and picked up his hat, 'but I'd have liked him to go to the Grammar School. I didn't go, because I was the youngest and my father had just died, but all my brothers went there. I know John's not over-bright, but he's a good lad and as bright as his uncles were. He'd have done well there.'

I said John would do well at Beech Green and wherever he went afterwards, but he was not to be comforted.

'There's something wrong somewhere,' he said, preparing to go. 'The Grammar School suffers in the end, as I see it; for it isn't always the cleverest boys that have most to give, is it? And why are the families with a bit more money than I have scraping up all they can to send their boys away to school? In the old days, they'd have been proud to send them to Caxley Grammar School. Why's that? I don't know much about schooling these days, but what I do know I don't feel happy about.'

Sadly he departed through the school gate, and I returned to collect my somnolent children from the elm tree's shade.

21. TERM IN FULL SWING

The last day of the month has a beauty of its own, for it is pay-day. Jim Bryant, a remote cousin of the Biblical Bryants, brings the post while I am still at breakfast, and the cheques arrive together in one envelope. There are four of them; one for Mrs Pringle's cleaning and washing-up ministrations, a smaller one for Mr Willet's unenviable but necessary duties, one for Miss Gray and the last for me.

Mrs Pringle never fails to remind me, in the most roundabout and delicate manner, that it is pay-day. She usually makes a remark about the post being late, or early, or has some information to impart about Jim Bryant, thus bringing the cheque to mind for me. Sometimes I am wicked enough to postpone handing over the money for a few minutes, in order to see what form the reminder will take. This morning, Mrs Pringle was standing up on a desk zealously flapping a duster round the top of the electric light shade, as I entered. She intended to let me see that she earned her money. Dust flew in clouds, and I felt it was a pity that her zeal was not spread more evenly through the month.

'Friday again!' was her greeting. 'Don't the time fly?' I said it did, unlocking the desk drawer. Mrs Pringle eyed the letters in my hand and I waited for the next move, my eyes averted.

'Midsummer Day past already!' said Mrs Pringle. I took out the register.

'Don't seem hardly possible that July's nearly here, do it?'

'No,' I said, and straightened the massive inkstand.

'Why, bless me, it's tomorrow!' gasped Mrs Pringle, with well-feigned astonishment. 'Last day of June today – last day of the month!' she continued with much emphasis.

I walked across to the piano and opened it. Mrs Pringle clambered down from the desk, with groans. 'Sometimes I wonder if I can stick this job out much longer, with my leg. The money's not all that good, though I must say it's regular.'

'Yes,' I said absently, turning over the leaves of the hymn-book.

There was a pause. Mrs Pringle changed her line of approach. 'Postman been yet?'

I gave in.

'Yes, Mrs Pringle, and he's brought your cheque.' I handed it over to her.

'Well, now,' said Mrs Pringle, with an affected laugh, 'and I'd forgotten all about it being pay-day!'

Mr Willet shows just as much delicacy of feeling over receiving his wages. He knows that I hand it over to him as soon as I can in the morning, but if, on the odd occasion, I have been unable to find him, he appears, without fail, in the afternoon of pay-day.

He would not dream of asking me outright for his rightful dues, but he finds some noisy job in the playground, close to the door or window, which focuses my attention upon him. He usually elects to scrape the coke up with a shovel – a perennial job in any playground – and, after a while, I realize what is happening and translate what I have dimly thought of as a passing nuisance into the cry for help which it really is. On one occasion, when coke was short, Mr Willet beat upon the iron shoe-scraper outside the lobby door, with a metal bar, and the clangour quickly brought me to my senses.

I always hurry out, overflowing with apologies, and Mr Willet invariably replies: 'No need to worry, Miss Read. It'd quite slipped my mind it was the last day of the month, but I'll take it now it's here.'

The ritual over, we part with compliments on either side.

*

As this day was not only the last day of the month, but also a Friday, it would be a busy one, for besides the disposal of cheques, there were attendance records to send into the office at Caxley, the dinner money accounts to check and send in with the cash in hand, and forms to be filled in stating the number of hours worked by Mrs Pringle and Mr Willet.

I was also engrossed in a lengthy document and numerous catalogues as this was the time to apply for the stock needed throughout the coming year. So much money is allocated to books, stationery and cleaning materials for each child, and it takes a considerable amount of time and heart-searching deciding how best to allot the stock. This year I felt that the infants' room should have the lion's share, for Miss Clare had never demanded much in the way of educational-play apparatus. In fact, I had had to introduce much there that she disapproved of and failed to use. Now that Miss Gray was in charge she had many good ideas for apparatus which I was only too glad to order. I only hoped that her successor would be as enterprising and enthusiastic.

Today she handed in her resignation from Fairacre School. Notice has to be given for three months, so that we should have her with us next term, as Mrs Annett, until the end of September. The marriage was to be at the beginning of August.

'And we both hope you'll be able to come to the wedding,' said Miss Gray, as I handed back the letter of resignation which she was posting to the office. 'We shall send you a proper invitation, of course, but do please come!'

I said that I should like nothing more, and was she wearing white?

'Not a *dead* white,' explained Miss Gray earnestly, 'I don't think I could take white satin, for instance; but I've decided on a cream chiffon, with a faille underslip, and a softly-swathed bodice.'

I was on the point of crying out that that was exactly what I had hoped she'd choose for her wedding dress when we were at Miss Clare's birthday party, but luckily I held my tongue in time.

'It sounds quite perfect,' I said enthusiastically; and we became engrossed in head-dresses, veils, bouquets, bridesmaids' ensembles and all the enthralling details of a well-equipped wedding, much to the pleasure of our classes, who took the opportunity to gossip happily among themselves, and had to be spoken to quite sharply.

John Burton and Cathy Waites were standing in front of the class, surveying their fellow-pupils with a judicious eye. They were picking sides for cricket, and as there were only nineteen children present I foresaw that I should be called upon to make up the number.

It was sultry weather. A hot little wind blew the dry grass and dust round and round the playground. The children scuffled their sandals in the dusty road as we crossed to Mr Roberts' field opposite, where we have his permission to play.

The wicket is not all it should be, but it is reasonably flat, and it is possible to give the children some elementary notion of the game and its rules. At the further end, Mr Roberts' house cow, a demure Guernsey named somewhat incongruously 'Samson,' was grazing peacefully.

She looked up at our approach, and advanced with tittupping gait and nodding head.

'It do seem wrong somehow,' observed Eric, 'to have that ol' cow round us cricket times.'

I pointed out that Samson had rather more right to the field than we had, and though no doubt the M.C.C. might look askance at our conditions of play, we were lucky to have any sort of pitch at all.

Eric and I were the opening batsmen, so that I should be able to take over my rightful duties as umpire with the least delay.

Cathy, a deadly under-arm bowler with a quite unpredictable pace, now rushed up to the wicket and hurled the ball at me. It flashed by me and Ernest, the wicket-keeper, and travelled at remarkable speed to Sylvia at longstop. She had been foolish enough to think herself too far away to be noticed and had squatted down happily by a grasshopper. They were surveying each other with mutual interest when the ball cracked upon her tender knee with the most fearsome report. Hubbub broke out.

'Serve you right! You did ought to be attending! It's your own fault!' said the hard-hearted ones.

'Do it hurt bad? Poor ol' Sylvie! Spit on it, mate, as quick as you can! Now, rub it well in!' said the more compassionate.

More scared than hurt, Sylvia struggled to her feet and the game was resumed. Cathy's second ball bowled me and I handed the bat to John Burton, with considerable relief.

The game wore on. Samson chewed the cud and watched our antics with a mild eye. In the next field the haycocks stood in rows and Mr Roberts' blue and red wagon had already started to collect them. Above us, black clouds were piling up ominously and I was wondering whether we should get our game finished and whether Mr Roberts would get his hay in before the rain came, when I noticed a stranger leaning over the gate, watching us with interest.

On seeing that he was observed, he opened the gate and crossed the grass towards me.

It transpired that the stranger was one of Her Majesty's Inspectors of Schools, newly appointed to this area. He had served before, he told me as we walked back to the school, in one of the home counties, where new estates had gone up rapidly since the war, and the new schools, despite their classes of forty or more children, were efficient in design and very well-equipped.

'You've no playing-field then,' he asked, 'although there are fields all round you? Do you think it's worth while trying to teach these children cricket under such conditions? Actually, you've not really enough people for two teams, I gather.'

I told him that I thought the effort was justified. At least the children knew the rules of the game, enjoyed it, and could, in their next school, feel that they could take part in the game with some knowledge and pleasure. Thanks to Mr Roberts, the children were able to get out of the small and badly-surfaced playground to take much of their exercise.

His gaze swept the lofty pitch-pine ceiling, the ecclesiastical high windows, and at last came to rest on the skylight.

'Do you find it dark in here?' he asked.

I said that I realized it was dark compared with the steel and glass schools of the present day, but that I didn't think the children's sight was impaired at all.

'Despite its architectural drawbacks,' I told him, 'there is something in this atmosphere conducive to quiet and to work. I know it is only right that children should have big, low windows that they can see through, but they can be very distracting.'

The inspector sighed, and I could see that he thought me prejudiced and a diehard, as he ambled round the room studying the wall-pictures. The children watched him furtively, their library books open but unread.

Outside, the wind had started to roar, and the black clouds which had gathered during the afternoon made the room murky enough to horrify any inspector. There was a flash of lightning, a few muffled squeals from the children, and then a long menacing rumble of distant thunder.

The rain suddenly burst upon us in torrents, lashing the windows and streaming down the skylight. In a few minutes the usual steady drip began into the classroom below. Without waiting to be told, Cathy went into the lobby, returned with the bucket, and folding a dishcloth neatly, she tucked it methodically in the base of the bucket to stop the clanging of the drops. Mr Arnold, the inspector, watched these smooth proceedings amusedly.

'How long has this been going on?' he nodded at the skylight.

'Seventy years,' I answered, and his laugh was drowned in another clap of thunder.

'Can I go through to the infants' room, before they go home?' he asked, and I took him in to meet Miss Gray, who was already buttoning children into coats and peering hopefully across the playground to see if any mothers had braved the rain with their children's mackintoshes. I left them discussing reading methods and returned to get my own class ready to face the weather.

There was a flurry in the lobby and the vicar burst in, his cloak pouring with silver streams from his dash across the playground.

'What a storm! What a storm!' he gasped, shaking his hat energetically. The children in the front row flinched as the cold rain splashed them, but otherwise endured this treatment with stoicism.

'I had to bring the hymn list and I thought I might stow some of the children who had no coats into my car and run them home.'

The children brightened up, sitting very straight with shining eyes. Here was adventure indeed! The prudent few, with mackintoshes waiting on the lobby pegs, cursed their own forethought which had deprived them of this treat.

'Some of their mothers may be coming,' I said, 'but, let's see . . . ! Who knows that their mothers won't be able to come? And who has no coat?'

John Burton and his little sister were in this category, and five more children. As they all lived roughly in the same direction along the Beech Green Road, they were called together, and under the vicar's outspread cloak it was decided to make a dash for his waiting car, when I remembered the inspector.

'Just a moment, children,' said the vicar, 'while I greet our visitor, and then we'll set off.' Cloak swirling, he sailed into the infants' room, and found Mr Arnold engrossed in a word-making game which he had found in the cupboard.

'Fat, mat, sat, cat, rat, hat . . .' he was muttering absorbedly to himself, turning a neat little cardboard wheel to make each new word. It seemed a pity to break in on his enjoyment, but I introduced the two men and left them while I interviewed a little knot of wet mothers who had just arrived.

The lobby floor ran with little rivulets from their mackintoshes and umbrellas. Outside, the playground streamed with water, and in the dip of the stone doorstep, worn with generations of sturdy country boots, a dark pool gleamed. The children who had been claimed were bright-eyed and garrulous, faces upturned and cheerful, as they suffered their heads to be shrouded and their collars buttoned. Those who still awaited rescue were anxious and forlorn, and their eyes, turned towards the school gate, were dark and mournful.

Mr Roberts' sheepdog, its coat plastered against its ribs, edged into the gateway and was implored by its urgent friends to come into the lobby for shelter.

'Bess, come on in!'

'Bess, Bess!'

'Poor ol' Bess. Soaking, ain't she?'

Hearing sympathetic voices, Bess joined the crowd in the lobby, her tail flicking drops as it wagged furiously, and confusion reigned supreme. Gradually the numbers thinned and the vicar, having made his farewells to Mr Arnold and Miss Gray, collected his charges on the doorstep, and with the black cloak outspread above them, they all set off across the playground. From the rear, the vicar looked like some monstrous black hen sheltering her chicks, as underneath each side of the outspread cloak a forest of little legs twinkled through the puddles to the car. With a parting toot they were off, heads and hands sticking out of all the windows, despite the downpour.

Mr Arnold engaged Miss Gray in conversation again, and I saw off those children who were well-equipped for the weather. Only Cathy, Jimmy and Joseph Coggs remained and I retrieved the old golf umbrella which shares a home with maps, modulators and other awkward objects in one of the cupboards, and opened it against the lashing rain on the doorstep.

'There you are, Cathy,' I said, handing over the red and green giant, 'hold it as low as you can over the three of you, and get to Tyler's Row in record time!'

I watched the umbrella bob along the lane at a smart trot, and then hurried back to my empty classroom.

Mr Arnold came through from the infants' room to make his farewells.

'I'm afraid I picked an unfortunate day for my first visit,' he said, 'but I should like to come again, quite soon, to see you all in action.'

He waved, and sprinted across to his car through the puddles and drove away through the downpour.

Mr Annett, with a solicitude for his future wife that was quite pretty to see, had deserted his schoolchildren promptly at four and dashed over in his car to collect Miss Gray. I prevailed upon them to share my tea and together we sat gossiping and eating home-made gingerbread in the school-house.

'As long as schools are dependent on local rates,' said Mr Annett decidedly, dusting far too many crumbs, for my peace of mind, from his lap to the carpet, 'there are bound to be serious disparities in buildings and equipment. My three little nieces started their schooling in Middlesex. Their first school was a model one, individual towels, combs, beds, and so on. There was a paddling pool, two chutes, stacks of first-class toys, mounds of

paper, chalks and everything else a teacher or child could wish
for. Now they've moved into this area, and their local village
school is not only as antiquated in design and as primitive in its
sanitation and water supply as this one, but is also looked upon,
as far as I can see, by the families with whom they play, as only
"good enough for other people's children." '

'Don't I know!' I agreed feelingly.

'My sister is looked upon as an oddity because her daughters
are going to the village school,' he continued, 'but, as she and her
husband point out, they have faith in our state education and
believe they are doing a wise thing. They live within a stone's
throw of the school and the girls are taught in small classes by
teachers who are all qualified and certificated, and any complaints made by their parents as ratepayers, about conditions,
have every chance of being considered and put right.'

'It's very difficult to argue about,' I answered, 'for in the end
it boils down to the liberty of the individual. If parents prefer to
pay for schooling, well, why shouldn't they? I, too, deplore this
"the-village-school-is-good-enough-for-them" attitude, but short
of state education for all, with no choice at all, what can be
done?'

'I don't quite know,' said Mr Annett thoughtfully, accepting
his fourth cup of tea in a preoccupied way, 'but there are one or
two things that will have to come before very long. The dis-
crepancies between different areas will have to be overcome to
begin with. Just as the teachers' salaries have been made equal in
different areas, so should the school conditions be evened up.
And if only more intelligent parents would make use of their local
school and take an interest in it, instead of complaining about the
rates they have to pay, plus school fees that they need not, it
might be a step in the right direction.'

'Owners of private schools won't think so,' I pointed out, as he
rose to help Miss Gray with her coat. We made our way to the
car. The storm had spent itself and the sides of the lane were
running with little rivers, bearing twigs, leaves and other flotsam
on their swirling surfaces.

The air was soft and fresh and a blackbird was singing its heart
out in the cherry tree.

'We're very lucky,' I observed, breathing in the damp earthy smell, but Mr Annett was gazing at Miss Gray. It was some time before he spoke.

'Very, very lucky,' he echoed soberly.

22. THE OUTING

The first Saturday in July is always kept free in Fairacre for the combined Sunday School and Choir Outing.

'At one time,' said the vicar, 'the schools here closed for a fortnight at the end of June for a fruit-picking holiday, and as they were paid at the end of that time the outing was held then. And now, somehow, we just stick to the first Saturday in July. It seems to suit us all.'

He beamed happily round the coach, which was filled with thirty-three of his parishioners, of all shapes and sizes, each one dressed in his best.

Behind us chugged another coach equally full, for mothers were encouraged to accompany their children on this expedition. 'For really,' as the vicar remarked, 'it would be far too great a responsibility for my wife and the two Sunday school teachers to undertake; and it does give some of these poor house-bound women a breath of fresh air.'

Mrs Pratt, as organist, was there with her two children and behind her sat Mr Annett, as choir-master, and Miss Gray. They were both making heroic efforts to be civil and attentive to their fellow-travellers, for they were at that stage of mutual infatuation when the mere presence of other people is a burden. I wondered how quickly they would abandon us when we reached the seashore. They would certainly need a breathing-space on their own for an hour or two, after behaving with such admirable self-control under the gaze of thirty-one pairs of eyes.

Miss Clare sat beside me. There had been a few seats to spare and she had agreed to come 'just to smell the sea and collect a fresh seaweed ribbon to hang in the back porch,' so that she could tell the weather.

'Years ago,' she said, 'we used to have our outing in a brake with four horses to pull it. Of course, we never went far, to the sea, or any great distance like that. But we had wonderful times. For several years we went to Sir Edmund Hurley's park, beyond Springbourne, and we all loved that journey, because we had to splash through the ford at the bottom of the steep hill there. It was before they altered the road and built the new bridge.'

'Was that Sir Edmund who gave Fairacre School its piano?' I asked, a vision of that fretwork-fronted jangler rushing at me from forty miles behind us.

'That's the one,' cried Miss Clare, delighted at my knowledge. 'He was a great friend of the vicar's at that time – the late vicar – Canon Emslie, such a dear, and so musical! He was shocked to find the school without an instrument and mentioned it to Sir Edmund one day when he was visiting at Hurley Hall. The upshot was that the present piano was sent over from the Hall. Most generous, but then all the Hurleys have been renowned for their generosity.'

'My grandfather,' boomed Mrs Pringle, swivelling round on the seat in front, 'the one as made the choir-stalls that come in for some uncalled-for criticism by them as is ignorant of such things – my grandfather did a tidy bit of carpentering for Sir Edmund.' She cast a triumphant look at Mr Annett from under the brim of her brown straw hat, as one who says, 'And if Sir Edmund was satisfied with my grandfather's handiwork, then who are you to point the finger of scorn at his choir-stalls?'

But Mr Annett was too busy adjusting the window so that no harmful gale should blow upon his life's love, and the shaft went by him and left him unscathed.

'And what's more,' continued Mrs Pringle's penetrating bellow, 'Sir Edmund asked his advice for some jobs actually in The House!' She nodded her head belligerently, the bunch of cherries on her hat-brim just a split second behind in time. This bunch of cherries is an old and valued friend, nodding from straw in summer and felt in winter, and now so far gone in years as to show, here and there, a little split, through which the white stuffing oozes gently, like some exotic mildew.

'In the house?' echoed Miss Clare. 'Where did your grandfather do the carpentering then?'

'Kitchen cupboards!' said Mrs Pringle shortly and bounced

round again to face the front, the cherries quivering, but whether with indignation or family pride no one could say.

Barrisford, as everyone knows, is a genteel watering-place with wonderful, firm, broad sands, which would cause a less refined borough to advertise itself as 'A Paradise for Kiddies.'

The children were ready to rush to the sea's edge the minute that the coaches shuddered to a standstill, but were restrained by the vicar, who, using his bell-like pulpit voice, made an announcement.

'We shall disperse, dear people, until four-thirty when we shall meet at our old friend Bunce's, on the Esplanade. I gather that an excellent tea is to be prepared for us there, with cold ham and other meats, salad, cakes, ices and so on. We shall leave here at half-past five sharp.' He looked severely at his flock, knowing that punctuality is not one of our Fairacre virtues.

'At five-thirty,' he repeated, 'and even so we shall not be home, I fear, until nearly nine, which is rather late for our very young members.'

'Never mind, vicar,' called a cheerful mother at the rear of the coach, 'it's only Sunday, tomorrow . . . nothing to get up for!'

This remark must have been instantly regretted, so scandalized was the vicar's expression on hearing it, for as well as its derogatory tone about the importance of the Sabbath, he would be celebrating Holy Communion at 8 a.m., Matins at 11 a.m., Children's Service at 3 p.m., and Evensong at 6.30 p.m.

'Four-thirty at Bunce's then,' he repeated, in a somewhat shaken voice, 'and five-thirty here.'

He stood aside, and with whoops of joy and rattlings of buckets, the youth of Fairacre swept on to the beach with a reckless disregard for kerb drill that made their teacher's blood, if not their parents', run cold.

Miss Clare had decided to take a turn about the shops before going down to the sea and asked me if I would like to accompany her.

'But not, of course, if you would prefer to be elsewhere. It's only that I am looking out for a blue cardigan, something between a royal and a navy, to wear with my grey worsted skirt in the winter.'

I said that there was nothing I should like better than a turn about the shops.

'It would be so useful too, for school,' went on Miss Clare happily, her eyes sparkling at this prospect, 'just in case, you know, I am needed, from the time Miss Gray leaves, until Christmas. The vicar has been so very kind about it all, and I feel so much better for my rest, that I hope I can come back, even if it is only for a few weeks.'

It was nice to see Miss Clare so forward-looking again, and I hoped, for her sake, that the vacancy at Fairacre School would not be filled before the end of next term.

We had a successful shopping expedition. '*Most* suitable, madam,' the girl had gushed, 'and if madam ever indulged in a *blue rinse*, the effect would be quite, quite electrifying.' Digesting this piece of intelligence we made our way to the beach, where, scattered among other families, the Fairacre children could be seen digging, splashing and eating with the greatest enjoyment.

The tide was crawling slowly in over the warm sand, and Ernest was busy digging a channel to meet it. His spade was of sharp metal and cleaved the firm sand with a satisfying crunch. I thought regretfully of my own childhood's spade, a solid wooden affair much despised by me, but nothing would persuade my parents that I would not chop off my own toes and be a cripple for life if I were given a metal one, and so I had to battle on with my inadequate tool, while more fortunate children sliced away beside me with half the effort, and, as far as my jaundiced eye could see, their full complement of toes.

Ernest paused for a minute in his work.

'Wish we could stay longer here,' he said, 'a day's not long, is it?'

We settled ourselves near him and agreed that it wasn't very long.

'You'd better make up your mind to be a sailor,' I said, nodding to a boat drawn up at the edge of the beach. People were climbing in ready for a trip round the harbour.

'Oh, I wouldn't like that,' responded Ernest emphatically, 'I don't reckon the sea's safe, for one thing. I mean, you might easy get drownded, mightn't you?'

'A lot of people don't,' I assured him, but his brow remained perplexed, working out the countryman's suspicions of a new environment.

'And there don't seem enough grass and trees, somehow. Nor animals. Why, I didn't see any cows or sheep the last bit of the journey. No, I'd sooner live at Fairacre, I reckons, but I'd like to have a good long holiday here.'

Having come to terms with himself he began digging again with renewed effort, and I looked about to see how the other children fared.

The sky was blue but with a fair amount of cloud, which kept the temperature down. Despite this, most of the children seemed content to be in bathing costumes, but it was interesting to see with what respect and awe they treated the sea. Not one of them, it appeared, could swim – not surprising perhaps, when one considered that Fairacre was a downland village and the nearest swimming water was at Caxley, six miles distant.

I wished, not for the first time, that I could see my way clear to taking my older children into the Caxley Swimming Baths once a week, but the poor bus service, combined with the difficulties of rearranging the time-table to fit in this activity, made it impossible at the moment. Paddlers there were, in plenty, but not one of the Fairacre children went more than a yard or two from the beach edge into the surf, and while they stood with the swirling water round their ankles, they kept a weather eye cocked on dry land, ready to make a dash for safety if this strange, unfamiliar element should play any tricks with them.

At digging they came into their own. Armchairs, sandworks, channels, bridges and castles of incredible magnitude were constructed with patience and industry. The Fairacre children could handle tools, and had the plodding unhurried methods of the countryman that produce amazing results. Here was the perfect medium for their inborn skill. The golden sand was turned, raked, piled, patted and ornamented with shells and seaweed, until I seriously thought of importing a few loads into the playground at home to see what wonders they could perform there.

One or two went with their parents for a trip in the boat, but they sat, I noticed, very close to the maternal skirts, and looked at the green water rushing past them with respectful eyes.

The day passed cheerfully and without incident. Tea at Bunce's was the usual happy family affair, held in an upstairs room, with magnificent views of the harbour.

'Our Mr Edward Bunce,' as the waiter told us, was in personal attendance on our needs, an elegant figure in chalk-striped flannel and bow tie. Soft of voice and smooth of manner, he swooped around us with the teapot, the living emblem of the personal service which has made Bunce's the great tea-shop that it is.

At five-thirty, we were back in our coaches, with seaweed, shells and two or three unhappy crabs awash in buckets in an inch or two of seawater. The vicar, quite pink with the sea-air, was holding his gold half-hunter and counting heads earnestly.

Mr Annett and Miss Gray mounted the steps in a dazed way and resumed their seat amidst sympathetic smiles, and only one seat then remained empty.

'Mrs Pratt, vicar,' called someone, 'Mrs Pratt and her two little 'uns!'

'I think I see one of them, coming across from the chemist's shop,' answered the vicar. A fat little girl in a pink frock stumped across to the coach, panted heavily up the steps and to her place, and sat, swinging her legs cheerfully. We continued to wait.

The driver flipped back his little glass window and said: 'That the lot?'

'No, no,' answered Mr Partridge, rather flustered, 'one more and a little boy to come. Peggy, my dear,' he said to the elder Pratt child, 'is your mummy still in the chemist's?'

'Yes,' said the child, smiling smugly. 'Robin's got something in his eye.' She sounded both proud and pleased.

The vicar looked perturbed, and sought his wife's support anxiously. She rose, bustling, from her seat, leaving her gloves and bag neatly behind her.

'I'll just run across to her,' said the good lady and trotted across to the open door of the chemist's shop.

Dimly, in the murk of the interior, we could see figures grouped around a chair, on which, presumably, sat the patient. There were head-shakings and gesticulations, and at length Mrs Partridge came hurrying back with the news.

'The chemist seems to think that the child should see a doctor. He suggests that we take him to the out-patients' department at the hospital. It's quite near here evidently.'

There was what reporters call 'a sensation' at this dramatic announcement. Some were all for getting out of the coach, rushing across to fetch Robin and Mrs Pratt away from all these foreigners, and taking them straight home to their dear familiar Doctor Martin; others suggested that the chemist was a scaremonger, and that 'the bit of ol' whatever-it-is will soon slip out. You knows what eyes is – hell one minute, and all Sir Garnet the next!' But all factions were united in the greatest sympathy for the unfortunate family.

'The child is in great pain,' went on Mrs Partridge, looking quite distracted. 'Cigarette ash evidently, and it seems to have burnt the eye. I really feel that he should go to the hospital.'

'In that case, my dear,' said the vicar, making himself heard with difficulty above the outburst of lamentation that greeted this further disclosure, 'you and I had better stay with Mrs Pratt and see this thing through, while the rest of the party go back to Fairacre.'

'But tomorrow is Sunday!' pointed out his wife.

'Upon my word,' said the vicar, turning quite pink with embarrassment, 'it had slipped my mind.'

'Shall I stop?' I volunteered.

At the same time, a voice said: 'What about little Peggy here? Had she better come with us or stay with her mum?'

Bedlam broke out again as everyone offered advice, condolence or reminiscences of past experiences of a similar nature. The driver, who had had his head stuck through his little window, and had been following affairs with grave attention, now said heavily, 'I 'ates to 'urry you, sir, but I'm due back at nine to collect a party of folks after a dance in Caxley; and we're running it a bit fine, if you'll pardon me mentioning it.'

The vicar said that, of course, of course, he quite understood, and then outlined his plan.

'If you will stop with Mrs Pratt and Robin,' he said to his wife, 'I'm sure our good friend Mr Bunce will be able to find you a night's lodging – I will hurry there myself, if the driver thinks we can spare ten minutes.' He looked inquiringly at the driver and received a reassuring nod. He produced his wallet, and there was a flutter of notes between him and Mrs Partridge, 'And then hire a taxi, my dear, to bring you all back tomorrow.' He looked suddenly stricken. 'I shall have to remember to set the alarm clock for early service, of course. I must tie a knot in my hand-kerchief to remind me.'

This masterly arrangement was applauded by all and we were sitting back congratulating ourselves on our vicar's acumen when a little voice said, 'And what about me?' We all turned to look at Peggy who sat, wide-eyed and rather cross, waiting to hear her fate. There was an awkward pause.

'There's no one at home,' said Mrs Pringle, 'that I do know. Mr Pratt's off doing his annual training with the Terriers.'

'Would you sleep in my house?' I asked her, 'I've got a nice teddy-bear in the spare room.'

This inducement seemed to be successful, for she agreed at once. Mrs Partridge hurried back to tell Mrs Pratt what had been planned, while the vicar sped at an amazing pace back to Bunce's tea-shop, to see if he knew where beds might be engaged for the night.

The coach buzzed with conversation as we waited for the vicar's return.

'Real wonderful, the vicar's been, I reckons.'

'Got a good headpiece on him . . . and kind with it, proper good-hearted!'

'I feels sorry for that little Robin. Must be painful, that. Poor little toad!'

Peggy elected to sit by me and Miss Clare obligingly took herself and her parcel containing the new winter cardigan to Peggy's vacated seat. In a few minutes a sad little group emerged from the chemist's shop. Robin had a large pad of cottonwool over one eye, securely clamped down with an eye-shade. Mrs Pratt was drying her tears as bravely as she could, while Mrs Partridge held Robin by one hand, and Mrs Pratt's shopping bag in the other. They approached the coach and made their fare-wells.

'You be a good girl now, Peg,' adjured her tearful mother, 'and do as Miss Read tells you. And if you'd be so kind as to keep a night-light burning, Miss, I'd be real grateful – she gets a bit fussed-up like if she wakes up in the dark. High strung, you know.'

I assured her that Peggy should have all she wanted, and amid sympathetic cries and encouragement the three made their farewells and departed in the direction of Bunce's.

In record time, the vicar reappeared. Mr Bunce's own sister had obliged with most suitable accommodation and had offered to accompany the Fairacre party to the hospital, in the kindest manner, said the vicar.

The driver set off at once and the great coach made short work of the miles between Barrisford and Fairacre.

Nine o'clock was striking from St Patrick's church as we clambered out and within half an hour, Peggy Pratt was sitting up in the spare bed, drinking hot milk and crunching ginger-nuts. A candle was alight on the chest of drawers, its flame shrinking and stretching in the draught from the open door.

'I likes this nightie,' said the child, looking admiringly at a silk vest of mine that was doing duty as nightgown for my small guest. There had been no tears and no pining for the distant mother and little brother left behind at Barrisford. I hoped that she would fall asleep quickly before she had time to feel homesick.

'I shall leave the door open,' I told her, tucking in the moth-eaten teddy beside her, 'in case you want me. And in the morning we'll have some boiled eggs for breakfast that Miss Clare's chickens laid yesterday.' I took her mug and plate and went to the door.

She wriggled down among the pillows, smiled enchantingly, sighed, and closed her eyes. She was asleep, I think, before I had reached the foot of the stairs.

23. Sports Day

'Mallets,' shouted Mr Willet, above the wind, looking with marked disfavour at the one in his hand, 'ain't what they used to be!'

He was standing on a school chair in Mr Roberts' field, driving chestnut stakes into the ground, so that we could rope off the track for the school sports which were to be held the next afternoon. His scanty hair was blown up into a fine cockscomb, and the rooks in the elms nearby were hurling themselves into the arms of the wind from the tossing branches.

A little knot of children, ostensibly helpers, watched his efforts. Eric had managed to get the rope into a tangle of gargantuan proportions, and the hope of ever finding an end among the intricacies on the grass at his feet, was fast waning.

'You ain't half slummered it up,' said Ernest admiringly, stirring the mess with his foot.

A despairing shout went up from John Burton who was counting sacks lent by Mr Roberts for the sack race. A malicious gust of wind had caught up half a dozen sacks and was whirling them towards the road. There was a stampede of squealing, breathless children after them.

The vicar's tent was being erected, slowly and hazardously in the shelter of the hawthorn hedge. Here lemonade and biscuits were to be sold. John Burton had executed a bold notice saying:

LIGHT REFRESHMENTS
(IN AID OF SCHOOL FUNDS)

and this was to be pinned on the tent just before the parents and friends arrived.

Samson, the house cow, had been moved to the next field, but showed a keen interest in the evening's proceedings, with her head protruding over the hedge and her eyes rolling. There were far more helpers offering her quite unnecessary meals than those who deigned to assist Mr Willet and me in our preparations.

Mr Willet drove in the last stake and looked at his watch. He held it at arm's length about a yard away from his stomach, and scrutinized it from under his lashes, frowning hard as he did so. His second chin settled on the stud which hung in the neck-band of his collarless shirt.

'Nearly seven,' he grunted. 'Better get a move on, miss. It's choir practice tonight and I reckons Mr Annett will be along pretty soon.'

He pocketed the watch and looked about him.

'Pity them moles saw fit to make their hills just where you're running tomorrow.' He turned to Eric and Ernest who were sitting on the pile of rope playing with plantains, one trying to knock the head off the other's, with much ferocity and inaccuracy.

'Here!' he bellowed, against the wind.

They looked up like startled fawns.

'You go and git spades and hit them molehills flat, else you'll be sprawling tomorrow. And let's have a hand at that 'orrible 'eap you made of that rope!'

Miraculously he found an end and handed it to me. Grumbling and grunting, puffing out his stained and ragged moustache, he slowly backed away from me; his tough old hands working and weaving among the tangle as though they had an independent life of their own, so swiftly and surely they moved.

I tied my end to the first stake, and though Mr Willet surveyed

it with some contempt he said nothing, but
worked down the line, leaning against the
wind and brushing stray children out of his
way without glancing at them, until the track
was roped off from the rest of the field.

The church clock struck seven and I
called the children.

'Best go and have a sluice I suppose,'
said Mr Willet, as we battled with the
gate, 'I'll see you're all straight tomorrow morning, miss.' He looked up at the
weathercock that shuddered in the wind
above the spire. 'If you races with this wind
behind you tomorrow,' he told the children,
'you'll break some records – mark my
words!'

I switched on the electric copper ready for my bath-water, when I
returned. In the dining-room stood large jugs of lemonade essence
ready for the morrow, but from the sound of the roaring wind
outside hot coffee would be more welcome. I sorted out coloured
braids for the relay race, and a basket of potatoes for the potato
race, and hoped that Mr Willet had looked out sound and hardy
flower-pots for the heavy-footed boys who had clamoured to
have a flower-pot race included in the programme. They had
seen this at Beech Green's Sports Day and had been practising in
the evenings for weeks, stumping laboriously along, placing one
pot by hand before the other, with their crimson faces bent
earthwards and their patched seats presented to the sky.

The kitchen was comfortably steamy when I put the zinc bath
on the floor and poured in buckets of rainwater from the pump.
As I lay in the silky brown water, too idle to do more than relax
and enjoy the heat, I listened to the rose tree which Dr Martin
had admired last autumn when he had come to visit Miss Clare
here. It beat, in a frenzy of wind, against the window-pane. To
drown the noise of its scrabbling thorns, I roused myself to switch
on the portable wireless set, which was within arm's reach, on the
kitchen chair.

'Strong westerly winds, reaching gale force at times, are

expected in all southern areas of the British Isles,' said a brisk, cheerful voice. Snarling, I switched off, and sank back into the comforting water.

Later, on my way to bed, I looked out of the landing window. Ragged clouds were tearing across the darkening sky, and over in Mr Roberts' field a dim, pale shape flapped against the hedge. Giving up the unequal struggle, the vicar's tent had sunk hopelessly to the ground.

Next morning, however, things looked brighter. The wind, though still strong, seemed less aggressive, and two of Mr Roberts' men erected the tent again. The sound of tent pegs being smitten reached us in school, where the children were much too excited to settle to any serious work.

The boys, as usual, were the more anxious about the afternoon. Fear of not doing well made them quite unbearable. They boasted of their own prowess and belittled that of their neighbours, while the girls looked on philosophically at this display of male exhibitionism.

'Look at John rubbing his legs! Thinks that'll make him run faster. Some hopes!'

'Tones up the muscles; that's what it does. All good runners does that before racing. Pity you don't try it. You was like an ol' snail last night down the rec.'

'Only 'cos I was a bit winded. Been overdoing the training, see!'

'You see ol' Eric, Saturday? Thought he was jumping high when he cleared that titchy little hedge down Bember's Corner. Coo, I've jumped twice that!'

'Me too. Easy, that hedge is. You should see me get over that electric wire Mr Roberts has put up in the heifers' field! Up I goes . . . and whoo . . . I bet it was over four foot I done!'

And so on. It seemed best to let them have their heads for a little while, but in the latter part of the morning they settled down to a history test, although I noticed a certain amount of secret muscle-flexing and leg-massage as the athletes prepared themselves for outstanding displays before the admiring gaze of parents and friends in the afternoon.

When Mrs Crossley arrived with the dinner van, the children

were washing their hands at the stone sink. I heard them cross-questioning her thoroughly.

'And what vegetables, Mrs Crossley?'

'Carrots and peas.'

'They blows you out too much. I shan't have they.'

'What for pudding, Mrs Crossley?'

'Some very nice currant pudding, with custard. You'll like that.'

''Twould have been best to have something lighter like. Fruit and that, wouldn't it, Eric?'

'I dunno. I'm hungry. Reckons I shall have some pudden, races or no races.'

'You hear him? Him what was so sharp on us last night eating sweets? Said us was in training? *Pudden*, he's going to eat! Fat chance we'll have in the relay!'

'We best eat summat,' said John Barton's placid voice, 'or we won't have no strength at all.'

'Well,' said Ernest grudgingly, 'it don't sound the sort of dinner that *real* runners would have, to me, but I s'pose us'll just have to stoke up best we can.'

They re-entered the schoolroom and settled themselves for grace. As far as I could see our athletes forgot their Spartan principles as soon as the food was put before them, and second, and even third, helpings of currant pudding were despatched with the usual Fairacre appetite.

There were plenty of people to watch the sports and patronize the refreshment tent. Miss Clare was in charge of the jugs of lemonade and the six biscuit tins and Mrs Finch-Edwards, looking very handsome in a classic maternity smock of polka-dot navy blue silk, with its inevitable white collar, sat beside her with an Oxo tin full of change.

'Yes, I'm keeping very well,' she responded to my inquiries, 'and I think hubby and I have got absolutely everything now. Even the pram's on order!'

There was a grunt from Mrs Pringle who had just brought in a tray full of glasses.

'Defying Providence!' she boomed. 'Never does to order the pram or cot till the little stranger's in the house. Times without number I've seen things go awry within the last three months. Seems to be the most dangerous time – particularly with the first. Why, there was a young girl over Springbourne Common—'

I broke in before Mrs Pringle could chill our blood further. Mrs Finch-Edwards' normally florid cheeks had blanched.

'That'll do, Mrs Pringle; and we shall need at least four tea-towels.'

'And lucky you'll be to get those, I may say,' said Mrs Pringle viciously, thwarted in the telling of her old-wives' tale. But she departed, nevertheless, and went back across the field to the school, limping ostentatiously to prove what a wronged woman she was.

Miss Gray was trying to keep the mob of children in order near the starting line which, being hand-painted by Ernest in yesterday's strong wind, wavered erratically across the width of the track.

A blackboard had been erected here showing the order of races, but so strong was the wind that, after it had capsized twice, nearly decapitating Eileen Burton on the second occasion, Mr Willet had lashed it to the easel. He looked very spruce this afternoon, in his best blue-serge suit as he stood with the vicar and Mr Roberts.

I had decided to be starter, and Miss Gray had the unenviable job of being judge at the other end. Mrs Roberts offered to help her and the two stood, with their hair blown over their eyes, waiting for the first race to start. It was 'Boys under 8: 50 yards.'

The young competitors crouched fiercely on Ernest's wobbly line, their teeth clenched and their lips compressed. 'On your marks, get set – go!' I shouted; and off they pounded, puny arms working like pistons and heads thrown back. The Sports had begun.

Everything went like clockwork. There were no tears, no accidents and the molehills were miraculously avoided by the children's flying feet. The parents and friends of Fairacre School, ranged on hard forms and chairs along Mr Willet's rope, applauded each event vigorously and made frequent trips, with the thirsty victors and vanquished, to the refreshment tent where trade was gratifyingly brisk. The fact that the tent was warm and peaceful after the tempest that blew outside may have helped sales, for the less warmly clad lingered in here, buying biscuits at four a penny, and filling up the Oxo tin with their offerings.

Mrs Moffat, in a becoming rose-pink suit, brought Linda in, flushed with success after winning the girls' sack race. Miss Clare noticed how much happier Mrs Moffat looked and how well she and Mrs Finch-Edwards agreed.

'If you like to go out for a bit, I'll manage the change,' offered Linda's mother, and Mrs Finch-Edwards, taking Linda by the hand, went out into the boisterous wind to see the Sports, leaving her friend in Miss Clare's company.

Perhaps the highlight of the afternoon was an unrehearsed incident. Mrs Pratt's white goat, attracted by the noise, had broken her collar and pushed through the hedge to see what was going on. Fastidiously, walking with neat, dainty steps, she approached the backs of the spectators and before anyone had noticed her, she picked up the hem of Mrs Partridge's flowered silk frock. Gradually, the goat worked it into her mouth, a sardonic smile curling her lips, tossing her head gently up and down, until at last a sudden tug caused the vicar's wife to look round and the hue and cry began.

Startled, the goat skipped away under the rope and charged down to see its friends, who were waiting, in pairs with their legs tied together, to run in the three-legged race. Squealing with excitement, and weak with laughter, they lumbered off in all directions, the goat prancing among them, bleating. Confusion reigned, some children sprawled on the grass, others attempted to capture the goat, and others rushed yelling to their parents. At last Mr Willet grabbed the animal's horns and slipped a rope noose over her head. Resigning herself to capture, the goat trotted meekly after him to the gate, accompanied by many young admirers.

By half-past four the Sports were over and the parents trickled away from the field with their children, some of them boasting of victory and some explaining volubly just how victory had evaded them.

Mrs Moffat, Mrs Finch-Edwards and Miss Gray had gone

home to the new bungalow to tea, and Miss Clare, Mrs Pringle and I collected the debris together in the shelter of the tent.

'It went very well,' said Miss Clare, mopping up lemonade from the table, while I counted braids and sacks, 'and how fit all the children look! I can see the improvement, in my lifetime, in the physique of the Fairacre children. Better conditions have a lot to do with it, of course, but I think less clothing and daily exercise play a great part. When I think how I was dressed at their age—' She broke off and gazed into the distance, seeing, I guessed, that little girl in high button boots, starched underclothes and stiff serge sailor dress complete with lanyard, whose photograph I had seen in the album at Beech Green.

Mrs Pringle's snort brought us back to earth.

'Never had such rubbishy things as sports in my young days,' she remarked acidly, 'making work for all and sundry, regardless! Never saw a jumping stand, or turned those 'orrible somersaults when I was a girl, and look at me now!'

We looked.

24. END OF TERM

It was the last day of term. Jim Bryant had brought the precious envelope containing our cheques; fantastically large ones this time, as they covered both July and August. Such wealth seemed limitless, but I knew from sad experience, how slowly September would drag its penniless length, before the next cheque came again!

Mr Willet was busy pulling up two roots of groundsel near the door-scraper, and expressed his customary surprise on receiving his cheque. Mrs Pringle was scouring the stone sink in the lobby and took her cheque grudgingly in a gritty hand.

'Little enough for the hours I puts in,' she said glumly, folding it and stuffing it down the front of her bodice. 'Sometimes I wonders if I can face next term, with fires and all. And the next few days will be nothing but scrub, scrub, scrub, with disinfectant, I suppose, all them cruel floorboards. Enough to make my leg flare-up, the very thought of it!'

'Well, give me good notice, Mrs Pringle,' I said briskly, 'when you do decide to give up. Then I can look round for somebody who'd like the job!'

There was an outraged snort from Mrs Pringle as she limped ostentatiously to the cleaning cupboard to put away her rags.

The morning was spent in a happy turmoil of clearing-up. Books were collected and counted, and then stacked in neat piles in the cupboards. Ernest and Eric sat at the long side desk, ripping out the remaining clean sheets of paper from the children's exercise books, to be put away for tests and rough work next term. The inkwells had been collected into their tray, and there was considerable competition among the boys as to who should have the enviable job of washing them, in an old bowl, out in the safety of the playground.

While the hubbub rose joyfully, I made my way painfully round the walls, prising out drawing-pins with my penknife and handing over dusty but cherished pictures to their owners. Through the partition I could hear the infants at their clearing-up labours, and when I reached the door I poked my head in to see how they were getting on.

Joseph Coggs was squatting by the big clay tin, tenderly tucking wet cloths over the clay balls to keep them in good order for next term. Eileen Burton was staggering to the cupboard with a wavering tower of Oxo tins, containing chalks, leant precariously against her stomach, her chin lodged on the top one to steady the pile. Some children were polishing their already emptied desks, others were scrabbling on the floor for rubbish, like old hens in straw, and a group besieged Miss Gray, holding such treasures as beads, coloured paper, plasticine and even used milk straws, all clamouring to know what should be done with them.

I clapped my hands to make myself heard above the din, and when it was a little less hectic I asked if any of them knew of any children likely to start school next term. This would give me some idea of numbers for ordering dinners for the first day.

There was a puzzled silence, and then Joseph said in his hoarse voice: 'My mum's coming up to see you about the twins.'

'How old are they?'

'They's five in November,' said Joseph, after some thought.

'Tell Mummy I should like to see her at any time,' I told him and looked to see if there were going to be any more newcomers, but there was no stir.

I returned to my own room, where the noise was deafening. No one seemed to know of any beginners next term, and it looked as though I should have room for the Coggs twins, although they were slightly under age, for John Burton and Sylvia would be leaving to go to Mr Annett's school at Beech Green, and Cathy would be going to the Grammar School at Caxley.

At last conditions became a little less chaotic. The overflowing waste-paper basket was emptied, the jam jars removed from the window-sills and put away, and the room wore a bleak, purged look, shorn of all its unessentials.

I put my old friend 'Constantinople' up on the blackboard, issued a piece of the rough paper and a pencil to each child, bullied them all into silence, and told them to see how many words they could make from it before Mrs Crossley arrived.

All was peaceful. From the playground came the distant splash of water as John Burton dealt with the inkwells, and nearer still, the clank of paint-boxes being cleaned at the stone sink by Linda Moffat. She pleaded so desperately to perform this filthy task, that I had given way, but now I was a prey to awful fears about the welfare of her crisp, piqué frock, and made haste to go into the lobby and envelop her in Mrs Pringle's sacking apron, much to the young lady's humiliation.

One Saturday previously I had taken several of the children into Caxley to buy Miss Gray's wedding present, for which the whole school had been collecting for weeks. I had managed to assemble all the children together, sending Miss Gray to the Post Office for more savings stamps. This manoeuvre was considered highly daring and the children were in a conspiratorial mood during her short absence, Eric going so far as to keep watch at the lobby door while we made our plans.

It was decided, in hushed whispers, that a piece of china would be appreciated, and the deputation, under my guidance, were given powers to make the final choice, not however, without plenty of advice.

'Something real good! Like you'd want for always!'

'And pretty too. Not some ol' pudden basin, say. A jam dish, more like!'

'Flowers, and that, on it . . . see?'

We promised to do what we could just as Eric thrust an agitated countenance round the door, saying: 'She's coming!'

With many secret giggles and winks they dispersed to their desks and all was unnaturally quiet when Miss Gray entered and handed over the savings stamps.

'What very good children,' she remarked; and then looked amazed at the gale of laughter that this innocent remark had released.

In Johnson's shop at Caxley, the business of choosing the present was undertaken seriously. We surveyed jam dishes, dessert services and fruit bowls, and I had great difficulty in steering them away from several distressing objects highly reminiscent of Mrs Pratt's collection. One particularly loathsome teapot fashioned like a wizened pumpkin exerted such a fascination over the whole party, that I feared Miss Gray might have to cherish it under Mr Annett's roof, but luckily, the man who was attending to us, with most commendable patience, brought out a china biscuit barrel, sprigged with wild flowers. It was useful, it was very pretty and it was exactly the right price. We had returned to Fairacre, after ices all round in a tea-shop, very well content with our purchase.

Excitement ran high, for the presentation was to be made at the end of the afternoon, just before breaking up for seven weeks' holiday. No wonder that eyes were bright, and fidgeting was impossible to control!

The vicar arrived in good time, bringing with him an unexpected end-of-term present for me – a bunch of roses from the climber which Mrs Bradley had admired on the day of the fête. Then the infants came into my room with Miss Gray shepherding them. They squeezed into desks with their big brothers and sisters, and the overflow sat cross-legged in the front, nudging each other excitedly.

The vicar made a model speech wishing Miss Gray much happiness and presented her with a carving set from the managers and other friends of the school. I gave Miss Gray my present next, as I guessed the children would like to see her receive it. As it was table linen they were not particularly impressed, and in any case they were far too anxious to see their own parcel handed over.

Joseph Coggs had been chosen to present the biscuit barrel. He advanced now, from behind my desk, holding the present gingerly in both hands. He fixed his dark eyes on Miss Gray's brogues and said gruffly: 'This is with love from us all.'

An enormous roar broke forth, hastily quelled to silence as Miss Gray undid the paper. Her delight was spontaneous and the children exchanged gratified smirks. She thanked us all with unwonted animation and then, putting her parcels carefully on the piano top, sat herself at the keys to play our last hymn of the term.

The vicar said grace; drawings and other treasures were collected, and with a special farewell to Cathy, John and Sylvia, general goodbyes were said and Fairacre School streamed out into the sunshine, free for seven long weeks.

Jimmy Waites could read now. He had had his tea and was sitting on the rag rug in his mother's kitchen, his fair head bent over a seed catalogue. There were certainly some formidable words in it, which he had had to ask his mother's help for . . . 'Chrysanthemum,' for instance, and 'Heliotrope' but 'Aster' and 'Anchusa' and even 'Sweet Alyssum,' he had worried out for himself, and he glowed with pride in this new accomplishment.

'You've done all right, this first year,' approved Mrs Waites who was pinning up her freshly-washed hair at the kitchen sink. She glanced through the window at Cathy, who was practising hand-stands by the wall, and whose mop of dark hair hung down into the dust of the yard. She noticed with pleasure how shapely and sturdy were her daughter's upthrust legs.

'Do her good to get more exercises and that at the new school,' she said aloud to herself. She let herself think for a brief, happy moment of Cathy's handsome father. Proper well-set-up he'd been, everyone agreed, a lovely dancer, and had played a sound game of football once or twice for Fairacre. If young Cathy took after him she'd be a real good-looking girl.

She leant forward anxiously to peer in the mirror. Now that

her hair was drying, the golden glints that the free shampoo (This Week's Amazing Offer) had promised its users were becoming apparent.

'As long as it don't get *too* bright,' thought Mrs Waite, in some alarm, 'I know it said "Let your husband look at you anew," but there's such a thing as making an exhibition of yourself.'

For a moment she was tempted to rinse her locks again in clear rainwater, but vanity prevailed. Anyway, she comforted herself, her husband would probably not notice anything different, even if she turned out auburn. Sometimes she wondered if those ladies up in London, who wrote the beauty hints, really had first-hand knowledge of husbands' reactions to their earnest advice.

Next door Joseph Coggs was submitting unwillingly to his mother's ministrations with the loathsome hair lotion.

'Prevention is better than cure!' Nurse had said dictatorially to the cowering mother. 'Once a fortnight, Mrs Coggs, or it will be the *cleansing station*!' If she had said the gates of hell, Mrs Coggs could not have been more impressed, and faithfully every other Friday evening, Joseph was greeted on his return from school with a painful dowsing and rubbing with 'the head stuff.'

'You ask Miss Read about the twins?' queried the mother, her fingers working like pistons in and out of the black hair.

'Ah!' jerked out Joseph. 'Her said you was to come and see her any time.'

'All right for her,' grumbled Mrs Coggs. 'Any time, indeed! The only minute I has to spare is while your father's wolfing down his tea afore making off to the "Beetle"!'

She released the child suddenly, and he made off, smoothing his greasy locks flat with his hands.

At the door he paused. 'Say! I give Miss Gray our present s'afternoon, and said a piece Miss Read learnt me!'

'Did you now?' answered his mother somewhat mollified at this honour to the family. 'What you give her then?'

'A biscuit barrel. Oh, and I forgot!' He fished in his pocket and produced sixpence. 'The vicar gave it to me for saying my piece all right.'

His mother's face softened a little.

'Well, that was real kind. You best put it where your father can't see it.' She went to the cupboard to find the evening meal. Once she'd got them all settled, she told herself, she'd slip up and see if Miss Read would have them two terrors after the holidays. Into everything, every blessed minute, and Arthur back at the 'Beetle' more than ever, and another baby on the way she'd bet a pound.

Joseph, lingering in the doorway, sensed the change in the atmosphere, and knew that his few moments of sympathy had flown. Sighing, he slipped into the garden and sought solace by the side of the baby's pram. Kicking and gurgling, his little brother looked up at him and Joseph forgot, in a moment, his unhappiness. With an uprush of joy he remembered his sixpence, his afternoon's triumph, and the fact that for seven long weeks he would be free to enjoy the company of his adored baby.

At that moment the future Mrs Annett was measuring the front bedroom at Beech Green for new curtains, happily unaware of the 'mortal damp' and Mrs Pringle's gloomy forecast of coming events in that ill-fated apartment. She was to be married in ten days' time, from the home of her Caxley friends, owing to the recent death of her mother. She wondered, as she strained upwards to the curtain-pole, if she would ever get all the things done that she wanted to do, in those few days.

Mrs Nairn, in her last fortnight as Mr Annett's housekeeper, was mounted on a chair, adjusting the tape-measure. A cloud of dust blew down from the ledge above the window.

Miss Gray gave a horrified gasp.

'Comes in a day, the dust, don't it,' remarked Mrs Nairn comfortably.

Miss Gray made no answer, contenting herself with the thought that in a week or two's time, under its new mistress's regime, their house would be clean from top to bottom for the first time for many years. What her poor darling had had to suffer, she thought to herself, no one could tell. But at least the future should make amends, and she was determined that her husband should be the happiest man in the kingdom.

*

Meanwhile, Linda Moffat, perched up on the dining-room table, listened to her mother and Mrs Finch-Edwards gossiping, as they adjusted the hem of her bridesmaid's frock.

'Four of them, there will be. Three little nieces and Linda. Wasn't it sweet of her to ask Linda too?'

'Very kind. What's her own frock like?'

Mrs Moffat told her at some length, and Linda lost interest as the technical details of ruching, darts, cut-on-the-cross and other intricacies were bandied between them.

At last the hem was pinned up, Linda was released from her half-made frock, and allowed to play in the garden while the two friends settled in armchairs, Mrs Finch-Edwards with her feet up, in approved style, on a footstool, embroidered by Mrs Moffat in earlier days.

'How will you manage without Miss Gray?' she asked. It was a delicate subject, and she decided that a plain approach might be best. Mrs Moffat seemed eager to be forthcoming.

'As a matter of fact, I thought I'd take in dressmaking in a small way. It might make the beginnings of a little business and then in time—' She faltered and Mrs Finch-Edwards came to the rescue.

'You mean, you still think we might, one day, go into this together?'

'I know with the baby coming and so on, you'll be tied; but it won't be many years before we both have more leisure. What do you think?'

Mrs Finch-Edwards put down the bib she was embroidering, and looked soberly at her friend.

'It would be a beginning. You know it's dress-designing we've both got a flair for. If we could persuade the customers to let us design for them, and we were recommended—'

Mrs Moffat broke in excitedly. 'We could get a team of dressmakers, couldn't we, if the thing worked?'

'I've got a little money coming to me in a few years' time from an aunt of mine in Scotland. It might just about set us up.'

The two women gazed at each other, half-fearful, half-enraptured. Little did they realize, on that summer evening, that the foundations of a flourishing future firm (named after Mrs Finch-Edwards' only daughter) were well and truly laid, and that the little girl, now skipping energetically outside in the garden, would become one of the most glamorous and publicized models in the world of fashion.

It was very peaceful in my garden. I sat shelling some peas which John Pringle had brought me, enjoying the warm evening sun.

In the elms, at the corner of the playground, the rooks cawed intermittently, and from the quiet schoolroom came the distant clank of Mrs Pringle's scrubbing-pail.

'Might as well make a start, first as last,' she had remarked morosely to me as she stumped in, limp accentuated, after she had had her tea. Occasionally, I could hear a snatch of some lugubrious hymn in Mrs Pringle's mooing contralto.

I thought, as the shelled peas mounted higher in the basin, of all the changes that had taken place in this last school year. We had parted with Miss Clare, enjoyed Mrs Finch-Edwards' boisterous session, welcomed Miss Gray, and, a rare thing indeed, seen a wedding planned for one of the staff of Fairacre School.

The three new children, who had entered so timorously on that far September morning, were now part and parcel of Fairacre School. Each had added something to the life of our small school; that little microcosm, working busily, within the larger one of Fairacre village.

I watched the swifts, so soon to go, swoop screaming over the garden, and wondered if Mr Hope, that unhappy poet-schoolmaster, who had lived here once, had sat here, as I was doing now, looking back. He, and, for that matter, all my predecessors, whom I knew so well from the ancient log-book, although I had never seen their faces, must have joined in the hotchpotch of fêtes, sales, outings, festivals, quarrels and friendships that make the stuff of life in a village.

The click of the gate roused me. There, entering, were Mrs Cogg and her two little daughters. They gazed about them with apprehension, with monkey eyes as dark and mournful as their brother's.

I put the past from me, and hurried down the path to meet my future pupils.

*

High above, on St Patrick's spire, the setting sun had turned the weathercock into a bird of fire. Phoenix-like, he flamed against the cloudless sky, looking down upon our miniature school world and all the golden fields of Fairacre.

Village Diary

To Jill,
the first reader

January

As I have been given a large and magnificent diary for Christmas – seven by ten and nearly two inches thick – I intend to fill it in as long as my ardour lasts. Further than that I will not go. There are quite enough jobs that a schoolmistress just *must* do without making this one a burden.

Unfortunately, the thing is so colossal that I shan't be able to carry it with me, as the adorable Miss Gwendolen Fairfax did hers, so that she 'always had something sensational to read in the train'.

It was a most surprising present for Amy to have given me. When we first taught together in London, many years ago, we exchanged two hankies each, I remember; and since she cropped up again in my life a year or so ago, it has been bath salts on her side ('To make you realize, dear, that even if you are a school teacher there is no need to let yourself go completely') and two-hankies-as-before on mine.

When Amy handed me this present she remarked earnestly, 'Try to use it, dear. Self-expression is such a wonderful thing, and so vital for a woman whose life is – well, not exactly abnormal, but restricted!' This smacked of Amy's latest psychiatrist to me, but after the first reaction of speechless fury, I agreed civilly and have had over a week savouring this *bon mot* with increasing joy.

Mrs Pringle, the school cleaner, told me yesterday that Miss Parr's old house at the end of the village has now been turned into three flats. The workmen have been there now for months; they arrived soon after her death, but I hadn't realized that that was what they were doing. A nephew of Miss Parr's now owns it, and has the ground floor. A retired couple from Caxley evidently move into the top floor this week, and a widower, I understand, has the middle flat.

'A very nice man too,' Mrs Pringle boomed menacingly at me. 'Been a schoolmaster at a real posh school where the boys have to pay fees and get the cane for nothing. Not in his prime, of course, but as Mrs Willet said to me at choir practice, there's many would jump at him.' Mrs Pringle eyed me speculatively, and I can see that the village is already visualizing a decorous wooing, culminating in a quiet wedding at Fairacre Church, with my pupils forming a guard of honour from the south door, with the aged couple hobbling down the path between them.

I said that I hoped that now that the poor man had retired, he would be allowed to rest in peace, and went out to clean the car. This is my latest and most extravagant acquisition – a small second-hand Austin, in which I hope to be able to have wonderful touring holidays, as well as driving to Caxley on any day of the week, instead of relying on the local bus on Tuesdays, Thursdays and Saturdays as heretofore. So far I have not been out on my own as I am still having lessons from an imperturbable instructor in Caxley, who thrives on clashing gears, stalling engines and a beginner's unfortunate confusion of brake and accelerator. Miss Clare, that noble woman, who taught the infants at Fairacre for many years, says that she will come out with me 'at *any* time, dear, whether you feel confident or not. I am quite sure that you can master anything.' Am touched, but also alarmed, at such faith in my powers, and can only hope that she never meets my driving instructor.

Miss Clare spent the evening with me recently and our conversation turned, as it so often does, to life in Fairacre in the early years of this century, when Miss Clare was a young and inexperienced pupil-teacher at this village school. I love to hear her reminiscing, for she has a tolerant and dispassionate outlook on life, born of inner wisdom and years of close contact with the people here. For Miss Clare, 'To know is to forgive,' and I have never yet heard of her acting in anger or in fear, or meting out to a child any punishment that was hastily or maliciously devised.

Her attitude to those who were in authority over her is as wide and kindly as it always was to the small charges that she taught for forty years.

We were talking of Miss Parr, who had died recently. She had been a manager of Fairacre School since the reign of King Edward the Seventh, and was a stickler for etiquette. It appears that one day she met Mrs Willet, now our caretaker's wife, but then a child of six, in the lane, and was shocked to find the little girl omitted to curtsy to her. At once she took the child to its mother, and demanded instant punishment.

'But surely—' I began to protest. Miss Clare looked calmly at me.

'My dear,' she said gently, 'it was quite understandable. It was customary then for our children to curtsy to the gentry, and Miss Parr was doing her duty, as she understood it, by correcting the child. No one then questioned her action. "Other days, other ways" you know. It's only that now, sometimes, looking back – I wonder—' She put down a green pullover she was knitting and stared meditatively at the fire.

'When you say that no one questioned the actions of his superiors, do you mean that they were automatically considered right or that verbal protestations were never made, or what?' I asked her.

'We recognized injustice, dear,' answered Miss Clare equably, 'as clearly as you do. But we bore more in silence, for we had so much more to lose by rebellion. Jobs were hard to come by, in those days, and no work meant no food. It was as simple as that.

'A sharp retort might mean instant dismissal, and perhaps no reference, which might mean months, or even years, without a suitable post. No wonder that my poor mother's favourite maxim was "Civility costs nothing." She knew, only too well, that civility meant more than that to people like us. It was a vital necessity to a wage-earner when we were young.'

'Was she ever bitter?'

'I don't think so. She was a happy, even-tempered woman, and believed that if we did our best in that station of life to which we had been called, then we should do well. After all, we all knew our place then. It made for security. And here, in Fairacre, the gentry on the whole were kindly and generous to those they employed. You might call it a benevolent despotism, my dear – and, you know, there are far worse forms of government than that!'

Miss Clare's eyes twinkled as she resumed her work and the room was filled again with the measured clicking of her knitting needles.

Tuesday was a beast of a day; foggy and cold, with the elm trees dripping into the playground. Two workmen arrived from Caxley to see to the school skylight over my desk: it must be the tenth time, at least, that it has received attention since I came here just over six years ago. Usually, it is Mr Rogers, from the forge, who has the job of clambering over the roof, but the managers decided to try the Caxley firm this time, hoping, I imagine, that it might be better done by them. The village, of course, is up in arms at this invasion of foreigners, and Mr Rogers wears a martyred expression when he stands at the door of his smithy. I am confident that he will soon be in a position to smile again, as the skylight has defied all comers for seventy-odd years – so the school log-books say – and I doubt whether any workmen, even if hailing from the great Caxley itself, will vanquish it.

One man, in Mrs Pringle's hearing, said loudly that 'it was a proper bodged-up job,' so that, of course, will inflame passions further. Mrs Pringle, who was scrubbing out the school dustbins at the time, drew in her breath for so long, with such violence, that I thought she would burst; but only her corsets creaked under the strain.

Tea, at Miss Clare's, was the bright spot of the day. We had a lardy cake which was wonderfully hot and indigestible, and conversation which was soothing, until I was putting on my coat when Miss Clare shattered me by asking if I had yet met a very nice man, a retired schoolmaster, who had come to live in Miss Parr's old house.

I am beginning to feel very, very sorry for this unfortunate man, and have half a mind to ring him up anonymously, advising his early removal from Fairacre if he wishes to have an undisturbed retirement.

The last day of the holidays has arrived, and, as usual, half the jobs I intended doing have been left undone. No marmalade made, no paint washed down, only the most urgent mending done, and school starts tomorrow.

It all looks unbelievably clean over there. I staggered back with the fish tank and Roman hyacinths, all of which have sheltered under my school-house roof for the past fortnight. Miss Gray – Mrs Annett, I mean – will have a smaller class this term, only sixteen on roll, while mine will be twenty-three strong.

The stoves are miracles of jetty brilliance. Mrs Pringle must have used pounds of blacklead and enough energy to move a mountain to have produced such lustre. Woe betide any careless tipper-on of coke for the next few days!

Term has begun. Everyone is back with the exception of Eileen Burton, who has, according to the note brought by a neighbouring child, 'a sore throat and a hard, tight chest.' Can only hope these afflictions are not infectious.

The workmen have found it necessary to remove the whole frame of the skylight, so that, having had a clear two weeks to do the job undisturbed, they now tell me that we must endure a flapping and smelly tarpaulin over the hole in the roof, while a new window-frame is made in Caxley. Straight speaking, though giving me some relief, dints their armour not at all as blame attaches, as usual, to other members of the firm 'higher-up and back in Caxley, Miss', so that I can see a very uncomfortable few days ahead.

The children appeared to have forgotten the very elements of education. Five-times table eluded them altogether, and my request to write 'January' on their own, met with tearful mystification. Having walked round the class and seen such efforts as 'Jamwy,' 'Ganeree' and 'Jennery' I wrote it on the blackboard with dreadful threats of no-play-for-a-week for those who did not master its intricacies immediately.

The vicar called, just before we went home, in his habitual winter garb of cloak, biretta and leopard-skin gloves. Surely they can't stand another winter? I only wish I had such a serene outlook as Mr Partridge's. He greeted us all as though he loved every hair of our heads, as truly I believe he does. I see that he has 'Jesu, Lover of my Soul' on the hymn list this week, but haven't the heart to tell him that I think it painfully lugubrious and quite unsuitable for the children to learn.

I invited him over to the school-house to tea and ushered him into the dining-room, where the clothes-horse stood round the fire bearing various intimate articles of apparel and a row of dingy polishing rags which added the final touch of squalor. Not that he, dear man, would have worried, even had he noticed the things – but that clothes-horse was whisked neatly into the kitchen in record time!

I have just returned from a day out with Amy. She rang me up last night to say that there was a wonderful film on, which I must see. It would *broaden* me. It was about Real life. I said that I'd looked through the *Caxley Chronicle* this week, but I thought that both cinemas were showing Westerns.

'Caxley?' screamed Amy down the wire. Did I think of nothing but Caxley and Fairacre? When she thought of what promise I had shown as a girl, it quite upset her to see how I'd gone off! No, the film she had in mind was to be shown in a London suburb – the cinema specialized in revivals, and this was a quite wonderful chance to see this unique masterpiece. She would pick me up at 10.30, give me lunch, and bring me back to the wilds again.

I mentally pulled my forelock and said that that would be lovely.

Amy's car is magnificent and has a fluid fly-wheel, which as a gear-crashing learner, filled me with horrid envy. We soared up the hills, passing everything in sight, while Amy told me that life, even for a happily married woman, was not always rosy. James, although utterly devoted of course, was at a dangerous age. Not that he was inattentive; only last week he gave her these gloves – she raised a gargantuan fur-clad paw; and the week before that these ear-rings – I bent forward to admire a cluster of turquoises – and this brooch was his Christmas present, and was fantastically expensive – but she found she was beginning to suspect the *reason* for so many costly presents, especially when he had been away from home, on business, so frequently lately.

I said: 'Why don't you ask him if there is anyone else?' Amy said that was so like me – it wasn't surprising that I stayed single when I was so – well, so *unwomanly* and *unsubtle*. No, she could handle this thing quite skilfully, she thought, and in any case it was her duty to stick by dear James through thick and thin. Unworthy thoughts crossed my mind as to whether she'd stick so nobly if James suddenly became penniless.

We arrived in the West End; Amy had no difficulty in finding a car park with an obsequious attendant who directed our footsteps to the hotel where Amy had booked a table. I was much impressed by the opulence of this establishment and said so. Amy shrugged nonchalantly: 'Not a bad little dump,' then, scanning the menu, 'James brings me here when he wants to be quick. The food is *just* eatable.'

We ordered ham and tongue, with salad, which Amy insisted on having mixed at our table, supervising the rubbing of the bowl with garlic (which I detest, but could see I must endure), the exact number of drops of oil, etc., and expressing horror that the whole was not being turned with wooden implements.

I would much rather have had my salad fresh and been allowed to ask for Heinz mayonnaise, in constant use at home, but realized that Amy was enjoying every minute of this worldly-woman-taking-out-country-mouse act, and would not have spoiled it for her for worlds.

Over lunch, Amy continued to tell me about James's generosity, and disclosed the monthly allowance which he gives her. This, she said, she just manages on. As the sum exceeds easily my own modest monthly cheque as a headmistress, I felt inclined to remind her of our early days together, teaching in a large junior school not many miles from this very hotel, when we thrived cheerfully on a salary of just over thirteen pounds a month, and visited the theatre, the cinema, went skating and dancing, dressed attractively and, best of all, were as merry as grigs all the time. As Amy's guest, however, I was bound to keep these memories to myself. As I watched her picking over her salad discontentedly I remembered vividly a meal we had had together in those far-off days. It must have been towards the end of the month for I know we spent a long and hilarious time working out from the menu which would fill us up more for eightpence – baked beans and two sausages, or spaghetti on toast.

The cinema was rather hard to find, in an obscure cul-de-sac, and the film which Amy had particularly come to see had just begun. It was so old, that it seemed to be raining all the time, and even the bedroom scenes – which were far too frequent for my peace of mind – were seen through a downpour. The women's hair styles were unbelievable, and quite succeeded in distracting my grasshopper mind from the plot; either puffed-out at the sides, like the chorus in *The Mikado*, or cut in a thick fringe just across the eyebrows, giving the most brutish aspect to the ladies of the cast. Waist lines were low and busts incredibly high evidently when this film first saw the light.

The supporting film was of later vintage, but, if anything, heavier going. Played by Irish actors, in Irish countryside in Irish weather, and spoken in such a clotted hotchpotch of Irish idiom as to be barely intelligible, it dealt with the flight of a young man from the cruel English. Bogs, mist, mountains, girls with shawls over their heads and bare feet splashing through puddles, open coffins surrounded with candles and keening, wrinkled old women, all flickered before us for an hour and a half – and then the poor dear was shot in the end!

We emerged into the grey London twilight with our eyes swollen. Drawn together by our emotional afternoon we had tea in a much more relaxed mood than lunch, and drove back in a pleasantly nostalgic atmosphere of ancient memories shared.

It was good of Amy to take me out. A day away from Fairacre in the middle of January is a real tonic. But I was sorry to see her so unhappy. I hope that I am not so wrong-headed as to blame Amy's recent affluence for her present malaise. As anyone of sense knows, money is a blessing and I dearly wish I had more – a lot more. I should have flowers in the classroom, and my house, all the year round, buy a hundred or so books, which have been on my list for years, and spend every school holiday travelling abroad – just for a start. I think the truth of the matter is that Amy feels useless, and has too little to do.

She used to be a first-class teacher and was able to draw wonderful pictures on the blackboard, that were the envy of us all, I remember.

School has now started with a vengeance, and I have heard all Mrs Annett's infants' class read – that is, those that can. She has done wonders since she came a year ago. The marriage seems ideal and Mr Annett has lost his nervous, drawn look and put on quite a stone in weight. He brings her over from their school-house at Beech Green each morning, and then returns to his duties there as headmaster. I was glad that the managers persuaded her to continue teaching. She intended to resign last September, but we had no applicants for the post, and as the Annetts had had a good deal of expense in refurnishing she decided to work for a little longer. The children adore her and her methods are more modern than Miss Clare's were. She has a nice practical grasp of infant-work problems too, as an incident this morning proved. I was sending off for more wooden beads for number work. 'Make them send square ones,' she said. I looked surprised. 'They don't roll away,' she added. Now, that's what I call intelligent! Square they shall be!

Joseph Coggs appeared yesterday morning with a brown-paper carrier bag. Inside was a tortoise, very muddy, and as cold and heavy as a stone. It was impossible to tell if it were dead or only hibernating.

'My mum told me to throw an old saucepan on the rubbish heap at the bottom of our place,' he told me, 'and this 'ere was buried under some old muck there.' He was very excited about his find and we have put the pathetic reptile in a box of leaves and earth out in the lobby – but I doubt if it will ever wake again. The children, I was amused to hear, were hushing each other as they undressed.

'Shut up hollering, you,' said Eric in a bellow that nearly raised our tarpaulin, 'that poor snail of Joe's don't get no rest!'

The weather is bitterly cold, with a cruel east wind, which flaps our accursed tarpaulin villainously. (The frame 'has been a bit held-up like, miss. Funny, really.') Scotland has had heavy snow, and I expect that Fairacre will too before long.

The vicar called in just before the children went home to check up numbers for our trip to the Caxley pantomime on Saturday. Two buses have been hired as mothers and friends will come too, as well as the school managers who generously pay the school-children's expenses. It is the highlight of dark January.

Mr Annett called to collect his wife – she won't be coming with us to the pantomime – and the vicar remarked to me on their happiness, adding that, to his mind, a marriage contracted in maturer years often turned out best, and had I met that very pleasant fellow – a retired schoolmaster, he believed – who had come to live at Miss Parr's?

An almost irresistible urge to push the dear vicar headlong over the low school wall, against which he was leaning, was controlled with difficulty, and I was surprised to hear myself replying politely that I had not had that pleasure yet. Truly, civilization is a wonderful thing.

I met Mr Bennett as I walked down to the Post Office the other evening. He is the owner of Tyler's Row, four thatched cottages at the end of our village. The Coggs live in one, the Waites next door to them, an old couple – very sweet and as deaf as posts – in the next, and a tight-lipped, taciturn woman, called Mrs Fowler lives in the last.

Mr Bennett had been to collect the rent from his property.

Each tenant pays three shillings a week and parts with it with the greatest reluctance.

'I gets to hate coming for it,' admitted poor Mr Bennett. He is beginning to look his seventy years now, but his figure is as upright and trim as it was when he was a proud soldier in the Royal Horse Artillery, and his waxed moustache ends still stand at a jaunty angle. He has his Old Age Pension and lives with a sister at Beech Green, who is ailing and as poor as he is.

'Every door's the same,' went on the old soldier. ' "Can't you set our roof to rights? Can't you put us a new sink in? Come and look at the damp in our back scullery. 'Tis shameful." And what can I do with twelve bob a week coming in? That's if I'm lucky. Arthur Coggs owes me for three months now. He's got four times the money coming in that I have, but he's always got some sad story to spin.'

The old man took out a pipe and rammed the tobacco in with a trembling finger.

'I shall have to give this up, I s'pose, the way things are. I went to get an estimate from the thatcher over at Springbourne about Tyler's Row roofs. Guess how much?'

I said I imagined it would cost about a hundred pounds to put it in repair.

'A hundred?' Mr Bennett laughed sardonically. '*Two* hundred and fifty, my dear. There's nothing for it, it seems, but to sell 'em for about a hundred and fifty while I can. Mrs Fowler would probably buy 'em. She's making a tidy packet at the moment. Pays me three bob, my dear, and has a lodger in that back bedroom who pays her three pound!'

'But can she?' I asked, 'Didn't you have a clause about sub-letting?'

'No. I didn't. When Mrs Fowler first come begging, all pitiful as a widder-woman, to have my cottage, I was that sorry for her I let her have the key that day. Now the boot's on the other foot. She earns six pounds a week up the engineering works in Caxley, gets three off her lodger, and greets me with a face like a vinegar bottle. "Proper hovel," she called my cottage, just now, "I sees you don't give me notice though, my dear," I says to her, "and, what's more, that's a real smart TV set you got on the dresser there." Ah! She didn't like that!'

The old man chuckled at the thought of his flash of wit, and blew out an impudent dart of smoke from under the twirling moustaches.

'I've just met Mrs Partridge,' he added. 'She asked me if I'd like to give something towards the Church Roof Fund. I give her a shilling, and then I couldn't help saying: "If I was you, Ma'am, I'd call along Tyler's Row for donations. There's something in the nature of forty or fifty pounds going in there each week. You should get a mite from that quarter."'

He leant forward and spoke in a conspiratorial whisper.

'And you know what she said to me? "Mr Bennett, I'm afraid

their hearts don't match their pay packets!" Ah, she sees it all – she and the vicar! Times is topsy-turvy. There's new poor and new rich today, but one and all has got to face responsibility, as I see it. You can't take out of the kitty and not put in, can you, Miss?'

The bus to Beech Green and Caxley drew up with a horrible squeaking of brakes. The driver, a local boy, from whom no secrets are hid, shouted cheerfully to Mr Bennett above the din.

'Been to collect them rents again? Some people has it easy, my eye!'

The old soldier cast me a quizzical glance, compounded of despair and amusement, mounted the steep step, and vanished among the country passengers.

I have been inflicted with a sudden and maddening crop of chilblains and can scarcely hobble around the house. No shoes are big enough to hold my poor, swollen, tormented toes and I am shuffling about in a pair of disreputable slippers which had been put aside for the next jumble sale, but were gratefully resurrected. A very demoralizing state of affairs, and can only put it down to the unwelcome appearance of snow.

The pantomime was an enormous success. Both buses were full, and Cathy Waites, looking very spruce in her new Grammar School uniform, sat by me and told me all about the joys of hockey. 'I'm right-half,' she told me, eyes sparkling, 'and you have to have plenty of wind, because if you're right-half you have to mark the opposing left-wing, and she's usually the fastest runner on the field.' There was a great deal more to the same effect, and in answer to my query about her prowess in more academic subjects, she said: 'Oh, all right,' rather vaguely, and went on to tell me of the intricacies of bullying-off.

Jimmy, her little brother, who sat by his mother opposite, was eating a large apple as he entered the bus, and in the six miles to Caxley consumed, with the greatest relish, a banana, a slab of pink and white nougat, a liquorice pipe, a bar of chocolate cream, and a few assorted toffees. This performance was only typical of many of his companions.

Joseph Coggs sat by me when we settled in the Corn Exchange. The pantomime was 'Dick Whittington,' and he was overawed by the cat, whose costume and make-up were remarkably realistic.

'How does he breeve?' he asked, in a penetrating whisper.

I whispered back. 'Through the holes in the mask.'

'But he don't have no nose,' objected Joseph.

'Yes he does. It's under the mask.'

'Well, if it's under the mask, how does he breeve?'

We were back where we started, and I tried a different approach.

'Do you think he's holding his breath all this time, Joseph?'

'Yes, he must be.'

'Then how can he talk to Dick?'

Still not persuaded of the cat's 'breeving,' or half-believing it to be a real cat all the time, Joseph subsided. He loved every minute of the show – which was an extraordinarily good amateur performance – and nearly rolled out of his seat with excitement, when I pointed out Linda Moffat to him on the stage. She was a dazzling fairy queen, in a creation of her clever mother's making, and her dancing was a pleasure to watch. I was glad that Mrs Moffat, with her friend Mrs Finch-Edwards, had been able to come with us this afternoon to witness Linda's success.

Several of the cast were known personally to the Fairacre children and storms of clapping greeted the appearance of anyone remotely known.

'Look,' said Eric, on my other side, clutching me painfully, 'there's the girl what drives the oil-van Tuesdays.' And he nearly burst his palms with rapturous greeting.

When we emerged, dazzled with glory, into the winter twilight, the snow was falling fast. Queen Victoria on her lofty pedestal wore a white mantle and a snow-topped crown. The lane to Fairacre was unbelievably lovely, the banks smooth as linen sheets, the overhanging beech trees already bearing a weight of snow along their elephant-grey branches, while the prickly hawthorn hedges clutched white handfuls in their skinny fingers.

St Patrick's clock chimed half-past five when we stepped out at Fairacre, after our lovely afternoon. Our footsteps were muffled, but our voices rang out as clear as the bells above, in the cold air.

Mrs Pringle asked me as we got off the bus if I had ever tried Typhoon tea? I successfully curbed an insane desire to ask her if it brewed storms in tea-cups? I enjoyed this *bon mot* all through my own tea-time.

A most peculiar thing happened today. A very loud knocking came at the door of my classroom, while we were chanting the pence table to 100, in a delightful sing-song that would make an ultra-modern inspector's hair curl – and when I opened it, a strange young man tried to push in. I manoeuvred him back into the lobby, shut the classroom door behind me, and asked what he wanted. He was respectably dressed, but unshaven. He said could he come in as he liked children? Thinking he was an eccentric tramp on his way from the Caxley workhouse to the next, I told him that he'd better be getting along, and shooed him kindly into the playground.

An hour later Mrs Annett came in from P.T. lesson, somewhat perturbed, because the wretched creature had hung over the school wall throughout the lesson making inane remarks. At this, I went out to send him off less kindly. By now, he had entered my garden and was drawing patterns on the snowy lawn with a stick.

When I asked him what he was supposed to be doing, he flummoxed me by whipping out a red, penny note-book and saying he'd come to read the gas meter. As we have no gas in this area, this was so patently silly that I made up my mind at once to get the police to cope with the fellow.

As I opened my front door he tried to come in with me, whining: 'I'm so hungry – so hungry,' and grinning vacantly at the same time. By now I was positive I had a madman on my hands, and very devoutly wished that I had not seen a gripping film about Jack the Ripper in Caxley recently, the horrider parts of which returned to me with unpleasant clarity.

'Go to the back porch,' I ordered him, in a stern school-marmish voice, 'and I will give you some food.' Luckily he went, and I sped inside, locked front and back doors, and rang Caxley police station in record time.

A reassuring country voice answered me, and I began to feel much better as I described the man, until the voice said, in a leisurely manner: 'That'd be the chap that ran off from Abbot-sleigh yesterday' – our local mental home.

'Heavens—!' I began, squeaking breathlessly.

'He wouldn't hurt a fly, miss,' went on the unhurried burr, 'he'll be scared stiff of you. Just keep him there if you can and we'll send a car out – it'll be with you in a quarter of an hour.'

I didn't know that I cared to be told that the man would be scared stiff of me, but I cared even less for the suggestion that I cherished him under my roof. Nor did I like the thought of the forty children, of tender years, for whom I was responsible, not to mention Mrs Annett, whose husband I should never dare to face, if aught befell her. All this I babbled over the telephone, adding: 'I'm just going to give him a drink and some bread and cheese, in the back porch, so please try and get here while he's still eating.'

'Car's gone out already. Never you fear, miss. Treat him like one of your kids,' said my calm friend, and rang off. I handed a pint of cider, half a loaf, and a craggy piece of hard cheese through the kitchen window, and with subtle cunning of which I was inordinately proud, supplied him with a small, very blunt tea-knife which should slow up his progress considerably. I couldn't make up my mind whether to dash back to the school and warn Mrs Annett, or whether to hang on in the house until the police car came. In the end I stayed in the kitchen, watching the meal vanish all too swiftly and edging my mind away from that pursuing film.

After the longest ten minutes of my life, the car drew up. Two enormous, cheerful policemen came to the back porch, and asked the man to come for a ride with them.

He went, without a backward glance, still clutching the plate and mug. Once inside the car he finished his cider, and I emerged from the front door and collected his utensils, wishing him a heartfelt good-bye into the bargain.

The policeman said: 'Thank you, miss, thank you!' and drove off, still beaming.

When I caught sight of myself in the mirror in the lobby I was not surprised. The most scared schoolmistress in the United Kingdom crawled thankfully back to her noisy class, and never breathed a word of reproach to the dear souls.

I really believe that my chilblains have finally gone, and wish I knew what had cured them – if anything particular, apart from Time-the-great-healer, I mean.

The various suggestions for their rout have ranged from (1) calcium tablets (Mr Annett); (2) painting with iodine (Mrs Annett) which I tried, but found tickly to do and so drying that the poor toes started to crack as well as itch; (3) treating with the liquid obtained from putting salt in a hollow dug in a turnip (Mr Willet, the caretaker); and (4) thrashing with a sprig of holly until the chilblains bleed freely (Mrs Pringle). Needless to say I did *not* attempt the last sadistic assault on my suffering extremities.

I am very worried about Joseph Coggs. His mother was taken to hospital last week with some internal trouble connected with the recent baby. Mrs Pringle, who usually describes any ills of the flesh in the most revolting detail, has seen fit on this occasion to observe an austere reserve about Mrs Coggs' symptoms, taking up the attitude that there are some things that the great army of married women must keep from their less fortunate spinster sisters. The twins, who usually adorn the front desk in Mrs Annett's room, and a toddler brother, have been sent to Mrs Coggs' sister in Caxley; but as she has no room for Joe he is living a hand-to-mouth existence with his father (who is completely useless) and with Mrs Waites, the next-door neighbour, 'Keeping an eye on him.'

It all sounds most unsatisfactory to me. The child is not clean, has not had his clothes changed since his mother's departure, and looks frightened. Mr Willet told me more this morning when he came to fill the two buckets for the school's daily drinking-water from my kitchen pump.

'I don't say nothing about Arthur Coggs' drunkenness,' announced Mr Willet, with heavy self-righteousness. 'Nor don't I say nothing about his hitting of his wife now and again – that's his affair. Nor don't I say nothing about an occasional lift round the ear for his kids – seeing as kids must be brought up respectful – but I *do* say this. That's not right to leave that child alone in that thatched cottage with the candle on, while he spends the evening at the "Beetle and Wedge." Why, my wife and I we hears him roaring along home nigh on eleven most nights.'

'But the candle would have burnt out by then,' I said, horror-struck. 'Joe would be alone in the dark.'

'Well, I don't know as that's not a deal safer,' said Mr Willet, stolidly. 'Better be frightened than frizzled. But don't you upset yourself – Joe's probably asleep by then.'

'I thought Mrs Waites was looking after him.'

'Mrs Waites,' said Mr Willet, with a return to his pontifical manner, 'is well-meaning, but flighty. Never room for more than one thought at a time in her head. Maybe she takes a peep at him, once in a while; maybe she don't.'

Discreet questioning of Joseph, later in the morning, revealed that the state of his home affairs was even worse than suspected. The candle *does* go out, Joseph is too terrified to get out of bed, so wets it, and Arthur Coggs on his return from the pub shows his fatherly disapproval by giving the child what Joe calls 'a good hiding with his belt.' (On seeing my appalled face, Joe added, reassuringly, that 'he didn't use the buckle end.') Joseph's stolid acceptance of this state of things was rather more than I could bear, and I went to Mrs Waites' house during the dinner hour to see what could be done.

She was sensible and helpful, offering to let Joe share her little Jimmy's bed downstairs. This sounded ideal, and I promised to see Arthur Coggs about the scheme after tea. He – great bully that he is – was all smiles and servility, and confessed himself deeply grateful to Mrs Waites, as well he might be.

Luckily, Mrs Waites, who is a confirmed novelette-reader, has just read in this week's number, she told me, a story about a friendless child who later becomes heir to a dukedom and landed estate (no taxes mentioned), and suitably rewards a kindly woman who befriended him in his early years. This has sweet-ened her approach to young Joe considerably, and though I can't see a dukedom looming up for him, he will doubtless never forget his own neighbour's present kindness. Flighty Mrs Waites may be, but thoroughly sweet-natured, and I can quite see how she has fluttered so many male hearts.

I seem to be more than usually financially embarrassed, and when I had paid the laundry man this morning, found I was left with exactly two shillings and sevenpence. Mrs Pringle brought me my weekly dozen eggs this afternoon, and I had to tip out my threepenny bits which I save in a Coronation mug, and make up the balance.

That's the worst of being paid for December and January just before Christmas! I shall have to take my Post Office Savings Book into Caxley on Saturday morning and withdraw enough to keep me going until the end of the month. It would be more than my reputation's worth to withdraw it here in the village. Mr Lamb, our postmaster, and brother to Mrs Willet, would fear I was either betting or keeping two homes. Meanwhile I must just embezzle the dinner money.

We have had pouring rain all day and – miraculously – the new skylight seems weatherproof.

I gave my class an arithmetic test. Linda Moffat did exceptionally well, and should go on to Caxley High School in two years' time if she keeps on at this rate. She grows prettier daily, and will doubtless become a heart-breaker.

All goes well with Joseph, thank heaven, and the child is cleaner than I've ever seen him. He and Jimmy are great friends and I can see that Mrs Annett is going to have to squash those two young gentlemen before long.

Joe's tortoise seems to have turned round in his box. At my suggestion that perhaps somebody lifted him round, there were hot denials, and I apologized hastily. He certainly looks less dead.

Jim Bryant, our postman, brought our cheques today. He was never more welcome. I gave Mrs Pringle and Mrs Annett theirs, but could not find Mr Willet. However, he had a noisy coughing attack in the lobby this afternoon, which reminded me of his rightful dues.

'There now,' he said, when I gave the cheque to him, 'this is a real surprise!'

Bless him, if anyone ever earned his humble wage it's Mr Willet! He copes with coke, water, dead leaves, dustbins, snow, intruding animals varying from Mr Roberts' cows to black beetles – not to mention the buckets from our primitive lavatories – with unfailing cheerfulness. May he endure for ever!

FEBRUARY

The village is agog. The engagement has been announced in *The Times* and the *Daily Telegraph* of John Parr – our Miss Parr's nephew, who now owns her house here in Fairacre. His bride, unfortunately, is not to be a Fairacre girl – what a wedding that would have been at St Patrick's – but lives somewhere in Westmorland. Mrs Pringle was somewhat disapproving this morning.

'Young enough to be his daughter! Man of his age – fifty-odd – with one foot in the grave, as you might say, to enter into 'oly wedlock with a kittenish bit like that! Don't seem respectable to me. A decent body, much the same age now, why, that's quite a different kettle of fish! I said as much to Mr Willet – which reminds me – that schoolmaster what lives on top of Mr Parr was in the Post Office yesterday. Looked lonely to me.'

We are all anxious to read about the engagement in 'the real paper,' the *Caxley Chronicle*, where we are bound to learn more details. For anyone in the news, who has the remotest connection with Caxley or its environs, must expect to face a detailed account of himself in the local paper.

In John Parr's case I think there will be some shortage of material, as he has lived almost all his fifty years in Hendon, only visiting his aunt at Fairacre as a child, until he took over her property recently. Still, it's a challenge to the paper and I shall look forward to next Tuesday, when it appears, as keenly as the rest of the village.

This avid interest of the countryman in his neighbours is a most vital part of country living, and is the cause of both pleasure and annoyance. I suppose it springs from the common and pressing need for a story. Books supply the panacea to this fever for those who read; but for the people who find reading distasteful, or are too sleepy after a day's work in the open air to bother with books, then this living drama which unfolds, day by day, constitutes one long enthralling serial, with sub-plots, digressions, flash-backs and many delicious aspects of the same incident as seen through various watchers' eyes.

The countryman, too, has more time than his town cousin, to indulge in his observations and speculations. To the lone man ploughing steadily up and down a many-acred field, the sporadic activity of the dwellers in the cottage on the hill-side acquires an enormous importance. He will see smoke coming from the wooden shed's chimney, and surmise that it is washing day. He will watch the old woman cutting lettuce from her garden and speculate on such things as cold meat for midday dinner – it all fits in. Later, as the garments billow on the line he will recognize the checked shirt that young Bill was wearing, American fashion, at the pub on Saturday night and wonder if his missus's first has arrived yet. And it may well be that it is he who first sees the brave white fluttering of new nappies and nightgowns which semaphore the tidings that a new soul has arrived to join in the fun and feuds of Fairacre.

Of course it is irritating at times to find that all one's personal affairs are an open book to the village, but, personally, I have two ways of mitigating the nuisance. The first is to face the fact that one has no real private life in a village and so it is absolutely necessary to comport oneself as if in the public gaze the whole time. The second is to let people know a certain amount of one's business so that their minds have a nice little quid, as it were, to chew on. There is then a sporting chance that any really private business may be overlooked. On no account, in a village, can one begin a sentence with: 'Don't let it go any further, but—' One has to face this consuming interest squarely. It doesn't worry me now, though it did in my early days here as headmistress; but I have reminded myself many times, that either – none must know, or all.

The vicar called in and said what delightful news it was about John Parr. A man needed companionship, particularly as he grew older, and would I be able to go to tea at the Vicarage one day next week (he had a note somewhere from his wife, but it seemed to have vanished – at times he half believed in poltergeists) to meet that charming fellow who lived above Parr? I said that I should look forward to it immensely.

I drove alone, for the first time today, to Caxley to do a little shopping. As I approached the bus stop, I overtook Mrs Pringle stumping along, black shiny shopping bag on arm, and offered her a lift.

'Most likely flying in the face of Providence,' she remarked morosely, as she settled her bulk beside me. 'I'll never forget going out with my old aunt the first time she took her car out alone. Phew! That was a nightmare, I can tell you! She started learning late in life, like you, and never had no consecration, if you follow me.'

I said I didn't, edging round a disdainful cat that was washing its legs in the road.

'Well, couldn't never do two things together like. Come she put one pedal down, she hadn't got consecration enough to put the other.'

'Is she all right now?' I asked – foolishly enough.

'Oh no!' said Mrs Pringle, with the greatest satisfaction, 'she lost the use of her right arm as a result of the accident. Not that the doctors didn't TRY, mark you. Speak as you find, I says, and it was months afore they really give her up. Pulleys, massage, deep-ray, X-ray, sun-ray—'

'Hooray,' I said absently, but luckily Mrs Pringle was well launched.

'Why, she was in that hospital for nigh on three months, and the doctors said theirselves that they'd never come across a woman what bore pain so brave before. Of course, she was only driving very slow at the time. Say she'd been driving this pace, now, she'd very like have killed herself outright. Having no consecration, you see, she couldn't stop quick.'

I was glad to reach Caxley and drop the old misery outside the Post Office.

I bought a very dashing pair of tan shoes, which cost far more than I can really afford, but I consoled myself with the thought that February is a short month – a specious piece of reasoning, which I shall not delve into. Also managed to get a new book from the library, much praised by the critics.

I felt rather wobbly on the drive home – probably lack of consecration – and so horribly tired this evening that I went to bed early with hot milk and the book.

I spent most of Sunday in bed, with what I can only think is a particularly unpleasant 'flu germ. My only nourishment was four oranges and about a gallon of lemon water, the thought of anything else anathema.

The book, of which I had read such glowing reports, I hurled from my bed of pain about 11 a.m., when the heroine – as unpleasant a nymphomaniac as it has been my misfortune to come across – hopped into the seventh man's bed, under the delusion that this would finally make her *(a)* happy, *(b)* noble and altruistic, and *(c)* interesting to her readers. Could have told the wretched creature by page 6, that, spinster though I am, this is not the recipe for contentment.

I am heartily sick of books from Caxley library – all termed 'powerful' by their reviewers (and in future I shall steer clear of any with this label), which give the suffering reader a detailed account of the bodily functions of their main characters. If the author has such a paucity of ideas that he must pad out his 300 pages with reiterated comments on his hero's digestive, alimentary and productive systems, I am sorry for him; but I don't see why he should be encouraged.

To have a heroine who does nothing but climb, regularly every thirty pages, from one bed into another, is, to my mind, not only inartistic. It is worse. It is tedious.

I spent the evening huddled over the fire, refreshing myself mentally with *The Diary of a Country Parson*, and physically with sips of lemon water. On opening the larder door, I nearly had a relapse, by being faced with a leering joint of fatty beef, some cold cooked sausages embedded in grease, and a pot of cod liver oil and malt.

Retired early to bed, and felt the greatest sympathy for James Woodforde who found 'Mince Pye rose oft' sometime in the 1790s. I lay awake for several hours and noticed, not for the first time, how peculiarly significant inanimate objects, such as chairs and tables, become when one's energy is low. It is almost as though they have some life of their own, a silent, immobile, waiting one, rather sinister – as though they were saying: 'Yes, we were here before you came. And we'll still be here, standing and watching when you – poor ephemeral creature – have gone.'

I suppose the logical reason is that all these things are used and taken for granted, and hardly noticed, as one bustles about with all sorts of plans to occupy one's mind. But when illness comes, then one becomes conscious of their presence, and imbues them with more power than is really theirs. I had worked out this interesting theory at about 2 a.m., and was toying with the idea of writing a letter to the *Caxley Chronicle* about it – with a rather well-turned aside, about the Romans' Lares et Penates – when I must have dropped off.

This has been Black Monday. The telephone rang at 8 a.m. and Mr Annett, who sounded quite beside himself with worry told me that Mrs Annett had a high temperature and was too ill to come to school.

'I'm so sorry,' I said, 'it's probably this ghastly 'flu.'

'Don't expect her this week at all,' said the harassed husband, 'I am insisting on her staying in bed for at least three days. She can't be too careful at a time like this.'

I should have liked to ask Mr Annett to explain this last remark. Did he mean, I wondered, that Mrs Annett was expecting a child?

Or did he mean, simply, that at this time of year one must take reasonable precautions? I forbore, as a respectable maiden lady, to cross-question the poor fellow, contenting myself with sending my love to the patient and a message to the effect that we should manage very well.

The distance from my house to the school is about fifty yards, but it seemed like half a mile to my shaky legs.

Mrs Pringle was nowhere to be seen and the stoves were unlit. Luckily they were laid and soon burnt up well, but the school was terribly cold.

Jim Bryant brought a note from her which read:

> *I am laid by with gastrick, and a flare-up of my leg. The doctor is comeing today and will let you know what he say.*
> *Matches is hid behind bar soap on top shelf. Mr Willet makes free otherwise. Hope you can manige.*
>
> *Mrs Pringle.*

Only ten of Mrs Annett's children arrived, so that with my own I had a class of twenty-nine – not too bad. Evidently this germ is fairly widespread in the village.

I felt too wobbly to do much active teaching, and the children worked cheerfully enough, from books, and the infants brought in their own number apparatus and reading books and got on very well.

Dinner turned out to be neck of mutton stew and mashed potatoes, which I served out with much nausea and as little lingering as possible. Figs and custard completed this – to me – revolting meal, but the children returned again and again for helpings, with true Fairacre appetites.

Mr Willet brought a message from Mrs Pringle during the afternoon, to the effect that Dr Martin recommended a week off, maybe more, and that her niece 'over to Springbourne' would oblige while she was 'laid by.' Mr Willet, after looking sadly at me for a long time, said that I looked a bit peaky to him, and suggested that I had a 'glass of stout and something substantial, like a good thick wedge of pork pie' for my supper. It was only the comforting support of the school fire-guard at my back that kept me from collapsing at the dear soul's feet.

Nevertheless, did manage to imbibe a glass of hot milk and two digestive biscuits, before going to bed, and felt very much better.

There appears to be no hope of getting a supply teacher while Mrs Annett is away. Mrs Finch-Edwards is fully occupied with her young baby and Miss Clare is nursing her sister, who is really very ill with this same wretched complaint.

Luckily, in a day or two, I felt perfectly fit again, and as there are so many absentees my class is not overwhelmingly large. The age range makes it rather difficult to choose a story that will interest them all, but the 'Ameliaranne' books are proving a great standby.

The *Caxley Chronicle* today carried an account of John Parr's engagement. As his fiancée is second cousin to a duke, the *Caxley Chronicle* has thrown poor John Parr to the lions with a casual 'who has always given generous support to the local branch of the League of Pity,' and concentrated on his bride-to-be's more glamorous connections. I foresee that Fairacre and particularly Mrs Pringle, will feel slighted.

Mrs Pringle's niece is doing her scatter-brained best to fill her aunt's place, but she is a sore trial. She has bright, rusty-red locks, very erratically cut, with no parting, and the back view of her head resembles a particularly tousled floor mop. Her eyes are of that very light blue, peculiar either to fanatics or feather-brained individuals, and her large mouth is curved in a constant mad grin. I don't mind admitting that I find her unnerving.

She wears a long, mauve hand-knitted woollen frock, which has been sketchily washed and pegged by the hem, so that it undulates in a remarkable fashion round her calves.

While I was looking out our morning hymn, before school, she dusted round me, and kept up a febrile chatter which I allowed to go in one ear and out of the other. However, she caught my attention suddenly by saying proudly: 'I've just had my third!' I had heard something about one moral slip, and had been inclined to take the usual tolerant village line, that it was regrettable, but might not perhaps be the girl's fault. When it comes to two, we villagers are not so sympathetic; and so, when Miss Pringle announced her third to me, I probably looked as taken aback as I felt.

'I said I've just had my third!' repeated the girl. I made no comment; and, probably, sensing from my lack of enthusiasm that all was not quite well, she added apologetically: 'I can't think how it happened!'

Amy rang up 'for a cosy chat' last night, just as I was going to bed. James had been called away on urgent business (unspecified} which would keep him engaged until Sunday. Amy said that he hated going, and couldn't tell her much about it as it was 'top-level and frightfully hush-hush'. (What 'top-level-hush-hush' stuff a director of a cosmetic firm meddles in, is no affair of mine, but it doesn't stop me thinking.)

I told her about the 'flu and no supply teachers, quite innocently and was amazed when she offered to come and help.

I had to ring the education office to get official consent, but as Amy has excellent qualifications, she was welcomed with open arms in this plague-stricken time.

She arrived in the luscious car, and I heard the children debating who it could belong to.

'That must be an inspector. Too posh for an ornery teacher. Look at Miss Read's car now!'

'More like the new head nurse – except there ain't no jars of head-stuff in the back.' (Luckily Amy was out of earshot.)

It was very cheering to have her here and we both enjoyed working together. She will stay until the end of the week.

I was to have gone to tea at the vicarage today, but Mrs Partridge rang up at morning play-time to say that we must postpone our tea-party as poor Mr Lawn (Pawn? Prawn? Line crackling badly as the 'Beetle and Wedge' is having a telephone installed at the moment) has succumbed to prevailing sickness. I expressed sincere sympathy.

I had a Thurberesque conversation with the mad Miss Pringle after school, about the third child of shame, which is to be christened on Sunday.

'Mr Partridge's coming over to Springbourne. I told him when he brought the hymn list this morning, I thought of Lance-a-lot Drick, for the baby's name.'

'Drick?'

'Like Bogarde. Drick Bogarde. But Vicar said Not-Too-Fanciful, but I think it's too much of a mouthful. So I said make it Hugh and Call-it-a-Day.'

Much shaken I said Hugh was a good name, and gave her five shillings for the baby. I have no doubt that it will buy a purple lipstick for its mother.

It will be a relief to see Mrs Pringle's glum countenance back on Monday.

I drove to Caxley after school, and met Mrs Martin, our doctor's wife, coming out of Boots', and enquired after his health.

'He's been run off his feet, poor dear, and now he's gone down with this horrible 'flu himself.'

I said I was sorry and was he a good patient?

'A fiend incarnate!' his wife assured me solemnly. 'But he must be in a really bad way.' She looked furtively about her, came very close to me, and dropped her voice to a conspiratorial whisper. 'He's been driven to taking his own cough mixture! That'll show you how bad he's been! He's just sent me in for a bottle from Boots' that doesn't taste quite so evil!'

On Monday we were all back at our posts. Mrs Annett arrived swathed in rugs and was supported to her room by her attentive husband. She assured me, when he had departed, that she was as fit as a fiddle.

Mrs Pringle's outraged expression when she saw the state of her beloved stoves was a real tonic.

'That Minnie Pringle!' she breathed menacingly. 'Black-lead and elbow-grease don't mean nothing to her!'

The weather had turned delightfully warm and spring-like. The lilac buds in my garden are as fat as green peas, and crocuses, daffodils and tulips are pushing through. Even the grass is beginning to smell hopeful again, as one walks on it.

Mrs Annett and I celebrated this return of joy by taking the whole school out for a nature walk in the woods, at the foot of the downs. They belong to Mr Roberts, the farmer, who lives next door to the school and is one of its most energetic managers, and he lets us go there whenever we please. This is a great privilege, for, like most country schools, Fairacre has a small playground with a stony, uneven surface, which means that any really riotous games in this confined space lead to skinned knees and hands. We consider ourselves very lucky to be able to use Mr Roberts's woods, and his meadow too, and so enjoy a wider world now and again.

The frogspawn was rising in the pond near the 'Beetle and Wedge.' The boys were anxious to take off their shoes and socks and wade in to fetch some for the classroom; but knowing the collection of tins, pieces of bedstead and other household junk which litters the bottom, I forbade this project.

The woods were awe-inspiringly quiet. Even the children hushed their sing-song chatter as they scuffled along in the beech leaves. Signs of spring were everywhere. The honeysuckle is already in small leaf, the primrose plants are sturdy rosettes, and we saw several birds with dry grass or feathers in beak, and a speculative glint in the eye.

At the edge of the wood is a small field, which is one of my secret joys. It always looks lovely. At this time of year it has a soft dewy greyness, which the line of pewter-coloured willow trees, at its boundary, enhances. Today a wood-pigeon, as soft and opal as a London twilight, winged across, and made the picture unforgettable. I once saw this field at eight o'clock on a fine May morning, when it was gilded with buttercups. A light breeze shivered the young willow leaves, and everything vernal that Geoffrey Chaucer and Will Shakespeare ever wrote was caught alive here.

We let the children run, while we sat on a dry log and rested. Mrs Annett, with her gaze fixed bemusedly on a cluster of heart-shaped violet leaves between her brogues, told me, in a dreamy tone in keeping with this enchanted place, that she was to have a child in August.

I said how very pleased I was, and we continued to sit, propped together, on the dry log in comfortable silence, savouring the niceness of this most satisfying affair.

Joseph Coggs' discovery of a very dead grey squirrel and his request for 'a lend of my penknife' to cut off the poor creature's tail in order to claim a shilling, brought this idyll to a close. We returned in great good spirits to Fairacre School.

Although we had had quite a long walk I was amazed to see how fresh and lively the very young children were on our outing.

The longer I teach, the more I am convinced that it is wrong for children in their first year at school to have to attend school for the whole day.

Perhaps, before long, morning school only for the five-, and even six-year-olds, will be the order of the day, and I am sure it would be welcomed by mothers, teachers and children. Most children have a big adjustment to make when they start school. The numbers alone are tiring, and new surroundings, new voices and a new, and perhaps more rigid, discipline all make for strain.

Before he went to school, the child probably had a rest before or after lunch, when, even if he did not sleep, he had a quiet period, on his own, with his feet up. After his rest, during the afternoon, he had his walk, when all the pleasures and richness of the outdoor world impinged on his young mind.

In a small country school it is difficult to provide a rest-time after school dinner for these really small people. It is not surprising that they frequently nod off to sleep in the afternoon, and I for one am only too pleased to let them. A refreshing nap will do them far more good than making a batch of plasticine crumpets – enthralling though that may be with the aid of a really sharp matchstick – and I am only sorry that I can't make them more comfortable, when I see a tousled head resting on two fat arms on the unsympathetic hard wood of an ancient school desk.

A new chant to the Psalms had us all bogged down, at church today, and I enjoyed watching the different methods of attack. My neighbour in the pew, Mr Lamb from the Post Office, preserved an affronted silence. Mrs Willet gobbled up three-quarters of each phrase on one uniform and neutral note, and then dragged out the last quarter in a nasal whine, somewhere near the printed notes. Mrs Pringle mooed slowly and heavily, a few beats behind the rest, but with an awful ponderous emphasis in the wrong places; while the vicar, with a sublime disregard for the organist's accompaniment, sang an entirely different chant altogether, and did it very well.

I drove to Caxley to have tea with Amy and James. She talked quite wistfully of her few days' teaching, and, I believe, would jump at the chance of coming again some time. She was perturbed about a rash which has come out on her face. I must confess that I could only see it when my eyes were two inches from her cheek. I suggested that the Caxley water which is villainously hard, might be responsible, and why didn't she use rainwater for a few days?

'Water?' screamed Amy. (If I had said vitriol, she couldn't have sounded more horrified.) Did I realize that she hadn't touched her face with *water* for over five years? Only the very blandest and most expensive complexion milk was dabbed on – with an upward movement – thrice daily, with an occasional application of an astringent lotion which was prepared in Bond Street to her own prescription. Her beauty specialist had forbidden – positively forbidden – the use of water on such a very sensitive skin.

I could only feel that layers of complexion milk over the years had probably formed a light cheese over Amy's face, which accounted for the rash; but as I was eating her delicious sponge-cake at that moment, was obliged, in common courtesy, to keep these thoughts to myself.

I am now the somewhat bewildered possessor of an engaging kitten. It all began with Jimmy Waites asking if he could go home during the dinner hour to fetch two kittens.

'So as Linda can choose which one she likes,' he said. Mrs Moffat had asked if Linda might keep it at school during the afternoon, and return home, with the pet of her choice, in time for tea.

This all seemed very agreeable, and the infants were delighted to hear that they would be entertaining two kittens for the afternoon session, and spent most of the morning preparing the doll's cradle for these much more exciting occupants. The doll, a cherished Edwardian beauty, from the vicarage nursery, was propped up on the cupboard, and surveyed her wanton young masters and mistresses with a glassy stare.

Mrs Annett had the greatest difficulty in persuading the children to drink their morning milk, but finally discovered that they were all hoarding it for the kittens' dissipation later. At length a bottle was put up on the cupboard, beside the slighted beauty, for the guests, and the milk bottles emptied rapidly.

Excitement ran high when Jimmy Waites entered with his basket. Mrs Waites had prudently tied a blue-checked duster over the top, and when this was removed two pretty kittens peered out from a nest of straw.

Linda Moffat, as pretty as a kitten herself, took the business of choosing her pet very seriously, and was given much unsolicited advice from her companions.

'Don't you take that black and white 'un, Lin. See his paws? Allus be filthy, them white paws.'

'I reckons he looks the best.'

'He do seem to stand up stronger, don't he? More push, like.'

'That other's the prettiest,' and so on.

The infants, who were in my room, milling round with their elders, while this great decision was being made, became querulous, for they were dying to put both to bed in the waiting cradle.

'Buck up, Linda.'

'They's both nice, Linda. Don't matter which one!'

Linda's troubled eyes met mine.

'I wish I could have them both. The other's got to be drowned.'

There was a shocked silence. I looked at Jimmy Waites.

'That's right, miss,' he said, his underlip quivering.

'My dad drowns them,' volunteered Joseph Coggs, with some pride. 'He does all the kittens down our end of the village.' He was stroking a fluffy head with a black stubby finger. He looked up into my face. What he saw there must have called forth his sympathy.

'He uses *warm* water,' he assured me earnestly.

'Can't you find a home for the other one, Jimmy?' I asked turning aside hastily from all the disturbing implications of Joseph's kindly remark.

'Mrs Bates up by the Post Office was going to have it, but she've got a puppy now, that Bill Bates give her for her birthday. No one else don't want it.'

'Who thinks they could have it?' I canvassed. The whole of Fairacre School instantly raised eager hands.

'Well,' I temporized, 'you'll have to ask your mothers, of course. Meanwhile, Jimmy, I'll keep the other one, and if someone wants it I will hand it over.'

At this happy outcome the noise was terrific. The infants showed their joy by jumping heavily, fists doubled into their stomachs, on to the resounding floor-boards. The older ones cheered and banged their desk lids, and we were all but deafened. Mr Willet, entering at this moment said: 'Mafeking relieved?' and was so taken with his own shaft of wit that he broke into gusty laughter, and I began to wonder if order would ever be restored.

The kittens, with remarkable composure, sat in the straw and washed their paws elegantly, despising disorder – and death itself – with the same fastidious good breeding that the French aristocrats showed in the shadow of the guillotine.

'Sweets for quiet children!' I roared above the tumult. It worked, as always, like a charm. The infants fled into their own room – being careful to leave the dividing door open so that I could see their exemplary demeanour – my own children melted into their desks, crossed their arms high up on their chests, put their sturdy country boots decorously side by side, and glared ahead at 'The Angelus' behind my desk, with unblinking gaze. Only when the sweet tin was in Patrick's grasp, and the fruit drops were being handed round, did they relax and breathe again.

There are some foolish and narrow-minded theorists who would condemn the use of a sweet tin in schools, dismissing this valuable and pleasant adjunct to discipline with such harsh words as 'bribery' and 'pandering to animal greed.' I stoutly defend the sweet tin. If the good Lord has seen fit to provide sweets and children's tastes to match them, then let us take advantage of the tools that lie at hand.

Linda carried the basket to the other room and introduced the kittens to their new bed.

'I think I'll have the tabby one,' she said, as she returned and closed the dividing door behind her. She brushed a straw from her immaculate grey flannel pinafore frock and resumed her place. The important business of the afternoon now over, we addressed ourselves to 'Poetry,' at the silent, but stern, behest of the time-table on one side and the school clock on the other.

I met Dr Martin as I was going to the grocer's after school. He said that he had quite recovered from his illness. I wondered if his own, or Boots', cough mixture was responsible for his return to health, but did not say this aloud.

He was just off, he said, to pay six calls on people he supposed he would find in better health than he was himself. He had never known his surgery so besieged. After he had rattled off, in his disreputable old car, I went on my errand, pondering, not for the first time, on the remarkable self-flattery of most doctors. Do they honestly think – always excepting the five per cent of humanity that is incorrigibly neurotic – that some people go to see them for pleasure? Do they seriously imagine that sensible men and women subject themselves to the miseries of doctors' waiting-rooms, of cold medical implements, and of colder medical fingers, with the further possibility of such horrors as injections and enemas to come, for the fun of the thing – or, as one would be led to believe from comments dropped by some doctors, for the express purpose of adding to the burden that already breaks the doctor's back? When one hears such a cheerful and sturdy medical man as our beloved Dr Martin talking in this fashion, it poses a number of unanswerable questions.

On Saturday, the village was shocked to hear of the death of young Peter Lamb. He was killed in a motor-cycle accident on the way home from a football match in Caxley in the afternoon. He was seventeen, and the only child of the Lambs, who keep the Post Office. The motor-cycle was their present to him on his last birthday. He spent hours polishing the gleaming monster on the lawn at the side of their house. I taught him for only a year, as he went on to Mr Annett at Beech Green at eleven, but I remember him as a very happy boy.

Mr Willet told me this ghastly news after morning service. He was pacing among the graves on his melancholy sexton's business of choosing a site for the grave he must dig.

'Terrible business,' he said, blowing out his ragged moustache with a sigh. 'The old slip away, and there's some left to grieve, but often their friends that would have taken it hardest have gone before. But a young fellow like this – well, miss, 'tis not just his own that loses him, 'tis every mortal in the village.'

('Send not to know for whom the bell tolls,' whispered a voice in my head, as Mr Willet echoed John Donne across the centuries.)

'Take the cricket team. Long stop he was. We've got no one like him to fill that place. I suppose, when it comes to it, John Pringle will have to move over from deep field and that lily-livered young Bryant that flinches at mid-on will have what he's always wanted and be put out in the field.' Mr Willet stepped round a tomb-stone. 'Take the bell-ringers. More shifting round to train up a new chap for Peter's place. Hard work for us all, you'll see. Ah! He'll be missed sadly!' ('It tolls for thee!')

Nowhere do John Donne's words, 'No man is an island' more poignantly apply than in a small community like a village. As a pebble in a pond spreads its ripples far about, so has this blow affected us all.

'Peter used to mend my bike for me,' nine-year-old Eric said, emerging from the vestry, where he had been blowing the organ.

'He always took my wireless batteries into Caxley to be re-charged,' said old Mrs Bates, among the knot of villagers at the church gate.

'He was going out steady with that girl at Beech Green. She'll take it hard, I don't doubt,' said another.

As the vicar said later, from the pulpit: 'We are indeed members one of another.'

But there was more to all this sober mourning than grief for one young man. The village was robbed, and we were all – every soul in Fairacre – the poorer for it.

Miss Clare came over to tea and spent the evening. The little cat, still with me – and, I imagine for good now – rolled ecstat-ically on the hearth-rug in the warmth of the fire. Miss Clare was knitting a green pullover and the ball of wool had to be rescued every now and again.

We had talked, naturally, of poor Peter Lamb and Miss Clare surprised me by saying that the pullover had been intended for him.

'He always dug over my vegetable patch every spring and autumn, and I could never get him to take any money. Sometimes he'd take cigarettes, but this time I thought I'd get on with the pullover for next winter.'

'What will you do with it now?' I asked.

She looked across at me with her wise calm gaze.

'I shall finish it,' she said composedly. 'A lot of work has gone into it, and I shall finish it as well as I can and give it to the cricket club.' She smoothed it lovingly. 'It will make a nice prize for their Whist Drive next winter when they raise money for the club.'

This eminently sensible and realistic approach I could not help but admire. So, surely, should all life's buffets be met – with dignity and good sense, but how many of us have Miss Clare's courage?

'I can't think what to call this kitten,' I said, to lighten our solemnity a little. 'What do you suggest?'

Miss Clare addressed herself to this problem with as much thought as she had to the right disposal of Peter's pullover.

'I have always called mine one after the other, plain "Puss",' she admitted, frowning with concentration, 'but you could think of something more interesting.'

I went on to enlarge on the difficulties of naming a cat. I abhorred the idea of anything – as dear Eric Blore (in 'Top Hat,' I think) said with a divine exhalation of breath – 'too *whumsical*.' None of your 'La Belle Fifinella' or even 'Miss Bertha Briggs' for my respectable Fairacre cat!

'And because he's black and white I'm not sinking to such obvious nonsense as "Whisky" or "Magpie",' I went on, now well launched. "Nor do I like Tom, Dick, Harry, Jane, Peggy, Betty, or anything, for that matter, which sounds as though I'm talking about a lodger, to people who don't know my circumstances.'

'It certainly is difficult,' Miss Clare agreed, and let her knitting needles fall into her lap.

We lapsed into silent thought. By the firelight I could see that Miss Clare was deep in meditation. Her face was so wistful that I imagined that her mind had strayed back to the all-pervading sadness of young Peter's death. Perhaps she too, I thought, is feeling the penetrating truth that Donne summed up for us.

She raised meditative eyes and looked earnestly at me.

'Come to think of it,' she said slowly, 'I did have *one* cat called Tom.'

Oh lovely, lovely life that can toss us from horror to hilarity, without giving us time to take breath! No matter how dark it may be, yet, unfailingly, 'Cheerfulness breaks in.'

MARCH

March has come in like a lion, with a vengeance, this year. The wind has whipped round to the east again, and hailstorms have been frequent and heavy. A number of the children were caught in one on the way to school and Joseph Coggs and his two small sisters were in tears with the painful rapping they had taken. Their clothes were quite inadequate – not a thick coat between them, and the two little girls in skimpy cotton frocks and layers of dirty jumpers and cardigans on top. Of course their legs are mauve with cold and they look chilled to the marrow.

It always surprises me to see how many of the mothers fail to clothe children consistently. The little things come to school in the winter with, perhaps, a snug woollen bonnet and scarf, a thick coat, and then there comes a long expanse of cold mottled legs, terminating, more often than not, in minute cotton socks. Mrs Moffat makes Linda neat tailored leggings, and of course a few of the children go into sensible corduroy dungarees for winter wear, but the common feeling seems to be that if they are muffled up above the waist, their legs can take care of themselves. The number of messages I get in the cold months explaining absences due to 'stummer-cake' or 'a chill inside' does not surprise me.

The battle of the wellingtons continues to rage through this bad spell. I will not allow the children to wear them all day in school and insist that a pair of slippers, or failing that, a thick pair of old socks, are brought to school to wear indoors.

'But my dad wears his all the time,' they protest. 'My mum says what's good enough for my dad's good enough for me!' One can hardly retort that the anti-social condition of dad's feet is only one of the reasons for insisting on changing one's rubber boots, but gradually, by dint of hygiene lessons and fulsome praise for those good children who do bring slippers as requested, we are slowly getting an improvement in this direction.

Mrs Annett has given in her notice, which means that she leaves Fairacre School at the end of April. We shall all miss her sorely. The vicar has already started drafting an advertisement for insertion in *The Teacher's World*, and is almost in despair about finding suitable lodgings for the new teacher in the village.

'I shouldn't cross that bridge yet,' I told him. 'We may not get any applicants for the post.'

'Oh my dear Miss Read! Please, please!' protested the poor man, beating his leopard-skin gloves together and creating a light shower of moth-eaten fur in the classroom. 'I cannot bear to think what the future holds for Fairacre School. Whatever happens it *must* not close! It shall not close!' Here the vicar looked and sounded as militant as Uncle Toby in Tristram Shandy when he too faced the extinction of a body much-beloved. 'But, sometimes, I wonder – poor Springbourne, you know. I hate to pass that little empty school, with its dreadful blank windows. And dear Miss Davis, they tell me, is finding that large school in Caxley much too much for her, and is struggling with nearly fifty six-year-olds!'

I said how sorry I was for her. She is an elderly gentlewoman, who smoothed the path of her little flock at Springbourne for many years. The bustle of Caxley, as well as a tiresome bus journey must exhaust her considerably.

'And I have heard,' added Mr Partridge, with horror darkening his benevolent countenance, 'that some of those children – young as they are – are Openly Defiant!'

He looked round at our own meek lambs who were busy colouring border patterns in a somnolent way, and his expression softened. I hoped that he would not notice the pronounced bulge in Ernest's cheek, which, I guessed, harboured a disgusting lump of bubble-gum. His eye travelled lovingly over the class, and he sighed happily.

'How fortunate we are here!' he said, 'they are dear, good children, all of them!' And, heavy with bubble-gum guilt, as some of them obviously were, I could not help but agree with him.

It would indeed be a tragedy if Fairacre School were to close, but I do not think it will happen here, as we maintain a steady number of about forty, which makes a good workable two-teacher school, with Mrs Annett taking the infants, and the juniors being taught by me, until the age of eleven. But alas! Springbourne's fate has been shared by several others in the neighbourhood, and more are scheduled to close within the next few years.

This closing of small village schools is a controversial and debatable problem. There is no doubt that some of the really small schools of, say, eighteen, or fewer, children on roll, under the sole charge of the head teacher, should be closed for several very good reasons. The biggest difficulty in these one-teacher schools is the age-range from babes of five years old to children ready for secondary education at the age of eleven. Conscientious teachers who have tackled this type of school single-handed, year after year, realize how impossible it is to do justice to every child. A newly admitted baby of five, homesick and mother-sick, can demand vociferously, urgent and immediate attention, for perhaps a week or more before he really settles in to his new environment. It is disconcerting, to say the least of it, to the rest of his schoolmates, some of whom may have the added anxiety of the eleven-plus examination hovering over them.

It is well-nigh impossible too, to organize team games, which junior children so much enjoy, and which will play so great a part in their later school life. Stories, poems and songs, broadcast programmes, films and classroom pictures must be chosen with the interests of five as well as eleven-year-old children in mind; but perhaps greater than all these teaching problems is the human one. It can be a very lonely life for a teacher, and the care of even such a tiny band of children can be a responsibility, which in some cases becomes too heavy to be borne. It is small wonder that these lonely women, devoted and conscientious, are often the prey of nervous disorders such as rheumatic pains, headaches and neuralgia. Maybe the cross-draughts that play so merrily between Gothic doors and ecclesiastical windows have something to do with it, but the mental strain is always there, and it takes a particularly robust and cheerful woman to cope successfully, and alone, for years on end, with these fascinating but exacting little schools, that are so much a part of our English village life.

The upkeep of some of these tiny places is, of course, out of all proportion to the number of children taught, which accounts for the transfer of pupils to one nearby, but it seems to me equally improvident to overcrowd one school by bringing busloads of children from others, and this may well happen.

Probably the ideal rural school is the three-teacher one, with a teacher for the infants, one for the younger juniors of seven to nine, and the head teacher taking the rest up to the age of eleven. (Though why the head teacher should not take the infants, I don't know. The longer I teach, the more positive I am that it is the first three years of the child's school life that really matter most). But village populations are not made to order, and local education authorities are not to be envied as they deal with children, parents, managers, rate-payers, the church and the Ministry of Education.

However, at a time like this, when harassed and nerve-wracked individuals rush to the countryside at every opportunity, there to revive their flagging energies and to find that 'balm of hurt minds,' fresh air and country sounds and scents – it seems decidedly odd to do away with village schools which are the very essence of country education. What a child may learn on his daily walk to school along a country lane will never be forgotten;

and to know intimately the changes that come to plants and trees, to birds and insects, as the full cycle of the four seasons turns, is a source of joy and wonder to the child who is the father of the man.

I have seldom had a more exasperating day. I began by smashing a Wedgwood coffee-pot, as I tried to hurry with the washing-up, which I had left in the most slatternly way from last night, before going over to the school.

At play-time Patrick fell heavily, took the skin from both knees, and worse still, a corner off a front tooth – his second, naturally. I was washing his knees in the school-house when the telephone rang, and an underling at the Caxley Education Office peremptorily demanded the return of a form 'with no delay.' This asinine document was devoted to the number, size, material, age, etc., of the various types of desk in Fairacre School, and as we have a motley collection it took me the rest of the morning, crawling round, ruler in hand, to measure the wretched things.

Mrs Crossley, 'the dinner lady' left two canisters of swedes, which the children abominate, and no gravy. I wonder what Beech Green School thought of two lots of gravy and no swedes! Mrs Pringle, rather more disgruntled than usual, reminded me so often of the combustible nature of her leg – 'proper flared up last night, no better today' that I would have welcomed her resignation, and said so. She retaliated by crashing the cutlery about in a deafening manner, all through my geography lesson.

I was thankful to get back to the peace of the school-house at tea-time, and decided to make some grape-fruit marmalade. Just as I was engrossed in a tricky bit of mental arithmetic about pounds of sugar and the weight of three grape-fruit, and waiting for my tea-kettle to boil, a knock came at the front door. A strange man stood on the doorstep holding a sheaf of tracts. I could hear the kettle's lid rattling in the kitchen, and knew, from bitter experience, that the floor would be swamped.

The strange man asked me, in a sepulchral tone, if I had found the Lord, thrusting a tract into my hand at the same time.

'Thank you, thank you! Yes indeed!' I answered, backing inside and shutting the door firmly. I returned to my swamped kitchen and began to mop up the floor in a very bad temper.

Really, Fairacre people must have a name for utter godlessness, judging by the number of earnest souls who present themselves at our doorsteps! Nothing puts me into a more unchristian state of mind than these unsolicited visitors, and yet I haven't the heart to tell them not to come again.

While I was regaining my composure over the tea-tray I noticed with horror that the tract was priced at sixpence. I could only hope that my cavalier and grasping behaviour would discourage further attentions; but, on the other hand, would not have been surprised to hear the stranger returning to demand his payment.

I was very glad indeed to climb into the sanctuary of my bed, and shelve life for nine hours.

The postponed tea-party at the Vicarage has taken place and I have at last met John Parr's tenant, about whom I have heard so much.

His name is Henry Mawne – ' "H. A. Mawne",' the vicar enlarged, and smiled hopefully at me. Seeing that I was still unenlightened, he added, 'Of the *Caxley Chronicle*,' and I remembered then that the Nature Notes have appeared recently over this name. I told Mr Mawne that I cut his notes out and put them up in the classroom for the children to read, and he was obviously delighted.

He is tall and very thin, and seems a pleasant, unassuming man. Since his retirement he has spent most of his time fishing and bird-watching, and is collecting material for a book about downland birds. He seems very well able to look after himself, and will no doubt continue to do so, despite village gossip to the contrary.

'What I particularly like about Fairacre people,' he said to the vicar, 'is their acceptance of a newcomer without a lot of unnecessary comment. I've found everyone so friendly, but not a bit inquisitive.'

I could not help feeling that Mr Mawne's ear must have been singularly far from Fairacre's bush telegraph, which has fairly hummed with such pertinent questions as:

Is Mr M. a widower? If so, what did his wife die of? And when? Is he a bachelor? How old is he? Who will he marry? And when? How much would his pension be from teaching? Would he have an old-age pension as well? How long has he known Mr Parr? What does he do with those field-glasses? Why is he always 'skulking about up the downs'? And much more, to the same effect.

He was very interested in the village school, and asked if he might call in to see the children. I said that we should love to see him, and if he would like to give us a nature talk some time, we should look forward to it immensely. It is good for our Fairacre children to hear someone else speaking in their classroom – heaven knows they have little enough variety. It is equally good for me to sit back and see a lesson taken by an expert in his subject.

At six o'clock Mrs Partridge took me upstairs to her bedroom for my coat. There is a wonderful view from the windows there, of the gentle swell of the downs beyond and the wooded hollow where Fairacre shelters. The spire of St Patrick's dominates the foreground, with the stubby little bell-tower of my school thrusting bravely up beside it.

On the bedside table lay a red leather-bound copy of the Bible and a photograph of an elderly man, with a mop of white hair, who smiled vaguely from his silver frame.

'Gerald's father,' said Mrs Partridge following my gaze, 'Gerald always says "He was a saint – if only I could do half as well!" '

The thought of our good vicar, whose life is as blameless as is humanly possible, sorrowing for his short-comings, made me wonder in what adverse light my own behaviour is thrown. I looked back, in that one swift moment, on innumerable child-slappings, hard words, black thoughts and a thousand back-slidings, and went downstairs in a sober mood.

Mr Mawne was examining a light horse-whip on the hall wall.

'My father used one like that on us on special occasions,' he said cheerfully.

'Really?' answered the vicar. 'Now, my father always shut us up in a dark cupboard under the stairs—'

I decided that values are strictly relative, and felt much more hopeful of my own shaky claims to divine mercy.

I decided to let the children write a poem about the spring. They have learnt Robert Bridges' 'Spring Goeth All in White' and

Thomas Nashe's 'Spring, the Sweet Spring' recently, and I thought it would be interesting to see what sort of attempts these most unbookish children would make. Their faces, when I suggested this mental exercise, were studies in stupefaction.

'What – rhyming and that?' asked Eric, appalled.

'Yes, rhyming,' I answered ruthlessly. There was a shocked silence. Linda Moffat was the first to find her breath.

'How many verses, Miss Read?'

'As many as you can think of.'

Patrick then piped up.

'Do us have to make it go thumpety-thumpety like that "Half a league, half a league" bit you read us?'

I said that rhythm would be expected, and they delved into their desks for their pens and English exercise books, with the doomed look of those that face the firing squad.

For half an hour the room was quiet, broken only by the solemn tick of the ancient wall-clock, and the sighs and groans of spirits in poetic travail. After the first few minutes, I had softened so far as to suggest that they could begin with:

In the spring

and go on from there. As drowning men clutch at straws, so did these Fairacre children clutch at these three words which could be copied from the blackboard.

After thirty minutes I collected their efforts and sent them tottering out to play. Never had their young minds been so sternly exercised, and the results were highly entertaining.

For sheer brazen effrontery and gross idleness, I think Ernest's takes the prize. He had shamelessly lifted, intact, a verse from one of the tombstones in the neighbouring churchyard. In his painstaking copperplate he had written:

> *In the spring*
> *She drooped and died.*
> *Now she sleeps*
> *By Jesu's side*

There is not one spelling mistake. Nor should there be,

considering that we pass and repass this inscription a dozen times a day.

Linda Moffat had very cunningly covered the maximum of paper with the minimum of effort. Her poem ran:

> *In the spring*
> *The swallows wing*
> *In the spring*
>
> *In the spring*
> *The flowers bring* (What? I wonder)
> *In the spring*
>
> *In the spring*
> *We all do sing*
> *In the spring*

Perhaps the most engaging poem was Eric's. He is a 'growler,' unable to sing in tune and incapable of keeping in step in dancing and other rhythmic work. Written in an appalling hand, with, apparently, a crossed nib dipped in black honey, his poem said:

> *In the spring*
> *I has my birthday and usually a hice*
> *cake which my gran makes. It is on March 20th*

I rather liked the gentle reminder about a fortnight before the great day, and felt inclined to give him a couple of extra writing lessons as a present.

But for brevity and charm, for a little snatch that reminds one of William Barnes's simplicity and use of dialect, I think the attempt of young bandaged-kneed Patrick takes the prize. His poem read thus:

> *In the spring*
> *It comes on worm* (sic!)
> *Us likes the spring*
> *Us has no storm*

Poor dears, how hard I made them work! Truly the mastering of one's own language is a major operation!

The kitten is still with me, and I hope that I shall never have to part with him. He answers to the deplorably plebeian name of 'Tibby,' while I still rack my brains daily for some other more inspired cognomen.

Now that the weather is warmer he plays outside and yesterday afternoon he ventured across the playground and found his way into the classroom, much to the children's delight. He settled himself in a patch of sunlight on the needlework cupboard, and I foresee many more such excursions to school, as he is a most companionable animal.

In any case, I see no reason why a good-tempered, steady-going cat should not be included in a country classroom. It adds a pleasantly domestic touch to our working conditions.

Amy came to tea and brought her sister, who is staying with her, as well. She is one of those people – all too common, alas! – who bore one to death with accounts of their important acquaintances. Never was a conversation so sprinkled with lords, ladies, admirals, generals, and what not, until I thought I should be driven to devising a game about them all, in order to keep my sanity. It could be done with points, I told myself, my glazed eyes on my visitor and a fixed smile on my lips. Two points, say, for peers of the realm and their ladies, and for top-ranking people in the services. One point for friends mentioned, who were working in:

a. The Foreign Office
b. Embassies
c. B.B.C. and
d. 'Little' shops in Bond Street;

and none, I decided, as I dropped sugar into my guest's cup, for nephews who had just written:

a. an enchanting collection of obscure verse – published privately,

b. a powerful novel or
c. a script for Midland Region.

However, she made a great fuss of dear Tibby, and didn't flinch when he ran cruel claws into her beautiful sheer nylons, so that I forgave her for her harmless delusions of grandeur, and made her a present of a pot of my grapefruit marmalade when she left. How far this generosity was prompted by my guilty conscience I should not like to say.

It has been a real spring day. The wind has turned due west and is as warm and soft as can be. I have a few crocuses out among the clumps of snowdrops, and there are fat buds on the japonica by the wall, which is all most heartening.

Mrs Pringle, to whom I made a blithe comment about the fine weather, did her best to turn the world sour for me.

'See the moon last night? Lying on its back?'

I said that I had. I had noticed it from my landing-window as I went to bed – an upturned silver slice, supporting the shadowy completion of its circle.

'Know what that means?' enquired Mrs Pringle, arms akimbo, and her voice heavy with foreboding.

Mr Willet, who was screwing up the catch on the wood-shed door, and had been listening to our conversation, now shouted across: 'Well, you tell us then. Seems you want to!'

'The moon on its back,' said Mrs Pringle, with much emphasis, 'is a sure sign of rain. "Moon on her back, with water in her lap." Ever heard of that? You see – we'll have a tempest before night – a proper downpour!'

She looked across to my garden where two pairs of stockings and two tea-towels danced in the breeze.

'You've chose the wrong day for washing,' she added, and returned into the lobby to scour the sink.

Mr Willet puffed out his moustache with disgust.

'Never heard such nonsense,' he said to me, in a carrying whisper, 'real old wives' tale that, about water in its lap. The ignorance! The stuff some of these folk believes, in the twentieth century! Lives in the dark ages some of 'em.'

He screwed another turn or two, grunting with effort. At

length he ceased, and wiped his brow with the back of his huge hand. He still looked disgruntled.

'"Moon on her back. Water in her lap,"' he quoted disgustedly. 'A downpour! Lot of nonsense! Why, any fool knows it means a high wind!'

Mrs Partridge called after tea to tell me about great goings-on in the W.I. world. Although I am a member of the Fairacre W.I., I can rarely attend the meetings, as they are held in the afternoon; but Mrs Partridge, who is President, keeps me *au fait* with the news.

Evidently the county as a whole is to stage a pageant. Each Institute, or group of Institutes, will have an historical scene to act, and the whole will tell the story of the people who have lived in this county, through the ages.

'When do we start?' I asked.

'As soon as we've had another meeting,' answered Mrs Partridge.

'No, I mean, at what stage of history do we begin? The Norman Conquest, or the Ice Age, or what?'

'For the life of me,' said Mrs Partridge, much perplexed, 'I don't know, but the County Office will send further particulars, I don't doubt.'

Neither did I, having seen some of the lengthy documents that flutter from that quarter every month.

'Do we choose which scene we like?' I asked. I was mentally casting Mrs Pringle as the seventeenth-century witch who was dumped in the horse-pond somewhere near Beech Green. My tone, I noted with regret, was eager.

'Now I come to think of it,' said Mrs Partridge, closing her eyes the better to 'consecrate,' 'the Drama Committee have drafted out so many scenes, about a dozen, I fancy, and the groups will draw for them. So much fairer, of course. After all, most women will prefer becoming costumes, and would plump for Stuart times with all those delicious silks and laces.'

'I rather fancy the Plantagenets,' I replied, wondering if Mrs Moffat could run me up a wimple. Really the whole project had endless possibilities for fun.

'Ah! now that *is* a good idea,' agreed Mrs Partridge. 'I've always had a feeling that I could wear long plaits with pearls entwined.'

We went off into a quiet reverie about wimples and plaits, until Tibby (name still evades me) brought us to earth by jumping through the window, knocking over a jar of catkins *en route*.

'Well, dear,' said Mrs Partridge, rising to her feet, and becoming her usual bustling self, 'that's how it is. The children, of course, will take part. It is to be held on a Saturday, in the grounds of Branscombe Castle; and I'll call an evening meeting for one day next week. We shall know then which scene we're to do and can arrange rehearsals and so on.'

'When is it to be?' I asked.

Mrs Partridge spoke patiently, as to a tiresome child. 'I've told you, dear. One evening next week.'

I began to feel that Fairacre's vicar's wife and its school-teacher might easily go on the halls in the near future as a pair of cross-talk comedians, Partridge and Read.

'No, no! The pageant. When does it come off at Branscombe Castle?'

'Oh, I'm sorry. In August, I understand.'

'Supposing it rains?'

'My dear,' said Mrs Partridge, with the utmost firmness, 'it will not rain! You should know by now, dear, that if one starts to take rain into consideration in village life – well – there just wouldn't be any village life!'

When she had gone I pondered over this direction of village activities which Mrs Partridge does so well. It is interesting to be living in this transition period between local, and in Fairacre's case enlightened, squirearchy, and whatever communal form may evolve in a village which is, perforce, part of a welfare state.

The older people, like Miss Clare and Mrs Pringle, shake their heads sadly over the departure of 'the good old days,' when the gentry did so much for the village, sparing neither advice nor practical and financial help. They looked to the families in the three or four large houses, not only for employment, but for guidance in matters spiritual and temporal; and now that death or the cold hand of poverty has removed this help, the older generation seems rudderless, and at times resentful, for the stability has gone from their lives.

'Why, when my father was working as gardener, up at the Hall,' said Mrs Pringle, one day, 'he broke a leg, falling out of the apple tree in the kitchen garden. And for all the weeks he lay up in our front room, regular as clockwork there came a basket of groceries sent down from the Hall kitchen. That's what I call being looked after.'

In vain was it to point out that an all-embracing state insurance has superseded this earlier happy relationship.

'All forms and stamps,' snorted Mrs Pringle, unimpressed, 'and some jumped-up jack-in-office in Caxley telling you how to get back what's been taken from you! Give me the old days!' It is the personal touch that these older people miss so sorely, the discussion of problems over a fireside, the confession, perhaps, of follies come home to roost, and the comfort of friendly advice and practical guidance. To have to board a bus, and sit, perplexed, as it rattles six miles into Caxley, to find an answer to one's personal problems at an office or a bureau or a clinic, comes hard to these people; and to be passed from the supercilious young lady in the outer office, from hand to hand, until the right person is encountered, means that the older countryman, more often than not, arrives even more tongue-tied than usual. How much simpler it all was, he will think dazedly, as he stares at the ledgers and typewriters and the man who waits with sheaves of forms in front of him, when he walked round to the kitchen door at the Hall with his troubles, confident that he'd be home again within half an hour, with his course set plain before him.

As Miss Clare put it: 'I know it's a great comfort, dear, to feel that one will never starve, and that sickness and madness and death itself are looked after. For an old woman in my position, the welfare state is a blessing. This national health scheme, for instance, has taken a great load off my mind. But I miss the warmth of sympathy – foolish perhaps, but there it is. It did both of us good – the one who told his trouble, and the one who tried to help – for, I suppose, we were both united in overcoming a problem and in sympathy with each other.'

I suggested that the present system might eventually be better. After all, advice from the Hall might be bad as well as good, depending on the mentality and disposition of the owner at any given time.

'Yes,' agreed Miss Clare, 'in the long run, I think each man will think out his own problems; but it is going to take him a very long time to realize that the machinery for coping with those personal problems is set up by his own hands. We in a village, my dear, can understand a small-community government – it's not much more than a family affair and we all appreciate our relationship. But when it comes to a nation – with ministries and councils and departments taking the place of the parish clerk and parish priest and squire – well, naturally, we're a little out of our depth, just at the moment!'

I had a wasted morning in Caxley trying to buy a light-weight coat for the summer.

As I was roaming round the coat department at Williams's, which styles itself 'Caxley's leading store,' followed by an assistant staggering under an armful of coats already rejected by me, I bumped into Amy.

'You look a wreck!' she said truthfully but unkindly.

'I *am* a wreck!' I replied simply, and went on to tell her of my hopeless quest.

'My dear, we are of the race of Lost Women,' said Amy dramatically. The wilting assistant stopped to listen to any more interesting disclosures. 'Clothes there are – beautiful clothes, magnificent clothes, inspired clothes – for those with thirty-six- or even thirty-eight-inch hips! For the forty-four inches and over there is a good range of comfortable garments, obviously designed by kind-hearted men who take pity on large problem-women. But for us, dear, for you and me – for you, with your forty-two hip measurement—' (she gave me no time to protest that I was only forty. Amy, in full spate, brooks no interruption) – 'and for me,' she continued, 'with my forty – well, thirty-nine really, but I prefer to be comfortable – what do we get?'

She waved a hand at the departing assistant who was returning a dozen or so coats to their show-case.

'Nothing?' I ventured.

'Nothing!' agreed Amy emphatically. Suddenly, her eye became fixed intently on my red frock that Mrs Moffat had made me. 'Turn round,' she commanded. 'Hmph! A zip right down to the waist, eh? That accounts for the fit. And that panel over the midriff is cut on the cross, I see. Who made it?'

I told her that Mrs Moffat designed and made it.

Amy continued to prowl round me, occasionally peering more closely at a particularly interesting seam. She even started to undo the zip 'to see how the back was faced,' until I protested.

'She's a marvel,' announced Amy, at length. Now Amy knows about clothes, and is an expert needlewoman as well as an astute buyer of really beautiful garments.

'Do you think she'd make for me?' she asked.

I said that I would ask her. I had to go for a fitting in the afternoon for two cotton frocks that she was making.

'But I'm having them buttoned down the front,' I told Amy. 'You can't believe how difficult it is for a woman living alone to cope with a zip down the back.'

'What you want,' said Amy, 'is a husband,' and without pausing to take breath added, 'How's Mr Mawne?'

I suggested, a trifle tartly, that coffee might restore both of us to our senses, and the question remained unanswered.

I had been invited to stay to tea at Mrs Moffat's bungalow after my fittings. I found Mrs Finch-Edwards, as handsome and exuberant as when she had taken charge in the infants' room over a year ago, sitting in the trim little drawing-room, while her baby daughter kicked fat legs on the rug at her feet.

She was an adorable baby, chubby and good-tempered, and Mrs Finch-Edwards had had her christened Althea.

'And she sleeps right through the night!' Mrs Finch-Edwards assured us. 'My hubby and I don't hear one squeak from six till six the next morning!'

'You just don't know how lucky you are,' Mrs Moffat answered, as she poured tea. 'Now Linda—' and the conversation became a duet compounded of such phrases as gripe-water, dreadful dummies, picking up, lying on the right side, kapok pillows, down pillows, no pillows – until it was enough to turn an old maid silly.

Mrs Moffat said that she would be delighted to make dresses for Amy, and I explained that, as she now lived at Bent, just the other side of Caxley and drove her own car, she could come whenever it was convenient for Mrs Moffat to have her. Mrs

Finch-Edwards and Mrs Moffat, I know, have high hopes of opening a shop one day, showing dresses that they have designed and made. In time they hope to have a substantial business, with a workroom of first-class sewing girls, while they attend to the designing and organization. They should make a success of such a venture, I feel sure, for they are both energetic, ambitious and particularly gifted at this type of work.

'I've made several children's frocks for that new shop in Caxley,' Mrs Finch-Edwards told me, 'but of course I can't do much while Althea's so young – but just wait!'

'Just wait!' echoed Mrs Moffat, and her eyes sparkled as she met the equally enthusiastic glances of her friend across the tea-cups.

The *Caxley Chronicle* today published a short article of mine about Lenten customs in Fairacre and other neighbouring parishes. This is my first appearance in the paper, and I must say it all looked very much more impressive in neat newsprint, than it did in pencil in a half-filled spelling-book from school.

The vicar began this project by showing me accounts in parish magazines of the last century, and Mrs Willet also told me of many interesting things that her father and mother did during Lent. The reaction to my appearance in print has been most amusing, and Mrs Pringle addressed me with something like awe this morning. To be 'in the papers' at all, is something. To be 'in The Paper,' is everything at Fairacre.

Less welcome were such comments as:

a. 'It is a real gift.' (The vicar)
b. 'I suppose it just flows out.' (Mrs Willet)
c. 'If it's in you, I suppose it's bound to come out.' (Mr Willet, rather morosely)
d. 'Wonderful, dear, and so effortless.' (Amy, on the telephone)

As I had spent six evenings at the dining-room table sitting on a hard chair with my toes twisted round its legs, chewing my pencil to shreds and groaning in much the same anguish as had my class when they composed their recent deathless verse, I found all these comments particularly souring.

On thinking over Mr Willet's gloomy comment I have come to the conclusion that he looks upon any kind of artistic urge as a sort of poison in the system, which is 'better out than in.' Perhaps this theory is more widely held than we realize, I thought to myself, as I knitted busily up the front of a cardigan this evening; in which case matters become very profound.

Instead of praising and envying artists, perhaps we should be sorry for them – victims as they are of their own pains. Is all art involuntary? Is it, perhaps, a bad, rather than a good thing? I paused to study the front of my cardigan, and found that I had decreased at both armhole and front edge, giving a remarkably bizarre effect to the garment, and involving two inches of careful unpicking.

I decided suddenly that literary fame had gone to my head, that the obscurer motives behind artistic impulses were beyond my comprehension, that a glass of hot milk would be a really good thing, and bed the best place for a bemused teacher.

April

In a week's time Fairacre School will have broken up for the Easter holidays. I, for one, am always glad to see the end of this most miserable of terms. In it we endure, each year, the worst weather, the darkest days, the poorest health and the lowest spirits. But now, with Easter in sight, and the sun gaining daily in strength, the outlook is much more heartening.

The return of the flowers and young greenery is a perennial miracle and wonder. The children have brought treasures from hedge, garden and spinney; and coltsfoot and crocus, violet and viburnum, primrose and pansy deck our classroom, all breathing out a faint but heady perfume of spring-time.

How lucky country children are in these natural delights that lie ready to their hand! Every season and every plant offers changing joys. As they meander along the lane that leads to our school all kinds of natural toys present themselves for their diversion. The seedpods of stitchwort hang ready for delightful popping between thumb and finger, and later the bladder campion offers a larger, if less crisp, globe to burst. In the autumn, acorns, beechnuts and conkers bedizen their path, with all their manifold possibilities of fun. In the summer, there is an assortment of honeys to be sucked from bindweed flowers, held fragile and fragrant to hungry lips, and the tiny funnels of honeysuckle and clover blossoms to taste. Outside the Post Office grow three fine lime trees, murmurous with bees on summer afternoons, and these supply wide, soft, young leaves in May, which the children spread over their opened mouths and, inhaling sharply, burst with a pleasant and satisfying explosion. At about the same time of year the young hawthorn leaves are found good to eat – 'bread and cheese' some call them – while the crisp sweet stalks of primroses form another delicacy, with the added delight of the thread-like inner stalk which pulls out from the hairier outer sheath.

The summer time brings flower games, the making of daisy chains, poppy dolls with little Chinese heads and red satin skirts made from the turned-back petals, 'He-loves-me-he-don't' counted solemnly as the daisy petals flutter down, and 'Bunny's mouth' made by pressing the sides of the yellow toadflax flowers which scramble over our chalky Fairacre banks. And always, whatever the season, there is a flat ribbon of grass blade to be found which, when held between thumbs and blown upon, can emit the most hideous and ear-splitting screech, calculated to fray the nerves of any grown-up, and warm the heart of any child, within earshot.

How fortunate too are country children in that, among all this richness, so much appeals not only to their senses of taste and smell, but to that most neglected one – the sense of touch. As they handle these living and beautiful things they run the gamut of texture from the sweet chestnut's bristly seedpod to the glutinous, cool smoothness of the bluebell's satin stalk. They part the fine dry grass to probe delicately with their fingers for the thread-like stalks of early white violets; and yet to pluck the strong ribbed stems of the cow parsley, they must exert all the strength of wrist and hand before its hollow tube snaps, with a rank and aromatic dying breath.

They leap to grasp the grey rough branch of the beech tree that challenges their strength near the school gate, and legs writhing, they feel the old rough, living strength of that noble tree in the very palms of their hands. Alas for their brothers in town who respond to the same challenge from a high brick wall! At its best it can but offer a dead stony surface, filthy with industrial grime, and, at its worst, the cruel shock and horror of vicious broken bottles.

For the most part country children say little of the joys that surround them. These are, rather naturally, taken for granted, and in the case of the boys they would think it vaguely effete to comment on the flowers and plants around them. The girls are less monosyllabic, and chatter interestedly about their latest finds. They enjoy finding the earliest violets – particularly a pinkish one that grows not far from 'The Beetle and Wedge' – and it is they who bring most of the contributions to the nature table. Their sense of touch is more sensitive and affords them greater satisfaction, and I remember Sylvia Burton's bunch of wild flowers, presented proudly one morning, with the comment: 'They've all got square stalks, miss. I've felt them.' Sure enough they had – it was a most satisfactory bouquet formed by members of the natural order *labiatae*.

The vicar called in to give his weekly talk. This time, as well as a little discourse on everyday Christianity, he told the children about Palm Sunday and the Easter festival, as is his wont before the school breaks up for the Easter holiday.

When he asked for pussy-willow to decorate the church, Joseph Coggs raised an eager, if grimy, paw.

'I can get a whole lot,' he said, eyes agleam. 'If I wriggles through the hedge down the bottom of Miss Parr's place, there's a pond and a pussy-willow tree.'

The vicar looked slightly taken aback.

'But I'm afraid that's a private tree, Joseph,' answered the vicar. 'It belongs to the people who live in the flats there.'

Joseph looked bewildered.

'But they never picks it,' he assured the vicar, 'and they'd never see me get in.'

The vicar drew in a sad breath, and very kindly and patiently gave an extra little homily about the sanctity of other people's property, and the promptings of one's own conscience, and the eye of the Almighty which is upon us all, even those who are but six years old and are wriggling on their stomachs through the long Fairacre grass. It was nicely put, and Joseph appeared to understand the vicar's words, but it was quite apparent to me that the principles behind the little homily were at war with the words of Joseph's feckless father, whose favourite maxims are 'Finding's Keepings' and 'What the eye doesn't see, etc.,' principles which, unconsciously, Joseph has imbibed. There is no doubt that innocent children, from such a slack and neglected home as Joseph's, need most positive guidance in right behaviour, frequently and firmly, if they are not to slide willy-nilly, into the clutches of evil companions and so to drift into the ranks of criminals.

This evening the meeting of the Women's Institute was held to hear more about the forthcoming pageant. We had had a heavy shower after tea, and the approach to the village hall, which stands not far from Mrs Moffat's spruce new bungalow, was very muddy. Someone's tractor had made deep squelchy ruts, which were full of rain water, and the women clucked their tongues with disgust, as they tried to wipe their shoes free of mud on the grass at the side of the door. Loudest in her protestations was Mrs Pringle.

'No need for all this muck,' she boomed, as she arched an elephantine ankle and poked mud from her instep with a stick. 'Time this place was built you could buy a load of good gravel for a few shillings – but it never was done. Now look at it. A pity poor old Sir Edmund's passed on. He'd have put down a good path for us.'

'I suggest we all put a shilling towards a load of gravel,' I said. Mrs Pringle snorted, and turned on me a glance so hostile that it was a wonder that I did not fall, withered, at her feet.

Inside the hall were about forty women, many of them with toddlers and young babies.

'My husband said fat chance he'd have of getting down to "The Beetle" if he had the children to look after – so I brought 'em too.'

'Ah!' agreed her neighbour comfortably. 'The men don't like the kids round 'em. 'Tis only natural, I s'pose!'

This charitable remark was endorsed by other women around, who, in the kindest and most indulgent tones, recounted various incidents of male selfishness, which made me feel very glad that, as a single woman, I was not called upon to endure such affronts to common justice.

'Oh, mine's very good,' said another. 'He never minded me coming up here this evening. "I'll have a sit and look at the paper," he says, as nice as you like, "and you can wash the dishes when you comes back, if you're a bit late now." Oh, he's easy!'

The murmuring grew in the hall as the late-comers arrived. The usual flicking of switches went on, as someone tried to find the best method of lighting the hall with the few bulbs remaining that worked.

The hall was erected about thirty years ago, and is a useful but ugly building of corrugated iron painted a dark red, which has, over the years, faded to a depressing maroon. The roof is also made of iron, and in very hot weather the building becomes stiflingly hot. If it rains heavily, the noise of the water drumming on the roof can successfully drown any speaker. If it is cold, the place is sketchily heated by means of four oil stoves, which frequently smoke and decorate the room, and its occupants, with black floating smuts which play havoc with clothes and complexions.

The lavatory, of the bucket variety, is housed, at some distance from the building, in a bower of elder trees, and is a constant annoyance to our Mr Willet, as he is frequently asked to look after it. Actually, Arthur Coggs is supposed to do it, but more often than not he forgets his duties. As he is away all day in Caxley working as a builder's labourer, and Mr Willet is on the spot here in Fairacre, it so happens that the urgent and outraged cries for help are answered by our school caretaker.

The hall itself is a fairly large building, with its inside walls lined with the sticky, ginger-coloured match boarding so beloved by our forbears. The First Fairacre Scout Troop, comprising about fifteen boys, holds its meetings here, and on one wall hang diagrams showing how to tie knots, a copy of Scout rules, a chart showing birds and their eggs and various other fascinating documents.

A little further along, hanging somewhat askew, are several photographs of past football teams. There is not one smile among the many grim countenances here displayed, but the biceps, forced up by judicious folding of the arms, are a wonder to behold. The manly forms of some thirty or forty years ago appear to have been much more corpulent than those of today, but perhaps there were more staunch and bulky garments underneath the red and white striped Fairacre jerseys then.

On the door, thoughtfully placed, is a small white card, on which is printed in uneven capitals:

HAVE YOU SWITCHED OF THE LIGHT?

The missing F tweaks at my schoolmistress's sensibilities so severely that I itch to be alone in the hall one day, when I shall give myself the exquisite satisfaction of adding the F. As it is, with possibly the perpetrator himself, or at least 'his sisters and his cousins and his aunts' all about me, I can do nothing, unless I am prepared to face a hornets' nest of buzzing family umbrage.

On the platform sat Mrs Partridge, our president, with Mrs Pratt, once Mrs Annett's landlady, beside her as secretary. The ink-stained deal table was covered with a magnificent cream linen cloth, embroidered by members of the institute. After each meeting it is folded into a clean piece of sheeting and borne away to Mrs Pratt's house and put safely into the first drawer of her sideboard, until it is time for it to see the light of day again. Mrs Pringle views this cloth with something of the low churchman's disapproval of the high churchman's elaborate ceremony.

'Made an idol of, that there cloth,' she told me once. 'I said at the time it was too fanciful and would show the dirt. What's more, I offered my mother's best tablecloth that she used year in and year out in her front parlour for as long as I can remember. As fine a piece of red chenille, with a good deep fringe to it, as ever you see in a day's march. A mite faded maybe, but that's no call for making personal remarks about my mother's care of it.

Mondays and Thursdays that was hung on the line and brushed lightly with an old clothes-brush dipped in cold tea. Come up beautiful. But no! 'Twasn't good enough for the W.I., so this fal-lal has to be made instead!' Mrs Pringle bridled at the memory of this rebuff to her offer, and I attempted to comfort her.

'Never mind. You must be glad that you've still got it at home.' Of course I had put my foot in it yet again.

'In a foolish moment,' began Mrs Pringle heavily, 'and believing that the girl would treasure it, I let that Minnie Pringle over at Springbourne have it for a Christmas present.' She paused, drew in a long and sibilant breath, and thrust her face within two inches of mine. 'And you know what? A fortnight later, as sure as I stand here and may I be struck down if I don't tell the truth of it, I saw that very same cloth on her aunt's table up the road. Called there one day I did, to give her my club money, and there was MY tablecloth on HER table. "Where d'you get that, pray?" I asked her. Civil, mark you, but cool. "Our Min she give it me," she said. "Why!" I told her, and you know what? She just laughed! *Just laughed!* I was proper wild, I can tell you. Never said nothing more to her, of course. Wouldn't demean myself. But when I next saw that Minnie Pringle, I give her the rough side of my tongue – the hussy!'

At last Mrs Partridge rose behind the tablecloth which had caused Mrs Pringle so much heart-burning, and the meeting began. The minutes were read, approved, signed and, as nothing arose from them, Mrs Partridge came straight to the point and told us the latest news of the pageant.

'The draw has been made,' she told us, 'and it is Fairacre's privilege to open the pageant. Ours is the first scene.' A gratified murmur arose from the hall, and proud smiles were exchanged. Mrs Partridge, astute in the handling of these affairs, allowed us to bask in this glory for a few happy seconds, before releasing the cold shower.

'It is a wonderful thing, of course,' she proceeded smiling expansively, 'and we are very lucky to get this scene. It also means that our part will be over first, and we can relax and enjoy the rest of the pageant. So less tiring for the children too.'

'I just ain't gonna be in it,' said an audible but obstinate toddler to his mother, at this juncture. Mrs Partridge continued without batting an eyelid.

'And now you'll want to know the title of Fairacre's scene.'

Mrs Moffat caught my eye across the room and mouthed the word 'Wimples' at me. I smiled back.

'It is "The Coming of the Romans",' went on Mrs Partridge.

'Romans!' said the members in one outraged breath. If they had been called upon to be earwigs, they could not have sounded more affronted.

Mrs Partridge gathered us up again. 'The Roman soldiers' costume will be most effective, of course. A lot can be done with gilt paint and good stout cardboard.'

After the first shock of losing wimples, pearls-in-plaited-hair, ruffs, buckled shoes and other flattering accoutrements, the meeting came round to the idea of even earlier times and their sartorial possibilities. Seizing her opportunity Mrs Partridge continued glibly.

'The scene opens with the native people of this country – Ancient Britons then – busy about their everyday work. The men shaping flints for tools, dragging logs back for the fire and so on, and the women nursing their babies and cooking over an open fire. After a time, there are sounds of distant voices and marching, and one of the Ancient Britons runs into the camp, pointing dramatically into the distance. A Roman cohort approaches – the natives flee terrified, but gradually creep back. The Romans give them small gifts, and we see that the régime of Roman rulers and British vassals will soon be set up.' Mrs Partridge paused, at the end of this swift résumé of our forthcoming task, and there was an ominous silence. At last Mrs Pringle broke it, in a voice heavy with foreboding.

'Madam President,' she began, becoming suddenly a stickler for etiquette, 'and fellow-members. Does this mean that some of us here have to be Ancient Britons?'

Before her relentless gaze even Mrs Partridge quailed a trifle. 'But naturally, Mrs Pringle,' she replied, doing her best to answer with easy grace. 'Some will be Ancient Britons, and others Romans.'

'Humph!' snorted Mrs Pringle. 'And what, may I ask – if anything, I mean – do Ancient Britons wear?'

It was an anxious moment. You could have run a satisfactory

heating system with the electricity generated in the hall at that quivering instant. Mrs Partridge, with the knowledge of past crises overcome and the rarefied blood of a vicar's wife beating in her veins, rose gamely to the challenge.

'We shall wear,' she said steadily, 'furs – probably mounted on old sacks.' There was a gasp from Mrs Moffat.

'And our hair,' she continued remorselessly, 'will be as rough and as dirty as we can make it.'

Mrs Pringle sat down with a jolt that made her companions on the bench shudder in sympathy. For once, she was speechless.

Mrs Partridge pressed home her attack.

'And our feet,' she said, with a hint of triumph, 'will be *bare*!'

There were faint sounds of dismay among the ranks before her, and the shuffling of feet clad, at the moment, in comfortable, if muddy, footwear. At this despondent moment, when dissension might so easily have reared its ugly head and wrecked our future revels, Mrs Moffat, a comparative newcomer to Fairacre, rose to her feet. Very pretty, very smart, an incomparable dressmaker and not much of a mixer as yet, she is still looked upon with a slightly suspicious eye by the old guard in the village.

'I don't know whether you want volunteers for the Ancient Britons,' she said, pink with her own temerity, 'but if you do, I'd like to be one of them.' It was a courageous statement, and made at a most strategic moment of the campaign. Moreover, it was a particularly noble one, when one considers that Mrs Moffat well knew that her own good looks would be hidden under sacks and old fur bits, which in themselves must be anathema to her sensitive clothes-loving soul. This unselfish gesture did not go unnoticed. There were sounds of approval, and one or two encouraging nods.

'Come to think of it,' said another woman, slowly, 'I don't mind being an Ancient Briton myself. I got a nice bit of ol' hearth rug—'

Mrs Partridge clinched the matter by saying: 'I'm looking forward to being one myself. For one thing the costume will be so easy to contrive.' Then with consummate generalship she drew her ranks of broken women together, at this precise moment which, she realized, would be the most propitious that she could hope for in these adverse conditions.

'I'm sure we shall be able to arrange Ancient Britons and Romans quite happily among ourselves; and I don't think we'll go any further with our plans tonight. It's getting late, and I know some of the mothers want to get these young people off to bed. I propose that we have a first rehearsal and allot parts one day next week. Shall we say at the vicarage?'

There were murmurs of assent, as people rose to their feet.

'Wednesday afternoon?' shouted Mrs Partridge above the noise.

'Clinic!' bellowed someone.

'Thursday then?' persisted Mrs Partridge, in a stentorian tone.

'Market day,' shrieked another.

'Monday?' bellowed Mrs Partridge indefatigably. The noise of scraping chairs and forms was unbelievable.

'Washday!' said someone; but she was howled down, by a self-righteous group near the door with lungs of brass.

'Did ought to be finished that by midday!'

'I gets mine done by eleven. And eight to wash for, my girl!'

'You can get there Monday afternoon, if you gets a move on!'

At last Monday afternoon was decided upon. The children would have broken up by then, and those that could be press-ganged into the pageant's service would be able to join their mothers in the fun at the vicarage.

Mrs Pringle, picking her way over the puddles, as we emerged in a bunch from the hall, voiced her feelings on the proceedings.

'Heathenish lot of nonsense!' boomed the familiar voice through the darkness. 'Furs and old sacks and bare feet! Why, my mother would turn in her grave to think of me tricked out so common. We was all brought up respectable. Our feet never so much as saw daylight except at Saturday bath-night and getting into bed. Catch me exposing my extremities to the gaze of all and sundry, and as like as not getting pneumonia into the bargain!'

In the brief pause for breath which followed this diatribe a would-be peace-maker broke in.

'Perhaps you could be a Roman soldier, Mrs Pringle.'

The snort that this meek suggestion brought forth would have done credit to an old war-horse.

'And what would my figure look like hung round with a few bits of gilt cardboard?' demanded Mrs Pringle majestically.

It seemed best to assume that this question was rhetorical and to be grateful for the merciful darkness which hid our faces.

The last day of term is over. It was spent in the usual jubilant muddle of clearing desks, tidying cupboards, searching for lost books and taking down pictures and charts from the schoolroom walls.

The last part of the afternoon was devoted to drawing a picture about Easter. Each child was given a very small piece of rough paper and a pencil, as everything else was packed securely away for three weeks, and had to do the best he could with this meagre ration.

I expected a spate of Easter eggs, chicks and the like, but was surprised by the various reactions to the word 'Easter'. The most striking use of paper and pencil came from Patrick, who had carefully folded his paper in half to form an Easter card, which he finally presented to me. It showed three large tombstones with crosses, and the letters R.I.P. printed crookedly across them, and inside was neatly printed 'HAPPY EASTER.' I accepted this gloomy missive as gravely as I could. It had taken the artist half an hour and a good quarter of an inch of blacklead pencil to execute it.

When the pencils too had to be yielded up to the cupboard, we were reduced to the game of 'Left and Right,' that incomparable standby of empty-handed and busy teachers. Linda Moffat supplied a hair-grip and called upon Anne, her desk-mate, to guess which fist it was secreted in. She guessed correctly, took Linda's place, and the game followed its peaceful course with little attention from me, as I was engrossed in adding up the attendances for the term in the register. This wretched record does not hold the same fears for teachers these days, as it did when I was a girl, but it still exercises a baneful influence over me, and early memories of trips to my first headmistress with a wrongly marked register in my trembling hand and instant dismissal hovering over me, have set up a horrid complex towards registers as a whole.

At the end of the afternoon we made our special farewells to Mrs Annett, and one of the Coggs twins presented her with a bouquet of daffodils, tulips, Easter daisies and narcissi, which the children had brought from their gardens. We shall miss her sorely. It has been decided by the managers to wait until after the summer holidays for the permanent appointment, when the newly-trained young teachers will be out from the colleges. Meanwhile, I was delighted to hear from the vicar that Miss Clare will be with us for next term. This is good news indeed.

I spent a very pleasant evening with the Annetts, after pottering happily about all day enjoying the freedom from school duties. I have turned out the cupboard under the stairs – one mad jumble of brooms, dusters, primus stove, and might-come-in-useful collection of pieces of brown paper, cardboard, carrier bags and the like – and feel much elated. From the schoolroom came sounds of Mrs Pringle at work scrubbing the floor-boards. Above the clanking of the pail and the groaning of heavy desks being shunted across the room, Mrs Pringle's carrying contralto voice could be heard raised in pious song, ranging from *A few more years shall roll* to *Oft in danger, oft in woe*.

It was very pleasant to take my time over tea and dressing. The little car goes well now, and gone are the days when I imagined knots of children playing marbles in the middle of the road round each corner, and held my breath when another car approached. In fact I felt quite a dashing driver as I swept into Beech Green school's empty playground, and slammed the car door shut, only to realize that I had left my keys inside. Luckily, the other door was unlocked, so all was well; but I went in a more humble mood across to the school-house next door.

It is very much more comfortable now that Mrs Annett is there to run the house, and I remembered my first visit there, when Mr Annett was officially looked after by a house-keeper, and how I had noticed the general neglect.

Now the furniture gleamed and fresh flowers scented the house. In the corner Mrs Annett's violin stood beside Mr Annett's 'cello. They are both keen members of the Caxley orchestra, but Mrs Annett will probably not be able to take part next season, when she has a young baby to look after. Their radiogram is a great joy to them and we played Mr Annett's new records until supper-time.

After supper we fell to talking about country schools and I was interested to hear that Beech Green is developing the practical farming side with even more vigour.

'If I have to have the children here until they are fifteen,' said Mr Annett, 'and I have no woodwork shop, no place for metal work and mighty little other equipment, then I must find something that is worthwhile for them to do, and from which they learn. Otherwise they'll be bored and surly. Luckily we've plenty of land here, enough for a large vegetable plot, and we've got permission to keep hens, ducks and pigs as well.'

I knew that Beech Green school had sent garden produce to Caxley market for some years, but the livestock was something quite new.

'We've been given a small grant from the county,' he went on, 'and our profit from the market has helped. The boys have made really fine coops and runs, which have involved quite a bit of practical arithmetic, and the way the accounts are kept is a miracle of book-keeping. The pigs have only just arrived. Brick-laying took longer than we thought for the sties, and we had a bit of trouble with the concrete yards, but they should bring us in a substantial profit later. The left-overs from school dinners form the major part of their diet. You must bring a party over from Fairacre School to see our farm when it's really working.'

I promised that I would, and as I drove home the sound good sense behind Mr Annett's scheme for these older rural pupils impressed me more and more. One thing that he had said I found particularly significant.

'I started by using these out-of-door and practical activities as a means to defeat apathy. After all, for generations most country children of fourteen and over have been out in the world earning their living. It is not surprising that today some still resent being kept at school, particularly if there's nothing new or absorbing to learn offered them. But the surprising thing is this. The defeat of apathy is only a by-product. For this itself is real education for the majority of the Beech Green children. Working with these methods brings out the patience, the endurance and the innate sagacity of the countryman; and, all the time, I am working WITH and not AGAINST the grain, as I so often felt I was when I urged them along reluctantly with book-work for which they had little sympathy.'

Mr Annett is a townsman by birth and breeding, so that it is all the more remarkable that he has stumbled on this truth, after a relatively short time as a country-dweller; but there are hundreds of rural schoolteachers from Land's End to John o' Groats who will endorse his views, and who know that the education of the countryman is a matter which must be given immediate and intelligent thought. Land today in England is more precious than ever before. It is our heritage and in trust for future generations. It is only right that it should be tilled and cared for by people who are not only capable and trained for this work, but who also are happy and contented to live among the farms and fields which give them their livelihood and – even more – a deep inner satisfaction.

Rural education must be tackled realistically if the drift to the towns is to stop. In this way village life will come into its own again, not as a picturesque setting for week-end visitors to enjoy, when they come down, in some cases, to see how a most satisfactory way of income-tax evasion is getting on, but as a vital working unit.

The first rehearsal at the vicarage went splendidly. Mrs Partridge said that she felt we really ought to get used to going barefoot, so that we removed our shoes, with varying degrees of reluctance, and left them on the veranda while we hobbled painfully over the gravel to the comparative comfort of the lawn, where we sat down to discuss casting plans.

It was decided that twelve of our more comely members would constitute the invading Roman force, and that the rest would be Ancient Britons of both sexes. I watched Mrs Partridge running an appraising eye over the legs of the assembled company, rather as the local trainers do as they watch their race-horses on the gallops above Fairacre.

Mrs Moffat, that brave volunteer to the Ancient Britons' ranks, was persuaded to be pack-leader, captain, or whatever the Roman equivalent might be for the one in charge, instead. She is tall and carries herself well, and her legs are impeccable. Mrs Partridge obviously feared that there might be an ugly rush for the other eleven places, for she spoke firmly to Mrs Pratt when she rose from her seat on the lawn.

'Now please, Mrs Pratt, I do so want you to be a rather influential Ancient Briton woman, with possibly a bundle of faggots, so will you forgo being a Roman?'

Mrs Pratt looked mildly surprised. 'I only got up because I was sitting on a thistle,' she said, in some bewilderment.

Mrs Partridge said she had quite misunderstood her gesture, and were there any volunteers?

As usual in Fairacre, the word 'volunteers' struck temporary paralysis upon its hearers, and we all sat, eyes glazed and limbs frozen, like so many flies in amber. It was quite apparent that far from there being an ugly rush to the Roman standard, Fairacre W.I. had elected to be Ancient Britons to a woman.

At last Mrs Partridge broke the silence.

'Miss Read, would you be a Roman?'

I said that I should be delighted to be called to the colours at my age. This seemed to break the ice a little, and two young women who cycle over from Springbourne to our meetings, offered to join the ranks too. Gradually our twelve were collected, and if some of us were a trifle long in the tooth, at least we were reasonably athletic.

There had been an awkward moment when Mrs Pringle had boomed a grudging offer of martial assistance, but Mrs Partridge had turned temporarily deaf, and as Mrs Fowler from Tyler's Row spoke up at the same time, all was well.

'Now,' said Mrs Partridge brightly, 'if you Romans would sit over here near the rose-bed – but do mind your nylons – we shall know where we are. We shall need to work out how much cardboard we shall require for armour; but that must wait for another time.'

'Breastplates and backplates should be enough,' said one of the Springbourne girls.

'And helmets,' said the other.

'And greaves,' said Mrs Moffat.

'Graves?' boomed Mrs Pringle from the Ancient Britons' camp opposite. 'Graves? We having a war then? If so, I tell you straight, my leg won't stand up to it!'

'Leg-pads – like in cricket,' volunteered a nephew of Mr Rogers at the forge, who attends Caxley Grammar School and is well up in greaves, helmets and other martial garments.

Mrs Pringle snorted her disgust.

'Got quite enough on me leg with me elastic stocking,' said that lady, 'without getting meself dolled-up in wicket-keeper's rubbish.'

With brilliant dash Mrs Partridge put all to rights.

'You won't need to be bothered with leg-pads, Mrs Pringle. As an Ancient Briton, I want you to be the mother of the chief warrior – a most important person – and you will sit on a kind of throne by the camp fire – which won't try your poor leg that you're always so brave about – and generally keep an eye on the rest of the tribe.'

Mrs Pringle allowed herself to be mollified, and something very like a gratified smirk spread over her dour features. It is no wonder that Mrs Partridge is elected annually as our president. No one else can touch her for spontaneous and inspired diplomacy.

As a nasty little wind had sneaked up, and the children were beginning to get restive, it was thought best to have a rudimentary rehearsal of the scene at once.

'You must pretend to have weapons and tools,' shouted Mrs Partridge, above the general movement. 'One of you boys fetch a stool for Mrs Pringle, and that flower-urn can be the camp fire.'

Slowly the Ancient Britons began to move shamefacedly about their occupations, their children tending to stand about with broad grins on their faces and with many a giggle behind hands. Mrs Pringle squatted in an unlovely attitude on her small stool, and folded her arms regally. Other women stirred imaginary pots, washed imaginary clothes, swept imaginary floors and occasionally cuffed far-from-imaginary children who crossed their path.

Meanwhile we Roman soldiers formed a ragged column behind the laurel bushes, awaiting our entrance. We waited until one of the tribesmen had returned to his fellows, showing by gestures that we were about to descend upon them. The Ancient Britons were then supposed to point towards us dramatically, making low uncouth cries at the same time as they bunched together in trepidation.

The low, uncouth cries they did rather well, as dramatically out-flung arms hit nearby bodies with considerable force. At a nervous command from our leader, Mrs Moffat, we marched into action from behind the laurels. The fact that some of us had started on the left, and some on the right foot, that we were all too close and tended to trip each other up, did not enhance our war-like aspect. But never can a Roman cohort have been so polite, and it was quite pretty to hear us all apologizing to each other as we stumbled along.

We approached our future captives, smiling faintly upon them. They beamed back, and we all mingled together in the happiest fraternity round the flower-urn and Mrs Pringle.

Mrs Partridge clapped her hands and we sat down thankfully.

'Very good indeed,' said she, with the greatest vigour. 'I think it's a wonderful beginning. When the soldiers have got their cardboard armour on, and their kilts,' (Mr Rogers's nephew, as a coming classics man, shuddered and turned pale) 'and the Ancient Britons are wearing their old fur and dreary hair, I think we shall all be quite—' she searched for the exact word, looked it over, found it good, and flung it at us triumphantly – 'quite *irresistible*!'

Flown with such heady praise we all returned, in great good spirits, to our homes.

MAY

As usual, the holidays slipped by in a golden haze. Apart from four crowded days in London, staying with a married friend with three young children, and having the excitement of an evening at the ballet, shopping and meals out, I spent the rest of the time here at the school-house. The garden is at its best, and the fruit trees, planted by those who taught at Fairacre long ago, are a mass of pink and white blossom. Mr Willet and all the other good gardeners pull long faces and say: 'Don't like to see it so early. Bound to get some late frosts, mark my words.'

A blackbird has built a nest in the lilac bush near the gate – so idiotically low that Tibby is much interested and spends her time glowering upon the foolish bird, from the top of the gate. I have tried to screen it with hazel boughs, but with small success. At my suggestion, to Mr Willet, that I might drape it with netting from the fruit cage, he looked at me pityingly, blew out his ragged old moustache, and said: 'Why not let the poor cat have a good meal? He's waited patient enough, ain't he?'

Mrs Pringle came to give me a hand with some spring-cleaning during the holidays, which she did with much puffing and blowing. To hear her disparaging comments on the condition of the backs of the bookcases, and the loot that she extracted from the sides of the armchairs, one might wonder why I hadn't died of typhus.

'Mrs Hope, what lived here in my young days, though an ailing woman with a child, and a husband with a Failing,' she told me, as she hauled out the loose cover from the crack of the sofa, 'never had so much as a biscuit crumb in her folds, they being brushed out regular twice a week, as is necessary for common cleanliness.' To add point to this stricture, she jerked out the last bit of the cover and projected a light shower of crumbs – biscuit and otherwise – two pencils, a safety-pin, a knitting needle and a liquorice allsort, upon the carpet. I was unrepentant.

Term is now a week old. The children look all the better for their freedom and fresh air, and it is very pleasant to have Miss Clare back again in the infants' room, where she reigned for so many years. However it is not without certain small difficulties. The children are used to Mrs Annett's more modern methods, and have been allowed to move about the classroom, to talk a little and to make much more noise than Miss Clare will allow. They are finding Miss Clare's more formal methods rather irksome.

'Can we play shops?' I heard Joseph Coggs ask, as I was collecting Miss Clare's savings money. 'Mrs Annett lets us play shops instead of writing down sums.' His dark eyes were fixed pleadingly upon her.

'I think we'll have table practice first,' was the kind, but firm, answer; and Joseph trailed back to his desk, with a pouting underlip.

'Do use all the apparatus that is here,' I said, waving to the desk-load of sugar cartons, cocoa tins and the like, that constitute 'the shop' at the side of the room, 'and don't worry about the noise – my children don't take any notice of a little hum next door.' But my gentle hints were of no avail. I could see from Miss Clare's quizzical glance that she knew exactly what was going on inside my head, and knew too that she was too old a dog to learn new tricks – even if she felt that they were the right ones, which, in this case, she doubts.

In a week or two the children will have become accustomed to a slower and steadier régime, and will respond to Miss Clare's methods as well as earlier generations of Fairacre children have done. Meanwhile, I have offered to take her class, as well as my own, for the games and physical training lessons, for not only is this too much of a strain on her elderly and delicate heart, but the small children revel in scampering and jumping and using the wealth of individual apparatus – balls, hoops, skipping ropes and the like – which they miss sorely in the formal four lines for head, arm, leg and trunk exercises which are used for the major part of Miss Clare's lessons.

It has not been easy to persuade Miss Clare to part with any of her duties, for she is the most conscientious woman alive; but after some demurring she acquiesced, not only in this matter but also in my suggestion that she rested for twenty minutes on my sofa during the dinner hour. It took some lurid word-painting on my behalf, of my own predicament if she should have an attack in school time, to make her agree to this measure, but a lucky thought of mine that she should make a pot of tea for us both, at the end of the twenty minutes, which would also be the end of my midday playground duty, just turned the balance, and the daily rest means that she returns to her afternoon session much refreshed.

My class this term has been enriched by the addition of an eight-year-old American boy. His parents return to the United States in what he calls 'the fall'. On first hearing this expression, Patrick, more scripturally-minded than most, began asking complicated questions about the Garden of Eden, which he was obviously confusing with Erle's native land, and was considerably surprised, and slightly disappointed, on being told that it was only another name for autumn.

The Fairacre children have taken Erle very much under their wing. He is a most attractive little boy, with a crew-cut, a cheerful grin and no trace of shyness. He appeared on the second morning with two pistols slung on a formidable, studded holster, round his checked jeans. I broke it to him, as gently as I could, that I did not allow guns, knives, bows and arrows or any other weapons on school premises, though, of course, he could do as he liked at home. I was conscious of the exchange of disgusted glances among my class, for this old sore still rankles, but Erle parted with his holster, with a grin that crinkled his eyes engagingly. He put it with a resounding clanking of pistolry on the old desk at the side of the room, among the paper bags containing elevenses, and the other, less lethal, toys, that had been brought for play-time.

There was an amusing sequel to this incident. At play-time I sat alone in the classroom, marking history test papers, when I became conscious of voices in the adjoining lobby.

'Never you mind, Erle,' said Eric earnestly, 'us'll play cowboys with you tonight down the rec. That ol' Miss Read—' he spoke witheringly, 'she treats us awful. Don't let us do nothin'. A proper ol' spoil sport!'

'Aw well,' came Erle's good-natured drawl, 'I guess teachers is teachers everywhere!' He spoke as one who has suffered in the past, and is resigned – fairly cheerfully – to suffering in the future.

'Don't you bring them no more, though,' warned Eric. 'The ol' girl locks 'em up in the cupboard till the end of term, and kicks up horrid.' His voice, dark with foreboding, suddenly took on a more jubilant note. 'Tell you what – come and play Indians up the coke-pile!' And with joyous whoopings, this enlightening conversation came to an end.

Mr Arnold, one of Her Majesty's Inspectors, spent most of the day with us. This is his second visit to Fairacre School. His first one was brought to an abrupt close by a violent thunderstorm last summer, when we had to get the children home as best we could by various means. The vicar, I remember, stuffed a record number into his car that afternoon, and the old golfing umbrella, that lives in the corner cupboard with the maps, had bobbed its way through the downpour with the Tyler's Row contingent.

He remembered Mrs Annett – Miss Gray, as she had been when he last visited the infants' room – and said that she appeared to have done an excellent job with the younger children; but didn't I feel that the reading was being pushed a little too hard? He put this point with the utmost delicacy, suggesting that perhaps Miss Clare was the person who was taking this subject a trifle too seriously, but I told him at once that this fault – if it were indeed a fault – was of my making.

This led us to a most agreeable and stimulating argument about children's reading. Mr Arnold sat inelegantly on the front desk, with his back to the class. Poor Patrick meekly wrote up his nature notes on the six square inches of desk lid which were not occupied by Mr Arnold's well-cut lovat tweed trousers. I sat at my desk and we argued over the massive brass and oak inkstand.

He maintained that children are not ready to read before the age of six, or even seven; and that all sorts of nervous tensions and eyestrain can be set up by too much emphasis on early reading.

I maintain that each child should go at its own rate, and that the modern tendency is to go at the rate of the slowest member of a reading group, and that this is wrong. There are, to my mind, far more bright children being bored and very frustrated because they are not getting on fast enough with their reading, than there are slow ones who are being harmed by too-rapid progress. I have known several children – I was one myself – who could read enough simply-written stories to amuse themselves at the age of four and a half to five. We were not forced, but it was just one of those things we could do easily, and the advantages were enormous.

In the first place we *could* amuse ourselves, and reading also gave us a quiet and relaxed time for recovering from the violent activity which is the usual five-year-old's way of passing the time.

Secondly, the amount of general knowledge we unconsciously imbibed, stood us in good stead in later years. Today, with the eleven-plus examination to face, this is particularly pertinent. Incidentally, I have known children who have come to reading so late in the primary school, that they have found real difficulty in reading the questions, let alone knowing enough to answer them. Even more important, the early poems and rhymes, read and learnt so easily at this stage have been a constant and abiding joy.

Thirdly, the wealth of literature written and presented expressly for the four to six age-group – the Beatrix Potter books are the first that spring to mind – can be used, loved and treasured to such an extent that is not possible to a late reader. The child who has never been taught until the age of seven or eight has missed the thrill of discovering a vast number of attractive books. He is beginning to want fairy stories, adventures, legends and so on, which may well be in language still too difficult for his retarded mechanics of reading.

The battle raged with great zest.

'I have never over-worked a child in my life,' I insisted. 'It always seems to me to be a most difficult thing to accomplish anyway, natural resistance to learning is remarkably resilient. There are some here who never will be able to read with ease – but, broadly speaking, I expect the average child to be able to read well enough to amuse and instruct himself by the time he is eight – and if he can't, then he is probably below average and will need a little extra encouragement. And if I get the odd infant who can rattle away at five – why then, good luck to him – and all the books in Fairacre School, and in Fairacre school-house, for that matter, are at his disposal.'

Mr Arnold twinkled, and said I was a renegade, but that he must admit that he had seen no cases of nervous disorders in my school. And after school, he, Miss Clare and I enjoyed a cup of tea in my garden, among the apple blossom, with the greatest goodwill, each knowing that he would never convert the other, but content to let it be so.

Erle and Eric have struck up a strong friendship and are quite inseparable. It dates, I think, from the day when I banished Erle's weapons from the school premises, and, united against stern tyranny, the pair flourish. Before prayers this morning, as I was wondering if I could manage five flats in the morning hymn and dusting the yellow piano keys, I listened to their conversation. Eric was giving out hymn books, dropping them with a satisfying smack on each desk, as the rest of the class wandered in, deposited their elevenses on the side table, or waited beside my desk with bunches of flowers or messages from their mothers.

Erle trailed behind him giving brief information about education in American schools.

'We don't have all this,' he said, touching a hymn book, 'we have the pledge.'

'The what?' said Eric, stopping dead. 'Like what you have in the Band of Hope?'

'Don't know nothin' about a Band of Hope,' replied Erle. 'The pledge is what we say every morning. We all look at the flag – our flag, Stars and Stripes – and promise to be real good Americans.'

Eric looked surprised and mildly disgusted.

'You tells all that to a *flag*?' he enquired.

Erle's good-natured face took on a perplexed expression.

'It's THE flag,' he explained. 'It's a real good flag, with gold fringe and all.'

Eric's reply was crushing. 'We got a flag too. But we don't keep all on about it.' He resumed his hymn-book slinging as though the matter were closed.

Erle was not to be side-tracked. 'Well, forget the flags,' he said doggedly, 'but we don't have hymns and prayers like you do. That's all I said. We just have this pledge – like I told you.'

Eric flicked the last hymn book on to the corner desk with a pretty turn of the wrist. Satisfied with the results, he dusted his hands down his shirt, and explained the position succinctly to this stranger from another shore.

'Well, that's all right where you come from, I don't doubt. But over here, Miss Read says we has a bit about God each morning – and rain or shine, a bit about God we has!'

Miss Clare invited me to her cottage for the evening. It only takes a few moments for me to drive the two miles between us; when she comes to me, she refuses to let me fetch her or run her home in the car, but cycles, very slowly and as upright as ever, on her venerable old bicycle.

The cottage is a model of neatness. The roof was thatched by her father, who was the local thatcher for many years. She has an early-flowering honeysuckle over her white trellis porch, and jasmine smothers another archway down the garden path.

As usual, the best china, the snowiest cloth and the most delicious supper awaited me. In the centre of the table stood a cut-glass vase of magnificent tulips, flanked by a cold brisket of beef on a willow-pattern dish garnished with sprigs of parsley from her garden, and an enormous salad. The freshly-plucked spring onions were thoughtfully put separately in a little shallow dish.

'It's not everyone that can digest them,' said Miss Clare, crunching one with much enjoyment, 'but my mother always said they were a wonderful tonic, and cleared the blood after the winter.'

Miss Clare's silver was old and heavy and gleamed with recent cleaning. How she finds time to keep everything so immaculate I don't know. Her house puts mine to shame, and she has no one to help her at all, whereas I do have Mrs Pringle occasionally to turn a disdainful hand to my affairs.

After we had consumed an apple and blackberry pie, the fruits of Miss Clare's earlier bottling, we folded our yard-square napkins – which were stiff with starch and exquisitely darned here and there – and washed up in the long, low kitchen, while the coffee heated on the Primus stove.

Miss Clare's larder is one of the pleasantest places I know. It is a long narrow room at the side of the kitchen and has a red brick floor and whitewashed walls. The wooden shelves have been scrubbed so often and so well that the grain stands out in fine ribs.

From the ceiling hang ropes of bronze onions, dried herbs in muslin bags, and ham, equally well-draped, which I know her brother gave her at his last pig-killing. Bottles of fruit, cherries, plums, blackberries, greengages and gooseberries, and jars of jam and jelly flash like jewels, as they stand in serried ranks: and on the floor stand bottles of home-made wine, dandelion, parsnip, sloe and damson, beside two large crocks containing salted runner beans. How Miss Clare ever gets through these stores I don't know, for she has little time for entertaining and has her main meal at school, more often than not; but as a true country-woman she bottles, preserves, salts and stores all the good things that grow in her own garden and are given her by kindly neighbours, and would count it a disgrace not to have a larder well-stocked for any emergency.

That she is generous with her possessions, I do know, from personal experience and from hearsay. No one goes away empty-handed; and I suspect that many of those bottles of fruit and wine will be carried away by visitors. Typical of her largeness of heart is the shilling which always waits on the corner of the mantelpiece in the dining-room.

'I keep one there for whoever calls,' she told me. 'They are all treated the same – Salvation Army, Soldiers and Sailors, Roman Catholics, Blind Babies, Red Cross, and all the rest.' When I think of Miss Clare's tiny pension and see how ready she is to give – not only these impartial shillings, but cakes to fêtes and bazaars, knitting to raffles, gifts to sales of work and the like, and always unfailingly, her time and little store of strength – to any good work in the village, I cannot help contrasting her attitude of mind with those others among us, earning perhaps five times as much, who never give one penny, one minute or one thought to others around them, but grab all, and grumble because it isn't more.

In the end, of course, it is Miss Clare, who scores, for she, *ipso facto*, is a happy woman, while their treasure turns to dust and ashes.

Mrs Moffat has undertaken to make Amy's costume for the forthcoming county pageant. Bent, the village where Amy lives, has been lucky enough to draw 'The Visit of Charles II and Queen Catherine of Braganza to Branscombe Castle' for its part in the series. Amy is to play the queen, and is full of enthusiasm. Her handbag was crammed with patterns of silks, satins, lace and brocade, and a number of small portraits of that royal lady, culled from the postcard stands at the National Portrait Gallery to snippets from the historical features in back numbers of *Everybody's*.

She had been to discuss the costume early in the afternoon, and called at the school as we were about to go home. She smiled kindly upon Linda, and took in, with an expert's eye, the cut of the tartan pinafore frock that Miss Moffat was wearing.

'She's going to be a beauty,' was her comment, when the children had trickled out into the sunshine. 'And with a mother like that to make her clothes, she's going to be a very lucky girl.'

She helped me to stack away the paintings which were draped around the room, on the piano top, the fire-guard, the side desk, window-sills – anywhere for that matter where the masterpieces could have ten minutes' peace in which to dry – and rattled on excitedly about Mrs Moffat's genius for dressmaking. Four or five other members of Bent W.I. had also enlisted her services, one of whom was an authority on costume and had worked, before her marriage, as an adviser on historical costume to a film company. Amy had high hopes that she would take an especial interest in Mrs Moffat's work and that this might lead to great things in the future, for the Moffat-Finch-Edwards partnership.

'And what might this be?' she enquired suddenly, holding up a damp painting by one corner. I said it was supposed to be Mr Lamb at the Post Office unlocking the post-box and taking out the letters.

'But it's a lilac letter-box,' objected Amy. 'There's not a spot of scarlet anywhere!'

'There's not a spot of scarlet in the whole wretched range of powder paint,' I told her. 'You can have anything from lime green to clover. We're all a bit greenery-yallery these days.'

'We had three good fat squeezes of red, blue, and yellow, when I was at school,' said Amy, looking back across the years. 'Primary colours, you know, and we made all the others from those three. Much more fun than these myriad pots of depressing paint.' She surveyed, with dislike, the large tray, laden with jam jars of paint, that stood on my desk.

I agreed heartily, and told her that in some painting lessons the children did exactly as she had done as a child, and that I believed they found the mixing of colours more absorbing than slapping on those already done for them.

'To have no really good red!' mused Amy sadly, as we locked up, and went across to the school-house. 'How you manage these days when it comes to buses and mail-vans and geraniums and poppies, I really can't think!'

I switched on the kettle, and washed my hands at the kitchen sink. I was amused to see how seriously Amy had taken this art problem. Her troubled gaze was fixed, unseeing, on the garden.

'Not to mention Chelsea pensioners and lobsters!' she added.

Mr Mawne has paid us his long-awaited visit. The children were delighted to have someone fresh to listen to, and a few of Miss Clare's older children were allowed to come in with their elders to hear his talk on our local birds. He had some excellent coloured pictures, some of which he had drawn and coloured himself, and these he has very generously handed over to Fairacre School. He had to hurry away, as he had promised the vicar that he would help him with the church accounts after an early tea, but he met Mrs Pringle as she was stumping in from the lobby with her broom. The arch smile that I was treated to, enhanced by the loss of her upper plate, broken earlier in the week, was so infuriating in its toad-like hideousness that I could cheerfully have floored her with my weighty inkstand, but alas! – common civility stayed my hand.

'A real gentleman that!' was her comment, as she watched his thin retreating back. 'Wouldn't stop to tea, I'll be bound. Wouldn't want people to start talking!' She bent, wincing, to pick up a milk straw from the floor. Her leg, I noticed, was dragging slightly, as she limped towards the waste-paper basket.

'Not,' she went on, 'that he'd take advantage of anyone!'

I could have wished that Mrs Pringle had used a less dubious phrase. But torn between amusement and irritation, I made my way to the house, there to order some films about birds for the first Wednesday in June, when the mobile film van pays us its next visit, to follow up poor misjudged Mr Mawne's excellent discourse.

This morning, while I was in the playground, directing litter-collecting in an unpleasantly cold wind, Mrs Partridge drew up in the ancient Ford. It was stuffed with spring cabbages, bunches of young carrots, spring onions and lettuces, for Mrs Partridge was on her way to Caxley to put her produce on the W.I. stall in the market.

She told me that Mrs Pratt's father had had a stroke the day before, and that Dr Martin was afraid that he would be completely helpless, perhaps for many months. Mrs Pratt had been obliged to give up the secretaryship of the W.I. and would I be willing to take over if the members agreed to this proposition.

I said cautiously that I would think about it, and let her know tomorrow, but if the meetings were to be held, as they always have been, in the afternoons, it was, of course, out of the question. The vicar's wife said: 'Of course, of course! How could I have forgotten! Well, we'll see what can be done! Perhaps Mrs Moffat might consider it. Linda's at school in the afternoon.' And with that, she drove off.

I collected my class, who had tidied the playground with such zeal that Erle was now dusting the shoe-scraper with his handkerchief, and we returned to the classroom, grateful to be out of the wind.

As the children worked at their arithmetic, my mind wandered back to the problem of running village activities. In Fairacre we manage fairly well owing to the small number of clubs and so on, and to the hard work of Mr and Mrs Partridge who are more than willing to undertake extra duties. But Beech Green, which is a much larger village and has a good bus service to Caxley, has great difficulty in finding people ready to take office in such things as their Women's Institute, the Scouts, and the Sports Club.

The vicar shakes his mild old head about dwindling numbers there and comments sadly on the flourishing men's clubs, glee clubs and the like, which had so many keen supporters twenty or more years ago. But then the buses to Caxley from Fairacre and Beech Green were non-existent and the villagers were thrown on their own resources. Families were much larger, and there were more people to each age-group than there are now. Bands of friends would join the appropriate activity and keep the thing going. Then too, there were leisured people, who willingly gave their time and money to support village affairs, who would come to the rescue when a financial crisis arose, who would lend houses and gardens generously, and would put their ideas and inspirations at the disposal of the village. This invaluable source of village richness is now no more.

When I think of those on Fairacre's and Beech Green's various committees I am struck by the fact that they are, in the main, outsiders, and not natives of the village. Now, why is this? Does it mean that organized activities are not needed by those for whom they are intended? Or does it mean that newcomers to a village enjoy running things, harking back perhaps to their own childhood in other villages, when such affairs were in their heyday? On one thing committee members are united. They lament the fact that they get little or no support from the bulk of the populace. Are they, perhaps, an anachronism in this transition period? Will organized activity come into its own again if and when the villages flourish again, when rural education is improved, and the drift from the countryside is halted?

That there is social intercourse is undeniable. We here in Fairacre are constantly visiting each other for tea parties, morning coffee, evenings at cards, or for watching television programmes, and we are always ready to stop and have delicious friendly gossips over our garden gates.

The 'Beetle and Wedge' is crowded nightly, and this is where the men really meet to exchange news and grumbles, and to relax after work. As P. G. Wodehouse truly says of the tap-room, 'The rich smell of mixed liquors, the gay clamour of carefree men arguing about the weather, the Government, the Royal Family, greyhound racing, the tax on beer, pugilism, religion and the price of bananas – these things are medicine to the bruised soul.'

There is a natural disinclination to go out on winter evenings, and in the summer our gardens occupy a major part of our time. Perhaps church-going, the visits to the pub, the occasional whist drive or fête, and the entertainment of neighbours is all that busy countrymen have time for at this stage of village life. With easy transport to Caxley and television in their own homes to supply entertainment, the people of our two villages certainly seem to find enough to occupy them, and whether one can expect large and flourishing clubs, admirable though they are, is a moot point.

We had a most unnerving accident here today. Eileen Burton, one of the infants, tripped over her own trailing shoe lace and fell like a log on to the metal milk crate. She hit her forehead on the sharp edge, concussing herself, and getting a horrible gash along the right eyebrow.

Joseph Coggs, who, once before, when Miss Clare was taken ill, was a harbinger of woeful tidings, was sent in to tell me of the catastrophe.

'Eileen Burton's busted 'er 'ead,' was his greeting and, as I hastened to the next room I heard him say, with relish to my round-eyed class: ''Er's prob'ly dead!'

You could have heard a pin drop in the infants' room. Miss Clare was mopping the child's head with a swab of damp cotton-wool. It was obvious that she would need stitches in the gash, and that we must get her to hospital.

'I'll get the car out and take her straight to Caxley, if you can manage both classes,' I said.

'Mr Roberts may not have gone to market yet,' said Miss Clare, looking up at the big wall-clock. 'Do you think he'd help?'

Mr Roberts farms next door to the school, is one of the school's managers and always a tower of strength. I sent a message over to the farm by Patrick, and returned to Eileen, still prostrate on the floor, but now with a cushion under her head and a rug over her from the school-house. My class surged ghoulishly in the partition doorway, and were dispatched to their desks with hard words and threats of no-play-for-nuisances.

Eileen began to come round as Patrick returned.

'Mr Roberts has gone, and Mrs Roberts too; so Jim's dad said.' He nodded to Jim in the back row. 'But he says if you wants a stretcher, he's got a hurdle he can send over.'

It was quite apparent that word would already have flown round the village grapevine that Eileen Burton – and probably a couple more – were lying with every limb broken and at the point of death, in Fairacre School.

'I must get a message to her mother,' I said hastily, 'before I take her into Caxley.'

'She's back at the fish-shop,' chorused the children. 'Sutton's, miss! At Caxley, miss! You'd see her there, miss! Market day, she's bound to be there, miss!' continued the helpful babble. I quelled them with that daunting glance which every teacher worth her salt keeps in her armoury, and when peace was restored helped Miss Clare to fasten the bandage round Eileen's head.

She had a drink of water and looked a little better. At last we propped her gently in the car, and I gave my children last-minute admonitions about helping Miss Clare, before setting off for the out-patients' department of Caxley hospital. I did not feel at all happy about leaving Miss Clare, for the shock had obviously upset her, and I hoped that the extra children would not be too much for her.

On the other hand, I told myself as we drove past Beech Green School, how fortunate that there was another teacher to leave in charge. If Fairacre had had a one-teacher school, as so many villages have, what would have happened in a case like this? Either the child must have been given second-best treatment, on the spot, or the services of a kindly neighbour with a car enlisted – as we had hoped to do when we appealed to Mr Roberts – with the possibility of no one being available. Otherwise the school must have been dismissed, while the patient was taken to hospital, or the children given work to do without supervision – both most unsatisfactory arrangements.

A telephone call to the hospital would have been the other alternative, but there are many schools without this service, and the time taken to send the message and to wait for the ambulance to arrive might be considerable. No, I decided, as I drew up at Sutton's fish shop to break the news to Mrs Burton – and to take her with us if possible – I was very glad that I did not have to face all these hazards alone, as so many country head teachers are obliged to do.

May has ended with a cold gusty day, which has shivered the young elm leaves, and whipped the windows with little whirl-winds of up-flung dust, twigs and straws. During afternoon play-time a vicious hail storm sent the children scurrying into school for shelter. It fell heavily, looking like slanting rods of steel, and the playground and adjoining churchyard were quickly white.

From the schoolroom window I could see Mr Willet, who had been trimming the grass paths, sheltering from the storm in the church porch. He had folded the sack, on which he had been kneeling, to make a hood to shelter his head and shoulders from the onslaught which had overtaken him, and as he stood there with his rough brown hood, and his drab trousers bound round the legs to stop them flapping, he might have been a figure from any century.

So must his forefathers have often stood, from Norman times on, dressed in sober serviceable cloth, waiting patiently for the weather to clear, gnarled old hands nursing elbows and long-sighted eyes fixed on the sky above the massive walls of their church.

JUNE

The Whitsun and half-term holiday combined gave Fairacre
School almost a week's break, which I spent, most agreeably,
at Cambridge, with an old college friend. The Backs, enchanting
at any time and season, seemed lovelier than ever, and Evensong
at King's College Chapel exerted the same magic as it did on my
first visit, with the same friend, many years ago.

What a hauntingly lovely place Cambridge is! It has a gentle-
ness, an ambience, a wistful elegance that is unique. A visit to
London, or Oxford, or any other great and ancient city for that
matter, exhilarates and stimulates me; but Cambridge always
gives something more – so deeply stirring, that I could not dismiss
it simply as nostalgia for my long-lost youth. Tentative questioning of other people has confirmed my suspicions, that Cambridge

has a quality, compounded of great skies, shimmering willows and water, ephemeral youth in age-old buildings and the loneliness of its setting in the desolate fens, which evokes a strangely powerful response from those who walk her ways.

The train journey back to Caxley was a tedious cross-country affair lasting over three hours. Luckily Mr and Mrs Annett were shopping near the station and gave me a lift to Fairacre, so that I did not have to wait another hour for the local bus.

The school-house was unnaturally quiet, when the sound of the Annetts' car had died away. I prowled round, savouring the joys of the newly-returned. The clock had stopped at four-twenty, the house was flowerless, and, in the kitchen, the dishcloth hung dry and stiff, arched over the edge of the sink, like a miniature canvas tunnel.

I put the kettle on for that first inspiring cup of tea, and resumed my prowling upstairs. Tibby, curled up comfortably in a patch of sunlight on my eiderdown, stretched out luxuriously, all claws extended, gave a welcoming yowl, half-yawn, half-mew, and resumed her interrupted slumbers again.

Mrs Pringle had been detailed to feed the cat, and when I returned to my singing kettle, I noticed that every morsel of food had been used. As I had left an imposing variety of delicacies, including cold meat, cold fish, dried cat-food and two tins of another variety much appreciated by Tibby, as well as half a pint of milk daily, my companion had obviously been living like a lord, and I could see that I should have the unenviable job of restoring her to a more humble way of life.

With all the windows in the house opened, I sat down with my tea tray and thought how lovely it was to be back. I feel like a sword in a scabbard, I told myself, and instantly decided that a sword was much too dashing. Perhaps a cup, hanging again on its accustomed hook on the kitchen dresser, would be a better simile. At any rate, to be a village schoolmistress, with a fine border of pinks just breaking before me, and the sound of rooks cawing overhead, seemed a very right and proper thing to be, and I envied no man.

The second half of the term has started in a blaze of sunshine. Yesterday the temperature was up in the eighties, and we had the schoolroom door propped open with the biggest upturned flower-pot that Mr Willet could find. The green paint on the doors and windows of Fairacre School has long since faded to a soft silvery green, like a cabbage leaf with a fine bloom on it. It is a most beautiful colour, and I regret that we are due to be repainted in the summer holidays. The managers have not decided on the new colour, I hear, but Mr Willet tells me that Mr Roberts, the farmer, favours a deep beetroot, Colonel Wesley 'a sensible chocolate,' and the vicar is pressing for green once again. I am doing a little subtle propaganda each time I see the vicar, and supporting his claim, as the least objectionable of the three colours.

The children spend their play-time and dinner hour in the shade of the elm trees, at the corner of the playground. The heat thrown up from our poorly-asphalted playground is unbelievable, and the two buckets of drinking water, which Mr Willet carries over from my kitchen daily, have been increased to three.

The distant clatter and hum of Mr Roberts' grass cutter at work, is a real high summer sound, and while the children loll in their desks, fidgeting as the backs of their knees stick uncomfortably to the edge of their wooden seats, they can hear the swifts screaming as they flash by St Patrick's spire next door, and the drone of a captive bee who has blundered through the Gothic window.

The flowers have burst into bloom in this heat, and the cottage gardens blaze with irises, lilies, cornflowers and peonies. Miss Clare brought a bunch of her white jasmine to the infants' room and Jimmy Waites brought me a bouquet of roses, but it is a pity to pick these lovely things while the weather is so phenomenally hot, for they dropped in a day.

I have never seen the elder bushes so covered in flowers, and, until this year, had never realized what beautiful trees they are with their hundreds of floating white faces, all tilted at the same angle, each composed of a myriad tiny flowers, each flower having five petals star-wise, with five golden stamens projecting above and looking like a *tremblant* piece of jewellery. The bushes in this summer heat are dazzling. Their luminous quality, compounded of their massed moons against young green leaves, which Sir Alfred Munnings has caught so brilliantly in paint, has never struck me so forcibly as during this vivid spell of weather.

The road through Fairacre, which the rural district council saw fit to tar and gravel a few weeks ago much to the joy of the schoolchildren – who arrived late because 'we was helping the steam-roller man' – is now a sticky black mess, which is ruinous to shoes, and is driving all the dogs in the neighbourhood mad, as the tar squelches between their paws.

Last night, as I returned from taking Miss Clare some gooseberries, I rounded the sharp corner into the village and nearly ran down Joseph Coggs and his two little sisters, who were squatting in the middle of the road, popping tar bubbles with leisurely forefingers.

The car screeched to an abrupt stop, and I lashed the amazed trio with my tongue. Joseph was as shaken as I was, and inclined to be tearful.

'We wasn't doing no harm,' he faltered, underlip quivering.

'You wasn't doing no good either,' I retorted wrathfully, letting the handbrake go – and it wasn't until I had changed into third gear, and was cooling down slightly, that my ungrammatical echo burst fully upon me.

Amy spent Saturday afternoon and evening with me, as James had been called away on a mysterious errand connected with the firm's business, which necessitated absence from home for the whole of the week-end.

As we sat in the shade of the apple trees, topping and tailing gooseberries for bottling, Amy surprised me by asking: 'Tell me, what do you do with your time when you're not in school?'

'Why, this sort of thing!' I replied, holding up a whiskery giant, 'I have to do all the things that other women do, I suppose. I wash my clothes, and iron them, and bake cakes, and mend things, and fetch in coal and clean the windows—' I could have continued the list indefinitely, but I could see that that was not really what Amy wanted to know. How did I use my leisure, and more particularly, was I happy here, living alone – a solitary woman, exposed to the interested gaze of my village neighbours and with virtually no private life of my own? Did I ever crave for city pleasures, for crowds, for shops, for excitement? Would I like to change my way of life? Wasn't I in danger of becoming a vegetable?

I don't know whether Amy believed me when I answered truthfully, that I was completely happy; for single women living alone like me – and there are thousands of us up and down the country – are often the object of pity and speculation. Amy had voiced the unspoken queries of many married people that I knew.

Amy said sternly that with the world in the state it was, and the misery that surrounded us on every side, she was surprised to hear me say that I was happy. To which jeremiad I replied sturdily that I knew just as much about the world's miseries as she did, but still remained incorrigibly content, and that nobody would find me apologetic for being so.

'But don't you feel you ought to be more ambitious?' persisted Amy, slightly nettled. 'Do you want to do nothing better than be schoolmistress at Fairacre School?'

'It suits me,' I said equably. Amy said: 'Tchah!' which I'd always hoped to hear somebody say one day, and flicked tops and tails off with a vicious snapping of scissors. I was mildly sorry that I had riled her, but I thought over our conversation when she had departed in the glorious car, and came to the conclusion that we should never see things in the same light. For Amy is the victim of today's common malaise – too much self-analysis; while I, finding myself remarkably uninteresting, am only too pleased to observe others and the natural objects around me. Thus I am spared the pangs of self-reproach, and, as my lot is cast in pleasant places, find endless cause for happiness and amusement.

One of Mr Roberts' calves strayed into the garden last night. The only damage it did was to lean heavily against a wooden post which supports a rose tree, while it scratched its back, leaving the post at a sad angle.

Mr Willet and I put it straight during play-time. I held it nervously, while Mr Willet, perched on a kitchen chair, smote it mightily on the top with a mallet. At every massive shudder I expected either to have my hand mangled or for Mr Willet to crash through the chair seat, but luck was with us.

'There!' he said at length, surveying his handiwork from aloft. He suddenly caught sight of someone in the lane, invisible to me on my lower plane.

'Now who might that be?' he pondered, eyes screwed up against the sun.

'The vicar?' I hazarded, picking a few pinks.

Mr Willet was applying all the fierce concentration of a villager confronted with a stranger. 'No. This chap's got a new panama hat on.'

'Mr Roberts?'

'No, no. I knows 'ee,' Mr Willet said testily. Silence fell. I picked a few more pinks, while Mr Willet remained rooted to the kitchen chair.

'Must be a gen'leman,' observed Mr Willet. 'Blows 'is nose on a 'andkerchief.' I found this social nicety very interesting, but did not like to pursue it further.

'He's coming this way,' continued my look-out. 'Why—' his voice fell an octave with disappointment, 'it's only that chap Mawne.' He checked suddenly, and added hastily: 'But there, I expect you'll be pleased to see him. You run along, miss. I'll put the chair back. You don't want to keep him waiting.'

Mr Mawne had called to see if I would go with him to the Caxley Orchestral Society's concert next week. He has tickets for Wednesday evening's performance, and I have offered to drive him in. The Annetts and other friends will be playing, and it should be a very pleasant evening.

Exactly twenty minutes after accepting Mr Mawne's invitation, Mrs Pringle arrived with a basket full of cleaning rags to store in her special cupboard in the lobby. She gave me an alarmingly coy smirk.

'Enjoy yourself on Wednesday,' said Mrs Pringle.

So much for Fairacre's efficient bush telegraph.

Miss Clare, Mr Willet and I were gossiping in the empty class-room after school today. Mr Willet was sitting on the old desk against the side wall.

'See this?' he said to Miss Clare. She went over and peered down at the desk, where his horny forefinger was pressed. There, carved in the ribby top were the letters A.G.W.

'Alfred George Willet,' said the owner, with pride. 'Done 'em in poetry once. Chipped away careful under my book. We was supposed to be learning some bit about Westminster Bridge with a dull soul passing by. Old Hope was a great one for poetry, wasn't he?'

Miss Clare, who is a few years older than Mr Willet, agreed. She was a pupil teacher in the same infants' room, when Mr Hope was headmaster at Fairacre. I have heard many tales of this interesting man, who used to live in the house I now occupy.

He was village schoolmaster for several years. His life was tragic, for his only child, Harriet, died at the age of twelve; his wife fell ill and he became addicted to drink. Soon after the First World War he left Fairacre and took a post in the north. He wrote verse himself, and his pupils were set inordinate amounts of poetry to learn weekly. I have often heard the older people in Fairacre tell of his powers of story-telling, and his pupils produced a play by Shakespeare annually, in the vicarage garden, no mean accomplishment in a small, unbookish village.

I should like to have known Mr Hope, that sad gifted man, whose small nervous handwriting fills so many pages in an earlier school log-book in my desk drawer. He was thought much of, but he was not beloved. As far as I can gather from latter-day comments, he was feared by many of his pupils, and looked upon as 'a crank' by their parents. One rarely hears of pity for him, which seems strange to me. I was interested to hear Miss Clare and Mr Willet exchanging memories as they surveyed the youthful Willet's handiwork of many years ago.

'Fine old temper he had,' observed Mr Willet. ' "Out in the lobby, boy," he shouted at me, when he saw this. And out I went, touched my toes and got six. You wants to try a bit more of that, miss,' he added, in a half jocular way that did not cloak his inner belief in the adequacy of Mr Hope's methods.

Miss Clare shook her white head slowly. 'There was too much of it, Alfred,' she said gravely. 'You bigger boys treated that far-too-frequent caning as a huge joke. You had to – otherwise you were afraid that your companions would think you cowardly. In fact it had two bad effects. Its frequency undermined Mr Hope's authority in the end – I'm sure that was one of the reasons that took him so often to "The Beetle". And secondly, the little ones in my room were terrified of him. They heard the shoutings and the canings, and I know for a fact that they dreaded him coming into the infants' room.'

'I don't think they minded that much,' said Mr Willet. 'We was all used to a tight rein then – big and little. Remember how we used to sit on these forms, with no backs to rest against? Got spoke to pretty sharp too if we sagged a bit.'

'It was quite wrong,' said Miss Clare firmly, 'to expect children to sit as they did then; and as for folding their arms across their backs – well, I told Mr Hope flatly, that I would not train the babies to sit so. It was one of the few things I did have words about. Mostly, he was very reasonable and helped me a great deal with the preparation of lessons.'

'Never made no friends, did 'ee?' mused Mr Willet, fingering his stained moustache. 'Looked down on us working class, and tried to keep in with the gentry too much.'

'Oh come,' protested Miss Clare, 'I'm sure he didn't look down on anyone! He found his home and family, and the school-house garden and his books and poetry, filled his free time. As for the gentry, don't forget that those that he had dealings with were his school managers, and it was necessary to see quite a bit of them, as a matter of school routine. No, you're not quite fair to Mr Hope.'

Mr Willet lumbered off the desk lid that had set so many far-off things stirring, and unconsciously summed up the enigma of Mr Hope.

'Fact is, I never understood the chap. He was a fish out of water in Fairacre, and to us folk – well, he smelt a bit odd.'

Mrs Pringle collects our metal milk-tops 'for blind dogs,' as she herself asserts. Despite careful explanation on my part to the children, I am quite sure that they imagine that Mrs Pringle purchases spectacles in various sizes to fit myopic pekes or bloodhounds, as this phrase is in general use. It was while she was stuffing these tops into her shiny black bag, that she told me a little more about education in Fairacre over forty years ago.

'Not all this playing about when I was in the infants' room,' she said flatly, 'we was kept down to pot-hooks and hangers on our slates, and then on paper, until we could do 'em absolutely perfect. Time I was six I could write a good copper-plate hand better than your top ones can these days.' Even allowing for Mrs Pringle's self-esteem, and the rosy veil which covers distant years, I could well believe this assertion. I have come across old exercise books, and 'fair copies' which have won prizes in their time, and certainly the standard of penmanship was far ahead of anything that I can get my own pupils to produce.

In arithmetic and reading too Mrs Pringle's generation, as a whole, reached a high standard, rather earlier than the present Fairacre pupils. Of course, there were the ineducable and, I suspect, several rather backward children who were dumped with the ineducables, and might have done better with more individual help which they would have had these days. Discipline was rigid, and almost all the hours of the timetable were devoted to the three R's in some form. I do not regret the somewhat lower standard of early attainment in the three R's – except for the modern *laissez faire* attitude to reading which is a personal hobby-horse of mine and on which I entered the lists against Mr Arnold recently – for there is no doubt that today's children have a much wider and better balanced grounding. Physical training, personal hygiene, school milk and meals, the medical services and better school conditions have all contributed to the wonderful improvement in their physique. The timetable embraces hand-work of every description, music – both to listen to and of their own making with the percussion band and singing – educational visits and much valuable material put out by the schools broad-casting service and the mobile film units, which range the countryside.

There is no doubt that the children today are much more responsible, friendly and alert, and though their ability and dexterity in the basic three R's may not compare favourably with their parents' at, say, the age of eight years, yet I am positive that they become as proficient in the end, and have a multitude of other interests in addition.

What I do feel that the modern child lacks, when compared with the earlier generation, is concentration, and the sheer dogged grit to carry a long job through. Teaching through play-ing is right. It is, in fact, the only way to teach young children. But as they get older they find that any attainment needs application, and fun alone will not bring completion to a project. This is the danger-point. The older generation, resigned to humdrum methods and a whacking here and there if there were any marked falling-off from hard work, got almost all their satisfaction from seeing the job completed and perhaps a word or two of approval as a titbit. They were geared, as it were, to low returns for much effort.

The child today, used as he is to much praise and encouragement, finds it much more difficult to keep going as his task gets progressively long. Helping children to face up to a certain amount of drudgery, cheerfully and energetically, is one of the biggest problems that teachers, in these days of ubiquitous entertainment, have to face in our schools; and the negative attitude, in so many homes, of 'How-much-money-can-I-get-for-how-little-work?' does nothing to help them in their daily battle.

I have been forced to have a day off from school – the first since I have taught here – as I have been the prey of rending toothache.

It began last night, soon after I had got to bed, and recurred every twenty minutes with awful intensity. I spent the night roaming the house, completely demoralized with pain, and quite powerless to overcome it with aspirin, oil of cloves, hot bottles or any other comforts.

It made me realize how much one's mind is at the mercy of one's physical well-being, as at times I felt quite demented. My admiration for people who withhold information under torture has increased ten-fold since this ghastly night, for I am certain that even the threat of such pain would be enough to make me blab out any secret, and even to make up further disclosures if I felt that these might mitigate the pain at all. Truly, a most shattering revelation.

My kind dentist in Caxley sees emergency cases at nine-thirty each morning, and having explained the position to Miss Clare, who was all sympathy and understanding, I left her in charge, drove to Caxley and presented my woebegone visage for inspection. Mr Chubb, that angel of mercy, decreed 'a little snooze, and they'll never hurt again.' Never was a patient so eager to breathe in gas, and within an hour I was back in Fairacre, minus two back teeth, and brimming with thankfulness.

Miss Clare insisted on my going to bed, brought me hot milk, and tucked me in. I am ashamed to admit that I slept like a top from eleven o'clock till four. I awoke to hear the children whooping and laughing as they ran out of school, and to hear the clock on St Patrick's spire striking. A most unusual day for a headmistress. Most assuredly, the blessing of good health, which I blithely take for granted, will be more esteemed by me in the future.

The vicar called in to bring me news of the Scripture examination which is to take place next week. This is an annual affair, under the auspices of the diocese, and usually a clergyman from a nearby village examines the children orally in the morning, and the afternoon is given as a holiday. The children usually enjoy this departure from school routine, and we have had some very interesting talks and sound teaching from most of our visiting examiners. This year, an old friend of Mr Partridge's, recently returned from Africa, and newly settled in the neighbourhood, has been selected by the board to visit Fairacre and to donate the Bishop's Bibles to the most worthy pupils here.

He also brought an invitation to tea from Mrs Partridge, so that after school, I put on one of my new frocks made by Mrs Moffat, and made my way to the vicarage.

The Gloire de Dijon rose which scrambles over the front of the vicarage was a mass of bloom, and bumbling with bees. I remembered how much Mrs Bradley had admired it at the fête last year, and enquired after the old lady's health.

'Excellent, excellent!' said the vicar plummily, through a mouthful of rich fruit cake. 'Told me to burn my gloves! Just think of that!' He beamed delightedly at the idea. Privately, I was in complete agreement with the irascible Mrs Bradley's direction, for the vicar's aged leopard-skin gloves moult far too often on my own desk for my liking.

'I laughed,' said the vicar, repeating the process heartily, 'I just laughed! "They'll do many a winter yet," I told the dear old lady. She will have her little joke, you know.'

'She has her likes and dislikes, as we all have,' commented Mrs Partridge, filling tea-cups placidly.

'Loves and hates, I should have said, in Mrs Bradley's case,' I added. 'She is a person of strong feelings.'

'Who isn't?' said Mrs Partridge, stirring her cup lazily. 'Even the mildest person has some particular private hatreds locked up like tigers inside him.'

'Oh come, my dear,' protested the vicar, and rushing in where angels feared to tread, 'I'm quite positive that you, for instance, have no such violent passions.'

'On the contrary,' replied Mrs Partridge, with the greatest composure, 'I have two great ramping, roaring hatreds, of which, happily, you are unaware, Gerald.'

The vicar's gentle countenance clouded over, and his mouth fell slightly open. His wife surveyed him blandly.

'They are – cruelty to animals and spitting,' she announced with decision, passing the sugar basin to her astounded husband.

'My dear! Really, my dear—' stammered the poor fellow. And so flustered was he, at his wife's shocking revelation, that he put a large lump of sugar into his mouth instead of his cup, and crunched unhappily while our conversation turned to the happier subject of the pageant.

Mrs Pringle, it appears, has taken umbrage because some malicious busybody saw fit to report Arthur Coggs's comments on Mrs Pringle's probable appearance in armour. A much bowdlerized version of Arthur Coggs's remarks was to the effect that Mrs P. would resemble a so-and-so bullet-proof tank and that she would be enough to make a cat laugh. This insult Mrs Pringle retailed to Mrs Partridge, and declared herself not only a deserter from the Ancient Britons but hinted at a possible removal from the low company of Fairacre altogether, drawing a gloomy picture of the village's future without her indispensable support.

Mrs Partridge had not batted an eyelid evidently, and had soothed the savage breast with honeyed words. Mrs Pringle had allowed herself to be persuaded against such a dire decision and returned to her cottage with honour avenged and an armful of flowers.

'I've asked her to count heads for us at the outing,' went on Mrs Partridge. 'She loves to be in charge of something, and Gerald finds counting two busloads of fidgety people almost impossible.'

'Where is it to be this year?' I asked. We have an annual church outing comprising the school children and their mothers, the choir, bellringers, and anyone else remotely connected with St Patrick's.

'Barrisford again,' said Mrs Partridge. 'It takes a lot of beating, and Bunce's always do such a good tea. Gerald says almost everyone has put Barrisford on the list in the church porch. Oh yes – and another piece of good news! Mr Mawne has asked if he can come with us! Now, isn't that nice?'

She smiled at me with a mixture of triumph and gratification which I found almost insupportable.

'Poor man!' she continued happily, 'he leads such a lonely life. So sad that he has lost his wife.'

'When did she die?' I asked.

Mrs Partridge looked momentarily disconcerted. 'Well, do you know, I've never quite found out. I gathered from John Parr that Mr Mawne had been alone for several years.'

'He has a portrait of her in his rooms,' vouchsafed the vicar. 'A handsome gel.'

'Of course he never mentions her,' went on Mrs Partridge, 'but naturally he wouldn't, would he?'

' "Thoughts that do often lie too deep for tears," ' quoted the vicar sadly, and was about to add a gusty sigh, which luckily took a wrong turning, and was transformed into a mighty sneeze, which considerably relieved the melancholy of the moment.

'Well, we must all do what we can to cheer him up,' said Mrs Partridge briskly, in her president-of-the-W.I. manner. 'I have promised him a seat by you, so that you can both enjoy a really long chat on the way to Barrisford. You do him a lot of good, you know.'

I felt quite unequal to responding to this alarming speech except in strong terms which I knew I should later regret; so I made my farewells as civilly as I could under such provocation, and returned through the golden evening to my own quiet house, debating meanwhile which was harder to bear – Mrs Pringle's roguish innuendos or Mrs Partridge's business-like and unwelcome forwarding of my affairs.

The Moffats are taking their summer holiday early this year

which means that Linda has to miss a fortnight at school. The little kitten has grown into a bigger cat than my Tibby, and I offered to feed him while they were away. Mrs Moffat was delighted, and refused to take her proper payment for a skirt she had altered for me.

'Shall I give you the key? Or shall I put it in the usual hiding place?' she asked. 'We always put it behind the oil-can in the shed.'

I decided to take the key with me, and walked home thinking of all the hiding places in Fairacre that I knew for our village keys.

Mrs Willet puts hers under the outside doormat. Mrs Pringle, who has a weighty monster which looks as though it belongs to Canterbury Cathedral, lodges hers on a beam under her front thatch. Miss Clare hangs hers by a loop of string inside her coal shed. Mrs Waites, in Tyler's Row, hides hers under a large white shell beside her front door; while slatternly Mrs Coggs next door puts hers under the old bucket that serves for a dustbin. Mrs Partridge drops hers inside the left gumboot of a pair that stand in her porch as a challenge to the weather, and my own is lodged on a jutting brick by the back door.

We all know each other's key places and it says much for Fairacre's honesty that there is remarkably little pilfering. If anyone's house were to be broken into the first cry would be: 'A stranger must've done it!'

The day of the Scripture examination dawned hot and cloudless. The children arrived looking fresh and expectant. Their mothers always take especial pains to dress them well for 'the Bishop's exam,' which they remember as an important event from their own schooldays. In many a Fairacre home the 'Bishop's Bible,' presented so many years ago, has pride of place on the front parlour table.

The boys had smoothed down their locks with wet brushes, and even Erle's crew-cut shone with some strange unguent. His normally vivid shirt had been exchanged for one of dazzling whiteness, and he presented a sober and sedate picture of American childhood. Even the Coggs family appeared to have met soap and water in a rather less perfunctory manner than was usual, and I felt sure that our visitor, even if he found our godliness a little deficient, could not find fault with our cleanliness.

At ten o'clock footsteps were heard and men's voices. Mr Partridge ushered in his friend, the Reverend James Enderby, the children leapt to their feet, and introductions were made.

Our examiner was in exact contrast to Mr Partridge, who is tall, thin and very gentle. Mr Enderby was a stocky man, short-necked and red-faced, and walked about the room with impatient strides. The children watched, fascinated.

Mr Partridge made his farewells, regretting that he could not persuade his friend to stay to lunch, and assuring him that the eleven-thirty bus to Caxley would connect comfortably with the twelve-fifteen bus, which was to carry him to a ruridecanal conference at the other end of the county.

'Now,' said Mr Enderby briskly, as the door closed behind the vicar's linen summer jacket, 'we'll put this where we can see it.' He pulled a large silver watch, with a fussy tick, from his pocket, and propped it up against the inkstand.

After a short prayer, during which I noticed many a half-shut eye peeping at this unusually business-like visitor, the children were settled in their seats, I retreated to a chair in the corner, and the Scripture examination began.

Our syllabus had included the story of Joseph in the Old Testament and John the Baptist in the New, and it was these two particular stories that Mr Enderby concentrated on.

He gave an admirably lucid and terse résumé of Joseph's history to refresh his hearers' memories, and then began more detailed questioning. It was doubtful to me if many of the children had followed his swift account clearly, for they are used to a much slower tempo, and in any case were somewhat over-awed by the visitor and becoming drowsy with the growing heat. Ernest and Eric, however, struggled nobly with the questions, and I wished that Linda Moffat had been present to answer with her quick intelligence, instead of being far away on the sunny beach at Bournemouth. Several of the younger ones slid lower in their seats and allowed the fire of questioning to go over their heads.

The door, propped open with Mr Willet's flower-pot, gave a

glimpse of the summer world outside. The distant downs shimmered in a blue haze, and the air was murmurous with myriad insects' wings. From my garden came the scent of pinks, and on the desk, hard by Mr Enderby's watch, a rose dropped fleshy petals now and again, with a little pattering. I watched Tibby swing indolently across the playground and collapse in the cool grass beneath the elm trees. A blackbird, motionless nearby, with beak half agape, watched him too, with no fear – confident that such heat killed all enmity.

Meanwhile the rapid questioning continued.

'And who was it ruled in Egypt at this time?'

There was a sluggish silence.

'Come now!' Mr Enderby glanced at his watch. 'Come along. Who ruled in Egypt?'

Patrick, in the front row, stirred uneasily.

'God?' he hazarded.

'No, no, not God,' said Mr Enderby with firm kindness. Silence fell again, and with a second glance at his time-piece, Mr Enderby was obliged to answer his question himself.

'Pharaoh. The ruler of Egypt was called Pharaoh. Who remembers that?'

As one man, Fairacre School raised sticky, and untruthful, hands.

'Good, good! Well, who remembers the name of the Egyptian man that Joseph worked for?'

Silence fell again. In the far distance a cuckoo called, and another rose-petal fluttered to join the pink shells on the desk.

'It begins with the same letter as "Pharaoh",' urged Mr Enderby.

Joseph Coggs let out a mighty yawn.

Ernest, who really was trying, said in a perplexed voice: 'Farouk, sir?' He was, very properly, ignored.

Mr Enderby's questing finger roamed around the class like a searchlight, but no one ventured any further revelation. He pounced again on poor Patrick.

'God?' said Patrick once more, with doubt, this time.

'*Potiphar*,' said Mr Enderby loudly. '*Joseph worked for Potiphar*.' He cast me a look, more in sorrow than in anger, and started afresh with the New Testament.

The clock crept on to eleven-fifteen.

The questions were as brisk as ever, but the answers came with increasing languor. Joseph Coggs had given up all attempts at listening, and with his head pillowed on his arms, and his eyes half-shut, hummed a tuneless lullaby to himself.

Ernest was our only mainstay, supported at times by Erle who was treating the occasion with unaccustomed solemnity, like some chance sightseer who, thrusting cheerfully at a cathedral door, finds himself in the midst of choral eucharist.

'And what sort of man was John the Baptist?' enquired Mr Enderby, of this freckle-faced listener.

'I guess he kinda reckoned the people needed noos, and he was the one who brought 'em the noos,' said Erle sagely. Mr Enderby smiled his approval.

'And who was he bringing news of?' persisted Mr Enderby.

Ernest opened his mouth to speak and shut it again. Erle was now grovelling under his desk for a dropped pencil. The rest of Fairacre School would have been better off in their beds for all the interest they were taking. Poor Patrick again fell prey to that probing finger. Jerked back from some private daydream, he gave his only answer.

'God?' he repeated.

Mr Enderby curbed his exasperation laudably and said: 'In a way. Yes, in a way.' Ernest, emboldened, gave the right answer, and all was well. I felt rather sorry for Patrick. His stock answer, so safe and so often right, had not stood him in good stead this morning.

At two minutes before the half-hour Mr Enderby congratulated the children and me on a good year's work, on their alert answering and their courteous behaviour. He promised to send the Bishop's Bible to Ernest, who was pink with delight, and stammered polite thanks. Mr Enderby then hurried away to catch his bus.

'Please, miss, can I have a drink of water?' pleaded Joseph Coggs, as the footsteps died away.

His cry was taken up by a thirsty chorus. The long-awaited Scripture examination was over for another year and Fairacre School looked forward after all its exertions, to a glorious half-holiday, amidst all the country delights of a June afternoon.

JULY

Arthur Coggs has been in trouble again, and the village is having a great deal of secret enjoyment at his expense. Mr Willet was my informant, punctuating his account with so many guffaws that I found myself roaring with laughter, long before the point of the story had been told me.

It appears that Jim Waites had been missing chicken food from his store at the end of the garden at Tyler's Row, on several occasions, and he strongly suspected that Arthur Coggs helped himself, under cover of darkness, to a few handfuls of corn and bran for his own bedraggled hens, that led a miserably-confined existence in a ramshackle run next door.

Jim Waites kept the chicken food in an old air-raid shelter. In the musty darkness bicycles jostled garden tools, ropes of onions swung overhead, firewood was stacked in one corner, and other awkward objects, too cumbersome to find a home in the little cottage, here found a resting place.

The shelter had been erected at the beginning of the war by a don from Cambridge who had taken over the cottage for his wife and young family. Two things keep his memory fresh in Fairacre – the incredible speed with which he had completed this air-raid shelter, and the looks of his progeny.

'Never seed a chap rush at a job so,' Mr Rogers, at the forge, told me once. 'Skinny little bit he was too, all teeth and glasses, but his arms was like flails waving round. One minute there was an ol' 'edge there – next minute this 'ere contraption. Cor! 'E fair flung 'isself at work, that chap!'

Mrs Pringle supplied details of his family.

'Four of them under six, all as thin as scarecrows, with braces on their teeth – those as 'ad 'em – and their clothes! Them open sandals, all weathers, and skirts and jerseys you'd have thought twice about sending to the jumble. Fed on health foods they was – and no advertisement for them neither. And she was a funny lot too. Said she'd been to an Economical School up in London somewhere, and she didn't have no objection to her kids playing with the village ones.' Mrs Pringle bristled at the memory, her three chins wobbling aggressively.

'I sorted her out proper. "Perhaps our village women," I says to her haughty, "has some objection to *our* kids playing with *yours*." She didn't like that, I could see! Why, if she washed once a month it was a miracle, and then the whites was as black as a crow – and I know for a fact she never done no boiling! Shameful, she were!'

One night recently, Jim Waites had been on the look-out for his shady neighbour. He had settled himself comfortably on an upturned wheelbarrow, behind the ivy-covered privy at the end of his garden, and patiently surveyed the stars above, as he listened for any suspicious sounds. In his pocket, the heavy key of the shelter door, which he had looked out, lay against his thigh.

The regulars, including Arthur Coggs, had returned from 'The Beetle,' when, about half an hour later, Jim Waites heard some furtive rustlings among the elder bushes which now overhung the building, and the soft clanking of a pail, which, presumably, was to carry home the stolen goods. Jim heard the scrape of the door on the stone floor, and cautiously peered round the corner of the privy. A flickering torchlight hovered about inside the shelter.

Swiftly, Jim Waites ran down the three rickety steps, drew the door to, and locked it securely. The torch had been switched off hastily, and there was no sound from the dark interior. Whistling jauntily, swinging the key round and round on his finger, Jim Waites made his way to bed.

He said nothing to his pretty wife about the matter until three o'clock in the morning. She had woken him saying: 'Jim, Jim! There's someone trying to get in! Listen!'

From a distance came the sound of heavy thumping, an occasional crash and outburst of invective. Arthur Coggs was getting belligerent and having thought up a story – thin enough, but he hoped plausible – was ready to bluff his way back to everyday life.

'Go to sleep,' counselled Jim Waites. 'It's only that fool Arthur Coggs. I've left him to cool his heels in the shelter.' He told his wife the story, and although she was worried about the poor wife next door, she recognized the rough justice of her husband's action, and even began to enjoy the distant rumblings from the end of the garden.

'Serves him right,' said Mrs Waites, plumping up her pillow, 'Cathy and me took a week to glean that corn. That'll teach him a lesson.' She slept again.

Mrs Coggs next door had also heard the rumpus, and knew instantly that her husband was the cause. She had known of these illicit excursions, although no words had passed, and she wondered now what she should do. The idea that Jim Waites had purposely trapped Arthur did not occur to her. She imagined that the door had blown to, imprisoning the malefactor, and she trembled at the thought of the Waites next door being awakened, and investigating the disturbance.

Should she creep down and release him before the Waites discovered him? A proper wife wouldn't think twice about it. A distant roar, as of a caged tiger, prompted a more prudent course. Many a bruise on poor Mrs Coggs' unlovely and neglected person had been bestowed there by her husband's heavy fist, when in just such a temper as he was now. Best let him cool off, thought Mrs Coggs, with seven years of married wisdom behind her. He put himself in there, didn't he? Well then, he could get himself out! Meanwhile, she stretched herself luxuriously amidst the frowsy blankets, enjoying the unwonted pleasure of plenty of room in the bed. Time enough to face the trouble when it came, she told her uneasy conscience grimly. There would always be plenty of that as long as she was Arthur Coggs' wife. She fell into a troubled sleep.

At half-past six she rose. All was quiet, and the summer sun warmed the dilapidated thatch of the cottages in Tyler's Row. She crept down the creaking stairs, lit the primus stove to heat the kettle for tea, put a packet of cereal on the table for the children's breakfast, and was about to set off for the shelter, when she heard the kitchen door of the Waites' house slam, and Jim Waites' cheerful voice.

'I'll feed the hens for you. Got to go down!'

Mrs Coggs was torn between fear and curiosity. The latter won. Snatching up a bowl of kitchen scraps, she too hurried down the garden to feed her own chickens. Unseen by Jim Waites, who was descending the steps to the shelter, she prudently hid behind her own hen-house, where she could hear what transpired.

Jim Waites pushed back the door, and stood, key in hand, smiling at his sullen prisoner. 'Had a good night, Arthur?' he asked.

A torrent of abuse greeted this mild opening. Arthur Coggs had had ample time to think up his story, and he presented it with all the righteous indignation of the born liar.

'I'll 'ave the law on you!' he blustered. 'I come round 'ere last night to see if my Leghorn had strayed in. Didn't want her eating up your corn.'

'Did you find her?' queried the unruffled Jim.

'No, I never!' said Arthur shortly, 'but her's missing. Only Leghorn I got too. Bet that ol' dog fox that's bin around has 'ad 'er.' He warmed again to his original theme, all the more annoyed because of this side issue which had distracted him. 'But you've no call to lock folks up all night – innocent folks too. What about me poor wife?'

'Glad to see the back of you for a bit, I daresay,' rejoined the other equably. The listener behind the neighbouring hen-house concurred silently. 'What did you bring that pail for? To carry your hen in?'

'If you must know,' said Arthur with cold dignity, 'I brought a bit of corn round to try and tempt her home!'

Jim Waites burst into loud laughter.

'You're the biggest liar I've ever met! Why didn't you tell me this yarn last night, when I turned the key? You was mighty quiet then! Hoping you could sneak out when I'd hopped it, eh? Found you couldn't, and worked up this rigmarole. There's not a soul in Fairacre will believe that lot of nonsense, Arthur Coggs, and you know it. Clear off home, will 'ee, and don't come in here pinching again, or *I'll* have the law on *you* next time!'

Still muttering dark threats, his tousled neighbour emerged into the sunlight, and pushed through the ragged dividing hedge, to his own cinder path.

'And take your rubbish with you,' shouted Jim Waites, who had just glimpsed his wife at the back door, and decided he must put on a more masterful display. The bucket sailed over the hedge, landing with a clatter among the squawking hens. Jim Waites saw the flutter of Mrs Coggs' crumpled skirt among the flying wings.

'Got your Leghorn there safely, Mrs Coggs?' he bellowed mischievously.

'Yes, thank you,' said Mrs Coggs timidly.

'You keep your trap shut!' growled her husband furiously, and stumped towards the kitchen door.

The Coggs entered together. The kettle had boiled over. The primus poured forth a hissing cloud of noxious paraffin vapour. Joseph Coggs stood by the table, his fist inside the cereal packet. He watched his father stamp blackly up the stairs.

'Where's Dad bin?' he asked his grim-faced mother.

'Making a fool of himself,' said she, giving herself the satisfaction of raising her voice so that it could be clearly heard above. It was one of her rare moments of triumph.

The first Saturday in July was set aside for Fairacre's combined Sunday School and Choir Outing, as usual. Miss Clare was unable to come with us this year as she had promised to go with her sister to visit an old friend, who had come from Scotland to spend a few days in the neighbourhood.

The vicar fluttered round the two coaches, which were drawn up in front of the church, like a mother-hen with straying chicks. Mrs Pringle, swollen with majesty as head-counter-for-the-day, had taken up her stance at the top of the steps inside the coach, and seriously impeded the entrances and exits of the party.

'If,' she boomed heavily, the cherries on her straw hat trembling, 'you was to sit quiet and steady in your own seats, it would be an insistence to me counting.' This reproof was ignored, as squeaking children changed places, excited parents bobbed up and down to put things on the rack, and relatives and well-wishers from the other coach constantly appeared, vanished, reappeared, and generally made themselves as ubiquitous as possible. As Mrs Partridge had foreseen, when bestowing this office on Mrs Pringle, it was going to keep that lady very busy.

Mr Mawne, looking vaguely about him, was the last to appear, and Mrs Partridge led him triumphantly along our crowded coach to the empty seat beside me. The hum of noisy chattering stopped suddenly, a pregnant silence taking its place, while knowing looks and nudges were exchanged.

'There we are!' said Mrs Partridge in the comforting tone of one returning a lost baby to its mother. It says much for civilization that Mr Mawne and I were capable of greeting each other with smiles, under such provocation.

'Thirty-two!' bellowed Mrs Pringle from the front. 'Thirty-two! Right?' she poked her head out of the door to shout this to the vicar, who stood on the steps of the coach in front.

'It should be thirty-three, dear Mrs Pringle!' the vicar's pulpit-voice fluted back.

A hubbub of counting began in our coach, half the travellers standing up, and the other half begging them to sit down. The din was appalling.

'I makes it thirty-one now!' said Mr Willet in a desperate tone. He looked uncomfortably spruce in his Sunday dark-blue serge, and his face shone red above a tight white collar.

'I was on the floor,' said a husky voice, and Joseph Coggs

emerged from beneath a seat, wiping his filthy hands on the front of his best jersey.

'Thirty-two!' boomed Mrs Pringle again, with awful finality. I wondered if it would be engraved on her heart when she died, and if so, would it be in letters or figures? This idle fancy was interrupted by Mr Mawne saying firmly: 'You have forgotten yourself, Mrs Pringle. Thirty-two – and you make thirty-three!'

Sourly Mrs Pringle intimated that this was, in fact, the case, waved her approval to the vicar, and then puffed her way down the aisle to the seat behind Mr Mawne and me. To rousing cheers the party set off to Barrisford.

Mr Mawne had an ill-assorted collection of luggage with him, for a day's outing. Three books, in an insecure strap, he put up on the rack, together with a small fishing net, and a rather messy packet, in greaseproof paper, which presumably held his lunch, and a very large green apple, obviously intended by the Almighty for baking, served with plenty of brown sugar and cream.

His magnificent camera, housed in a leather case which gleamed like a horse chestnut, he held carefully on his thin knees, occasionally whizzing the strap round and round, in an absent-minded fashion, perilously near my face.

For the first part of the journey he seemed content to gaze about him silently, but after we had stopped for coffee at a roadside café and resumed our seats, he became quite talkative. Mrs Pringle leant forward behind us, the better to hear the conversation.

'Do you go out much in the evenings?' asked Mr Mawne politely. 'Or do you have school work – marking, and so on – to occupy you?'

I told him that I usually spent a little time on school affairs, chiefly correspondence with the local education office, ordering new stock, checking school accounts and so on, but that otherwise household matters and the garden filled up most of my time.

'And I read a lot,' I added.

'Excellent, excellent,' said he, 'but surely you find your life a little lonely at times?'

I was conscious of Mrs Pringle's heightened interest behind me.

I was obliged to tell Mr Mawne, quite truthfully, that I had never felt lonely in my life.

'It seems, if I may say so, a very – er – *restricted* life, for a woman. Particularly an attractive woman.' He essayed a small bow, but was somewhat impeded by the camera. Mrs Pringle's breathing became more marked by my left ear.

'I can assure you,' I said, acknowledging the compliment with a polite smile, 'that it's a very full life. Too full at times. The days don't seem long enough.'

Mr Mawne dropped his eyes to his lap, and spoke sadly.

'I find them too long, I'm afraid. Particularly cold, long summer evenings.'

By this time Mrs Pringle's face was almost between our heads, and I could see the agitated cherries from the corner of my eye. Ignoring the pathos of poor Mr Mawne's tone, I hurled myself into an over-bright description of making jam on just such a cold, long summer evening as Mr Mawne disliked, steering erratically, and perhaps a trifle hysterically from the particular to the general, while Mrs Pringle's breathing stirred the hair on my neck.

When at last I paused for breath, Mr Mawne gave me a gentle, sad smile.

'You are very lucky,' he said slowly. 'I think, perhaps, a man needs companionship more than a woman does.' He relapsed into dreamy silence, and we both watched the outskirts of Barrisford rushing past the windows.

Mrs Pringle released the iron grip she had held on the back of our seat, and, well content with her eavesdropping, settled her bulk back on her own cushions, and gave a gusty sigh.

To my relief and, no doubt, to Mrs Pringle's disappointment, Mr Mawne bade me a kindly farewell at Barrisford and set off, with brisk, purposeful strides, along the beach, to some far distant rocks which were awash with a lazy tide. The children rushed seawards whilst we older Fairacre folk settled ourselves on the warm sand, and screwing up our eyes against the dazzle, watched the sea-gulls swooping and crying in the vivid blue sky.

Mrs Moffat watched Linda setting off to the water, clad in a dashing yellow sun-suit of her making, then sat herself down beside me. She obviously had something of importance to say.

'Do you mind?' she began. 'I wanted to speak to you on the coach, but I didn't like to interrupt your conversation with Mr Mawne. He looked so happy.' This was all very hard to bear, I thought, and could only hope that the recording angel was ready, with pencil, to note with what fortitude and long-suffering I was enduring these mortifications.

'I wanted to thank you for sending your friend to me. She's introduced several more people from Bent, and Hilda and I are making nearly a dozen costumes for the pageant.'

I said that that was wonderful, and did Hilda – Mrs Finch-Edwards – find she could manage this work with the baby?

'She's marvellous!' said Mrs Moffat with fervour. 'She's borrowed dozens of books about costume from the County Library, and Mrs Bond who is in charge of the organizing of the pageant is coming over to see us both next week to see how we're getting on. The costumes must be historically correct, of course. It's fascinating work.'

I asked her if Amy had been able yet to introduce them both to the film producer.

'Not yet,' she replied, 'but I believe Mrs Bond knows him well. She may tell us more when we see her.'

She rose in answer to a distant shout from her daughter, who was gazing, fascinated, at something in the surf that swirled about her ankles.

I leant back against a sunny breakwater, and dozed off.

'Our Mr Edward' at Bunce's, the famous tea shop, was elegant in a light fawn worsted suit, exquisitely cut. He showed us to our tables in an upper room, and personally supervised the serving of delicious ham and salad, swooping round with plates ranged up his arm. Mr Mawne did not appear at tea, but we found him when we returned to the coach, busily making notes in the margin of one of his three books. It was, I saw, a book about birds. His face was bright pink with the sunshine and salt air, and he greeted me almost boisterously. I was glad to see that his spirits had revived.

Mrs Pringle bared her teeth at us in a ghastly, sickly leer as she sidled by to her place.

'Now you two will be all right,' she said, as though bestowing a blessing on a bridal pair. Mr Mawne appeared not to hear, and continued with his animated account of the purple sandpiper.

'I knew it!' he said emphatically, slapping his book gaily. 'When I heard that Barrisford was the place, I thought, "Now's my chance!"'

Mrs Pringle, catching the last few words, inclined the cherries a little nearer.

'I saw quite a dozen sandpipers – the *purple* sandpiper—' he added, peering anxiously into my face. 'There are a number of sandpipers, you know.'

I went into a pleasant trance while he rattled on. 'The purple sandpiper,' I said silently to myself, 'and the *lesser* sandpiper, and the *crested* sandpiper, and the *continental* sandpiper, and, of course, the *English speaking* sandpiper . . .'

The coach roared on, and we must have been half-way to Fairacre before he finished, triumphantly.

'And I've taken twenty-three photographs, both wading and on the wing, so I've really accomplished more than I set out to do today! I shall set this fellow Huggett to rights!' Here he slapped the book again. 'A pompous ass! We were at school together, and what he knows about the purple sandpiper could be written on a pin head!'

And with this charitable remark he settled back with the evening paper, and read, with the closest attention, a very sordid account of a young girl drug-addict who had been found murdered on one of the ugliest divans ever to find its way into the photographs of the evening press.

The Monday following an outing often brings some absentees from school, and today was no exception. The twins, Helen and Diana, were reported to have nettlerash and colds – which sound suspiciously like chicken-pox to Miss Clare and me. Several others look decidedly mopey, and Ernest, in my room, has spent most of his school day rubbing his back against the desk behind him, in order to gain relief from 'an itching sunburn, miss, done Saturday.'

Miss Clare confessed over her morning tea that it was a relief not to have the twins in her classroom.

'There they sit,' said she sadly, 'breathing away through their mouths, eyes glazed, and nothing in their heads after five terms! They still choose a penny instead of sixpence, because it's bigger – although I've put out six pennies for sixpence, and explained it time and time again.'

I sympathized with her.

'And, mark my words,' continued their far-seeing teacher, 'they'll both have anything up to six children apiece, and as dull as they are themselves! Just you wait and see!'

In the evening I drove Mrs Annett to Springbourne to see if Minnie Pringle would come daily to Beech Green school-house when Mrs Annett is confined.

'There just seems to be no one else to ask,' she said as we wound along the narrow lane from Fairacre. 'There are no nice spare women these days – no kind single aunts to step into the breach, and I've no sisters who might spare a few days.'

She looked rosy and cheerful despite it all, and trotted very nimbly up the brick path to the thatched cottage which housed Minnie, her three illegitimate children and her virago of a mother. I drove up the cart track, just off the narrow road, to wait till the business was over.

It was an oppressive evening, with a stillness that held the threat of thunder. The trees were beginning to look over-heavy and shabby, and, in the field beside the car, there spread into the hazy distance, the sullen khaki shade of July wheat.

It was so quiet that small sounds, usually unheard, were quite clear. A dead bramble leaf, swinging brown and brittle on a thread nearby, cracked dryly as it touched a twig. A pigeon rocketed over the hedge, and clapped its wings shut, with the hollow, bony snap of a closing fan.

I felt as though I had been worlds away by the time Mrs Annett returned to the car, all her arrangements as satisfactorily made as would ever be possible with such a scatter-brained creature as Minnie Pringle. We drove home together under the lowering sky, and were safely indoors before the storm broke.

A spell of fine weather, following the storm, has kept us all happy and indolent in the village. Apart from the growing frenzy of pageant preparations – the great day is only a few weeks distant – everyone agrees that it is too hot to do any gardening, or to go shopping in Caxley, or to wash the blankets, or to do the outside painting, or, in fact, to cope with any of the jobs which we have been postponing for weeks 'until we get a fine spell.'

My garden is looking lovely, and the new potatoes and peas are at their best. There is nothing I enjoy more than turning up a root of pale golden potatoes, in the warm crumbly earth, secure in the knowledge that treasure so freshly dug will mean easy skinning.

The peas have done well, and I sit on the lawn shelling them for my supper, and enjoying the scent of a freshly popped pod, packed with fat moist peas, as much as the delicious eating later.

The new teacher, who has been appointed straight from college to take up her post in the infants' room here next term, called to see us yesterday. Her name is Hilary Jackson, and she is nearly twenty-one. She seemed a conscientious, rather earnest young woman, squarish in build, with a shaggy hair-cut and horn-rimmed glasses. She was dressed in a crumpled blouse and a gathered skirt of glazed chintz, and she wore aggressively tough sandals.

I hope she settles down with us, but at the moment she is well above all our heads.

'Have you read *A Little Child's Approach to Relativity?*' she asked me. I admitted that, so far, I had not met this work.

'But you should!' she insisted, looking rather shocked. 'It's the text of the Heslop-Erchsteiner-Cod lectures, which he gave last autumn.'

'Who?' I asked, with genuine interest.

'Why, Professor Emil Gascoigne,' she replied, eyes wide behind the glasses. 'He gave the Heslop-Erchsteiner-Cod series at Minnesota – no, I'm wrong!' She stopped, appalled at her own mistake, and stared fiercely at Ernest and Patrick in the front desk, who were supposed to be pasting a geometrical pattern, but had done very little, I noticed, preferring to read one of Mrs Waites' magazines which had been spread on their desk lid to catch the paste drops.

'Could it be Minneapolis?' she asked, turning a distraught face to me.

'Or Minnehaha perhaps,' I returned, beginning to get a little tired of it all, in this heat.

'Oh no!' she assured me earnestly, 'not Minnehaha. I think you're confusing it with Longfellow.'

Suitably and deservedly crushed, I bore her off to Miss Clare's room, where her new class surveyed her, round-eyed.

Miss Clare greeted her very kindly and took her to the large cupboard in the corner to show her the number apparatus.

'But surely,' I heard Miss Jackson remark, in ringing tones, as I returned to my own class, 'those out-of-date old bead frames aren't *still* in use. Child psychologists *everywhere* have agreed for *years*, that the inch-cube is the only possible medium for basic number . . .'

I left them to it, closed the dividing door gently behind me and walked round my own desks, where the children snipped and pasted with unusual industry now that my eye was upon them.

The reason for Ernest and Patrick's paucity of work was readily apparent when I saw the page at which Mrs Waites' favourite weekly was opened. Scissors held idly in their laps, mouths open and eyes bursting from their heads, they sat engrossed – Ernest in an article headed 'How to Wean Baby,' from which no intimate details were spared, and Patrick in an outspoken dissertation on family-planning, on the opposite page.

The vicar called in, as is his custom on a Friday afternoon, and after his talk with the children, asked me if I thought that Mrs Moffat would be able to give Miss Jackson accommodation next term, as she had once done for Mrs Annett, then Miss Gray.

I knew that she was now so busy with her needlework that the chances were slight. The spare room, which had been Miss Gray's, was an enchanting mass of rich costumes, at the moment, in preparation for the pageant, but after that great day, it was doubtful if Mrs Moffat would be any less busy, for her name, as an excellent and imaginative dressmaker, was getting widely known, thanks to Amy's recommendation.

We discussed again the difficulties of obtaining suitable lodgings for young women in a village. The cottages are crowded, and often have no bathroom. The people with large houses, like the vicar, seem strangely averse to letting a room, and as most of them are elderly, it would not be easy for them or for their lodger. On the other hand, I sometimes think that perhaps this possibility never enters their heads. I have been present when the managers have met together, cudgelling their brains for somewhere to put an innocuous and respectable young woman – who would be delighted to do for herself, and quite probably be away every week-end – and have been amused to hear them suggesting that Mrs So-and-So (who has a husband, four children and no help whatsoever), might be delighted to let that little slip room of hers that looks out on to the wall of the village bakehouse; whilst large empty rooms in their own houses, inhabited by a moth or two and a stray mouse, cry out for a bit of fire and an airing.

There was no other hope but Mrs Moffat, as we both well knew, and as the vicar's kind old face began to pucker into ever-growing anxiety, I rose to the occasion and said that Miss Jackson could stay in my spare room for the time being, until she found somewhere that she really liked. It is not an ideal arrangement, but it is the only way out of the difficulty; and the vicar, breathing relief and thanks, departed a much happier man.

As we suspected, it was chicken-pox which reared its ugly head just after the outing, and nearly half the school is down with it. Dr Martin, whom I met at the school gate, said that the attack was very mild.

'As I hope it is!' I rejoined, waving a hand to a bunch of my spotty pupils, playing near the church gates. 'What's the point of excluding them from school, if their mothers let them mix with all and sundry?'

'Won't hurt them,' responded Dr Martin, with that fine careless rapture with which so many present-day doctors dismiss children's infectious diseases. He drove off hastily, before the tart remarks that trembled on my tongue had time to fall.

It was the day after this encounter that Miss Clare and Arthur Coggs crossed swords. I had driven into Caxley during the dinner hour, to drop in some forms at the Education Office. Unfortunately I had forgotten that it was market day, and the town was jammed with traffic. Cattle vans jostled farmers' cars, while my battered little Austin tried to nose along in their wake. Country ladies, indistinguishable in their market-day uniforms of grey flannel suit, white blouse, marcasite clip, dark glasses and classic grey felt hat (jay's feather at side), gave tongue to each other across the traffic, and exchanged news of their families in tones which would have filled the Albert Hall comfortably.

The children were already in school when I returned. My pox-free few were busy with a spelling game, the infants with bricks and jig-saw puzzles. Miss Clare told me of her adventure as they worked.

We had sent Joseph Coggs home again, on his arrival at school that morning, for he was obviously suffering from chicken-pox. Arthur Coggs, who had elected to have the day off work, was furious about this, and had marched him up again for afternoon school, breathing fire and threats. School was compulsory, wasn't it? he had blustered at Miss Clare, the children, half-frightened, half-thrilled gazing on. Soon complained if the kid was kept away, that there office, and now here young Joe was packed off home. There was much more to the same effect, while poor Joe drooped beside him, shaken with fever and fear.

'Have you called in Dr Martin?' asked Miss Clare.

'No, nor shall I!' retorted Arthur. 'That kid's got nothing wrong with him, but a few gnat bites.'

'He also said that Joe "ate too rich,"' added Miss Clare to me.

'Ha-ha!' I commented mirthlessly.

Miss Clare had then watched the tears pour hotly down Joe's flushed cheeks, and had taken decisive action.

'The child is ill and must have medical attention,' she said firmly. 'If you refuse to call in Dr Martin, I shall do so!' And grasping Joe's hand she walked swiftly to the school-house, followed by Arthur Coggs, bellowing and gesticulating. She adjured the child to lie on the sofa, ignored Arthur's vociferous shoutings about a father's rights and what happened to kidnappers, and rang Dr Martin's house.

Luckily, he answered the telephone himself, heard the rumpus in the background, and came to the rescue within a few minutes. He had diagnosed chicken-pox, taken poor Joe's temperature, which now stood at 103°, and had told Arthur Coggs, in good round terms which had delighted and shocked Miss Clare, his opinion of him. He had now taken Arthur back to his cottage, keeping up a rapid fire of advice and threat of 'taking-it-to-the-police' under which the craven Arthur soon wilted, and was there now, seeing that a decent bed was prepared for his patient and that the parents knew what to do for him.

'Well done!' I said heartily to Miss Clare. 'I'll go over and see Joe. And then I think you'd better have a rest yourself after all that bother!'

'Nonsense!' said my assistant rebelliously. 'Stuff and nonsense! It's done me a world of good to have a battle with that wretched Arthur Coggs. And as for Dr Martin's language—!' Her old eyes sparkled at the recollection. 'It was quite wonderful! So fluent and so *really dreadful*!' Her voice was full of admiration and awe.

Within an hour Dr Martin returned, carried the now sleeping Joe wrapped in a rug, to his car, and settled him on the back seat. I had picked the finest roses I could find in my garden for Dr Martin, for I knew that roses were his first love.

'And the best one's for your button-hole,' I told him, fixing it through the car window. 'We can't thank you enough!'

'You're a good girl – despite your crotchety-old-maid ways,' retorted Dr Martin, blowing me a kiss as he drove slowly away.

'*Well!*' said an outraged boom behind me, and I turned to confront Mrs Pringle, purple with stupefaction. 'Such goings-on—!'

I concealed my mirth as best I could, and shook my head regretfully.

'I'm afraid Dr Martin is hopelessly susceptible!' I said. And assuming the air of a *femme fatale* I returned, in great good spirits, to the children.

Miss Clare's bouquet, on the last day of term, was even larger than Dr Martin's, for all the children had contributed from their gardens, and southernwood and lavender added their aromatic, spicy scent to that of the roses and carnations which formed the largest part of the massive bunch.

Joseph Coggs was not there, as he was still in the throes of chicken-pox, but Mrs Coggs had sent some madonna lilies to swell the bunch, and we recognized them as a silent tribute to her son's champion.

The schoolroom was very quiet when they had all gone. Bereft of pictures, piles of books, and flowers, it looked bare and forlorn. The floorboards sounded hollowly as I made my way to the door.

Mrs Pringle had told me that she would start 'that back-breaking scrubbing' the next day, so I locked the school door, admiring the soft, old green paint, so soon to be burnt off and replaced.

The sun scorched my back as I bent to the lock. Swinging the massive key round and round on my finger, I went to hang it up in its allotted place on the nail in the coal cellar.

Dazzled with sunshine I hummed my way back to the school-house. The swifts screamed excitedly round St Patrick's spire and seven glorious, golden weeks stretched ahead.

AUGUST

The first few days of the holiday were gloriously hot, but the weather broke during the first week in August and steady relentless rain has covered the country. I spent ten days with an old friend at the sea – luckily during the fine spell – and returned to Fairacre to find the garden sodden, and farmers beginning to look gloomily at their corn.

'It can't keep on at this rate,' I said to Mr Roberts, when I encountered him in the lane. 'It's much too heavy to last.'

'You'd be surprised!' he rejoined grimly, surveying his farm-yard, which looked more like a lake. Rain drummed steadily on the corrugated-iron roof of the barn, and pattered on my umbrella. Little rivulets, carrying twigs and leaves, coursed down each side of the lane, and the heavy sky looked as though it held plenty of rain in reserve.

'Don't suppose it'll be fit for the pageant,' said Mrs Pringle, with gloomy relish. 'Muck things up a treat, this will. 'Twouldn't be safe to have the children running about the grounds at Branscombe Castle, in this lot – the river's fair rushing through, I'm told, and there's many a life been lost by that weir there.'

The pageant overshadows everything. Nothing is safe from the marauding hands of pageant-producers and actors. We are all busy sticking gummed labels on the undersides of old pieces of furniture, which have been requisitioned for the day, and our wardrobes have been ransacked – not only for fur for our own simple Ancient Britons' costumes, but for hats, cloaks, velvet jackets, feathers, jewels, buckles and belts for the rest of the county. I quite dread Amy's visits at the moment, as I see her predatory eye ranging round my house, and even over my person, for any little titbit that might further Bent's glory on the day of the pageant.

'You can't need that great pearl ring,' she insisted, on her last foray, eyes agleam. In vain to protest that it was a bridesmaid's present years ago, and that I was much attached to it. After five minutes of Amy's browbeating, I found myself taking it off and handing it over, having to content myself with awful threats if any ill befell it.

So it goes on all over the county, and many an old friendship is cracking under the strain, I surmise.

I drove through squelching lanes to Beech Green school-house yesterday to have tea with the Annetts. They are not going away this summer, as the baby is due to arrive next week.

Mr Annett was in the throes of revising his time-table. His farming project is going well, but the difficulties in arranging other school activities are great.

'I shall have a hundred and forty next term,' he said, 'from five to fifteen – and only four teachers for the lot.'

I knew that Miss Young took the infants' class and that it involved teaching thirty-odd infants aged from five to eight. Miss Hodge had the juniors, from eight to eleven, which meant that they took the eleven-plus examination from her room. Mr

Hopgood and Mr Annett took the older boys and girls, having about forty in each class. Several neighbouring schools – mine included – send their children on to Beech Green School, at the age of eleven, so that the top two classes are usually large and the children do not know each other as well as do those in the lower two classes.

'It's arranging games that is giving me a headache,' confessed Mr Annett, running his fingers through his hair. 'Miss Young can take netball with the girls on Wednesday afternoon, while I take football with the boys from the top two classes, but that means we have about forty apiece to cope with, and it's too much. It means that Miss Young has three netball games to supervise, and I have two football teams. It also means that Hopgood has to go into the junior room to free Miss Hodge who takes the infants while Miss Young's out, and frankly, Hopgood's no earthly good with young children.'

'Can't he take the football?' I suggested.

'Got a gammy leg,' said Mr Annett, running an ink-stained finger round the inside of a nice white collar. 'Can you wonder,' he went on, 'that I've had two visits from parents who are trying to get their children accepted at that new secondary modern school this side of Caxley? In theory we're offering their children the same education – but are we? Here I have forty children, from thirteen to fifteen in my class, ranging from complete duffers to bright ones. True the girls have a day at the cookery and house-wifery centre once a week, and the boys have a day at carpentry. But what facilities have I got here at Beech Green to offer them, compared with the schools in Caxley?

'The parents know as well as I do that there are two, if not three, streams there, and the bright ones will get the chance to get along at their own pace, instead of being held back by the dim-wits. They will have a gymnasium, a metalwork room, a woodwork room, decent sanitation – and what's more, properly-trained specialist teachers to take them in different subjects – not a poor old hack like me who has to teach everything, in between filling in the forms and interviewing the hundred and one callers who come during the day.'

I protested that he was doing a difficult job very well.

'But that's not enough,' said he vehemently, making the

tea-cups jump as he banged a bony fist on the table. 'I often think the children would be better off staying in their own small schools. Take Springbourne, that closed recently. Miss Davis's fifteen children come here now; the school-house has been sold to somebody "up-the-atomic," and I see that the school itself is for sale, advertised in this week's *Caxley Chronicle* as "a commodious building suitable for conversion".'

'But it would have cost an enormous amount to repair properly – and for fifteen children—' I began.

'But *why* for fifteen children?' argued Mr Annett. 'I know as well as you do that a one-teacher school is uneconomic, but there were two good classrooms there, and a school-house. Why not let dear old Miss Davis stay on, give her an assistant for the infants, and take some of the children who now burst our walls apart, over there to make up a worth-while little two-class school? As it is, I have ten children from Badger's End, only a stone's throw from Springbourne School, and there are a dozen council houses just finished on the other side – I expect all the children there will come driving gaily past empty little Springbourne School and squash in here with all the rest.'

Mr Annett sounded so bitter that I felt quite guilty when I remembered that three of my old pupils would be adding to the congestion at Beech Green next term. Mrs Annett tactfully changed the subject by asking me if I would like to see the baby's layette, and thankfully we climbed the stairs to happier things, leaving Mr Annett to tear himself to shreds over the injustices of present-day rural education.

Tibby has become a renowned mouse and rat catcher, doubtless an admirable trait in a country cat, but one which gives me many a pang, for rats and mice I just cannot endure, and Tibby insists on dragging home her dead trophies to display proudly before me.

There is something about rodents – possibly their long, ghastly, naked tails – which fills me with the deepest revulsion, and I am quite unable to cope with these dreadful offerings which Tibby lays at my door. Imagine, then, my horror when, on reaching down for a saucepan from the cupboard under the sink, a *live* rat bolted across the kitchen. Obviously the cat had let it escape and being unable to get it out from its retreat, had sauntered off in search of further prey. I gave a yelp and fled upstairs.

After a few minutes' shuddering I tried to decide how on earth I could get rid of the wretched thing. To touch it at all – let alone kill it – was beyond me, and I was just working out a plan whereby I would go out of the front door, open the kitchen one, and pray that it made its own way out, when I heard the oil van stop outside.

Leonard, who drives it, was one of my pupils when I first came to Fairacre. A weakly, adenoidal boy, and not over-bright, he appeared, on this occasion, to have the attributes of Apollo himself.

'Leonard!' I called in quavering tones, from the bedroom window. He looked dimly about him, at ground floor level, until I was forced to call: 'I'm upstairs, Leonard!'

His gaze slowly travelled upward.

'Never saw you, miss!' he responded. 'Want anything?'

'The usual gallon,' I answered, 'and a dozen matches – not those dreadful things I had last time, but Bryant and May's.' He began to open the van doors at the back, as I screwed up my courage to ask for help.

'And Leonard—' I pleaded, 'could you possibly see to a rat that's in my kitchen? Get rid of it for me somehow?' I very nearly added, so low was my morale, that I was sorry that I had kept him in so often as a child, but a teacher's blood, even though at its lowest ebb, still trickled in my veins, and I forbore.

Leonard became positively brisk. His eye lit up and his manner became energetic.

'Got a stick?' he asked, advancing swiftly up the path.

'In the hall—' I faltered, and sat on the bed with my fingers in my ears as the first blood-curdling whacks began.

Five minutes later Leonard appeared underneath my bedroom window.

''E's finished!' he said with great zest, 'I've chucked him out the back – over the far ditch. Made a bit of a mess, but I've mopped up with a bit of old clorth!'

Trying not to let my horror at these words show in my face, I thanked him deeply.

'That's all right, miss. I likes a bash at a rat!' said my

bloodthirsty ex-pupil. I thought wryly of the numberless talks I had given the children on kindness to animals – but who was I to criticize? He waved good-bye, climbed into the rickety van, and roared off.

Shaking, I crept down to the scene of carnage. It was all very quiet. A new tea-cloth, gruesomely stained, was draped along the sink. Shuddering, I picked it off with the fire-tongs and dropped it in the dust-bin. It seemed a small price to pay for Leonard's services.

Throughout the rest of the day I found I had a marked aversion to opening cupboards and even drawers, and I made a mental note to be less severe with the children, in future, when they fussed about wasps, gnats and so on in school.

I decided that an early bath and bed would be a good idea, having sampled a radio play, so obscure and so full of people with dreadful allegorical names like Mr Striving and Lady Haughtyblood as to drive one mad.

The kitchen is also the bathroom at the school-house. The rain-water is tipped, bucket by bucket, into an electric copper and while it heats, I spread a bath-mat, fetch the zinc bath that hangs in the back porch and pour in two buckets of cold rain-water in readiness. There are quite a few preparations to make for a rain-water bath – including skimming out a few leaves – but the result is well worth it, and the soft scented water really gets one clean.

The telephone rang as I was soaking, but I ignored it. At ten o'clock I was in bed, and at half-past ten, asleep. To my alarm, the telephone rang shrilly again, in the middle of the night – or so it seemed to my befuddled brain, as I crossly grabbed my dressing-gown, and groped downstairs. I managed to get one arm in a sleeve on the way. The rest trailed behind.

'Hello, hello!' said an exuberant voice, 'George Annett here. Thought you'd like to know that Isobel's had a boy. Five pounds!'

I said that that was wonderful and how were they both? There was a cruel draught under the door and my feet were frozen. I attempted to put my other arm in the second sleeve behind my back, found the sleeve was inside out, and gently put the receiver down, in order to arrange myself.

'Hi!' said an alarmed voice. 'Have you rung off? What's that click? You there?'

I put my mouth down to the table and spoke with what patience I could muster with both arms behind me, and my nightclothes twisted all round, and no shoes on, at a quarter to twelve at night.

'Yes, I'm here!'

'We're so pleased about it being a boy. Isn't it amazing? We wanted a boy, you see. And five pounds! Pretty good for a first attempt, isn't it? It's got a lot of black hair – doesn't seem to grow any particular way. Can't think how we'll part it!' Mr Annett sounded concerned.

With a super-human effort I wrenched my second sleeve out, to a nasty snapping of stitches, and inserted my second arm. 'What are you going to call him?' I asked.

'Well, my father's name was Oswald—' began Mr Annett, and rattled gaily on, as I hitched my frozen feet on the chair rail out of the draught, and made fruitless efforts to wrap them in the bottom of my dressing-gown.

At last the voice slowed down. The clock stood at midnight, and pleased though I was to hear such very good news, my bed called me seductively.

'Now you must go to bed,' I said to Mr Annett. 'You must be very tired after all this excitement.'

'Funnily enough,' said the tireless fellow, 'I feel fine. I'm just going to ring one or two more friends – I've done the relatives!'

Feeling that I should drop asleep at the table if I stayed there one minute more, I promised to come and see Isobel and the baby in a day or two's time, rang off firmly, and took my icy feet to bed.

'I hope to goodness they think of something better than Oswald,' I thought to myself, as I crept into bed. 'Such a pursed-lips-and-Adam's-appley sort of name.' I racked my brain to think why I disliked it. The only Oswald I could think of was an old friend, of whom I have always been very fond, a man of great charm and vivacity, but even this fact could not reconcile me to the name.

I heard St Patrick's clock strike two before I finally fell asleep.

On the day of the pageant, I woke to hear the rain gurgling merrily down the pipe from the gutter to the rain-water butt, by the back door. Large puddles lay in the hollows of our uneven playground, and Tibby, rushing into the kitchen, shook drops disdainfully from her paws, and mewed her complaints.

We were due to start off for Branscombe Castle at eleven sharp. The coach was to appear outside the church well before that time, and Mrs Partridge had impressed upon us the great need for punctuality.

'And bring packed lunch,' she had said at the end of our last rehearsal, 'and don't let the children have anything too rich, *please*!'

Our costumes had been packed the night before in two enormous wicker hampers, one labelled A. BRITONS and the other ROMANS. Mrs Moffat kept guard over these. Mrs Finch-Edwards was coming over later when she had settled her young daughter after lunch.

By ten o'clock the rain was getting lighter, though an unpleasantly chilly wind still blew. I could see from my bedroom window, as I was dressing, little knots of women and children converging upon the church. The coach arrived soon after.

By the time the excited mothers and children had sorted themselves out, there seemed to be remarkably little space left for the properties. The two hampers were piled, one on top of the other, at the front of the coach, but we had a collection of ungainly 'props,' including a squat pouffe, which, covered with grey crayon paper (from the school cupboard), represented a boulder on which Mrs Pringle was to be seated by the fire. Worse still was a stuffed deer, which was to be slung on a pole and brought in by the Ancient Briton hunters. No one who has not attempted to travel in a modern coach with a stuffed deer can have any idea how much room the animal needs. We found that it was too long to be propped up on end. It was too fat to go on the rack. Its rigid legs were an insuperable obstacle, and it was only by lodging the poor thing athwart the back of one seat, with its front legs down one side and its rear ones down the other, that we got it in at all.

The younger children were scared of it – as well they might be, for its glass eyes had not been set in quite straight and it had the most horrific and malignant squint.

A strong smell of raw fish pervaded the coach as we drove the ten miles to Branscombe Castle. This came from a brown-paper bag, of which I had unhappy charge, and was given off by a pound of sprats, due to be cooked at the Ancient Britons' camp-fire. There had been a certain amount of argument as to the menu and cooking facilities of Ancient Britons.

'A big black cauldron, surely,' someone had suggested. 'Fixed on a tripod.'

Mrs Willet had offered her coal scuttle, which, she assured us, was just like a cauldron, and Caxley had had it when the Methodist witches did *Macbeth* last autumn.

Mrs Partridge said that she was positive that tripods and hanging cooking-pots came much later, and that she thought that something naked, on its own as it were, in the embers, would be the thing.

'Potatoes?' suggested Mrs Pringle.

Mrs Partridge said surely potatoes hadn't been introduced as early as that?

Mrs Pringle, taking umbrage, said she hadn't had the schooling that some had had – mentioning no names – as she had been sent out to bring in an honest penny to as hard-working a pair of parents as ever a girl had. She then added that her potatoes were excellent bakers and no one had ever sniffed at them before.

Mrs Partridge, who can cope with this sort of thing with one hand tied behind her, said she had no doubt that Mrs Pringle's potatoes were fine specimens, as everyone who attended Harvest Festival could testify, but that that was quite beside the point.

Rushing in where angels fear to tread, I said I thought that Raleigh had something to do with bringing potatoes back from America.

Mrs Partridge said: 'Of course, of course! And his servant thought he was on fire, when he was smoking. Or am I confusing that with Drake and singeing the King of Spain's beard?'

(Which only goes to show how competently Messrs Sellar and Yeatman have summed up the common man's grasp of his country's island story.)

After much discussion, equally hazy and misinformed, it had been decided to settle for fish.

'*Small* fish!' said Mrs Partridge, as though someone had been pressing for whale steaks. I had offered to be in charge of the fish-buying, and only hoped that they would smell better cooked than they did now in their raw state.

It was nearly twelve o'clock when the coach drove through the gates of Branscombe Castle, and up the long avenue of limes which leads to the castle itself. The rain had stopped, and everyone was feeling much more cheerful.

We turned out of the coach, hampers, stuffed deer, and all, and made our way to a large barn at a little distance from the house, which had been prepared for use as a dressing-room.

Long trestle-tables were placed at intervals down its length and the place was already humming with activity. Large notices had been stencilled in green and white, and these showed which part of the barn we could claim as our particular niche. Fairacre W.I. was at one end, next door to a marquee which had been erected to give extra room. In here were two pier-glasses, hand-mirrors, and two wash-stands, for final adjustments to make-up and costume.

As is usual, in affairs run by Women's Institutes the world over, everything had been methodically and painstakingly organized. Six large dustbins, bearing the stencilled word LITTER, were ranged along the length of the barn. Hooks had been screwed to beams, and coat-hangers, in generous bunches, awaited the costumes. I wandered about, still clutching the sprats, admiring these detailed preparations.

In the marquee I was taken aback by a peremptory notice over the door which said: 'PLEASE LEAVE THIS PLACE.' But whilst I was still pondering this inhospitable request, a tall woman came in, bearing another long strip of cardboard, which she pinned securely below the first. 'AS YOU WOULD WISH TO FIND IT' it read triumphantly.

My faith restored, I went back to the Fairacre contingent, who were now swarming round the two wicker hampers, and greeting their costumes of old sack and moulting fur with as much affection as they would have bestowed on new hats.

Enormous tiers of seats had been erected in a semi-circle in front of the castle itself, which was to form a most impressive setting for the pageant's scenes. By midday, people were beginning to fill up the rows, prudently spreading newspapers and mackintoshes along the wet benches, before settling themselves. The car park at the rear of the castle filled rapidly and it was apparent that despite the damp weather our county pageant would be presented to a full house.

The castle is now open to the public, but the present owner, Lady Emily Burnett, lives in its sunniest corner. Now in her seventies she still takes an active part in W.I. work, and bustled about among us in great good spirits – a little rosy bundle of a woman, with very bright eyes and short, curly, white hair. She was particularly interested in Fairacre's costumes, admiring the ingenuity which had turned rabbit skins, old muffs and even hearthrugs into passable garments.

She caught Joseph Coggs by the chin, turned his face up to hers and looked silently at his dark, amazed eyes.

'Pure Murillo!' said she decisively, releasing him gently; then bustled on to the next point of interest.

The members from Bent were further down the barn and took much longer to dress in all their finery than we did. Amy and I took chairs outside to have our lunch, for by this time a watery sun had emerged, and, out of the wind, it was almost warm.

She looked magnificent in deep-blue satin and cream lace and I noticed that my pearl ring was being worn.

Amy's lunch was put up in a very dashing tartan case. Her chicken sandwiches had the crusts trimmed off and were cut into neat triangles. There was a small blue plate and a mug to match. A tube of mustard and a small cut-glass salt-shaker were tucked into corners, and a snowy napkin lay folded over it all. Her flask was a magnificent affair of leather with a silver top, and I admired this well-appointed meal openly.

My own consisted of some Ryvita, two wrapped cheeses, a hard-boiled egg, a hearty-looking apple and a squashed piece of fruit cake, and my napkin had served to tie it all up and now acted as my plate. The salt was in a serviceable but homely screw of greaseproof paper – and I could not help feeling that the serving of my meal lacked Amy's polish.

'You might just as well have put a hunk of cheese and a raw onion in a red-spotted handkerchief,' said Amy severely. 'You're much too inclined to Let Yourself Go.' Meekly I agreed, and Amy, relenting, offered me some of her very good coffee, which I accepted with proper humility. Once I had safely downed it, I pointed out that she had a dab of mustard perilously near my pearl ring, and that Gone As I Had I still fed myself cleanly.

At this childish retort Amy and I both broke down into uncontrollable laughter, which took us back twenty years and made us feel very much better.

After lunch the fun began. As Fairacre's scene was the first on the programme, we crowded into the marquee to put on our make-up and collect our properties. The children milled about under our feet, patting the stuffed deer – now in an advanced state of moult – pulling each other's rabbit skins, jeering at each other's appearances and generally making nuisances of themselves.

Mrs Pringle, matriarchal in a piece of grey blanket and an inconsequent strip of fur which she wore as a tippet, was sitting on a chair in front of one of the mirrors, thus successfully blocking the way for anyone else who might wish to use it.

Mrs Partridge was energetically shaking talcum powder into Mrs Pringle's scanty hair, rather as a cook dredges flour over a joint.

'Just enough to give it a touch of grey,' shouted Mrs Partridge above the growing din. Mrs Pringle nodded grimly from her scented cloud.

'And have you all taken off your shoes?' shouted Mrs Partridge to the Ancient Britons, who were now twittering around the marquee in a fine state of nerves. Mrs Moffat had dragooned her self-conscious Roman cohort into a column near the tent-flap. We stood wriggling our gold-painted dishcloths into more comfortable positions and easing our cardboard bootees from our sore ankle-bones. The Roman standard had taken a beating on the way, and the eagle was apt to collapse forwards, displaying the cereal carton of which it was made, with horrid clarity. Mrs Moffat had effected hasty repairs with tape and gummed paper, but we trembled to think of the effect of a strong wind on our proud emblem.

'Nobody gets these boots off my feet until I'm settled,' announced Mrs Pringle with awful deliberation. She rose from under Mrs Partridge's ministrations and stumped heavily towards her tribe. One of the twins darted across her path as she ploughed inexorably onward. There was a squeal of pain, the child hopped round in a frenzy, and Mrs Pringle, majestic in grey blanket and tousled locks – like some foreshortened Lear – checked in her advance.

'Should of looked where you was going,' she said sourly. 'Good thing I'd kept me boots on, or me corns would have been done in proper.'

By two-fifteen, when the pageant was due to open, the excitement was feverish. All the stands were packed and ground sheets had been spread in front to take the overflow. A number of schools had brought coach-loads of children. They chattered like starlings and were only silenced when, with a fine rolling of drums and a fanfare of trumpets, two heralds strode on to the stage to deliver the prologue.

Fairacre W.I. was now divided into two parties. The Ancient Britons were on one side awaiting their entry, complete with paraffin-drenched sticks for the camp-fire, a few noisome sprats, and the scuffed deer, which had now split across the neck and lost one glass eye.

Nerves already strained to breaking-point had almost snapped when Mrs Willet had said idly whilst they waited: 'Wonder where that eye's got to?' and was answered by Eileen Burton who said smugly that 'one of the kids had swallowed it!'

'*Which?*' screamed a dozen frenzied mothers, converging upon their informant menacingly.

'Don't remember,' confessed the child, and was spared further recriminations by the trumpets' brazen cry which announced that Fairacre's greatest hour was upon it.

We Romans, huddled behind a hurdle on the other side of the lawn, watched our fellow-members at their primitive tasks. Mrs Pringle was an awe-inspiring sight, as, boots removed, she settled her great bulk on the groaning pouffe. Regally she made signs to

Mrs Willet, unrecognizable in a moth-eaten tiger-skin from the vicarage landing, to light the fire.

This Mrs Willet knelt to do, braving the dampness to her bare knees. She vigorously rubbed two sticks and then artfully dropped a lighted match into the paraffin-soaked twigs. A blazing yellow flame shot into the air, amidst great applause, and shouts of 'What-ho! The atom bomb!' from a hilarious party of preparatory school boys sitting on the ground-sheets.

The sprats were put to sizzle, Ancient Briton mothers tended their grinning children, the stuffed deer luckily hung together to be borne in by Mrs Pratt and one of the members from Springbourne, and at last came the moment when tidings were brought of the Romans' approach.

Near-panic broke out behind our hurdle, as one of our number was suddenly stricken with stage-fright. Surprisingly enough, it was staid Mrs Fowler from Tyler's Row.

'I just can't go on,' she fluttered, 'my stomach's turned right over. I'm all ashake!'

We all did our best to encourage our weaker brother, though our own knees were knocking.

'You'll be all right as soon as you're on,' one insisted.

'Put your head between your knees,' said another.

'No don't,' advised a third, 'you'll have your helmet off!'

Mrs Moffat proved herself a born leader. Advancing with our wobbly eagle, she said fiercely: 'Mrs Andrews has been waving at the other Ancient Britons for a full two minutes. We MUST go on. Come on Mrs Fowler, follow me!'

And with standard upraised she marched valiantly from behind the hurdle, while, with hearts aflutter beneath our gilded cardboard armour, we stumbled in her wake.

We Romans got through the scene very well once we had overcome our initial stage-fright, and we even jostled, in a lady-like way, for the best places near the camp-fire, which was roaring away merrily. The sprats were done to a turn by the time we arrived, and I wished I could secrete a few about my Roman garments, for Tibby's supper.

The children, who were supposed to flee with their parents at our coming, had become very interested in the schoolboys, and had to be poked sharply in the back to recall them to their actors' duties, but otherwise there was no hitch. Mrs Pringle, shuffling crab-wise and picking her barefoot way carefully over damp patches, was a sight I shall long remember.

Storms of applause greeted our bows, and we hastened off full of relief. Behind the hurdles waited a motley set of Saxons, hiding behind large cotton-wool beards and adjusting their cross-garters. They, poor dears, were as frightened as we had been ten minutes before.

'It's nothing!' we told them airily, as we swept by to the changing-room. We could afford to be blasé now.

During the interval Mrs Bond, who had organized the pageant, collected Mrs Moffat and Mrs Finch-Edwards and took them along to meet Andrew Beverley, a very famous film-producer indeed. He was a small, diffident individual, and from a distance looked far too fragile for the hurly-burly of the film world. It was only when one caught sight of his grey and glittering eyes, as compelling as those of the Ancient Mariner himself, that one realized the latent power that lay in his diminutive frame.

When he had returned to his seat the two friends, much awed, showed me the card that he had given them.

'And he's written the name of his wardrobe mistress on the back,' breathed Mrs Moffat.

'With his own pencil!' echoed Mrs Finch-Edwards, her eyes like stars. 'And we can call at his studios any time while he's shooting his new film, to see the costumes.'

'Isn't it wonderful!' whispered Mrs Moffat, sitting down heavily on the pouffe. Mrs Finch-Edwards sat beside her. Together they gazed before them at that rosy world which lay ahead. There was nothing more to say, and they sat there together in blissful silence.

I tiptoed quietly away, leaving them to their dreams.

The sun was setting behind St Patrick's spire when we arrived at Fairacre. We were all tired, but proud of our efforts. There, in the wicker hampers, lay the battered remains of our past splendour. The eagle had fallen long ago, and had been left behind in one of the litter bins at Branscombe Castle. The stuffed deer, much the worse for wear, had been used as a pillow by three children asleep on the back seat, throughout the journey.

Stiffly we clambered down from the coach, tired and dirty. Only the dabs of gilt about our persons gave any hint of the brief Roman glory that had been ours. We could scarcely believe that, at last, the pageant was behind us.

SEPTEMBER

Erle arrived on the doorstep at nine-thirty this morning, armed with a box of chocolates, a bouquet of pink carnations and a note of thanks and farewell from his parents. It was a typically American gesture of generosity and courtesy, and I was much touched.

'We're off to Southampton right now,' said Erle, when I asked him in, 'so I mustn't.' He offered me his hand solemnly. 'Well, I guess it's good-bye,' he said, pumping mine energetically up and down.

He nodded his crew-cut across at the little school. 'That's the best school I've ever been teached at!' he said warmly.

I watched him run up the lane, somewhat comforted by this compliment. I shall not forget Erle. He and his classmates at

332

Fairacre School have been living proof of Anglo-American friendship.

Mr Roberts brought me over a basket of plums this evening – the
first, I suspect, of many which will find their way from generous
neighbours to the school-house.

He told me that Abbot, his cowman, is leaving him at
Michaelmas.

'He's got a job at the research station evidently,' said Mr
Roberts. 'His brother's there already, and he's found them a
house nearby. Another good man leaving the village – I don't
like to see it.'

I asked him why he was going.

'Well, the hours are shorter, for one thing. Cows have to be
milked, Sundays and all, and there's no knowing when a cow-
man may not have to spend a night up with a sick cow. It's heavy
work too. I think the women have a lot to do with their menfolk leaving the land. They look upon farmwork as something
inferior. If they can say: "My husband works at Garfield"
instead of "at Roberts' old farm", they feel it's a step up the
social ladder.'

'Will he get more money?' I asked.

'Yes, he will. But his rent will be three times what it is now –
and though I says it as shouldn't – he will be lucky to find as easy
a landlord.' I knew this to be true, for Mr Roberts's farm cottages
are kept in good repair.

'Oh yes, his pay will go up,' said Mr Roberts somewhat
bitterly, 'but what a waste of knowledge! It's taken forty years
to make that good cowman; I'd trust him with a champion, that
chap – and all that's to be wasted on some soulless routine job
that any ass could do. And where am I to get another? The days
have gone when I could go to Caxley Michaelmas Fair and give
my shilling to one of a row of good cowmen waiting to be hired –
as my father did!'

I felt very sorry for Mr Roberts, as he stood, kicking morosely
with his enormous boots at my doorstep, pondering this sad
problem. This is only one case, among many, of old village
families leaving their ancient home and going to bigger centres
to find new jobs. There must be some positive answer to this drift

from the country to the town. It cannot be only the promise of high wages that draws the countryman, though naturally that is the major attraction, offering as it does an easier mode of living for his wife and family.

'I picks up five pound a week for doing nothing,' boasted one elderly villager recently. Sad comment indeed, if this is true, on the outlay of public money and of his own starved mental outlook.

Perhaps, for a family man, the advantages of bigger and more modern schools for his children are an added incentive; and I thought again of Mr Annett's outburst about his own all-standard country school, which, he is clear-sighted enough to see, runs a poor second to the new secondary modern school which can offer so much more to his older children.

The new school year started today, and we have forty-three children in Fairacre School.

Miss Jackson is ensconced in the infants' room with twenty children, aged from five to seven; and I have the rest, up to eleven years of age, in my class.

Among the new entrants is Robin Pratt, who created such a dramatic stir one year, when we went on our outing to Barrisford, by suffering an accident to his eye. His sister Peggy has been promoted to my class this term, and as Robin was rather tearful on his first morning, he was allowed to sit with her until he felt capable of facing life in the infants' room, without any family support. His eye has suffered no permanent damage, and he is going to be a most attractive addition to the infants' class.

Miss Jackson has been unable to get lodgings in the village, and is with me at the moment. She is rather heavy going, and inclined to 'tell me what' in a way which I find mildly offensive. However, I put it down to youth and, perhaps, a little shyness, though the latter is not apparent in any other form. Getting her up in the morning is going to be a formidable task, I foresee, if she sleeps as heavily as she did last night. It was eight o'clock before I finally roused her, and my fifth assault upon the spare-room door.

The wet weather, which persisted through the major part of the holidays, has now – naturally enough – taken a turn for the better. The farmers look much more hopeful as they set about getting in a very damp harvest, and Mr Roberts' corn-drier hums a cheerful background drone to our school day.

To my middle-aged eye, the new entrants appear more baby-like than ever, and my top group more juvenile than ever before; but this I find is a perennial phenomenon, and I can only put it down to advancing age on my part. For I notice too, these days, how irresponsibly young all the policemen look, and on my rare visits to Oxford or Cambridge I find myself looking anxiously about to see who is in charge of the undergraduate innocents, dodging at large among the traffic.

Yesterday evening Mr Mawne called at the school-house, bearing yet another basket of plums. This makes the seventh plum-offering to date, and really they are becoming an embarrassment.

Miss Jackson and I were about to start our supper of ham and salad, and we invited him to join us. This he seemed delighted to do, making a substantial meal and finishing up all the cheese and bread in the house, so that we were obliged to have our breakfast eggs this morning without toast, but with Ryvita.

He told us, in some detail, about his correspondence with his friend Huggett on the subject of the purple sandpiper, and it was eleven o'clock before he made a move to return to his own home. Miss Jackson bore up very well, taking a markedly intelligent interest in all Mr Mawne's exhaustive (and to my mind, exhausting) data on birds; but I was in pretty poor shape by ten o'clock, answering mechanically 'Oh!' and 'Really?' between badly-stifled yawns. Although I am not averse to Mr Mawne, and realize that his life is – as he himself has frequently told me – a trifle lonely, yet I must confess that, to put it plainly, I find him a bore.

'What an interesting man!' enthused Miss Jackson, as I closed the front door thankfully upon him. 'He's just what you need – a really stimulating companion!'

More dead than alive, I crawled to bed.

This morning Mrs Pringle said that she hoped I'd enjoyed my evening with Mr Mawne, and it was shameful the way his underclothes wanted mending.

'I'm doing for him while his housekeeper's having her fort-night's break,' she told me. 'If ever a man needed a woman to look after him, that poor Mr Mawne does. He sits about, moping in an armchair, with me dusting round him, as you might say. And not a rag has he got to his back that doesn't need a stitch somewhere!'

I said, with some asperity, that that was no concern of mine, and had she removed my red marking pen from the inkstand.

Ignoring this retreat to safer ground, Mrs Pringle sidled nearer, dropping her usual bellow to an even more offensive lugubrious whine.

'Ah! But there's plenty thinks as you should make it your concern. He's fair eating his heart out – and the whole village knows it, but you!'

This was the last straw, I had suffered enough, heavens knows, from hints and knowing glances lately, but now that Mrs Pringle had the temerity and impertinence to bring this into the open, I had the chance to put my side plainly.

I pointed out, with considerable hauteur, that she was doing a grave injustice to Mr Mawne and to me, that to repeat idle gossip was not only foolish, but could be scandalous, in which case I should have no hesitation in asking for my solicitor's advice and recommending Mr Mawne to do the same.

At the dread name of 'solicitor' even Mrs Pringle's complacency buckled, and seeing her unwonted abjection, I hastened to press home my attack.

'Understand this,' I said in the voice I keep for those about to be caned, 'I will have no more behind-hand tittle-tattle about this poor man and me. I count upon you to give the lie to such utter rubbish that is flying about Fairacre. Meanwhile I shall write for legal advice this evening.'

Purple-faced, but silent, Mrs Pringle positively slunk back to her copper in the lobby; whilst I, full of righteous wrath, looked out our morning hymn. *Fight the good fight* seemed as proper a choice as any, and my militant rendering so shook the ancient piano that quite a large shred of red silk fell from behind its fretwork front and landed among the viciously-pounded keys.

Throughout the day Mrs Pringle maintained a sullen silence and, as I expected, arrived at the school-house after tea to give in her notice. This is the eighth or ninth time she has done this and, as usual, I accepted it with the greatest enthusiasm.

'I am delighted to hear that you are giving up,' I told her truthfully. 'After this morning's disclosures, it's the best possible thing for you to do!'

Mrs Pringle bridled.

'Never been spoke to so in my life,' she boomed. 'Threatened me – that's what you done. I said to Pringle: "I've had plenty thrown in my face – but when it comes to solicitors – Well!" So you must make do without me in the future.'

I said that we should doubtless manage very well, wished her good night and returned to the sitting-room.

Miss Jackson looked up with a scared expression. 'I say! What an awful row! What will you do without her?'

'Enjoy myself,' I said stoutly. 'Not that I shall get the chance. She'll turn up again in a day or two, and as there's really no one else to take the job on, we'll shake down together again I expect. It'll do her good to lose a few days' pay and to turn things over in her mind for a bit. Offensive old woman!'

Much exhilarated by this encounter I propped up on the mantelpiece the grubby scrap of paper – torn from the rent book I suspected – on which Mrs Pringle had announced her retirement, and suggested that we celebrated with a bottle of cider.

'Lovely!' said Miss Jackson, catching my high spirits and beaming through her unlovely spectacles, 'and if you like I'll make tomato omelettes for supper!'

And very good they were.

I have paid my promised visit to the Annetts to see Malcolm (not Oswald, I am relieved to know). He is a neat, compact, little baby, who eats and sleeps well, and is giving his mother as little trouble as can be expected from someone who needs attention for twenty-two hours out of the twenty-four.

I felt greatly honoured when I was asked to be godmother and accepted this high office with much pleasure, for although I have two delightful goddaughters, this will be my only godson. The christening is fixed for the first Sunday in October and I am looking forward to a trip into Caxley to find a really attractive silver rattle and coral, worthy of such a fine boy.

'My brother Ted is to be one of the godfathers,' said Mr Annett, 'and Isobel's cousin, who is in the Merchant Navy, is the other. With any luck he may have shore leave just then. If not, I'll stand proxy.'

He rubbed his hands gleefully.

'I must say I enjoy a party,' he went on. 'We'll have a real good one for every baby we have. Will you take it as a standing invitation?'

I said indeed I would, and that I looked forward to many happy occasions. But Mrs Annett, I noticed, was not so enthusiastic.

As is customary in Fairacre at harvest time, the children at the school helped to decorate the church for Harvest Festival.

Mr Roberts sent over a generous sheaf of corn and the children had a blissful morning tying it into small bundles to decorate the ends of the pews. The floor was littered with straw and grain, and I was glad that Mrs Pringle had given in her notice and that we could make as much mess as we liked without hearing many sour comments when that lady passed through the classroom.

Miss Jackson was inclined to be scathing about our efforts and also about the use to which we should apply the fruits of our labours.

'Straw,' she announced, 'is a most difficult medium for children to work in. Why, even the Ukrainians, who are acknowledged to be the most inspired straw-workers, reckon to serve an apprenticeship – or so our psychology teacher told us.'

One of the Coggs twins held up a fistful of ragged ears for my inspection at this point.

'Lovely!' I said, tying it securely with a piece of raffia, 'that will look very nice at the end of a pew.'

Flattered, she swaggered back to her place on the floor, collecting her second bunch with renewed zest.

Miss Jackson looked scornful. 'And I don't know that it's not absolutely primitive – all this corn and fruit and stuff! Makes one think of fertility rites. I did a thesis on them for Miss Crabbe at college.'

'Harvest Festival,' I said firmly, 'is a good old Christian custom, and we here in Fairacre put our hearts into it. If you object to such practices, I don't quite know why you have accepted an appointment in a church school.' She had the grace to look abashed, and the preparations went forward without further comment, except for one dark mutter about it being a good thing that Miss Crabbe – the psychology lecturer, who seems to have exerted a disproportionate influence on my assistant – doesn't live in Fairacre; with which statement I silently concurred.

In the afternoon we all trooped over to the church, bearing our corn bundles, about two bushels of plums, six bulbous marrows and some rather dashing cape gooseberries.

The children love decorating the church and do their part very well. The boys lashed the corn to the pew ends while the girls threaded cape gooseberries through the altar rails, and put a neat little row of plums – with a marrow at regular intervals – along the foot. It all looked very formal and childlike – and none the less effective for that.

The tranquil atmosphere of the church did much to soothe our nerves, after the excitement of the morning, and we returned much refreshed in spirit, to practise *We plough the fields and scatter* ready for the great day. And so busy were Miss Jackson and I trying to wean our charges from singing: *But it is fed and wor-hor-tered* that it was time to send them home before we knew where we were.

I usually do my washing on Saturday morning and iron, if I've been lucky with the weather, just after tea. With the kitchen door propped open I have a very pleasant view of the garden. I find ironing one of the less objectionable forms of housework, for it is quiet, clean and warm, three attributes which rarely come together in other household activities.

Miss Jackson manages to get home most week-ends, which gives me time to catch up with all the little jobs which a schoolmistress has to leave until then, without bothering over-much about Saturday's meals.

This week-end she relieved me of two large vegetable marrows, which, she said, her mother would welcome for jam. The spate of plums has begun to slacken, but marrows – alas! – are arriving in a steady stream at the back door. As Miss Jackson and I can only cope with about half a marrow between us in a week, I can see that I shall have to start digging, under cover of darkness, and inter the unwieldy monsters. To give them away again, in

Fairacre itself, might cause the greatest offence, and in any case, every garden seems to boast a fertile heap swarming with flourishing marrows. Oddly enough, the majority of people who grow them in Fairacre say, as they hand them over: 'Funny thing! I don't care for them myself. In fact, none of the family likes them!' But still they plant them. It must be the fascination of seeing such a wonderful return for one small seed, that keeps marrow-growers at their dubious task.

As I ironed, I amused myself by watching a starling at the edge of the garden bed. He was busy detaching the petals from an anemone, conscious that I was watching, and half-afraid, but persisting in his destruction. His iridescent feathers, as smooth and sleek as if oil had been stroked over them, gleamed like chain-mail in the level rays of the sinking sun. Having finished with the anemone, he began to run, squawking, about the lawn, his feet thrown rather high and forward, which gave him a droll, clown-like air. In time, others joined him, and I realized that they had found the remains of Tibby's cornflakes which I had thrown out. Chattering, quarrelling and complaining, they threw themselves energetically into this job of self-nourishment. As suddenly as they had arrived, they checked, and then whirred away over the house.

This short scene, I thought as I pressed handkerchiefs, is typical of the richness that surrounds the country dweller and which contributes to his well-being. As he works, he sees about him other ways of life being pursued at their own tempo – not only animal life, but that of crops and trees, of flowers and insects – all set within the greater cycle of the four seasons. It has a therapeutic value, this awareness of the myriad forms and varied pace of other lives. Man, particularly the town dweller, scurrying to catch up with what he considers the important jobs, which none but he can do, presses himself onward at a crueller pace daily. He scuttles from stone and steel office to arid tube-station. If he sees a blade of grass, prising its way between the paving stones, it only registers itself to his overwrought brain as something which should be reported to the corporation. Small wonder that sleeping pills lie within reach of so many tousled beds, when man has lost sight of the elementary fact that he must go at his own pace, or face the consequences.

Two other benisons are more generously bestowed in the country – solitude and handling earth. Not to be alone – ever – is one of my ideas of hell, and a day when I have had no solitude at all in which 'to catch up with myself' I find mentally, physically and spiritually exhausting.

When one is alone one is receptive – a ready vessel for the sights, the scents and sounds which pour in through relaxed and animated senses to refresh the inner man.

As for the healing that lies in the garden, let Mr Willet's wise words be heard. 'Proper twizzled up, I was after that row at the Parish Council. I went and earthed up my celery, on my own. That sorted me out a treat!'

While Mrs Pringle has been preserving a dignified silence at her cottage for the past week, Minnie Pringle has called in after school, 'to give us a lick-round,' as she so truly says.

It is convenient for her at the moment, as she spends most of the day at Mrs Annett's, leaves there at half-past three, and arrives here at about ten to four ready for her labours. She then cycles on to Springbourne.

We finish our last lesson of the day, and sing our grace, to the accompaniment of Minnie's clatterings in the lobby as she washes up the dinner things. In theory, Miss Jackson, whose room leads into the kitchen-lobby, switches on the copper at three-fifteen, but for three days it slipped her mind and Minnie arrived to find a copper full of cold rain-water, in which swam half a dozen hardy earwigs.

'Good thing you never switched on,' was her comment. 'Think of they poor little dears being boiled alive like lobsters!'

Miss Jackson, when I reminded her about the copper, said that her mind was so engaged with the Harvest project in her class-room and in making out a case-history for each child (which she was amazed to find had never been done in Fairacre – despite the strong recommendations of the Perth-Pullinger investigating committee as long ago as 1952), that she very much doubted if she could wrench it from the sort of work for which she imagined she had been trained, in order to deal with a domestic trifle of such a lowly nature.

I said that in that case I would give Ernest the job of walking through her room at three-fifteen each afternoon, and she must put up with the interruption. Various biting retorts, which rose to my lips, I forbore to utter, which made me feel unwontedly virtuous.

We have dusted our own classrooms each morning, and things have gone very smoothly, but with the colder weather coming I can see that we shall have to accept Mrs Pringle's return. Minnie finishes at Mrs Annett's in a week's time, and the tortoise stoves, which have so far remained unlit, will soon be roaring away.

Meanwhile, fired by the accounts from Miss Jackson of the excellent preserve which her mother concocted from the two marrows and at my wits' end to know just what to do with yet another monster which had appeared on the back doorstep, I decided to turn it into marrow jam.

I collected a most delectable mass of ingredients on the kitchen table; lemons, ground ginger, sugar and a small screw of grease-proof paper, which Minnie Pringle had brought from the chemist in Caxley, containing knobbly pale lumps of root ginger.

'It says: "Bruise the ginger",' I remarked to Miss Jackson, who was busy filling up the copper for her bath. We pored over the recipe together. 'How did your mother do that?'

'Just banged it, I think,' said she vaguely, 'with a rolling-pin, or something.'

I carried my screw of greaseproof paper out on to the back step. There was a cold wind blowing, and I anchored the ginger with a large flint while I found a hammer.

I was busily pounding at my little parcel when Mr Willet arrived, bearing a brown-paper carrier-bag.

'Don't like the way the wind's turned east,' he said, blowing on his fingers. 'Fair shrammed I am, I can tell 'ee. Vicar said would I tell you he won't be able to get over this Friday after all. Got a funeral over at Springbourne.'

I said was it anyone we knew?

'Oh no, no one what matters,' said Mr Willet airily. 'Some old boy from London what only lived there two or three months. Just come to die, so to speak.' He peered down at my little parcel and the large hammer.

'And what are you up to?'

'I'm bruising ginger,' I replied. Busily I unwrapped the folds of greaseproof paper and displayed the flattened contents. I looked at them anxiously.

'Would you say I'd bruised that?' I enquired.

Mr Willet broke into a guffaw. 'Bruised it? You've dam' well pulverized it!' He laughed until he had to lean against the wall for support, while I collected the squashed remains carefully together, out of the wind's harm.

'Ah well!' he said, recovering at last. 'I'll get back to my supper. Steak and kidney pudden my old woman's had on the hob all day – with a dozen button mushrooms inside it. Proper sharp-set I be – I'll do justice to that!'

I wished him good-bye and accompanied him to the corner of the house.

'Oh!' I said, looking back. 'You've left your carrier-bag.'

'That's all right,' replied Mr Willet cheerfully. 'It is for you. A marrow!'

This morning, with the wind still in the east, I decided that the school stoves ought to be lit. In theory, they are supposed to wait until October 1, but with the vagaries of the British climate we could often do with them in June. Mr Willet has chopped a neat stack of kindling wood, ready for the cold weather, and the coke pile in the playground looms over all.

'I'll light these 'ere for you each morning,' volunteered Mr Willet, 'until her ladyship turns up again. Fancy it won't be long now. Heard her telling my old woman yesterday that it was hard times for the unemployed and she wouldn't be going to the Whist Drive this week. It's a Fur and Feather too – so she must be hard pressed to miss that!'

Sure enough, in the evening, I found Mrs Pringle at my front door, her face set in a series of down-turned arcs, which made her look like a disgruntled tortoise.

'Come in,' I said politely, and settled her in the armchair by the fire. She looked at the flames with disgust.

'Fancy having a fire as early as this!' was her comment. 'Some has money to burn, seemingly!' I let this charitable remark go by, and asked if there was anything I could do for her.

'I've made up my mind to come back,' announced Mrs Pringle majestically. I was on the point of answering that no one wanted her back, but prudence restrained me. After all, Minnie would be leaving on Friday, and the school must have a cleaner. And funnily enough, though the wicked old woman before me drove me quite mad at times with her sulks and her downright rudeness – yet somehow, I had a soft spot for her. It had cost her something, I could see, to pocket her pride this evening and offer to come again – even if it were to suit herself in the long run. For never before had our 'little upsets,' as the vicar calls them, had quite such personal point as this one, and never before had I been quite so fierce with her.

'Minnie will be here until Friday,' I pointed out. 'She came to help us over a difficult patch, so I can't turn her away immediately.'

'Suits me,' said she, rising with some difficulty from the depths of the chair. 'I'll be along Monday.' I noticed with some amusement, that there was no word of apology. What was past was now past, I supposed.

She hung her black shiny shopping bag, from which she is never parted, over her arm, and stumped towards the door.

On the doorstep she turned. Her face was grimmer than ever.

'I see them chimneys smoking today,' she said, jerking her head towards the school. 'I don't let no one else meddle with my stoves – even if they has been lit days before the Office gives the word. We'll be needing a new tin of blacklead, and a new blacklead brush. Mine's worn right down to the board. I'll bring 'em with me Monday – and the bill.'

She fished inside the black bag, withdrew a paper one and pressed it upon me. Before I could find words, she had trudged off to the gate.

'See you Monday!' she boomed threateningly, and vanished round the bend of the lane.

When I opened the paper bag I found six brown eggs, double-yolkers to a man, and with the bloom of that day's laying on them.

It was Mrs Pringle's peace-offering and silent apology.

Michaelmas Fair at Caxley is an enormous affair, held in the market-place, where it causes the greatest disturbance possible and utter confusion to normal traffic conditions. The inhabitants of Caxley and the surrounding countryside curse roundly about the noise and the congestion, but look forward to its advent as soon as the dahlias are out, and would be the first to fight, with jealous pride, if anything were done to stop its coming.

'Livens things up a bit!' remarked the girl in Budd's knitwear department to me, as I chose a twin-set. She stood by the window gazing bright-eyed at the swarthy men who were erecting helter-skelters and swing-boats. Customers reckon to take second place in the shops overlooking the fair-ground, and no one would be so pernickety as to complain about inattention from the staff. We all face the simple fact that if you want whole-hearted and devoted service in the choice of purchases, then to choose to shop in Fair Week is asking for trouble.

The children have talked of nothing else, and the infants' room which is the scene of Miss Jackson's fair-ground project is a jumble of stalls with trays of plasticine toffee-apples, candy-floss made of dyed cotton-wool, and a table laid out with a model fair with roundabouts, switch-backs and all, contrived from cardboard and paper. It is the joy of the whole school; and my class have to be routed out from there at playtimes, as they stand entranced – and full of suggestions for further delights – forgetting to drink their milk, eat their elevenses, call at the lavatory, find their handkerchiefs and generally do all the things that very properly should be done at play-time.

It was their delight in this project that first gave me the idea of taking a party of children to the Michaelmas Fair this year.

'Most of them will go with their parents or with "Caxley aunties",' I told Miss Jackson, as we sipped our tea in the school-house, 'and I don't think we can take the real babies – those who have just entered – it's too big a responsibility. But would you be willing to help me with those that are left? Probably eight or ten of them?'

Miss Jackson was most enthusiastic. We decided that we would discreetly make a list of all those definitely going, and then see how many were left. If the parents in the village knew of our scheme we guessed that they would cheerfully let us take the lot, and that was rather more than we could face.

'Miss Clare will give us a hand I know,' I said, 'and perhaps Mrs Partridge. It seems a pity for the children to miss it, especially as you've fired them so with your project. It's been most success-ful.'

Miss Jackson said that she felt it had eased many nervous tensions in the less well-co-ordinated members of her class, and she welcomed the idea of the visit to Caxley. She would take a note-book, she said, so that she could make up the case-histories after the event, as it would give her an excellent opportunity of observing the children's individual emotional reaction to the stimulus of strong colour, noise and movement.

'I can tell you that,' I said. 'They just shout. Or are sick.'

About six o'clock on the great day, almost the whole of Fairacre School stood outside St Patrick's. Although only twelve were coming with Mrs Partridge, Miss Jackson and me, the rest had come along to see us safely on the 6.10 bus. The din was terrific.

Our charges included Linda Moffat whose mother had a heavy cold and was unable to take her, and Joseph Coggs. They were all unbelievably clean and neat, with faces as shiny as apples.

Joseph had on his best jersey, and Linda was most suitably dressed for the fair in a chic ensemble of dark-green tartan dungarees and a thick red sweater.

'I don't usually wear trousers to an evening outing,' she assured me, 'but Mum thought they'd be better than a skirt on the roundabouts.' Her ideas on the sartorial fitness of things is already strongly advanced.

We waved good-bye to our well-wishers from the bus, and then settled down to a rousing journey to Caxley. Miss Clare was waiting outside her gate, just before the road bends to Beech Green. She looked very neat and trim in her navy-blue coat and sensible felt hat. Not one of her white hairs was out of place, and I knew that, however tousled the rest of us would look after an hour or two at the Michaelmas Fair, Miss Clare would be as tidy as when she boarded the bus.

She was greeted with the greatest affection by the children, who all besought her to let them sit by her, and she made the journey into Caxley with one on her lap and two other lucky ones squeezed beside her on the seat.

The evening was a great success. The Fairacre party wandered enchanted among the blaze of electric lights, the pounding engines and the coils of oily cable that snaked across the market square.

Pink and white candy-floss vanished like magic. One minute a child would be waving a billowing cloud of it on a stick, and the next he would be licking the stick itself with fervour.

Joseph Coggs spent most of his time at the helter-skelter plodding patiently up the narrow stairs with his mat to reappear again, feet first, at the bottom of the corkscrew chute. His hair was on end, his hands black and his face transformed with bliss.

The other children seemed to prefer the games of chance, rolling pennies down grooved slopes and trying to manoeuvre horses into loose boxes, ducks into ponds and the like. The prizes, in many cases, were goldfish, and Eileen Burton was the envy of all when she walked away with two, thrashing madly, in a jam jar.

Mrs Partridge and I enjoyed the roundabouts and switch-backs, and had quite a job to get the children to join us.

Mrs Partridge showed herself a most intrepid rider, electing to sit on the outside of the fastest roundabout, and at one stage sitting sidesaddle in the most dashing and insouciant style.

Miss Clare preferred the swing-boats. From my perch on a mad-looking horse with enraged nostrils, I could see her blissfully floating up and down pulling gently on her furry caterpillar of a rope, whilst Linda Moffat hauled more energetically on the other. They were both, I noticed, as immaculate as when they started out, which could not be said about the rest of the party. My own skirt was inelegantly twisted round the ribs of my uncomfortable steed, my shoes had been stood on, and I could feel a ladder, of alarming magnitude, creeping steadily down one leg.

We caught the last bus back to Fairacre, arriving at half-past nine, gloriously dirty and tired. Even Miss Jackson looked young and happy, and had a prodigious mass of notes which she looked forward to incorporating into the case-histories.

The next morning the usual mob of admirers stood round the fairground model in her room, discussing the excitement of the night before.

'And that candy-floss,' said one with rapture. 'Coo! Didn't half taste good!'

'But this 'ere,' said another indicating the dyed and dusty cotton-wool substitute before him, '*looks* more like it!'

Could loyalty go further?

OCTOBER

'Adjer!'

'Adjerback!' came floating through the window from the playground this morning. These cryptic sounds, suggesting some exotic mid-European dialect, are readily construed by the initiated into 'Had you' and 'Had you back!' and are a sure indication that autumn is really upon us and that the weather is cold enough for a brisk game of 'He' before school begins.

Mrs Pringle, austerely reserved in her conversation at the moment, is back in full force. The stoves gleam like black satin, the kitchen copper steams cheerfully and such dirge-like hymns as *Oft in danger, oft in woe*, mooed in Mrs Pringle's lugubrious contralto, once again sound among the pitch-pine rafters.

349

Mr Mawne's name has not passed her lips, but the vicar told me that he is in Ireland with friends, for a short holiday.

'Do you know that he is thinking of buying a small house, somewhere in the neighbourhood?' added the vicar. He has resurrected the leopard-skin gloves now that the weather is cooler, and he beat them gently together, filling the air with floating pieces of fur which Patrick and Ernest caught surreptitiously as they fluttered near the front desk.

I said that I had not heard the news.

'A good sign, I think,' went on the vicar. 'It looks as though he intends to settle here. That place of Parr's is all very well in its way, but really only suitable for a bachelor.' He looked at me speculatively.

I was about to ask if Mr Mawne proposed to change his status, but thought better of it.

'Not that I can see him as a family man,' mused the vicar, half to himself. 'Not a *large* family man, anyway!' He pondered for a moment, and then shook himself together.

'But a wonderful head for the church accounts,' he finished triumphantly. 'I do so hope he stays!'

Amy spent the evening with me and was unusually preoccupied.

It was a cold, blustery evening. The rose outside the window scrabbled at the pane. Every now and again a particularly fierce gust shuddered the door in its frame; and the roaring in the elm trees at the corner of the playground compelled us to raise our voices as we talked.

Amy surprised me by saying that she hoped I realized how lucky I was in being a single woman. As Amy's usual cry is: 'How much better you would be if only you were married,' I was a little taken aback by this *volte-face*. Before I could get my breath, she said that she had been thinking a lot about the married state recently, as a friend of hers was having some trouble.

It appeared, said Amy, that her husband was much attracted to a young woman in his office, that his wife knew of it, but could not make up her mind if it would be wiser to ignore the whole thing – despite her great unhappiness – or if it would be better to tax the man with it.

At this point Amy put her knitting in her lap, with such a

despairing gesture, that I was glad the twilight veiled both our faces. There was nothing that I could say to help, and after a few minutes' silence, Amy continued.

It wasn't as if her friend were a young woman, she pointed out. Twenty years ago she would have been able to snap her fingers in the man's face, go out and earn her living, and have thought herself glad to be shot of such a wastrel. But now it wasn't so simple. She was older, was not so keen on, or so capable of making a good living on her own. And in any case, he was *her* husband, after all, and she was fond of him, they were accustomed to each other, and her friend could easily forgive, if not forget, these little peccadilloes.

Amy's voice faltered slightly towards the end of this narrative, and she rummaged in her sleeve for her handkerchief. For what it was worth I gave my spinsterish advice.

'If I were your friend,' I began cautiously, 'I should say nothing. It's bound to blow over, and there's no point in breaking up twenty years of comfortable married life for a week or two's nonsense. "Least said soonest mended" I should think.'

'My feelings entirely,' said Amy, blowing her nose briskly. She stuffed her handkerchief away, and talked of some new rose bushes that she had just ordered, and her plans for their arrangement.

So we passed the evening, and I was careful not to put the light on until Amy had completely regained her composure.

At half-past nine she rose to go and I accompanied her to the gorgeous car, by the hedge. The wind still roared, and the trees groaned, as they were wrenched this way and that. Round our feet the dead leaves scurried in whispering eddies.

To my surprise Amy gave me a sudden and most unexpected kiss, then entered her car.

'Lucky old maid!' she said, but I was relieved to hear the laughter in her voice. And with a final toot, she drove away.

The storm raged for hours, and to sleep right through the night was, even for me, quite impossible.

A terrific crack woke me soon after two o'clock and I lay wondering if I could be bothered to get up and investigate. By the time I had persuaded myself that it might only be the chest of drawers giving one of its occasional gun-like reports, it was almost three o'clock, and by that time I was ravenous.

I wished I were as provident as Miss Clare, who kept by her bedside a tin of biscuits, and a smaller one of peppermints, for just such an occasion as this. Downstairs I knew were such delicacies as fruit cake, apples, cream cheese, eggs and a hundred and one delights – but that would mean getting out of my warm bed. I had fought for an hour, I told myself, I could fight again. Doubling my fist, I lay on it and wooed slumber, trying to ignore the clamours of my hunger.

By a quarter to four I had mentally cooked myself scrambled eggs on toast, bacon and tomato, grilled chop and Welsh rarebit. I had also opened a tin of peaches, mandarin oranges, Bartlett pears and some particularly luscious pineapple rings, all of which floated round my bed in the most tantalizing fashion.

At ten to four I rose, cursing, thrust my feet into slippers, descended to the kitchen, frightening poor Tibby out of her wits, collected a most unladylike hunk of fruit cake and took it back to bed – furious with myself for not doing the whole thing hours before. I was asleep in ten minutes.

This morning I discovered the source of the crack which woke me. A branch of one of the elms had split from the trunk, and lay, amidst a mass of twigs, leaves and part of the roof of the boys' lavatory, across the playground. Two tiles had slipped from my own roof, and lay askew in the guttering.

The garden was wrecked. Michaelmas daisies lay flattened, and the rose had been torn from the wall. It waved long skinny arms across the doorway.

Mrs Pringle surveyed the untidy playground sourly, as if such confusion were a personal affront.

'And only swep' up two days ago!' was her comment, 'Mr Willet'll have something to say to that!'

Her reactions to the soot which had been blown down the flues and covered the stoves and the surrounding floor, were even more violent.

'As if ash wasn't bad enough, and bits of coke scattered all round by them as should know better – mentioning no names – without this filth!' Her leg presumably burst into flame at this point, for she hobbled, with many a sharply indrawn breath, to fetch the dustpan and brush.

The children were joyously garrulous about the gale's damage when they arrived.

'A great old 'ole up Mr Roberts' rick !' reported one gleefully.

'My dad says there's a tree right across the Caxley road, and half the Beech Green kids can't get to school,' said another, with the greatest satisfaction.

'My auntie's next-door neighbour's baby had a slate fall on its pram!' announced a third, 'and if it hadn't been sitting up, and a bit too far from the porch, and the wind had been stronger, it might have been in hospital!'

Altogether we had a pleasurably dramatic morning, for there is nothing like the sharing of common danger, with the added spice of others' misfortunes, to give one a sense of cosiness, and, in a village, these excitements provided by nature, give us the same stimulus as 'This Week's Sensational Programme' for our town cousins at their local cinemas.

Furthermore they stir old memories, for the countryman's recollections go back a long way. Reading little, they remember the tales passed down from father to son, tales which lose little in the telling. Mr Willet had a wonderful story to add to the general excitement today.

'It happened in the seventies,' said Mr Willet, who had come in to the classroom to borrow a boy to steady the ladder while he effected repairs to the lavatory roof. The children quietly put their pens in the grooves of their desks. I turned my history book face downward, and we all prepared to listen. Mr Willet, when wound up, goes on for a long, long time – and anyway still, in the country, thank God, there is always tomorrow.

'My old dad remembers it well. He was doing a job for old Sir Edmund up the Hall, and Mrs Pringle's old dad was up there too, doing a bit of carpentering in the back parts.' He stopped suddenly and looked round, puffing out his stained moustache. 'Here! You say if I'm interrupting. Don't want to stop the work, you know!'

I assured him that we were all keen to know the rest of the story. The children, seeing that their eavesdropping had been legalized, relaxed somewhat and flopped forward comfortably on to their desks. Mr Willet resumed.

'Well, it was about this time of year – soon after Michaelmas Fair, because Sir Edmund had got several new hands just come to work for him, and this 'ere old gale blew up. Did it blow!' Mr Willet swivelled his eyes quite awfully, and we all shivered.

'The gals – the maids that was – fair screeched, and run about like a lot of chickens with their necks half-wrung. The cook got burnt with some sparks what blew out of the fire and give up doing the dinner, and there was a proper panic. Some of the chaps, with my dad, was sheltering in a bit of an old outhouse where they kept the firing and that, when all of a sudden—!' Here Mr Willet, with a proper sense of drama, paused and lifted his gnarled fingers. The children's eyes grew rounder, and the suspense was almost unbearable.

'All of a sudden—' repeated Mr Willet, with relish, 'there was a groanin' and tearin' and crashin' you could 'ear as far away as Springbourne. A 'orrible roarin' sort of commotion, and then the biggest crash of all! One of Sir Edmund's big old lime trees fell across the glass house! Coo – that were a crash! And after the crash my dad said you could 'ear the tinkle-tinkle of bits of glass as they fell on the tiles in the greenhouse floor. Poor old Jeff Radge what looked after the stuff in there, he was crying, my dad said; and when they could fight their way through the wind to go and see the damage, he said there was tomatoes and cucumbers all hanging up with splinters of glass sticking out of 'em like a lot of hedgehogs!

'And this Jeff,' he finished triumphantly, 'he put his hands up over his face, and swayed about and cried 'orrid!'

Here Mr Willet did the same, much to the consternation of the children. 'And he kep' on saying, "I can't bear no more! I can't bear no more!" Poor chap—' commented Mr Willet compassionately, lowering his hands and speaking in his normal voice again. 'And old Sir Edmund had him in the kitchen and give him some of his own brandy to get him round again! Ah! That was a gale and no mistake!'

He stood silent for a few moments, his old eyes looking out across the heads of the children, as though he could see those cucumbers and tomatoes bristling with glinting glass, and the sorrow of the man who had tended them. The children watched him solemnly.

'Ah well!' he said, returning to this century with a jerk. 'I'd, best choose a good stout boy for the ladder!'

At once, the children pulled themselves upright, and with chests outflung and breath held to bursting point, tried to look as stout and trustworthy as they knew Mr Willet would expect them to be, if they wanted to escape from the dull classroom to the joys of the playground and remain in his august company.

Eric was chosen and, grinning joyfully, followed Mr Willet through the door. Deflated, the rest sighed sadly and returned to their books.

Since the gale the weather has turned soft and warm. Mr Willet tells me it is Saint Luke's little summer, and very welcome it is.

Miss Jackson and I decided to take the whole school out for a nature walk, to enjoy it all. We made for the little lane that turns off by the 'Beetle and Wedge' and rises steadily until it peters out high up on the windy downs.

The children dallied in the lane, scrambling up the high banks to collect the hazel nuts which flourish there.

'Gi'e us a bunk up!' rang the cry, and one would obligingly put his shoulder down and hoist his friend higher in the hedge. We meandered along eating nuts and blackberries and even sloes and damsons which grow thickly, powdered with a blue bloom, among their spikes.

We found a patch of dry grass half-way up the slope, sheltered by a clump of stunted thorn bushes, and here we sat to rest. The view of Fairacre below us was clear in the limpid October air. There is a unique atmosphere about a fine October day. The sky is a burning blue, which combined with the golden and auburn glow of the trees creates a sparkle and glory unseen at other more-vaunted periods of the year.

From this distance the yellow elm trees by the school looked like the chubby pieces of cauliflower that one spears from picca-lilli; and in the field beyond we could see Samson, Mr Roberts' house cow, placidly grazing.

Blue smoke plumes waved from cottage chimneys, and Joseph Coggs was delighted to see his mother pegging washing on her line, far below. Some of the fields were still bright with stubble, but most of them had already been ploughed, and lay, clean and brown, awaiting next year's crops.

We spent a long time there, gazing and speculating, drinking in great draughts of the scented air. I was brought to earth by a vicious blow across the back.

Startled, I turned to see Ernest grinding something fiercely into the grass.

'A dummle wasp!' he explained. 'Crawling up you, miss. They always stings worse if they're sleepy. Ah well! He've had it now!'

I thanked him, and called to the children that we must return. They came reluctantly, bearing all sorts of treasures with them. Rose hips, feathers and toadstools were among their souvenirs, but Eric was struggling along with a colossal knobbly flint, whose weight threatened to age him considerably.

When I remonstrated with him he turned an accusing eye upon me.

'It's a meatright!' he told me. 'Saw one just like it on the telly!' And shouldering his burden he bore it painfully back to Fairacre School.

Malcolm Annett's christening party was a great occasion. The sun shone through St Patrick's windows, catching the gleaming brass on the altar and the tawny chrysanthemums which Mrs Partridge had arranged.

Mrs Moffat had made the christening gown – a miracle of tiny stroked gathers and finely-pleated tucks, with a froth of old lace at the hem. Apart from making a few popping sounds as he withdrew a wet thumb from his mouth, the baby behaved with the greatest decorum, even suffering his pink forehead to be doused with water, from a silver scallop, in quite large quantities.

Ted, Mr Annett's brother, was resplendent in his best grey suit and the other godfather was in uniform. They spoke their responses in manly tones, undertaking to renounce the works of the devil on behalf of the infant I held, as I as godmother did too. It was hard to believe that the angelic bundle was 'conceived and born in sin,' I thought privately, watching a Red Admiral butterfly hovering in the church porch, as the vicar's beautiful voice fluted benignly on.

Mrs Pringle had come to the service with her cherry-decorated hat on, and a very dashing white organdie blouse which had once been Mrs Partridge's and had been the *pièce de résistance* at a recent jumble sale. Outside, whilst brother Ted fussed with his camera and we squeezed obediently together in order to make a compact group, she came up to admire the baby.

'It's a wonder either of you are here to tell the tale,' she told Mrs Annett, 'that front room of yours is nothing better than a morgue – facing north and dripping damp. You mind you has all the rest in your back bedroom where the hot tank is!'

Mrs Annett assured her that she would give the matter her attention, and invited her to join in the historic group, which she did with the greatest pride.

The christening party at Beech Green school-house was a hilarious affair. Miss Clare had come over from her cottage and we found a corner together.

'I didn't come to the service,' she explained, 'as Dr Martin insists that I have a little rest in the afternoon.'

I thought that this sounded ominous and enquired if she had had any more attacks.

For a moment she was silent, and then confided: 'Well, yes, my dear, I have. Doctor says I shall be quite all right if I rest more, so I'm being sensible and lying down every afternoon.'

There was not time to say much, for the cake was being cut and toasts drunk to the future felicity of young Malcolm Annett, but for me, at least, a shadow had fallen over the festivities.

Mr Annett implored me to come over to talk to brother Ted who is a mathematics professor, and who had just been honoured by an invitation to lecture at Cambridge, and was very pleased about it all.

With becoming modesty Ted admitted that his subject was to be 'The Triangulate Isotopic Hebdominal and its Associated Quotients' (or something very like it), and would I care to be present?

Though decidedly flattered by his kindness, I was secretly glad that I was already engaged to go with Amy to the theatre on the same day, so that with polite sounds of regret we passed to other and more intelligible topics.

As six o'clock approached and young Malcolm, after patiently waiting for us to finish our refreshments, was now vociferously demanding his own, we made our farewells. I looked around for Miss Clare, hoping to take her back with me, but she had slipped away unobserved, and I determined to call on her before many days went by.

On Monday morning Miss Jackson did not arrive until nearly eleven o'clock. She had been away for the week-end and had missed the evening train.

I was inclined to be sympathetic at first, despite the difficulty I had had in collecting dinner money and savings money, reading parents' notes and marking two registers during the first part of the morning. However, it gradually came out, through chance remarks, that Miss Jackson had had no intention of catching the Sunday evening train, as she had had the opportunity to visit Miss Crabbe who happened to be staying in her neighbourhood.

So engrossed had they become in educational and psychological affairs that they had stayed talking until past eleven o'clock. On hearing this, my own flabbergasted rage gave way to the deepest sympathy for Miss Crabbe's long-suffering hosts, who could never have bargained for such verbosity when they invited Miss Jackson to tea to renew their guest's acquaintance.

I said nothing during school hours about this behaviour, thinking it better to cool down; but after supper I pointed out, as mildly as I could, that the school must come first and that it was essential that she appeared at the correct time after a week-end.

To my astonishment I was given to understand that I was old-fashioned, narrow-minded and petty. Furthermore, the inestimable advantage of listening to Miss Crabbe's wisdom far outweighed such mundane affairs as collecting dinner money and the like – all of which could be performed by those with inferior minds (like mine, I supposed!), thus giving the more visionary educationalists (presumably Miss Jackson!) a chance of using their talents for the good of the community.

When I had regained my breath I said that I had never heard such utter nonsense, that I would have preferred a straightforward apology, that an early night might be a good thing, after her late session, that she appeared over-heated and if she cared for a dose of milk of magnesia there was a bottle in the medicine cabinet.

At this, she flounced towards the door, saying that no one had ever understood her except Miss Crabbe, that it was no wonder that English education was in the state it was when prosy old women with antediluvian ideas still ruled the roost, and that she didn't want any supper.

With that she slammed the door, pounded up to her bedroom, slammed that door too and was seen no more by me. I was amused to find, later, that the top of a loaf and a hunk of cheese had vanished from the larder – and that the milk of magnesia had been used.

In all fairness to Miss Jackson I must record that she appeared very humbly at the breakfast table, apologized handsomely and brought me back a melon from Caxley, on her next visit, as a peace-offering. Moreover she went out to do her playground duty much more promptly and even got up a little earlier in the mornings, so that the outburst had good results.

A day or two after this, I was busy putting in some tulip bulbs, under the front windows, when I heard a hoot and saw Dr Martin driving by. I waved and he drew up.

'What are you putting in?' he asked, seeing my trowel. I told him that I had treated myself to two dozen pink tulips and that he must look out for them in the spring.

At this moment Mrs Pringle appeared, on her way to sweep the school out. Dr Martin hailed her.

'How's that leg!'

Mrs Pringle's gait, which had been normal, took on a shuffle-and-hop action, rather like a wooden-legged person essaying the polka. She drew a great shuddering sigh.

'Oh, doctor! If you only knew what I went through! Mighty little sympathy I gets, or asks for, for that matter, but if you was to realize the way it sometimes burns – then sometimes prickles – then sometimes jumps – then sometimes twitches – you'd wonder I didn't go down on my bended knee – always supposing I *could* go down on my bended knee, which is well nigh impossible, as the vicar can vouch for, me having to lean forward in the choir stalls, prayer-time – and beg of you to cut it off for me!'

Dr Martin said: 'Oh rats to all that! Got your elastic stocking on?'

Mrs Pringle nodded haughtily.

'Then get a bit of weight off,' said her unsympathetic medical adviser. 'You must be three stone too heavy. No starch, no fat and no sugar! That'll do it!'

'*Some people*,' began Mrs Pringle with awful deliberation, 'has a hard day's work to do, every day that God sends. Scrubbing, sweeping, carrying buckets, and cleaning up after others – who shall be nameless! And hard work can't be tackled on an empty stummick, as my mother could have told you any day. I don't suppose I eats more than a butterfly – but a woman with my job needs a trifle of cold bacon or bread puddin' to keep her going, if she's to do all she's asked!'

'Try skipping then,' suggested the doctor, as she paused for breath. Mrs Pringle ignored this facetious interruption, and boomed inexorably on.

'Them as does their work – so-called – a-setting in a chair, writing rubbish what no one understands in a hand what no one can read; or at best getting ailing folks to strip out when the wind's in the east, so's they can poke 'em about sharper with their cold fingers – them, I says, has no need for half the food that finds its way down their gullets. Gentry food at that too! Pheasants, partridges and other dainties I sees hanging up in the back porch as I passes.'

Dr Martin here let out a delighted guffaw, but Mrs Pringle finished her tirade unperturbed.

'And if them that *sits* to work needs that lot, stands to reason that them that *stands* and *bends* and *kneels* to labour, needs a fat lot more!'

'You're a wicked old tartar,' said Dr Martin affectionately, 'and I'll come to your funeral when you pop off with a fatty heart. Get along with you, you fascinating hussy!'

Bridling, Mrs Pringle limped ostentatiously towards the school, her stout back registering extreme disapproval.

Dr Martin watched her go. 'How I do love that old termagant!' he said.

Just then my kettle let off a shrill whistle.

'Going to make one?' asked the doctor hopefully, getting

smartly out of his car, and opening the front door for me, before I could answer.

Meekly I took off my gardening gloves, and we went into the kitchen.

Over the tea-tray I broached the subject of Miss Clare.

'I didn't think she looked at all well last week,' I said. 'Is there anything else wrong besides her heart?'

Dr Martin looked steadily across the table at me.

'Do you really want to know?'

'Of course I do.'

'Well,' said the doctor, replacing his cup very carefully. 'To be blunt, she doesn't get enough to eat'

'Good God!' I cried, appalled. My own cup crashed on to the saucer. 'You don't mean that?'

I thought of Miss Clare's larder, with the gleaming rows of jam and chutney of her own making. I thought of the onions hanging up, the carrots and parsnips in an old well-scrubbed wooden rack. I thought of my last supper party there – of the cold brisket, the tart, the salad, the glinting silver and snowy cloth.

As if he could read my mind Dr Martin spoke again.

'Yes, I know she keeps a good store cupboard. There's not a morsel of waste there. She uses every bit of produce from her garden that she can. But she can't afford to use it all. She was giving baskets of windfall apples to the neighbours last week. Before, she would have turned them into jelly – but three pounds of preserving sugar costs half a crown or so, and that wants finding.'

'This is awful—' I began.

Dr Martin went on ruthlessly. 'She gets next to no butcher's meat, and things that she should have, like liver and cream and a drop of Burgundy, are beyond her these days. It stands to reason. She's got the old age pension and a minute teaching one; and though she owns that little cottage she still has to keep it in repair. She told me last week that the repairs to her well came to over five pounds. Her shoes cost between ten and fifteen shillings to mend. God knows how long she wears her clothes. Her house linen was her mother's, and when it goes she can't afford to replace it. Her father thatched the roof just before he died – what, twenty years ago now – and it'll need doing again before long. How's Miss Clare ever to get two hundred pounds together for that?'

'Fool that I am!' I said passionately. 'I should have thought of all that. But somehow – she's always so neat, and the house is so beautiful, and she's always given me such good meals—' I couldn't go on.

'Oh she'd give her guests a good meal!' agreed the doctor brutally. 'You'd have butter too. But I noticed there was only margarine in the larder when I went there last week for a teaspoon.' Indeed, I thought, there's mighty little that this wise old man misses about his patients' background. 'Mind you, she's got a kind of instinctive knowledge of nutrition, handed down from peasant forbears. She sprinkles parsley around pretty heavily. She makes herself rough oatmeal porridge – but she doesn't have all the sugar and milk with that, that she should have. She bakes a bit of bread now and again, when the oven's on; but naturally she's sparing with the firing these days.'

'You don't mean she's going cold, as well?' I said piteously.

'Hardly surprising,' rejoined the old man. 'And she can't work as she did in the garden. Peter Lamb, poor fellow, used to dig it for nothing. That idle neighbour of hers will condescend to turn it over for three bob an hour – which she can't afford anyway. I noticed that last year's potato patch is left rough this year. Less food again.'

He pushed his chair back from the table as if the matter were closed. I leant across and caught his wrist.

'Now sit down. You're not going till we've thought something out. We must help her. Besides,' I admitted, 'I can't stick this out alone, until I can see some way round it.'

The doctor smiled, hitched his chair up again and passed his cup across to be refilled.

'For a tough old schoolmarm with a good caning arm, you've got a remarkably soft heart,' he commented. 'Good Lord, girl, Miss Clare's only one of hundreds! They're the new poor; fighting a rear-guard action and keeping the standard flying. I'll bet Miss Clare puts a shilling in the collecting tin next Poppy Day, and that chap next door who's picking up twelve pounds a week, won't be able to put his hand on a bit of change!'

'I know all that,' I said, 'but come on now. Let's be practical. How can we help?'

'She won't let you. She's too proud.'

'Don't be such a *maddening* man!' I almost shouted. 'You come in here torturing me, and making me give you cups of tea – oh sorry, I forgot to fill it up—' I pushed it across hastily. 'And you put me into an absolute fantod and fever—'

'You wanted to know,' he pointed out.

'And now I do know, we must do something, or I shall go clean out of my mind, and the children will find me sitting with straws in my hair, drooling, when they come tomorrow – and you'll have another patient on your hands.'

This outburst appeared to sober him, I was glad to see; for no doctor, however zealous or impoverished, cares to hear of another patient being added to his burdens these days.

'The answer, I think,' he said slowly, 'is a nice easy-going lodger. Like your Miss Jackson.'

'I'd be delighted for Miss Clare to have her,' I said, 'but I don't know that she's exactly easy-going.'

'Well, someone like that,' pursued the doctor. 'She's got a spare bedroom and that front parlour too, that's hardly ever used. Then she'd eat more. She'd be most conscientious about giving a lodger a nourishing meal and she'd have some as well.'

'It's sounds a good idea,' I agreed. 'But could she stand the extra work?'

'Speaking from a medical point of view, I think any extra work involved – and there needn't be much, I'd have a word with the prospective lodger and tell her to pull her weight with bed-making and lifting and so on – would be offset by the advantages. She wouldn't be anxious about making ends meet – and there's nothing more fraying than that, week after week – she'd have someone else to think about, which would take her mind off her own ills a bit; solitary people can't help dwelling on 'em a bit too much, and she'd have more money to spend on food. And that's the main thing!'

He drained his cup, and then rose.

'Now I must be off. Think it over, and think about Miss Jackson going there. I'll tackle Miss Clare. I shall tell her I'd feel happier if she had someone in the house with her. I'll suggest her sister. That'll properly put her back up – and she'll consider a lodger much more readily!'

'Honestly,' I said, flabbergasted, 'I'd no idea you were such a Machiavelli! But I will suggest to Miss Jackson that she might like to make a change. But somehow – I don't know if she's quite right for Miss Clare.'

'She'll be better off with Miss Clare than with you,' said the doctor shrewdly, 'Cooped up together all day – why, you don't want to hear her news when she gets back here to tea – you know it all! Give her Miss Clare to pour her troubles out to, and she'll blossom like a rose; and so will her landlady! She'll look forward to her coming in to hear all the school gossip. Do all three of you good, I know that.'

We proceeded to the front door and I surveyed my tulip bed, still unfinished.

'And what does Miss Jackson give you for board and lodging?' he asked. I told him three pounds, which seemed to suit us both.

He threw up his hands in mock horror. 'You bloated profiteer!' he exclaimed. 'On top of your fat salary too! You pass her over to Miss Clare, my girl, and put that three pounds into her pocket.' This bit of by-play I recognized for what it was – a subtle way of relieving the tension of the past hour, and of bringing us back to a more normal plane.

He pointed to my tulip bulbs. 'Bought with your ill-gotten gains, I suppose.' He could not resist one final stab. 'Miss Clare makes her garden pretty with slips that friends give her. She might be able to afford bulbs if she had a lodger!'

At this moment, Mrs Pringle, her work completed, came limping back, bucket in hand.

'You are the most cruel, heartless creature I've ever met,' I told him, and hailed Mrs Pringle. 'Don't you agree?' I asked her, above the noise of the car's engine.

'Ah!' said Mrs Pringle with much satisfaction, 'that he is. He's a walking monument of vice!' We stood, side by side, waving good-bye to him. For once, Mrs Pringle and I were united.

Having given the children an earnest little homily on thrift, and the wisdom of putting some part of their money away, however small, for a rainy day, I was shocked to find that I have one and sevenpence only in my own purse.

When I think of what I earn, and my 'profiteering' three pounds a week in addition, I am ashamed of myself, for nearly every month I seem to spend the last few days of it counting out pennies and shamelessly embezzling needlework money or dinner money, until Jim Bryant brings the cheque.

This is another painful reminder of Miss Clare's plight, which is constantly in my mind. Since the doctor's visit, I have approached Miss Jackson, who seemed unflatteringly delighted to quit my portals if she could find another resting-place, so that that is one step forward.

I have no doubt that before half term is here, in another week's time, Dr Martin will have his well-laid plans in working trim.

NOVEMBER

It is wonderful to be solvent again, if only for the first week of the month. Shaken by my former extravagance, and determined to organize my expenditure, I have started an account book, and I intend to put down my daily spendings. How long this good resolution will last I can't tell.

Today's entries make disagreeable reading:

	£	s.	d.
Electricity bill	3	6	0
Coal bill	3	18	0
Garage's bill	2	4	0
Weekly grocery bill	1	12	6

I comfort myself with the thought that the first three will not appear again for a little while, and I certainly hope that the entry which follows these four will never appear again – though I have serious doubts about that. It says: 'Repayment to needlework money tin, and dinner money tin . . . 8s. 9d.'

I am going to put an elastic band round each of those Oxo tins and remove them only when the exigencies of rightful duty make it necessary.

'Always put a little by!' as I told my children firmly last week, when the savings' money had fallen below average. Sometimes I wonder that a bolt from heaven doesn't strike me.

We have had our first fog of the winter. Here, in open country, we are spared the sulphurous, choking fog that makes everything filthy, but the thick, white mist that rolls down from the hills, or that creeps up from the valley where Caxley lies, can be equally disconcerting.

It was very, very still. Drops of moisture hung in the hedges and cobwebs. From the school playground it was impossible to see the church, my house and the great elm trees. Only the occasional spattering of heavy drops from the elms showed where they were. In the distance Samson, Mr Roberts's cow, lowed in bewilderment.

Tibby dislikes these damp mornings, and has taken to accompanying me over to the classroom. Here, his doting admirers have placed a chair from the infants' room near the stove, furnished it with an old woollen jacket from the dressing-up box, and Tibby deigns to ensconce himself there for most of the day. At play-time he accepts offers of milk, cake, and occasionally chocolate from the children.

'Don't 'e purr nice?'

'Pretty little dear, ennit?' they say fondly to each other, as they pet him, and this adulation is, of course, exactly what his lordship likes best.

It grew so thick by midday, that I wondered if Mrs Crossley would be able to find her way along with the dinner-van. But all was well, and our canisters of stew, mashed potato, apples and custard arrived safely, only ten minutes later than usual.

'It's even worse in Caxley!' she told us. 'It seems to be general everywhere.'

The children elected to play indoors during the dinner hour, and as the weather was so appalling, it seemed the best thing to do. Jigsaw puzzles, beads, picture books, crayons and paper, and plasticine modelling kept them all engrossed, and they begged to be allowed to hear 'Listen with Mother' at a quarter to two. As a special treat I switched it on. It is, as everyone knows, a programme intended for children under school age, but most of the Fairacre children listen with attention to it. This does not surprise me with the infants, for our children are remarkably unsophisticated and appreciate stories, games, songs and so on intended for much younger people; but I am astonished that some children of eight or nine, in my own class, should still get satisfaction from this excellent programme. I should be interested to know if other teachers find that their children are equally responsive, for I should have thought that the natural reaction of the older child to 'Listen with Mother' would have been impatience. In any case, it is a compliment to the planners of this programme, which I am happy to pass on.

Joseph Coggs has brought his tortoise to school. This animal has been lost dozens of times during the summer, but has been found in various parts of the parish and returned to Joe. Now, it is comatose and ready to hibernate, and Joseph's mother has asked if we can find it accommodation in school. Today, the children put it in a box of dry earth and leaves, and it is back in the corner of the lobby. With any luck, it should survive, and will certainly be less disturbed there, despite forty-odd children's attention, than it would be in the Coggs' crowded and ramshackle cottage.

We sent the children home ten minutes earlier this afternoon, much to their jubilation. The classroom was already too dark to see properly, and the four inadequate bulbs, which hang naked from the ceiling, did little to help. The children ran off into the mist, squealing like piglets, and shouting joyfully to each other.

Miss Jackson and I stoked up a roaring fire, drew the curtains to shut out the first dismal, dispiriting day of November, and made anchovy toast for tea. I only hoped that all our pupils were as happily and snugly sheltered.

I am appalled at the amount of litter lying about in Fairacre's once tidy lane. I suppose it is more noticeable since poor old Bannister, the road man, died a few weeks ago, for no one can be found to take the job on.

At this time of year, too, the leaves are thick in the sides of the roads and any rain carries them along to the drains which soon get blocked. Then again, far more things are wrapped in paper these days; but litter baskets stand outside the grocer's shop, the butcher's and the 'Beetle and Wedge' and one would have thought that three would have been ample in a little place like Fairacre. I can't help feeling that this nuisance shows complete callousness towards the look of the place, and also an unpleasant trait in the public's attitude to the welfare state. As Mrs Pringle horrified me by saying, when commenting on the rubbish blowing about near the church: 'We pays to have it done, don't we! In rates and that!' Presumably, that should be enough!

I have been having an extraordinary anti-litter campaign at school, but with only partial success. Linda Moffat, of all people, peeled a mint sweet free from its wrappings in the playground, and let each wisp flutter delicately to the ground. When the last had fallen, I pounced upon her, and drove her into picking each minute piece up.

She obeyed, with a mixture of one-humouring-an-idiot and genuine bewilderment, which made me give yet another blistering lecture to Fairacre School, which the children listened to with great resentment, as it should have been a percussion band period, and they felt themselves most hardly used.

Mrs Willet commented on this problem too when I went down to her cottage to leave a message for Mr Willet.

'Not much good ticking off the children,' she remarked, 'when the parents are behaving like that!' She nodded through the window towards Mrs Coggs who was passing. The latest baby was blissfully clawing a newspaper and dropping the pieces over the side, while its mother gazed at it with fond pride.

Mrs Willet was busy making sloe gin when I called. She sat at her kitchen table, pricking the sloes diligently with a stout darning needle, and dropping them into a bottle half-full of gin.

'Ready at Christmas!' she said proudly. 'I do a bottle every year, and sometimes wine as well!'

She opened her larder door and displayed the riches inside. It was as well-stocked with jars and bottles as Miss Clare's, and I was struck – not for the first time – with the versatility and energy of the average countrywoman.

Mrs Willet can tackle a hundred jobs, without having been specifically *taught* any of them. She can salt pork or beef, make jams, jellies, wines, chutneys and pickles; she can bake pies – with all manner of pastries – cakes, tarts and her own bread, which is particularly delicious. She makes rugs, curtains, and her own clothes. She can help a neighbour in childbirth and – at the other end of life's span – compose a corpse's limbs for decent burial. She is as good a gardener as her husband, can distemper a room, mend a fuse, and sings in the choir.

She is, in fact, typical of most countrywomen, and with them she shares that self-reliance which is the heritage of those who have had to face tackling daily jobs of varied kinds.

Mrs Willet is small and pale and yet she is 'always on the go,' as she herself will tell you. The fact that she can do so many things, and takes enormous pride in doing them well, is, I think, the secret of this apparently inexhaustible energy. There are so many different activities to engage her, that when she tires of one, there is another to which she can turn and get refreshment. From turning her heavy old mangle in the wash-house, she will come in and sit down to stitch a new skirt. She will prepare a stew, and while it simmers on the hob, filling the little house with its fragrance, she will practise her part in Mr Annett's new anthem, ready for the next church festival. And – this perhaps is the most important thing – she sees a satisfying result from her labours. The clothes blow on the line, the skirt is folded and put away in the drawer ready for next Sunday; Mr Willet will come in 'sharp-set' and praise her bubbling stew; and, with any luck, Mr Annett will congratulate her on her grasp of that difficult passage just before the basses come in.

It is a creative life. There is something worthwhile to show for energy expended which engenders the desire to accomplish more. Small wonder that the Mrs Willets of this world are happy, and deserve to be so.

Mr Willet, as the school's shipshape condition testifies, is equally resourceful. There are very few jobs that are beyond Mr Willet's powers. He replaces hinges, panes of glass, roof tiles, fence palings, and other casualties of school life. I have seen him giving a hand with thatching, cleaning out a well, felling a tree, and catching a frightened horse. He can build a shed or a garage, laying bricks and smoothing cement with the best of them, fashion a pair of wooden gates, or erect a bird bath or sundial. He knows how to prune any shrub that grows, how to graft, how to lay a hedge, where to get the best manure, pea-sticks, bean-poles and everything else necessary to maintain a flourishing garden. To me and to the managers of Fairacre school he is beyond price, saving many a repair bill and foreseeing any possible trouble and forestalling it with his capable old hands.

And yet, when his modest cheque arrives at the end of the month, he receives it with a bashfulness which puts my own eagerness to shame.

Two days before half term I received a note from Miss Clare inviting me there for the next evening.

Dr Martin had hailed me from his car, soon after his visit, and told me that he'd 'had a word with Miss Clare about having someone in the house.' With that he had driven off – so that I wondered how much Miss Clare knew, when I approached her door.

She greeted me as warmly as ever, and before long, introduced the subject of lodgers herself.

'Dr Martin suggested that I joined forces with my sister Ada, but of course that's out of the question. He insists that someone should be with me – foolishly, I think – but I feel that I must do as he says. Do you think my spare bedroom and the little front parlour would be suitable?'

I said that any lodger would be lucky to get them. Then I took a deep breath, and said that I believed Miss Jackson would be prepared to make a change.

'But I must warn you,' I said, 'that she's not awfully easy in some ways. Getting her up is a dreadful job each morning. She sleeps like the dead – and you shouldn't have to run up and down stairs after her with your wonky heart.'

'I shouldn't dream of doing so,' answered Miss Clare, 'and in any case Dr Martin said that she would have to understand, from the first, that I could not do all I should wish to do for her—' She broke off and began to laugh. 'There! Now the cat's out of the bag! Yes, my dear, I'm afraid the doctor and I have been discussing this business. Quite unforgivable of us, behind your back!'

'Don't worry,' I said. 'I can guess who started the conversation, and, frankly, I should be glad to be relieved of my lodger. We see too much of each other for the thing to work properly – and I'm probably a bit irritable after school, and let things rile me unnecessarily.'

'As we're being honest, I'd better tell you that Dr Martin said as much. His words were: "If you want to see Miss Read staying sane, you'll take pity on her and remove her assistant. That poor girl gets a pretty thin time of it, living with her headmistress"!'

'Well!' I exclaimed, flabbergasted at Dr Martin's duplicity. He'd certainly seen the best way to get Miss Clare to fall in with his machinations! I wouldn't mind betting, I thought to myself, that the harrowing tale he had pitched me was all part of his low cunning! However, I could not help feeling amused at the skilful way in which he had worked on us both, and could do nothing of course to let Miss Clare know of his conversation with me, which had led up to the present situation.

'I'm sure he's right,' I said, swallowing my bitter pill. 'She'll be much happier with you, if you feel up to coping with the extra work. Why not write to her? I'll take a note back, if you like.'

She fetched her old red leather writing-case, which the Partridges had given her one Christmas, and sat down at the table. The room was very quiet as she wrote. A coal clinked into the hearth and the tabby cat stretched itself on the rug. I leant back and closed my eyes and thought wryly of the lengths to which conscientious doctors will go for their favourite patients.

At last the letter was finished, and Miss Clare handed it over for my perusal. It said:

Dear Miss Jackson,
I understand from Miss Read that you are still looking for permanent lodgings. Would you care to come here? I can offer

*you a bedroom and a separate sitting-room, and should be very
glad to welcome you.*

*If this interests you perhaps you could come to tea one day
soon, to see if the accommodation is suitable and to discuss
other arrangements.*

*Yours sincerely,
Dorothy Clare*

It was written in her beautiful, flowing, copper-plate hand,
which has been Fairacre's model for forty years, and, with its
even spacing and equal margins was a work of art, most pleasing
to the eye.

'I'm sure she'll jump at the chance,' I told her, handing it back
to be put in its envelope, 'and I shall be able to revert to my
pleasant solitary state, and talk nonsense to the cat without being
afraid that I'm overheard.'

And so Miss Jackson's future was settled, to the great comfort
of Miss Clare, Dr Martin, Fairacre's headmistress – and, most
important, to the happiness of Miss Jackson herself.

'Heard about that chap Mawne?' asked Mr Willet, the next
morning. 'They were saying after choir practice that there's two
places he's trying for. That pair of old cottages on the road to
Springbourne, where Mr Roberts' old shepherd lived some while
ago, afore he moved up to the council houses; and Captain
Whatsisname's – you knows, up the back there.' He waved a
massive thumb in the direction of the 'Beetle and Wedge.'

'Bit big, aren't they?' I said, and then wished I hadn't.

'They says as he's settling down here,' said Mr Willet stolidly. I
was grateful for his sober face. 'Maybe he's having relations, and
that, to live there too.'

'Quite likely,' I said.

'It do seem wrong to me,' went on Mr Willet thoughtfully, 'the
way that folks with a bit of money buys up these old cottages
us village chaps have always lived in. Don't leave nothing for
us.'

'But everyone's bursting to get into a council house,' I protested. 'You know the heart-burning that goes on, every time a few
are allotted to different families.'

'Ah!' said Mr Willet, nodding sagely. 'They all WANTS a council house – but not at the rents they asks for them.'

'Good lord!' I expostulated, 'the houses are subsidized now! They're living partly at other ratepayers' expense. They get the amenities they ask for cheaper than they would in a private house. What more can they want?'

'Take old Burton, that used to be shepherd. He used to pay three bob a week for that cottage. Now his rent's nearer thirty-three.'

'And how can you expect any landlord to keep a cottage in repair for three bob a week! I should have thought you'd have seen the sense in that!'

Mr Willet was not at all put out by my heat. He stropped his chin thoughtfully, as he replied.

''Tisn't that I don't see the sense. *Of course*, three bob's not enough. *Of course*, thirty-three don't cover the proper cost of them new council houses – I knows that. But, you think again. What is a chap like old Button to do, on his bit of money! Where is he to live, if he's to stay in Fairacre?'

I pondered this problem. Mr Willet, who had obviously given this matter much more earnest thought than I had ever done, spoke again.

'If the council could build some real *little* places – nothin' elaborate, mind you – as could be let fairly cheap, why, they'd go like hot cakes. That's the thing – some real *little* places for us old 'uns.'

He switched to another aspect of rural housing.

'Mr Roberts gave young Miller the rough side of his tongue evidently.'

'Oh? What's the trouble there?'

'Well, you know his old dad is the main tractor driver and his old mum does a turn mornings for Mrs Roberts? That cottage has got four rooms, and when young Ern got married he hadn't got no place to go, so home he comes, wife and all, to live with the old people. Mr Roberts told him flat he was to find somewhere – but you know how it is – he just never! Now the baby's come, and it grizzles all night and fair drives the old folks dotty. Young Ern works up the atomic and gets good pay. He's got no business in a tied cottage and he knows it. It's been that awkward. Mr Roberts don't want to lose his best tractor man, by being too sharp, and yet why should that young Ern live off of him?'

I said it was certainly unjust.

'Looks as though this baby'll settle things. The old chap's getting proper fed-up and Mr Roberts told Ern he wasn't going to have one of his best workers upset, because his son was "a selfish lout". Ah! that was his words, miss! Ern says he ain't stopping to be insulted, so I reckons he'll sling his hook – and a good job too.'

He seized the broom he had leant against the wall during this interesting gossip, and stumped off to resume sweeping the scattered coke in the playground.

'How all you ladies does run on!' he called wickedly over his shoulder.

The half-term holiday flew by, and a week later Miss Jackson left the school-house to take up her new quarters with Miss Clare. I must say she seems very much happier, and has been remarkably punctual, despite her journey, each morning.

It was soon after her departure that Amy called to insist on taking me to a play, being performed nightly at the Corn Exchange in Caxley, by a repertory company.

'But it's so cold in the evenings,' I protested weakly. 'All I want to do after school, is to settle in here by the fire and doze with Tibby.'

'*Exactly!*' said Amy vehemently. She was back in her old dictatorial form, I noticed, quite unlike the unhappy Amy who had told me of her mythical friend's matrimonial sorrows, on an earlier visit.

'You live in this *backwater*' – here she waved a disdainful hand round my comfortable sitting-room, with such effect, that I could almost imagine the reeds standing in muddy water and the whirring of wild duck around us – 'and dream your life away! This play will pull you up sharply, my girl!'

I began to say that I didn't want to be pulled up sharply, but Amy swept relentlessly onward.

'It deals with Problems of the Present. I admit it's Sordid and Brutal – but life's like that these days. Even the décor is symbolic.

The first set shows a back alley in a slum. It could be anywhere, the Gorbals, or New Orleans, or Hong Kong – and the windows are shuttered, symbolizing Blank Weariness. In the centre of the stage is a dustbin, symbolizing Filth and Hopeless Waste and Rejection.'

'You don't say!' I interjected, trying to restrain my mounting hysteria.

'If you are going to be *flippant*,' said Amy severely, 'I shall think twice about taking you, I haven't forgotten your disgraceful behaviour at that Moral Rearmament meeting!'

I said that I was sorry, and begged her to forgive me. She looked somewhat mollified.

'The actors speak in blank verse – the language is rather strong, naturally, but when the play is dealing with such things as rape, homosexuality, betrayal and lingering death, both of spirit and body, one must expect it!'

I said it sounded quite delightful, so fresh and wholesome, but that they were reviving *Genevieve* at the local cinema, and could we go to that instead? Amy ignored this pathetic plea, and was about to continue, when I capitulated.

'All right, I'll come,' I said sighing. 'But I warn you! If any old Father This or Brother That comes wailing on to the stage – as I feel in my bones he must – I shall walk straight out, stating in a clear, carrying voice that I am taking my custom to a nice, clean, cheerful entertainment at the cinema opposite!'

I gave Mrs Partridge a lift to Caxley on Saturday morning. I was off to buy some really thick winter gloves, despite the reproaches of my account book which makes gloomy reading. Mrs Partridge was about to buy Christmas presents for relatives abroad.

'Have you heard the good news about Mr Mawne?' she asked, as we passed Beech Green school. My godson, I noticed, was taking the air in his perambulator in the front garden of the school-house.

'I heard that he was trying to find a house,' I said guardedly.

'Well, it's all settled. He's renting Brackenhurst, where Captain Horner and his family were. He has been posted to Nairobi or Vancouver, or one of those places out East,' said the vicar's wife with a fine disregard for geography, 'and will be away for five years, poor dear. Still, it's very nice for Mr Mawne. Now, he really will be able to settle down in Fairacre, and look for a place to buy if he feels like it. He's a great asset to the village, you know.'

I said yes, I did know – the church accounts, for instance.

Mrs Partridge laughed and said that she didn't suppose that it was for the sake of the church accounts that Mr Mawne was making his home in Fairacre, and added that I was apt to belittle myself.

With this cryptic and uncomfortable remark still echoing in my ears, I drew up by the kerb, and allowed Mrs Partridge to alight.

As I made my way through Caxley's jammed High Street to the car park – which is ignored by most of the residents, who prefer to drive themselves mad by attempting to wedge their cars outside the shops rather than carry a basket for five minutes – I wondered how much longer I should have to endure Fairacre's romantic and ill-founded conjectures about my private life, in silence.

In the Public Library I was delighted to come across Mrs Finch-Edwards. She was looking through an enormous book, with plates showing eighteenth-century costumes. We had a sibilant but eager exchange of news under the SILENCE notice. Luckily, we were alone in the non-fiction department, and apart from a glare from a tousled young man in a spotty duffle coat who passed through, carrying an aggressive-looking book with a Left-Wing coloured jacket, we were undisturbed.

'We're making costumes for the Caxley Octet's concert after Christmas,' she whispered excitedly. 'It's to be a period programme. Eighteenth-century music and clothes and furniture. Isn't it lovely? Mrs Bond plays the viola and it was she who asked us to design and make the costumes. Isn't it fun?'

I said it certainly was, and that she and Mrs Moffat would be famous in no time, and that Mr Oliver Messel and Mr Cecil Beaton would have to look to their laurels.

'Oh, I don't think so!' protested Mrs Finch-Edwards seriously. 'I mean, they're *really* good. It will be some time before we can compete with them!'

On which satisfactory note we parted.

*

Mrs Pringle staggered in with a bucket of coke this morning, puffing and blowing like a grampus, and limping with great exaggeration whenever she remembered.

'If them as uses this coke so heavy-handed had to lug this 'ere bucket in, day in and day out,' she remarked morosely, dumping it noisily on a well-placed *People* by the guard, 'it might be an eye-opener to them! Flared up again, my leg has.'

I said I was sorry to hear that, and perhaps Minnie would help out again. As I had intended, this touched Mrs Pringle's pride. She drew in her breath sharply.

'What? And let her ruin my blackleading again? Not likely! I'll struggle on, thank you!'

She settled herself on the front desk, folded her arms upon her black woollen jumper, and embarked on a short gossip, before the school bell summoned the children.

'I hear there's going to be more changes in the village,' she began circumspectly. This, I suspected, referred to Mr Mawne's plans, but since our altercation over that gentleman, Mrs Pringle has been most careful not to mention him by name.

'That poor young Captain Horner's been took off to Siberia or Singapore – some place anyway – where the army's looking for trouble,' she continued. From her tone one would have imagined that the army had nothing better to do than stir up strife in a desultory way, with the ends of their bayonets, and solely for their own idle pleasure.

'So his house, I understand,' went on Mrs Pringle delicately, 'has been LET to someone!'

I said shortly that I knew that Mr Mawne had taken it.

'Oh, Mr Mawne is it?' said Mrs Pringle, feigning extreme surprise. 'There now, that will be nice!'

'What other changes are there?' I asked, leading her, I hoped, to safer ground.

'That empty cottage, where old Mr Burton used to live years back – that's being done up.'

'Who for?'

'Well, now, it's for a distant relation of mine. My old auntie married again, on the passing of her first husband to higher things, the second one being quite a young man, but steady. They had two children, pretty sharp, and this girl's the daughter of the second one. No! I'm telling a lie! He had but the two boys. Gladys was Tom's girl. Very refined she is – has her hair permed and all that, and speaks ladylike – and marrying a nice young chap at a baker's in Caxley. She was over last week. We had a nice set-down with the teapot and she told me all about him. "Auntie," she said, "he's wonderful! Love is the most important thing in the world!"'

Mrs Pringle's sour old face wore a maudlin simper which astonished me.

'And what did you say?' I asked, fascinated.

'I said: "Glad," I said, "you're right," I said, "it's only True Love that matters!" Don't you reckon that's right, Miss Read?'

Thus appealed to I found myself saying cautiously that I supposed it was important, but agreed privately with the Provincial Lady's secret feeling that a satisfactory banking account and sound teeth matter a great deal more.

'Believe me,' said Mrs Pringle, rising from the desk to continue her labours, 'there's nothing like it! Let it come early, let it come LATE—' Here she fixed me with an earnest and slightly watery eye – 'it's love that makes the world go round!'

Walking almost jauntily, and without a trace of a limp, she went, humming romantically, on her way.

The children came rushing in a few minutes later, in the greatest excitement.

'Joe Coggs, miss!'

''E's fell over!'

'Cut his head open, miss!'

I quelled them as best I could as I made my way into the playground, thinking, not for the first time, how very much I disliked that word 'OPEN', added to these statements of injury. Somehow, 'He has cut his head,' sounds the sort of injury that I can cope with. Add that unnecessary and obnoxious word, and at once I visualize a child's head cloven in half, and looking like a transverse section in a botanical drawing. It is unnerving, to say the least of it, and I must admit that I am a squeamish woman at the best of times.

We met Joseph in the porch, surrounded by a crowd of garrulous well-wishers, who were almost tearing the clothes off his back in their anxiety to assist his passage. Luckily, the wound turned out to be a minute cut on his forehead, which was soon put to rights with a piece of adhesive bandage.

Prayers were over, and the children were just settling down to arithmetic, when the vicar called with the hymn list. He seemed disposed to chat and I brought another chair and set it by my desk.

He had just come from old Mr Burton's council house, where he had lived since giving up his regular shepherding.

'I'm afraid he's sinking,' said the vicar sadly, looking down at the leopard-skin gloves on his thin knees. 'It was a pity he ever left that little cottage of his. He's ailed ever since he went up to the council house. He was too old to uproot himself, you know.'

'It was jolly damp and uncomfortable in that cottage,' I replied, 'and the only water available was from that stand pipe out in the lane. I should have thought he would have been much more comfortable in the new house.'

'More comfortable in his body perhaps,' said the vicar slowly, 'but not in his spirit. In the first place he has little privacy there, in full view of his neighbours. And then, that little old cottage was like a snail's shell to a snail. He'd lived in it all his life, and it had vital associations. The mantelpiece, for instance, with its rest above it for whips, and the bracket below for his old gun, the peg on the back door where he hung his canvas lunch bag – it was an old A.R.P. gas-mask holder, I remember – the kitchen shelf still showing grooves where his wife screwed the mincer, and where his children had nicked the edges with their penknives – why, the whole place was a record of his life! Take him from that at the age of seventy-odd, and how can you expect him to flourish? One might just as well tear up a primrose plant from the wood and expect it to flower in concrete!'

I agreed and said that I'd heard he had become very morose lately and inclined to be querulous.

'Naturally,' went on the vicar, 'he feels lost and without value there. Have you read *Lucy Bettesworth* by George Bourne?'

I said that I had not.

'I'll lend it to you,' said the vicar, 'he sums up this problem so well in one of the essays in the book. "Whatever is agreeable and kindly in his nature" – I quote from memory – "is kept alive by the intimate touch of homely possessions. They are the witness of his life's work, and surrounded by them he still feels a man." So true, so true!' sighed the vicar, reaching for his biretta.

By this time the children were getting restless. I could see that Ernest had contrived a warlike weapon from his ruler and an elastic band, and was busy making ammunition with pellets of pink blotting-paper, which he was ranging with military exactitude along the groove of his desk. The next stage, I knew, would be to dip each pellet in the inkwell before letting it fly gloriously abroad, and I was anxious to see the vicar comfortably to the door before this last and lethal step was taken.

On the threshold he paused again, and said more cheerfully: 'Young Captain Horner is off to Malta, I hear, and has let his house to Mr Mawne. So that's quite settled. I have written to him, and my wife and I hope you will both come to tea as soon as he is back. I must say I shall be glad to see him. The Free-Will Offering Fund has somehow become inextricably involved with the Altar-Flowers and Church-Fabric Accounts – most mystifying. They're all together in a chocolate box, but I can't find enough money to tally with the three accounts.'

I said that he should have an Oxo tin for each. His mouth dropped open with admiration.

'What an excellent idea! I shall go straight to the vicarage and do it at once. Really, Miss Read, what a grasp of business affairs you have!'

Much cheered, he bustled off, and I returned in the nick of time to prevent the first ink-dipped pellet from being projected, and to direct that the entire arsenal be put forthwith into my waste-paper basket.

As tomorrow will be the first day of December, I settled down this evening with my account book.

I am delighted to find that I have £1 4s. 9d. left in the bank from this month's salary, and twelve shillings and fourpence in my purse. Greatest triumph of all is the fact that the dinner money and needlework money tins are untouched.

The account book makes depressing reading, however, for I really cannot see that I can spend less than I do, unless I cut out such pleasant items as 'Anemones – 9d.' and 'Sweets for Children

– 2s. 3d.', which I don't intend to do. If only I lived in the kind of exalted circles where champagne parties, two yachts, diamond dog-collars and so on are normal – if such circles still exist, which I doubt – I believe I could cut down a bit. Say, *one* yacht, and *topaz* dog-collars . . .

Meanwhile, remembering Mr Micawber's well-known maxim about expenditure, I feel exceptionally smug, and having decided to abandon my gloomy and tedious account-keeping, I threw the book on the back of the fire, and Tibby and I ate our supper by the light of its flames.

It was only when I was snug in bed, still glowing with thrift and virtue, that I remembered that the grocer's bill was as yet unpaid. Another of life's little tweaks!

DECEMBER

Miss Jackson arrived at school this morning, pink-cheeked and starry-eyed, and clutching a bulky envelope.

'It's from Miss Crabbe,' she told me, her voice trembling with awe. 'A copy of the lecture she gave to a W.E.A. meeting somewhere near Middlesbrough. Isn't it wonderful?'

I said I had not heard it – but I expected that it was.

'Oh, not just the *lecture*,' said Miss Jackson, slightly shocked. 'I meant isn't it wonderful that she's sent me a copy? It's terribly enthralling!' Here she withdrew, with some difficulty, a wad of crumpled and flimsy typed literature, which bore the unlovely title of 'Some Psychological Interpretation of Play-Behaviour in the Under-Fives'.

'And in her letter,' continued Miss Jackson, sorting among the litter feverishly, and finally abstracting a grubby piece of paper, covered with large angular writing in green ink, 'she says that she wants me to read her notes with particular attention, as she hopes one day to start "an enlightened school of her own" based on her studies, and perhaps I may like to help her with it, when I have had a little more "work-a-day experience with the hum-drum". Doesn't she express herself well?' sighed my assistant ecstatically.

The school bell, lustily pulled by Ernest, now reminded us that the children would be with us almost at once, and I said that the future looked most hopeful for her, but would she mind reverting to the hum-drum present for the moment, and go outside into her lobby where a vicious and strongly-worded fight appeared to be going on.

So exalted was Miss Jackson this morning that this request was met with a happy smile, instead of the scowl and flouncing with which she so often obeys my behests, and Fairacre School was lapped in bliss and peace all day, thanks to Miss Crabbe's benign influence from afar.

'Heard about poor old Burton?' asked Mr Willet at play-time. 'Went early today. His son and daughter was up there with him. Nice old fellow – be missed he will. Knew all there was to know about sheep, and did some lovely carving too.'

I said I had not realized that he was so clever.

'Ah! Them pew ends in Springbourne church – they're his work; bunches of grapes and hops and that. A fair treat. Those old chaps was good with their hands. Miss Clare's father now – he was a wonder with straw. You should see the straw ornaments he made for his ricks; birds and little old men and women, 'twere wonderful! My missus said last night, "These young chaps don't seem able to make like their fathers." And Mrs Partridge said the same, only yesterday. "'Tis a pity to see the old crafts dying out, Willet!" I told 'em both the same!'

Here he paused, pursing his lips up under his ragged moustache, and I took up my cue.

'And what was it you told them?'

'I said to 'em both: "There's no one disputes that 'tis a pity the old crafts is dying, but you never hears people say how clever the youngsters has been picking up all the new ones. I bet old Burton couldn't drive a combine-harvester, or a tractor, and dry the corn or milk the cow by electric, like his boy can!" That's true, you know, Miss. There's new skill taking the place of the old, all the time, and I don't like to hear the youngsters becalled, just because they does different!' said Mr Willet sturdily.

He looked across the playground and raised his voice to a formidable bellow.

'Get you off that there coke! Let me catch one o' you little varmints on that pile again, I'll give 'ee a lift under the ear that'll take 'ee clean over the church spire!'

Notices have been posted at strategic points in the village for the last fortnight announcing a meeting to discuss the possibility of reviving the annual Flower Show, which has not been held in Fairacre for a number of years.

Evidently, before I came here, the Flower Show was an event of some magnitude, and people came from miles around to enjoy a day at Fairacre. It was usually held in the field at the side of the Vicarage.

It was a frosty starlit night, and the muddy approach to the Village Hall was hard and rutty. I had decided to go, as the children, I knew, used to play quite a large part in this village excitement, in earlier days, and there was a number of special classes, such as wild flowers, pressed flowers, dolls'-house floral decorations and so on, included in the programme, for their particular benefit. Also, fired by Mr Annett's horticultural efforts at Beech Green, I had been considering for some time, a modest school garden of our own, and this village show should give our efforts an added fillip.

By the time I arrived there were about ten people already in the hall. The vicar was in the chair, Mrs Partridge in the front row, talking to Mr and Mrs Roberts from the farm, and Mr Willet, Arthur Coggs and a few other men were warming their hands over the rather smelly oil stove, which was trying, inadequately enough, to warm the room. There was a strong smell of paraffin, mixed with the smoke from shag tobacco, and a few black smuts, trailing gossamer threads behind them, floated across the scene.

The meeting was called for seven-thirty – a most uncomfortable time in my private opinion – as it successfully throws the evening into confusion and plays havoc with one's evening meal. By a quarter to eight, only fifteen people had arrived. The vicar looked at his watch, then at his wife, and having received a nod, rose to his feet.

'I think we must begin,' he said, turning his gentle smile upon us. 'If you could shut the door, Mr Willet?'

Mr Willet shut the door with such firmness, that the oil stove belched forth a puff of smoke which reinforced the army of smuts already abroad. The vicar gave a brief little speech about the past glories of Fairacre's Flower Show, and his hopes that it might flourish again.

'Perhaps someone would propose that the Flower Show be revived?' he suggested. There was a heavy silence, broken only by the shuffling of boots from the bench at the back. All fifteen of us, I noticed, were elderly. John Pringle, Mrs Pringle's only child, must have been the youngest among us, and he is a man of nearly thirty. It was John who, at last, sheepishly answered the vicar's plea.

'I'll do it,' he said. 'Propose we has a Flower Show, then.' He sat down, pink and self-conscious, and the vicar thanked him sincerely, his thoughts, no doubt, fluttering about his postponed supper.

'Could we have a seconder?'

Again that painful silence. It was as though we sat in a trance.

'I'll second it,' I said, when I could bear the suspense no longer.

'Good! Good!' beamed the vicar. 'Those in favour?'

All fifteen raised hands unenthusiastically. To look at our faces, an outsider might reasonably have thought that we were having the choice of hanging or the electric chair.

Slowly the meeting ground on. It was uphill work for the chairman, as indeed it is for any chairman at Fairacre's public meetings. Eight o'clock chimed from St Patrick's church, and then eight-thirty. The vicar by that time had squeezed from his reluctant companions that they were in favour of reviving the Flower Show, that it should be held in the Vicarage meadow next July, and that there should be classes for outsiders to enter as well as for Fairacre folk, and a number of special classes for the children.

'Well now,' said the vicar, in an exhausted tone, 'are there any questions, before we close the meeting? Do please speak out now so that we can have a discussion while we're all together.'

This sensible appeal had its usual effect of casting everyone into utter silence again. Mr Willet coughed nervously, and we all looked at him hopefully. He looked unhappily at the ceiling, and fingered his stained moustache. Mrs Roberts made a slight noise as she moved in her chair, and the vicar turned courteously towards her.

'Yes?' he enquired hopefully.

'Nothing – oh, nothing!' replied Mrs Roberts in near-panic, and looked as unhappy as Mr Willet at this publicity. The pall of silence fell upon us again. No one dared to move in case our chairman should suppose us anxious to spring to our feet with brilliant suggestions for the success of the Flower Show – which would have been unthinkable.

At last the vicar rose to his feet again.

'That seems to be all that we can do, at the moment then. I suggest that we call another meeting before Christmas, when we'll hope to see more people with us, and perhaps some of the younger generation. We'll leave the setting-up of a Flower Show committee until then. Thank you so much, everyone.'

Like so many released birds the men on the back bench hastened through the door. Once outside, in the fresh air, under the stars, they seemed to breathe more freely, for they gathered there and wagged the tongues which had for so long remained locked behind sealed lips.

The vicar collected his papers, and he and Mrs Partridge and the Roberts left the hall amid a chorus of cheerful 'Good nights' from the knot at the door. Mr Willet and I remained in the building.

From the wall glowered the long-dead footballers, flanked by a copy of the Scout Rules. Mr Willet turned out the oil-stove, which gave a last malicious belch before it expired.

'That the lot?' queried Mr Willet looking round the hall, and rubbing a smut across his nose thoughtfully.

'Looks like it,' I replied, as we made our way to the door.

'HAVE YOU SWITCHED OF THE LIGHT?' asked that maddening notice severely.

'Us has now!' said Mr Willet, snapping the switch in answer to this silent enquiry, and plunged the hall into darkness.

He locked the door behind us, and we all set out for our own hearths again.

Mr Willet and I proceeded homeward, a few steps in front of the backbenchers, who were now as vociferous as they had formerly been tongue-tied.

'I don't hold with outsiders coming in on our Flower Show. We gets it up – has to pay through the nose for a marquee and that – and then, like as not, some foreigner gets the prizes!' said one.

'Ah! You're right there!' agreed another energetically. Little sparks, struck from the flinty road by his metal-tipped boots, accompanied this statement. All Fairacre meetings really start in the lane after the official meeting has been formally closed.

'And another thing,' said Arthur Coggs morosely, 'where's all the youngsters tonight? Don't know what'd become of the village if us older chaps didn't take an interest.'

'Never seems to care if Fairacre goes hang, does 'em?' commented the spark-maker. 'Why, when I was a boy, it was us young 'uns that turned up to all the meetings, and helped to get this ol' Flower Show up every year, and a Glee club in the winter, and them tableaus for the Red Cross, and a Nativity Play every Christmas in the church—'

'Ah! We made our own fun then! Fairacre always had something going on. But look at the young 'uns today! Take tonight – not one of 'em interested enough to turn up to this meeting and speak out like the rest of us!'

I remembered the abysmal silence of a few minutes before, and was glad that it was dark. Mr Willet spoke beside me, throwing his words back over his shoulder at the dark figures behind us.

''Course we made our own fun when we was young. 'Twas a case of have to, with no buses to Caxley, and no wireless or telly. We'd have gone plumb crazy setting about twiddlin' our thumbs. But times is changed. You can't expect young folk to want what we did. They've got all the world to amuse 'em now, and if you asks me they're a sight more civilized than we was! I ain't forgot the gangs of lads that used to lounge outside the "Beetle", kicking their heels, and not above chucking mud at folks passing, and swearing at any strangers as dared to come into Fairacre! You don't get them louts about now in this village, say what you like. They've got something better to do!'

By now we had reached Tyler's Row and Arthur Coggs wished us good night before kicking open his ramshackle gate.

'Well,' he said unctuously, 'I suppose us old stagers'll have to put our shoulders to the wheel again for this 'ere Flower Show!'

We proceeded through the village, the lighted cottage windows throwing a homely flicker across our path.

'That Arthur Coggs!' burst out Mr Willet testily. 'He fair gives me the pip – un'oly 'ypocrite! Great useless article! Why the Almighty saw fit to put waspses and adders and Arthur Coggs into this world, is beyond me! Good night, Miss Read – see you bright and early.'

Preparations for Christmas are now in full swing. For weeks past the shops in Caxley have been a blaze of coloured lights and decorated with Father Christmases, decked trees, silver balls and all the other paraphernalia. Even our grocer's shop in Fairacre has cotton-wool snow, hanging on threads, down the window, and this, and the crib already set up in the church all add to the children's enchantment.

It has turned bitterly cold, with a cruel east wind, which has scattered the last of the leaves and ruffles the feathers of the birds who sit among the bare branches. The tortoise stoves are kept roaring away, but nothing can cure the fiendish draught from the sky-light above my desk, and the one from the door, where generations of feet have worn the lintel into a hollow.

Yesterday afternoon the whole school was busy making Christmas decorations and Christmas cards. There is nothing that children like more than making brightly-coloured paper chains, and their tongues wagged happily as the paste brushes were plied, and yet another glowing link was added to the festoons that lay piled on the floor. All this glory grows so deliriously quickly and the knowledge that, very soon, it will be swinging aloft, above their heads, among the pitch-pine rafters – an enchanting token of all the joys that Christmas holds in store – makes them work with more than usual energy.

In Miss Jackson's room the din was terrific, so excited were the chain-makers. The only quiet group there was the one which was composed of about eight small children who had elected to crayon Christmas cards instead. Among them was the little Pratt boy. I stopped to admire his effort. His picture was of a large and dropsical robin, with the fiercest of red breasts, and very small and inadequate legs, as there was only a quarter of an inch of space left at the bottom for these highly-necessary appendages. His face was solemn with the absorption of the true artist.

'It's for Miss Bunce,' he told me. 'You knows – the one at Barrisford what took me to the hostipple to have my eye done. She writes to me ever so often, and sometimes sends me sweets. D'you reckon she'll like it?'

He held up his masterpiece and surveyed it anxiously at arm's length.

I told him truthfully that I was sure she would like it very much, and that all sensible people liked robins on Christmas cards. With a sigh of infinite satisfaction he replaced it on the desk, and prepared to face the horrid intricacies of writing 'HAPPY CHRISTMAS' inside.

The afternoon flew by amidst all this happy turmoil, and we were clearing up hastily when Mrs Partridge arrived. She stayed with us while we sang grace, and helped to tie scarves, and button up coats, before sending the children out into the bleak world. I wondered vaguely why she had called, for she is such a direct and bustling person that it was unusual for her not to have stated her business on arrival. I invited her into the school-house for tea.

Miss Jackson was wheeling her bicycle across the playground, and Mrs Partridge asked her how she was faring at Miss Clare's.

'It's lovely!' said my assistant with enthusiasm, 'I'm absolutely spoilt and she lets me do a little cooking if I want to, and we gossip away about school and the children—' It was the first time that I had seen her genuinely happy, and I thought how shrewdly Dr Martin had summed up the position when he had meddled so successfully in the affairs of Fairacre School.

Mrs Partridge seemed ill at ease as I made up the fire and put on the kettle. She followed me into the kitchen as I set out cups and saucers, and she began to pleat the dish cloth that hung along the sink's edge.

'Gerald asked me to call,' she began, her eyes fixed on her handiwork. 'He felt that I should have a word with you.'

'Well, I'm very glad to see you,' I said cheerfully. 'Was it about the hymn list?'

'No, no. Nothing to do with the school!' She left her pleating abruptly and asked if she could carry anything. I gave her the biscuit barrel, picked up the tray, and followed my unhappy guest into the dining-room.

After a few sips of tea, she made a second attempt to broach this painful subject, of which I was completely in the dark.

'We've had some very unsettling news,' she said at last. 'About Mr Mawne.'

I said I was sorry. I hoped that he wasn't ill? Mrs Partridge gave a heavy sigh.

'No, he's not *ill*—' she said, and stopped.

'Perhaps he's decided not to come back to Fairacre?' I said, trying to help her, and thinking that perhaps she was worried, on my account, about this matter.

'Yes, he's coming back. That's partly the trouble,' said the vicar's wife, stirring her tea meditatively. 'Gerald had a letter this morning from him.'

'I should think that's good news,' I said. 'I know he's an enormous help to the vicar.'

'But, my dear,' Mrs Partridge broke out in anguished tones, 'I really don't know how to tell you! To be blunt, he's bringing his wife back with him!'

The relief which this thunder-burst brought to me cannot be described, but Mrs Partridge looked so distraught that I could hardly let out a cheer and caper round the room, when she had suffered so much on my behalf. I did the next best thing.

'Believe me,' I said earnestly, 'that's the best news I've heard since Mr Mawne came to live here. Now I hope I shall be left in peace!'

I wished that I hadn't added the last sentence, when I saw poor Mrs Partridge wince.

'We've all behaved insufferably,' said she, 'and I hope you will forgive us. Really I've been greatly to blame. It seemed such a very good thing—' She faltered to a stop.

'I'm delighted to know that he still has a wife,' I told her, 'and to be honest, I rather suspected it from the first. So you see I am not at all upset by this disclosure – in fact I am greatly relieved. He was sorely in need of companionship.'

Now that the first breach had been made Mrs Partridge's words rushed out in spate.

'They separated about two years ago evidently. That was why he took John Parr's flat, and his wife went to relations in Ireland. There was never any question of divorce, I understand – which makes me feel that if any overtures were made to you, he behaved very badly.'

'I can assure you,' I said, 'that I never for one moment imagined that Mr Mawne had designs on me; and if he had been free to offer marriage I should not have hesitated to refuse him. I am – quite honestly – much happier as I am. Fairacre's romantic heart is the only one that is going to be broken when the news leaks out.'

Much relieved, the vicar's wife accepted a second cup of tea, and our conversation turned to less painful topics. It was only when she departed that she returned again to the subject.

'You've taken it so well,' she said. 'You put us all to shame. I shall never be able to forgive myself for being so thoughtless, and such an old busybody.'

I assured her again that she was forgiven, and that I felt as though a great weight were lifted from my back.

I closed the door behind her, and waltzed gaily back to the kitchen, cutting the caper that had been pent-up for so long.

Tibby was not amused.

On Saturday morning I met Amy in Caxley. She was busy shopping for Christmas presents and had already accumulated half a dozen neat little parcels.

'I'm buying small things this year,' she said, 'that are easy to pack. Costs so much less in postage too.' I thought, not for the first time, how efficient and sensible Amy was. My own presents included a large cushion, and an adorable, but fragile, fruit set, and I was already beginning to wonder how on earth I was going to prepare them for the post.

'Let's have some coffee,' I suggested, shelving this problem for a moment, and we entered the doorway of 'The Buttery.'

A blast of hot thick air, and a noise like the parrot-house at the zoo greeted us, and we settled ourselves comfortably among the oak beams, settees, warming-pans, chestnut roasters and other archaic domestic utensils which have witnessed the shredding of many a Caxley reputation. The coffee, as usual, was excellent, and over it Amy told me that she wanted a particularly nice present for James this year.

'I usually give him cigarettes,' said she, 'but he's had rather a worrying time lately at the office and I think he needs cheering up.'

I said I hoped that all was well now.

'Oh yes,' answered Amy, lighting a cigarette, and keeping her gaze carefully upon the flame, 'he has had to get rid of a number of his staff; and things should go much more smoothly. He's buying me a garnet bracelet that I've wanted for some time, and so I'd like to give him something rather special.'

'Cuff-links?' I suggested vaguely.

'We went through the cuff-links stage when we were courting,' said Amy, somewhat impatiently, 'and talking of that – is Mr Mawne back yet?'

'Mr Mawne,' I said, with relish, 'is coming back almost immediately, and is bringing his wife with him!'

'*Never!*' said Amy, dumbfounded. Then she began to laugh. 'Snooks to Fairacre, I suppose you think – you heartless hussy! Well, it's best as it is!'

I agreed wholeheartedly, and Amy returned to the pressing business of James's present.

'There's a rather nice paisley dressing-gown next door. Let's go and look at that.' We gathered our parcels together, while Amy continued.

'James said last night that he thought it would be fun to go away for Christmas this year. It's been pretty hectic at the office, I gather, and as he said, we haven't seen much of each other lately, with so much business to attend to.'

I said that a little holiday would do them both good. Amy seemed to be far away in her thoughts. She stood in the crowded restaurant, amidst the chattering Caxley folk, and an impatient waitress tried in vain to pass her with a loaded tray.

'He said,' she said slowly, oblivious of her surroundings, 'that old friends were best!' She looked very happy, and much as I remembered her twenty years ago. The waitress gave a final heave to her tray, and struggled past.

'Let's go and buy that dressing-gown,' I said.

The news of Mr Mawne's early return, and of his married state, has now leaked out in Fairacre. That it has been a shock, no one can deny, but I have been amused – and also touched – by the sympathy and staunch support which have been shown me, in the most delicate and unobtrusive manner.

Mr Willet took a long time working round the subject to try and find out if I knew yet of Mr Mawne's perfidy. At last I took pity on him and told him that I hoped to meet Mr Mawne's wife before long, and that it would be pleasant to have new people settled in Fairacre.

A great gusty sigh blew from under Mr Willet's stained moustache.

'Ah! Well now – glad you've heard about it! My old dad used to say "Speak the truth and shame the devil," so here goes! I never took to that chap Mawne myself, and I don't know as I ever shall. But there, we must all shake down together, I s'pose – so "Least said, soonest mended!" '

He plodded off across the playground comforting himself with this homely philosophy of well-tried tags which serves him so well. In fair weather or foul, in joy or adversity, Mr Willet can always find an age-old snatch of country wisdom to guide him in his wanderings. His conversation is sprinkled with salty maxims, adding not only savour, but support, to his daily progress.

The first intimation I had that Mrs Pringle had heard the news was the discovery of a small parcel, wrapped in grease-proof paper, on my desk.

The classroom was empty, for it was only twenty to nine, but Mrs Pringle was already moving ponderously about her dusting, behind the closed door of the infants' room. I recognized her handwriting on the parcel.

'To Miss Read,' it said, in careful copperplate, and smudgy indelible pencil.

I undid it carefully, and found inside a partridge, trussed and dressed ready for the oven, even to the refinement of two fat streaky rashers across its dusky breast. This gift, I realized, was a tribute of sympathy, and I was more touched than I should have cared to admit.

Sitting alone, in that quiet classroom, with only the tick of the wall-clock and the faint shouts of my approaching pupils to be heard, I felt, perhaps more keenly than ever before, just what it means to be a villager – someone whose welfare is of interest (sometimes of unwelcome interest) to one's neighbours – but always to *matter*. It was a warming thought – to be part of a small, living community, 'members one of another,' so closely linked by ties of kinship, work and the parish boundaries, that the supposed unhappiness of one elderly woman affected all.

The opening of the partition door disclosed Mrs Pringle looking sombrely upon me. I thanked her, most sincerely, for her present.

'My John had a brace from Mr Parr's week-end shoot,' she said, 'I thought it'd make you a bit of supper. It's a change from butcher's meat.'

She bent down, corsets creaking, to dust the rails of the front desks. With her face thus hidden from me, she spoke again.

'You've heard the news, I don't doubt?'

I said that I had heard about Mr Mawne. She puffed along to the last desk and then straightened up cautiously.

'Wild horses wouldn't drag that name across my lips after what's been done between us, Miss Read, as well you knows! But in all fairness, I must say that I wasn't the only one in Fairacre as thought he was hanging his hat up to you. He ain't thought much of in the village, I can tell you – and him having the sauce to come back and live here too!'

Her face was red with indignation. She sat herself heavily on the front desk, arms folded majestically, and gazed grimly at me over the brass and mahogany inkstand.

I felt laughter welling up inside me, which would not be checked.

'Mrs Pringle,' I said, 'you can let it be known discreetly, that I'm as pleased as Punch about the news. Believe me, a heart as old as mine takes a lot of cracking!'

Her belligerent countenance softened, and a rare smile curved those dour lips. For a moment we sat smiling across the inkstand, and then Mrs Pringle heaved herself to her feet.

'Ah well! That's done with!' was her comment, and she retreated again to the infants' room, to finish her dusting. I could hear her singing a hymn in her usual gloomy contralto.

It was only when I had repacked my partridge, and looked out my register and red and blue pens for marking it, that I realized she was singing:

'Let us with a gladsome mind
Praise the Lord, for He is kind!'

By right and ancient custom at Fairacre School the last afternoon of the Christmas term is given up to a tea-party.

The partition had been pushed back, so that the two class-rooms had been thrown into one, but even so, the school was crowded, with children, parents and friends. Mrs Finch-Edwards was there, showing her baby daughter Althea to Miss Clare. Miss Jackson, who had dressed the Christmas tree alone, was receiving congratulations upon its glittering beauty from Mrs Partridge. Mr Roberts's hearty laugh rustled the paper-chains so near his head, and the vicar beamed upon us all, until Mrs Pringle gave him the school cutting-out scissors and reminded him of his responsibilities. For it was he who would cut the dangling presents from the tree before the party ended.

In the quiet of the school-house across the playground my godson slept peacefully, too young yet for the noise and heat engendered by forty-odd hilarious schoolchildren. Mrs Annett was with us, busily discussing clothes with Mrs Moffat, her former landlady. Mrs Coggs and Mrs Waites had walked up together from Tyler's Row, and now sat, side by side, watching their sons engulf sardine sandwiches, iced biscuits, sponge cake, jam tarts and sausage rolls, all washed down with frequent draughts of fizzy lemonade through a gurgling straw. Mr Willet, at one end of the room, had the job of taking the metal tops off the bottles, and with bent back and purple, sweating face, had been hard put to it to keep pace with the demand.

It was a cheerful scene. The paper-chains and lanterns swung from the rafters, the tortoise stoves, especially brilliant today from Mrs Pringle's ministrations, roared merrily, and the glittering tree dominated the room.

The children, flushed with food, heat and excitement, chattered like starlings, and around them the warm, country voices of their elders exchanged news and gossip.

After tea, the old well-loved games were played, 'Oranges and lemons' with Miss Clare at the piano, and Mr and Mrs Partridge making the arch, 'Poor Jenny sits a-weeping,' 'The Farmer's in his Den,' 'Nuts and May' and 'Hunt the Thimble.' We always have this one last of all, so that we can regain our breath. The children nearly burst with suppressed excitement, as the seeker wanders bewildered about the room, and on this occasion the roars of 'Cold, cold!' or 'Warmer, warmer!' and the wild yelling of 'Hot, hot! You're REAL hot!' nearly raised the pitch-pine roof.

The presents were cut from the tree, and the afternoon finished with carols; old and young singing together lustily and with sincerity. Within those familiar walls, feuds and old hurts forgotten, for an hour or two at least, Fairacre had been united in joy and true goodwill.

It was dark when the party ended. Farewells and Christmas greetings had been exchanged under the night sky, and the schoolroom was quiet and dishevelled. The Christmas tree, denuded of its parcels, and awaiting the removal of its bright baubles on the morrow, still had place of honour in the centre of the floor.

Joseph Coggs' dark eyes had been fixed so longingly on the star at its summit, that Miss Clare had unfastened it and given it into his keeping, when the rest of the children had been safely out of the way.

The voices and footsteps had died away long ago by the time I was ready to lock up and go across to my peaceful house. Some of the bigger children were coming in the morning to help me clear up the aftermath of our Christmas revels, before Mrs Pringle started her holiday scrubbing.

The great Gothic door swung to with a clang, and I turned the key. The night was still and frosty. From the distant downs came the faint bleating of Mr Roberts' sheep, and the lowing of Samson in a nearby field. Suddenly a cascade of sound showered from St Patrick's spire. The bell-ringers were practising their Christmas peal. After that first mad jangle the bells fell sweetly into place, steadily, rhythmically, joyfully calling their message across the clustered roofs and the plumes of smoke from Fairacre's hearths, to the grey, bare glory of the downs that shelter us.

I turned to go home, and to my amazement, noticed a child standing by the school gate.

It was Joseph Coggs. High above his head he held his tinsel star, squinting at it lovingly as he compared it with those which winked in their thousands from above St Patrick's spire.

We stood looking at it together, and it was some time before he spoke, raising his voice against the clamour of the bells.

'Good, ain't it?' he said, with the utmost satisfaction.

'Very good!' I agreed.

Storm in the Village

To Douglas

PART ONE

Straws in the Wind

* * * *

1. THE TWO STRANGERS

Miss Clare's thatched cottage lay comfortably behind a mixed hedge of hawthorn, privet and honeysuckle, on the outskirts of Beech Green. The village was a scattered one, unlike its neighbour Fairacre, where Miss Clare had been the infants' teacher for over forty years, only relinquishing her post when ill-health and the two-mile bicycle journey proved too much for even her indomitable courage.

The cottage had been Miss Clare's home for almost sixty years. Her father had been a thatcher by trade, and the criss-cross decorations on the roof still testified to his skill, for they had been braving the weather for over twenty years, and stood out as clearly now, on the greying thatched roof, as they had on the first day of their golden glory. It was true that here and there, particularly round the squat red-brick chimney, the roof was getting a little shabby. Miss Clare often looked at it ruefully, when she went into the back garden to empty her tea-pot or to cut a cabbage, but as long as it remained weather-proof she had decided that it must stay as it was. It would cost at least two hundred pounds, she had been told, to rethatch her home; and that was out of the question.

One breezy March morning, when the rooks were tumbling about the blue and white sky, high above the cottage, Miss Clare was upstairs, making her lodger's bed. A shaft of sunlight fell across the room, as Miss Clare's thin, old hands smoothed the pillow and covered it squarely with the white honeycomb quilt which had once covered her mother's bed.

No one would call Miss Jackson tidy, thought Miss Clare, as she returned books from the floor to the book-shelf, and retrieved shoes from under the bed. It was one of the few things that grieved her about her young lodger. Otherwise she was thoughtful, and very, very clever with the children.

Miss Clare imagined her now, as she tidied the girl's clothes, standing in front of her class of young children, as she too had done for so many years, at Fairacre School. Prayers would be over, and as it was so fine, no doubt they would be getting ready to go out into the playground for physical training. Often, during the day, Miss Clare would look at the clock and think of the children at Fairacre School. The habits of a lifetime die hard, and to have the present infants' teacher as her lodger, to hear the school news, and the gossip from the village which, secretly, meant more to her than the one in which she lived, was a source of great comfort to her.

She picked a small auburn feather from the floor. A Rhode Island Red's feather, noted Miss Clare's country eye, which must have worked its way from the plump feather bed.

Outside, the birds were clamorous, busy with their nest building, and reconnoitring for likely places in the loose parts of the thatched roof. Miss Clare crossed to the window and let the feather float from it to the little lawn below. Before it had time to settle, three excited sparrows threw themselves upon it, squabbling and struggling. Miss Clare, sunning herself on the window-sill, smiled benevolently upon them, and watched her feather borne off in triumph to some half-made nest nearby.

It was then that she noticed the men.

There were two of them, pacing slowly, side by side, along the edge of Hundred Acre Field which lay on the other side of Miss Clare's garden hedge.

It was one of several unusually large fields which formed part of old Mr Miller's farm. Harold Miller had lived at the farmhouse at Springbourne all his life, and had farmed the same land as his father before him. Now, at eighty, he was as spry as ever, and nothing escaped his bright, birdlike eye. His two sons, much to his sorrow, had shown no desire to carry on the farming traditions of the family, but had sought their fortunes, with fair success, elsewhere, one as an engineer and the other as an architect.

Hundred Acre Field and its spacious neighbours were among the more fruitful parts of Mr Miller's farm. Many of his acres were on the bare chalk downs which sheltered his home from the northerly winds. Here he kept a sizeable flock of sheep, rightly renowned for many miles around. At the foot of the downs the plough soon turned up chalk, and on a dry day, the white, light dust would blow in clouds from these lower fields. But those which lay furthest from his farm, near Miss Clare's cottage, had at least two feet of fertile top soil, and here old Mr Miller grew the oats and wheat which Miss Clare watched with an eye as keen and as appreciative as their owner's.

At the moment, Hundred Acre Field was brushed with a tender green, the tiny spears of wheat showing two or three inches above the soil. Beyond this field had lain a large expanse of kale, on which Mr Miller had been feeding his flock during the hardest months of the winter.

The two men walked slowly towards the kale stumps, stopping every now and again, to bend down and examine the soil among the wheat rows. Miss Clare's long-sighted eyes noted their good thick tweeds approvingly. The wind was still keen, despite the bright sunlight, and she liked to see people sensibly clad. But their shoes grieved her. They were stout enough, to be sure; but far more suited to the pavements of Caxley than the sticky mud of a Beech Green field. And so beautifully polished! Such a pity to mess them up, thought Miss Clare; and what a lot of mud they would take back into that neat little car that stood on the green verge of the lane, quite near her own front gate!

What could they be doing? she wondered. There they stood, with their backs to her, gazing across the grand sweep of the fields to the gentle outline of the hazy downs beyond. One had drawn a paper from his pocket and was studying it minutely.

'What a busybody I'm getting!' said Miss Clare aloud, pulling herself together.

She took a last look round Miss Jackson's room, then crossed the little landing to her own at the front of the cottage.

She had just finished setting it to rights, and was shaking her duster from the window, when she saw the two men again. They were standing now by the car and, Miss Clare was glad to see, they were doing their best to wipe the mud from their shoes on the grass.

'Though why they don't pick a little stick from the hedge and dig it all away from their insteps, I really don't know,' said

Miss Clare to herself. 'They *will* make a mess in that nice little car!'

She watched them climb in, turn it adroitly, and move off in the direction of Fairacre.

'Curiouser and curiouser!' quoted Miss Clare to the cat, who had arrived upstairs to see which bed had a pool of sunlight on it, and would be best suited to his morning siesta. But his luck was out, for his mistress headed him firmly to the stairs, and followed him into the kitchen.

'Ministry of Agriculture, I should think,' continued Miss Clare, lifting the cat on to his accustomed chair near the stove, from which, needless to say, the outraged animal jumped down at once, just to assert his independence.

His mistress was gazing, somewhat uneasily, out of the kitchen window. She was still preoccupied with the arrival of the two strangers.

'I wonder who they can be? And what are they going to do in Fairacre?'

At that moment, in Fairacre, as Miss Clare had surmised, Miss Jackson and her young charges were pretending to be galloping horses in the small, stony playground of Fairacre School.

'Higher, higher!' she urged the leaping children, prancing among them spiritedly, and her excited voice floated through the Gothic window, which was tilted open, to my own class.

As headmistress of Fairacre School I have taken the older children now for several years; while Miss Clare, then Miss Gray (now Mrs Annett), and finally Miss Jackson, held sway in the infants' room. Miss Jackson, to be sure, could be a thorn in the side at times, for she was still much influenced by her college psychology lecturer and apt to thrust that good lady's dicta forward for my edification, much too often for my liking. But she had improved enormously, and I was inclined to think that her serene life with Miss Clare had had a lot to do with this mellowing process.

My children were busy with sums, working away in their exercise books, with much rattling of nibs in inkwells and chewing of pen holders. I walked to the window to watch the progress of Miss Jackson's galloping horses.

The sun was dazzling. The weather cock glittered, gold against the blue and white scudding sky, on the spire of St Patrick's church, which stood, a massive neighbour, to our own small, two-roomed building. The children cavorted madly about, their faces rosy and their breath puffing mistily before them in the sharp air. Their short legs worked like pistons and their hair was tossed this way and that, not only by their own exertions but also by the exhilarating wind which came from the downs. Miss Jackson blew a wavering blast on her whistle, and the galloping horses stopped, panting, in their tracks.

It was at this moment that the little car drew cautiously alongside the school wall, and one of the two men inside called to Miss Jackson.

I could not hear the conversation from my vantage point at the window, but I watched the children edge nearer the wall, as Miss Jackson, leaning well over, waved her arms authoritatively and presumably gave directions. Inquisitive little things, I thought to myself, and then was immediately struck by my own avid curiosity, which kept me staring with fascination at the scene before me. There's no doubt about it – we like to know what's going on in Fairacre, both young and old, and there's precious little that happens around us that goes unobserved.

The men smiled their thanks, appeared to confer, and Miss Jackson turned back to her class, who were now clustered about her, well within earshot of her conversation. One of the men got out of the car and made his way towards the centre of Fairacre, Miss Jackson resumed her lesson, and I, with smarting conscience, set about marking sums, much refreshed by my interlude at the school window.

'They had a flat tyre,' vouchsafed Miss Jackson, over our cup of tea at playtime, 'and wanted to know if they could get some coffee anywhere while they had the wheel changed. I told them to try the "Beetle and Wedge", and to call on Mr Rogers at the forge about the wheel. They seemed very nice men,' she added, a trifle wistfully, I thought.

I felt a slight pang of pity for my young assistant, who had so little opportunity of meeting 'very nice men'. There are very few young men in Fairacre itself, and not many more at Beech Green, and buses to Caxley, the nearest town, are few and far between, even if one felt like making the effort to join the Dramatic or Musical Society there. Occasionally, I knew, Miss Jackson went home for the weekend, and there, I sincerely hoped, she met some lively young people with her own interests. Unfortunately, it appeared from her chance remarks that Miss Crabbe still held first place in her heart, and if she could ever manage to visit this paragon I knew that she did so.

When I took my own class out for their P.T. lesson, later in the morning, the little car was still there, and both men were busily engaged in changing the wheel themselves; so, presumably, no help had been forthcoming from Mr Rogers at the forge. Before the end of my lesson, the job was completed. They wiped their hands on a filthy rag, looked very satisfied with themselves, and drove back on their tracks towards Caxley.

'See them two strangers?' shouted Mrs Pringle, an hour or so later, crashing plates about in the sink. Mrs Pringle, the school cleaner, also washes up the dinner things, and keeps us in touch with anything untoward that has happened in Fairacre during the morning.

I said that I had.

'Up to a bit of no good, I'll bet!' continued Mrs Pringle sourly. 'Inspectors, or something awkward like that. One went in the butcher's first. I thought p'raps he was the weights and measures. You know, for giving short weight, They has you up pretty smartish for giving short weight.'

I said I supposed they did.

'And so they should!' said Mrs Pringle, rounding on me fiercely. 'Nothing short of plain thieving to give short weight!' She crashed the plates even more belligerently, her three chins wobbling aggressively, and her mouth turned down disapprovingly.

'*However*,' she went on heavily, 'he wasn't the weights and measures, though his suit was good enough, that I must say. But he was asking for the forge. My cousin Dolly happened to be in the shop at the time, and she couldn't help overhearing, as she was waiting for her fat to be cut off her chops. Too rich for her always – never been the same since yellow jaundice as a tot. And the butcher said as he knew Mr Rogers was gone to Caxley, to put a wreath on his old mother's grave there, it being five years to the day since she passed on. As nice a woman as I ever wish to meet, and they keep her grave beautiful. So this fellow said was there anywhere to get a cup of coffee? And the butcher said no harm in having a bash at the "Beetle", but it all depended.'

She turned to the electric copper, raised the lid, letting out a vast cloud of steam, baled out a scalding dipperful of water, and flung it nonchalantly into the flotsam in the sink.

'I passed him on my way up to the post office. Nicely turned out he was. Beautiful heather mixture tweed, and a nice blue shirt with a fine red line to it – but his tie could have done with a clean – and his shoes! Had a good polish first thing, I don't doubt, but been tramping over some old ploughed field since then! Couldn't help but notice, though I hardly give him a glance; I never was a starer, like some in this parish I could mention!'

She bridled self-righteously and dropped a handful of red-hot forks, with an earsplitting crash, on to the tin draining board.

'Was that his car?' she bellowed, above the din. I nodded.

'They'd got a new-fangled thing – brief-case, ain't it? – in the back. Two strangers, poking about here with a brief-case and a lot of mud on their shoes,' she mused. 'Makes you think, don't it? Might be Ag. men, of course. But you mark my words, Miss Read, they was up to a bit of no good!'

Mr Willet, the school caretaker, verger and sexton of St Patrick's next door, and general handyman to all Fairacre, had also noted the strangers.

'Nice little car that, outside here this morning. Them two chaps from the Office?'

The Office, which is always spoken of with the greatest respect, referred in this case to the divisional education office in Caxley, from which forms, directions and our monthly cheques flutter regularly.

'No,' I said, 'I don't know who they were.'

'Oh lor'!' said Mr Willet, blowing out his moustache despairingly. 'Hope it ain't anything to do with the sanitary. They're terrors – the sanitary! Ah well! Time'll tell, I suppose – but they looked uncomfortable sort of customers to me!'

He trudged off, with resigned good humour, to sweep up the playground.

But it remained for the Reverend Gerald Partridge, vicar of Fairacre and Beech Green, to say the last word on this mysterious subject.

'Did you have visitors this morning?' he asked, after he had greeted the children. I told him that we had not seen anyone strange in school.

'I noticed two men in a little car outside here, as I drove over to see about poor old Harris's funeral at Beech Green. Now, I wonder who they could have been?'

I said that I had no idea.

'Who knows?' said the vicar happily. 'We may look forward to having some new people among us perhaps?'

As it happened, the vicar had spoken more truly than he knew.

2. FAIRACRE'S DAILY ROUND

By next day, of course, the two strangers were forgotten. Life, particularly in a village, has so many interests that each day seems to offer more riches than the last.

Miss Clare turned her attention to a magnificent steak and kidney pudding, which simmered gently on her stove from two o'clock onwards, for her lodger's, and her own, supper together at eight o'clock. It filled the little house with its homely fragrance, and Dr Martin, who called in hopefully about half-past three for a cup of tea with his old friend and patient, noticed it at once.

'That's the stuff!' he said approvingly, rubbing his hands, and he cast a glance at Miss Clare's spare frame. 'You're putting on weight since that girl came. Good idea of yours to have a lodger!'

It had not been Miss Clare's idea at all, as they both knew very well, but Miss Clare let it pass. It was Dr Martin who had engineered Miss Jackson's removal from her headmistress's house to Miss Clare's; and he could see that young company as well as an addition to her slender housekeeping purse was doing his patient all the good in the world.

'Have a ginger nut,' said Miss Clare, pushing the massive biscuit barrel across to him.

'I'll have to dip it. My new bottom set's giving me hell!' said the doctor, with disarming frankness. 'We're getting old, Dolly, that's our trouble.'

They smiled across at each other, and sipped their tea in comfortable silence. The steak and kidney pudding sizzled deliciously on the stove. The fire warmed their thin legs, and though indeed, thought Miss Clare, we're both old and white-haired, at least we're very happy.

Mrs Pringle was busy washing out the school tea cloths at her own sink. This was done every day, but on this occasion Mrs Pringle was particularly engrossed, for it was the first time that she had used what she termed 'one of these new-fangled deterrents.'

A staunch upholder of yellow bar soap, Mrs Pringle had set her face against the dazzling array of washing powders which brightened the grocer's shop. On a wooden shelf, above her sink, were stacked long bars, as hard as wood, which she had stored there for many months. This soap was used for all cleaning purposes in the Pringle household. The brick floors, the stout undergarments and Mrs Pringle's dour countenance itself were all scoured with this substance, and when one piece had worn away, Mrs Pringle fetched her shovel, laid a bar on a piece of newspaper on the kitchen floor and sliced off another chunk to do its work.

But the gay coupons, all assuring her of their monetary value, which fluttered through Mrs Pringle's letter-box from time to time, gradually found a chink in her armour. The day came when, slightly truculent, she handed one across the counter, and put the dazzling packet in her basket. She was careful to cover it with other packages, in case she met neighbours who, knowing her former scorn of these products, would be only too pleased to 'take a rise out of her' if they saw that she had finally fallen.

And so, on this day, Mrs Pringle washed her tea cloths with a critical eye. The packet had been tucked away behind the innocent bars of soap, for Mrs Pringle had no doubt that her husband and grown-up son could be as equally offensive as her neighbours about this experiment, if they caught sight of the soap powder.

'Hm!' said Mrs Pringle grudgingly, as she folded the wet tea towels, and put them into her laundry basket. 'It don't do so bad after all!'

With some pride, she trudged up the garden and began to peg out the cloths on the line. When she had done this, she propped the line up with a sturdy forked hazel branch, and surveyed the fluttering collection.

'Might be something to be said for these deterrents, after all!' she told herself, returning to the cottage, 'and it do save chipping up the soap – that I will give 'em!' It was, indeed, high praise.

Miss Jackson, in the infants' room at Fairacre was embarking on the most elaborate and artistic frieze yet attempted by her class. It was to go all round the room, fixed with drawing pins to the green-painted matchboarding, and it was to represent Spring.

The children were busy snipping with their blunt-nosed little scissors – which were always much too stiff for small children to manage properly – at gummed paper, in all the colours of the rainbow.

'Make just what you like!' Miss Jackson had exhorted them. 'Flowers, leaves, lambs, birds, butterflies – anything that makes you think of Spring!'

Most of the class had flung themselves with abandon into this glorious snipping session, but there were, as always, one or two stolid and adenoidal babies who were completely without imagination, and awaited direction apathetically.

'Make grass then!' had said Miss Jackson, with some exasperation to the Coggs twins, who sat with glum, dark eyes fixed upon her. Ten minutes later, she found that a large mound of green snippings lay on the desk between them, while, with tongues protruding, and with a red ring round each hard-working thumb, the grass-makers added painfully to their pile.

Anyway, thought Miss Jackson, that's far better than making them go, step by step, drawing round tobacco tins and paste jars to make horrid little yellow-chicks-in-a-row, for an Easter frieze! For she had found just such a one – made by her predecessor Mrs Annett – and had looked scornfully upon its charming regularity. The children, needless to say, had loved it, but Miss Jackson favoured all those things which were written in capital letters in her own teaching notes – such as Free Art, Individual Expression, Untrammelled Creative Urge, and so on, and anything as formal and limited as poor Mrs Annett's despised chicks were anathema to her.

And so the children snipped and hacked and tore at a fine profusion of gummed papers. Mrs Annett's and Miss Clare's frugal eyes would have expressed concern at the large pieces which fell to waste on the floor. But Miss Jackson, seeing in her mind's eye the riotous glory which was to flower around her walls so soon, and with a fine disregard for the ratepayers' money, smiled upon her babies' efforts with approval.

In the churchyard, next door to the school playground, Mr Willet was having a bonfire. He had made himself a fine incinerator by knocking holes in a tin tar barrel. This was set up on three bricks, so that the draught fairly whistled under it, and inside Mr Willet was burning the dead flowers from the graves, stray pieces of paper, twigs, leaves and all the other rubbish which accumulates in a public place.

He had had some difficulty in getting the fire to start, for the débris was damp. But, having watched Mrs Pringle returning to her home after washing up the school's dinner plates, he had made a bold sortie to the school woodshed, and there found a paraffin-oil can, which Mrs Pringle fondly imagined was known to her alone.

He sprinkled his languishing bonfire lavishly, and stood back to admire the resulting blaze.

'Ah! that's more like!' he said with satisfaction. He bent to retrieve the oil-can and stumped back to the woodshed.

'And if the old Tartar finds out, 'tis all one to me!' he added sturdily, tucking it behind the sack which shrouded it.

Meanwhile, the vicar was polishing his car, and doing it very badly. It wasn't that he was lazy about it. In fact, he was taking the greatest pains, and had an expensive tin of car-polish, half-a-dozen clean rags of various types, ranging from a soft mutton-cloth to a dashing blue-checked duster which he had found hanging on the banister.

Mrs Willet, who was helping with the spring-cleaning at the time, was much perplexed about this duster. It had vanished while she had fetched the feather mop for the top of the spare room wardrobe, and was never seen by her again.

But despite his armoury and his zeal, the vicar's handiwork was a failure.

'I must admit,' said the vicar aloud, standing back on his gravel path to survey the car better, 'that there are far too many smears.'

'Gerald!' called his wife, from the window. 'You did remember to ask the Mawnes to call in for a drink this evening?'

'Well, no!' answered the vicar unhappily. 'To be truthful, it slipped my mind, but I have to take a cheque to Mawne for the Church Maintenance Fund. I'll ask them then.'

'Good!' said his wife, preparing to close the window.

The vicar forestalled her. 'My dear!' he called. The window opened again. 'What do you think of the car?'

'Smeary!' said his wife, closing the window firmly.

'She's right, you know,' sighed the vicar sadly to the cat which came up to rub his clerical-grey legs. 'It definitely *is* smeary!'

With some relief he turned his back on the car, and went into the house to fetch his biretta. He would visit the Mawnes straight away. An afternoon call would be much more satisfying than cleaning the car.

The smoke from Mr Willet's most successful bonfire began to blow into my classroom during history lesson, and I went to the window to close it.

I could see Mr Willet, his shirt-sleeves rolled up, forking dead vegetation into the smoking mouth of the incinerator. He turned, as he heard the window shut, and raised his hands in apology and concern.

I shook my head and smiled, waving my own hands, hoping that he would accept my grimaces and gestures as the verbal equivalent of 'Don't worry! It doesn't matter!'

It appeared that he did, for after a minute or two of further dumb show, he saluted and returned to his fork; while I gave a final wave and returned to my class.

The slipshod spelling in the older children's history essays had roused me to an unaccustomed warmth and I had been in the midst of haranguing them when I had broken off to close the window. I returned to the fray with renewed vigour.

'Listen to this Patrick, "There were four Go-urges. Go-urge the Frist, Go-urge the Scond, Go-urge the Thrid, and Go-urge the Froth." And to make matters worse, I had put "George" on the blackboard for you, and spent ten minutes explaining that it came from a Greek word "Geo" meaning earth.'

Patrick smiled sheepishly, fluttering alluring dark lashes. I refused to be softened.

'Who remembers some of the words we put on the blackboard, beginning with "Geo"?'

There was a stunned silence. The clock ticked ponderously and outside we could hear the crackling of Mr Willet's bonfire. Someone yawned.

'Well?' I said, with menace.

'Geography,' said one inspired child.

'Geology,' said another.

Silence fell again. I made another attempt to rouse them.

'Oh, come now! There were several more words!'

Joseph Coggs, lately arrived in my room, broke the silence.

'Je-oshaphat!' he said smugly.

I drew in a large breath, but before I could explode, his neighbour turned to him.

'That's Scripture, Joe!' he explained kindly.

I let out my breath gently and changed the subject. No point in bursting a blood-vessel, I told myself.

Mrs Annett had asked me to tea that afternoon.

'And stay the evening, please!' she had implored on the telephone. 'George will be going into Caxley for orchestra practice, and I shall be alone. You can help me bath Malcolm,' she added, as a further inducement.

The thought of bathing my godson, now at the crawling stage, could not be resisted, so I had promised to be at Beech Green school-house as soon after four as my own duties would allow.

It began to rain heavily later in the afternoon. I saw Mr Willet, his bonfire now dying slowly, scurry for shelter into the church. By the time the clock stood at a quarter to four, the rain was drumming mercilessly against the windows, and swishing, in silver shivers, across the stony playground.

We buttoned up the children's coats, turned up their collars, tied scarves over heads, sorted Wellington boots on to the right feet, and gloves on to the right fingers, before sending them out to face the weather. One little family of four, somewhat inadequately clad, had the privilege of borrowing the old golfing umbrella from the map cupboard. So massive is this shabby monster that all four scuttled along together, quite comfortably, in its shelter.

'I'll give you a lift,' I said to Miss Jackson. 'I'm going to Beech Green for tea, and you'll get soaked if you cycle.'

I sped across to the school-house to put things to rights before leaving my establishment. Tibby, my black and white cat, turned a sour look upon me, as I shovelled small coal on to the fire, and put up the guard.

'And is this meagre warmth,' his look said, 'supposed to suffice? Where, pray, are the blazing logs and flaring coals best suited to the proper warming of a cat's stomach?'

I escaped from his disapproving eye and got out the car.

The downs were shrouded in rain clouds, and little rivers gurgled down each side of the lane as we drove along to Beech Green.

'Betty Franklyn told me that she was going to live with an aunt in Caxley,' Miss Jackson said, speaking of a six-year-old in her class. 'I wonder if that's right? Have you heard?'

'No,' I answered, 'but it would be the best thing, I should think. She'll be looked after properly, if it's the aunt I'm thinking of.'

Betty's mother had died early in the year, and the father was struggling along alone. I felt very sorry for him, but he was a man I had never taken to, sandy-haired, touchy and quick-tempered.

He was a gamekeeper, and lived in a lonely cottage, in a small copse, on the Beech Green side of Fairacre. He brought the child to school each morning on the cross-bar of his bicycle, and sometimes met her, when his work allowed, after school in the afternoon.

It must have been a cheerless home during the last two or three months, and the child had looked pathetically forlorn. I hoped that this rumour would prove to be true. The aunt had always seemed devoted to her little niece, and, in Caxley, the child would have more playmates. I felt certain that the aunt had offered to have the child as soon as her mother had died; but the father, I suspected, was proud and possessive, and would look to his little daughter for company. He was certainly very fond of her, and probably he had realised that she would be far happier in Caxley, and so given in to persuasion.

I said as much to Miss Jackson, as we edged by a Land-Rover which was drawn up on the grass verge by Hundred Acre Field. Despite the sweeping rain, old Mr Miller, a small, indomitable figure in a trench coat and glistening felt hat, was standing among his young wheat surveying his field. He appeared oblivious of the weather, and deeply preoccupied.

'It will be a good thing for Betty,' I said, 'I shouldn't think her father's much company.'

To my surprise, Miss Jackson replied quite sharply.

'I should imagine he's very good company. He's always very nice when he brings Betty in the mornings. I've found him most interesting, and very well read.'

I negotiated the bend near Miss Clare's house in silence.

'And what he doesn't know about trees and birds and wood-land animals!' continued Miss Jackson warmly. 'He's suggested that I take my class to the wood for a nature walk one day, and he'll meet us there.'

'Will he, indeed?' I said, somewhat taken aback.

'And when you think of the lonely life he leads, since his poor wife's death,' went on my assistant, her face quite pink with emotion, 'it really is quite shattering. How he must have suffered! And he's a sensitive man.'

I drew up outside Miss Clare's cottage. She waved through the window from behind a pink geranium, and beckoned me in.

'I'm going to tea with Isobel,' I bellowed in an unladylike way, 'so I mustn't stop!' She nodded and smiled, and watched her lodger, who was alighting, still pink and defensive.

'Good-bye, and thanks!' said Miss Jackson, somewhat shortly, pushing open the wet gate.

I drove off slowly and thoughtfully.

'It looks to me,' I said aloud, 'as if Miss Crabbe will soon be supplanted in Miss Jackson's heart. But not, heaven forbid, by that Franklyn fellow! I know a scamp when I see one!'

3. Mrs Annett has Doubts

'Hello, hello!' called Mr Annett, bursting out from his school door as he heard my car forge its way slowly into the playground.

'Put it under cover! Up in the shed,' he shouted, through the pouring rain. I edged carefully under the corrugated iron roof of the playground shelter. The drumming of the downpour was thunderous under here.

Two small boys, ostensibly tidying up some gymnastic apparatus, watched my manoeuvres with interest.

'Best leave 'er in gear, miss,' advised one. 'Nasty slope back if the 'and brake give up the ghost!'

'I'll stick a brick by your back wheel,' said the other. 'Don't do no harm, if it don't do no good! And don't forget your ignition keys, miss!'

By this time Mr Annett had joined us, and overheard my mentors.

'Those two,' he told me, when we were out of earshot, 'are supposed to be educationally sub-normal.'

'They may not know how many beans make five,' I returned, 'but they know a good deal more about my car than I do. You see, they'll find a niche, soon enough, when they leave school!'

We made our way across the streaming playground, to a little gate let in the side fence of Mr Annett's garden. As he closed it behind us I looked at his trim beds and lawn and compared it sadly with my own.

A fine clump of white crocuses, sheltered from the rain by a glossy rhododendron bush, were a joy to see; their pure white cups lit from within by their dazzling gold stamens. Nearby, a speckled thrush was diligently hammering a snail on a large knobbly flint, that glistened in the rain. He was far too engrossed with his task to bother about us, although we passed close to him as we made our way to the back door.

A warm odour of freshly-baked scones met us from the kitchen. Isobel, flushed and cheerful, was busy buttering them, while Malcolm, strapped securely in his high chair, out of temptation's way, was shaking a bean in a screw-topped jar, and singing tunelessly as an accompaniment.

'The tympani chap in a jazz band,' said his father, nodding towards him. 'That's what he's going to be!'

'And very nice too,' I said. 'I've always wanted to have a go at that myself.'

Tea was set in the dining-room, which looked out on to the back garden. Beyond the lawn lay Mr Annett's kitchen garden, and I could see that his broad beans were already standing in sturdy rows. In the distance, I had a glimpse through the budding hawthorn hedge, of the school pig sties and chicken houses in the field beyond; for Mr Annett was a firm believer in rural pursuits for his older boys, and his practical methods had become much admired, and emulated, by other local teachers.

Tea was a hilarious meal, much enlivened by young Malcolm, who preferred to eat his neat strips of bread and butter by squeezing them well in his plump hands. When the food emerged, as a revolting squish between his fingers, he devoured it with the greatest relish, covering his face and his duck-decorated bib with rather more than half. His father watched with disgust.

'Loathsome child!' he said sternly.

'Take no notice!' said his wiser mother. 'He wants us to make a fuss about it.' She passed the scones to me, her face carefully averted from her offspring, and I tried to wrench my own gaze away from my godchild's unpleasant handiwork.

'It must be very hard work,' I observed. 'All that kneading and squeezing. I wonder if it's nicer that way?'

'Don't you start, for heaven's sake!' said Mr Annett with alarm. 'Here, have some honey, and don't go getting ideas in your head!'

He began to talk about the two boys who had been so interested in my car.

'The smaller one tells me that there's talk of a housing estate in Hundred Acre Field,' said he. 'Heard anything about it?'

I said I hadn't.

'There was a tiny paragraph in the *Mail* or the *Telegraph* a week or two ago,' said Mrs Annett. 'Something about two or three thousand new workers coming to the atomic place. They've had some new plant put in, haven't they?'

'And is this housing estate for them?' I asked, somewhat alarmed. 'Good lord, it surely won't be built at Beech Green. It's miles from the atomic station!'

'Well, I don't know. There'd be work buses, I suppose.'

'Not that we're likely to have a huge estate here,' said Mrs Annett. 'That field is excellent farming land. Surely, it wouldn't be built on?'

We ate, for a few minutes, in silence, turning over this uncomfortable rumour in our minds. Mr Annett broke the silence.

'Come to think of it, there were two men sizing things up over there one morning last week—'

'So there were!' I broke in. 'We thought they were just Ag-men!' For it is by this euphonious terms that officials of the Ministry of Agriculture are known here.

'Never mind,' said Mr Annett boisterously. 'Think of all the children! Beech Green Comprehensive School, we'd have here, and Fairacre would have a couple of new wings and a bathing pool and a nursery block—'

'And if Mrs Pringle's going to look after that lot, my life won't be worth living!' I retorted. 'Let's pray that we hear no more of housing estates in this peaceful spot!'

Alas! My prayer was not to be answered.

When Mr Annett had driven off to his orchestral practice in Caxley, in his shabby little car with the 'cello propped carefully in the back, Isobel and I enjoyed ourselves putting young Malcolm to bed.

We enveloped ourselves in mackintosh aprons for bathing the energetic baby, for he was a prodigious splasher, screaming with joy as he smacked the water, and drenched the bathroom.

When we had dried him and tucked him firmly into his cot, we tiptoed downstairs.

'Not that we need to bother,' said his mother, 'he'll be standing up again by now, ready for half an hour's jumping! He's just like George – never still. I'll go and cover him up when he's fallen asleep with exhaustion, but that won't be yet!'

Sure enough, we could hear the rhythmic squeaking of Malcolm's cot springs as he jumped spiritedly up and down, letting off the final ounce or two of energy that still quivered in his plump frame.

'Let's forget him!' said his mother, leading the way into the drawing-room, where a bright fire burned.

'George is looking very well,' I said, when we were settled.

'I'm so glad to hear you say that,' said young Mrs Annett earnestly. 'You know, I often wonder if he's really happy. It's not easy to be a second wife. One always imagines – wrongly, I'm sure – that the first wife was a paragon of all the virtues, and that one is a very poor second best.'

'What an idea!' I exclaimed.

'Well, there it is! I can't talk about it to George, naturally, and there's really no one else I've ever felt I could say anything to; but it doesn't stop these nagging doubts, you know, just to keep quiet about them.'

I felt very sorry for the girl. She was obviously worrying about a non-existent problem, as I set about explaining. But, once she had started to tell me her confidences, more came in quick succession and I began to wonder, with some trepidation, what further disclosures Isobel might make. As an incorrigible spinster

I very much dislike being the confidante of married ladies, and marital troubles, imparted to me in low tones whilst their husbands are temporarily from the room, fill me with the greatest alarm and foreboding. Fortunately, Isobel's good sense and reticence spared me any major discomfort.

'Of course, I know I'm foolish to think such things,' went on Mrs Annett, poking the fire vigorously. 'And I should feel better about it if George and his first wife had been married long enough to have had a few healthy rows. But to be killed – when they'd only been married six months – well, it does cast an odour of sanctity over the whole thing, doesn't it? And George really did adore her. You must admit that a second wife's got a good bit of leeway to make up!'

She sat back on her heels, brandishing the poker and looking so fierce that I burst into laughter.

'Listen!' I said. 'If you've got the sense to see it all as squarely as that, then you must also have the sense to see that you're an addle-pated ass! And why not give George credit for a little intelligence too? He married you because he wanted to – and the first wife just doesn't come into the picture now, poor soul!'

'I do see that really,' admitted Isobel, 'but I'm here alone such a lot that I think too much and imagine things. You see, I've always had people round me – at school, at college, and then when I taught with you at Fairacre. The day seems quite long with George over at the school, and although I'm terribly busy with Malcolm and the house and meals – somehow one's mind goes rattling on, and I get these idiotic ideas.'

It was the first time that I had realised the possibility of young wives being lonely, but I saw now, in a flash, that that very simple circumstance was, possibly, the reason for a number of troubles in early married life. Isobel went on to tell me more.

'And then, of course, I worry far too much about our finances. When I was earning, I bought anything I took a fancy to – within reason – and if I were short at the end of the month, well, that was my own affair and I took the consequences. But now I feel that it is George's money, and that I must use it to the best advantage for the three of us. It really is shattering at times! And there are so many things I see when I go to Caxley – pretty things, you know, like flowers and china and blouses and bracelets – that

I would have bought for myself before, and had no end of a thrill from – but now, I feel it's extravagant and go without, and it is distinctly depressing!'

I was becoming more enlightened, each minute, about the terrific adjustments that a young female of independent means has to make when she throws aside her comfortable job and takes on the manifold duties of a wife and mother.

'And another thing,' continued Mrs Annett, now in full spate, 'I enjoyed teaching and knew that I could do it well. I felt sure of myself – but now, I can't tell whether I'm making a good job of housekeeping or not. There's no one to tell me if I am, and, I must say, I feel full of doubts.'

'Don't forget,' I said, 'that you've suddenly taken on about six skilled jobs and have got to learn them all at the same time. Catering, cooking, looking after Malcolm, keeping George happy, laundry work, entertaining, and all the rest of house-keeping will take months and years to learn. I think you're doing jolly well. The only thing is – I feel you do it all for twenty-four hours out of the twenty-four, seven days a week, and have no time to stand away from the job and see how nicely it's getting along.'

'I suppose that's it, really. It's impossible for us both to go out together unless we get a reliable sitter-in, and Malcolm's a bit of a handful at the moment, so we don't do it often. But I do miss the orchestra!'

'Then I'll come definitely every orchestra night,' I promised. 'I should have thought of it before. It's the least a godmother can do.'

Mrs Annett's face lit up.

'Do you mean it? Won't it be an awful tie to you? I'd just love to go, but I feel it's too much to ask anyone.' She broke off suddenly.

'Listen!'

We sat rigidly, mouths open. I could hear nothing but the gentle gurgling of the rain down an outside guttering, and an occasional patter on the pane.

'He's stopped jumping!' said Malcolm's mother, leaping to her feet. 'Let's go and cover him up.'

Collapsed, face downward, at the end of his cot lay Malcolm

Annett. With bated breath we turned back his blankets, scooped the warm bundle to the right end, and covered him up all over again. This time he lay still, and we tip-toed downstairs again, leaving him to his slumbers.

When I returned home, I found that a note had been put through the door. It said—

'FAIRACRE FLOWER SHOW
A committee meeting of the above will be held in the school at 7 o'clock on Friday next, March 30th. Your attendance is requested.'

'Well, Tibby,' I said to the cat, who was curling round my legs luxuriously, 'that'll be a nice comfortable evening, cramped up in small wooden desks.'

But, as it happened, Fate decided otherwise.

The rain which had been so torrential on the Tuesday when I had visited Beech Green, gave way to clear skies and high winds.

The children were excited and boisterous, as they always are when the weather is windy. Doors slammed, windows rattled, papers blew from desks, and the gale roared so loudly in the elm trees that border the playground that at times it was difficult to make my voice heard in the classroom.

On Friday morning the wind reached unprecedented force. The weathercock shuddered at the top of St Patrick's spire, my lawn was scattered with petals torn from the prunus and almond trees, and the gay clumps of crocuses lay battered in the garden beds, like bowed dancers in satin skirts.

I was busy correcting Eric's arithmetic at his desk at the back of the classroom when the rumbling began. The children looked up in alarm, for the noise was terrifying. I had only just time to realise that it must be a tile slipping down the roof, when, with a deafening crash, it reached the skylight, smashed the glass into a hundred tinkling fragments, and fell thunderously on to my desk below. It was, in fact, a large piece of the curved ridge of the roof, and had I been sitting in my accustomed seat, would doubtless have caused me a trip to Caxley hospital.

The children were much shaken – and so was I, for that matter.

Miss Jackson burst in from the infants' room to see what the trouble was, and stood appalled on the threshold. It was Joseph Coggs who first recovered.

'Best clear the mess up,' he growled huskily, and set off for the lobby, returning with the dust-pan and broom. I lifted the heavy lump of masonry and staggered with it to the playground, while Miss Jackson wielded the broom, and the children, having recovered from their fright, began to cluster round and thoroughly enjoy this sensational interruption to their peaceful labours.

Mr Willet, who had been setting out his seed potatoes ready for sprouting in shallow wooden boxes, in his own quiet kitchen, had somehow been informed of the disaster, by the mysterious bush telegraph which works so well in every village, and had rushed straight to the scene, pulling on his jacket as he pounded up the village street.

'Accident! Up the school!' he had puffed to curious questioners, without slackening his pace.

It was not surprising, therefore, to find that Mr Willet was accompanied by four agitated mothers when he arrived, in an advanced state of breathlessness, at the school door.

'You all right?' he gasped out.

I assured him that we were all unharmed and indicated the smashed skylight.

'Lord!' breathed Mr Willet, with awe. 'That's done it!' The four mothers edged round the door, their eyes goggling. I let them feast on the scene before them for a minute, and then decided that it was time for them to depart.

'No harm done!' I said firmly. 'And now that Mr Willet's here we shall soon clear up the mess!' I shepherded the reluctant quartet towards the lobby.

'Poor little mites! Might have been struck dead!' said one, with relish.

'I always said that skylight was a danger!' asserted the next.

'Tempting Providence to have glass in a roof!' said the third.

'Proper upset I be!' said the fourth, somewhat smugly. 'And if our Billy has nightmares, I shan't wonder! Poor little toad, and him so high strung! I've a good mind to take him back home with me!'

She glanced sidelong at me to see how I would take this display of maternal concern.

'Take him by all means!' I said. 'But I think you're being very silly. It will only make Billy think he's been in far more danger than he has. We shall all finish our lessons in the infants' room, while the skylight is being seen to.'

'Maybe that's best,' agreed the woman hastily. It was quite obvious to me, and to the rest of the mothers, that she had no real intention of being burdened with her son's presence for the rest of the day. Now that she had paraded her maternal rights she was prepared to give way.

'Perhaps you'd be good enough to tell the other mothers, if you happen to see them, that all's well here, and there's nothing to worry about.'

Full of importance, and heavy with the dramatic tales which they would be able to unfold, they hastened away, chattering among themselves, and I returned to Mr Willet.

He was standing on my desk, surveying the ugly splinters of glass which protruded from the edges of the skylight's frame.

'I'll have to pull they out,' he said slowly. At every shuddering blast of wind, the skylight rattled dangerously, and it was obvious that we should have another shower of glass before long.

'Best do it from the roof,' advised Joseph Coggs, who had taken a workmanlike interest in these happenings. 'If us doos it underneath us'll get glass cutting us!'

Mr Willet surveyed the small boy with respect.

'You're dead right, son.' He turned to me. 'I'll get down to Rogers at the forge and we'll bring his long ladder and get up on the roof.'

'I'll take the children out of your way,' I said, opening the dividing door in the partition, and shooing my children into their younger brothers and sisters.

' 'Twould be best to nail up a bit of sack, I reckons,' continued Mr Willet, still gazing aloft. 'Catch the bits, like, and keep some of the weather out. Cor! What a caper, eh? What actually done it?'

I told him about the lump of tiling and he stumped out into the playground to inspect it. His face was full of concern when he returned.

'You shouldn't 'ave lifted that, miss! Might've raptured your-self. Easy enough to get a rapture, heaving rocks like that!'

I said meekly that I was only trying to clear the place up.

'Ah! I daresay,' said Mr Willet gravely, 'but you wants to give a thought to your organs now and again.'

I promised that I would give my organs every consideration in the future and Mr Willet seemed mollified.

'I'll get this straightened up, and old Rogers and I'll fix some-thing up on the roof this afternoon, till them Caxley chaps can do their bit of glazing.'

He bustled away, and I thought as I watched him go how fully he was enjoying our small upheaval. To Mr Willet, with all the time in the world, this was no annoying interruption to his potato sorting. It was an exciting happening, a bizarre quirk in the gentle pattern of his day, and a challenge to be met with courage, common sense and joyful zest.

It was Mrs Pringle who reminded me about the committee meet-ing in the evening.

'Can't have it here, in this glory-hole,' she said, looking at the débris with distaste. 'All catch your deaths! The vicar's bronical enough as it is!'

'That's all right,' I said, 'we'll have it at my house. I'll put a notice on the door here, and we'll send messages after school by the children. There's only about six of us on the committee.'

'At *your* place?' exclaimed Mrs Pringle. If I had suggested the school coke-pile for our rendezvous she could not have sounded more taken aback.

'Yes,' I said, 'in the dining-room. The fire's going, and there's plenty of room, and I've even got a drop of sherry some-where.'

Mrs Pringle surveyed me morosely.

'I'd best come over and put your place to rights, when I've done this lot,' she said, as one who knows where her duty lies, no matter how unpleasant 'Can't have the gentry in that dining-room, with that brass of yours in the state it's in. Noticed it through the windows – and they could do with a wipe over!'

I rallied as best I could under this blow, and thanked her humbly.

427

'That's all right,' she answered graciously. 'Flared-up leg, or no flared-up leg, I'll do you!'

'And it isn't as dirty as all that,' I felt compelled to point out, still smarting slightly from this surprise attack. 'Anyone would think I lived like a pig!'

'Hm! There's pigs and pigs!' boomed Mrs Pringle enigmatically. And limping heavily, she made a triumphant exit, before I could retaliate.

4. REVIVING THE FLOWER SHOW

By seven-twenty the committee members of the Fairacre Flower Show were assembled in my freshly furbished dining-room, enjoying, I hoped, some of my sherry, and the dazzle of my unusually clean brass.

'This really is most pleasant – most pleasant,' said the vicar from the head of the table. 'We really are indebted, Miss Read, for your hospitality.' He dropped his leopard-skin gloves, now in an advanced state of moult, on to the table, and I watched a light shower of fluff settle gently on Mrs Pringle's newly polished surface.

'Nice to be able to stretch your legs,' agreed Mr Roberts, the farmer, who is over six feet tall and has to sit on, and not in, the school desks at most committee meetings.

John Pringle, Mrs Pringle's only son and a keen gardener, made the third man, and Mrs Bradley, Mrs Mawne and I made up the rest of the committee.

Mrs Bradley, in her eighties and a person of determined character, might have been known as the mother of Basil Bradley, a popular novelist, if she had not been such a dominant personality in her own right. It was she who had pressed for the revival of Fairacre's Flower Show, and it was apparent that, despite her age and deafness, she intended to play a vital part in its organization.

Mrs Mawne was a newcomer to Fairacre, although her husband, a retired schoolmaster and keen ornithologist, had lived in the village for a year or two. They had lived separately for some years, but had recently composed their differences and appeared to be peaceably settled (somewhat to the village's disappointment!) among us.

She was a large woman, as used to getting her own way, I suspected, as Mrs Bradley, and I surmised that a clash would soon arise between these two ladies. We did not have long to wait.

We had safely sketched out the different classes, such as 'Six Roots' and 'Six Onions' and so on, and had come to the more delicate task of deciding on the specific requirements of the Table Decoration class.

'Vawse of sweet peas,' said Mr Roberts. 'Can't beat sweet peas for the table.'

Mrs Bradley snorted.

'No scope! We must give people a chance to show their talents. What about a colour qualification? Say, in blue and pink?'

Mrs Mawne smiled deprecatingly and spread her hands.

'A little obvious, don't you think?' she suggested.

Mrs Bradley fell back upon her invaluable weapon of deafness.

'What say? I didn't hear you, Mrs Mawne!' she bellowed, though the dangerous glitter in her beady eyes belied her words.

Mrs Mawne, though a trifle discomfited, joined battle.

'I said,' she shouted menacingly, 'that I thought the colour idea a little obvious!'

'Oh! You did!' replied Mrs Bradley, her neck growing very red. 'Well, have you any better suggestion?'

'Indeed I have,' answered Mrs Mawne, with maddening composure. 'Several, in fact. When I was in Ireland I organized a most successful Flower Show and the table decorations fell into three classes—'

'Pshaw!' muttered Mrs Bradley testily, and fidgeted with her gloves. The vicar began to look very unhappy, and Mr Roberts and I carefully avoided each other's eye.

'One decoration to be not higher than four inches,' swept on Mrs Mawne, enunciating with infuriating emphasis close to Mrs Bradley's unwilling ear, 'the second to be composed of the flowers of one natural order – *ranunculaceae*, I believe it was; and the third to be made entirely of dead flowers.'

'*Dead* flowers?' jerked out Mr Roberts, with extreme surprise. 'Oh, I don't like *dead* flowers! They smell, for one thing.'

Mrs Mawne ignored him. As a sweet pea lover he had damned himself as a Philistine for ever in her eyes.

'That sort of thing may impress the Irish,' retorted Mrs Bradley, with octogenarian vigour. 'Poor, ignorant peasants as they are – but for enlightened Fairacre folk, it just won't do. In any case,' she added, switching abruptly, 'whatever could you get, in July, four inches high?'

'Chickweed!' suggested Mr Roberts, guffawing at his own shaft of wit. Both ladies glared at him, but he was oblivious of their fury, as with his huge head tipped back he roared out his merriment.

'Perhaps we'd better leave—' began the vicar timidly, just as I was saying: 'Annuals in a soup-plate?' in an apologetic query. The vicar fell upon this well-worn suggestion avidly.

'Excellent!' he said cheerfully, and scribbled on his little pad. 'Table decoration then, "Annuals in a Soup Plate". All agreed?'

Six hands were raised in silence, and the rest of the programme was completed in outward harmony.

'Have you heard anything about this housing estate?' queried Mr Roberts, as the ladies were collecting their gloves and handbags, and the vicar was putting his papers away in an envelope much too small for them.

'Housing estate?' said he, looking up from his task. 'Where?'

'Only a rumour, I expect,' said Mr Roberts. 'Heard it in "The Bell" at Caxley last market day. Wasn't there a bit in the papers, about new houses being needed for the atomic station?'

'But that's miles away,' said Mrs Mawne.

'Ugly great rubbishy thing!' pronounced Mrs Bradley. 'Spoiling the view!'

'And are they building a new estate there?' pursued the vicar.

'More likely here,' answered Mr Roberts.

'*Here!*' squeaked the assembled company in five different keys.

The vicar was the first to find his breath. 'My dear Roberts, are you serious?'

Mr Roberts began to look uncomfortable.

'Look! I shouldn't have said anything. It's just a rumour I heard that the atomic people may choose a site near Fairacre. Someone said that Miller's land might be picked on. Hundred Acre Field, I believe – but don't spread it round.'

John Pringle now spoke in his slow, measured burr.

'I heard that too. There was two chaps looking at it recently – and it's my belief all the tittle-tattle started from that. Nothing in it, I don't suppose.'

'I certainly hope it's not true,' said the vicar decidedly. 'It's a wonderful piece of country just there – a real beauty spot.'

'Dan Crockford made one of his best pictures of the downs from the edge of Hundred Acre Field,' said Mrs Bradley, naming a local artist of some fame, who died a few years ago.

'Dan Crockford!' commented Mrs Mawne, with some scorn.

'It is a most beautiful picture, Mrs Mawne,' the vicar assured her earnestly, 'and hangs now in the Caxley Town Hall. It was in the Royal Academy early in the century.'

'And so were dozens of other quite dreadful things,' responded that lady decisively, pulling on a glove with great vigour. Mrs Bradley seized this golden opportunity.

'Dan Crockford,' she began with deadly precision, 'was one of my dearest friends, and once did me the honour of proposing marriage.' She omitted to add that this had happened after the

Hunt Ball of 1902 when the exuberant young Dan had offered his heart and hand to no fewer than six ladies within an hour.

Mrs Mawne had the grace to look abashed.

'I'm sorry, Mrs Bradley. I withdraw my remarks!'

Mrs Bradley gave a stiff nod, and turned to say her farewells to me, when the vicar spoke.

'If this dreadful business does come to anything, perhaps your son might be willing to draft a few strong letters to the papers—'

'Basil would do all he could to protect his native land,' asserted the old lady militantly, and I felt extremely sorry for the unsuspecting novelist, who, I had heard, was engaged on his seventeenth historical novel and would doubtless loathe to be dragged from some elegant and urbane past century to struggle with the affairs of the twentieth.

Basil Bradley's novels had steady sales for he mixed love, duels and history in very unequal proportions, and had the whole displayed in attractive dust jackets, showing ladies in Empire gowns reclining on those uncomfortable bolster-ended sofas which are usually upholstered in striped damask in pastel shades.

The ladies were invariably unhappily married to squat, square men, much older than themselves, with purple complexions and the gout. By about page 352, however, each heroine in turn decided that she must renounce her lover and tread the stony path of duty with her unloved husband, thus leaving four or five pages for a tearful scene written in unbearably tender prose. As all Basil Bradley's books were illustrated by a man who had been a friend of his at Oxford, this touching finale gave the artist a chance to let himself rip over the intricate wrought-iron balcony from which the heroine, with draperies fluttering, waved good-bye to the gallant and diminishing figure on horseback. Unkind critics of the artist's work had not failed to point out a noticeable feature – that of horses so far distant as to be almost incapable of recognition, the animals either being held by grooms in murky shrubberies while the hero was duelling, or else cantering with such speed that a cloud of dust obscured all but the rider's wig. They had further observed, in the captious way that critics will, that the artist was incapable of drawing a horse at all. But these waspish comments luckily made no difference to Basil Bradley's admirers, who as soon as they saw the latest reclining lady in dampened muslin, swooped upon the book and, horses' or no horses, knew that here they would find several hours' pleasant entertainment.

'Well, let's hope there'll be no need for letters to the papers,' said Mr Roberts heartily, 'but if you do get a few hundred people coming here to live, you'll have some fine congregations, vicar!'

The vicar's face glowed.

'Of course, they would be in my parish! It would mean a great deal of visiting, but most interesting, most interesting. I wonder how they would get on with the village folk?'

'They'd never mix!' said Mrs Mawne. 'Nothing in common. Town dwellers mainly, and would spend their time in Caxley.'

'They'll have to have a few more buses running then,' commented Mr Roberts. 'Liven us all up, wouldn't it?'

Mrs Bradley had the last word.

'There won't be a housing estate on Dan Crockford's landscape. There could never be the slightest possibility of such a monstrous project!'

We made our farewells in the little hall, and Fairacre's Flower Show Committee made its way out into the windy night.

But despite Mrs Bradley's brave words a most unsettling occurrence was taking place at that very moment.

Far away, beyond the roaring elms and the wind-swept young wheat of Hundred Acre Field, old Mr Miller stormed vigorously up and down his firelit drawing-room. He had just returned from an evening with friends in Caxley, and had found a letter, in a long official envelope, on the doormat.

It was the contents of this letter which had thrown the peppery little man into such fury. His wife, still in her coat and hat, watched him with concern from her armchair.

'Come to bed! Do now, dear. Sleep on it!' she urged.

'Sleep on it! I'll never sleep!' shouted her enraged husband. He shook the letter in her face as he passed.

'Lot of jumped-up jacks-in-office! "Might come to some fair agreement", they dare to say! Hundred Acre Field's been in our family for over a century. Do these people think I'll part with it? That they'll ever get it, while I'm alive?'

He stopped his agitated pacing and eyes blazing, he shook a fist at the ceiling.

'Let 'em try!' he roared. 'Let 'em try!'

5. Rumours Fly

News of Mr Miller's letter from the Atomic Energy Authority spread rapidly. People shopping in Caxley High Street shook their heads over the affair, and the folk of Fairacre and Beech Green, between whose two villages the new housing estate would be, dropped their everyday discussion of births (unduly premature), marriages (not before time) and deaths (always whole-heartedly regretted), and turned to this more meaty fare.

Mr Miller had written a spirited reply to the letter, flatly refusing to part with an inch of land and adding a page or two of scurrilous remarks about the authority concerned, that made Mr Miller's cautious solicitor blench when he showed it to him. By the time it had been recast into language comprehensible only to the legal mind, and Mr Miller's plain refusal had been hedged about with clauses, parentheses and a whole hatful of 'heretofores', 'whereases' and 'inasmuchases', the reply ran into four pages of typing on quarto-sized paper, and was enough to make poor, frustrated Mr Miller beat his octogenarian brains out on his solicitor's desk.

'All I wanted was "No! And damn you!",' protested the fiery little man. Mr Lovejoy, who, to tell the truth, had had a most trying morning with this client, smiled placatingly.

'I can assure you,' said Mr Lovejoy, spreading his pink, smooth hands, 'that this is worded in the strongest possible manner.' He would like to have pointed out that he had just saved Mr Miller from almost certain charges of defamation of character, slander, libel and quite a dozen other obnoxious things, but he did not feel up to it. Gratitude he was not so silly as to look for from this elderly firebrand, common civility he hardly dare expect in his present state of mind, and personal assault would not have surprised him.

He was relieved when Mr Miller, glancing at the clock, said he had an appointment at eleven, and made for the door.

'We'll do our very best for you in this matter, Mr Miller,' said Mr Lovejoy as his client shot through.

Exhausted, he returned to his desk, and rang for his morning coffee.

'Black, today!' he said.

April was being as warm and lovely as March had been rough and wet. The gardens in Fairacre were at their best, full of colour and fragrance, and Mr Willet's little cottage garden was one of the loveliest.

I had spent the first part of the Easter holidays with friends by the sea, but returned to Fairacre about a week before term started to do a little spring-cleaning, with Mrs Pringle's grudging assistance, some gardening and odds and ends of shopping which are difficult to fit in during term-time.

Amy, my old college friend, who lives at Bent on the other side of Caxley, spent two days with me, whilst James, her husband, was away on business, and we talked so much that we were quite hoarse.

'The trouble with you,' said Amy severely, watching me look up Mr Roberts' telephone number in the book, 'is that you don't train your mind. In some ways, you've got quite a *good* mind,' she continued, more kindly, 'but you don't apply it.'

I said I didn't quite follow this.

'Well, fancy wasting all that time looking up a telephone number that you must want dozens of times during the year! You should remember it!'

'But I can't !' I protested.

'You could!' insisted Amy, prodding me quite painfully with her knitting needle.

'Two, one, three!' I said, having found Mr Roberts' name.

'There you are,' said Amy triumphantly, 'what a simple one to remember! Two, halve the first number, and add the two together for the third! Child's play!'

'But I've got to remember "Two" to begin with,' I argued. 'Supposing I thought of six, and halved that, and added it, and all the rest! Why I'd probably get Caxley Swimming Bath!'

'Tchah!' said Amy. 'It's just a matter of association. For instance, I always remember my mother's number 237, because the 23 bus goes by the door, and the house is number seven.'

'Well, Mr Roberts doesn't have any buses passing his house, and the farm's called "Walnut Tree Farm," so that doesn't get us very far!'

'Of course, if you're going to be plain *naughty*—' said Amy loftily.

'There's always the book,' I pointed out.

'What's your car number, d'you know?' shot Amy at me.

'Yes,' I said promptly, 'It's—' I stopped short. 'No, I don't know. I would have known if you hadn't put it out of my head by asking.'

'And what would you do,' said Amy, with heavy sarcasm, 'if a policeman asked you?'

'I'd get out and walk round to the back of the car and tell him,' I responded.

'If you hadn't *got* the car,' shouted Amy rudely.

'Then I doubt if the occasion would arise,' I answered with maddening insouciance.

Amy was on the point of gibbering, when the idiocy of the conversation overcame us both, and we laughed so much that it was some minutes before I could ring Mr Roberts. By that time I had to look his number up all over again.

We walked down to Mr Willet's cottage after tea. It was a perfect evening, sunny and still. The young leaves were more golden than green in the evening sunshine, and the birds were singing their hearts out.

Mr Willet's cottage is a thatched one, and has an uneven old brick path from the gate round to the back door. The bricks have weathered to a soft rose colour, and have brilliant emerald streaks between them where the moss grows, smooth and close as velvet ribbon. The path to the front door is seldom used. The knocker is encrusted with paint and is difficult to lift, but I remembered the story told of Arthur Coggs, our village reprobate, who had wielded that knocker energetically late one night, when, afire with beer and missionary zeal he had attempted to arouse Mr Willet's religious conscience and had only succeeded in rousing his fury.

Mr Willet, with true peasant frugality, scorns to put his precious land down to grass anywhere. The whole of his patch is dug over, with the narrowest of paths threaded here and there, and only where absolutely necessary. But he likes growing flowers as well as vegetables – unlike some of his neighbours – and his small front garden this evening was thick with velvety wallflowers of every colour, from palest yellow to deep blood red. Their scent was heady, and mingled with the clean, waxy smell of the small box edging which lined the brick path.

We found him bent double over the box edging, carefully parting the stubby branches with his gnarled hands. He was collecting snails, and dropping them, with a satisfying plop, into a pail of salt water which stood on the path beside him.

'Kills 'em in a minute,' he told us, stirring the revolting frothy mixture with a stick. 'Snails loves a bit of box! Ten minutes' steady snailing along the box, saves a mort of damage in the garden. Come round the back, Miss Read, and see mother. She's doddlin' about there somewhere.'

We followed him to the back of the house, admiring his neat rows of vegetables as we went. A narrow strip, bordering the path was devoted to flowers, and rosy double-daisies, grape hyacinths and early pansies flourished here.

'Look,' I said, 'your apple tree's breaking already!' The tight little knots of buds were beginning to show pink streaks, and it was plain, that if this warm weather lasted, Mr Willet would have his blossom within a week.

'Much too early,' said Mr Willet, screwing up his eyes against the sun as he scrutinised this forward fellow. 'Don't like to see it! Plenty of frosts to come yet!'

He gave the grey, hoary trunk a reproving slap, and led us to the back door.

Mrs Willet was busy with her ironing, and her kitchen was filled with the comfortable smell of fresh linen.

'Take a seat, do, Miss Read,' she said, indicating two broad wooden chairs against the wall. She smiled at Amy, and I made introductions.

'I'll just finish off this shirt, and then we'll have a glass of wine,' said Mrs Willet, holding the iron to one side of her and spitting delicately upon it. A tiny ball of spittle sizzled across the surface and vanished for ever floorwards.

'Just right!' commented Mrs Willet with immense satisfaction, and plunged the iron into the depths of an arm-hole.

We talked while she worked, and I gave Mr Willet the message I had brought about small school repairs. Naturally, the topic of the proposed housing estate soon arose.

'I heard as 'twasn't just Hundred Acre they wanted, but a goodish bit of the downs behind,' said Mr Willet, as he leaned against the doorpost. ''Tidn't right, you knows, to take farm land like that. They say old Miller's in a fair taking about it all!'

'Well, I don't know,' said Mrs Willet, hanging the shirt carefully over the clothes horse. 'You hears a lot about spoiling the view and that – but I knows one or two thinks it's a good idea!'

'And who might they be?' enquired Mr Willet, puffing out his moustache belligerently.

'Mrs Fowler, the Coggses—' began Mrs Willet.

'Faugh! That old Tyler's Row lot!' scoffed Mr Willet with scorn. 'I suppose they thinks there'll be some pickings for them out of it! Does Arthur Coggs reckon he'll get a jammy job there when they starts building? Plenty of overtime and skedaddle home when it starts to rain?'

'I suppose it would bring plenty of work,' said Amy.

'Not only work,' replied Mrs Willet. 'They reckons us'd get more buses through this way – probably some every day, not three times a week like we has it now.'

Mr Willet snorted his disgust. 'Be everlasting traipsing to Caxley then, I s'pose, wasting time and money. I don't see no sense in it at all.'

'The Caxley shopkeepers might welcome the scheme,' I said doubtfully.

'They most certainly would!' said Amy with conviction, 'I was talking to Bob Lister at the ironmonger's and he reckons that a new housing estate would probably bring half as much trade again to that end of Caxley.'

'Not only Caxley,' pointed out Mrs Willet. 'They was saying down the baker's yesterday, that Tom Prince was thinking of getting another delivery van for the bread, if all these new people come. Bring trade to Fairacre and Beech Green, it would.'

'Miss Clare seemed to think that the young people in the village would welcome the buses to Caxley,' I observed. 'I know Miss Jackson hopes it will come. I must say it would give much more scope to the boys and girls who have just left school.'

'Well, I don't like to hear it even talked of,' said Mr Willet decidedly, 'I prays it won't come, and I'll back old Miller up, any day, in his fight. Why should the poor ol' feller give up his ground? He's farmed it well, ain't he, all his life? And his father before him? There's plenty of scruffy land, between here and the atomic, fit for houses to be built on, without picking on as fine a bit of farming land as Hundred Acre!'

He shook his head, like a spaniel emerging from a stream.

'Ah well!' he continued, more mildly, as though this energetic shaking had rid him of all tiresome worries, 'What about that drop of wine, mother? Which d'you fancy, ladies? Cowslip or dandelion?'

'You know,' said Amy, when we were back at the school-house, 'most people will agree with your Mr Willet. I can foresee a real battle about this wretched project. I know people in Caxley are furious about it, on the whole – particularly the *avant-garde* of the artistic group,' added Amy shrewdly.

'Are they all admirers of Dan Crockford?' I asked in some surprise.

'Dear me, no!' exclaimed Amy, 'but when you've gone to the expense of papering one wall different from the rest and buying a Degas to put on it, you're not going to see *any* artist's landscape defiled for the sake of a mere atomic power station. You see, they'll be firmly on Mr Willet's side.'

'It was the farming value of the land that weighed with Mr Willet,' I objected.

'It's the aesthetic value that will tell in the end,' forecast Amy, 'just wait and see!'

'I hope you're right,' I said fervently.

Term started, and the children returned looking fit and brown, having been able to play outside during the fine sunny days of the holiday. I was sorry to see that three children – all from one family – had left the village and that our numbers were down to thirty-two, seventeen in my class and only fifteen in the infants' room.

'It's the smallest that the school has ever been,' I said to Miss Jackson, looking sadly at her little class. The children were drinking their bottles of milk, sucking steadily through their straws, and gazed owlishly over the top at us as we talked. 'There were over forty here when I first came.'

'People don't have so many children these days,' explained Miss Jackson kindly, as though I had been speaking of mid-Victorian times. 'They have fought for a higher standard of living, and intend to maintain it, which means that the family must be a more economic size. With the overthrow of the tyranny of church superstitions, and the setting-up of family-planning clinics—'

'All right! All right!' I broke in testily, 'there's no need to talk to me like some pink left-wing paper, and in any case, it isn't so much the size of the family, but the move to the towns that's depleting us here. This makes the third family within a year to leave Fairacre. They've all gone nearer the atomic station. Mr Roberts is still looking for a really reliable cow-man.'

'We shall get an influx when the new housing estate goes up,' observed Miss Jackson, 'or will they all go to Beech Green School?'

'I should think the children would go to either,' I said, shaking my head at a very naughty little boy who had decided to empty the dregs of his milk bottle into the ear of his neighbour. 'I wonder if we shall have to have any new buildings?'

'More likely to have a colossal new school on the estate,' hazarded Miss Jackson, rescuing the milk bottle.

I felt uncomfortably jolted.

'I never thought of that !' I answered slowly.

I drove over to the Annetts' house that evening for my weekly baby-sitting session.

Young Malcolm was having his jumping practice at the end of the cot, singing a tuneless and breathless accompaniment to this exercise. To his mother and to me, peeping through the crack of the bedroom door at this bundle of energy, it looked as though he would be at it for at least another hour.

The usual thousand-and-one last minute injunctions were given me by the departing mother, while her husband brought in coal and logs, for the evening was turning chilly, and gave me the *Telegraph, The Times Educational Supplement, The Farmer's Weekly* and *Eagle* – the last, I suspected, confiscated from one of his pupils. I decided to read that first, whilst giving an ear to Isobel's directions.

'Let him jump until he falls asleep, and if you can get him into the right end of the bed, all the better. If not, tuck him up where he's asleep. If he stirs, you'll find the old shawl he takes to bed with him, somewhere among the covers, unless he's thrown it over the side. If he's wrinkled up his mackintosh sheet and you can possibly straighten it without waking him, it would be a help.

'I've left some boiled water in a blue jug on his bunny tray in the kitchen – not the white jug – that's got orange juice in it. And if he really seems hungry he can have some warm milk, preferably in his mug, but if he's really being frantically naughty put it into his bottle and he may drop asleep as he takes it that way. I'm trying to break him of the bottle, but he has it occasionally at bed time.'

I said I would remember all this, reaching for Dan Dare.

Mr Annett called anxiously from the hall. 'It's past seven, Isobel!'

'Coming!' said she, throwing a scarf round her neck and grabbing her violin. 'Oh! And one last thing, take the bottle away as soon as he's asleep!'

I said I would. Dan Dare appeared to be in a most awkward predicament, having been hoisted on a crane of some sort, by green-faced men with claws and legs like birds. I was dying to read about his adventures.

'You are a dear,' said Isobel, giving me a hasty kiss, and knocking Dan Dare to the floor unnoticed. She rushed from the room and I heard the front door slam. I bent down to retrieve *Eagle* and heard the front door open again. Isobel's head appeared round the door. She looked extremely agitated.

'Of course, if he's *emptied* the bottle *before* he's asleep, take it away in any case, or he'll get the *frightful* wind!'

She vanished before I could reply. The door slammed again, the car gave a distant and impatient hoot, and finally drove off towards Caxley.

I listened to my charge. He was still jumping rhythmically in the distance.

Sighing luxuriously, I leant back in my chair and put my feet up on a footstool. In ten minutes' time, I reckoned, I should insert my young god-child into the right end of his bed, put his comforting old shawl into his sleeping hand, and forget him.

Meanwhile, I turned my attention to Dan Dare, who, I was sorry to see, was in an even worse plight in the last picture than in the first with the green-faced crane operators.

Peace descended on Beech Green school-house as I read *Eagle* avidly from cover to cover, to the accompaniment of the distant squeakings of cot springs. Gradually, the squeaking grew less frequent, and finally stopped.

Heaving myself from the chair, and throwing Dan Dare aside, I made my way upstairs to attend to my duties.

6. TROUBLE AND LOVE

Miss Clare was busy putting the last minute touches to the supper table. It had been a lovely day, and she had been pleased when Miss Jackson had said, at tea-time, that she thought she would cycle into Caxley and call on a friend there.

'We might go to the pictures,' she had said, 'so don't wait supper for me if I'm a little late. It just depends how we feel.'

Miss Clare had been delighted to hear about the friend. She knew that she had met one or two young teachers in the town, but had feared that her lodger's unswerving devotion to Miss Crabbe, the psychology lecturer, might stand in the way of any warm friendship elsewhere. With great delicacy Miss Clare refrained from asking the sex of the Caxley friend, but hoped, for Miss Jackson's sake, that it was male, and that he was young, single and good-looking. She was inclined to think, however, that the friend was much more likely to be female, and if it were that new gym mistress, she, alas, was no more prepossessing than Miss Jackson herself, thought Miss Clare sadly.

By ten o'clock Miss Clare was beginning to think of bed, for she had risen at half past six as was her custom. She looked out of the window at the clear sky, and breathed in the fragrance from her garden. The lilac was in flower, and she could see the plumy pyramids of blossom outlined against the stars.

It was nearly eleven before Miss Jackson arrived. Miss Clare heard her calling good-bye, and a muffled voice replying in the distance. Then came the sound of Miss Jackson's bicycle thrown, with a clatter, into the shed. The back door burst open, and Miss Jackson with flushed face and shining eyes, stood before her. She looked very happy.

'Oh! You shouldn't have waited up,' she said reproachfully. 'I was later than I meant to be. We went to the pictures after all.'

Miss Clare enquired about the film. Yes, she was told, it was most awfully good, but rather a short programme. They had come out at a quarter to ten.

Miss Clare looked a trifle surprised, and Miss Jackson rattled on.

'We were so thirsty that we went into "The Bell" for a drink,' she explained, somewhat defiantly. 'Anything wrong with that?'

Miss Clare felt vaguely uncomfortable. It was obvious that Miss Jackson was very much on the defensive and Miss Clare was beginning to wonder why. So far no name had been given to the friend, and whether it was male or female Miss Clare did not really know – but she was beginning to suspect that the friend was a man, and one that Miss Jackson felt she would not approve of.

'I don't know that "The Bell" is a very pleasant place for two girls to enter unescorted,' answered Miss Clare mildly, 'I see from the *Caxley Chronicle* that it is frequented by a number of Irish labourers who appear regularly before the magistrate.' She had chosen her words with some guile, and her manner was pleasant.

Miss Jackson bolted her last mouthful of pie, and placed her knife and fork across her plate, with exaggerated deliberation. 'As it happens,' she said, raising her thick eyebrows, 'I was

443

accompanied by a man.' Miss Clare congratulated herself privately upon eliciting this information. 'And what's more, he saw me home, so I was well looked after.'

'I'm glad to hear it,' said Miss Clare gently, pushing the cheese dish towards her lodger. 'Would you take some of my dark purple lilac to Miss Read in the morning?' she continued, skating gracefully away from thin ice. 'She has a lovely pale one, I know, but no deep purple.'

'Of course I will,' said Miss Jackson heartily. She seemed relieved that the subject had been changed, and Miss Clare's misgivings grew. Who on earth could it be? She pondered the question as she made her way wearily up the little staircase.

Although it was late, it was some time before Miss Clare fell asleep. Her lodger had gone, singing, to bed. Miss Clare had waited for the two thumps which were the sign that Miss Jackson's shoes had been kicked off, for the click of the light switch, and the final creak as Miss Jackson clambered into the high feather bed.

Somewhere, in the velvety darkness, a nightingale throbbed out his song from a spray of blossom. He was urgent and languorous in turn, now brittle and staccato, now pouring forth a low, steady ripple of bubbling sound. Miss Clare lay in her shadowy room, listening to him, and thinking of the girl beyond the wall, so young, so very ignorant, and so pathetically sure of herself.

'She's really old enough to know what she's about,' Miss Clare told herself, 'And yet – how I wish her parents were here.'

She heard the church clock at Beech Green strike two before she fell asleep. And still the nightingale sang of love and trouble, trouble and love, as though his heart were full to overflowing.

It was Amy who first told me that Miss Jackson and the Franklyn man had been seen about together, on several occasions, in Caxley.

'They were in the cinema the other night,' said Amy, 'holding hands and with eyes only for each other. I wonder why courting couples pay good money to sit through films which must be a great interruption to them?'

'Nowhere else to go, I expect,' I said, trying to sound less concerned than I felt. 'But Amy, are you sure it was Franklyn?'

'How do I know?' said Amy reasonably enough. 'But Joy Miller was with me, and she said that she thought it was her uncle's gamekeeper from Springbourne. He was a biggish fellow with sandy hair and white eyelashes. Most unattractive I thought, but there – love is blind, they say.'

'It certainly sounds like him,' I observed. Amy and I had met this Saturday morning and were now having coffee together. We stirred our cups in silence.

'Isn't it the limit?' I said, after a bit.

'Jealous?' asked Amy slyly.

'No, I'm blowed if I am!' I responded inelegantly, and with sudden warmth. 'The older I get, the more delighted I am that I'm single. Love seems a frightful nuisance.'

'Sure you're not having a reaction from Mr Mawne's perfidious attentions?' suggested Amy. 'Is this the brave front put on by an unfulfilled female of uncertain age?'

I looked at her acidly across the rickety oak table.

'If you're going to act the goat, and talk like that ghastly Crabbe woman Miss Jackson's always thrusting down my throat,' I said coldly, 'I shall leave you at once – and what's more, you can pay the bill!'

'Pax, pax!' said Amy hastily, crossing her fingers. 'Take back all I said! See my finger wet, see my finger dry, may I slit my throat, if—'

'All right, all right!' I broke in upon her gabbling. 'But talk sense for a moment. Do you really think Miss Jackson is serious about this man?'

'Looked like it,' said Amy.

'But he must be nearly forty – and his wife's only been dead a few months,' I objected.

'Just when he'd feel the need for a little sympathy and feminine company,' replied Amy, 'and dozens of men are at their most attractive at forty. What's against him? Do you think that his intentions are *not* matrimonial?'

'I don't think he'd marry Miss Jackson for a minute,' I said. 'And a very good thing too. It would be quite unsuitable. They've absolutely nothing in common. He's already got a daughter, he has a bad name in the village, and Miss Jackson's such an utter fool that she'd never see anything until she was in a complete mess, and then she'd be too pigheaded to ask for help. I don't like this business at all. If you ask me, he's a thoroughly bad lot!'

Mrs Pringle thought so too. I had wondered how soon the rumours would begin to fly, after Amy's disclosure over the coffee-cups. I had not long to wait.

Within three days Mrs Pringle broached the subject, obliquely, and with nauseating self-righteousness.

I was alone in the classroom after school. The children had gone home, and Miss Jackson had pedalled off towards Beech Green. Mrs Pringle, trudging through to the infants' room, with two brooms under one arm and a dust pan clutched across her stomach, stopped, ostensibly to pick a toffee paper from the floor, but in fact to impart and receive any news of Miss Jackson's affairs.

'Seems to have settled down nicely, she do,' said Mrs Pringle, in such dulcet tones that I was instantly on my guard. 'I like to see a girl happy.'

I made a non-committal noise and continued to look for a form which the office had told me (with some irritability) I had been asked to return three weeks ago. It did not appear to be in the drawer allotted – on the whole – to forms.

'A good day's work when Miss Jackson moved in with Miss Clare,' went on Mrs Pringle, raising her voice slightly. 'Not that she wasn't well looked after with you, I don't doubt,' she said, with the air of one telling a white lie, 'but she do look a bit more cheerful. Plumper too!' she added, with some malice, annoyed that I still turned over my papers busily.

'I didn't starve her, you know,' I observed mildly, opening the gummed paper drawer. The thing must be somewhere!

Mrs Pringle gave a high forced laugh.

'The very idea! We all knows that – but Miss Clare seems to suit her best, and of course, being young she's soon finding friends.'

'Naturally,' I said shortly, slamming in the gummed paper drawer, and opening the one with the log books and catalogues from educational publishers. It looked like being a hopeless search.

Mrs Pringle began to close in upon her subject.

'Not that I'm one to criticise. It's not my place, as I said to my husband when he repeated some gossip he'd heard about her down at "The Beetle" last night – but we've all got our own ideas, and say what you like, there's still such a thing as class.'

The form was not to be found in the log book drawer. I armed myself with a ruler, and set about getting into the drawer which holds envelopes full of cardboard money, packets of raffia needles, a set of archaic reading cards embellished with pictures of bearded men, ladies with bustles and little girls in preposterous hats and buttoned boots, and various other awkward objects known to all schoolteachers. By pulling the drawer open a crack, thrusting in the ruler upon the seething mass within, and bearing down heavily, it was just possible to jerk it open. (Every teacher who is not soullessly efficient has at least one drawer like this. I have several.)

Mrs Pringle warmed to her theme as I struggled.

'She's got all the world before her. A young girl like that, speaks nice, been to college, can read and write – why, she could have anyone! They do say there's someone interested. *Someone*, I won't say a *gentleman*, because that he isn't, not by any manner of means! But we all hope that that young thing won't have her head turned, and by someone no better than he should be.'

447

I felt that it was time to speak.

'Mrs Pringle, do try and scotch any gossip about Miss Jackson. She's quite old enough to choose her own friends.'

'Ah! but do her parents know who she's going round with? Their only daughter, I understand.' Her tone grew lugubrious, and she assumed the pious look that the choir boys mimic behind her back.

'Their one tender chick,' she continued, with an affecting tremor in her voice. I thought of Miss Jackson's sturdy frame and attempted to keep my face straight. 'How would you like it, if she was your daughter? Think now, if she was!'

I did. But not for long.

'Look, Mrs Pringle,' I replied, 'I think you're all making far too much of Miss Jackson's innocent affairs. She is in Miss Clare's care – and mine, for that matter – and writes regularly to her parents, and frequently goes home to see them. There are far too many busy-bodies in this village!' I ended roundly, thrusting the last drawer back. Heaven alone knew where that form had vanished!

Mrs Pringle drew in a long, outraged breath. Hitching up her burdens, she continued her journey into the infants' room. Her leg, I noticed, was dragging badly.

Soon after this brush with Mrs Pringle, I was invited to tea at the vicarage.

The tea was set out on the verandah, sheltered from the wind and bathed in warm sunshine. Mrs Partridge had spread a very dashing cloth of red and white checks over the spindly iron table. This round table was painted white; and its legs were most intricately embellished with scrolls, fleur-de-lys and flourishes, with here and there a spot of red rust, for the table stood outside in all weathers.

A motley collection of chairs helped to furnish the verandah. Mrs Partridge, presiding over the tea-pot, sat in a creaking wicker chair which had once been cream in colour, but had weathered to grey. The vicar lay back in a chaise-longue, with his stomach skywards, until he was passed his cup of tea, when he straightened up, planted a leg on each side of his perch, and sat well forward, nearly split in half.

Mr and Mrs Mawne, who were also of the party, were more comfortably placed in canvas armchairs of a more upright nature. They sat very straight, to avoid knocking their cups off the narrow wooden arms, and looked remarkably careful and prim.

I think I was the worst off, for my seat was a basket chair, very close to the floor so that my legs could either be stretched straight ahead or pulled in with my knees just under my chin. No compromise seemed possible, and I feared that my best nylon stockings were taking a severe tousling from the wicker-work which caught them maliciously from time to time.

Despite our discomforts, however, the tea was excellent, the sun shone and we chatted away cheerfully enough. Mr Mawne told the vicar about a whitethroat's nest he had discovered, built in a most extraordinary position; Mrs Mawne told me how the Women's Institute should be run, and Mrs Partridge, who is President of Fairacre W.I., listened unperturbed and poured tea for her critic, in the kindest manner.

It was Mr Mawne who first mentioned the proposed housing site.

'A scandal if that land is taken for building!' he said, chopping up a piece of chocolate cake viciously. 'More larks there to the square yard than anywhere else in England!'

'Have you heard any more?' asked Mrs Mawne, deflected momentarily from her account of the lost splendours of former W.I.s run by herself.

'I was on the telephone this morning,' said the vicar, 'to Miller – about an address I needed – and evidently things are moving.'

'Which way?' asked Mrs Mawne.

'As far as I could gather – and I must say he was so very – er – *cross* about the whole affair, that it was difficult to hear him clearly – it seems that he has had a letter pointing out that the land can be purchased compulsorily, if need be, and that the proposals are now in the hands of the County Council.'

'But we just *can't* have a great, ugly, housing estate on our doorsteps!' exclaimed Mrs Partridge, voicing the feelings of us all.

'Think what an enormous parish you'd have!' said Mr Mawne to the vicar, who had gently tipped back to his prone position, with his legs up.

'Think of the visiting!' said Mrs Partridge. There was a touch of horror in her tone.

'They might,' said the vicar, in a small voice, addressing the roof of the verandah, 'I say it is *just* possible that they *might* have a small church of their own.'

There was a shocked silence. It was broken by Mr Mawne, who shifted his canvas chair nearer to the vicar, with a horrible scraping noise on the tiles, and looked down upon him.

'You mean, it's going to be *that big*?' he enquired.

The vicar heaved himself upright again and straddled his leg-rest as though he were riding a horse.

'No one knows, but there's no doubt that five or six hundred workers are to be taken on. Then there are their families. They'll need a lot of houses, and I believe a row of shops is envisaged. Miller gave me to understand that the preliminary layout provided for a playing field as well.'

'Shall we have enough room at Fairacre School – and Beech Green – for all the children?' I asked.

The vicar turned his gentle gaze upon me. His face was troubled.

'It's possible,' he began slowly, 'that a school is planned for the estate as well.'

We looked at each other in silence. You could have heard a pin drop on the verandah.

'And my school,' I answered, equally slowly, 'is dwindling steadily in numbers—'

The vicar jumped to his feet, and smote me on the shoulder.

'It shall never close!' he declared militantly, his eyes flashing, 'Never! Never!'

PART TWO

The Storm Breaks

* * * *

7. MISS JACKSON'S ERRAND

The early summer months were bathed in sunshine, and Fair-acre shimmered in the heat. The shining days followed, one after the other, like blue and white beads on a string, as every morning dawned clear.

The hay crop was phenomenal, and was carried with little of the usual anxiety at this time. Wild roses spangled the hedges, buttercups gilded the fields, and even in such raggle-taggle gardens as the Coggs' beauty still flowered, for the neglected elder bushes were already showing their creamy, aromatic blossoms.

The shabby thatch, which served the four cottages comprising Tyler's Row, was bleached to ash-blonde with age and the continued heat. In the garden of the second cottage Jimmy Waites, now nearly eight years old, was having the time of his life.

His mother, worn down at last by repeated entreaties, had allowed him to have the family zinc bath on the minute grass patch, and had let him put two inches of water in the bottom.

'But no more, mind!' she had said firmly. 'The well's getting that low, and us all shares it as you know. And don't tell your father as I let you have it – or there'll be no supper for you tonight!'

She spoke more sternly than she felt, for she was smarting from a guilty conscience not only about the use of precious water, but also of the bath itself. She was a good-natured mother, and had sympathised with her young son's craving for cool water on such a day. She watched him indulgently, through the kitchen window, as he splashed and capered in the bath, clad respectably in an old bathing suit of his sister's, that clung hideously to his brown legs.

To a gap in the hedge came the three eldest Coggs children,

Joseph and his younger twin sisters. They watched enviously, their eyes and mouths like so many O's, as the bright drops glittered in the sunshine around the capering form of their lucky neighbour.

'Can us come?' growled Joseph, in his husky gipsy voice. The capering stopped. Jimmy advanced towards the trio, with delicious cool runnels of water trickling down his legs.

'Dunno. I'll ask my mum,' responded Jimmy.

Mrs Waites heard this exchange, and was torn between pity and exasperation. She had become very fond of Joseph whilst his mother had been away in hospital some time before, but did not care to encourage the family too much, for there was no denying the dirtiness and slap-dash ways which might undermine her own child's more respectable upbringing. She had, since Mrs Coggs' return, become a little more intimate with that dejected lady, lending her the weekly magazine which she took regularly, and occasionally handing over outgrown garments for Joseph. Arthur Coggs was notorious in Fairacre. 'A useless article,' was Mr Willet's summing-up of the head of the Coggs family, and Fairacre agreed.

Mrs Waites heard the padding of bare feet at the kitchen door, and opened it hastily. No need to have a clean brick floor all messed-up, she told herself, looking down into the upturned face of her youngest child. His blue eyes, bluer than the cloudless sky behind his fair head, melted her heart as usual.

'All right,' she said good-naturedly, 'let 'em come for a bit.'

With squeals of delight the three children squeezed through the ragged hedge, and hurled their battered sandals aside. Mrs Coggs hurried from her back door to see what caused this commotion and stood, nonplussed, at the sight that met her eyes. Mrs Waites hurried from her own cottage to reassure her. They stood, one each side of the hedge, and watched the four children jumping ecstatically up and down in the zinc bath.

'They likes a drop of water,' said Mrs Coggs indulgently. 'Pity there ain't no ponds much round here. The Caxley kids has the swimming bath, of course. They's lucky!' Her tone was envious.

'From what I hear,' said Mrs Waites, with some importance, 'Fairacre might get a swimming bath before long if that new estate comes along.'

Mrs Coggs looked suitably impressed.

'My! I hope it does then,' she said emphatically. 'That's what us wants for our kids, ain't it?'

Mrs Coggs' tacit assumption that she and Mrs Waites were united, jarred upon Mrs Waites considerably. She at once disassociated herself from such low company.

'Not that there won't be plenty against a new estate,' she said, as one explaining matters to a backward child. 'The high-ups is in a fine old fever already. And quite right too!' she added righteously. 'That's a real pretty view over there to Beech Green!' In a few sentences she had ranged herself on the side of those who Lead Affairs in Fairacre, and poor Mrs Coggs looked bewildered, and, once again, an outcast.

'But 'tis only a field!' she protested.

'It won't be if they builds houses all over it,' pointed out Mrs Waites.

'Well, I don't know, I'm sure,' said Mrs Coggs miserably, and faltered to a stop. It was obvious that she had put her foot in it somewhere, but just where and how, she could not determine. She made a fumbling attempt to get matters right again.

'Still, us might get a few more buses and that. 'Twould make it easier for shopping to be able to go to Caxley any day like.'

Mrs Waites agreed graciously.

Somewhat emboldened, Mrs Coggs continued diffidently. 'Which reminds me! I wanted to slip up the shop for half a pound of broken biscuits. Would the kids be in your way?'

Mrs Waites, still in her role of great lady, was about to grant permission for Mrs Coggs' temporary absence, in suitably cool terms, when a cry from the zinc bath attracted her attention.

'Look at Jim!' crowed Joseph Coggs admiringly. Jimmy stood poised on his hands, in the water. His fair hair hung like a mop and his wet shining legs pointed towards the vivid sky.

'Ain't he *clever*!' squealed Joseph, beside himself. Touched by this tribute Mrs Waites' warm heart melted entirely. She cast a compassionate glance upon the bedraggled mother beside her.

Some life she had of it, poor toad, thought Mrs Waites. She spoke gently, jettisoning the refined accent she had used during the conversation, and using her homely country burr.

'You be off, m'dear! Us'll be all right here. Yours can have a bite of tea with our Jimmy in the garden. You take your time!'

On an equally hot day, during the following week, Miss Clare and her lodger sat at tea in the cottage garden. A sycamore tree threw a welcome patch of shade across the sunny lawn and here the two sat eating bread and butter spread with lemon curd of Miss Clare's own making. A massive fruit cake, well stuffed with plums, stood on the table before them, and would have delighted the heart of Dr Martin had he been there to see it.

A bumble bee fumbled about the flower border nearby, and his droning added to the languor of the summer afternoon. Miss Clare, watching him, spoke slowly.

'I quite forgot to give you the jumble sale parcel this morning,' she said. 'Do you think the eldest Kelly boy is reliable enough to take it over to Springbourne?'

Miss Jackson appeared to give the matter some thought, and then replied quite excitedly.

'Would you like me to take it this evening? It is no distance on a bicycle, and I think it might be rather heavy for Tim Kelly.'

'But it's so hot, my dear,' protested Miss Clare, 'and quite a pull up through the wood. And then you don't know where Mrs Chard lives, do you? She's collecting the jumble at her house.'

Miss Jackson waved aside these little difficulties.

'You can easily tell me, and I'd really like to go out for a little while. I wanted to collect some twigs for the nature table, in any case, and the wood will be quite cool for doing that.'

Miss Clare was pleasantly surprised at her lodger's readiness to undertake this errand. The jumble sale was to take place on the following evening and she had promised Mrs Chard that her contribution would be delivered in good time.

'If you're sure—' she began diffidently.

'Quite sure!' replied Miss Jackson, putting her plate on the tray, and rising with unaccustomed animation. 'I'll just go and change into a cooler frock and then set off.'

She ran into the cottage, omitting to carry anything with her, noted Miss Clare sadly. She saw her head bobbing about in the bedroom window as she opened and shut drawers. Miss Clare stacked the tea things methodically on the tray. The magnificent cake remained uncut and Miss Clare, though still a trifle hungry, would not think of broaching it for herself alone. The shade of Dr Martin seemed to approach and speak to her. 'Eat something else, Dolly!' it said authoritatively. Obeying her conscience, and smiling as she did so, Miss Clare meekly ate the last slice of bread and butter before gathering up her tray and returning, across the shimmering lawn, to the kitchen whose cool shadows fell like a benison around her.

She heard the girl above singing as she clattered about the ancient floorboards. Miss Clare washed the cups and saucers carefully in the silky rainwater, and dried them lovingly with a linen cloth that was thin but snowy-white.

Miss Jackson burst in upon her as she was replacing the china on the kitchen dresser. Her lodger's face was shining, her hair carefully dressed, and she wore a becoming yellow cotton frock.

'How pretty you look!' cried Miss Clare. 'Don't spoil that lovely dress picking twigs.' She indicated the parcel which stood on the kitchen chair. 'Are you sure you can manage it?' she asked earnestly.

Miss Jackson swung it up easily and made for the door.

'Don't worry, I'll enjoy it! Just tell me where Mrs Chard lives, then I'll be off.'

The two of them walked together to the shed to collect the bicycle and then to the front gate. Miss Clare gave her directions clearly and slowly. Miss Jackson appeared impatient to be off.

At last she mounted the bicycle, waved erratically, and pushed steadily along the lane towards the rough track that led from the Fairacre road over the hill to the little valley where Springbourne lay.

It was only when Miss Clare had settled herself once again in the deck chair that something occurred to her.

The lonely track which Miss Jackson must traverse ran close beside the cottage belonging to John Franklyn.

Hilary Jackson, with the sun full upon her face, zigzagged laboriously up the chalky cart track. She had to keep carefully to the middle of the pathway for the ruts made by farm carts and tractors were deep and dangerous. Ahead she could see the welcome shade of the wood. Behind her rose a light cloud of chalky dust sent up by her bicycle wheels.

The path grew steeper, and some distance before it entered the wood the girl gave up pedalling and dismounted. It was very quiet. The fields sloped down to the Fairacre road which shimmered in the distance. The warm air was murmurous with the humming of myriad wings, and beside her, as she wandered with one hot hand on the handlebars, two blue butterflies skirmished together above the tall pollen-dusty grass.

Her head throbbed with exertion but also with excitement. Very soon she knew she would be approaching the cottage where John Franklyn, the gamekeeper, lived. His daughter Betty was now safely with the aunt in Caxley and he would be alone in the little house. She looked at her watch. It said twenty minutes past five. With any luck he would be at home, and perhaps he would speak to her. She quickened her pace, steadied Miss Clare's parcel which swayed across the bicycle basket, and entered the woods.

It was like stepping into an old, old church from a sunny field. The sudden chill raised gooseflesh on the girl's scorched arms, and the sudden quiet gloom, after the singing brightness of the chalky fields, created a feeling of awe. The companionable murmuring of insects had gone and silence engulfed her. The trees stood straight and tall, menacingly aloof, and to the girl, in her high-strung state, they appeared like watchful sentinels who passed and repassed each other in the distance as she moved nervously between them.

On each side of the path festoons of small-leaved honeysuckle draped low branches of hazel bushes, and the cloying sweetness of its perfume blended with the moist fragrance compounded of damp earth, moss and the resinous breath of many close-packed trees. The path was damp beneath her feet and muffled the sound made by her sandals and the wheels of the bicycle. To give herself courage Miss Jackson looked at her watch again. Why, it was still really afternoon! Nothing to fear in a wood at five-thirty! If the watch had said midnight, now! She had a sudden terrifying picture of inky trees, a slimy path, and a furtive, leering, sickening moon sliding behind crooked branches. Owls would be abroad, screeching and cackling, and bats, deformed and misshapen, would leave their topsy-turvey slumbers and swoop out upon their horrid businesses. She took a deep, shuddering breath, pushed such fancies resolutely behind her, and in two minutes had reached the bend of the lane which brought her within sight of the gamekeeper's cottage.

It stood quite close to the path, tucked into the side of a steep slope which rose sharply behind it. The garden was narrow, and lay to the side of the house bordering the track through the woods. The currant bushes were heavy with fruit, and the acid smell of blackcurrants was wafted to the girl as she dawdled past. She noticed the tidy rows of vegetables, the two apple trees, sprucely pruned, and already bearing a crop of small green apples. A rough shed, painted with tar to protect it from the dripping of the surrounding trees, stood at the far end of the garden. Hilary could see that the door was shut and the padlock fastened as she passed by it.

She looked at the cottage hopefully, but her heart sank as she noticed the closed windows and door. She could see no movement anywhere. The windows were dirty and the curtains looked grubby. Clearly the mistress of the house was here no more, and the neglected dwelling place contrasted strongly with the trim garden in which it stood.

Disappointment flooded the girl's heart, but relief too, for she half-realized that she felt fear as well as infatuation for this odd soft-spoken man who had noticed her. She was now past the house, rising steadily, until in a few moments she could stop and look down upon its tiled roof, stained with lichens and bird-droppings and streaked with murky tears shed by the trees overhead. In a dappled patch of sunlight at the side of the house she could now see a small tabby kitten rolling luxuriously in some dry earth beneath a jutting window-sill. It looked up, startled, as she chirruped to it, and fled helter-skelter out of sight.

At the top of the hill Hilary Jackson paused for breath and looked down upon the hamlet of Springbourne scattered below in the valley. Ah, there was Mrs Chard's white house, with the pine tree at its gate, just as Miss Clare had said.

She smoothed her yellow frock, adjusted the parcel once more, and clambered up into the saddle. The wind rushed past her, cooling her flushed face and quieting her restless heart. Within five minutes she was pushing open Mrs Chard's green gate and approaching the open door.

8. THE GAMEKEEPER'S COTTAGE

While Hilary Jackson sat in Mrs Chard's cool green and white drawing-room sipping a glass of lemon squash and listening to her hostess's ecstatic comments as she unpacked the parcel of jumble, the vicar of Fairacre was talking to Mr Mawne.

The two men lay back in deckchairs in the shade of a fine copper beech tree which John Parr's great-grandfather had planted. Upon Mr Mawne's chest were lodged his binoculars which he frequently clapped to his eyes the better to observe some distant bird on the far side of the garden. Upon the vicar's chest lay his folded hands, pink and damp with the heat, and above them his mild old face looked aloft worriedly.

'And Philpotts should know,' he was saying. 'He is one of the chaps on the rural district council, and a most reliable fellow.'

'Sh! Sh!' hissed his companion, adjusting his binoculars, and making his deckchair emit noises far more violent than his friend's gentle voice. The vicar was obediently quiet until the binoculars were lowered again.

'And it means,' continued the vicar in a gusty whisper, 'that the rural district council have seen the plans, and there's no doubt about it that a school will be needed on the site.' He sighed heavily, and a blackbird rattled from a hawthorn tree, scolding and squawking madly. The vicar looked penitent.

'I'm so sorry, my dear Mawne! Another bird that I've scared, I'm afraid.'

'That's nothing,' said Mr Mawne indulgently. 'Carry on. So what's worrying you?'

'Why! My school!' said the vicar sitting suddenly bolt upright and turning his wide-opened eyes upon his friend. 'Don't you see, it may mean that our children are taken by bus to this new school, and Fairacre School may close!'

'I don't believe it!' said Mr Mawne with conviction. 'Fairacre school won't be closed as long as the parents want it to stay open.'

'I hope you're right. Indeed, I hope you're right,' said Mr Partridge, in a troubled voice, 'but the numbers have dwindled to almost thirty – and I don't know—' His voice trailed away unhappily. Silence fell between the two men. Far away a cow lowed, and a tiny stealthy sound from the hawthorn tree made Mr Mawne raise his binoculars again and scrutinise it for some minutes. Finally he lowered them, pulled the strap over his head and replaced them in the leather case which lay on the grass at his feet. He spoke with decision.

'I think you're worrying yourself unnecessarily, but to put your mind at rest why don't you go and see someone at the county council offices, and see what the plans are for your school and Beech Green's?'

'It's an idea,' responded the vicar slowly.

'The local authority will have the job of providing the new school,' went on Mr Mawne, snapping the clasp on his binoculars, 'and they'll know what's happening to the existing schools if this business goes through.'

He looked at his old friend and clapped him on the shoulder. 'Cheer up!' he said, struggling from his deck chair. 'Come and have a glass of sherry. These gnats are getting me.'

He held out his hand to the vicar and hauled him to his feet.

'You've given me new heart,' confessed the vicar, as they made their way into the house. 'I'll do that.' A sudden jangling of church bells broke out in the distance.

'Bless my soul!' exclaimed the vicar. 'Half past six already! The bellringers have started practising promptly tonight.'

He sank back into an armchair and accepted the glass of sherry, which his friend carried over to him, with great care.

'You're a good fellow, Mawne,' he said. 'You've comforted me with words, and now with wine.' He raised his glass to his host before he sipped.

The sound of the bells ringing floated across the warm evening air to Hilary Jackson as she made her return journey. The slope up from the Springbourne valley was shorter but steeper than that from the Fairacre road and the girl was obliged to go on foot, wheeling her dusty bicycle. Her thoughts raced ahead of her slow feet. Would he be back yet? Should she knock at his door? She was torn between a wild strange excitement which drove her on, and nagging doubts, half-fearful, which held her back. Hilary Jackson was in love for the first time.

For a girl of twenty-odd she had very little experience of men. An only child, educated at a girls' school and going from thence straight on to a women's training college, where the redoubtable Miss Crabbe had engaged her affections and admiration, she had had little occasion to mix with the opposite sex. John Franklyn's casual attentions had lit a greater fire than he would ever guess in the foolish heart of this girl. Despite the rumours which rumbled round Fairacre, and which were causing Miss Clare and Miss Read such heart-burning, the meetings of the two had been by chance, except on the occasion of the visit to the cinema. John Franklyn had been pleasantly surprised by the ardour with which his casual invitation had been accepted. He flirted, as a matter of course, with any woman, but with young Miss Jackson he had tempered his usual bonhomie with a certain amount of reserve due, he felt, to the teacher of his daughter. He had not bargained for the response which he had received and, truth to tell, was half-embarrassed by it. Like all countrymen he wished to avoid trouble, and he disliked the sly teasings which he feared might get to the ears of his sister in Caxley who was giving a home to his child. It would 'look bad' to have this girl tagging after him, he told himself, but at the same time his vanity was flattered. He had loved his wife, and he missed her sorely; and though he had no intention of asking Hilary Jackson to become his second, he was in need of comfort and tempted to accept it, at the moment, from any source.

As Hilary Jackson approached the cottage she became conscious of the homely smell of frying onions. The door of the tarred shed now stood open and the little cat was lapping at a saucer of milk set out on the brick path near the back door. The girl stood irresolute and called softly to the cat. At that moment John Franklyn emerged, with an armful of sticks, from the shed. Hilary called out joyfully.

'Hello! Your supper smells good!'

'Want some?' replied the man, half jocularly.

Construing this as an invitation to the house, Hilary propped her bicycle against the fence, and entered the garden. John Franklyn watched her with mingled dismay and pleasure. She was an awkward great lump of a girl, he told himself, his eyes on her thick ankles and broad flat sandals, but her feelings seemed warm enough. He motioned her to enter the kitchen and followed her in.

'What have you been up to?' he asked, dumping the sticks on the top of an old copper which stood in the corner. His tone was bantering. Hilary told him breathlessly of her errand, her eyes roaming round the little room.

Sizzling on a primus stove stood a gargantuan frying pan full of onions. On a white enamel plate nearby lay two freshly-cooked rashers, the biggest and thickest that the girl had ever seen. A three-pronged small fork and a pointed knife with a horn handle flanked the plate, and a bottle of sauce and a bottle of beer stood before it.

'Take a seat,' said John Franklyn, nodding towards a kitchen chair by the table. It was obviously little used for it was thick with dust. Too flustered to bother about its effect on her yellow frock the girl settled herself and watched the man turning the onions over and over with the small fork.

The room, after the brilliant sunshine outside, was murky, but as her eyes became accustomed to the gloom Hilary noticed that the dust was general. The window sill was thickly coated, and a dead geranium, whose leaves crackled under her touch, was a silent sad memorial to the dead mistress of the house. The window looked out upon a damp wall made of flints, which acted as a barrier against the shifting soil of the steep slope of the wood against which the cottage had been built so snugly. The wall was so close that even short-sighted Hilary could see the holes in the ancient flints quite clearly. All her senses seemed acutely sharpened. She noticed, as she had never done before, that the chalky covering of each grey flint caused a milky edge round the transverse section, and that many of the jagged holes in the flints were filled with a glistening granulated substance that looked like thick honey.

Tiny ferns grew in the crevices and some small mauve flowers, unknown to the girl, cascaded down the damp surface. A little movement attracted her notice. Close beside a ribbed hart's tongue fern, which lolled from the mouth of a miniature cavern, squatted a toad. She saw his coppery eyes gleaming above the pulsing throat. Shivering, the girl turned again to the domestic scene before her. John Franklyn was now lifting the onions from the pan, and a second plate lay beside the first.

'Oh please,' begged Hilary, 'I don't really want any of your supper! I thought you were joking!'

'Plenty here,' said the man, ladling it out carefully.

'I couldn't, honestly!' protested the girl. Her eye lit on the bottle. 'But I'd love something to drink.'

'Beer do?' he asked, pausing in his operations. She nodded. He put down the frying pan and made his way out of the kitchen along a corridor to the front parlour. The girl could hear him opening and shutting doors and moving furniture. At last he returned bearing a florid china mug with a picture of King Edward VII and Queen Alexandra on the side. He set it before her and filled it, then poured the rest of the bottle into his own battered enamel mug.

Hilary felt better after the first draught. She watched the man tackle his supper heartily, and though the noise which he made in eating would have revolted her had it been anyone else, so besotted was she that his hungry gulpings perturbed her not a whit. He finished the plateful, scraped his knife carefully across the surface, then between the prongs of his fork, ate this last morsel, wiped his mouth on the back of his hand, and leant back in his chair. He looked at the girl from beneath his sandy eye-lashes and smiled.

'Ah, that's better! A chap gets sharp set out in the air all day.'

'I expect so,' said Hilary, gazing at him fondly through her thick glasses. Half-remembered descriptions of strong earthy men from the works of D. H. Lawrence and Mary Webb floated bemusedly through her head. She sipped her beer again.

'Haven't seen much of you lately,' continued John Franklyn, raising his own drink. 'What's up?'

'Why, nothing,' said Hilary. 'I just haven't been to Caxley lately.' She set her mug very carefully on the table, unable to meet his eyes, and John Franklyn putting his hand over hers bent across the table. Even the smell of onions could not quell the uproar in Miss Jackson's romantic heart.

'You enjoyed our last evening there?' asked John Franklyn softly.

'Very much,' faltered Hilary. The room seemed darker and hotter than ever. She lifted her mug with her free hand and drank deeply.

'What about next Wednesday?' said the man. His face seemed amazingly close and very pink. 'Good film on at the same place.' He gripped Hilary's hand in a hot and rather painful grasp. Muzzy with unaccustomed beer and bliss she leaned gently towards him.

'Hi!' said a shrill voice from the doorway, 'What yer want done with this lot?'

A small boy, with a roll of wire netting lodged across his shoulder, gazed interestedly upon them. Miss Jackson recognized him, with instant dismay, as one of Miss Read's pupils although she did not know his name. She leapt to her feet and smoothed her dress nervously.

Without any trace of embarrassment John Franklyn rose slowly from his chair and came to the door.

'I'll give you a hand with it to the shed, son,' he said mildly. 'Tell your dad I'll settle up with him when I see him.'

The child stared at Hilary unblinkingly, his mouth slightly open. He lowered the wire netting and between them he and the man carried it down the garden path. Hilary, trying to overcome her discomfiture, emerged into the sunlight as they returned.

'You don't have to go yet,' muttered John Franklyn urgently.

The child gazed from one to the other. The girl spoke primly and rather loudly.

'I really must. Thank you very much for giving me a drink.'

John Franklyn looked quizzically at her. The sun was getting low now and his light sandy hair was turned to a fox-like tawny red by its rays. She knew that he was amused by her clumsy acting for the benefit of the child who gaped beside her, and this upset her. Even more upsetting was the breaking of that charmed spell, now shattered beyond hope of regaining. For one dreadful moment, the girl felt tears rise behind her thick glasses, and prayed that they should not fall. John Franklyn saw all and pressed home his advantage.

'You're welcome to the drink,' he said with loud heartiness. He turned to the boy. 'Time you got back, Jim. Off you go!'

The child, still staring, edged slowly towards the gate, and Hilary, shaken with love and hurt pride, went with him. The man ambled slowly behind him and leant over the gate as he watched the girl lift her bicycle from the fence where it rested. He spoke very low and with his face averted from the laggard boy.

'Wednesday then? You'll come?'

The girl could only trust herself to nod, her eyes downcast.

'Same time, same place?' he persisted. His voice gained a new urgency which was music to her. 'You'll come?'

'I'll come!' replied Hilary.

The boy, who had come over the hill from Springbourne, walked back up the slope from the gamekeeper's cottage with slow thoughtful steps, his eyes fixed on the fast-moving figure of one of his school teachers. A light cloud of chalk dust rose from behind her skimming wheels as she swooped down to the distant Fairacre road.

He remembered the scene in the murky cottage kitchen and his eye brightened.

'Coo-er!' he said rapturously, aloud. For in matters of the heart, despite his tender years, he was not 'as green as he was cabbage-looking,' as his mother would have said.

As for Hilary Jackson, careering headlong towards Miss Clare's cottage with her slightly dizzy head awhirl with dancing anticipation, what a pity it was that she had not taken heed of the moral to be found in the story that she had been reading to her infants that very afternoon! It was the tale of that foolish creature Jemima Puddleduck, who was so easily – so easily – beguiled by a certain foxy gentleman.

9. The Vicar Does His Duty

Rumours about the proposed housing estate continued to fly about Fairacre, Beech Green and the busy streets of Caxley. To begin with, opinions had been almost equally divided. Many of the Caxley shopkeepers, seeing a considerable source of income in the scheme, approved the idea. A number of the inhabitants of Beech Green and Fairacre agreed with Mrs Coggs that a more frequent bus service to Caxley, which must inevitably result from a greatly increased village population, would be of great advantage to them.

The opponents of the scheme included those who disliked change of any sort – and certainly the change brought about by hundreds more people in their own secluded corner of the country – those who were shocked at any desecration of Dan Crockford's landscape, and those who had the foresight to see that a great number of urban dwellers set down suddenly in a small rural community could cause more commotion than just the despoiling of a much-loved scene.

But when the rumour of the new school and possibly the closure of Fairacre's own village school began to be bruited abroad, the opponents of the scheme found their numbers swelling.

'Been up our school all my schooldays and my father afore me! Catch me sending our two little 'uns all that way – bus or no bus!' was the sort of comment one heard, delivered in a robust burr, by staunch Fairacre worthies. One such remark particularly amused me. Mrs Partridge overheard two parents discussing the project heatedly, and retailed it to me.

'Well,' said one, with decision, 'our Miss Read ain't much to look at, poor toad, but her learns 'em fair enough. And I will say this for her – she don't bring 'em up in the weals old Hope did us, do she now?' With which modest tribute I was well content.

The vicar had pondered Mr Mawne's advice about getting some official light on the matter of the school's closing. He was very much perplexed over the way he should go about it. Should he ignore the rumours and wait until an official declaration was made, as it must be, if there were any truth at all in the proposal?

Should he call a meeting of the school managers to discuss things? Or should he say nothing, but approach someone in the Education Office at the County Hall, and feel the way?

After much earnest thought he had decided that he would go privately to his county town, seek an interview with the Director of Education, and let his fears either be put to rest or confirmed, before meeting his managers.

Accordingly, one overcast morning, the vicar set off in his shabby car, along the shady lanes, to his appointment. He drove alone, for not even his wife knew his business that morning, and he pondered many things as he rolled sedately along, hooting gently when he approached any bend, cross-road or, more frequently, any newly-fledged bird which sat, fearless and innocent, on the hard highroad. Apart from his conjectures about the forthcoming interview, he was also sorely perplexed about a more personal matter.

He had in his wallet a book token for one guinea, treasured from a recent birthday. Should he be extravagant and add yet another guinea to it and buy the new volume on the subject of George Herbert, the parson-poet, for whom he had such a high regard? He feared that it might be an indulgence. His stipend was very small and a guinea's expenditure was not to be undertaken lightly. His wife, he knew, would not hesitate to encourage him to buy it, selfless soul that she was; yet only that morning she had told him that saucepans would have to be replaced and that yet another sheet had been ripped from top to bottom by his own careless big toe. The vicar sighed heavily, discovered that he was now in a built-up area, dropped the speed of his car from 35 miles an hour to 25, and cautiously approached the Education office.

His appointment was at eleven o'clock and at five minutes to the hour the vicar was ushered into a waiting-room by a pretty young typist.

'If you'll wait,' she said, turning such a dazzling smile upon the vicar, that he felt quite young again, 'I'll tell Mr Temple that you're here.'

The room was oppressively quiet when she had gone. Mr Partridge, crossing to a table which held an imposing spread of magazines and newspapers, was conscious of the noise that his black shoes made on the bare linoleum. He felt acutely nervous and looked, with lacklustre eye, at the literary fare set out for his refreshment. *The Teachers' World, The Times Educational Supplement, The Schoolmaster, The Journal of Education* he supposed were the right and proper things to find here, but his eye brightened as it fell upon the local paper.

The first thing he saw, when he opened it, was a photograph of a fellow parson who was noted for his outspoken dicta on subjects of which he had the scantiest knowledge.

'Dear, oh dear!' said the vicar aloud, folding back the paper, 'And how has poor old Potts put his foot in it this time?'

Completely engrossed, his own troubles for the moment forgotten, Mr Partridge was unconscious of the Town Hall clock which boomed eleven times and was the signal for hundreds of coffee cups to appear on desks all over the county town.

The pretty girl reappeared.

'Mr Temple can see you now,' she said. The vicar dropped the paper, and his head awhirl with poor Potts, inadequate book tokens, sheets, saucepans and the plight of his adored village school, followed her to the door of the Director's office.

Meanwhile, the vicar's wife was paying a call at Fairacre School. The Flower Show was imminent and she had come to see how the children were progressing with their dancing.

The infants only were taking part in this particular activity, and I had given Miss Jackson a free hand in choosing some simple song and dance to amuse the onlookers. Somewhat to my dismay, she had unearthed a quite dreadful thing, called 'The Song of the Roses,' whose inane words echoed and re-echoed through our two classrooms as the interminable practising went on. The words had been printed up on a blackboard, for the past month, in the infants' room.

> 'We are little rosebuds gay,
> Nidding, nodding through the day.
> Some are pink, and some are white
> Some are clad in scarlet bright
> See us scatter petals sweet,
> Like confetti, at your feet.'

After this had been chanted with various halts, cries of despair from Miss Jackson, false starts, and so on, the floorboards would begin to quake to the ensuing dance, as the roses wove their way, thunderously, between each other. A light dust would rise from between the ancient cracks, and my class would groan heavily next door.

This morning, however, Miss Jackson was taking a rehearsal in the playground.

'I want someone to take a message to Miss Jackson,' I said. Mrs Partridge and I watched the effect of this innocent remark on the posture of all the children in my room. Shoulders were pulled back, chests thrust out, and eyes of every hue raised to mine with looks of mingled pleading and responsibility.

Patrick was chosen to ask Miss Jackson if we might all watch the rehearsal, and as he skipped joyfully doorwards the rest of the class relaxed their fierce posture and breathed again quite naturally.

While we waited for Patrick's return Mrs Partridge told me of a further complication in the dancing programme planned for the Flower Show.

'Mrs Waites has asked if Cathy can do her scarf dance again,' she said in a worried voice. 'It really is difficult.'

'What's the problem?' I asked. Cathy Waites had performed her scarf dance at more village functions than I cared to remember and I wondered what the objection could be to her repeating it yet again.

'Well, dear,' said Mrs Partridge, in a very low voice, carefully turning her back to the class to foil any astute lip readers, 'the last time Cathy did it was two years ago, and even then Gerald – and a great many other people too – felt that her costume was – well – *inadequate*, shall we say? And Mrs Waites showed me the new one, and really—!' Mrs Partridge's normally rosy face took on a deeper hue.

'Nothing, my dear, but a few wisps of chiffon,' she continued gravely, 'and poor quality chiffon at that. And yet she's so keen, and a good church-goer! It does make things difficult!'

Patrick returned as Mrs Partridge sighed, and we all trooped out into the playground where the fifteen or so infants stood about in positions of acute self-consciousness. At Miss Jackson's

command they shuffled into a faint resemblance of a crescent. Miss Jackson raised a plump arm, fingers daintily extended, and fixing her eyes upon her inattentive class she sang very loudly: 'Ready? "We are little—"'

A ragged bashful chorus took up the ditty in true country burr:

> 'We are li'l rawse buds gy-ee
> Nidd'n, nodd'n all the dy-ee.'

Here the children shook their heads stolidly, their expressions wooden. A few fierce nudges and shovings resulted in five or six unhappy little girls stepping forward to say:

'Some are pink—' Here they stepped back, with disastrous results, among their fellows, whilst a few more were projected forward to recite:

'And some are whoite.'

A group of bigger boys then took their place, shouting cheerfully:

'Some are clad in scawlet broight.'

After this there was a short embarrassed silence, until Miss Jackson, throwing herself forward and up again in an unlovely way, reminded them of the final couplet. Wielding their arms as though they were pitching bricks into a well, and panting with their exertions, the infants gasped out their last two lines:

'See us sca'er pe'als swee'
Like confe'i a' your fee'.'

We all clapped heartily at this performance, whilst I made a mental note to speak to Miss Jackson about curing the glottal stops which our children much prefer to the sound 't'.

'Absolutely splendid!' said Mrs Partridge enthusiastically. The children preened themselves and exchanged smug smiles.

'It's only just over a week to the Flower Show,' she continued, 'and I'm sure everyone will enjoy the dancing.'

Miss Jackson smiled graciously at this kind remark, but had a gleam in her eye which dismayed me.

'It is for the *children's* benefit primarily,' she began. 'It is a wonderful release from the rigid type of exercise which they were accustomed to, and gives them freedom for true imaginative expression.' She had just drawn a deep breath, preparatory to embarking – as I knew from bitter experience – on a tedious rehash of Miss Crabbe's half-baked psychology notes, when St Patrick's clock saved us by striking twelve.

The children broke into cries of pleasure, Mrs Partridge remembered that she had cutlets to egg-and-bread-crumb, the dinner lady approached the schoolroom door, and Miss Jackson's monologue mercifully remained unsaid.

The vicar had returned much relieved in his mind, and sitting on the verandah with a comforting pipe in his mouth, he had confessed the main purpose of his trip to his wife.

'A most pleasant fellow,' commented Mr Partridge on the Director of Education, 'an uncommonly pleasant fellow – sympathetic, intelligent – and gave me a very good cup of coffee too!' In the vicar's gentle eulogy there sounded a faint note of bewilderment as though he had expected Directors of Education to have small horns and cloven hooves and a whiff of sulphurous fumes emanating from them.

'He has heard indirectly of the housing scheme and says he feels sure that our Parish Council will know more about it before long.'

'But what about the school?' asked his wife anxiously. 'Is it likely to close?'

The vicar leant across and patted her knee comfortingly.

'Evidently not, my dear. But if a new school were to be built on the site it's quite likely that Fairacre School would take infants only, and the juniors would go by bus to the new building.'

Mrs Partridge put down a hideous straw hat she was embroidering with fearsome raffia flowers for the fancy stall of the Flower Show, and gazed thoughtfully across the garden. 'It's a relief of course,' she said slowly, 'to know that much. But the village won't like the idea. Anything touching the children rouses the village at once. I wish we knew more about this wretched business!'

The villagers of Fairacre and Beech Green had not long to wait before more was known about 'the wretched business.'

Caxley Rural District Council having been notified of the proposed scheme decided that here was a matter which might well prove contentious.

'Best let the Fairacre and Beech Green Parish Council know of this,' said burly Tom Coates, the retired estate agent. 'Let's hear what the feeling is out there before we send word back to the planning committee.'

It was agreed, and within two days Mr Roberts the farmer, one of the Parish Councillors, was propping up on his kitchen mantelpiece the notice of the meeting to be held in the near future in Fairacre School.

'And that should set 'em all talking!' he observed to his wife. 'If the fur don't fly from Mrs Bradley I'll eat my hat!'

His gigantic laugh rustled the paper spills on the shelf before him. The formidable and ancient Mrs Bradley was a fellow councillor. They together represented their Parish Council on the Caxley Rural District Council, and if parley were to be made Mr Roberts could ask for no better ally than Mrs Bradley beside him.

'Bless my soul!' he continued, slapping his breeches with a hand like a ham, 'that'll be a meeting worth going to!' His eye was bright at the thought, for Mr Roberts dearly loved a scrap, and it looked as though plenty of trouble were brewing somewhere.

His wife observed his relish with misgiving.

'Now don't go saying anything you'll regret,' she cautioned.

'You remember that business over collecting the pig-swill! You're too hasty by far!'

'I shall speak the truth and shame the devil!' declared Mr Roberts roundly. 'And 'tis the truth that old Miller should keep what's his own! And 'tis the truth, too, that that's some of the finest growing land in the county and should never be built on!'

'Well, speak *quietly* then,' implored his wife, as her husband's voice shook the bunches of herbs which hung from the kitchen ceiling.

'I shall speak as mild as milk!' roared her husband, his hair bristling. 'I shall coo at 'em, like a turtle dove, but I'll coo the truth!'

He thrust his arms into his jacket, shrugged his massive shoulders into it, and made towards the door. His wife watched him go with a quizzical look. From across the yard she heard his voice raised in cheerful song. He was singing: 'Onward Christian soldiers, marching as to war,' with all the zest in the world.

10. The Flower Show

The day of the Flower Show dawned with a brilliance which enchanted most of Fairacre, but which caused the weather-wise minority to shake its head.

'Don't like the look of it,' said Mr Willet, mallet in hand. He was putting the final touches to the stakes which supported the ropes of the bowling-for-the-pig site.

Mr Roberts was busy building a sturdy wall of straw bales near him.

'Keep your fingers crossed, Alf,' he answered. 'If the wind turns a bit by noon we may miss the squall.'

Mrs Partridge and a bevy of helpers were pinning bunting round the produce and sweet stalls, and Miss Jackson, Miss Clare and I were straining our thumbs by pinning notices at various vantage points to some of the hardest wood I had ever encountered.

'Come out of Sir Edmund's old stable roofs,' said Mr Willet, when I commented on our difficulties, 'and weathered to iron almost. When this lot's over, I'm having a few of these beauties to make a little old gate. I'm looking forward to working with a bit of good wood.'

And a fine job he would make of it, I knew, looking at those sinewy old hands that gripped the mallet. They were probably the most skilled and useful hands in the village, I thought, cursing my own inadequate pair which had just capsized the tin full of drawing pins into the long grass. I had seen Mr Willet's hands at work daily on wood, stone, iron, earth and tender plants. They were thick and knobbly, with stained and ribby nails edged with black, but I never ceased to marvel at their deftness and precision as they tackled the scores of different jobs, from lashing down a flailing tarpaulin in a howling gale to pricking out an inch-high seedling in fine soil.

The great marquee which dominated the vicar's garden was full of hustle and bustle, as people carried in their entries for the Flower Show, and walked round to admire – and sometimes to envy – the other exhibits.

Mrs Pringle had left the smaller tea tent, conveniently placed near the vicarage so that boiling water was available from the kitchen, and had come to look at her son John's entries. She gazed with pride upon the six great bronze balls of onions, each with its top neatly trimmed and laid to the side at exactly the same angle. His carrots, placed with military precision upon their tray, glowed with fresh-scrubbed beauty, and a plate of white currants gleamed like heaped pearls. Mrs Pringle's heart swelled with maternal pride, until her eye fell upon Mr Willet's entries which lay beside her son's. There was little to choose between the size, quality, and colour of both displays, but Mr Willet had covered his tray with a piece of black velvet, a remnant from an old cloak of his mother's, and against this dramatic background his exhibits looked extremely handsome.

'Black velvet indeed!' exclaimed Mrs Pringle scornfully to her neighbour. 'Funeral bake-meats, I suppose. About all them poor things are fit for!'

Huffily she made her way back to the tea tent, with her limp much in evidence.

*

475

By half past twelve all the preparations were completed. Mr Willet's mallet had tapped every stake and the stalls fluttered their bunting above sweets, jam, bottled fruit, raffia hats, wool-embroidered egg-cosies and all the other paraphernalia of village money-raising. In the marquee the air was languorous and heady with the perfume from sweet peas, roses and carnations, and in the tea tent rows and rows of cups and saucers awaited the crowd which would surely come.

The sun still shone, but fitfully now as the clouds passed lazily across it. Mr Willet surveyed the weathercock on the spire of St Patrick's church with a reproachful eye.

'Git on and turn you round a bit!' he admonished the distant bird, shaking his mallet at it, and making Miss Clare laugh at his mock ferocity.

She and Miss Jackson came back to lunch at the school-house with me, and within ten minutes Miss Jackson was setting the table and Miss Clare grating cheese whilst I whipped up eggs for three omelettes.

'Though I says it as shouldn't,' I shouted above the din, 'I can cook a good omelette.'

'And I can't!' confessed Miss Clare sadly. 'I think I must get the pan too hot.' She watched my preparations intently, as I buttered the frying pan and finally swirled the mixture in.

'You're probably too gentle,' I told her. 'You must be bloody, bold and resolute when dealing with eggs. Master them, or they'll master you.' Luckily, my demonstration of egg-management was thrice successful and we sat down to a cheerful lunch party.

Our conversation turned, naturally enough, to the Flower Show. Miss Jackson was anxious that the infants' dancing display should go without mishap. Miss Clare, as so often before, was going to play the accompaniment to the rose song-and-dance, which I so heartily detested, on the vicarage piano. My two guests discussed the intricacies of timing and the best position for Miss Jackson to take up on the lawn so that both the children and their accompanist could see her.

'Who's turning the music for you?' I asked. 'Shall I ask Ernest to help you? He's a sensible boy.'

'Betty Franklyn is doing it,' answered Miss Clare. On hearing the name Miss Jackson dropped her fork with a clatter. It rebounded from the edge of her plate and fell to the floor. Muttering apologies, Miss Jackson dived headlong after it. Her face remained hidden from view as she grovelled. Miss Clare continued calmly.

'I met the child with her aunt in Caxley last market day. They said they were coming out to the Flower Show and I asked her then. She seemed a bit disappointed because she wouldn't be dancing with her old friends, of course, and I thought that turning the pages might be some comfort.'

By this time Hilary Jackson had emerged from under the table, with a very red face. Miss Clare, observing her discomfiture with one swift glance, turned the subject to the matter of the new housing estate.

'Of course those two men must have been surveyors, I suppose,' she said, 'and what a long time ago it seems since I saw them walking up and down poor old Miller's field! I hear that it's going to be a really big affair.'

'With a site for a school already planned,' I observed. I began to serve the raspberries which I had picked early in the morning, but I felt Miss Clare's wise gaze upon me.

'And Fairacre's plans?' she queried softly. There was the very faintest tremor in her voice, and I remembered with a sudden pang the forty odd years which Miss Clare had spent under that steep-pitched roof and of the scores of Fairacre men and women who had learnt their letters, their manners and their courage from this devoted school-mistress.

'The vicar tells me that it won't close,' I assured her. Her sigh of relief was music to hear. 'But it may become "infants only".' I passed her the sugar and cream, and set about filling Miss Jackson's bowl.

'And your own plans?' she continued gently. For a moment I was at a loss to know what to answer, for my own plans, in face of this project, had been perturbing me more than I had cared to admit.

'I should like to stay,' I said slowly, 'but I haven't had much experience with infants. The managers may prefer to get someone who is better qualified to teach young children.'

'What utter rubbish!' declared Miss Clare roundly, 'Fairacre will never let you go! Never!'

And with these few stout words my long-sore heart was com-forted.

When we had washed up Miss Jackson vanished across to the school to collect music and other odds and ends for the dancing display. Miss Clare and I sat in the garden, resting before the fray.

'Of course,' I said, turning back to Miss Clare's own problems, 'this housing estate will be bang next door to your cottage. Will it make much difference, do you think?'

'I can't believe that it will ever happen,' replied Miss Clare, 'and even if the plans go through I imagine it will be some time before building actually begins. I doubt if I should live to see it.'

These last few words were uttered in such a matter-of-fact tone that at first I could hardly take in their importance.

'But surely,' I said, shocked, 'you are stronger now! You look much better than when you were teaching. I sincerely hope that you'll flourish for at least another thirty years.' It was my turn to be comforter now, but Miss Clare brushed aside my words, with a shake of her white head that had never had a shred of self-pity in it.

'I've had a good life, and a useful one too, I hope. And I've loved every minute of it,' she continued soberly. 'But, to tell you the truth, my dear, I'm getting tired now, and I shall be happy and ready to step aside whenever the time comes. I like to think of someone else teaching the children here, someone else picking my roses and sitting under the apple tree I watched my father plant. I've had my party, said my party piece, and I shall be glad to give my thanks and go quietly home.'

St Patrick's clock chimed a quarter past two. Miss Clare patted my knee and said briskly: 'But the party's still on, you know! It's time we went across to the vicarage and took our place in the revels!'

We took the short cut through the churchyard. Across the silent tombs and cypresses came the sound of a dance tune played through the loudspeaker.

Hardly daring to look to left and right, I hurried with Miss Clare towards the gaiety and safety of the Flower Show, as though ghosts were at my heels – as, in very truth, they were.

*

In the vicarage garden the scene was colourful and gay. Despite the overcast sky and a threatening line of black clouds which advanced from the south-west, the women and children were in their prettiest summer frocks and the men in open-necked shirts. Mrs Finch-Edwards, who had once taught with me at Fairacre School, was one of the most beautifully dressed women there, in a lilac creation of her own making, and her daughter Althea, now at the toddling stage, was in a froth of white frills. She was to present the bouquet to the opener of the Flower Show, who was a friend of Mrs Bradley's, and a famous gardener, and Mrs Finch-Edwards was having some difficulty in preventing her daughter from squatting down on the ground the better to eat worm-casts.

'Althea, please!' implored the distracted mother, dusting down the dozen frills tossing around the child's hind parts. She had grown into a chubby attractive child, with dimpled arms, and a mop of auburn curls like her mother's. The bouquet of roses was being secreted under a nearby stall, guarded by Joseph Coggs, and Mrs Finch-Edwards hoped that Lady Sybilla would soon make a start on her speech, that the speech would be very, very brief, and that her daughter would do her credit, and neither hurl the bouquet from her en route to the dais nor stop to pick it to pieces.

'I'd rather work a fortnight at the shop!' she confessed to me. 'This is agony!' But she looked very gratified, despite her agitation, at this honour done to the family.

I enquired after the shop in Caxley, which she and Mrs Moffat had recently opened and was not surprised to hear that they had already enough orders for clothes to keep them occupied until the late autumn.

At this moment Lady Sybilla was led to the microphone and introduced. She was a large, vague, charming old lady, wearing a black cartwheel hat which gave her some trouble. One white-gloved hand rested upon its crown, and in the other she held her notes. A nasty little wind fluttered her silk draperies as she leant forward to speak into the microphone.

'It is indeed a pleasure—' she began, in a sweet light voice, when a mumble of thunder sounded overhead, there was a crackling from the microphone and we heard no more. Quite unaware that four-fifths of her audience were unable to hear a word Lady Sybilla continued with her speech, and the people of Fairacre watched this dumb show with docility. Mrs Finch-Edwards was terrified that she might not know when the speech was over, but all was well. With a charming smile and much nodding of the cartwheel hat to left and right, Lady Sybilla stepped back from her non-co-operative microphone, and Althea Finch-Edwards was propelled forward, bearing the bouquet which was nearly as big as herself. She acquitted herself well, handed over the bouquet, and turned to rush back to her mother, but remembering, in time, her curtsey, turned back, some yards away from the dais, to make a wobbly bob.

The crowd dispersed to the various stalls. The Bryant boys, dour-visaged and clad, despite the warmth, in Sunday black, made straight for the bowling-for-the-pig where they would stay for the remainder of the Flower Show. It was a foregone conclusion that either Amos, Malachi, Ezekiel or Gideon Bryant would bear away the prize.

Inside the giant marquee the judges, among them Lady Sybilla, walked thoughtfully about with their notebooks in their hands, and their brows furrowed. They pinched gooseberries, smelt roses, tasted jelly and cut cheeses, giving to every case that concentration of wisdom and experience which they knew was expected at Fairacre Flower Show. Many an anxious eye was cast upon them when at last they emerged, having left the tickets 1st, 2nd and 3rd, which would cause such joy or despondency to the exhibitors.

The rumbling of thunder became more ominous as the black cloud arched over Fairacre. It was decided to put forward the dancing display which was to be held on the lawn, in case the rain came, and the vicar announced through the badly-crackling microphone, that Miss Cathy Waites would open the proceedings, followed by Miss Jackson's children.

There was desultory clapping as Cathy came skipping from behind the vicar's laurel bushes, and one lone wolf-whistle from a rude Beech Green boy.

Cathy, her dark hair blowing in the breeze, was clad in the flimsiest of garments as Mrs Partridge had feared. Luckily, she appeared to be wearing her High School knickers of a commendable staunchness and a brief but adequate brassiere, but over these basic necessities floated a yard or two of green chiffon of the most diaphanous nature.

In her hands Cathy held a long strip of the same material which she tossed from side to side as she bent and capered gracefully between the cedar tree and the produce stall. Occasionally, she fell on to one knee, cupping her ear as if listening to the horns of Elfland. In actual fact, the voice of one of the Bryant brothers who had just missed two skittles whilst bowling for the pig, was deplorably audible, whilst Miss Waites remained, wide-eyed and expectant, in her listening attitude, and the words used must have given a more innocent nymph considerable revulsion.

'That girl would do better with more clothes to her back,' observed Mr Willet to his neighbour, in a carrying whisper.

'Flaunting herself in next to nothing,' boomed Mrs Pringle from the door of the tea tent, 'Catch me looking like that at her age!' She wobbled her three chins aggressively, but remained to goggle as the scarf dance wound its airy way to its end.

I hurried round the edge of the crowd to the shrubbery where Miss Jackson and the children awaited their entry. Roses of every hue, the children were in a fine twitter of excitement.

'Why can't us wear our shoes? I've been and stood on a prickle!'

'Can I be excused? I can't wait.'

'I can't remember the words.'

'I feel sick.'

'My knicker elastic's busted.'

With such ominous phrases well known to teachers in all school crises, the children greeted me. Miss Jackson, flushed and heated, was doing her best to calm her flock.

'Would you remind Miss Clare that we'll have the first part twice?' she implored me, and I made my way to the drawing-room where Miss Clare was visible sitting at the piano by the open french windows.

As I threaded through the edge of the crowd I noticed a man, with a woman and a little girl, also approaching the french windows. Betty Franklyn was arriving at her page-turning appointment with her father and the aunt from Caxley. We greeted each other and I made enquiries about Betty's new school in Caxley. The aunt was a pleasant, fresh-faced person, who chattered away about her little niece, but John Franklyn stood slightly apart, eyeing the crowd and looking self-conscious.

'You run along to Miss Clare now,' said the aunt, pointing to the piano, and as the child stepped over the threshold the woman turned to me as though she were about to speak, but stopped short.

From among the crowd a large young woman, in a bright yellow beach frock which matched her brassy hair, stepped purposefully towards John Franklyn who watched her approach with obvious amusement.

'Fancy seeing you, Johnny,' said the plump beauty, looking at him sidelong from under well-plastered lashes. She edged a little nearer.

'And what are you doing anyway at Fairacre?' he responded jocularly.

'I've got an auntie lives this way. At Tyler's Row. Mrs Fowler, she is.'

I remembered suddenly that Mrs Fowler had a niece who was barmaid at 'The Bell' in Caxley. This must be the girl. The two began to stroll slowly away towards the shrubbery where the Fairacre children still waited for Cathy to finish fluttering her draperies on the lawn.

Betty was listening to Miss Clare's directions by the piano, and the aunt turned to me in some agitation.

'John was a good husband to my sister – but there, he's like all of 'em, needs company. Sometimes, I think—' But here her voice faltered to a stop.

Her eyes were fixed on a little scene near the shrubbery, and my gaze followed hers.

Hilary Jackson had come running out, presumably to give Miss Clare another last-minute direction, and had encountered John Franklyn and his brazen companion face to face. She grew as red as a poppy, and stopped short, her mouth open.

John Franklyn, with all the assurance in the world, inclined his head politely as he passed by her.

'Got a nice crowd here today,' he commented, without pausing in his leisurely progress.

Speechless, Hilary Jackson rushed past them, and past Betty's aunt and me, stumbling towards Miss Clare. Her face was suffused and her eyes were full of tears. Once she was well inside the aunt put an appealing hand on my arm, and spoke in a low whisper.

'He's a bad lot with women. If you don't tell her, Miss Read, then I shall!'

After this unnerving incident I watched the rose dance with even more detachment than usual. Miss Jackson was visibly upset, but luckily the children remembered their steps and the words perfectly, and encouraged by the applause of the onlookers, excelled themselves.

As they made their way from the lawn, bobbing breathlessly along with a fine disregard for Miss Clare's accompaniment, a wicked tongue of lightning flickered across the black sky, followed by an ear-splitting crash of thunder. Within a minute huge drops began to fall, the rain drumming down upon the baked lawn and bouncing dizzily from its surface like a myriad spinning silver coins.

Covers were hastily thrown over the stalls, and the crowd ran for shelter, either to the marquee or the tea tent. I found myself wedged by the table bearing a score of entries for 'Annuals in a Soup Plate' and remembered that spring evening when I had humbly suggested this class. First prize I noticed had gone to Mrs Willet who had massed nasturtiums in a deep plate with green dragons on it.

In the corner behind the vegetable stall I caught a glimpse of John Franklyn and his companion. They seemed quite engrossed in each other and as I was contemplating the outcome of this affair, a voice spoke behind me.

It belonged to Mr Willet, and the innocent words, delivered in his slow country voice, seemed pregnant with meaning to me.

'Been stewing up a long time this 'ere storm,' commented Mr Willet.

11. Parish Council Affairs

The Fairacre Parish Council meeting was held in the village school. Mr Roberts had seated himself on a long ancient desk which stood at the side of the room. His tall, burly frame was too big to cram itself into juvenile desks, but Mrs Bradley, small, alert and ready for battle, looked quite at home in the front desk usually occupied by Joseph Coggs.

Two members from Beech Green sat nearby, for although that village was larger than Fairacre it came in the latter's parish. Mr Annett had unashamedly rummaged in his desk, abstracted Ernest's arithmetic book and was studying his work with a censorious eye. Beside him sat the Beech Green butcher's wife, a large, florid lady, looking as succulent as her husband's joints.

Mr Lamb, from Fairacre Post Office, who was Clerk to the Council, had set out his papers on the teacher's desk and was now roaming round the classroom looking at the children's pictures which decorated the walls.

'Too much paint slopped on this one,' he remarked to anyone who cared to listen. 'Shocking waste of material! And never had these durn great lumps of paper when I was here! Half a sheet of small white, just big enough for a sprig of privet, and then shade the lot in careful!'

At this point the vicar bustled in, breathless and full of apologies, and took his seat as chairman. Mr Lamb sank on to the chair beside him, and applied himself to his papers.

'Apologies from Colonel Wesley, laid up with lumbago, I'm sorry to say,' began the vicar. At once remedies were suggested by all present.

'Nothing like old-fashioned brown paper ironed on!' asserted Mr Lamb.

'Nothing but heat and rest does any good!' vowed Mrs Bradley.

'Plenty of exercise and forget about it!' said Mr Roberts, at the same moment. He had never suffered an ache or pain in his life.

The vicar raised his voice slightly.

'And from Mrs Pratt who can't leave her poor old father, I fear. He's at his most trying as the moon waxes.'

There were murmurs of sympathy. Mr Annett, stuffing away Ernest's arithmetic book, looked sceptical.

'And now to the main business,' said the vicar, opening out a very long typewritten document, which had so many pages that even the stoutest heart among the parish councillors quailed a little as thoughts of supper grew sharper. 'I'd better read this straight through. The letter attached is from the Clerk of the Rural District Council who says that he encloses the proposed plan for an estate to house workers at the atomic establishment and he would be glad of our comments.'

'Unprintable!' said Mrs Bradley vehemently.

'Please, please,' begged the vicar, 'let us keep an open mind until we have studied this document.'

'Poor Mr Miller,' sighed the butcher's wife, 'he came into our shop last week, and he looked proper broken up!'

'We don't know, officially, that Mr Miller is involved in any way,' said the vicar patiently. No one appeared to hear him.

'Talk about Russia!' commented Mr Roberts with a snort.

'Taking first-class farmland for a pack of townees to ruin!' exclaimed Mr Annett warmly. 'And five times too many children swarming into my school!'

'And what's to happen to our own kiddies?' asked Mr Lamb, thumping the desk to emphasize his point.

The vicar thumped beside him, and the parish council looked with surprise and some disfavour at this display of officiousness on the part of its chairman.

'Ladies and gentlemen, please!' protested the vicar, his mild old face quite pink with effort. 'You are all jumping to conclusions! I must beg of you to listen to the proposals here set out, and we will discuss them – impartially, I hope – after we have heard them!'

The councillors settled themselves more comfortably in their cramped quarters, and turned attentive faces to the vicar. He began to read in his beautifully sonorous voice and his audience listened intently. Outside, the swifts screamed past the Gothic windows and, now and again, the lowing of Samson, Mr Roberts' house cow, was heard. From the window-sill the scent of honeysuckle wafted down from a fine bunch which had been stuffed by a child's hand into a Virol jar.

The wall clock, whose measured tick had acted as a background to the vicar's monologue, stood at ten to eight when at last he put the papers down on the desk, removed his reading glasses, and gazed speculatively at his thoughtful companions.

'Well?' he asked. Mr Roberts shifted his long legs.

'Can't say I took it all in,' he confessed.

'Nor me,' admitted Mr Lamb sadly.

Mr Annett caught his chairman's eye and spoke in his brisk, light, schoolmaster's voice. 'It seems to me that it all boils down to this. Perhaps you'll correct me if I'm wrong?' He turned to the vicar questioningly and received a gentle nod.

'The atomic energy authority proposes to purchase – compulsorily, if necessary, and it looks as though it will be – a site between our two villages comprising about a hundred and fifty acres. This will take in Miller's Hundred Acre Field with about half the slope of the downs behind. Provision, is made for a school, playing fields for the community, and a row of shops. In other words this township would be a self-contained unit.'

'There is no church,' put in the vicar. His tone held a mild rebuke.

'No. No church,' agreed Mr Annett. 'But presumably there would be room for more people in Fairacre or our own church.'

The vicar nodded his agreement rather sadly.

'Plenty of room!' he admitted. 'Yes, my dear fellow, plenty of room!'

'Water and sewage is also proposed, and these services would probably be extended to include Fairacre and Beech Green. As I see it this means that although the atomic energy authority pays a considerable part, our local authority will also have to pay, which means that our rates will go up again.'

'Impossible!' said Mrs Bradley. 'There's not a soul will stand for it!'

'And anyway,' pointed out Mr Roberts, 'who wants to pay for something he doesn't want?'

'Exactly,' said Mrs Bradley vehemently, turning her back on the meeting and settling herself face to face with the farmer for a really downright argument.

The vicar thumped the desk again.

'Thank you, my dear Annett, for summing-up so neatly. Now, ladies and gentlemen, your opinions, please!'

'Not a brick to be laid on Dan Crockford's landscape!' snapped Mrs Bradley.

'I think poor Mr Miller should keep what's his own!' asserted the butcher's wife.

'I'm not sure that the people themselves won't be a confounded nuisance,' said Mr Annett decidedly. 'I can see them making trouble about shocking rural schools—'

'But they'll have their own!' protested Mr Roberts.

'Not for years, if I know anything about school-building,' replied Mr Annett feelingly, 'and I'll have a procession of out-raged urbanite parents inspecting my school's sanitary arrange-ments, and telling me that my teaching methods are archaic.'

'I don't know that that water idea isn't attractive though,' said Mr Roberts meditatively. 'Getting water up to the sheep on those downs has always been a problem.'

'What's the matter with the dew-pond?' demanded Mrs Brad-ley. 'One of Dan Crockford's best pictures that was, "The Ancient Dew Pond".'

'My husband had it on his trade almanack one year,' began the butcher's wife conversationally. 'He said those sheep drinking were as fine a flock of Southdowns as he'd ever seen, and would've ate beautiful!'

'Nothing to touch a good saddle of mutton!' agreed Mr Lamb.

'With onion sauce,' added Mr Annett.

The vicar, seeing his meeting getting out of hand again, coughed gently.

'The business, my dear people! The planning committee asks for our observations. Can I have firm proposals, please?'

Mr Roberts suddenly stood up, partly because he was getting cramped and partly because he felt that the time had come for a decision. His great figure dominated the room.

'I propose that we have an open village meeting here in Fairacre and tell the people just what we've heard tonight, and get their reactions.'

'Stout man!' ejaculated Mr Annett, 'I'll second that proposal.'

Mr Lamb scribbled busily in his minute book.

'Agreed?' asked the vicar. Everyone raised a hand.

'The only thing to do,' said Mrs Bradley, gathering her belongings together fussily. 'There's much too much at stake for just the parish council to dispose of. Let's make it soon.'

'Next Monday?' suggested the vicar.

'No good for me,' said Mr Roberts.

'Friday?' said someone.

'Choir practice,' said Mr Annett.

At last, after various village engagements had been sorted out, the following Thursday was chosen, and Mr Lamb guaranteed that he would put up notices in Fairacre, and Mr Annett offered to put up more in Beech Green and let his pupils copy a notice each to take home to the parents, as well.

St Patrick's clock chimed eight-thirty as the members of the Parish Council emerged into the playground. From a nearby lime tree came the fragrance of a thousand pale flowers, hanging creamy and moth-like beneath the leaves.

'Smells good!' said Mr Lamb, sniffing noisily, 'but I'd sooner it was my supper!'

He spoke for all of them.

It was on the following day that Miss Jackson burst into school in a state of great excitement. I was glad to see her so happy, for ever since the day of the Flower Show she had gone about her affairs in an unnaturally subdued manner and I had felt extremely sorry for the girl. I was also much perturbed in my own mind about speaking of her infatuation for John Franklyn until I had learnt more from Miss Clare, and as that lady was looking so frail I felt diffident about worrying her unduly. As I have a horror of stirring up emotional upsets and very much dislike receiving confidences from overwrought individuals who will doubtless regret their own disclosures as soon as they have come to their senses, I had so far kept silent on this matter, but it had given me many uneasy moments and I wished to goodness that either Miss Jackson's affections could be engaged elsewhere or that John Franklyn could find employment at a distance, preferably in another hemisphere. 'I've had such a wonderful letter from Miss Crabbe,' exclaimed Miss Jackson ecstatically. 'She wants to come and spend next weekend here. Isn't it lovely?'

I said that that would be very pleasant indeed for them both, and where was she going to stay?

'Of course, Miss Clare can't manage it,' said Miss Jackson. 'I wondered if "The Beetle and Wedge" would put her up? Or "The Oak" at Beech Green?'

I suggested that she should go down to 'The Beetle' during the dinner hour and see what could be done. It was already nine o'clock, the children were milling about the classroom talking at the tops of their voices, someone had knocked over an inkwell, and from the infants' room a young finger was picking out 'The Teddy Bears' Picnic' on the piano with excruciating inaccuracy.

After we had dispatched cold pork and salad and a very sticky date pudding which the children greeted with cries of joy, Miss Jackson set off for 'The Beetle'. But within ten minutes she had returned with a glum face.

'No good,' she announced, sinking on to the front desk. 'They've got a friend coming for the fishing that weekend.'

'Try "The Oak",' I said. 'Go and ring up now, if you like, then you'll feel more settled.'

She went across the playground to my house, and at once a new child burst into the room to tell me.

'That other one,' she said accusingly, 'has busted into your place.' She was a plump red-haired infant, obviously a sensationalist, and dying for me to take instant recriminatory action. She watched my motionless figure with growing annoyance.

'Ain't you going to do *nothing*?' she demanded shrilly.

'No,' I said equably. 'I said she could go in.' The child looked suddenly deflated.

'Oh well!' she said, shrugging her shoulders, as if dismissing the whole incomprehensible affair, 'if you *said*!' She vanished round the door and a minute later Miss Jackson reappeared.

'Hopeless! Don't take in people. Now what's the next move? Caxley, I suppose?'

I pointed out that she and Miss Crabbe would waste a lot of time in trying to meet. Miss Jackson grew even more melancholy.

'I suppose I could ask Miss Clare if I could use the sofa in the sitting-room and Miss Crabbe could have my bedroom,' she sighed.

'It means that Miss Clare would have more work to do,' I said as kindly as I could.

'Oh, I'd help!' responded Miss Jackson vaguely. A horrid thought had entered my head. My spare room stood ready for just such an emergency, but my heart sank at the idea of having the redoubtable Miss Crabbe at such close quarters. I knew only too well that if Miss Clare were appealed to she would readily agree to have Miss Jackson's guests and undertake bed-making, extra cooking and shopping without a tremor. Steeling myself, I took the plunge.

'Would Miss Crabbe care to stay in my house?' I suggested. I could almost feel the draught from my guardian angel's quill as he eagerly scribbled down this rare good point in my record. Miss Jackson's dazzling smile would have been ample reward for a better-natured woman. Although I was pleased to cheer the girl after her recent misery, I was beginning to feel that the price might prove too much for me.

'It would be perfect,' she said. 'We won't be in your way, I promise you. I know Miss Crabbe wants to go for a long tramp across the downs on Saturday, and of course she'll have to go back on Sunday.'

'Then that's settled,' I said. 'Tell her that I am looking forward to meeting her.' And in a way, I commented to myself, that is true, for my curiosity about Miss Jackson's paragon had frequently been whetted by my assistant's eulogies.

Further discussion was cut off by the entry of a mob of children surrounding a very large, shaggy, smelly dog which had obviously been rolling in something extremely unpleasant.

'Miss, he's lost!' exclaimed Ernest, flinging his arms round the creature, which stood wagging its tail at the sensation it was causing. Another child proffered a piece of biscuit and two infants patted its matted flanks with loving hands. The din was as appalling as the odour.

'Take that animal out!' I directed, in a carrying voice. Casting sorrowful, shocked looks over their shoulders the children and their noisome friend departed. I opened the Gothic windows to their fullest extent.

'Mean old cat!' floated up a low voice, from outside. 'She wouldn't give a home to no one, I bet!'

Oh, wouldn't she! I thought, as the memory of my noble, but rash, invitation came home to me once more.

12. MISS CRABBE DESCENDS UPON FAIRACRE

Mrs Pringle came, as she said, 'to straighten me out,' after school on Thursday, in readiness for Miss Crabbe's visit.

'These sheets will soon need sides to middling,' she observed dourly, as we made the spare bed together. 'Pity you didn't buy better quality while you was about it. Always pays in the end!' I let this comment on my parsimony go by me.

'And this 'ere white paint everywhere,' continued my helper morosely, 'shows every speck of dust, don't it? Now, when Mrs Hope lived here – and she was what I'd call a really CLEAN woman – it was all done out a nice chocolate brown that never showed a mark. But there, Mrs Hope had a FEELING for house-work and dusted regular after breakfast and after tea, day in and day out.'

I remarked, a little shortly, that Mrs Hope didn't teach all day, and then felt sorry that I had risen so easily to Mrs Pringle's bait.

We heaved the blankets up together.

'Fair strains me back!' groaned the old misery, laying one plump hand there.

'If this is too much for you, Mrs Pringle,' I said firmly, 'you must let me do it all alone. I don't want you laid up on my account.'

Mrs Pringle's mouth took on the downward curves I know so well.

'I can manage!' she said, with a brave, martyred sigh. 'Always was a one for giving of my best cheerful!'

We worked together in silence for a little and then Mrs Pringle, changing the subject tactfully, asked me if I had heard the news about Minnie, her niece. Minnie Pringle lives at Springbourne and is the young and inconsequent mother of three small children. She has no husband.

'She's getting married,' volunteered Mrs Pringle, with pride.

'Good heavens!' I said, startled. 'Who to?' It seemed odd to me that Minnie, having got along for all this time without the encumbrance of wedlock, should suddenly decide to regularise her position.

'You wouldn't know him,' said Mrs Pringle complacently. 'He's a widower chap, very steady, getting on a bit, but can still enjoy a pipe and a read.' This conjured up a picture of a doddering individual on the brink of the grave, and I was at a loss to think how the lively young Minnie had been attracted to him. Further disclosures enlightened me.

'He's got five children of his own, so with Min's three, it'll make a nice little family to be going on with,' said Mrs Pringle. 'And Min's mother has been that awkward with her lately, it'll be best for all parties if our Min has a place of her own.'

'Does she seem fond of him?' I felt impelled to ask. Mrs Pringle's answer held a wealth of worldly philosophy.

'He's got a nice bit put by, and he's getting on. Min'll do right by him for the few years she has to, I don't doubt, then there's plenty of children to look after her later.'

It certainly sounded reasonable enough, I thought, if not wildly passionate. I smoothed the counterpane while Mrs Pringle puffed about the room with a duster.

'D'you want this great chest of drawers heaved out?' she asked. There was a menacing streak in her voice which I chose to ignore.

'Yes, please,' I said. Mrs Pringle leant gloomily against the piece of furniture, which glided easily away before such an onslaught.

'One thing *does* worry me,' confessed Mrs Pringle as she flicked her duster. 'I've been invited to the wedding and I think I must put my hand in my pocket for a new hat.'

'What about the one with the cherries?' I suggested. The hat with the cherries is an old and valued friend of Fairacre's, and I felt a pang at the thought of it being put from sight for ever.

'Just that bit past it!' announced Mrs Pringle. 'It's been a good hat, bought up in London first by Miss Parr, and given to the Primitive Jumble Sale for the Welcome Home Fund after the war. It's done me well, I must say, but I fancy a navy myself. Navy with white – say a duck's wing like, or a white lily laid acrost – always looks smart.'

I said that it sounded just the thing.

'It's to be a fairly dressy wedding,' went on Mrs Pringle. 'Min was all for a long white frock and having the children as attendants, but her mum made her see reason, so she's got a pale-blue that looks quite a treat.'

I agreed that it would be more suitable for Minnie.

'And I'm giving an eye to Min's three at the back of the church while my sister sees to his five,' continued Mrs Pringle. 'Should go off very nicely. I always enjoy a wedding.'

She stood motionless in the middle of my spare bedroom, duster in hand, and a faraway look in her eye, as she gazed across the playground. A rare and maudlin smile played across her normally grim visage.

'Ah, Love!' she sighed gustily. 'It rules the world, Miss Read, it rules the world!'

It transpired that Miss Crabbe was coming by car and would arrive at Fairacre in the early evening, so that I prepared a cold supper for Miss Jackson, our guest and myself, and went upstairs to make quite sure that fresh rainwater filled Miss Crabbe's ewer, that her bed was turned down, and everything in readiness in the spare room.

I had put a vase of my choicest roses on the bedside table, and spent some time in deciding on a variety of books. After much thought I had selected *Country Things* by Alison Utley, *The Diary of a Provincial Lady* by E. M. Delafield, *Winnie the Pooh* by A. A. Milne, an anthology of modern verse, and one of Basil

Bradley's novels bearing a reclining Regency beauty on its dust jacket.

'And if she can't find something there to enjoy, she must be very hard to please,' I told myself.

At seven o'clock Miss Jackson arrived looking very spruce in a new pink linen suit. She was happy and excited, the wretched John Franklyn forgotten for once.

It crossed my mind that Miss Crabbe might be able to help in discouraging this affair, but it remained to be seen what manner of woman she was before approaching her.

'She's always terribly punctual,' said Miss Jackson ardently. 'She said half past seven in her letter, so she won't be long.'

She followed me down the stairs and I noticed her searching scrutiny of the supper table. All must be perfect for the approaching goddess. She appeared satisfied with what she saw, and we walked out into the school-house garden which was still warm in the July sunshine.

Before long St Patrick's struck the half hour and Miss Jackson began to look anxious. But within ten minutes we heard a car approaching. There was a tooting which sent Miss Jackson flying from my side to the gate, and I followed her more slowly, wondering if my mental portrait of the unknown psychology lecturer would bear any resemblance to my newly-arrived guest.

During supper, whilst Miss Crabbe and Miss Jackson exchanged news of college friends and I cut innumerable slices of bread for my visitor's side plate which seemed constantly empty, I thought how wrong I had been about Miss Crabbe's looks.

I had imagined a massive woman about six feet in height, with flashing eyes, a resonant voice and an overpowering presence. In fact Miss Crabbe was a wispy five-foot-three with thin faded hair dragged back into a skimpy bun, and her most noticeable feature was a long thin nose with a pink flexible end which always appeared in need of attention. Her voice was slightly nasal and whining, but very soft. It was, however, never silent, I was beginning to discover. It flowed ruthlessly on, brooking no interruption, and appeared to function whether she were in the process of eating or not.

With considerable forethought for my own catering arrangements over the weekend I had cooked a piece of gammon and
one of Mrs Pringle's chickens. These cut cold, with salad, or with
new potatoes and peas from the garden, I had proposed to rely on
for the main meals. Miss Crabbe, with one devastating sentence,
knocked all my plans askew as soon as I picked up the carving
knife to attack the cold bacon.

'I'm not a flesh eater,' she said in a low voice, as though
discussing something of an intimate nature. I felt at once that to
be a flesh eater was to be put on a par with all the less pleasant
carnivores of the animal world, and I wondered which of them,
the vulture, the wolf or the carrion crow, I most resembled.

'Let me cook you an egg,' I offered. 'Or I've plenty of cheese.'

Miss Crabbe smiled in a resigned fashion.

'A little of this delicious salad,' she said, 'is all that I shall need.'

But I very soon found that it wasn't. Miss Crabbe's con-
sumption of bread was alarming, and I began to fear that I should
not have enough left for breakfast. Fresh fruit followed, and
when Miss Crabbe had demolished a banana, some grapes, a
Beauty of Bath apple and a generous helping of raspberries from
the garden, she and Miss Jackson agreed to my suggestion that
coffee in the sitting-room would be pleasant. They both rose from
the table, still talking, and with never a backward look at the
mound of dirty crockery, left me to it.

I set the coffee on the stove and cleared the table as it heated.

'This is going to be lively, Tibby,' I said to the cat. We
exchanged morose glances.

Miss Jackson was listening entranced to Miss Crabbe's monologue when I took in the coffee.

Its theme, I gathered, as I set about pouring out was the
regrettable manifestations of cruelty among children and how
best to avoid them.

'It must be something lacking in our own approach as teachers,' asserted Miss Crabbe.

Miss Jackson nodded owlishly.

'Black or white?' I asked, for the second time.

Miss Crabbe continued, brushing aside this interruption. 'Fun-
damentally, the Good should predominate in the normal child.

Certain maladjustments do occur, of course, but with the right kind of environment—'

'Black or white?' I said loudly.

'Black, please,' muttered Miss Jackson.

Miss Crabbe droned on. 'Which we should be able to make for them if we, as teachers, are appropriately adjusted, they should be non-existent. It is, to a large extent, a question of Aura. Now, I personally have an Ambience which, I am told by my professional friends, suffuses a room and creates an atmosphere conducive to a ready flow between the children and myself—'

'Black or white, Miss Crabbe?' I repeated fortissimo, handing Miss Jackson hers.

Miss Crabbe looked at me coldly. 'White, please,' she said, speaking more in sorrow than in anger. Now that she had noticed my presence in the room she seemed to feel that some conversational sop should be thrown to me. Speaking with maddening condescension she continued with her face turned towards me.

'We were discussing the little outbursts of spite which one still comes across in the classroom. Petty pinchings and so on. The children, of course, are the victims of their own dominating impulses, and Hilary and I were trying to find a solution to this problem. It calls for very great delicacy in approach, I feel – an application of psychological knowledge which helps the child who has had this emotional outburst without upsetting its ego. What do you do in these cases?'

'Smack!' I said briefly, and at last passed the coffee.

The evening wore on. By a quarter past eleven Miss Crabbe had told us about her recent lecture tour in the northern counties, her argument with a colleague about comprehensive schools and their influence on future political developments, the reactions of the press to her recently-published thesis on 'Play Behaviour in the Under-Fives,' and her suggestions for the complete re-organisation of Fairacre School. Overcome as I was with mingled amusement, irritation and fatigue, I could not help admiring the lady's amazing command of the English language. She flowed on remorselessly, her voice soft and faintly nasal. She paused neither for breath nor thought, but let her monologue stream forth like some smooth, never-ceasing, steady river which washed impassively about Miss Jackson and me as we sat helpless in our seats.

'Loungin' around and sufferin'!' I thought, echoing Uncle Remus. Finally, I rose to collect the coffee things, and suggested to Miss Jackson that she should set out on her cycle ride to Miss Clare's. She went with the greatest reluctance, after making complicated plans about the morrow's arrangements, and I conducted Miss Crabbe to her bedroom.

I showed her how to work the switch of the bedside lamp and indicated the books. She studied them briefly, with a sad smile.

'Juvenilia!' she said, dismissing my darlings in one word. 'In any case, I like to spend an hour jotting down notes on my reactions to the day's affairs. I find that people take so much out of me – one gives and gives and gives! My little hour before I sleep restores my spiritual resources, then I am refreshed enough to face the next day's demands on me.'

I hoped privately that my own depleted ration of sleep would refresh me enough to remain civil to my exhausting guest during the next day. Aloud I wished her good night, closed the door gently upon her, and tottered thankfully to my own bed.

The weekend slowly crawled by. Luckily, Saturday was a fine day and the two friends set off for their walk along the downs bearing packets of sandwiches – carefully non-flesh in Miss Crabbe's case – and flasks. Miss Clare had invited them to tea and so I was able to get through the usual weekend jobs undisturbed.

Miss Crabbe's unceasing conversation continued unabated for the rest of the time. She had changed her plans and decided to depart during Monday morning instead of on the Sunday evening as first arranged. After tea on the Sunday, she and Miss Jackson set off again for a walk. The sky looked threatening, but they refused to take mackintoshes with them.

'I am unduly sensitive to weather conditions,' announced Miss Crabbe, 'and it certainly won't rain.'

It gave me some satisfaction to see the heavens open an hour or so after their departure, but I sincerely hoped that they would find shelter, for the shower was heavy, and lasted a good half-hour.

They reappeared at about eight and I was careful to avoid any reference to the weather. Miss Crabbe volunteered the information that they had sheltered in a cottage in the woods and so had missed getting wet, but I did not press for further details. It was apparent, however, that something was amiss between the two. Miss Crabbe's aura was anything but benign as we sat down to supper and Miss Jackson was visibly upset. Somewhat to my relief she made her farewells considerably earlier than on the previous nights, and seemed anxious to get away.

Miss Crabbe too seemed unduly thoughtful, and though she more than held her own in our civil exchanges there was an occasional pause when the silence fell heavily about us.

As half past ten struck from St Patrick's Miss Crabbe ascended the stairs. On the landing she paused and confronted me.

'What is between this Franklyn man and Hilary?' she demanded. Her neck had flushed an ugly red, and I was quite relieved to see that the impregnable Miss Crabbe could feel emotion as sharply as her neighbours.

Before I could reply she continued. Her voice was shriller than usual, and by the glint in her eye I guessed that Miss Crabbe, behind that impassive veneer, had a very nasty temper.

'Hilary knocked there for shelter, and it didn't take me two minutes to sum up that situation! The little fool's in love with him, and he's willing too!'

Could it be jealousy that had brought an angry tear to this furious woman's eye, I wondered? I was soon to know.

'I won't stand for it, I tell you!' she almost screamed, and flounced into the bedroom, slamming the door behind her.

13. FAIRACRE SPEAKS ITS MIND

The Thursday of the parish meeting was also the last day of term. The children were excited, chattering like starlings, and bustling between their desks and the wastepaper basket as they put all in order.

The cupboards gaped open as Ernest and Eric packed away the books for their seven weeks' rest. Linda Moffat was removing pictures from the partition between the two rooms, Patrick was cleaning out the fish tank at the stone sink in the lobby, and holding a noisy conversation with Joseph Coggs who was washing inkwells in the playground. Miss Jackson's infants were equally busy and vociferous and we were only too thankful when playtime came and we could refresh ourselves with a cup of tea.

Miss Jackson had been in a black mood ever since Miss Crabbe's visit. The friends had parted civilly enough on the Monday morning, and my guest's outburst had not been mentioned again. I had received a thank-you letter in which, I was relieved to find, there was no reference to Miss Jackson. That young lady was going about her affairs with a stony face and, I suspected, an equally stony heart. She was in a pitiable plight, and I was glad to hear of her holiday plans.

'My parents have taken a house by the sea for a month,' she told me. 'I didn't know quite what I should be doing, but I've decided to go there. They always like me with them,' she added, with the breathtaking assumption of the young that their parents find them indispensable.

I remembered that a holiday with Miss Crabbe, in Brittany, had been mooted earlier in the term, but obviously this had fallen through. The month by the sea, I thought, should give poor Miss Jackson time to sort out her tangled emotions, but I felt very sorry for her parents.

The vicar called in to take the final day's prayers and to wish everyone a happy holiday.

'And the same to you, sir!' bellowed Fairacre School in a combined roar. Their faces beamed and their eyes shone so brightly that an outsider might suppose that their school hours normally consisted of back-breaking labour and physical tortures devised by their two sadistic teachers, so obvious was their relief at having a holiday.

Clutching their possessions to them they scrambled headlong to the door and out into the sunny playground. The vicar smiled benignly as their excited cries floated back to us.

'Good children!' he commented. 'All *good* children! Shall I see you at the meeting, Miss Read?'

The meeting to discuss the proposed housing site was held in the village hall, an unlovely corrugated iron building which had faded from a hideous beetroot red to a colour resembling weak cocoa.

There was an unusually large number of Fairacre people in the hall when I arrived. On most occasions a village meeting consists of a dozen or so, but this evening there were about four times that number, and seats were getting scarce.

Mr Willet seemed to be in charge of the seating arrangements and led me towards the front where Mr and Mrs Mawne were already seated. One chair stood vacant, beside Mr Mawne, at the end of the row. We greeted each other, and Mr Willet politely held my chair while I sat down.

'Between two fires!' commented Mr Willet, with misplaced gallantry, to Mr Mawne, who smiled vaguely. Mrs Mawne, however, turned a frosty glance upon Mr Willet and another, hardly less cold, upon her innocent husband and me. I remarked feebly that the evening was dark, and was not answered.

At this moment there was a stir by the door and the vicar and his wife entered. He made his way briskly to the chairman's seat, followed by Mr Lamb bearing a sheaf of papers.

'Lor!' said someone at the back of the room, in an awed voice, 'I hopes us ain't got to sit through that lot!'

The vicar rose to his feet.

'Could we have the lights on?' he asked. Several people

crowded round the switches by the door, and frantic clickings began. Sometimes one of the four hanging bulbs lit up, but never the one nearest to the chairman's table.

'Do seem to be a bit awkward-like tonight, sir,' admitted one of the operators. 'Wants a new bulb, or summat o' that.'

'A power cut, I expect,' boomed Mrs Pringle gloomily. Several people started to explain to her, in a fine confusion, that this could not be the case. Mrs Pringle, arms folded across her massive bosom, remained unconvinced.

'Never mind, never mind!' said the vicar benignly. 'We may be able to get through our business before it gets too dark. Mr Lamb, would you care to read the letter from the Rural District Council.'

Mr Lamb arose and read, first, the letter, and then, at a nod from the vicar, the proposals of the United Kingdom Atomic Authority. His voice sawed steadily up and down, and though many an eye glanced at watches, the people of Fairacre listened in attentive silence. The vicar came round from his chair, when Mr Lamb had finished, and sat on the front of his table instead. He had ruffled his fine white hair as he had listened, and his lined, kindly face wore a look of perplexity. He appeared, at that moment, particularly vulnerable and endearing to his parishioners.

'You see why the Parish Council has invited you to hear about this proposal. We are asked if we have any observations to make, and I do earnestly beg you to consider just what these proposals will mean.

'We shall have, between our two villages, a third new one, larger by far than either Fairacre or Beech Green. The people living there will have come, in the main, from towns. They may take some time to adapt themselves to our ways. They may, in some cases, never become adapted.

'Hundred Acre Field and a considerable area beyond that will be built over.

'We are told, in the proposals, that new roads will have to be built, that provision has been made for street lighting, sewage, a school, playing fields and shops. These plans are only in rough, as it were, and may be modified.

'There is no doubt that our two villages would benefit by the electricity and sewage schemes and by more frequent bus services between here and Caxley and the atomic station. But it remains for you to say what you feel about this project.'

At the end of this very fair and unbiased account the vicar walked round the table again and resumed his seat. Mr Willet was the first to take the floor.

'Mr Chairman,' he began, 'I'm a plain man and don't pretend to have understood all the rigmarole the Parish Clerk has just read us. But this I do say. I for one don't want to see Fairacre swamped by another young town—'

'Here, here!' muttered several of his neighbours.

'And I don't see paying out good money in rates and that for a lot of street lights and waterworks what we've done without long enough. I'm a plain man, and I reckons it's best to speak out plain.'

Mr Willet, puffing out his stained moustache, reseated himself heavily.

Beside me Mr Mawne shifted uncomfortably.

'If that fellow keeps saying that he's a plain man,' he whispered to me, 'I fear that someone will shortly get up and agree with him.' I was having some difficulty in controlling my enjoyment of this dry statement, when I caught Mrs Mawne's eye, and sobered up immediately.

Mrs Bradley, a diminutive figure in black, hoisted herself upright by prodigious clawing at her neighbour's shoulder, and added her views.

'I feel that someone should point out to the meeting that the land scheduled for building purposes is a particularly valuable local heritage.'

'Jest ol' fields, ain't it?' breathed someone in the row behind me, in a bewildered whisper.

'Our great local artist, Dan Crockford—'

'Ah now! He were a one for the girls!' commented the voice behind appreciatively.

'—immortalised that part of the country, which will be ruined,' went on Mrs Bradley.

'Two-penny halfpenny dauber!' muttered Mrs Mawne viciously to her husband.

'I should like to protest, most strongly, against the idea of houses being built on one of the most beautiful parts of our country. A part which has proved an inspiration to generations of our countrymen, and to the great Dan Crockford in particular.'

Applause greeted this robust statement and Mrs Bradley resumed her seat, flushed with success.

'And what about this school?' boomed Mrs Pringle before the clapping had died away. 'Am I to be out of a job at Fairacre School if the kids go to the new one? Or are that lot all to come tramping over my floors making double the work?'

'There appears to be no doubt that the school here would remain open,' said the vicar hastily, 'only its status might be altered.'

'*Meaning?*' queried Mrs Pringle, in a menacing crescendo.

'It might take just the very young children,' admitted the vicar, 'and the juniors would perhaps attend the proposed new school. But, of course, nothing is definite—'

A hubbub arose in the hall.

'What? Send our Bert off in a bus?'

'And who'll take the little 'uns to school if their brothers and sisters goes elsewhere?'

'And have a headmaster, like as not, caning 'em cruel.'

'Ah! Us had enough o' that ourselves, with old Hope, way back.'

'And do Miss Read stop on? Or do she get the push? Like Miss Davis?'

' 'Tis proper upsetting for the children.'

The meeting, until then, had been quiet, but this murmur of change affecting the children roused it amazingly. The vicar thumped on his table.

'Please, please! I think the time has come when a few proposers and seconders are needed, so that Mr Lamb can get down his points in order. Mrs Bradley, would you care to put your motion?'

Mrs Bradley climbed precariously to her feet again.

'I propose that this meeting protests strongly against the taking of a noted local beauty spot – the subject of many of Dan Crockford's pictures – for building purposes.'

'I second it!' said Mr Mawne beside me. His wife cast up her eyes significantly.

'And I propose us protests on the grounds of expense – rates and that,' put in Mr Willet.

'Voting first, please, on Mrs Bradley's proposal,' said the vicar gently. All hands were raised.

'Now, Mr Willet?'

Mr Willet put his proposal, in rather better terms this time. Mrs Pringle seconded it, and it was passed unanimously.

Mrs Moffat, chic in a coral-coloured coat, rose to frame her protest against the possible alteration in status of Fairacre School and its effect on the pupils and village life in general. It was seconded, surprisingly enough, by Joseph Coggs' father. Mr Lamb scribbled busily at the table, his tongue slightly out and writhing as he wrote.

'And tell 'em,' shouted an unknown stalwart from Beech Green, who appeared to be under the impression that Mr Lamb was taking down a letter direct to the authority involved and was hurrying to catch the post, 'tell 'em we're all right as we are and don't want the place mucked up with a lot of toffee-nosed types from town!'

'Could that be put a little more formally?' suggested the chairman.

After a certain amount of murmuring a proposal was put forward in more orthodox terms and it was seconded and carried. At that moment there was a disturbance by the door, and in stumped the figure of old Mr Miller, the owner of the land under discussion.

'Sorry to be late,' he barked. 'How far are we, chairman?'

'We are putting down our protests,' the vicar told him.

Mr Miller took a deep breath, and his eyes flashed fire. 'Then here's the biggest one,' he roared. 'That's been my farm, and my family's farm, for generations. I do more than protest against good farm land being put under buildings! I'll see them damned first!'

There were one or two indrawn breaths from those ladies of refinement, including Mrs Pringle, who objected to such strong language. Mr Miller, red in the face and brandishing his arms, was about to continue his diatribe, when the vicar broke in gently.

'Perhaps you would put that in the form of a proposal?' he suggested.

Mr Miller was attacked by a paroxysm of coughing and some-one helped him to a chair.

'You do it!' he gasped to Mr Roberts who approached him.

And so it was a fellow farmer who added Mr Miller's heartfelt protest to the list which lengthened under Mr Lamb's hand, while the irascible originator lay back in his chair and nodded his shaky head vehemently as he listened.

'Poor old chap!' whispered one woman to another. ' 'Tis too bad he's got this to put up with at his age! Right's right, after all, and he should keep what's his!'

The meeting drew briskly to its close, and I had never seen Fairacre so stirred. The people, normally so docile and mono-syllabic, were unusually heated, and spoke up bravely. Slow to kindle, once their hearts were fired they blazed strongly. The vicar spoke again.

'If there are no further comments I think we will ask Mr Lamb to send our protests to the Rural District Council, and close the meeting. I do so hope that we have been guided aright, and I thank every one of you who has come here tonight to put his wisdom and experience at the disposal of his neighbours. May the hand of the Lord guide our path!'

'Amen!' said a number of people fervently, and the vicar stepped down from the platform.

Soberly the villagers made their way out into the summer twilight.

The vicar had hurried directly to Mr Miller after the meeting and was insisting that he rested at the vicarage before returning to his home. We watched the two white-haired men, one so fiery and the other so mild, make their slow progress arm-in-arm towards the haven of the vicarage drawing-room.

'I shall go home and make a nice cup of tea,' announced a woman to her neighbour. 'I feel fair twizzled up inside after all that!'

The first day of the holidays dawned bright and fair. I made up my mind to spend it alone, savouring to the full the exquisite pleasure of being free.

To those who have never had to undergo regular employment with set hours of work, the glory of not being clock-bound cannot be truly appreciated. I looked gleefully at my kitchen clock as I took a leisurely breakfast at nine o'clock, and thought to myself, 'Ah! Yesterday at this time I was marking the register!'

I wandered round the dewy garden, admiring the velvety dark phlox just coming into flower, and getting an added fillip from the thought that normally I would be setting about an arithmetic lesson at the stern behest of the timetable on the wall. It is heady stuff, freedom – this cocking-a-snook at clocks, bells, whistles, timetables, syllabuses and all the other strait-jackets curbing the gay flow of time.

I sauntered through the village, swinging my basket, as St Patrick's clock struck eleven o'clock. ('Time to bring them in from play!' warned my teacher-shadow. 'And rats to that!' chortled my exuberant holiday-self.) What bliss it was to be at large in Fairacre on a Friday morning, instead of cooped up in a dark school!

It was fun to see the difference in the village at this time of the morning. The sun slanted from a different angle, winking on the brass knocker of Mr Lamb's door, a beautiful lion's head with a ring in its mouth, which I had not noticed before when the sun had slipped further round. In a cottage window stood a cactus plant which I had noticed before, but now, with the sun shining full upon it, two vivid orange flowers gaped like young birds' beaks in its warm benison.

On the other side of the village street a topiary hedge, finely clipped into towers and battlements, cast its black shadow upon the sun-drenched road, and a young thrush with jewelled eyes sheltered in the cool shade there.

Other Fairacre folk were still about their everyday business. From the Post Office came the irregular thumping of Mr Lamb's date-stamp as he hastened to get the mail ready for the van. The clinking of brass weights came from the grocer's and the whirring of the coffee-grinder, accompanied by the most seductive of all food smells.

Dusters flapped from upstairs windows as the bedrooms received their morning toilet. Here a woman bent in her vegetable garden cutting a lettuce or pulling spring onions for the midday meal. A baby lay kicking in its pram, eyes squirrel-bright as it crowed at the fluttering leaves about it.

From the bakehouse at the rear of the grocer's shop wafted the homely fragrance of new bread. In there, I knew, the great tables had been scrubbed clean and the white-overalled baker, with his short sleeves rolled up, would be waiting to rap the top of his loaves to see if the batch were done. And at the far end of the village, near Tyler's Row, I caught a glimpse of Mr Rogers, the blacksmith, in dusky contrast to his equally hot bakehouse neighbour, standing at the door of his forge to get a breath of fresh air.

Nothing can beat a village, I thought, for living in! A small village, a remote village, a village basking, as smug and snug as a cat in morning sunlight! I continued my lover's progress, besotted with my village's charms. Just look at that weeping willow, plumed like a fountain, that lime tree murmurous with bees, that scarlet pimpernel blazing in a dusty verge, the curve of that hooded porch, the jasmine – in fact, look at every petal, twig, brick, beam, thatch, wall, pond, man, woman and child that make up this enchanting place! My blessing showered upon it all.

It was the first day of the holidays.

14. A DAY OF CATASTROPHE

I was to look back with longing upon that first halcyon day, in the week that followed, for the clouds gathered with alarming speed.

On that Friday evening, I had driven to see Miss Clare and was shocked by the change in her. She looked suddenly old. Her hands shook uncontrollably as she poured out a glass of her home-made parsnip wine for me, and she seemed to move more slowly about her little cottage.

'It's a touch of rheumatism,' she said, dismissing my anxious enquiries. 'And I haven't slept well lately.'

'Is it that wretched girl?' I asked.

'Hilary? No, not really. She hasn't mentioned that Franklyn fellow again, but I think that little tiff with Miss Crabbe upset her more than she'll admit. I don't know what it was all about, and didn't enquire.'

I did not enlighten Miss Clare either, but a vision of Miss Crabbe's distorted and furious countenance flashed into my mind uncomfortably.

'Anyway,' continued Miss Clare, 'the child went off very happily this afternoon to her home. And the family go off to the sea for a month on Monday. I believe it will do her good.'

I pressed her to come and stay with me for a few days and have a rest. I had a clear week at Fairacre before I went away for my own holiday, and I knew I should go more happily if Miss Clare were less frail. But she would have none of it.

'No, no, my dear, though it's sweet of you to offer to have me. Now that I'm alone, and can get up a little later and not bother with quite as much cooking and shopping, I shall soon pick up.'

She agreed to come to tea during the following week and I had to be content with this. But I drove back to Fairacre far from easy in my mind about my old friend's health and happiness.

I woke the next morning still worried about Miss Clare, and within an hour or two had yet another disturbing incident to perturb me.

Mr and Mrs Mawne were in the butcher's shop when I went there to buy my weekend joint. Amy was coming over from Bent to have lunch with me and I was out early to do my shopping.

Mrs Mawne, never particularly affable to me, was even less amiable than usual. Mr Mawne, to my surprise, was in a bantering mood, quite unlike his normal vague daze, and I could sense that the couple were on edge with each other. Mrs Mawne prodded a piece of beef with a disdainful finger as Mr Mawne greeted me with unnaturally high spirits.

'Well, well, well, Miss Read! What a morning, eh? Just right for a trip to the sea!'

Mrs Mawne sniffed and I said guardedly that it was indeed a fine morning.

'Another trip to Barrisford would be just the thing!' said Mr Mawne with one eye on his wife. I disliked this teasing very much, particularly as he was using me to annoy his wife. The butcher looked at me as though I were Jezebel.

'We had a most enjoyable trip together last year,' continued Mr Mawne, addressing his wife, 'I really believe Miss Read would come again if I asked her nicely!' Mrs Mawne grew red and her mouth tightened. I was no more pleased than she was and looked steadily at her facetious little husband.

'I fear that you flatter yourself, Mr Mawne,' I said, and then felt a brute as his face fell under this pin-prick to his self-esteem.

'I'll call later,' I said to the butcher, and left the shop and the Mawnes as quickly as I could.

Amy was in one of her what-a-pity-you-aren't-married moods, when she arrived for lunch, particularly irritating after Mr Mawne's earlier exhibition of male conceit.

'Now James,' she told me, attacking the beef with gusto, 'is absolutely devoted and seems to get fonder of me as the years go by.' With a heroic effort I desisted from reminding her of several unhappy occasions when she had endured James's lapses from strict fidelity. '*Sour grapes*' is the phrase that readily trips from the lips of married ladies when reminded by their single friends about male frailty, and behind this two-word shield many a married man or woman has evaded a spinster's straight aim.

'You see what a waste of talent all this is,' continued Amy, as I bore in a plum pie, a little later. 'You're quite a good cook really, and a man would appreciate it.'

'I appreciate it too,' I said, cutting the crust.

'But with two of you,' persisted Amy, bent on furthering the cause of matrimony, 'you would enjoy it all far more.'

'I should have to do twice as much cooking,' I pointed out, 'and that might pall.'

'Really!' said Amy exasperatedly, 'you are the most trying, awkward, maddening, *unfeminine* woman I've met, and thoroughly deserve to be single!'

'Have some cream,' I suggested consolingly. 'It covers the nerve endings.'

'Tchah!' exclaimed Amy, and took a generous helping with a smile.

The shock came as we were washing up. Amy wandered to and fro in the kitchen drying up for me and occasionally returning a piece of china for a second wash. Amy's standards are much higher than mine and she scrutinized each article with an eagle eye.

'I know two adorable sisters,' I told her as she flung back a spoon into the washing-up bowl 'who work on the principle that one wets the things and the other wipes. And a very nice co-operative job they make of washing-up with never a harsh word between them!'

Amy was not impressed.

'I don't wonder Mrs Pringle ticks you off. Look at this smear of mustard! Must be ages old! It's a wonder you don't pop off with typhus!'

I surveyed the plate which she held out to me with interest.

'That,' I said, with pardonable smugness, 'happens to be gilding.'

Amy had the grace to laugh, and returned it to the dresser. As she lodged it she said: 'And when is Hilary Jackson going away?'

'She's gone,' I answered, busily scouring the sink.

'Well, I saw her last night, with that dreadful Franklyn fellow. They were just going into "The Bell"!'

I felt as though I had been hit. Could that foolish young woman really be in the neighbourhood? Was she really so infatuated with

Franklyn that she could deceive Miss Clare and her parents and also hope to evade the all-seeing eye of Fairacre and its environs? Or could Amy have been mistaken? I clung, for one endless second, to this forlorn hope, but in my heart I knew immediately that Amy was far too sharp-eyed to be deceived. And I knew too, with a sudden sickness, that Hilary Jackson was quite silly enough to imperil her good name, the happiness of her friends and her teaching career, at the promptings of this ill-fated infatuation.

In a flash I decided that Amy must not know of my doubts. There was still a chance that I might be able to get in touch with the girl and get her to see sense before the tongues started wagging in the neighbourhood.

'She must have gone off this morning then,' I said, trying to sound casual.

Luckily, Tibby created a most welcome diversion by bringing in a squeaking shrew. In the following few frantic minutes, whilst Amy and I tried to rescue it from the outraged cat, Miss Jackson and her affairs were shelved.

At two o'clock Amy drove off. I had found the time from her disclosure until her departure agonisingly long, and could only hope that my anxiety was not too apparent.

I waved good-bye with relief, and before the car was round the bend of the lane I had fled up the stairs, two at a time, to get myself ready for my visit to the cottage in the woods, where I hoped to find Miss Jackson.

It seemed best to go on my bicycle, for the steep track would tax my ancient car's asthmatic powers, and would be more readily noticed. A bicycle, leaning against John Franklyn's fence, could be anybody's, but the car could belong to me alone.

The day was close and sticky. Clouds of minute thunderflies wafted about in the warm air, tormenting and tickling sensitive places like one's neck and eyes. I was seriously perturbed, as I pushed along, about the best way to handle this uncomfortable interview. It might be easier, though perhaps more painful for Hilary Jackson, if Franklyn were there, for I had no doubt that the craven fellow would be only too pleased to back out of an awkward situation, and would side with me in persuading the girl to return. No gallant hero, this Franklyn, I suspected, but the sort of man who would let a girl break her heart rather than endanger his own skin.

Hilary alone might be a different proposition, full of fervid and misplaced loyalties and seeing herself as the Passionate Woman Who Dared All for Love. A middle-aged headmistress, plain, and untouched by romance, stood a small chance of succeeding against such formidable odds, I told myself.

The track grew steeper and dustier and I dismounted. So far I had not met a soul. I stood on the slope of the downs and looked back to the peaceful valley. The still heat was all-enveloping and shimmered on the road so far below. In the dry fine grass, which whispered at my bicycle wheel, a cricket chirruped tirelessly, and away above, a speck against the dark clouds which gathered ominously above the wood, a lark trickled out his clear song, like sparkling drops from a fountain. With that awareness which comes from a state of heightened emotion I could hear each separate liquid note, and smell the aromatic tang of the small thyme bruised under my feet. From a tall dock plant nearby hung a dying scarlet leaf, a neat and elegant triangle, fluttering like a pennant from a mast. It was as though these small lovely things held out their beauty for the comfort of my sad heart. How easy to succumb, to sit upon this thymy bank and to lose oneself in the company of these old and ever-faithful friends! What business was it of mine to meddle with Hilary Jackson's affairs, whispered a small siren's voice?

Sighing, I resumed my uphill pushing, and with a throbbing head and heavy heart approached the cottage in the woods.

Hilary Jackson was alone. She had answered my knock at the kitchen door, her face was flushed and her eyes bright but wary. She had invited me into the dim interior, cool after the heat of the climb, and we sat now, one each side of the grubby kitchen table and surveyed each other.

'John,' said the girl, throwing the Christian name across at me like a challenge, 'John has gone to Caxley and should be back for tea. Perhaps you'll stop?' Her air was studiedly insolent and she was more nervous than she cared to admit. I decided that a plain approach would be best.

'Miss Clare is under the impression that you returned home yesterday. Only by chance I heard that you had been seen in Caxley yesterday evening.'

'And what have my affairs to do with Miss Clare? Or anyone else, for that matter?' demanded the girl, tossing her head.

'Only this – that the way you behave is noticed by everybody in a small community. By consorting with John Franklyn, whose affairs have been watched for many years, I may say, you are giving yourself a bad name. As a teacher you should be doubly careful of the example you set and by flaunting the conventions – which are, after all, only the commonly accepted modes of decent living – you are not only making a fool of yourself but jeopardising your whole career. One silly slip now may mean much future unhappiness.'

Hilary's face had darkened as my homily unwound.

'I don't care a row of pins for what people think of me – back-biting, narrow-minded, evil-thinking country bumpkins, as stodgy as you are yourself! John Franklyn is a fine man and I'm proud to be seen with him. I suppose a withered old spinster like you thinks that love doesn't matter! Well, it does – and for me everything else must take second place!'

Her eyes flashed behind her thick spectacles and she thumped vehemently upon the kitchen table.

I answered her quietly. 'The world is never "well lost for love" in my opinion. And this is not even love, I'm afraid, but a foolish infatuation on your part which I am positive John Franklyn does not share.'

'You'd never dare to say that to his face!' she flared.

'Indeed I would, and I hoped that he would be here when I called. I think that you might have seen him in his true colours.'

There was a pause in the heat of the battle. Through the open door came soft woodland scents that cooled my warm blood. I tried again.

'Look, Hilary. Please come back to the school-house with me for the night. I'll take you to the station early tomorrow and you can get home with no one knowing any more about this business.

I shall say nothing to Miss Clare, or anyone else, and we can scotch any rumours started by people yesterday.'

The girl rounded on me furiously.

'Do you think I'm ashamed to be seen with him? Why, I'm *glad* that people saw us together yesterday! I suppose your beastly mind thinks that we spent the night here. Well, it's wrong! I stayed at John's sister's in Caxley, and she thinks I've gone home today!' Her voice was strident and triumphant, and her eyes glittered with dangerous excitement. She thrust her face close to mine. 'And where I spend tonight is my own business! I'm old enough to look after myself!'

'Old enough,' I said sadly, rising to my feet, 'but not wise enough. I can see you're in no mood to see reason. Someone will have to make you – but I can't obviously.'

I drew the door further back and made my way unhappily into the green and gold glory of the wooded garden.

Hilary Jackson stood in the doorway, pink and panting from the tussle, and exalted with her own fine, but foolish, outpourings. She looked immensely young and silly, and whilst I was very worried, I couldn't help but feel sorry for her.

'I'll be in Fairacre if you want me,' I called back, lifting my bicycle from the fence. 'Don't be too proud to ask for help if you need it. And *please do* think over what I've said!'

'*Amor omnia vincit!*' quoted Miss Jackson, loudly and soulfully. And, distressed as I was, I noted that my assistant's pronunciation of Latin was execrable.

It was hotter and more oppressive than ever as I rode back down the steep slope to the Fairacre road. I must get in touch with her parents at once, I told myself, my head throbbing and eyes half-closed against the myriad flies that bombarded my face.

I did not know the Jacksons' address and nothing would make me worry Miss Clare for it, ill as she was. Luckily, by the time I was pedalling along the road towards the spire of St Patrick's, I remembered the name of Hilary's home town in the Midlands, and also that her father's Christian name was Oliver.

Black clouds were gathering swiftly overhead and there were

ominous rumblings from the Caxley direction as I entered the school-house and made straight for the telephone.

'Enquiries, please,' I said to the girl and sat down thankfully, cradling the receiver. The line crackled as the thunder grew nearer. There was a rushing sound outside as the wind which precedes a storm lifted the branches of the elm trees that stand at the corner of the playground. A fierce eddy twirled a few dead leaves and dust round and round, in a miniature whirlwind, outside the window.

The girl was a long time in tracking down the Jacksons' telephone number from the few poor clues that I could supply. As I waited I was torn with anxiety. Supposing that they had already gone to the house by the sea and that there was no one at home? This was Saturday, and people generally took over a holiday house on that day of the week. And if I did get through – how on earth could I word the dreadful news which I must transmit? Confound the wretched girl, I thought wrathfully, ruining my own and her parents' holidays!

A jagged orange streak split the black sky behind St Patrick's, and a crash like a ton of coals let down upon the school-house roof, rocked the room.

A faint voice spoke through the hubbub. 'You're through!' it said.

Mr Jackson listened to my somewhat incoherent remarks with commendable patience.

'I'll come straight away,' he said decisively. 'I can be there in two hours and I'll bring her back with me. Don't worry, and many thanks!'

I said I was so relieved to find them at home.

'My wife had an attack of migraine,' he answered, 'so we postponed the journey until tomorrow.'

Another fearful crash shattered the air around me, and must have penetrated to the telephone.

'Are you all right?' said Mr Jackson. He sounded alarmed. I explained that we were in the midst of a violent thunderstorm.

'Oh!' said he, 'that all? For a moment I thought you'd fainted! I'll ring off now, and be on my way!'

Through the teeming rain which now lashed against the

window I saw the church clock. The hands stood at half past four. On trembling legs I made my way to the kitchen and filled the kettle.

I spent the next few hours making plum jam, with a quarter of my mind on the operation and the other three-quarters imagining the happenings at the game-keeper's cottage. Would Hilary refuse to go? Would there be any violence? Would the cottage have been struck by lightning and the sorrowing and vengeful father arrive only to find two charred bodies among the smoking embers? I did my best to curb these morbid fancies and to concentrate on the jam, but it was uphill work.

The storm still raged and muttered, following the line of the downs. At times it died away in intensity, but returned again periodically with renewed vigour. The playground streamed with water and I guessed that the skylight would be letting through a regular steady trickle into my classroom.

At nine o'clock the telephone rang. It was Mr Jackson's comfortable deep voice at the other end.

'All's well! A few tears on the way, and now the girl's in bed. I thought you might be worrying. We'll write from the other house. Meanwhile, all our thanks.'

What a day, I thought, as I climbed the stairs to bed two hours later. The gutters still gurgled and the thunder still growled in the distance. I looked out upon Fairacre's glistening church and a few steaming roofs among the tossing trees.

This was the halcyon village I had mooned over so sentimen-tally early in the holidays, I thought grimly. Where now was the tranquil sunshine, the serenity, the innocent-hearted populace going about its honest business?

I thought of the misplaced passion of Hilary Jackson, the cupidity of John Franklyn, the evil gossiping of neighbours, the sad injustice of Miss Clare's ill-health, the misery of the Coggs family at the mercy of their drunken father under the broken dripping thatch of Tyler's Row, of the chained unhappy dogs in back gardens, bedraggled hens cooped all too closely in bare rank runs, and, over all, the tension engendered by the housing scheme and the ugly passions it aroused.

A flash of lightning illuminated the landscape in quivering

mauve and yellow lights, distorting its normal lovely colouring to something livid and sinister.

Sick at heart, with the noise of the storm still raging round me, I sought in vain for the comfort of sleep.

PART THREE
Thunder and Lightning

* * * *

15. DR MARTIN IS BUSY

On the hottest day of the year Dr Martin drove on his rounds along the winding lanes of Fairacre. Heat throbbed from the dusty road, the cows were gathered into any patch of shade that they could find, and the distant downs shimmered under a burning sky.

He had just paid a visit to old Mr Miller who had not fully recovered from his paroxysm at the parish meeting. He had aged considerably since this infernal business about the housing estate had blown up, thought Dr Martin. In a long life Mr Miller had had many troubles, but usually he had had his own way. The possession of his farm and his beloved acres, inherited from his family and in trust for the next generation, had given him confidence and joy. With that threatened he was a lost man, and though he fought bravely and his spirit burnt as fiercely as ever, his ageing body paid the price. He no longer slept the deep dreamless slumber of the healthily tired man who has spent the day working in the open air. His appetite had dwindled, and his sturdy compact little figure now had a pathetic droop. Dr Martin knew well that his medicines could do little against this spiritual canker. He doubted very much if they were taken at all, and though he had prescribed sleeping tablets for his crusty patient, he had been told by poor tearful Mrs Miller that her husband would not countenance them. Ah, it was a wretched threat that hung over them all! And until the thing was settled, one way or the other, Dr Martin supposed that he and his country neighbours would have to continue from day to day feeling as though a weight lay upon their chests.

He drew his car into the side of the lane, switched off the engine and filled his pipe meditatively. Through a wide gap in the hazel hedge beside him he had a clear view of Hundred Acre Field and the threatened landscape, which lay now with a heart-lifting serenity before him. How long those lovely lines had endured, thought the doctor, blowing out a fragrant blue cloud of tobacco smoke!

How many troubled and heavy-hearted men before him, clad in homespun, silks and lace, doublet and hose . . . ay, and rough furs too . . . had looked, as he did now, at those immemorial downs and had there found comfort? 'I will lift up mine eyes unto the hills, from whence cometh my help,' the psalmist had said, in plain, sober, simple words, as lovely and as refreshing as clear water. And as vital too, the doctor mused, his mind now running on his patients. In these last few months he had had far more cases suffering from nervous strain than ever before. His advice was generally, 'Get out into the fresh air. Look at the life about you. Look out and not in. Nature can cure you where I can't. I can only give her a hand.'

Dr Martin was a wise man and took his own advice. His observant eye watched now a bee pushing its way busily in and out among the velvety toad flax flowers that flared beneath the hedge in the hot sunlight. Along the edge of the open window crawled a ladybird, so recently alighted that its underwings were untidily folded under their red enamelled case, and protruded gauzy black snippets. It was moments like these, precious, quiet, contemplative breaks in the doctor's busy day that revived him, and gave him the happiness and power to inspire his patients.

'Did me good just to see him,' people said. 'Always got time to listen to you. That chap at Caxley, as is always buzzing about like a blue-bottle, fair puts you in a tizzy when he comes tearing into the room, and don't appear to listen to half you says. Now our Dr Martin he can speak sharp if need be, but you know it's for your own good and he intends to get you well again. He's a real gentleman!'

The doctor took a last refreshing look at the view through the gap. In the distance he could see the humped thatch of Miss Clare's cottage, his next calling place. He'd better get along, he supposed, switching on the engine. Do the job before him and not linger too much on the misty future.

The engine came to life, but before moving off the doctor

rested his hot sticky hands on the wheel and gazed unseeingly before him. He was drowsier than usual, in this heat, and say what you like this housing estate was deuced unsettling for a man of his age. What would become of him and his wife and all his great family of patients? He looked forward to retiring very soon, to spending more time with his much-loved wife, to tending his roses which were among the finest in the county, to pottering about in Fairacre – but the Fairacre he loved and worked in for so many years, not some raw new suburb of Caxley, smearing his beloved hills. It might be better to move if this came about. But why on earth should he? Lord, it was little enough to ask after a long life, surely? Just a few years' rest in the same place, with the same friends, the same pastimes and hobbies – and the same, please God, the same downs!

The doctor blinked rapidly and let in the clutch.

'Let's see if Dolly Clare can give me a cup of tea,' said he to the ladybird. 'If I go on like this I shall be in bed with poor old Miller!'

Miss Clare, in Dr Martin's opinion, had gone back in health during the past few weeks and he knew, as well as the rest of Fairacre knew, just why. The indiscretions of her lodger had not passed completely unnoticed, though no one quite knew how far the affair had gone. Miss Clare had been blaming herself needlessly for not warning the girl against the Franklyn fellow, whose name was a byword. Could she have helped her more? The question remained unanswered in the days that followed Hilary Jackson's adventure, and sadly troubled Miss Clare.

Mr and Mrs Annett had evolved a plan of which Dr Martin thoroughly approved.

'We're taking a little house for three weeks in August, by the sea, near Barrisford,' George Annett had said to the doctor when he had called in with young Malcolm's tonic.

'Though why he needs a tonic, I really don't know,' observed the doctor, eyeing his young patient, who was bouncing energetically up and down in his pram to the detriment of its springs.

'But you ordered it!' protested Mrs Annett, wide-eyed. She looked up from buckling her exuberant son into his harness.

'Should have been bromide,' returned the doctor, smiling.

'Push him into the garden and then come and tell me all about the holiday plans.'

It appeared that the Annetts were as perturbed as the doctor himself was about Miss Clare's frail health, and had invited her to spend the three weeks with them by the sea, but she had gently declined.

'There's a spare bedroom,' went on Mrs Annett earnestly, 'and we truthfully would love her to be with us, and I'm sure the air would do her a world of good—'

'But she feels she may be in the way; that she would be an added expense, that you three young things should be together alone, and so on, and so on. I know. You don't have to tell me what's in Dolly Clare's mind. She's a living saint and as obstinate as a mule,' responded Dr Martin.

'Can you do anything to help?' asked Mr Annett.

'I should think I might try,' said the doctor, his eye taking on that gleam which meant that he was up to his tricks. 'I shall tell her that you two could get out together if she weren't such a selfish old woman as to refuse to do an hour or two's sitting-in—'

'*Please*,' begged Mrs Annett, horrified, 'don't say anything so wicked!'

'And then I could tell her that I am having sleepless nights because she is such an obstinate patient and won't do as she's told, and my health is suffering,' he continued, warming to his theme. 'And finally, I could threaten her with Sister Ada who has offered, somewhat grudgingly, to have her there if need be. That should settle it nicely,' said this incorrigible meddler in the affairs of others, with a satisfied smile.

The Annetts gazed at him aghast. George was the first to find his breath.

'I don't really think there's any need for such wholesale lying,' he began in a schoolmasterish voice, but he was cut short.

'There's no need at all,' agreed the doctor with a disarming smile, making his way to the door, 'but I enjoy a thundering good lie if it makes my patients see reason. Remember your Kipling?'

He stood in the doorway, his white hair standing out like an aureole, and his eyes twinkling.

'Not a little place at Tooting—
But a country house with shooting,
And a ring-fence, deer-park lie!'

he quoted triumphantly, and vanished into the sunshine.

The door of Miss Clare's cottage stood ajar on that throbbing hot afternoon. Dr Martin put his head round, but there was no one to be seen.

He stepped down into the brick-floored living-room. It was cool in here, under the sheltering thatch, and a fine bouquet of mixed roses caught his eye. Their reflection gleamed in the polished table on which they stood.

He looked around him, noting the freshness of the curtains, the gleam of copper on the mantelpiece and the crystal clearness of Miss Clare's leaded panes. These silent objects stood as proof of their mistress's zeal and devotion to them. They might be older than, and as frail as, their owner, but they were as full of grace.

'An hour's less polishing, and one more hour in bed,' thought Dr Martin, 'would be ideal, but I'll never get her to do that, I fear.'

A small noise above attracted his attention. He went to the door of the box staircase, opened it by its latch, and called aloft.

'Anybody there?'

There was a creaking of a bed and Miss Clare's voice answered.

'I'll be down in just one moment, doctor. I was having a rest.'

'You stay there then. I'll be up,' said the doctor, stooping for his black bag.

'But I'm in my petticoat—' began Miss Clare.

'All the better,' responded Dr Martin, mounting the narrow stairs sturdily, 'I want to listen to your chest, anyway.'

He entered the bedroom to find his patient propped up against two fat feather pillows, with the eiderdown over her legs. Miss Clare's top half was decorously clad in a pale-grey lock-knit petticoat with a modestly high neckline. A novel lay, face downwards, upon the bed.

Miss Clare smiled at her old friend.

'It was too hot for anything round my shoulders,' she said.

'Well, you won't shock me, my dear, I can assure you. That petticoat's a sight more decent than Minnie Pringle's sun top she was flaunting in the lane just now.'

He fetched a cane-bottomed chair, set it by the bedside, and adjusted his stethoscope. It was very quiet in the cottage bedroom. Outside a faint rustling came from the jasmine at the window, and a sparrow, who lived in the thatch above, glanced in, upside down, with a beady eye and, with a frightened chirrup, flew away.

'Humph!' said the doctor grimly, folding up his instrument and stuffing it in the black bag. 'You're not doing as well as you should.'

'I'm sorry,' said Miss Clare contritely, and patted the doctor's hand, as though it were he, and not she, who needed reassurance.

Dr Martin saw his opening. 'I must admit it worries me. Here I am doing all I can for you – and I do honestly believe you are eating more and resting more often – but you don't quite get on as I'd like. I don't mind telling you, Dolly, I'm beginning to wonder if I'm past my job.' He shook his white head slowly. For such a burly fellow he really had a very nice line in pathos. Miss Clare watched him quizzically.

'You can't be expected to replace worn-out hearts,' she said gently.

Dr Martin continued to look sad. 'I wonder if you ought to join forces with your sister Ada,' he said, with such sweet, spontaneous reasonableness, that even he was surprised to hear his own voice.

'Never!' said Miss Clare firmly. 'Not even for your comfort, doctor!'

Dr Martin now rose and paced restlessly about the diminutive bedroom, his head narrowly missing the beam that ran across the whitewashed ceiling. He had thrust his hands into his pockets, and with shoulders hunched he prowled thoughtfully, wearing an expression of extreme perplexity. Miss Clare watched him affectionately.

'If only you could get away somewhere – have a change of air, preferably by the sea – say, for two or three weeks, I believe it would set you up completely.'

'Would it?' said Miss Clare, with suspicious meekness.

'Indeed it would. Otherwise, I must see about a nursing home or something of that nature for you, for a spell before the winter.'

There was a slightly threatening note in this last sentence, which did not elude Miss Clare.

'And what about my lodger?'

'Your lodger,' burst out the good doctor, standing stock-still and glaring at his patient over the bedrail, 'could do with a dam' good spanking, and I hope her father's given her one by this time!'

'She's only young and silly—' Miss Clare began to protest; but she was cut short.

'I won't waste my breath on such a fool, but she's responsible for your set-back, and that I cannot forgive.'

'I shall get better now that the holidays are here. Don't worry about me.'

'You won't unless you get away. Everything here reminds you of her, and in your present low state it will take more than half an hour under the eiderdown to cure you, my girl.' There was a pause, and doctor and patient looked steadily at each other across the quiet room. The doctor broke the silence first.

'Dolly, I shan't feel at ease until you have a holiday. What about it?'

Miss Clare gave him a slow, lovely smile, but her eyes were mischievous.

'You've been talking to the Annetts,' she said.

Dr Martin threw his head back in a gusty laugh.

'Well, what of it?' he protested, 'I did just have a word—'

'And planned all this after that word!' smiled Miss Clare. 'And how well you do it too! I was beginning to feel quite anxious about your failing powers!'

'But, Dolly,' said the doctor, suddenly grave. 'Will you go? It isn't all humbug, you know. I'd like you to be well again. This offer means health for you, and a chance for those two young people to get out on their own without that baby, if you'd feel up to coping with it occasionally.'

This aspect of it, as the wily doctor had foreseen, touched Miss Clare at once.

'If I really can be of help,' she said slowly, 'then I will go with the greatest pleasure.'

'You will!' shouted Dr Martin, with delight. 'That's the best news I've heard today. Now mind you keep your word!'

'Of course I shall,' said Miss Clare indignantly. 'And now, if you'll wait downstairs I'll get dressed and we'll make a pot of tea.'

'Put your legs straight back under the eiderdown,' ordered her medical adviser, 'and *I'll* make the tea and bring it up here.'

Whistling discordantly, the doctor clattered cheerfully downstairs.

His last call of the day was at Fairacre school-house where he found a most interesting operation going on.

Mrs Pringle had for many months deplored, loudly and bitterly, the condition of the spare-room feather bed.

'One heave,' she had said to me, 'and the room's thick with feathers! As soon as we gets a fine still day I'll tip the lot into a new ticking I'll run up for you.'

She had been as good as her word, and the new striped mattress cover, with its inside seams carefully sealed with a dampened piece of that yellow bar soap which was Mrs Pringle's household stand-by, lay spread on the lawn awaiting its contents.

Mrs Pringle and I had spread an enormous sheet on the grass and together had emptied out a mountain of feathers, white, speckled and coppery brown, upon it. Mr Willet, who had come to clip the hedges, had abandoned his job and joined us on the lawn. He greeted the doctor boisterously.

'Us only wants the tar, doctor, then us be all ready for you!'

'Not in this heat, Willet. Have pity, man,' said Dr Martin, settling himself in the shade. He looked at Mrs Pringle who was busy turning the feathers over and over, 'to get a bit of clean air into the poor things,' as she so tactfully told me.

'That leg any better?' he enquired.

'Torture!' said that lady implacably. 'Simple torture. Flaring, burning, twitching, jumping, itching, throbbing—'

'No better then, I take it,' said the doctor calmly. He lay back upon the grass and closed his eyes. Mrs Pringle cast a disgusted glance at his peaceful figure.

'What if a wind come up?' asked Mr Willet suddenly.

'Come wind, come rain, come fair, come foul,' announced Mrs Pringle majestically, 'my leg's still torture to me.'

'Wasn't speaking of your leg, gal, but the feathers,' responded Mr Willet without gallantry. 'You wants to thank the Lord you're not worse. Remember last Sunday's psalm?'

'I know as well as you do,' answered Mrs Pringle sourly, 'and I remember some pretty botched-up singing too, in the new chant.'

Mr Willet was stung.

'There wasn't one of us in that choir could sing that agrarian chant,' he said wrathfully. 'I don't say Annett don't know his job at teaching, but for a choir-master he's got pretty rum ideas. Too popish by half, if you ask me! Might just as well go to St Peter's over the other side of Caxley!'

'And what, pray,' began Mrs Pringle loftily, 'is wrong with St Peter's? I went there a time or two when I was courting and we had some real beautiful services.'

'I been there,' said Mr Willet heavily, 'but the once. Never again, I said, never again! Pictures all round the walls, curtains hanging up, candles blazing away all over the place, people bobbing up and down – I tell you!' Mr Willet's sturdy Calvinistic frame shook at the very remembrance of the place.

Dr Martin rolled over on to his front, giving me a slow wink on his course.

'And that minister of theirs,' continued Mr Willet warmly, 'a beardless boy, young enough to be me son, told me to call him father when I spoke to him! I tell you it's against nature – and so's that agrarian chanting, to my mind; no proper tune at all!'

'Maybe you just don't know real music when you hears it,' suggested Mrs Pringle sarcastically. She bent over the feathers, corsets creaking, and began to stuff handfuls into the new mat-tress cover. I knelt down beside her, and Mr Willet and Dr Martin set to with us.

The sun beat on our heads and the white sheet reflected the light blindingly. Despite the heat and energetic thrusting of feathers Mr Willet rose to the challenge.

'I heard the Messiah at the Corn Exchange last year,' puffed

Mr Willet, 'and that's what I call real music. Good, plain, God-fearing, English-sounding music that you can sing out hearty! It done you good! Plenty of up and down, and soft and loud, and everyone having a rattlin' good time of it!'

'Takes some beating,' agreed the doctor, sneezing some feathers from his nose. 'Here, why don't we lift the lot up in the sheet and ram it all in?'

This sensible suggestion was welcomed. Mrs Pringle and I folded the sheet carefully, imprisoning the rest of the ubiquitous feathers some of which had floated far and wide in the summer garden, while the two men held open the gaping mouth of the ticking.

Coughing and spluttering we finally made the transfer. The sheet still bore a mass of fluff, and the lawn looked as though a snowstorm had passed over.

'Fiddlin' stuff!' observed Mr Willet, 'but it give us all a nice set-down and chat. I'll be back to my hedges.'

He stumped off, swinging the shears and humming to himself. Mrs Pringle watched him go.

'What that chap lacks,' said she slowly, 'is soul!'

Dr Martin refused all refreshment, picked himself a rosebud and returned to his car.

'Nearly forgot,' he said. 'I called to tell you that Miss Clare is going to have a break with the Annetts, by the sea.'

'That's absolutely wonderful!' I cried. 'How did they manage to persuade her?'

'They didn't,' answered Dr Martin smugly. 'I did!' The car moved slowly forward.

'And what farrago of arguments did you concoct this time?' I shouted, after the departing car.

Two derisive hoots were my answer, and I returned, smiling, to my feathered garden.

The heat continued. A few days after Dr Martin's visit I went to Devonshire to spend three weeks with two sisters, friends of mine since childhood, who owned a cottage by the sea. Sunshine, sea, bathing, boating, walking and the cheerful companionship of old friends dispelled my Fairacre worries about Miss Clare, the future of the school, the housing estate and the problem of Hilary Jackson's affairs of the heart.

The holiday was almost at an end and I was spending an hour doing a little leisurely shopping for gifts to take back with me, when I decided that the blazing sunshine reflected from the tiny market-square's cobbles, called for an ice.

I turned into a small café and on opening the door came face to face with Miss Crabbe. Our mouths dropped open in surprise.

'On holiday?' I enquired weakly. Miss Crabbe assured me that she was combining business with pleasure, attending a summer course at a nearby manor house recently taken over for this purpose.

I persuaded her to return to her table and eat another ice while she told me all about it. My invitation was not completely altruistic, as I welcomed this opportunity of finding out how matters stood between this lady and my unfortunate assistant.

'The course is most imaginatively conceived,' began Miss Crabbe, and I felt that dreadful ennui overtaking me as she got into her stride. 'It deals with every possible means of self-expression, and we have tackled pottery-making, miming, finger-painting and stick printing. Some of us have attempted some really worthwhile work in music, making our own instruments first, as a matter of course, and I have made a set of most satisfying bamboo pipes.'

The voice droned on whilst I demolished my ice. As I had noticed during Miss Crabbe's visit to my house she had the ability to eat and talk at the same time, and even quite large portions of strawberry ice seemed to glide down, whilst an endless flow of words streamed up, from the same orifice. I was fascinated.

No mention was made of Miss Jackson and I determined to broach the subject myself. There was no doubt about it, Miss

Jackson might well be influenced by the woman who now sat with me, and it was worth asking for her help. Hilary's reckless behaviour with this undesirable man had dated from her clash over him with Miss Crabbe, for before that time, as far as I knew, she had been a little more circumspect. What Miss Crabbe thought really mattered to the girl, and I suspected that their estrangement was a secret source of great grief to both of them, but that neither would give way.

Miss Crabbe's countenance flushed an unlovely pink when I spoke of Hilary Jackson.

'I have had no word from her since we met at Fairacre,' she said stiffly. 'We had made tentative plans for visiting Brittany, but as I heard nothing, I applied to come on this course at the last minute. She seems to have become a very silly girl since she left college. We all had great hopes of her there.' The last two sentences were spoken so primly that she could only infer that Hilary's shocking state of silliness was due to the influence of those foolish people whom she had met since leaving college! I did not rise to this bait.

'To be frank,' I said, 'I think Hilary Jackson has always been a silly girl, but she has two great qualities, warm-hearted affection, and loyalty to her friends. In this affair with Franklyn it is these two qualities which have led her astray.'

I paused for a moment, wondering whether I dared to go on. Miss Crabbe's mouth, now mercifully free from food, was set in a stubborn line. I decided that I might as well hang for a sheep as a lamb and continued.

'If only she could have continued to direct this affection and loyalty to you, I think all would have blown over between Hilary and this fellow, but when she saw that you – er – felt so strongly about it she was forced to take sides. Unfortunately, she took the wrong side, and because she was so thoroughly miserable she flung herself at this man.'

'Then she's only herself to blame,' remarked Miss Crabbe decidedly, but to my watchful eye she appeared slightly molli-fied.

'Loyalty to him,' I went on, 'won't allow her to get in touch with you as she knows that you don't approve; but, believe me, she has been desperately unhappy about this break, and I know she'd give the world to make things up if only you'd give her a sign.'

Miss Crabbe began drawing geometrical patterns on the table-cloth with the handle of her spoon. Her face was set and thoughtful. She too, I guessed, had suffered considerably from the withdrawal of her young friend's adulation. Jealousy of John Franklyn was merely the outcome of her own overweening pride.

'It would be so much easier for you to make the first move,' I went on. 'You are an older, wiser woman, and if you left John Franklyn's name out of it for a bit I'm positive that the whole wretched affair would die a natural death. The man does not want it, I feel convinced. Meanwhile Hilary makes herself unhappy, and Miss Clare and her parents, and all her friends.'

'She does indeed,' said Miss Crabbe slowly and softly. She looked up from her drawing and took a deep breath.

'I'll think it over. It might be a good thing for the girl,' she said.

'It would be a great service to everyone,' I responded. Particularly to Miss Crabbe herself, I surmised privately. 'I should be very grateful indeed. She is at the start of a very promising career. A word from the right person now means such a lot.'

Miss Crabbe inclined her head graciously.

I looked at my watch.

'Would you like to come and meet my friends?' I asked. 'They have a little house in Fore Street, just round the corner.'

But Miss Crabbe excused herself, saying that she must get back to a percussion band class after tea.

We parted amicably in the hot sunshine.

'I'm glad we met,' I said truthfully, 'and do please help if you feel that you can!'

'I shall sleep on it,' Miss Crabbe assured me solemnly, 'but I think I may say, here and now, that I shall extend the olive branch to that poor misguided child.'

And so we parted, she to her percussion band class and I to my friends' cottage, where I celebrated this minor victory with scones, strawberry jam and a large dish of clotted Devonshire cream.

The countryside, as I approached Fairacre on the return drive, slept peacefully in the heat. Things were getting their shabby end-of-August look. The trees were heavy and dusty, the grassy banks parched by the prolonged sunshine, and already the farmers were busy harvesting. In the fields of one or two of the smaller farms the stooks of corn waited in neat rows for the farm carts which would take them to the ricks, but on Mr Miller's Hundred Acre Field, a combine-harvester crawled busily along, an enormous red monster that poured the grain from its gaping mouth into a truck that drove slowly beside it collecting the rich harvest. This was the crop that Miss Clare had watched growing beside her garden, throughout the year, and the one which two strangers had studied on that spring morning, so long, it seemed, ago.

The school-house at Beech Green was shuttered, I noticed, as I drove by, and Miss Clare's little house too. They would all be returning at the weekend, for school began on Tuesday morning. I sincerely hoped that Miss Clare's health would have benefited from the sea air and sunshine.

My own house greeted me with a wonderful aroma of furniture polish. Mrs Pringle had been left in charge of my household matters, the cat Tibby being the most important of her duties. This disdainful animal came down the stairs as I entered and greeted my own effusive cries with a glassy stare, never pausing in his progress to the garden.

A bottle of milk stood on the kitchen table and under it lay a note in Mrs Pringle's hand. It said:

Dear Miss Read,
Hope you have had a good time. Milk here six eggs in safe lettuce and tomattos in basket and bread in bin. Young Prince had not no holemeal but only this coberg (white).
Cat have et like a horse.

Mrs Pringle.

I boiled one of the eggs for my tea, for I had made an early start and was hungry, and carried my tray into the sunny garden. How lovely it was to be back, I thought! The garden was drooping sadly in the drought, the lawn was scorched and the garden beds were baked hard, but it still smelt fragrant and lapped me in peace, and the air from the high downs blew softly upon it all.

Tibby, seeing food, approached me lovingly and gave me, at last, a belated welcome.

I was still sitting in the garden, reading back numbers of *The Times Educational Supplement* which had piled up in my absence, when Mrs Partridge called bearing the Parish Magazine.

'Well, well, my dear!' she greeted me affectionately. 'It is so nice to see you again.'

'Tell me all the news,' I begged, pushing a deck chair towards her. She settled herself in it gingerly.

'I never quite trust them,' she confessed. 'As a child I caught my finger in one once, and the nail went quite black and had to be taken off at the hospital—'

'Please don't tell me,' I pleaded hastily, 'I'm a squeamish woman, and anything like that makes my back open and shut like Mrs Pringle's!'

Mrs Partridge smiled kindly.

'Then I won't tell you, my dear, for the sequel was perfectly horrid.' She licked her lips ghoulishly, and took a breath.

'It went septic—' she began, but I cut her short.

'DON'T!' I protested, putting my hands over my ears.

Mrs Partridge opened her eyes very wide, and I saw her lips moving. Very cautiously I took my hands away.

'So of course I won't mention it again,' she was saying. Breathing a sigh of relief I put my hands back in my lap.

'What's happened in Fairacre?' I pursued. 'Any births, deaths or marriages?'

'No. No, I don't think so,' said the vicar's wife in a slow, considering voice. Then her eyes brightened.

'But Mrs Pringle tells me that Minnie is expecting her fourth in the New Year.'

'Make a nice change to have one born in wedlock,' I said comfortably, closing my eyes against the sun's lowering rays. Mrs Partridge agreed.

'And the estate?' I ventured.

'Not a word more directly. We've heard that the Planning Committee of the County Council object to the idea. It doesn't fit in with their ideas for that area any more than it does with ours. So we're all unanimous on that point. But that's not to say there isn't plenty of strong feeling in Caxley and elsewhere. I suppose that the County Planning people will register their objections and then we all wait to see what happens.'

'All most unsettling!' I said.

'Don't let it worry you,' said Mrs Partridge gently. She leant forward and patted my knee. 'Fairacre School will always be here, and you with it, I hope, for many, many years.'

She departed very soon after this, leaving me to relish my much-loved little house and garden, the sight of the village school awaiting the new term's activities, while her comforting words rang in my head.

17. JOSEPH COGGS LEAVES HOME

Joseph Coggs was locked out. The shabby wooden door of Number 2 Tyler's Row, from which the faded paint was flaking fast, was firmly shut against him, and the little house was empty.

Mrs Coggs and the two youngest children had gone to Caxley to buy shoes for the winter, and she had forgotten, in the last minute helter-skelter rush for the bus, to put the door key in its usual hiding place.

Joseph had pelted home from school through pouring rain, had flung open the rickety gate and heaved up the old pail which served as a dustbin by the door, to find the key. It was not there. He tried the door, found it locked, shrugged his wet shoulders philosophically, and wandered down the garden path to seek shelter in the shed.

This was not the first time that Joseph had found himself locked out. His mother, poor, feckless, overworked creature, all too often forgot to put the key out in 'the secret hiding-place,' and Joseph prepared now to wait for almost an hour, when he knew the bus from Caxley was due back.

The shed was a flimsy construction of corrugated iron sheeting, and the rain drummed relentlessly and deafeningly upon it. Joseph upturned a bucket, usually used for mixing the chickens' mash and heavily encrusted with the remains of long-past meals, and sat himself down with his elbows on his knees and his chin cupped in his cold hands.

He wondered idly where his little sisters had got to. They had set off from school a few minutes before him, but he had run past them in the lane where they were blissfully paddling in a long, deep puddle with sticks in their hands with which they stirred the murky depths, quite oblivious of the rain which soaked their flimsy clothes.

'Come on 'ome !' Joseph had directed hoarsely. 'Mum won't half go on at you! Look at your shoes!'

The twins had scarcely spared a glance either for their brother or for their canvas-topped plimsolls which were almost hidden by water. They had answered him boldly: 'Don't care! Tell her then! Don't care!' they had said tauntingly.

> *'Don't care was made to care,*
> *Don't care was hung!*
> *Don't care was put in a pot*
> *And boiled till he was done!'*

shouted their brother threateningly; but seeing that they took no notice he had sped away home.

Apart from the drumming of the rain above his head and the trickling of a little stream that ran in the ditch which separated the Tyler's Row gardens from the field beyond them, Joseph found the shed very peaceful. It was a dirty place, but that did not worry Joseph unduly, for he was well acquainted with dirt. The floor was of hard earth and upon it lay an assortment of objects, poor enough in themselves, but of great service to the Coggs' family. A treacle tin, with a loop of wire for a handle, stood half full of creosote. Arthur Coggs had purloined this in order to 'do the fowl house sometime,' but so far that time had not come.

Strips of boxwood, which had once housed oranges and margarine, lay in a heap ready for kindling wood, beside a heavy bar of iron which had once been part of Mr Roberts's harrow but had 'been found' by Arthur Coggs who had prudently put it by for future use. Joseph idly turned this over and watched innumerable wood lice scurry for shelter.

He picked one up, a scaly, grey, little creature, with its myriad legs thrashing wildly. Gently, he turned it over on his palm, fascinated to see it roll itself up into a tight ball no bigger than a goose grass seed. It was like a minute football, with its even lines round and round it. Joseph tipped his grimy palm this way and that, watching his treasure roll.

At last it rolled between his fingers to the ground. The legs reappeared as if by magic and away the wood louse scuttled to find its own again. It vanished beneath a sack containing dusty straw, a sack which gave forth a strong odour of dog-biscuits and stale corn which reminded Joseph of his own stomach.

He rose and pulled out an ear or two from the musty wheat straw, and began to roll the grains between his palms. Four hard grains rewarded his labours and he chewed them contentedly enough, his old posture with elbows on knees resumed, and his gaze fixed upon the chicken run which he could see through the open door.

The bare earth there was a slimy mass of mud, starred with the marks of chickens' claws. The unhappy birds stood hunched beside their rickety house, a converted tea chest. They were in an advanced state of moult, several without tail feathers, and most showing areas of pink pimply flesh here and there.

They were sadly bedraggled and half starved, but Joseph loved them. It grieved him to see them now, almost shelterless, without food, enduring the pitiless rain upon their bare backs with such humility and hopelessness. Tears sprang to his dark eyes as he looked upon these pathetic prisoners. It wasn't fair, thought young Joseph passionately, that some birds should be able to fly wherever they liked and have all the food that they could eat and be warmly wrapped in thick feathers, while others had come out of the eggs only to find a naked hungry world awaiting them!

It did not occur to Joseph that he himself could be compared with his own unhappy hens, the victim of poverty, neglect and callous indifference, equally hungry, cold and without shelter.

He sat there as hunched as the hens, beneath his glistening ragged clothing, comforting himself by squelching his bare wet toes up and down inside his soaking canvas shoes, and watching the small bubbles bursting from their sides.

Four miles away the bus from Caxley crept slowly towards Fairacre through the puddles that swirled around its wheels.

Term was now several weeks old. An unusually silent and subdued Miss Jackson reigned in the infants' room and relations between us were strained, which was not surprising. I did not blame her for resenting my intrusion into her private affairs, and I had no knowledge of her father's handling of this delicate matter, after he had summarily removed her from Franklyn's cottage.

I had received a letter from Mr Jackson at the beginning of term thanking me for my care of his daughter and asking me, in effect, to keep an eye on her movements. This letter gave me some uneasy moments and I really wished that Mr Jackson could have quelled his very natural parental anxieties and not placed me in the dubious position of 'policeman'.

I disliked the feeling of conspiring with her father behind Hilary's back, but, after some thought, I decided to say nothing to her about the letter, and contented myself with a brief reply to the effect that Hilary seemed more settled.

The girl vouchsafed nothing about either Franklyn or Miss Crabbe, and I began to wonder whether that lady had ever written to Hilary as she had said she would. I told Hilary of our encounter in Devon, of the heat and the ices, but nothing, naturally, of our conversation. The girl's response was off-hand, and if indeed Miss Crabbe had proffered the olive branch I began to wonder if it had been spurned.

Altogether it was being a most uncomfortable term. The heat wave had given way to a long dreary spell of rainy weather, which meant that the children lacked fresh air and proper exercise, and were nearly as crotchety as their much-tried teachers.

The one bright spot was the return to good health of Miss Clare. The three weeks' rest by the sea in glorious weather had restored her considerably and she returned with a most becoming tan that showed off her white hair beautifully. Her lodger's low spirits had not gone unnoticed, but I gathered from her comments on them that the girl was genuinely more cheerful at Miss Clare's than she was in my damping presence at school.

'I think her father has written a pretty straight note to Franklyn,' she said to me, 'and forbidden Hilary to see him.' She paused, and shook her head sadly. 'But whether she does or not, I really don't know. She goes into Caxley quite often, but I can't bring myself to cross-question the child about her comings and goings. It's really not my affair at all, and I'm sure the girl has learnt her lesson now.'

'I hope so,' I answered. 'But I can't help feeling that a teaching post well away from this part of the world would be the best thing for everybody. She's a capable girl, but she needs young company. As one of a large mixed staff she'd get her corners rubbed off, and a lot of fun into the bargain!'

Our conversation was interrupted by some peremptory thudding at the door. On opening it I discovered Miss Clare's imperious cat, who deigned to enter only when I had held the door aside for a full two minutes. After this, rather naturally, our conversation turned to happier things.

But very soon afterwards an incident occurred which gave me food for thought. I had taken the car into Caxley to be overhauled after school one day, had stayed there for my tea and caught the six o'clock bus, in driving rain.

I sat in the front of the bus watching the raindrops course down the window in front of me. We made various stops, the driver good-naturedly drawing up near roadside cottages where he knew certain of his passengers lived. The bell tinged as we approached the long, lonely track up to John Franklyn's house and the bus pulled up in a sheet of water, milky with the chalk which it had collected in its journey down the side of the downs.

A man stepped off first and turned to help his companion over the puddles. It was John Franklyn, and I recognized the woman whose arm he tucked so protectively under his own. She was the same person who had accompanied him to the Flower Show – the barmaid from 'The Bell' at Caxley.

It was on this same wet day that Joseph Coggs had taken shelter in the shed. His sojourn there, surveying the wretched hens before him, had been a prelude to unsuspected drama.

Mrs Coggs had returned from Caxley wet and cross. The shoes had cost far more than she had ever imagined, and she found that a mere six shillings and a few coppers remained in her shabby purse to last her until the following Saturday night when Arthur Coggs would hand over a grudging three pounds for house-keeping.

The sight of her three older children, waiting by the rickety gate and drenched to the skin, did nothing to mitigate her despair. More firing needed to dry that lot of dripping clothes by morning, she thought bitterly, as she fished at the bottom of her basket for the key.

A reek of paraffin oil met her nostrils as she grated the door back over the grubby brick floor. It overwhelmed the usual aroma of the Coggs' household which was compounded of stale food, damp walls and unwashed clothing. The oil lamp, overturned by the cat, lay across the table, its glass chimney shattered and its precious oil seeping steadily into half a loaf of bread which had been left beside it.

Another woman, facing this final blow after so many, might have sat down and wept. Not so Mrs Coggs, who gave one piercing hysterical shriek, dropped her basket to the floor, and set about cuffing her children out of the way to relieve her feelings.

'Git on upstairs out of it, you little 'uns,' she screamed. 'Out o' this mess till we've cleared up! Git a cloth, Joe, you great ninny standing gawping!' She gave him a resounding box on the ears which sent him reeling into the diminutive scullery where the floor cloth lay. He returned with it to the dusky room, his eyes full of tears. It wasn't that he minded the box on the ears, although it had been a particularly vicious one, but he hated to see his mother in a mood like this. His father's blusterings and heavy blows he could endure equably, for he expected him to behave in that way; but that his mother should shout, and banish the youngest ones for no fault of their own, hurt Joseph.

He retrieved the bread from the floor whilst his mother set

about mopping up the oil, scolding and railing all the time. The baby, a smelly bundle still wrapped in its shawl, had been thrust into a sagging armchair, and now began to wail pathetically. It was more than tenderhearted Joe could bear. He picked a piece of bread from that part of the loaf which was still free from oil, stepped across his mother's swirling floor cloth and handed it to the baby. He himself was now faint with hunger and hoped, under cover of the darkness which was gathering quickly, to break himself a piece too. But his luck was out.

Whether he stood accidentally on his mother's hand, or whether she jerked her arm and overturned him, Joseph never knew; but he heard a scream of rage and found himself falling towards the chair. He hit his head with a crack, while behind him his mother, beside herself by this time, let fall a torrent of yelling abuse.

For Joseph, as for his poor tormented mother, this was the breaking point. Confused images of the unhappy innocent hens, of his equally innocent and helpless young brothers and sisters floated before him. Not fair, not fair! rang in his dizzy head. His mother might be cold, might be hungry, might be sad. Weren't they all? Weren't they all as wretched, sunk in the same deep pit? And more than that, he and the little 'uns and the hens were small, weak, and had to do as they were bid. They couldn't even answer back like the grown-ups could!

He struggled to his feet. He felt as though he were battered by his mother's shouting, the baby's wailing, the snufflings of his frightened sisters, and his own intense hunger and dizziness. He lurched unsteadily towards the door.

'Don't you go out!' warned his mother. 'There's plenty for you to do here, and you've ruined enough clothes for today!' Her voice grew shriller as she saw the child wrench the door open.

'Where you going?' she screamed.

'I'm clearing out of here!' growled Joseph, and ran out thankfully into the pitiless rain.

18. THE PUBLIC ENQUIRY

Fairacre tongues wagged busily one Monday morning early in October. Three notices had appeared in the village. One was fastened to the wire grille in Mr Lamb's Post Office, another was displayed by the bus stop, and the third was fixed to the notice board outside the village hall.

The notice had been issued by the Caxley Rural District Council and it announced that the Ministry of Housing and Local Government had fixed a date for a public enquiry into the proposed plans for a housing estate to be built in that area, following the objections already received to the said scheme, as put forward by the County Council.

'I'll bet Mrs Bradley's got summat to do with this,' said Mr Willet sagely to me. 'There's been talk down at "The Beetle" – and more in Caxley – about her harrying the Planning Committee with tales of Dan Crockford. And some other chap's got a bee in his bonnet about them downs.'

He knitted his brows in an effort to remember and tossed a small screwdriver thoughtfully from one horny hand to the other.

'Lor'! I'll forget my own name next!' said Mr Willet, exasperated with his own shortcomings. 'But he comes from some lot that keeps all on worrying about beauty spots and old monuments and that. Begins with a C.'

I looked blankly at him.

'Not C. of E.,' he explained, throwing the screwdriver even faster, 'but that sort of thing.'

'C.P.R.E.?' I hazarded. 'Council for the Preservation of Rural England?'

'Ah! That's it!' said Mr Willet triumphantly. 'I'll bet he's there, and old Miller, of course, and someone from the Office about the schools.' He checked suddenly, and put the screwdriver in his pocket. His expression grew embarrassed.

'If this did come, God forbid,' said he more slowly, 'would you feel like staying on, Miss Read?'

I looked from the massive brass and mahogany inkstand to the wheeling rooks that I could see through the Gothic window.

'I'd feel like staying on,' I answered.

The same notice appeared next morning in the *Caxley Chronicle*. The enquiry was to be held on the Thursday of the following week in the premises of the Caxley Rural District Council.

'And some very uncomfortable chairs they've got there,' said the vicar sadly to Mr Mawne, who was taking coffee with him that morning. 'And we're bound to take a long time.'

'Everything official takes a long time,' said Mr Mawne, shamelessly fishing out his lump of sugar and eating it with the greatest relish. 'Dash it all, all this began last spring. The R.D.C. saw the plans last June, we had our village meeting way back in July, and here we are in October, just putting the whole boiling before the Inspector from the Ministry of Whatsit! Heavens alone knows when we get the Minister's ruling!'

He helped himself to two more sugar lumps, the vicar obligingly pushing the bowl to his elbow.

'Have you any idea,' asked the vicar, 'how long we shall have to wait?'

'Might be a couple of years,' said his friend airily.

'No!' exclaimed the vicar. 'Surely not as long as that!'

'Well – might be three months,' admitted Mr Mawne grudgingly, 'but we'd be lucky! I bet the Inspector's report will find a resting place in many a tray and pigeon-hole before any decision is made.' He paused, and peered into the sugar bowl.

'I say,' he said anxiously, 'I seem to have finished the sugar!'

'No matter, my dear fellow,' answered the vicar genially, 'I don't believe it is rationed now.'

The chairs in the offices of Caxley Rural District Council were indeed uncomfortable, as the vicar had said, but that had not deterred a large number of local people from attending.

The room in which the enquiry was to be held had first been the principal bedroom of a hard-riding, wealthy merchant who had built this solid Georgian house in 1730. Three long, handsome windows, looking over Caxley High Street, let in a watery sun that flickered over wide oak floor boards, highly polished in the merchant's day by a posse of mob-capped maids, but now dull and scuffed by many feet, and grudgingly swept by one overworked old man.

At one end of the room the Inspector from the Ministry of Housing and Local Government sat, with his secretary beside him, at a big table. He was a large man, with a pendulous dewlap and heavily lidded eyes, which gave him a deceptively sleepy appearance. His manner was ponderously formal, but an astute and lively mind lay hidden behind his slow movements.

The chairs were arranged in arc-shaped rows before the table, and supported, in varying degrees of discomfort, according to the clothing and natural padding of their occupants, about sixty people.

At one side, in the front, sat various people who would be called to put forward the case for the United Kingdom Atomic Energy Authority, and on the other side were a number of people, including old Mr Miller and his solicitor, who would be called as witnesses to support the objections which had caused this public enquiry. About a dozen Fairacre folk, including the vicar, Mr Mawne, Mr Roberts and his wife, and Mrs Bradley were also present.

There was an air of expectancy in the room. The smoke from pipes and cigarettes spiralled in the sloping rays of sunshine. People spoke urgently to each other. The months of waiting, the many heart-searchings, arguments, wild rumours and distressing suspense had now reached a climax. Here, in this once-lovely room which had witnessed so much history, so many 'old, unhappy, far-off things,' yet another battle would be fought. It would be fought politely, with decorous words read from innocent slips of paper held in unbloodied hands, and the account of that battle would be jotted down in neat shorthand by the Inspector's imperturbable secretary and, in the fullness of time, would reach headquarters.

But a battle it would be, as everyone present sensed, and the Minister could be likened to a General in those headquarters, who would read the communiqué, sum up the situation and give his decision on the issues at stake.

The Inspector opened the proceedings and invited the representatives of the Atomic Energy Authority to put forward their case.

Mr Devon-Forbes, Q.C., counsel for the authority, was a tall, cadaverous individual with sardonic dark eyebrows that rose to a sharp point in the middle, like a circumflex accent. In a deep, resonant voice that rang round the room he put forward the desirability of this site for the housing of the authority's workers. He spoke feelingly of the exhaustive survey carried out as a preliminary measure to find an area which would not only prove suitable for the scheme, but would give the absolute minimum of disturbance to the local inhabitants and their environs. The scheme, if carried through, he added, his voice taking on a note as soft and seductive as black velvet, would bring many long-sought amenities to the area involved.

Mrs Bradley, at this point, wriggled on her hard chair, and said 'Tchah!' very loudly. The Inspector cast her a look from under his heavy lids, but Mr Devon-Forbes continued quite unruffled.

His first witness, he said, would be the Planning Consultant of the authority, and he bowed politely to a short sandy-haired man who came forward thrusting a pair of horn-rimmed glasses against his face and clutching a sheaf of papers. Yes, indeed, he agreed, answering counsel's suave questions, the matter had been discussed at top-level with the greatest attention. He began to unfurl a large scale map, and dropped his papers. Several people scuttled to retrieve them.

Might he pin up the map in full view, he asked? The Inspector said, 'By all means, by all means,' and indicated the beaver-boarding behind him. The map was pinned up and became the centre of attention.

The Planning Consultant then pointed out the present atomic centre, the distance involved in travelling to work from the nearby towns, the need for more workers, and the impossible congestion this would cause on towns already overcrowded, and the perfect position of the site under discussion for a new, and, he emphasised, *attractive* small township which could bring added prosperity to the neighbourhood. The authority would do every-thing in its power to see that the countryside remained unspoilt and that the project would not industrialize or urbanize the area.

Mr Devon-Forbes nodded gravely at this pronouncement and his witness was about to sit down when the Deputy Clerk of the County Council jumped up and asked if he might cross-examine.

Had the planning consultant considered the value of the area in terms of agricultural worth?

Mr Devon-Forbes said that his next witness would answer that question if the opposing counsel would allow. The Deputy Clerk sat down, and counsel called his second witness who was as he said, 'an agriculturist in general, and a soil surveyor in particular.'

Samples of the soil had been taken and statistics of the crop-yield from this area over the last twenty years had been made available, and it had been decided, after exhaustive discussion, that, agriculturally speaking, the loss would be negligible compared with the material advantages of using the site as a housing estate for people of the highest importance to the national effort.

Mr Miller here muttered something to his solicitor, who affected not to hear, but turned a very unbecoming beetroot colour.

The enquiry wound on. A formidable number of technical men were called and stated the case for the authority in varying degrees of clarity and audibility. Mr Devon-Forbes conducted his part in the affairs with firm politeness, keeping his witnesses very much to the point, but it was, as Mr Mawne had foreseen, a lengthy business.

Fidgeting became more general as the clock on the wall passed noon, and at half past, with still two more speakers to be called by Mr Devon-Forbes, and several more who had asked to be allowed to add their comments, the Inspector rose and adjourned the enquiry until after lunch.

'Terrible ol' chairs, ennum?' growled old George Bates who had worked for Mr Miller until last Michaelmas, to his crony, as they limped down the stairs. 'My bottom's fair criss-crossed!'

'Ah!' agreed his companion. 'You coming back after dinner?'

'Got to go to the dentist. He's taking out my last three, and I shan't be sorry to see they go, I can tell 'ee! One thing, I bet his chair'll have a sight more padding, whatever he does to me t'other end!'

But most of those who had attended in the morning turned up again for the afternoon session. One or two had prudently brought a cushion or a rug from the car and sat in comparative ease as the witnesses gave their testimony.

At ten to three the last speaker for the authority came forward. She was a welfare worker in one of the neighbouring towns which at present housed a large number of the employees at the power station. She spoke of the difficulties of overcrowded clinics and schools, the lack of proper playground facilities, and the incidence of childish diseases in these places. Gangs of young children, sent out to play in the streets, were already causing the local authorities headaches, and if this new estate could be built, some of the pressure in the towns could be relieved, with the consequent benefit for all concerned.

Mr Devon-Forbes then rose, cast a look around the room from under his distinguished eyebrows, and then made a short speech stating that the enquiry had now heard the authority's case, and that its evidence was now completed.

The Inspector adjourned the enquiry until the next day, and the assembly emerged into the grey October drizzle, with tea in mind.

The vicar drove Mr Mawne home to Fairacre in his rattling Ford. The drizzle became a downpour as they edged out of Caxley on to the road to Fairacre and beat in upon the vicar's clerical grey as he drove.

'Really I should have seen to this window, too,' said the vicar to his companion, 'but I so often need it open for signalling. What a good thing yours is staying up!'

He looked with pride at Mr Mawne's side of the car. A large knobbly flint, weighing two or three pounds, dangled from the end of a stout string. This was attached to the bottom handle of the window and exerted enough force to hold up the rattling pane against the weather.

'I thought of it myself,' said the vicar modestly.

Mr Mawne, who had received several vicious blows already from the swinging stone, feigned respectful surprise.

'Worthy of Leonardo da Vinci,' he assured the vicar, who glowed at the kind words.

They passed beneath the tunnel of great trees that gives Beech Green its name. The nutty autumn smell of wet leaves mingled with the rain that came through the open window. They drove in silence, occupied with their own thoughts, until the vicar stopped with a flourish at Mr Mawne's gate.

'Coming in?' asked Mr Mawne. 'Oh, I forgot! My wife's got the Ladies' Sewing Circle here, I believe.'

'Thank you, thank you, no!' said the vicar hastily. 'I must be getting back.' He rested his arms across the wheel and looked at his friend. His expression was troubled.

'What do you make of it? They had a good case, you know. Very fair, I thought, really very fair.'

Mr Mawne straightened his shoulders.

'Our turn tomorrow, with a case as good as theirs! We'll rout them, never fear. Hope and pray for the best, my dear fellow!'

'I always do that,' said the vicar simply.

There were more people than ever, next morning, willing to endure the hardship of the R.D.C.'s chairs in order to hear the case put forward by the Deputy Clerk to the County Council, who was acting counsel for the local side of the affair.

He was a large, cheerful man, with a florid complexion and a merry blue eye. His bald, pink head fringed with silky white hair, shone with health and energetic soapings. He was clad in a shepherd's plaid suit, a blue shirt and blue spotted bow-tie, and looked hearty enough to take on all comers. Those about to be called as witnesses, and others who hoped for a reprieve for the downs, felt their spirits rise as they watched their spokesman.

He called first the County's Planning Officer who made a long and thoughtful statement about the objections to the scheme. The Planning Committee were not happy about the water supply for such a large number of people, probably used to urban life where water was more freely used. (Here a few eyebrows were lifted, as several country dwellers wondered if this might be an aspersion on their cleanliness.) The disposal of sewage was another problem. At the moment a fleet of up-to-date lorries adequately coped with the present need. (Long-suffering glances were exchanged by some Fairacre folk.) But if an estate, of the size envisaged, were to be built, a sewage system on a large scale must be faced.

The roads between Caxley and other nearby towns would need to be widened, and possibly lighted, to ensure safety for the increased traffic, and he was asked by the Finance Department to state that the expense involved could not reasonably be met, even in part, from the ratepayers' pockets.

He would like to point out too, that the Planning Committee had most definite ideas for that particular site. It was an area of great beauty, scheduled as an open space, and set on canvas many times by the noted local artist Daniel Crockford. (Here a pleased hum ran round the room and Mrs Bradley thumped vigorously on the floor with her umbrella. 'Order, please,' said the Inspector mildly.)

It should be kept as an open area for all to enjoy. An ancient road – of the Iron Age, he believed, but he was a bit hazy about this – it might be Bronze, he was open to correction – but *ancient* anyway, ran along the top of the downs, and he believed that more would be said about this by another speaker. He looked questioningly at counsel, who nodded his pink-and-white head vigorously, and said, 'That is so! Yes!'

The Planning Officer then folded his notes and added that the Education Department had viewed the scheme with concern, especially in the light of their own commitments already under-taken for the next financial year, and that the Director of Education would give further particulars. He turned towards the Inspector, who was making notes, steadily.

'I do assure the Ministry, sir, that great hardship will come if this scheme goes through. Not only financial hardship, which will be heavy enough, but in losing a well loved beauty spot to all, a valuable area of agricultural land and a certain gentleman's home for several generations. The whole balance and harmony of the two small flourishing villages will be thrown out. The repercussions on farming conditions will be serious and the social life of the present population will be hopelessly disturbed. I do honestly beg the authority to reconsider their siting of the estate.'

He sat down, and the people stirred upon their uncomfortable chairs and felt that he had spoken well for them.

Mr Devon-Forbes, on being invited to cross-examine, intimated that he would prefer to do this at a later stage, and the second witness, the Director of Education, was called.

The proposed new school on the housing site, he said, had given rise to alarm in the area affected, and he had had several visits from both parents and managers who had expressed their very deep concern at the possible closing of local village schools. He had been able to assure them that the schools in question would not close, but that if the new school were built, Fairacre School would have a different status – becoming a school for infants only, with but one teacher.

The closing of any village school was not welcomed by the Committee any more than the parents. In this case, Fairacre School had already lost its 'over-elevens' to Beech Green, an adjustment not without some feeling at the time, but if all the children of eight and over were to be taken from the village daily to the new school, which was what was envisaged, he had the greatest sympathy for the parents, managers and present staff of that admirable little school.

Apart from the humane side, the cost of the new establishment would be fabulous. He had estimates with him which would make painful reading to an audience already taxed beyond endurance. The Finance Committee had already passed plans for substantial improvements to Beech Green School, to be undertaken during the next six months, and any further expense would be out of the question.

He must stress too, he added, the importance of the two present schools to the existing communities. They were perfectly suited to the needs of the villages in question. Both Beech Green and Fairacre took a lively interest in their schools, pride in their children's attainments and had expressed every confidence in the educational arrangements made for them. He would be betraying their trust if he overthrew their wishes and attempted to force a comfortably working machine to a gear beyond it.

It might be as well to make one last point, went on the Director, studying his nails minutely. The dwellers on the new estate would doubtless be drawn from urban areas, where educational conditions were different. '*Different*,' he stressed, 'but not necessarily *better!* However, they will have seen magnificent buildings, ample stock, a formidably large staff, and all the rest of it. For that reason alone, I am glad that they cannot, for reasons of space, send their children to Fairacre or Beech Green, for they would have made a great fuss about those two somewhat elderly buildings – and been as vociferous in their scoldings as they would have been silent about the excellent teaching and individual care possible with their relatively small classes. But even so they will bring a different standard to the area. They will want things – cinemas, a dance hall, a fried-fish shop possibly, which those who have lived there all their lives have not felt necessary or even desirable. They may well be difficult people to digest into the slowly grinding system of village life, and I fear that they will not add to the sum of happiness which already exists there. They may cause resentment with their larger pay-packets. They may be bored with the sort of social life that a village can offer. They will be neither flesh, fowl, nor good red herring, but just a lost tribe on a lost, once-lovely hill. In my opinion, it would be better for the authority to make several smaller estates on the outskirts of existing towns, such as this one, where the children can take advantage of the present schools, and they and their parents can be assimilated into a way of life to which they are more accustomed.'

There was a considerable amount of throat-clearing and whispering as the Director resumed his seat. The room was growing very dark, as black clouds gathered outside, and the air grew uncomfortably close. The enquiry continued, the chairs grew harder, and it was with a feeling of general relief that they saw the inspector glance at the clock, rise, and say, 'We will adjourn now for lunch, ladies and gentlemen.'

The vicar and Mr Mawne made their way to 'The Buttery' which stands conveniently near the R.D.C.'s offices.

A blast of hot air met them as they pushed their way against the heavy door.

'Beastly stuffy!' muttered Mr Mawne, undoing his coat and slinging it over the back of a pseudo oak settee. 'Hope there's something cold to eat.' He put his hand on the radiator beside the table, withdrew it with a regrettable exclamation, which the vicar affected not to hear, and called to a waitress 'to open a window and let in a bit of air.'

The vicar was studying the menu.

'Could you eat haricot mutton?' he asked.

'Good God, no!' exclaimed Mr Mawne, shuddering. 'Nothing hot, for pity's sake!'

'Then I fear it must be ham and salad,' said the vicar.

'Suits me,' said Mr Mawne. 'And an iced lager. For you too?'

'Yes, yes! Admirable!' agreed the vicar. 'It really is uncommonly close. Almost like thunder. Amazing in October.'

'Kept warmish most of the year,' answered his friend. 'The swallows were particularly late migrating this season. Ah! Here it comes!' He attacked his ham with relish, and neither spoke until he had finished.

But while the vicar ate a coffee ice, and Mr Mawne crunched celery with his biscuit and cheese, they turned to the business of the morning.

'A great deal of good sense spoken,' said the vicar. 'I wonder who is still to come?'

'The Ag. man,' said Mr Mawne elegantly, 'to tell us that that particular field is like gold-dust to the nation agriculturally. Then we're bound to get some old fogey for an hour or two about that prehistoric road along the top.'

'Heavens!' said the vicar, in some alarm. 'Do you think it might drag on till tomorrow? I've an early communion service and two churchings.'

'Never can tell!' said Mr Mawne, rummaging in his pocket for some money. 'Come on. We'd better be getting back.'

As it happened, old Mr Miller was the next to put his case, or rather Mr Lovejoy, his much-tried solicitor, did his best, by judicious questioning of his client, to set Mr Miller's various losses before the Inspector. He had an uphill job. It had taken him twenty minutes to make his points about material losses in crops, and hard cash, and the depreciation of Mr Miller's remaining property if this estate were to be built, and he was flagging a little. Mr Miller, seated by him, looked about with button-bright eyes. He had missed his usual nap, but he was still fighting fit.

Mr Lovejoy had already given a heart-rending account of his frail client being wrested from his birthplace and tottering sorrowfully towards his grave, leaving a homeless family behind him. Mr Miller had listened with barely concealed impatience, drumming on his knee in a way which his solicitor found peculiarly tiresome. He took a deep breath and embarked on the last part of his case.

'Is it any wonder?' he asked, 'that my client's health has given way, his appetite has gone, and he can no longer get about as he did?'

'Fiddlesticks!' rejoined the crusty old gentleman, rising to his feet. 'I've just ate a partridge, drunk a pint of porter, and walked to "The Blackbird" and back, my boy!'

Mr Lovejoy did his best to retrieve the situation, amidst some laughter.

'As you can see, my client is a courageous man, as full of spirit as he is full of years. But, I can assure you, and his doctor can testify, if need be, that he is not the same man since the shadow of this project fell across his birthright!' He gave a polite bow and put a solicitous hand under Mr Miller's elbow, much to that gentleman's annoyance. Together they resumed their seats.

The 'Ag. Man,' as Mr Mawne had so euphoniously called the officer of the Ministry of Agriculture and Fisheries, spoke next, and if he did not actually mention gold-dust he certainly made it clear that this was indeed a valuable agricultural area, farmed intensively by an enlightened owner who kept the land in good heart, and was a national asset. It would be a crime to see it built upon. He was sure too, that taking the long view, the building of a new town in this agricultural area would create a great deal of unemployment troubles for the farmers, already harassed by the shift to the towns of their erstwhile farm workers. It would be an unsettling influence for all concerned. He agreed with the Director of Education that these people would be better placed near the existing towns.

Outside, the rumbling of thunder made itself heard above the steady drone of the traffic in Caxley High Street. The room was so dim that the lights had to be switched on, and despite the open windows the room was oppressively hot. The list of speakers lying before the inspector gradually shortened as the afternoon wore on.

Mrs Bradley had her say, and a very spirited one it was. No one, in her opinion, had really stressed the important point, which was that this was *artistically* one of the most important landscapes in England. She reminded her hearers, forcefully, of all Dan Crockford's many pictures of the spot. She adjured them to look once again at the splendours that hung – in far too dim a light, to be sure – in their own Town Hall. It would be a lasting disgrace to Caxley if this generation sold its birthright to a pack of – to the authority, for a pot of message – a mess of pottage, and denied its children their rightful inheritance. She sat down amidst some applause.

The proceedings wound on, statements, cross-examinations and answers, and nearer and nearer grew the thunder. The rain began to beat down, like straight steel rods, and the windows had to be shut. It was stifling as the last speaker rose. He was an official from the Council for the Preservation of Rural England and he was young, ardent and appallingly long-winded.

He agreed, at length, with Mrs Bradley. He reiterated, at length, the beauties of the range of downs involved, and he pointed on the map that still embellished the wall behind the Inspector's head, to the ancient green road that ran clean through the proposed site. That alone, surely, made the whole project impossible. He sat down as Mr Devon-Forbes rose to answer. The authority had as much feeling for the historic past as had the council which Mr Brown had the honour of representing. If he had troubled to look more closely at the map he would have seen that the ancient road was to remain as it had always been, with no building within a number of specified feet. If he remembered rightly, just such a situation had arisen in Berkshire, at Harwell, where the authority had taken the greatest pains to preserve a stretch of ancient roadway – the Icknield Way, he understood – for posterity, although it ran through quite a large portion of the authority's property. His tone implied that the recalcitrant roadway, like a wayward child, had had every consideration from a much-tried nursemaid.

The inspector looked at the Deputy Clerk, who rose and said that that brought the case for the County Council to a close.

The inspector thanked all those who had attended this necessarily lengthy enquiry, promised to put his report before the Minister with all possible speed, and began to put his papers together.

A devastating crack split the sky. There was a sizzling noise, and the lights went out. Through the murk came laughter, the clatter of those wicked chairs, and above all the voice of the inspector.

'And that,' he said loudly, 'ends our enquiry.'

There was a certain amount of confusion in the twilit hall below. The vicar waited for Mr Mawne, from whom he had become parted, and saw a very young man approach Mrs Bradley. They stood together at the head of the steps down to the pavement, and effectively held up the flow of traffic.

'I thought you were wonderful!' said the young man, flushing pink. 'I'm Dan's great-nephew. Another Dan – but Dan Johnson!'

'*No!*' squeaked Mrs Bradley, in delight 'Not Lucy's boy?'

'Lucy Crockford was my grandmother.'

'Wonderful! Yes, I can see you have her eyes. Come home to tea, won't you? Stay to supper. Stay the night. Stay a week or two—'

'I can't do that, I'm afraid,' he laughed. 'I'm due in Oxford next week. I go up on Tuesday.'

'Which college?'

'Worcester.'

'Near Mac Fisheries?'

The young man wrinkled his brow with mental effort.

'I don't think so.'

'No matter. I often shop in Oxford. You must have lunch with me at the Eastgate. Heavens, how rude people are, pushing like that!'

'We'd better move,' agreed the young man, and they walked together down the steps, and out of the vicar's earshot.

'What a scrum!' gasped Mr Mawne, arriving. 'I got cornered by some ass who wanted minute instructions on how to feed a captive tawny owl!'

'The price of fame,' said the vicar benignly, leading the way to the car park.

Rivulets chortled along the gutters of Caxley, and the good citizens picked their way among the puddles. The downpour had stopped with the same dramatic suddenness with which it had started, and, although black clouds still hung in the sky over the distant downs, the sun shone.

Sparkling raindrops slid along the telegraph wires, and awnings were beaded with diamonds. The vicar and Mr Mawne drove up Caxley High Street, splashing sedately through the water, and heading towards the black cloud that hung, like the threat which still lowered, above the two villages.

'Look at that!' exclaimed Mr Mawne, ducking his head and peering up into the sky above the windscreen. The vicar followed his gaze.

Arched above them, a flamboyant and iridescent arc across the dark cloud, shone a rainbow. The vicar smiled at his friend.

'Let us hope it is an augury,' he said. And, stepping on the accelerator, he set the nose of his rattling car on the road to Fairacre.

PART FOUR

Calm After Storm

* * * *

19. Mrs Coggs Fights a Battle

When Joseph Coggs fled, in frantic despair, from the domestic hell of Tyler's Row, he had no plan in mind but escape from intolerable conditions. The wind howled in the trees above the road as he ran headlong, through the rain-swept darkness, towards the centre of the village.

He still burned with injustice, and was as frightened by the magnitude of his own rage as he was by the fury of the storm around him. Habit led his steps towards the school, and, still sobbing, he found himself at the school gate with the bulk of St Patrick's looming blackly against the dark sky.

All was in darkness, except for a faint ruddy glow from behind the red curtains of the school-house. But Joseph was in no mood to approach authority. Authority meant his mother, his father, scoldings, railings, and forced obedience to unbearable circumstances.

Joseph turned his back upon the light and looked, with awe, at the church. It would be dry in there, but nothing would induce him to find shelter in a building which, to his superstitious mind, might house the dead as well as the living. What should he do?

He became conscious for the first time of his own position. His clothes were so wet that he could feel the cold trickles running down his shivering body. He was dizzy with hunger and fatigue. He had left home and there was no going back. He walked slowly and hopelessly to the school door. It was locked, as he had expected. The great, heavy ring which acted as handle to the Gothic door lay cold and wet in Joseph's hand, denying him entrance.

Joseph leant his head against the rough wood and wept anew. Tears and rain dripped together upon his soaked jersey, but as he rested there, abandoned to grief, a small, metallic sound revived his hopes. The rain was making music upon the empty milk crates beside the door-scraper. Those two milk crates, piled one on top of the other, would enable him to reach the lobby window and Joseph knew full well that that window had a broken catch.

He dragged the crates noisily along by the wall and struggled up. Sure enough, the tall narrow window tilted up under pressure and Joseph struggled through into the lobby closing the window behind him. Breathlessly, he made his way into his classroom, not daring to switch on the light lest he should be discovered.

It was warmer in here, for the tortoise stove still gave out a dying heat, but it was terrifyingly eerie. The floorboards creaked under Joseph's squelching canvas-topped shoes as he approached the stove. He held his thin hands over its black bulk and looked fearfully about him at the shadowy classroom. The moon-face of the clock gleamed from the wall. Its measured tick was the only companionable sound in the room. The charts and papers pinned to the partition glimmered like pale ghosts, and the ecclesiastical windows, gaunt and narrow, filled Joseph with the same super-stitious terror that St Patrick's had done. He turned again to the comfort of the homely stove, and remembering the little trap-door at its foot which he had seen Mrs Pringle adjust, he bent to examine it through the bars of the fire guard.

He lifted up the metal flap and was enchanted to see a red spark fall from the embers. He crouched down beside it and with growing wonder watched the grey cinders glow again as the air blew through. His spirits rose as the warmth began to grow, and he set about making himself more comfortable.

He crept back into the windy stone-floored lobby and collected two coats which had been left there. He stripped off his wet jersey, his poor shirt and his heavy wet trousers, wrung them out into the coke scuttle and spread them to dry along the fire guard. His ragged vest was almost as wet, but modesty made him continue to wear it. He fought his way into a coat much too small for him, spread the other on the floor by the stove, and lay down, well content, where he could look straight into the minute cavern of glowing cinders inside the trap-door.

He was almost happy. In the arrangements he had made for his own comfort he had forgotten the past miseries which had led to his flight. Only one thing bothered him, an all-invading hunger beside which every other trouble dwindled into insignificance. His mind bore upon this problem with increasing urgency. What was there to eat in school?

He remembered Miss Read's sweet tin, but knew that the cupboard would be locked. Earlier in the evening he would have wept at this remembrance, but he was past tears now. To survive he must eat. To survive, to eat, he must think.

He sat up, looked around him, and relief flooded over him, for there in the shadows near the door was the nature table, and he himself had helped Miss Read to arrange 'Fruits of the Autumn'. He scrambled to his feet and ran towards this richness. A shiny cooking apple, as big as his baby brother's head, was the finest prize the table yielded, but there were a few nuts and a spray of blackberries.

Gleefully he returned to his coat on the floor and sat cross-legged. In the shadowy school room, his tear-strained face gilded in the glow from the stove, Joseph Coggs thankfully munched his apple, while the storm raged furiously outside.

In ten minutes' time, with every scrap of food gone, he lay curled up, sleeping the sleep of the completely exhausted.

He woke once during the night. The rain had ceased and a pallid moon shone fitfully between the ragged clouds that raced across the sky. A mouse, disturbed by his movement, scurried across the floor to its home behind the raffia cupboard, and Joseph caught a glimpse of its vanishing tail.

The stove had gone out and the room felt much colder. The draught from the window stirred the papers on the walls, and there was a little sibilant whispering from a straw which had escaped Mrs Pringle's broom, as it moved to and fro across the floorboard in which it was caught.

Joseph lay there quite unafraid. What had happened was too big, too important, too far-away to take in. He was drained of all feeling. Nothing really mattered now except the fact that he was safe and at peace. Someone else must bother about his mother, the howling babies, the upturned lamp, the wretched chickens. He was too tired.

He rolled over again upon his hard bed, conscious only of the relief of being alone with enough room to stretch himself, in quietness and shelter.

It was there, fast asleep on the floor before the cold stove, that Mrs Pringle found him at eight o'clock the next morning.

At Tyler's Row Joseph's flight had had unexpected consequences. Before Mrs Coggs had had time to collect her scattered wits, her husband had entered. Work had stopped early on the building where Arthur Coggs was engaged because of the torrential rain. The overturned lamp was now upright and burning, but the children continued to whimper, awaiting their tea, and the house still reeked of paraffin oil.

'Where's the grub?' growled Arthur Coggs, slinging his wet cap and coat on to that same chair which had upset his first born. 'And shut your noise!' he bawled at the snivelling youngsters.

It was too much for Mrs Coggs. Years of abuse, hard words and hard blows, culminating in this disastrous day, made her suddenly and loquaciously bold.

'Shut your own!' she screamed at her flabbergasted husband. He began to raise a massive fist, but she advanced upon him, with such fire sparking from her eyes, that he stepped back.

'Joe's run off and I don't blame him. Any more of your tongue and I'll go after him, and you can look after the kids yourself!'

'Now then! Now then!' began Arthur Coggs, in a menacing growl. 'Mind what you're—'

'I mean it – straight!' panted his distracted wife. 'I can't stand no more. I'm off to the police!' She meant to ask for their help in finding Joseph, but her husband's guilty conscience construed this last remark as a reflection on his own wrong-doing. Alarmed at this fresh independence displayed by his wife, he became conciliatory.

'Here, don't take on like that! What if Joe has gone off? He'll be back for his tea, you see.'

'That he won't,' responded Mrs Coggs. 'I'm off after him!' She began to push past him to the door but Arthur Coggs stopped her.

'You make us a cup o' tea, gal, and I'll have a look round,' he said, gently. He put on his coat and cap again and went thoughtfully out into the downpour.

His wife watched him go grimly, arms akimbo. The worm had turned.

He returned fifteen minutes later. The children were seated at the table demolishing thick doorsteps of bread and margarine. His own plateful of baked beans and rasher stood ready for him.

'Anyone seen him?' cried his wife anxiously, hand on heart.

'No. But I told old Lamb at the Post Office and he said he'd keep a lookout.'

'Fat lot of good that was!' commented his wife.

Arthur Coggs lied quickly. 'And I saw the copper on his bike. Going on home he was, so I let him know our Joe were out somewhere!' His wife looked at him suspiciously.

'It's the truth!' protested Arthur, beginning to bluster. 'And I'll tell you another thing – if he ain't home before bedtime we'll leave the doors unlocked so's the kid can get in.'

'I'll go out meself,' answered his wife resolutely, 'as soon as this lot's finished with.' She looked at her gobbling brood, at the poor, scanty meal, the cracked plates, the meagre fire and at her shifty, lying bully of a husband. The new-found fire burnt steadily within her and gave her unquenchable courage. She turned upon him again furiously.

'You've driven our Joe to this,' she told him shrilly, 'I went for him, I knows that, but only because I was that worried and fed-up. If I'd had a good man behind me all these years, there'd be no need for us all living worse than pigs. Things is going to alter here, Arthur Coggs, or, mark my words, you faces the lot on your own! I'm off otherwise, back to service, with good meals and decent people. I been a fool too long I reckons!'

The tears were running down her cheeks as she ended this tirade. The children watched her open-mouthed and Arthur Coggs, for once, was beyond speech.

Mrs Pringle presented Joseph Coggs to me just as I was about to lift my breakfast egg out of the saucepan. I had never seen a child look so exhausted.

'Asleep on the floor!' said Mrs Pringle dramatically. 'Lord! That give me a start! "What on earth can that old bundle of rags

be adoing down there?" I thought to myself – when, all of a sudden, it moved!'

Mrs Pringle threw her hands up in astonishment.

'And been there all night, he says. What'll his poor ma be doing?'

'Be a dear and take a message down,' I begged. 'The stoves can wait. I'll give him breakfast while you're gone.'

Pleased to be the bearer of such momentous tidings Mrs Pringle hurried off with not the slightest trace of a limp, whilst I returned to my visitor.

'Do you like boiled eggs?' I asked him. He nodded dazedly. His eyes were puffy, his face and hands filthy and I led him to the sink while his two eggs boiled.

I stripped the child's dirty clothes from his waist up and gave him a thorough wash, as he stood silently impassive. He was pathetically thin, every rib showing and his ebony shoulder blades protruding like a fledgling's wings. Here and there was an ugly bruise and the poverty-stricken smell of accumulated dirt and neglect hung around his fragile form. I wished that I had time to bath him properly, but after redressing him and combing his matted hair, I looked upon my breakfast guest with pride.

I let him eat before doing a little tentative questioning. The child seemed too listless, too dazed and too bewildered to do more than grunt a 'yes' or 'no' to my few queries, but it was enough to give me a true and heart-breaking glimpse of all that Joseph had endured throughout his short life.

By the time his mother arrived I had already decided that someone in authority would have to tackle this family problem. I had foreseen a forlorn, negative hopelessness from Mrs Coggs, but was pleasantly surprised to find that, though red-eyed with weeping, she was in fighting trim. To my suggestion that the County Medical Officer should take a look at Joseph and his sisters in the school, and that he might be able to give some help, her face lit up.

'I only wants a hand,' she said. ' 'Tis that ol' house and all the kids. And Arthur's no help, as you knows, miss. If he brought his money home regular, us might've had a real house by now.'

I said that the Medical Officer might be able to pass their case forward to the housing committee. Something should be done, I promised her.

'I wouldn't know where I was!' she said wonderingly. She looked bemusedly about my kitchen, at the sink, the electric kettle, at the checked tablecloth and the breakfast food.

Joseph returned with his mother to Tyler's Row, there to sleep in his own bed.

'Let him come up to school dinner if he's awake by then,' I said to Mrs Coggs as they went down the path. 'And I won't forget to do what I can to help.'

And I should have done it long ago, I scolded myself, as I collected a pile of books and made ready to go over to the school. I made up my mind to get in touch with the vicar that same day. Two heads would be better than one, as Mr Willet no doubt would tell me, and between us the desperate conditions of Tyler's Row should be lightened by some hope from the county authorities.

Yes, I thought, remembering Mrs Coggs, the worm had turned indeed, and as it later transpired, the fortune of the whole Coggs family too. For before the end of the year the council house, which had been the home of old Shepherd Burton's family, became vacant, and the Coggs family was immediately moved in.

Mrs Coggs' new-found spirit glowed steadily in these surroundings. Arthur Coggs, in flabbergasted obedience to a court order, found himself handing over a fixed sum of money to his wife each week, and the whole of Fairacre voiced its approval. It was generally agreed that Joseph's rebellion on that stormy autumn evening had been 'a real blessing in disguise.'

20. MISS JACKSON HEARS BAD NEWS

The autumn term slipped by. The elm trees, overshadowing the school, now stood in gaunt majesty, the wind from the downs blew breathtakingly cold and the first signs of Christmas were abroad.

The children were busy preparing a nativity play, and during handiwork lessons the pile of Christmas presents for parents, such as smudgy calendars, bumpy raffia mats and little hankies bearing here and there a needle-prick of blood from some hard-worked fingers, grew apace.

In the village shop delicious boxes of crackers glowed on the shelves and further delights were to be found at the Post Office, which also sold sweets.

Cheek by jowl with the red sealing wax and foolscap envelopes stood pink and white sugar mice with string tails, chocolate watches and tiny jars filled with minute satin cushions, all waiting to deck some cottage Christmas tree.

The younger children, under Miss Jackson's care, grew daily more excited, and I dreaded to think of the pandemonium which would greet the ceremony of 'hanging up the paper chains.' These grew at an incredible rate, scarlet linking yellow, yellow blue, blue silver, silver green, cascading down the sides of desks, lying in great rustling heaps on the floor and sending the makers into ecstasies. They plied their paste brushes madly, their faces flushed and their eyes sparkling. But Miss Jackson seemed unmoved.

I spent an evening with Miss Clare and our conversation turned to the girl. Miss Clare was busy knitting a pair of blue dungarees for Malcolm Annett's Christmas present.

'I hear that John Franklyn has found another attraction,' she told me, as her busy needles clicked. 'Mrs Fowler's niece who works at "The Bell".'

'Is it true, do you think?' I asked.

Miss Clare lowered her knitting and looked steadily across at me. 'I'm quite sure it is. It seems to be general knowledge that the two are about together everywhere. Frankly, it seems the best thing for everybody. They are neither of them particularly like-able people, but they would suit each other very well and I'm sure she is a good-hearted woman who would welcome little Betty Franklyn if the aunt wanted to part with the child.'

'And what about Hilary?' I asked. 'Does she know?'

'I think she must have an inkling. I'm pretty sure that she doesn't see the man as often as she did. But she says nothing.'

'Well, if she doesn't know now,' I said, 'she will pretty soon, if I know anything about village life!'

Mrs Pringle had more to say on the subject as she washed up after school dinner. Miss Jackson had taken the savings money to the Post Office to buy stamps, and Mrs Pringle took advantage of her absence to probe into this delicate matter.

'Seems as though the wedding bells'll be ringing out again,' she said, with ponderous jocularity. She swilled down the draining board with a sizzling hot dish-cloth that would have scalded a less asbestos-like hand.

'Mrs Fowler was telling me she helped her niece write out an advertisement for her engagement for The Paper.' The *Caxley Chronicle* is always spoken of in this way for it commands well-deserved respect from its few thousand loyal readers.

'Be a shock to some, I dare say,' continued the old harpy, with morose relish, 'but best in the end. The Lord giveth and the Lord taketh away!'

I always find Mrs Pringle's invoking of divine support par-ticularly irritating, especially when her mind is working mali-ciously. I tried to pin her down.

'Who do you think will find the engagement a shock?'

Mrs Pringle bridled self-righteously, tucking her three chins firmly against her black jumper.

'It's not my place to say. But this I do know. The gentleman – so-called – has been paying attentions to someone not a hundred miles from here. And there's no knowing what *she* might feel about it – the poor, put-upon, innocent soul!'

Mrs Pringle uttered this last with an affecting tremor in her voice and with her eyes upraised piously to the clouds of steam near the ceiling.

Luckily, the entry of Miss Jackson with the savings stamps called a halt to our discussion.

Nothing more had been heard officially about the new housing estate, but the matter hung ominously at the back of people's minds.

Dr Martin stood at Miss Clare's window looking at the brown furrowed beauty of Hundred Acre Field.

'I'd hate to think this is the last winter we'd see it like that,' said the doctor thoughtfully.

'Sometimes,' answered his patient in a far-away voice, 'I think I'd like this winter to be my last one.'

Dr Martin turned and looked swiftly at her. Her blue eyes gazed serenely into space. He crossed to the chair where she sat, and looked down with mock severity.

'Now, none of that, Dolly. You'll see eighty yet!'

Miss Clare smiled at him.

'What a bully you are! I'm very, very tired you know. I often sing that little bit of Handel to myself.

> "Art thou weary?
> Rest shall be thine,
> Rest shall be thine".'

Miss Clare sang in a small voice, as sweet and clear as a winter robin's.

The doctor stood in silence, watching his old friend meditatively. When he spoke it was with more than usual robustness.

'Tonic for you tomorrow, my girl! A *large* bottle, with plenty of iron in it!'

'We must move,' said Mrs Mawne decisively to her husband, 'if this estate comes. The place won't be fit to live in!'

'I fear that we shall have to face much more responsibility,' said the vicar soberly to his wife, 'if our parish houses so many more souls. It is a very great trust – and we're neither of us getting younger, my dear.'

'Pretty well double my turnover, this will,' said Mr Prince, the baker at Fairacre.

'I shall have to give over the dining-room to Christmas cards next year,' commented Mr Lamb at the Post Office, surveying his cramped stock.

'This hanging about will dam' well kill me!' exploded old Mr Miller in his threatened farm house.

And thus spoke many in Fairacre and Beech Green as they chafed under this intolerable burden of suspense.

It remained for Mr Willet to sum up the matter.

'Ah! It's a bad time for us all, waiting and wondering. Which reminds me. I've chose my words for my gravestone. What d'you think of that, Miss Read?

> "Good times
> Bad times
> All times
> Pass over".'

'For last words on a subject, Mr Willet,' I said, 'you couldn't do better.'

On the Saturday morning following my conversation with Mrs Pringle, I went to Caxley to buy Christmas cards.

As usual this was no light task. After overcoming the initial shock of staggeringly high prices (unconsciously I still expect something rather distinguished for fourpence!) I found further difficulties confronting me. Despite the plethora of cards on view in the stationer's they seemed to fall into comparatively few classes – arch poodles, ladies in crinolines and ringlets accompanied by mawkish verses, stage coaches hurtling through cheering spectators waving beaver hats, and cards of a religious nature bearing three camels and a star embossed in gold.

Whilst I was turning over morosely a pile of cards showing puppies in hampers and kittens in boots, someone spoke. It was John Franklyn's sister-in-law, the woman who was looking after his daughter Betty, in Caxley.

'I haven't seen you for a long time,' she said, and my mind flew back to the scene in the vicar's garden on the day of the fête. As though she could read my thoughts, she went on.

'Have you heard that my brother is engaged to the young lady we saw him with at the fête?'

I said that I had heard, but had wondered if it were just a rumour.

The woman's eyes grew troubled. 'No, it's no rumour. It'll be in The Paper this week.' She put her hand, in a sudden confiding gesture, on my arm.

'Break it to that poor girl,' she pleaded urgently. 'She was in a fair taking about him. Not that it's not all for the best, as it's fallen out – but it'll come hard if she sees it without warning.'

I promised to do what I could, shelved the comparatively simple problem of Christmas cards and left the shop pondering on this knottier one.

As any teacher will tell you, Monday morning is a hectic time. What with notes from mothers, dinner money, savings money, returned absentees, new children and other distractions, affairs of the heart, however pressing, have to take second place.

I was considerably perturbed about the best way to approach this delicate subject, and decided that after midday dinner would perhaps be a good time to make as casual a mention of it as I could. But it was not to be. Linda Moffat complained of severe stomach pains and looked so wretchedly ill at dinner time that Miss Jackson took her home to her mother.

It was not until school was over for the day and the children had run and skipped their way through the school gate to the lane that the opportunity occurred for an uninterrupted conversation.

Hilary Jackson came across to the school-house to borrow a book and, taking a deep breath, I made a cautious approach. I remembered our last catastrophic clash over John Franklyn, on that distant thundery day. The sound of that storm still echoed in my ears as I began reluctantly.

'I hope you will forgive me for asking you something very personal,' I said gently.

Hilary Jackson looked round from the bookshelves, wide-eyed. 'Good lord, no! What's that?'

I began to feel like a babykiller, but I stuck to it doggedly. 'It was about John Franklyn—' I began. Hilary drew in her breath so sharply, that I knew at once that I had no need to break any news to the girl. She already knew the truth.

She dropped the book she was holding, and with a dreadful despairing cry crumpled down on to the floor, pillowing her head in my armchair. Her shoulders shook with her sobbing and I stood there watching her, feeling powerless to help.

At last she lifted a blotched, woebegone face to me.

'Yes, I know, I know! And what's to become of me?' she burst out tragically. 'What's to become of me?'

21. THE PROBLEM OF MISS CLARE

The *Caxley Chronicle* carried the notice of John Franklyn's engagement the next day, and Miss Jackson went sad-eyed about her affairs, the object of much sincere pity in the village. Although she had never made much effort to be pleasant to the parents and friends of the school she was young and in love, and the romantic heart of the village was stirred. It rose to her support to a man.

'Enough to make your heart bleed!' announced Mrs Pringle lugubriously, laying a hand upon her afflicted member. Mr Willet, who was present, was much too delicate-minded to have mentioned the subject on his own, but was stung into speech by Mrs Pringle's dramatic excesses.

' 'Tis good riddance to bad rubbish,' he asserted sturdily, 'whatever you old women says, making sheeps' eyes over something that's none of your business. She'll get over it, and thank her lucky stars she's rid of him!'

Mrs Pringle bridled and looked to me for support. 'Broken hearts don't mend so easy, do they, Miss Read?' she said with dreadful meaning.

I could only think that she was harping back to the long-forgotten affair of Mr Mawne and I replied with some tartness. 'I agree with Mr Willet,' I said with finality and watched Mrs Pringle retreat, registering extreme umbrage by her rigid back and severe limp.

But comfort was in store for Hilary Jackson.

The next day had dawned clear and bright, one of those sparkling December days all the more precious because they are so rare.

The bare black elm trees looked as though they were drawings in charcoal sketched delicately against the wintry pale blue sky. The smoke from the village chimneys rose in straight columns, the larks sang as though spring itself had burst upon them, and our spirits soared with them.

At morning playtime the children scampered eagerly outside with no prompting from their teachers. Cowboys, Indians, mothers-and-fathers, horses, spacemen and an occasional idle dreamer disported themselves in the playground, revelling in the warm sunshine.

Miss Jackson was taking playground duty, and even her sad heart appeared to be a trifle cheered by the weather.

I went indoors to put on the kettle for our elevenses and found the telephone ringing.

'I have a call for you,' said a distant voice. The line crackled and buzzed whilst I waited. Should I make a quick dash for the kettle, I wondered? It would be getting hot while I sat there.

'Have you finished?' asked a peremptory woman.

'No,' I answered aggrieved. 'I haven't even started!'

'Hold on!' commanded the voice. I held on whilst some violent clicking noises exploded against my eardrum. By this time I had imagined the worst. All my relatives had been taken ill, met with serious accidents, been wrongly imprisoned, and were, each and all, in urgent need of immediate help. I had mentally rearranged the timetable, enabling the school to be taught for the rest of the day by Miss Jackson alone, chosen a suitable wardrobe for travelling at a moment's notice in all directions, composed a note for Mrs Pringle about the household chores, and made arrangements for the cat's welfare, when another voice broke through the crackling.

It was, unmistakably, Miss Crabbe's.

'Is Hilary there?' she asked, sensibly going to the point at once and not spending ninepence on fatuous enquiries after my own health. I said I would fetch her at once, and fled to the playground.

'Miss Crabbe's on the telephone,' I said breathlessly, 'and wants a word with you.' If I had expected Hilary Jackson's face to light up I should have been disappointed. A distinctly sullen look was added to her dejected appearance.

'Oh! I'd better go, I suppose,' she answered resignedly, and departed into my house, while I remained outside among the hurtling bodies and ear-splitting shrieks of my pupils.

In a few minutes she returned, transfigured.

'She's wonderful—' she began.

'Miss,' shouted a child deafeningly, his face upturned by my waist. 'Miss, ol' George says there ain't no Father Christmas! NO FATHER CHRISTMAS!' he reiterated in an appalling crescendo.

'I'll see about it later,' I shouted back, above the din. With any luck, I thought cravenly, the dispute will be forgotten by then.

'Let's get the kettle on,' I said to Miss Jackson, 'and you can tell me in peace!'

'She's asked me to go to Switzerland with her, for the Christmas holidays,' burst out my assistant, and now her eyes were like stars, I noticed. 'The friend she was going with has been taken ill, and has had to cry off. I've always wanted to go to winter sports! Isn't it simply marvellous?'

It was a tonic to see the poor child in such good heart again, and I was glad too that at last she had made her peace with Miss Crabbe. This reconciliation and the wonderful holiday to look forward to should cure effectively the wounds made by John Franklyn.

'I'm absolutely delighted!' I told her honestly, and we fell to discussing ski clothes and kit, what to buy outright and what to hire, how much money one might need, the best method of travel and a hundred and one other matters whose discussion is as much part of the fun as the holiday itself.

I put the sugar and milk in our two cups, still chattering, and with one eye on the children whom I could see through the dining-room window. I raised the tea pot and poured a stream into Miss Jackson's cup. Shaking with laughter, she directed my attention to the liquid. It was crystal clear. In the excitement of the moment we had forgotten the tea.

*

The last few days of term sped by in an atmosphere of mounting excitement. The spring term, which normally lasts from January until early April, is acknowledged by the teaching profession to be the most gruelling of the three, but the two weeks at the end of the Christmas term, particularly in the infants' school, run a close second, from a class teacher's point of view.

The climax came with the customary Christmas party in the schoolroom on the last afternoon. Parents and friends joined in the time-honoured games. 'Cat and Mouse,' 'Hunt the Thimble,' and 'Oranges and Lemons,' and Miss Clare came to play the ancient piano, a period piece with a filigree walnut front through which one had a glimpse of once-scarlet pleated silk. It must have been an object of great beauty in its early Victorian days, and even now adds an archaic dignity to our schoolroom, standing against the wall like a well-bred, elderly chaperon watching over our revels.

The yellowing keys tinkled plangently under Miss Clare's fingers as she played. Her face was pink with happiness at being among the children once more, and I began to wonder, for the first time, if loneliness perhaps, was the major cause of her general decline in health. Certainly, on the afternoon of the party, she glowed like an autumn rose. I determined to give the matter more attention during the holidays.

The vicar cut the presents from the sparkling Christmas tree, we all sang carols together, wished each other a Merry Christmas, and went out into the darkness.

Miss Clare, Miss Jackson and I watched the torches bobbing away down the lane, like fireflies, before we locked the school door upon the débris within, which was to await tomorrow's ministrations.

Later that evening I drove the two back to Beech Green and accepted an invitation to tea the next day.

It would be Miss Jackson's last meal at Beech Green before catching the night plane with Miss Crabbe to Switzerland, and she was as excited and as whole-heartedly happy as the children had been at their party.

As she chattered, Miss Clare and I exchanged secret smiles compounded of relief and extreme satisfaction. Franklyn was forgotten!

I spent the next day packing Christmas parcels and sending off my Christmas cards, jobs which have to be left until the whirl of end-of-term festivities are over. The house was refreshingly peaceful, and I pottered about enjoying my leisure and solitude.

It is deeply satisfying to me, after spending so much of my time among a number of energetic young people, to hear the clink of a hot coal and the whisper of flames in my own chimney, the purring of Tibby delighting in company, and the chiming of the clock on the mantelpiece. All these domestic pleasures tend to be taken for granted by the normal housewife, for they are her working conditions as well as her home, but they have an added appealing charm for the woman who is forced by circumstances to spend only part of her time at home. As I went happily about my small affairs I turned over in my mind the problem of Miss Clare. It seemed right to me that I should offer her a home with me at Fairacre school-house if she would like to come. I was beginning to see that she should not live alone, and that even if she had a lodger for some time to come, it would not be many years – or perhaps months – before that would become too much for her.

There were many factors to consider, I knew. Miss Clare would not want to give up her independence and her life-long home any more than I, or anyone else, would. She would hate to feel that she was imposing on anyone, and I certainly might prove an awkward person to live with. I remembered wryly, with what relief Miss Jackson had quit my portals, not so long ago! But I intended to make the offer. She would have companionship, someone in the house at night when she might be in urgent need, be within sight and sound of the children during the daytime, and have a house which would be probably more comfortable, if not as dear to her, as her own cottage.

A small faint regret about my own precious solitude I thrust resolutely and fiercely from me. I was getting downright selfish and it would do me a power of good to have someone else to consider. I went off to the tea party hoping for a chance to put my suggestion forward.

Miss Clare had drawn her round table close by the crackling

fire. There were hot buttered crumpets under a covered dish and a very fine dark fruit cake covered with nuts.

As we ate the crumpets, with butter oozing deliciously over our fingers, Miss Clare poured tea. She had brought out the family silver teapot for this state occasion, a wonderful fluted object with a yellowed ivory knob like a blanched almond.

'I've made a large Christmas cake,' said Miss Clare nodding at the one before us, 'from the same mixture. You must sample this and tell me if it's good.' She began to recite the recipe, a list of so many mouth-watering ingredients including raisins, cherries, brown sugar and brandy, that it was like listening to a particularly luscious and fleshly poem.

Miss Jackson, resplendent in a new dark red suit, watched the clock eagerly. Mr Annett, who was going to meet his father-in-law at the county town, had offered to take her in to catch a fast train. He was due at half past five.

'Remember me to Miss Crabbe,' said Miss Clare, 'and I hope that she'll come down here again when the evenings are lighter.'

'I'm sure she'd like to,' responded Miss Jackson, warmly. She paused while she cut a piece of cake carefully into fingers and then looked from one of us to the other. 'She means a great deal to me. I'm beginning to realize that trouble shows you your real friends.'

Miss Clare nodded gravely, and it was at this moment that we heard the hooting of Mr Annett's car at the gate.

Miss Jackson fled upstairs for her things and we all escorted her down the garden path to the gate.

'Enjoy yourself!'

'Have a lovely holiday!' we called into the darkness, as we waved good-bye to the back of the disappearing car.

We washed up the tea things and settled thankfully one on each side of the roaring fire. The wind was rising outside, and though I should dearly have loved a holiday in Switzerland, I was glad that I was not setting off on such a long journey. An aeroplane seemed a very flimsy little thing to be conflicting with the mighty winds which were at large, sweeping the dark heavens.

I steered the conversation to the state of Miss Clare's health and her hopes for the future.

'Everyone worries far too much about me,' she said gently. 'I think I shall be able to manage here for some time yet. And I must say, that with Miss Jackson looking more cheerful, the outlook is much more hopeful for me. It's just at night sometimes—' Her voice died away and she looked into the fire. Taking a deep breath I unfolded my proposals.

Miss Clare listened in silence. When I had finished, she leant forward and took my hand.

'I can't thank you enough, but I'm going to tell you something. George Annett has promised that if ever Miss Jackson leaves me he will find a really easy lodger from his own school to take her place – so that I have no financial worries. And if my health should fail, and I have to leave this little house, he and Isobel have another plan. But I won't speak of that. I hope I may be here for many years.'

She bent down and put two logs of apple wood on the fire. Their sweet outdoor fragrance began to creep about the firelit room.

'For a woman who loves solitude as much as you do,' she continued, 'and who gets so little of it – I think you have made a superhuman offer. But I don't think the need will arise for me to accept such kindness.'

'It will stand anyway,' I told her truthfully.

Miss Clare stood up. 'Have a glass of home-made wine,' she said briskly. She went to a corner cupboard, high on the wall, and produced a deep red bottle that glowed like a ruby.

'Plum,' she said with satisfaction, 'and two years old!'

She trickled it into two wine glasses, brought mine over to me, and then raised her own.

'I'm thinking of Hilary's remark,' she said. 'To our friends!'

We sipped, smiling at one another.

22. Fairacre Waits and Wonders

The Nativity Play, which took place in St Patrick's church three days before Christmas, had occasioned almost as much comment as the proposed estate. This was the first time such a thing had been attempted and the innocent vicar, whose only thought had been of his parishioners' pleasure in praising God in this way, would have been flabbergasted could he have heard some of the criticisms.

'Nothing short of popery!' was Mr Willet's dictum. 'Play acting in a church! I don't hold with it!'

'It's been going on for years,' I pointed out mildly. 'Churches were used quite often to perform plays for the people.'

'When?' asked Mr Willet suspiciously.

'Oh, a few hundred years ago,' I replied.

'Then it's about time we knew better,' was Mr Willet's unanswerable retort.

The children had been practising their part in it for several weeks, and I knew that Mr Annett as choirmaster had been busy with the singing which was to form part of the play. Several parents had spoken to me, rather as Mr Willet had, expressing their grave concern about what one called 'doing recitations in the Lord's House.' The singing passed without comment.

But on the evening in question Fairacre's villagers turned up in full force and it was good to see the church packed. A low stage had been erected at the chancel steps and the setting was the stable at Bethlehem.

The church looked lovely, decorated for Christmas with holly wreaths and garlands of ivy, mistletoe and fluffy old-man's-beard. On the altar were bowls of Christmas roses and white anemones. Only candlelight was used that evening, and the golden flames flickered like stars here and there in the shadows of the ancient church.

The play was simple and moving, the country people speaking their parts with warm sincerity, but it was the unaccustomed beauty of the boys' singing that was unforgettable. Mr Annett had wisely set aside several passages for the boys alone and their clear oval notes echoed in the high vaulted ceiling, with thrilling beauty. Whatever may have been said about such goings-on in church before the play, everyone agreed, as they stopped to talk afterwards in the windy churchyard, that it was a moving experience.

'The vicar could've done a lot worse,' conceded Mr Willet. And that indeed was high praise.

The holidays slipped by with incredible speed and early in January I was facing the school again at our first morning of the New Year.

There were thirty-six children now on roll and I wondered, as I watched them singing, how many I should see before me at the same time next year. Would all these older children, now making the partition rattle with their cheerful voices, have been wrested from Fairacre and be adding their numbers to those at the new school, standing on what had once been Hundred Acre Field? Would I have a handful of infants, and remain here, the sole member of staff, with one of the rooms empty of children after nearly eighty years? It was a depressing and disturbing thought and it had occurred to me more often than I cared to admit to anyone. This was my life, as satisfying and rewarding as ever a woman could ask for, and the thought of change distressed me.

Mr Willet would say 'Cross that bridge when you get to it!' I told myself, and I put these upsetting conjectures from me resolutely and determined to live for the day alone, although it was not easy.

Miss Jackson had returned in high spirits. Miss Crabbe was now in the ascendant, and had evidently done her best to make the girl forget the unhappy love affair which had so unsettled her. She told me some interesting news.

'Miss Crabbe is starting a small school this summer. It's to be a kindergarten school quite near the college and she's running it on progressive lines, of course.'

'Of course,' I echoed gravely.

'She's got two other friends who are helping her with the money – people who are *quite sure* that her teaching methods are revolutionary – and she's asked me if I would like to be appointed to the staff.'

'And would you?' I asked unnecessarily.

Hilary's face was radiant. 'I can't think of anything that I'd like more. There will be a house attached as there are going to be a few boarders – the really difficult cases – and I should live there with Miss Crabbe. Won't it be lovely?'

I said that it sounded a most hopeful venture and thought, privately, what a good thing it would be for the girl to get into another new post after all that had happened in Fairacre.

'She wants to open it next September and is already getting out prospectuses.'

'Then you'll have to give in your notice here about Eastertime,' I said.

'That's right,' agreed Hilary ecstatically. 'It will all fit in quite well, because by that time I expect the older children will have been sent on to the new school, and you won't need an assistant with just the infants.'

I was a trifle shaken by this calm acceptance of Fairacre's future plans, and hastened to point out that even if the estate were built, the school could not possibly be ready to house children by next September.

'In that case,' said Miss Jackson off-handedly, 'they would have to get another teacher in my place.'

'I suppose so,' I agreed. For one dreadful minute my old doubts engulfed me again. Supposing that there was no assistant to be had this time? Could I tackle the whole school for any length of time? Could I even tackle the infants if the older children had been whisked away – to Beech Green perhaps – if the new school were not ready? Would it be best for everyone if I tendered my resignation too? I thought of all the tedious business of writing out testimonials, filling in endless forms, asking people if they would stand as referees. I thought too of all that Fairacre and its folk had come to mean to me. No, I told myself firmly, I couldn't face it. For Fairacre's good or not, I should do my best here, and be happy to stay if I were deemed fit for the job. I came back to earth from this swift day-dream to hear Miss Jackson speaking with great earnestness.

'I couldn't let Miss Crabbe down, you know. It would be unthinkable!'

It seemed to me, in the weeks that followed, that Miss Jackson's acceptance of the housing scheme, as a foregone conclusion, was shared by others in Fairacre and the neighbourhood. It was as though the prolonged waiting had numbed the anti-estate feeling which had been so ferocious earlier in the affair. The people had lived with the idea for so long now that a fatalistic resignation to what might transpire had affected quite a number of them.

'We must get a more efficient heating system in the church if we have to house the new people,' said the vicar to his wife. 'The back of the church is never really warm.'

'I'll have to think of an extra delivery van and an extra driver, this time next year,' said Mr Prince, the baker, to his assistant.

Even Mrs Pringle was beginning to soften towards the project.

'Poor things must live somewhere!' she pointed out reasonably. 'Do 'em good to get out into decent houses and a bit of fresh air!' From the way she spoke one might imagine that they were living, at the moment, huddled together in sewers.

But the flame still burned brightly in some breasts. Over at Springbourne old Mr Miller looked out at his unchanged view and the first tiny spears of his new crop in Hundred Acre Field.

'They'll not shift me!' he said grimly to his wife, wagging his frosted head. 'We'll still be here when they've gone elsewhere, mark my words!'

The vicar, on hearing that Mr Miller had planted his field as usual was much impressed and said so to old Mrs Bradley who was present at the time.

'It is an act of faith, dear Mrs Bradley. A true act of faith!'

'Plenty of spunk there,' agreed Mrs Bradley spiritedly. 'Keep fighting! That's the way to gain your ends, and fight with all the weapons you can find! I myself sent a telling Christmas card to the Minister at his home address.'

'Really?' said the vicar, somewhat alarmed. He would not have put sending a bomb past this fierce old lady.

'A reproduction of "The Dew Pond on the Downs",' continued Mrs Bradley. 'One of Dan's best pictures. And I signed it "Adelaide Bradley – Lover of Fair Play and Our Downs" and added "Remember Dan Crockford!" for good measure!'

'It may well have helped,' said the vicar politely.

'Too much waiting about is making far too many fainthearts,' announced Mrs Bradley shrewdly. ' "Up and at 'em" is my motto! We'll see 'em off yet!'

Amy brought much the same news of Caxley's reaction to the scheme when she came to spend an evening with me. Resentment had largely been replaced by a philosophic acceptance of the affair as a necessary evil, and, in fact, the shopkeepers were beginning to speculate on the increase in their business which so many extra families must inevitably bring.

Amy herself, however, was as militant as Mrs Bradley.

'I've sent four letters already to the *Caxley Chronicle* and two more to *The Times* about this business,' she asserted.

'I haven't seen them,' I said innocently.

'For some reason they haven't been published yet,' replied Amy, not a whit disturbed, 'but it's the *writing* that matters. We mustn't give way and let things slide. Which reminds me!'

She scrabbled in her large crocodile handbag, a gift from James after a week's absence at a mysterious conference at a place unspecified, and handed me a book.

'It's a lesson to you!' said Amy firmly. 'It's about a woman, living alone, just as you do, on a small income with a regular working day, who never Lets Herself Go! It impressed me very much. Quite a nice little love-story too,' added Amy, in a patronising tone.

'Any picture strips?' I asked acidly, putting the book on my shelf.

'It's that sort of remark,' said Amy coldly, 'that reveals what a frustrated woman you really are!'

'That be blowed!' I answered inelegantly. 'Don't come the Integrated-Married-Woman over me, my girl. I've known you too long. What about scrambled eggs on toast for supper?'

United in common hunger we went cheerfully together to raid the larder.

23. THE VILLAGE HEARS THE NEWS

March that year was one of the coldest that Fairacre had ever known. The nights were bitter, and cottage fires were kept in overnight with generous top-sprinkling of small coal dampened with tea leaves, and stirred into comforting life first thing the next morning.

All growth was at a standstill. The small buds on the hedges were brittle to the touch and the spearlike leaves of those hardy bulbs which had already sent them aloft grew not a whit. The birds were particularly hard hit and not a day passed without a child bringing in a small pathetic corpse, its frail claws clenched stiffly in its last agony.

The vicar grieved over the inadequate heating of St Patrick's. Mr Roberts, Mr Miller and all the neighbouring farmers chafed at the delay to their crops, the children came to school wrapped up like cocoons in numberless coats and scarves, and I suffered my seasonal stiff neck from the draught from the skylight above my desk.

Despite continuous stoking, on my part, of the tortoise stoves, the school seldom seemed really warm because of villainous draughts from ill-fitting doors and windows. The coke pile in the playground began to dwindle visibly and Mrs Pringle was affronted.

'Good thing the Office can't see the rate we're using up the fuel!' she said darkly.

'Must keep warm,' I replied equably.

'What some calls *warm*,' replied Mrs Pringle, loosening the buttons at her neck, 'others calls *stifling*. Proper unhealthy in here with the stoves blazing away like that! Shouldn't be surprised if we had the chimney afire.' She limped off, outraged, before I could answer.

'It won't get no warmer till the snow's down,' said Mr Willet, surveying the iron-grey sky behind St Patrick's spire. 'And that won't be long now. You take your shovel indoors with you tonight, Miss Read. Wouldn't mind betting us has a bit of digging out to do tomorrow.'

Mr Willet was right. The first flakes began to flutter down early in the afternoon. I was putting a writing copy on the blackboard, and wishing that my own handwriting were as elegant as Miss Clare's had been, when I heard the excited whispers behind me.

'Snowing! Look, 'tis snowing!'

'Smashing!'

'Reckon it'll settle?'

' 'Tisn't *half* snowing too! Coming down a treat!'

The children were bobbing up from their seats the better to see this wonder through the high windows. Their faces were radiant. Here was drama indeed, and, with any luck, they might be sent home a few minutes early! Their day was made.

Within ten minutes the snow was falling steadily, whispering sibilantly along the window sills outside and covering the playground, the coke pile and the roofs with a white canopy. As the children finished their writing, they were allowed to go to the window to watch. They gazed entranced, looking up at the whirling flakes as they swirled down and making themselves deliciously dizzy with the sight.

'Miss!' burst out Eric, 'they's black coming down! *Black* snow flakes! Come and look!'

The scene outside might have come from a Christmas card. The bare black trees stood out starkly against their grey background and the bulk of the church loomed larger then ever against the heavy sky. The church windows glowed with lights within the buildings and I guessed that Mr Willet was stoking up the stove again. Along the lane I could see two small figures bent against the onslaught. They each carried a shopping bag and I suspected that the Coggs twins, ostensibly absent from school with unspecified ailments, had been sent 'up shop' by their mother. I watched their red coats vanish round the bend and realized that the only spot of vivid colour had now gone. The thatched roofs, the gardens, hedges and ground were all in muted shadings of grey, black and white.

At playtime the children had a few delirious minutes out among the flakes, I watched Patrick scoop up a handful of snow from the window ledge and eat it rapturously.

'S'lovely!' he shouted to the others, looking up with sparkling eyes and a thick white fringe round his wet, red mouth. The rest skimmed round and round like swifts, screaming as shrilly, and kicking up the wonderful stuff with their flying heels.

When they came in they stood apple-cheeked, warming their pink hands over the stove and chattering away about the joys in store for them, 'if it only lays.'

It continued to snow heavily and Miss Jackson and I sent the children home ten minutes early. It was settling, even then, to a depth of two or three inches and I feared that it would be over the top of some of the smaller children's shoes. We wrapped them up as best we could. They stood, chafing at the delay, as we buttoned coats and tied bonnet strings, and the minute that they could break away from our grasp they rushed ecstatically out into this glorious new world which had miraculously been transformed from everyday Fairacre.

There was an orchestral rehearsal that evening and I made my usual trip to Beech Green to mind Malcolm Annett while his parents went to Caxley. The snow lay thickly on the verges of the road, in the crooks of the trees and along their branches, but the road itself was easily traversed.

Malcolm had become a vivacious toddler with only one thing in mind – farm machinery. He was as elated as the school children were about the snow, but this did not deflect him from his usual obsession and whenever the sound of passing vehicles was heard he bolted to the window, shouting hopefully: 'Tractor!'

His dearest possession was a red model tractor which accompanied him everywhere. Teddies, golliwogs, soft animals and all the other former loves now languished in the toy cupboard. To my enquiries after their well-being and his own health and interests, he answered brightly: 'Tractor!' holding up the object for my inspection.

'I must say it's a bit tedious,' said his mother plaintively, 'and when I mislaid it the other day I thought he'd have apoplexy.'

The conversation turned to Miss Clare, while Malcolm shunted the tractor blissfully back and forth between our feet on the hearthrug.

'We loved having her with us on holiday last summer,' said Isobel, 'and George and I talked it over with Dr Martin when she was groggy again later on, and we suggested that she might like to come and live here, if ever she found her own house too much for her.'

'I'm very glad,' I answered, 'but did she accept the idea?'

'Not at first,' said George. 'In any case it is far better for her to manage on her own in her own home for as long as she can comfortably do so. I hear Miss Jackson's likely to go.'

I said it looked as though she would be leaving Fairacre at the end of the summer and told them what I knew of her plans.

'Lord!' said George Annett, with profound awe, 'think of Miss Jackson *and* Miss Crabbe on one staff!'

They went on to tell me about the provision of a suitable lodger for Miss Clare, as long as she wanted one.

'I can never find enough decent accommodation for my young staff,' said George. 'Any one of them would jump at the chance of being with Dolly Clare.'

'And we're keeping a room ready here where she can have all her things and make her home,' continued his wife. 'She could let her cottage probably and that would bring her in a little income. It's all very much in the future we hope, but she has promised to come if she needs to, and we are all of us – and Dr Martin too – very much relieved.'

I said that it was a most satisfactory arrangement, and thought what thoroughly good hearted people these two Annetts were.

'Look at the clock!' exclaimed George, jumping to his feet. 'Come on, Isobel, we'll be late!'

The usual scurrying began with Isobel shouting last-minute injunctions about her son's needs as she dressed.

'Let him have plenty of supper – he won't bother to eat during the day. And when he goes to bed, don't forget that he always takes—'

'Don't tell me,' I said, 'I can guess!'

'Tractor!' said my intelligent and besotted godson.

The snow continued intermittently for over a week, much to the joy of the children and the annoyance of their parents as they struggled about their affairs in a white world.

It was during this bleak period that a meeting was held of the Rural District Council at the offices in Caxley. Muffled in thick overcoats and scarves, and beating their leather gloves together, the members made their way up the stairs to the committee room, among them Mr Roberts from Fairacre accompanied by a cheerful young reporter from the *Caxley Chronicle*. They little realized what momentous news they would hear, for although the agenda lay in their pockets, the Clerk to the R.D.C. had received that morning a missive from the Minister of Housing and Local Government, sharing that honour with the Clerk to the County Council and the representative of the Atomic Energy Authority who had also received similar messages. It was this delicious letter which the Clerk looked forward to reading to his fellow councillors.

Within an hour the meeting was over and down the stairs tumbled the councillors with most gratified expressions. Mr Roberts' great laugh shook some flaking plaster from the hall ceiling as they emerged and the young reporter tore along the snowy streets to the offices of the *Caxley Chronicle* with the biggest scoop of his brief career. This, surely, he could sell to a national daily and win himself, not only approval from his own local editor, but a guinea or two from the lords of Fleet Street!

Mr Roberts drove through the black and white lanes to Fairacre in roaring good spirits. As he passed Hundred Acre Field, a sheet of unsullied whiteness stretching to the misty obscurity of the downs behind, Mr Roberts gave it an affectionate wink and a smile.

His wife was making dripping toast for tea when he entered the farmhouse kitchen. He kissed her boisterously, told her the good tidings, and inspected the toast. It was a delicacy of which Mr Roberts was a connoisseur.

'Plenty of that brown goobly from the bottom, my dear, and a good sprinkling of salt,' he directed, as he made his way to the telephone. Anxious as he was to let one or two intimates know his good news, Mr Roberts recognized that there was a time and place for everything. Dripping toast has as much right to respect as parish affairs, and at tea-time on a winter afternoon it must take pride of place.

'I'll go,' said the vicar, when he heard the telephone bell. He heaved himself from his shabby leather armchair by the fire and hurried into the draughty tiled hall where the vicarage telephone was housed.

'I can hardly believe it!' Mrs Partridge heard her husband say. 'Indeed, Roberts, it's almost more man I can take in! Thank you a thousand times for telling me.' She heard the tinkle as the vicar replaced the telephone, and a moment later he appeared in the doorway. He held out both hands to her and looked strangely moved.

'There is to be no housing estate. The Minister has made his decision known. It will be in the *Caxley Chronicle* the day after tomorrow.'

Mrs Partridge gripped her husband's hands thankfully. Tears, which did not come easily to the robust Mrs Partridge, filled her eyes as she felt relief flooding her.

'It is a direct answer to prayer,' said the vicar gently. 'I shall give public thanks in church next Sunday.'

'If that's a baby arriving,' said Dr Martin, setting down his unsipped tea as he heard the telephone, 'it can dam' well wait half an hour.' He lifted the receiver that lay within arm's reach on top of the bookshelf.

'Ah, Roberts,' he smiled across at his wife. 'Stand back a bit from the blower, man. You're deafening me!'

The roaring noise which Mrs Martin could hear subsided slightly. The doctor's face grew more and more pleased as he listened.

'Best news I've heard this year!' exclaimed the doctor delightedly. 'It solves a lot of my problems as well as everyone else's. Many thanks for letting me know!'

He put down the receiver and beamed at his wife.

'You can put all those plans about moving out of your head, my dear. The housing scheme is off!'

He took a long, satisfying draught from his tea cup.

'Thank God for that!' said Mrs Bradley when she heard the news. 'If anything had happened to Dan Crockford's field I think it would have killed me.'

She paused to listen to Mr Roberts's booming voice giving further particulars of the Minister's decision.

'Well, all I can say is this,' cackled the old lady mischievously, 'it was that Christmas card of mine that did the trick! I told you we must keep fighting – and now, you see, we've won!'

George Annett heard the news later that evening when the vicar telephoned to him about some arrangements for the next Sunday's anthem.

He rushed at once to the sitting-room where his wife and Miss Clare sat listening to the news on the wireless.

'Switch that off,' ordered Mr Annett excitedly, 'and I'll tell you some *real* news that'll make that international stuff look pretty silly!'

The two women gazed at him in surprise, but Isobel obediently switched off.

'Now then, it had better be good,' she said warningly.

'It is!' responded her husband proudly. '*We're not going to have a housing estate!*'

And snatching two knitting needles from Miss Clare's lap, he set them crosswise on the carpet and executed a lively sword dance, complete with triumphant, blood-curdling cries, much to the delight of the ladies.

Over at Springbourne late that night, Mr Miller filled four glasses. He had heard the wonderful news earlier that day by letter from the Rural District Council, and he looked upon it as a personal reprieve.

His two distinguished sons were at home when the news came, and they agreed that their father had shed twenty years from his eighty, as he had perused the letter. They stood now, glasses in hand, smiling warmly upon their sprightly father.

Old Mr Miller raised his glass to his wife.

'To our home!' he said simply.

24. FAREWELL TO FAIRACRE

During the night a warm westerly wind blew across the downs and Fairacre folk woke to find that the thaw had started. The thatched roofs dripped under a warm sun, little streams began to trickle in the gutters, the thirsty birds rejoiced in the puddles and life began to stir again.

The thermometers rose steadily, and as the news of the Minister's findings began to circulate with the village's customary briskness, the spirits of all who lived in Fairacre and Beech Green rose too. Many a village quarrel was patched up that morning. With such sunshine and such news, such relief from iron-hard frost and restricting suspense, it was impossible to pass a neighbour, even if one had been on 'no-speaking' terms for months, without stopping for a lively gossip. At backdoor steps, over hedges, in the village street, in the grocer's shop and at the post office the loosened tongues wagged. A great burden had been lifted and life in Fairacre rattled on all the more lightly and merrily.

' 'Twould never have done,' repeated Mr Willet. 'I said at the time that 'twould never have done! Fairacre takes a bit of beating as it is!'

'I'll believe it when I sees it,' was Mrs Pringle's comment. 'I've heard too many rumours flying about lately for me to put much store by a lot of idle chitter-chatter. I'll wait till I sees it put plain in the paper!'

We had not long to wait, for the *Caxley Chronicle* came out the next morning and had given pride of place to the youthful reporter's notice of the meeting.

'In view of the government's recent decision for stringent cuts in expenditure, and having given the objections raised by local bodies his earnest attention, the Minister has decided, with reluctance, that the present housing-estate scheme must be abandoned.'

As everyone in Fairacre, Beech Green and Caxley pointed out to his neighbour the Minister had put the less important factor first. Naturally, it was the fighting spirit of the local inhabitants that had forced the issue, but as the Minister had seen reason in the end no one was going to quarrel with him over this relatively minor point.

'And give the chap his due,' Mr Willet pointed out, reasonably enough, 'he do seem to have sat up there cudgelling his brains over this 'ere business ever since last October. Say what you like, after six months' honest thinking he's pretty well bound to have got the right answer.'

'And that he have!' agreed Mr Lamb from the Post Office with conviction. And all the neighbourhood, with rejoicing hearts, concurred.

The spring term had ended in a spell of warm sunshine which looked as though it might well stay for the Easter holidays.

The children had run home, on that last afternoon, hugging their bright Easter eggs carefully to their chests, and chorusing cheerfully.

'Good-bye, Miss. Happy Easter, Miss!'

When I answered with 'Be good children and help your mothers,' and some wag had called, with well-simulated innocence, 'Same to you, Miss!' their delight knew no bounds. It was a retort which would doubtless go down into Fairacre history.

The first morning of the holiday was so fair and sweet that I readily turned my back upon household affairs and set out for a walk on top of the downs. I chose the narrow little-used lane that winds steeply up the slope of the downs, beginning among trees which form a leafy tunnel in the summer and now showed the first small fans of breaking leaves, and later emerging into the bare open downland.

The scent of spring was everywhere, heady and hopeful, and as I gained the upper slopes I could hear the numberless larks carolling. I remembered Mr Mawne's remark: 'More larks to the square yard on those downs than anywhere else I know.'

Puffed by now, I arrived at a five-barred gate at the side of the lane, and leant gratefully upon it, looking down at the view spread below me. What an escape we had had, when the housing scheme had been abandoned!

A fine blue haze lay over the valley. Away to my right lay Beech Green. Miss Clare's cottage, tucked in a fold of the downs, was hidden from my view, but the reprieved Hundred Acre Field lay spread there tinged with tender green. Mr Miller had weathered his storm bravely, I thought. And for that matter, hadn't we all, during this last year? I remembered the anxiety of the vicar, of Mr Willet and Mrs Pringle and of all those among us whose lives would have been shaken by the advent of the new town. I remembered too Hilary Jackson's stormy passage, Miss Crabbe's brief passion, dear Miss Clare's fight for health, and Joseph Coggs' rebellion.

But that was behind us now. The storm had passed, the sunshine warmed my bare head, and I remembered, with an uprush of spirit, that the barometer had said *Set Fair* when I had tapped it that morning.

I took a last look at Fairacre away below me. There it lay in a comfortable hollow of the sheltering downs, ringed with trees that hid many of the thatched roofs from sight. But the spire of St Patrick's pierced the greenery like an upthrust finger and, at its tip, the weathercock, glinting in the morning sunlight, seemed to crow a challenge to all comers.

Well-satisfied, I turned my back upon Fairacre, happy in the knowledge that however far I journeyed, it would always be there waiting for me, timeless and unchanged.